In 2010, Justin Cronin's *The Passage* was a phenomenon. The unforgettable tale that critics and readers compared to the novels of Cormac McCarthy, Michael Crichton, Stephen King, and Margaret Atwood became a runaway bestseller and enchanted readers around the globe.

Justin Cronin is also the author of *Mary and O'Neil* (which won the PEN/Hemingway Award and the Stephen Crane Prize), and *The Summer Guest*. Other honours for his writing include a fellowship from the National Endowment for the Arts and a Whiting Writer's Award.

A Distinguished Faculty Fellow at Rice University, he divides his time between Houston, Texas, and Cape Cod, Massachusetts.

Also by Justin Cronin

The Summer Guest
Mary and O'Neil

The Passage Trilogy
The Passage
The Twelve
The City of Mirrors

ROYAL BOROUGH OF GREENWICH

Follow us on twitter 🐦 @greenwichlibs

Please return by the last date shown

Thank you! To renew, please contact any
Royal Greenwich library or renew online or by phone
www.better.org.uk/greenwichlibraries
24hr renewal line 01527 852384

'There are enough human themes to raise it well above the average **horror**'

Independent on Sunday

'Cronin writes with verve and versatility ... and his **future world** is richly imagined'

Sunday Times

'Cronin's sprawling epic, the first of a trilogy, is insanely elaborate, with a huge amount of thought given to the world. It's immersive, nuanced and **splendid** (in a terrifying way) – it **draws you in** and refuses to let you go'

Sci Fi Now

'Older lads of the Stephen-King adoring type ... can **devour** the doorstep *du jour*: Justin Cronin's novel *The Passage*, with its apocalyptic plague of the **viral undead**'

Independent

'I turned *The Passage*'s pages **feverishly** to find out what happened next'

Observer

'A **gripping** story and a richly drawn cast'

Daily Mail

'This epic tale is truly **exhilarating** stuff'

Daily Express

THE PASSAGE

JUSTIN CRONIN

ORION

First published in Great Britain in 2010
by Orion Books
This paperback edition published in 2015
by Orion Fiction,
an imprint of The Orion Publishing Group Ltd,
Carmelite House, 50 Victoria Embankment
London EC4Y 0DZ

An Hachette UK Company

1 3 5 7 9 10 8 6 4 2

Copyright © Justin Cronin 2010

Map copyright © David Lindroth, Inc. 2010

The moral right of Justin Cronin to be identified as the author
of this work has been asserted in accordance with
the Copyright, Designs and Patents Act 1988.

Grateful acknowledgement is made to Carcanet Press
Limited for permission to reprint five lines of 'The Wild Iris'
from The Wild Iris by Louise Gluck,
copyright © 1992 Louise Gluck. First edition 1996.

All the characters in this book are fictitious,
and any resemblance to actual persons, living
or dead, is purely coincidental.

A CIP catalogue record for this book
is available from the British Library.

ISBN 978 1 4091 9098 1

Printed and bound in Great Britain by
Clays Ltd, Elcograf S.p.A

MIX
Paper from
responsible sources
FSC® C104740
FSC
www.fsc.org

www.orionbooks.co.uk

For my children.
No bad dreams.

When I have seen by Time's fell hand defac'd
The rich proud cost of outworn buried age;
When sometime lofty towers I see down-raz'd,
And brass eternal slave to mortal rage;
When I have seen the hungry ocean gain
Advantage on the kingdom of the shore,
And the firm soil win of the watery main,
Increasing store with loss, and loss with store;
When I have seen such interchange of state,
Or state itself confounded to decay;
Ruin hath taught me thus to ruminate
That Time will come and take my love away.

—WILLIAM SHAKESPEARE, Sonnet 64

I

THE
WORST DREAM
IN THE WORLD

5–1 B.V.

The road to death is a long march beset
with all evils, and the heart fails little by little
at each new terror, the bones rebel at each step,
the mind sets up its own bitter resistance and
to what end? The barriers sink one by one,
and no covering of the eyes shuts out
the landscape of disaster, nor the sight
of crimes committed there.

– KATHERINE ANNE PORTER,
Pale Horse, Pale Rider

ONE

Before she became the Girl from Nowhere – the One Who Walked In, the First and Last and Only, who lived a thousand years – she was just a little girl in Iowa, named Amy. Amy Harper Bellafonte.

The day Amy was born, her mother, Jeanette, was nineteen years old. Jeanette named her baby Amy for her own mother, who'd died when Jeanette was little, and gave her the middle name Harper for Harper Lee, the lady who'd written *To Kill a Mockingbird*, Jeanette's favorite book – truth be told, the only book she'd made it all the way through in high school. She might have named her Scout, after the little girl in the story, because she wanted her little girl to grow up like that, tough and funny and wise, in a way that she, Jeanette, had never managed to be. But Scout was a name for a boy, and she didn't want her daughter to have to go around her whole life explaining something like that.

Amy's father was a man who came in one day to the restaurant where Jeanette had waited tables since she turned sixteen, a diner everyone called the Box, because it looked like one: like a big chrome shoe box sitting off the county road, backed by fields of corn and beans, nothing else around for miles except a self-serve car wash, the kind where you had to put coins into the machine and do all the work yourself. The man, whose name was Bill Reynolds, sold combines and harvesters, big things like that, and he was a sweet talker who told Jeanette as she poured his coffee and then later, again and again, how pretty she was, how he liked her coal-black hair and hazel eyes and slender wrists, said it all in a way that sounded like he meant it, not the way boys in school had, as if the words were just something that needed to get said along the way to her letting them do as they liked. He had a

3

big car, a new Pontiac, with a dashboard that glowed like a spaceship and leather seats creamy as butter. She could have loved that man, she thought, really and truly loved him. But he stayed in town only a few days, and then went on his way. When she told her father what had happened, he said he wanted to go looking for him, make him live up to his responsibilities. But what Jeanette knew and didn't say was that Bill Reynolds was married, a married man; he had a family in Lincoln, all the way clean over in Nebraska. He'd even showed her the pictures in his wallet of his kids, two little boys in baseball uniforms, Bobby and Billy. So no matter how many times her father asked who the man was that had done this to her, she didn't say. She didn't even tell him the man's name.

And the truth was, she didn't mind any of it, not really: not the being pregnant, which was easy right until the end, nor the delivery itself, which was bad but fast, nor, especially, having a baby, her little Amy. To tell Jeanette he'd decided to forgive her, her father had done up her brother's old bedroom as a nursery, carried down the old baby crib from the attic, the one Jeanette herself had slept in, years ago; he'd gone with Jeanette, in the last months before Amy came, to the Walmart to pick out some things she'd need, like pajamas and a little plastic tub and a wind-up mobile to hang over the crib. He'd read a book that said that babies needed things like that, things to look at so their little brains would turn on and begin to work properly. From the start Jeanette always thought of the baby as 'her,' because in her heart she wanted a girl, but she knew that wasn't the sort of thing you should say to anyone, not even to yourself. She'd had a scan at the hospital over in Cedar Falls and asked the woman, a lady in a flowered smock who was running the little plastic paddle over Jeanette's stomach, if she could tell which it was; but the woman laughed, looking at the pictures on the TV of Jeanette's baby, sleeping away inside her, and said, *Hon, this baby's shy. Sometimes you can tell and others you can't, and this is one of those times.* So Jeanette didn't know, which she decided was fine with her, and after she and her father had emptied out her brother's room and taken down his old pennants and posters – Jose Canseco, a music group called Killer Picnic, the Bud Girls – and seen how faded and banged up the walls were, they painted it a color the label on the can called 'Dreamtime,' which somehow was both pink and blue at once – good whatever the baby turned out to be. Her father hung a wallpaper border along the edge of the ceiling, a repeating pattern of ducks splashing in a puddle, and cleaned up an old maple rocking chair he'd found at the auction hall, so that when Jeanette brought the baby home, she'd have a place to sit and hold her.

The baby came in summer, the girl she'd wanted and named Amy Harper Bellafonte; there seemed no point in using the name Reynolds, the last name of a man Jeanette guessed she'd never see again and, now that Amy was here, no longer wanted to. And Bellafonte: you couldn't do better than a name like that. It meant 'beautiful fountain,' and that's what Amy was. Jeanette fed and rocked and changed her, and when Amy cried in the middle of the night because she was wet or hungry or didn't like the dark, Jeanette stumbled down the hall to her room, no matter what the hour was or how tired she felt from working at the Box, to pick her up and tell her she was there, she would always be there, you cry and I'll come running, that's a deal between us, you and me, forever and ever, my little Amy Harper Bellafonte. And she would hold and rock her until dawn began to pale the window shades and she could hear birds singing in the branches of the trees outside.

Then Amy was three and Jeanette was alone. Her father had died, a heart attack they told her, or else a stroke. It wasn't the kind of thing anyone needed to check. Whatever it was, it hit him early one winter morning as he was walking to his truck to drive to work at the elevator; he had just enough time to put down his coffee on the fender before he fell over and died, never spilling a drop. She still had her job at the

5

Box, but the money wasn't enough now, not for Amy or any of it, and her brother, in the Navy somewhere, didn't answer her letters. *God invented Iowa,* he always said, *so people could leave it and never come back.* She wondered what she would do.

Then one day a man came into the diner. It was Bill Reynolds. He was different, somehow, and the change was no good. The Bill Reynolds she remembered – and she had to admit she still thought of him from time to time, about little things mostly, like the way his sandy hair flopped over his forehead when he talked, or how he blew over his coffee before he sipped it, even when it wasn't hot anymore – there was something about him, a kind of warm light from inside that you wanted to be near. It reminded her of those little plastic sticks that you snapped so the liquid inside made them glow. This was the same man, but the glow was gone. He looked older, thinner. She saw he hadn't shaved or combed his hair, which was greasy and standing all which-away, and he wasn't wearing a pressed polo like before but just an ordinary work shirt like the ones her father had worn, untucked and stained under the arms. He looked like he'd spent all night out in the weather, or in a car somewhere. He caught her eye at the door and she followed him to a booth in back.

—*What are you doing here?*

—*I left her*, he said, and as he looked at where she stood, she smelled beer on his breath, and sweat, and dirty clothes. *I've gone and done it, Jeanette. I left my wife. I'm a free man.*

—*You drove all this way to tell me that?*

—*I've thought about you.* He cleared his throat. *A lot. I've thought about us.*

—*What us? There ain't no us. You can't come in like you're doing and say you've been thinking about us.*

He sat up straight. —*Well, I'm doing it. I'm doing it right now.*

—*It's busy in here, can't you see that? I can't be talking to you like this. You'll have to order something.*

—*Fine*, he answered, but he didn't look at the menu on the

6

wall, just kept his eyes on her. *I'll have a cheeseburger. A cheeseburger and a Coke.*

As she wrote down the order and the words swam in her vision, she realized she had started to cry. She felt like she hadn't slept in a month, a year. The weight of exhaustion was held up only by the thinnest sliver of her will. There was a time when she'd wanted to do something with her life – cut hair, maybe, get her certificate, open a little shop, move to a real city, like Chicago or Des Moines, rent an apartment, have friends. She'd always held in her mind a picture of herself sitting in a restaurant, a coffee shop but nice; it was fall, and cold outside, and she was alone at a small table by the window, reading a book. On her table was a steaming mug of tea. She would look up to the window to see the people on the street of the city she was in, hustling to and fro in their heavy coats and hats, and see her own face there, too, reflected in the window, hovering over the image of all the people outside. But as she stood there, these ideas seemed like they belonged to a different person entirely. Now there was Amy, sick half the time with a cold or a stomach thing she'd gotten at the ratty day care where she spent the days while Jeanette was working at the Box, and her father dead just like that, so fast it was as if he'd fallen through a trapdoor on the surface of the earth, and Bill Reynolds sitting at the table like he'd just stepped out for a second, not four years.

—*Why are you doing this to me?*

He held her eyes with his own a long moment and touched the top of her hand. —*Meet me later. Please.*

He ended up living in the house with her and Amy. She couldn't say if she had invited him to do this or if it had just somehow happened. Either way, she was instantly sorry. This Bill Reynolds: who was he really? He'd left his wife and boys, Bobby and Billy in their baseball suits, all of it behind in Nebraska. The Pontiac was gone, and he had no job either; that had ended, too. The economy the way it was, he explained, nobody was buying a goddamn thing. He said he had a plan, but the only plan that she could see seemed to be him sitting in the house doing nothing for Amy or even cleaning up the breakfast dishes, while she worked all day at the Box. He hit her the first time after he'd been living there three months; he was drunk, and once he did it, he burst out crying and said, over and over, how sorry he was. He was on his knees, blubbering, like *she'd* done something to *him*. She had to understand, he was saying, how hard it all was, all the changes in his life, it was more than a man, any man, could take. He loved her, he was sorry, nothing like that would happen again, ever. He *swore* it. Not to her and not to Amy. And in the end, she heard herself saying she was sorry too.

He'd hit her over money; when winter came, and she didn't have enough money in her checking account to pay the heating oil man, he hit her again.

—*Goddamnit, woman. Can't you see I'm in a situation here?*

She was on the kitchen floor, holding the side of her head. He'd hit her hard enough to lift her off her feet. Funny, now that she was down there she saw how dirty the floor was, filthy and stained, with clumps of dust and who-knew-what all rowed against the base of the cabinets where you couldn't usually see. Half her mind was noticing this while the other half said, You aren't thinking straight, Jeanette; Bill hit you and knocked a wire loose, so now you're worrying over the dust. Something funny was happening with the way the world sounded, too. Amy was watching television upstairs, on the little set in her room, but Jeanette could hear it like it was playing inside her head, Barney the purple dinosaur and a song about brushing your teeth; and then from far away, she heard the sound of the oil truck pulling away, its engine grinding as it turned out of the drive and headed down the county road.

—*It ain't your house*, she said.

—*You're right about that.* Bill took a bottle of Old Crow from over the sink and poured some in a jelly jar, though it was only ten o'clock in the morning. He sat at the table but didn't cross his legs like he meant to get comfortable. *Ain't my oil, either.*

Jeanette rolled over and tried to stand but couldn't. She watched him drink for a minute.

—*Get out.*

He laughed, shaking his head, and took a sip of whiskey.

—*That's funny*, he said. *You telling me that from the floor like you are.*

—*I mean what I say. Get out.*

Amy came into the room. She was holding the stuffed bunny she still carried everywhere, and wearing a pair of overalls, the good ones Jeanette had bought her at the outlet mall, the OshKosh B'Gosh, with the strawberries embroidered on the bib. One of the straps had come undone and was flopping at her waist. Jeanette realized Amy must have done this herself, because she had to go to the bathroom.

—*You're on the floor, Mama.*

—*I'm okay, honey.* She got to her feet to show her. Her left ear was ringing a little, like in a cartoon, birds flying around her head. She saw there was a little blood, too, on her hand; she didn't know where this had come from. She picked Amy up and did her best to smile. *See? Mama just took a spill, that's all. You need to go, honey? You need to use the potty?*

—*Look at you*, Bill was saying. *Will you look at yourself?* He shook his head again and drank. *You stupid twat. She probably ain't even mine.*

—*Mama*, the girl said and pointed, *you cut yourself. Your nose is cut.*

And whether it was what she'd heard or the blood, the little girl began to cry.

—*See what you done?* Bill said, and to Amy, *Come on now. Ain't no big thing, sometimes folks argue, that's just how it is.*

—*I'm telling you again, just leave.*

—*Then what would you do, tell me that. You can't even fill the oil tank.*

—*You think I don't know that? I sure as by God don't need you to tell me that.*

Amy had begun to wail. Holding her, Jeanette felt the

9

spread of hot moisture across her waist as the little girl released her bladder.

—*For Pete's sake, shut that kid up.*

She held Amy tight against her chest. —*You're right. She ain't yours. She ain't yours and never will be. You leave or I'm calling the sheriff, I swear.*

—*Don't you do me like this, Jean. I mean it.*

—*Well, I'm doing it. That's just what I'm doing.*

Then he was up and slamming through the house, taking his things, tossing them back into the cardboard cartons he'd used to carry them into the house, months ago. Why hadn't she thought it right then, how strange it was that he didn't even have a proper suitcase? She sat at the kitchen table holding Amy on her lap, watching the clock over the stove and counting off the minutes until he returned to the kitchen to hit her again.

But then she heard the front door swing open, and his heavy footsteps on the porch. He went in and out awhile, carrying the boxes, leaving the front door open so cold air spilled through the house. Finally he came into the kitchen, tracking snow, leaving little patches of it waffled to the floor with the soles of his boots.

—*Fine. Fine. You want me to leave? You watch me.* He took the bottle of Old Crow from the table. *Last chance,* he said.

Jeanette said nothing, didn't even look at him.

—*So that's how it is. Fine. You mind I have one for the road?*

Which was when Jeanette reached out and swatted his glass across the kitchen, smacked it with her open hand like a ping-pong ball with a paddle. She knew she was going to do this for about half a second before she did, knowing it wasn't the best idea she'd ever had, but by then it was too late. The glass hit the wall with a hollow thud and fell to the floor, unbroken. She closed her eyes, holding Amy tight, knowing what would come. For a moment the sound of the glass rolling on the floor seemed to be the only thing in the room. She could feel Bill's anger rising off him like waves of heat.

10

—You just see what the world has in store for you, Jeanette. You remember I said that.

Then his footsteps carried him out of the room and he was gone.

She paid the oil man what she could and turned the thermostat down to fifty, to make it last. *See, Amy honey, it's like a big camping trip we're on,* she said as she stuffed the little girl's hands into mittens and wedged a hat onto her head. *There now, it's not so cold, not really. It's like an adventure.* They slept together under a pile of old quilts, the room so icy their breath fogged the air over their faces. She took a job at night, cleaning up at the high school, leaving Amy with a neighbor lady, but when the woman took sick and had to go into the hospital, Jeanette had to leave Amy alone. She explained to Amy what to do: stay in bed, don't answer the door, just close your eyes and I'll be home before you know it. She'd make sure Amy was asleep before creeping out the door, then stride quickly down the snow-crusted drive to where she'd parked her car, away from the house, so Amy wouldn't hear it turning over.

But then she made the mistake one night of telling someone about this, another woman on the work crew, when the two of them had stepped out for a smoke. Jeanette had never liked smoking at all and didn't want to spend the money, but the cigarettes helped her stay awake, and without a smoke break there was nothing to look forward to, just more toilets to scrub and halls to be mopped. She told the woman, whose name was Alice, not to tell anyone, she knew she could get in trouble leaving Amy alone like that, but of course that's just what Alice did; she went straight to the superintendent, who fired Jeanette on the spot. *Leaving a child like that ain't right,* he told her in his office by the boilers, a room no bigger than ten feet square with a dented metal desk and an old easy chair with the plush popping out and a calendar on the wall that wasn't even the right year; the air was always so hot and close in there Jeanette could barely breathe. He said, *You*

11

count your lucky stars I'm not calling the county on you. She wondered when she'd become someone a person could say this to and not be wrong. He'd been nice enough to her until then, and maybe she could have made him understand the situation, that without the money from cleaning she didn't know what she'd do, but she was too tired to find the words. She took her last check and drove home in her crappy old car, the Kia she'd bought in high school when it was already six years old and falling apart so fast she could practically see the nuts and bolts bouncing on the pavement in her rearview mirror; and when she stopped at the Quick Mart to buy a pack of Capris and then the engine wouldn't start up again, she started to cry. She couldn't make herself stop crying for half an hour.

The problem was the battery; a new one cost her eighty-three dollars at Sears, but by then she'd missed a week of work and lost her job at the Box, too. She had just enough money left to leave, packing up their things in a couple of grocery sacks and the cartons Bill had left behind.

No one ever knew what became of them. The house sat empty; the pipes froze and split like bursting fruit. When spring came, the water poured from them for days and days until the utility company, realizing nobody was paying the bill, sent a couple of men to turn it off. The mice moved in, and when an upstairs window was broken in a summer thunderstorm, the swallows; they built their nests in the bedroom where Jeanette and Amy had slept in the cold, and soon the house was filled with the sound and smell of birds.

In Dubuque, Jeanette worked the night shift at a gas station, Amy sleeping on the sofa in the back room, until the owner found out and sent her packing. It was summer, they were living in the Kia, using the washroom behind the station to clean up, so leaving was just a matter of driving away. For a time they stayed with a friend of Jeanette's in Rochester, a girl she'd known in school who'd gone up there for a nursing degree; Jeanette took a job mopping floors at the same hospital where the friend worked, but the pay was just minimum wage, and the friend's apartment was too small for them to stay; she moved into a motel, but there was no one to look after Amy, the friend couldn't do it and didn't know anyone who could, and they ended up living in the Kia again. It was September; already a chill was in the air. The radio spoke all day of war. She drove south, getting as far as Memphis before the Kia gave out for good.

The man who picked them up in the Mercedes said his name was John – a lie, she guessed, from the way he said it, like a child telling a story about who broke the lamp, sizing her up for a second before he spoke. *My name is . . . John.* She guessed he was fifty, but she wasn't a good judge of these things. He had a well-trimmed beard and was wearing a tight dark suit, like a funeral director. While he drove he kept glancing at Amy in the rearview mirror, adjusting himself in his seat, asking Jeanette questions about herself, where she was going, the kinds of things she liked to do, what had brought her to the Great State of Tennessee. The car reminded her of Bill Reynolds's Grand Prix, only nicer. With the windows closed you could barely hear anything outside, and the seats were so soft she felt like she was sitting in a dish of ice cream. She felt like falling asleep. By the time they pulled into the motel she hardly cared what was going to happen. It seemed inevitable. They were near the airport; the land was flat, like Iowa, and in the twilight she could see the lights of the planes circling the field, moving in slow, sleepy arcs like targets in a shooting gallery.

Amy, honey, Mama's going to go inside with this nice man for a minute, okay? You just look at your picture book, honey.

He was polite enough, going about his business, calling her baby and such, and before he left he put fifty dollars on the nightstand – enough for Jeanette to buy a room for the night for her and Amy.

*

13

But others weren't as nice.

During the night, she'd lock Amy in the room with the TV on to make some noise and walk out to the highway in front of the motel and just kind of stand there, and it didn't take long. Somebody would stop, always a man, and once they'd worked things out, she'd take him back to the motel. Before she let the man inside she'd go into the room by herself and carry Amy to the bathroom, where she'd made a bed for her in the tub out of some extra blankets and pillows.

Amy was six. She was quiet, barely talked most of the time, but she'd taught herself to read some, from looking at the same books over and over, and could do her numbers. One time they were watching *Wheel of Fortune*, and when the time came for the woman to spend the money she'd won, the little girl knew just what she could buy, that she couldn't afford the vacation to Cancún but could have the living room set with enough money left over for the his-and-her golf clubs. Jeanette thought it was probably smart of Amy to figure this out, maybe more than smart, and she guessed she should probably be in school, but Jeanette didn't know where there were any schools around there. It was all auto-body-repair and pawn shops and motels like the one they lived in, the SuperSix. The owner was a man who looked a lot like Elvis Presley, not the handsome young one but the old fat one with the sweaty hair and chunky gold glasses that made his eyes look like fish swimming in a tank, and he wore a satin jacket with a lightning bolt down the back, just like Elvis had. Mostly he just sat at his desk behind the counter, playing solitaire and smoking a little cigar with a plastic tip. Jeanette paid him in cash each week for the room and if she threw in an extra fifty he didn't bother her any. One day he asked her if she had anything for protection, if maybe she wanted to buy a gun from him. She said sure, how much, and he told her another hundred. He showed her a rusty-looking little revolver, a .22, and when she put it in her hand right there in the office it didn't seem like much at all, let alone something that could shoot a person. But it was small enough to fit in

14

the purse she carried out to the highway and she didn't think it would be a bad thing to have around. —*Careful where you point that*, the manager said, and Jeanette said, *Okay, if you're afraid of it, it must work. You sold yourself a gun.*

And she was glad she had it. Just knowing it was in her purse made her realize she'd been afraid before and now wasn't, or at least not so much. The gun was like a secret, the secret of who she was, like she was carrying the last bit of herself in her purse. The other Jeanette, the one who stood on the highway in her stretchy top and skirt, who cocked her hip and smiled and said, *What you want, baby? There something I can help you with tonight?* – that Jeanette was a made-up person, like a woman in a story she wasn't sure she wanted to know the end of.

The man who picked her up the night it happened wasn't the one she would have thought. The bad ones you could usually tell right off, and sometimes she said no thanks and just kept walking. But this one looked nice, a college boy she guessed, or at least young enough to go to college, and nicely dressed, wearing crisp khaki pants and one of those shirts with the little man on the horse swinging the hammer. He looked like someone going on a date, which made her laugh to herself when she got into the car, a big Ford Expo with a rack on the top for a bike or something else.

But then a funny thing happened. He wouldn't drive to the motel. Some men wanted her to do them right there, in the car, not even bothering to pull over, but when she started in on this, thinking that was what he wanted, he pushed her gently away. He wanted to take her out, he said. She asked, *What do you mean, out?*

—*Someplace nice*, he explained. *Wouldn't you rather go someplace nice? I'll pay you more than whatever you usually get.*

She thought about Amy sleeping back in the room and guessed it wouldn't make much difference, one way or the other. *As long as it ain't more than an hour*, she said. *Then you got to take me back.*

But it was more than an hour, a lot more; by the time they

15

got where they were going, Jeanette was afraid. He pulled up to a house with a big sign over the porch showing three shapes that looked almost like letters but not quite, and Jeanette knew what it was: a fraternity. Some place a bunch of rich boys lived and got drunk on their daddy's money, pretending to go to school to become doctors and lawyers.

—*You'll like my friends*, he said. *Come on, I want you to meet them.*

—*I ain't going in there*, she said. *You take me back now.*

He paused, both hands on the wheel, and when she saw his face and what was in his eyes, the slow mad hunger, he suddenly didn't look like such a nice boy anymore.

—*That*, he said, *is not an option. I'd have to say that's not on the menu just now.*

—*The hell it ain't.*

She threw the door of the truck open and made to walk away, never mind she didn't know where she was, but then he was out too, and he grabbed her by the arm. It was pretty clear now what was waiting inside the house, what he wanted, how everything was going to shape up. It was her fault for not understanding this before – long before, maybe as far back as the Box on the day Bill Reynolds had come in. She realized the boy was afraid, too – that somebody was making him do this, the friends inside the house, or it felt like it to him, anyway. But she didn't care. He got behind her and tried to get his arm around her neck to lock her with his elbow, and she hit him, hard, where it counted, with the back of her fist, which made him yell, calling her bitch and whore and all the rest, and strike her across the face. She lost her balance and fell backward, and then he was on top of her, his legs astride her waist like a jockey riding a horse, slapping and hitting, trying to pin her arms. Once he did this it would all be over. He probably wouldn't care if she was conscious or not, she thought, when he did it; none of them would. She reached into her purse where it lay on the grass. Her life was so strange to her it didn't seem like it was even her own anymore, if it had ever been hers to begin with. But everything made sense to a gun. A gun knew what it was, and she felt the cool metal of the revolver slide into her palm, like it wanted to be there. Her mind said, *Don't think, Jeanette*, and she pushed the barrel against the side of the boy's head, feeling the skin and bone where it pressed against him, figuring that was close enough she couldn't miss, and then she pulled the trigger.

It took her the rest of the night to get home. After the boy had fallen off her, she'd run as fast as she could to the biggest road she could see, a wide boulevard glowing under streetlights, just in time to grab a bus. She didn't know if there was blood on her clothes or what, but the driver hardly looked at her as he explained how to get back to the airport, and she sat in the back where no one could see. In any case, the bus was almost empty. She had no idea where she was; the bus inched along through neighborhoods of houses and stores, all dark, past a big church and then signs for the zoo, and finally entered downtown, where she stood in a Plexiglas shelter, shivering in the damp, and waited for a second bus. She'd lost her watch somehow and didn't know the time. Maybe it had come off somehow when they were fighting and the police could use it as a clue. But it was just a Timex she'd bought at Walgreens, and she thought it couldn't tell them much. The gun was what would do it; she'd tossed it on the lawn, or so she remembered. Her hand was still a little numb from the force of it going off in her fist, the bones chiming like a tuning fork that wouldn't stop.

By the time she reached the motel the sun was rising; she felt the city waking up. Under the ashy light, she let herself into the room. Amy was asleep with the television still on, an infomercial for some kind of exercise machine. A muscled man with a ponytail and huge, doglike mouth was barking silently out of the screen. Jeanette figured she didn't have much more than a couple of hours before somebody came. That was dumb of her, leaving the gun behind, but there wasn't any point worrying over that now. She splashed some water on her face and brushed her teeth, not looking at herself in the mirror, then changed into jeans and a T-shirt and took her old clothes, the little skirt and stretchy top and fringed jacket she'd worn to the highway, streaked with blood and bits of things she didn't want to know about, behind the motel to the reeking dumpster, where she shoved them in.

It seemed as if time had compressed somehow, like an accordion; all the years she had lived and everything that had happened to her were suddenly squeezed below the weight of this one moment. She remembered the early mornings when Amy was just a baby, how she'd held and rocked her by the window, often falling asleep herself. Those had been good mornings, something she'd always remember. She packed a few things into Amy's Powerpuff Girls knapsack and some clothing and money into a grocery sack for herself. Then she turned off the television and gently shook Amy awake.

'Come on, honey. Wake up now. We got to go.'

The little girl was half asleep but allowed Jeanette to dress her. She was always like this in the morning, dazed and sort of out of it, and Jeanette was glad it wasn't some other time of day, when she'd have to do more coaxing and explaining. She gave the girl a cereal bar and a can of warm grape pop to drink, and then the two of them went out to the highway where the bus had let Jeanette off.

She remembered seeing, on the ride back to the motel, the big stone church with its sign out front: OUR LADY OF SORROWS. If she did the buses right, she figured, they'd go right by there again.

She sat with Amy in the back, an arm around her shoulders to hold her close. The little girl said nothing, except once to say she was hungry again, and Jeanette took another cereal bar from the box she'd put in Amy's knapsack, with the clean clothing and the toothbrush and Amy's Peter Rabbit. Amy, she thought, you are my good girl, my very good girl, I'm sorry, I'm sorry. They changed buses downtown again and rode for another thirty minutes, and when Jeanette saw the sign for the zoo she wondered if she'd gone too far; but then she remembered that the church had been before the zoo, so it would be after the zoo now, going the other direction.

Then she saw it. In daylight it looked different, not as big, but it would do. They exited through the rear door, and Jeanette zipped up Amy's jacket and put the knapsack on her while the bus pulled away.

She looked and saw the other sign then, the one she remembered from the night before, hanging on a post at the edge of a driveway that ran beside the church: CONVENT OF THE SISTERS OF MERCY.

She took Amy's hand and walked up the driveway. It was lined with huge trees, some kind of oak, with long mossy arms that draped over the two of them. She didn't know what a convent would look like but it turned out to be just a house, though nice: made of stone that glinted a little, with a shingled roof and white trim around the windows. There was an herb garden out front, and she thought that must be what the nuns did, they must come out here and take care of tiny growing things. She stepped up to the front door and rang the bell.

The woman who answered wasn't an old lady, like Jeanette had imagined, and she wasn't wearing a robe, whatever those things were called. She was young, not much older than Jeanette, and except for the veil on her head was dressed like anybody else, in a skirt and blouse and a pair of brown penny loafers. She was also black. Before she'd left Iowa, Jeanette had never seen but one or two black people in her life, except on television and in the movies. But Memphis was crawling with them. She knew some folks had problems with them, but Jeanette hadn't so far, and she guessed a black nun would do all right.

'Sorry to bother you,' Jeanette began. 'My car broke down out there on the street, and I was wondering—'

'Of course,' the woman said. Her voice was strange, like nothing Jeanette had ever heard, like there were notes of music caught and ringing inside the words. 'Come in, come in, both of you.'

The woman stepped back from the door to let Jeanette and Amy into the front hall. Somewhere in the building, Jeanette knew, there were other nuns – maybe they were black, too – sleeping or cooking or reading or praying, which she guessed nuns did a lot of, maybe most of the day. It was quiet enough, so she supposed that was probably right. What she had to do now was get the woman to leave her and Amy alone. She knew that as a fact, the way she knew she'd killed a boy last night, and all the rest of it. What she was about to do hurt more, but it wasn't any different otherwise, just more pain on the same spot.

'Miss—?'

'Oh, you can just call me Lacey,' the woman said. 'We're pretty informal around here. Is this your little girl?' She knelt in front of Amy. 'Hello there, what's your name? I have a little niece about your age, almost as pretty as you.' She looked up at Jeanette. 'Your daughter is very shy. Perhaps it is my accent. You see, I am from Sierra Leone, west Africa.' She turned to Amy again and took her hand. 'Do you know where that is? It is very far away.'

'All these nuns from there?' Jeanette asked.

Standing, the woman laughed, showing her bright teeth. 'Oh, goodness no! I'm afraid I am the only one.'

For a moment, neither of them said anything. Jeanette liked this woman, liked listening to her voice. She liked how she was with Amy, the way she looked at her eyes when she talked to her.

'I was racing to get her to school, you see,' Jeanette said, 'when that old car of mine? The thing just kind of gave out.'

The woman nodded. 'Please. This way.'

She led Jeanette and Amy through the hallway to the kitchen, a big room with a huge oak dining table and cabinets with labels on them: CHINA, CANNED GOODS, PASTA AND RICE. Jeanette had never thought about nuns eating before. She guessed that with all the nuns living in the building, it helped to know what was where in the kitchen. The woman pointed to the phone, an old brown one with a long cord, hanging on the wall. Jeanette had planned the next part well enough. She dialed a number while the woman got a plate of cookies for Amy – not store-bought, but something some-body had actually baked – then, as the recorded voice on the other end told her that it would be cloudy today with a high temperature of fifty-five degrees and a chance of showers moving in toward evening, she pretended to talk to AAA, nodding along.

'Wrecker's coming,' she said, hanging the phone back up. 'Said to go outside and meet him. Said he's got a man just around the corner, in fact.'

'Well, that's good news,' the woman said brightly. 'Today is your lucky day. If you wish, you can leave your daughter here with me. It would be no good to manage her on a busy street.'

So there it was. Jeanette wouldn't have to do anything else. All she had to do was say yes.

'Ain't no bother?'

The woman smiled again. 'We'll be fine here. Won't we?' She looked encouragingly at Amy. 'See? She is perfectly happy. You go see to your car.'

Amy was sitting on one of the chairs at the big oak table, with an untouched plate of cookies and a glass of milk before her. She'd taken off her backpack and was cradling it in her lap. Jeanette looked at her as long as she would let herself, and then she knelt and hugged her.

'You be good now,' she said, and against her shoulder, Amy nodded. Jeanette meant to say something else, but couldn't find the words. She thought about the note she'd left inside the knapsack, the slip of paper they were sure to find when Jeanette never came back to get her. She hugged her as long as she dared. The feeling of Amy was all around her, the warmth of her body, the smell of her hair and skin. Jeanette knew she was about to cry, something the woman – Lucy? Lacey? – couldn't see, but she let herself hold Amy a moment longer, trying to put this feeling in a place inside her mind, someplace safe where she could keep it. Then she let her daughter go, and before anybody said another word, Jeanette walked from the kitchen and down the driveway to the street, and then kept right on going.

TWO

From the computer files of Jonas Abbott Lear, PhD
Professor, Department of Molecular and Cellular Biology,
    Harvard University
Assigned to United States Army Medical Research Institute of
    Infectious Diseases (USAMRIID)
Department of Paleovirology, Fort Detrick, MD

From: lear@amedd.army.mil
Date: Monday, February 6 1:18 p.m.
To: pkiernan@harvard.edu
Subject: Satellite linkage is up

Paul,
Greetings from the jungles of Bolivia, landlocked armpit of the Andes. From where you sit in frigid Cambridge, watching the snow fall, I'm sure a month in the tropics doesn't sound like a bad deal. But believe me: this is not St. Bart's. Yesterday I saw a snake the size of a submarine.

The trip down was uneventful – sixteen hours in the air to La Paz, then a smaller government transport to Concepción, in the country's eastern jungle basin. From here, there aren't really any decent roads; it's pure backcountry, and we'll be traveling on foot. Everybody on the team is pretty excited, and the roster keeps growing. In addition to the group from UCLA, Tim Fanning from Columbia caught up with us in La Paz, as did

Claudia Swenson from MIT. (I think you told me once that you knew her at Yale.) In addition to his not inconsiderable star power, you'll be happy to hear that Tim brought half a dozen grad assistants with him, so just like that, the average age of the team fell by about ten years and the gender balance tipped decidedly toward the female. 'Terrific scientists, every one,' Tim insisted. Three ex-wives, each younger than the last; the guy never learns.

I have to say, despite my misgivings (and, of course, yours and Rochelle's) about involving the military, it's made a huge difference. Only USAMRIID has the muscle and the money to pull together a team like this one, and do it in a month. After years of trying to get people to listen, I feel like a door has suddenly swung open, and all we have to do is step through it. You know me, I'm a scientist through and through; I don't have a superstitious bone in my body. But part of me just has to think it's fate. After Liz's illness, her long struggle, how ironic that I should finally have the chance to solve the greatest mystery of all – the mystery of death itself. I think she would have liked it here, actually. I can just see her, wearing that big straw hat of hers, sitting on a log by the river to read her beloved Shakespeare in the sunshine.

BTW: congrats on the tenure decision. Just before I left, I heard the committee voted you in by general acclaim, which didn't surprise me after the department vote, which I can't tell you about but which, off the record, was unanimous. I can't tell you how relieved I am. Never mind that you're the best biochemist we've got, a man who can make a microtubule cycloskeletal protein stand up and sing the 'Hallelujah Chorus.' What would I have done on my lunch hour if my squash partner hadn't gotten tenure?

My love to Rochelle, and tell Alex his uncle Jonas will bring him back something special from Bolivia. How about a baby anaconda? I hear they make good pets as long as you keep them fed. And I hope we're still on for the Sox opener. How you got those tickets I have no idea.

—Jonas

From: lear@amedd.army.mil
Date: Wednesday, February 8 8:00 a.m.
To: pkiernan@harvard.edu
Subject: Re: Go get 'em, tiger

Paul,
Thanks for your message, and of course for your very sage advice re: pretty female postdocs with Ivy League degrees. I can't say I disagree with you, and on more than one lonely night in my tent, the thought has crossed my mind. But it's just not in the cards. For now, Rochelle is the only woman for me, and you can tell her I said so.

The news here, and I can already hear a big 'I told you so' from Rochelle: it looks like we've been militarized. I suppose this was inevitable, at least since I took USAMRIID's money. (And we're talking about a lot of money – aerial recon doesn't come cheap: twenty thousand bucks to retarget a satellite, and that will buy you only thirty minutes worth.) But still, it seems like overkill. We were making our final preparations for departure yesterday when a helicopter dropped out of the sky at base camp and who should step off but a squad of Special Forces, all done up like they were ready to take an enemy pillbox: the jungle camo, the green and black warpaint, the infrared scopes and high-power gas-recoil M-19s – all of it. Some very gung ho guys. Trailing the pack is a man in a suit, a civilian, who looks to be in charge. He struts across the field to where I'm standing and I see how young he is, not even thirty. He's also as tanned as a tennis pro. What's he doing with a squad of special ops? 'You the vampire guy?' he asks me. You know how I feel about that word, Paul – just try to get an NAS grant with 'vampire' anywhere in the paperwork. But just to be polite, and because, what the hell, he's backed by enough firepower to overthrow a small government, I tell him, sure, that's me. 'Mark Cole, Dr Lear,' he says, and shakes my hand, wearing a big grin. 'I've come a long way just to meet you. Guess what? You're now a major.' I'm thinking, a major what? And what are these guys doing here? 'This is a civilian scientific expedition,' I tell him. 'Not anymore,' he says. 'Who decided this?' I ask. And he tells me, 'My boss, Dr Lear.' 'Who's your boss?' I ask him. And he says, 'Dr Lear, my boss is the president of the United States.'

Tim was plenty ticked off, because he only gets to be a captain. I wouldn't know a captain from Colonel Sanders, so it's all the same to me. It was Claudia who really kicked up a fuss. She actually threatened to pack up and go home. 'I didn't vote for that guy and I'm not going to be part of his damned army, no matter what the twerp says.' Never mind that none of us voted for him either, and the whole thing really seems like a big joke. But it turns out she's a Quaker. Her younger brother was actually a conscientious objector during the Iran War. In the end, though, we calmed her down and got her to stay on, so long as we promised she didn't have to salute anyone.

The thing is, I can't really figure out why these guys are here. Not why the military would take an interest, because after all, it's their money we're spending, and I'm grateful for it. But why send a squad of special ops (they're technically 'special reconnaissance') to babysit a bunch of biochemists? The kid in the suit – I'd guess he's NSA, though who really knows? – told me that the area we were traveling into was known to be controlled by the Montoya drug cartel and the soldiers are here for our protection. 'How would it look for a team of American scientists to get themselves killed by drug lords in Bolivia?' he asked me. 'Not a happy day for US foreign policy, not a happy day at all.' I didn't contradict him, but I know damn well there's no drug activity where we're going – it's all to the west, on the altiplano. The eastern basin is virtually uninhabited except for a few scattered Indian settlements, most of which haven't had any outside contact in years. All of which he *knows* I know.

This has me scratching my head, but as far as I can tell, it makes no difference to the expedition itself. We just have some heavy firepower coming along for the ride. The soldiers pretty much keep to themselves; I've barely heard any of them even open their mouths. Spooky, but at least they don't get in the way.

Anyway, we're off in the morning. The offer of a pet snake still stands.

—Jonas

_____

From: lear@amedd.army.mil
Date: Wednesday, February 15 11:32 p.m.
To: pkiernan@harvard.edu
Subject: See attached
Attachment: DSC00392.JPG (596 KB)

Paul,
Six days in. Sorry to be out of touch, and please tell Rochelle not to worry. It's been hard slogging every step of the way, with dense tree cover and many days of constant rain – too much work to get the satcom up. At night, we all eat like farmhands and fall exhausted into our tents. Nobody here smells very nice, either.

But tonight I'm too keyed up to sleep. The attachment will explain why. I've always believed in what we were doing, but of course I've had my moments of doubt, sleepless nights when I wondered if this was all completely harebrained, some kind of fantasy my brain cooked up when Liz became so sick. I know you've thought it too. So I'd be a fool not to question my own motives. But not anymore.

According to the GPS, we're still a good twenty kilometers from the site. The topography is consistent with the satellite recon – dense jungle plain, but along the river, a deep ravine with cliffs of limestone pocketed with caves. Even an amateur geologist could read these cliffs like the pages of a book. The usual layers of river sediment, and then, about four meters below the lip, a line of charcoal black. It's consistent with the Chuchote legend: a thousand years ago the whole area was blackened by fire, 'a great conflagration sent by the god Auxl, lord of the Sun, to destroy the demons of man and save the world.' We camped on the riverbank last night, listening to the flocks of bats that poured out of the caves at sunset; in the morning, we headed east along the ravine.

It was just past noon when we saw the statue.

At first I thought maybe I was imagining things. But look at the image, Paul. A human being, but not quite: the bent animal posture, the clawlike hands and the long teeth crowding the mouth, the intense muscularity of the torso, details still visible, somehow, after – how long? How many centuries of wind and rain and sun have passed, wearing the stone away? And still it took my breath away. And the resemblance to the other images I've shown you is inarguable – the pillars at the temple of Mansarha, the carvings on the gravesite in Xianyang, the cave drawings in Côtes d'Amor.

More bats tonight. You get used to them, and they keep the mosquitoes down. Claudia rigged up a trap to catch one. Apparently, bats like canned peaches, which she used as bait. Maybe Alex would like a pet bat instead?

—J

From: lear@amedd.army.mil
Date: Saturday, February 18 6:51 p.m.
To: pkiernan@harvard.edu
Subject: more jpgs
Attachment: DSC00481.JPG (596 KB), DSC00486 (582 KB), DSC00491 (697 KB)

Have a look at these. We've counted nine figures now.

Cole thinks we're being followed, but won't tell me by who. It's just a feeling, he says. All night long he's on the satcom, won't tell me what it's all about. At least he's stopped calling me Major. He's a youngster, but not as green as he looks.

Good weather, finally. We're close, within 10K, making good time.

From: lear@amedd.army.mil
Date: Sunday, February 19 9:51 p.m.
To: pkiernan@harvard.edu
Subject:

_____

From: lear@amedd.army.mil
Date: Tuesday, February 21 1:16 a.m.
To: pkiernan@harvard.edu
Subject:

Paul,

I'm writing this to you in case I don't make it back. I don't want to alarm you, but I have to be realistic about the situation. We're less than five kilometers from the gravesite, but I doubt we'll be able to perform the extraction as planned. Too many of us are sick, or dead.

Two nights ago we were attacked – not by drug traffickers, but bats. They came a few hours after sunset while most of us were out of our tents doing the evening chores, scattered around the campsite. It was as if they had been scouting us all along, waiting for the right moment to launch an aerial assault. I was lucky: I had walked a few hundred yards upriver, away from the trees, to find a good signal on the GPS. I heard the shouts and then the gunfire, but by the time I made it back the swarm had moved downstream. Four people died that night, including Claudia. The bats simply engulfed her. She tried to get to the river – I guess she thought she could shake them off that way – but she never made it. By the time we reached her, she'd lost so much blood she had no chance. In the chaos, six others were bitten or scratched, and all of them are now ill with what looks like some speeded-up version of Bolivian hemorrhagic fever – bleeding from the mouth and nose, the skin and eyes rosy with burst capillaries, the fever shooting skyward, fluid filling the lungs, coma. We've been in contact with the CDC but without tissue analysis it's anybody's guess. Tim had both his hands practically chewed to pieces, trying to pull them off Claudia. He's the sickest of the lot. I seriously doubt he'll last till morning.

Last night they came again. The soldiers had set up a defense perimeter, but there were simply too many – they must have come by the hundreds of thousands, a huge swarm that blotted out the stars. Three soldiers killed, as well as Cole. He was standing right in front of me; they actually lifted him off his feet before they bored through him like hot knives through butter. There was barely enough of him left to bury.

Tonight it's quiet, not a bat in the sky. We've built a fire line around the camp, and that seems to be keeping them at bay. Even the soldiers are pretty shaken up. The few of us who are left are now deciding what to do. A lot of our equipment has been destroyed; it's unclear how this happened, but sometime during the attack last night, a grenade belt went into the fire, killing one of the soldiers and taking out the generator as well as most of what was in the supply tent. But we still have satcom and enough juice in the batteries to call for evac. Probably we should all just get the hell out of here.

And yet. When I ask myself why I should turn back now, what I have to go home to, I can't think of a single reason. It would be different if Liz were still alive. I think for the past year some part of me has been pretending that she'd simply gone away for a while, that one day I'd look up and see her standing in the door, smiling that way she did, her head cocked to the side so her hair could fall away from her face; my Liz, home at last, thirsty for a cup of Earl Grey, ready for a stroll by the Charles through the falling snow. But I know now that this isn't going to happen. Strangely, the events of the last two days have given my mind a kind of clarity about what we're doing, what the stakes are. I'm not one bit sorry to be here; I don't feel afraid at all. If push comes to shove, I may press on alone.

Paul, whatever happens, whatever I decide, I want you to know that you have been a great friend to me. More than a friend: a brother. How strange to write that sentence, sitting on a riverbank in the jungles of Bolivia, four thousand miles away from everything and everyone I've ever known and loved. I feel as if I've entered a new era of my life. What strange places our lives can carry us to, what dark passages.

From: lear@amedd.army.mil
Date: Tuesday, February 21 5:31 a.m.
To: pkiernan@harvard.edu
Subject: Re: don't be dumb, get the hell out, please

Paul,

We radioed for the evac last night. Pickup in ten hours, which is the nick of time as far as everyone's concerned. I don't see how we can survive another night here. Those of us who are still healthy have decided we can use the day to press on to the site. We were going to draw straws, but it turned out everyone wanted to go. We leave within the hour, at first light. Maybe something can still be salvaged from this disaster. One bit of good news: Tim seems to have turned a corner during the last few hours. His fever's way down, and though he's still unresponsive, the bleeding has stopped and his skin looks better. With the others, though, I'd say it's still touch and go.

I know that science is your god, Paul, but would it be too much to ask for you to pray for us? All of us.

From: lear@amedd.army.mil
Date: Tuesday, February 21 11:16 p.m.
To: pkiernan@harvard.edu
Subject:

Now I know why the soldiers are here.

30

THREE

Situated on four thousand acres of soggy East Texas piney woodland and short-grass prairie, looking more or less like a corporate office park or large public high school, the Polunsky Unit of the Texas Department of Criminal Justice, a.k.a. Terrell, meant one thing: if you were a man convicted of capital murder in the state of Texas, this was where you came to die.

On that morning in March, Anthony Lloyd Carter, inmate number 999642, sentenced to death by lethal injection for the murder of a Houston mother of two named Rachel Wood whose lawn he had mowed every week for forty dollars and a glass of iced tea, had been a resident of the Administrative Segregation Block of Terrell Unit for one thousand three hundred and thirty-two days – less than many, more than some, not that in Carter's sense of things this made a lick of difference. It wasn't like you got a prize for being there the longest. He ate alone, exercised alone, showered alone, and a week was the same as a day or a month to him. The only different thing that was going to happen would come on the day the warden and the chaplain appeared at his cell and he'd take the ride to the room with the needle, and that day wasn't so far off. He was allowed to read, but that wasn't easy for him, it never had been, and he had long since stopped fussing with it. His cell was a concrete box six feet by ten with one window and a steel door with a slot wide enough to slip his hands through but that was all, and most of the time he just lay there on his cot, his mind so blank it was like a pail with nothing in it. Half the time he couldn't have said for sure if he was awake or still sleeping.

That day began the same as every other, at 3:00 a.m., when they turned on the lights and shoved the breakfast trays through the slots. Usually it was cold cereal or powdered eggs or pancakes; the good breakfasts were when they put peanut butter on the pancakes, and this was one of the good ones. The fork was plastic and broke half the time, so Carter sat on his bunk and ate the pancakes folded up, like tacos. The other men on H-Wing complained about the food, how nasty it was, but Carter didn't think it was so bad on the whole. He'd had worse, and there were days in his life when he'd had nothing at all, so pancakes with peanut butter were a welcome sight in the morning, even if it wasn't morning in the sense of being light out.

There were visiting days, of course, but Carter hadn't had a visitor in all the time he'd been in Terrell except for the once, when the woman's husband had come and told him that he'd found Christ Jesus who was the Lord and that he'd prayed on what Carter had done, taking his beautiful wife away from him and his babies forever and ever; and that through the weeks and months of praying, he'd come to terms with this and decided to forgive him. The man did a lot of crying, sitting on the other side of the glass with the phone pressed to his head. Carter had been a Christian man himself from time to time and appreciated what the woman's husband was saying to him; but the way he spoke the words made it seem like his forgiving Carter was something he'd chosen to do, to make himself feel better. He certainly didn't say anything about putting a stop to what was going to happen to Carter. Carter couldn't see how saying anything on the subject would improve the situation, so he thanked the man and said God bless you and I'm sorry, if I see Mrs Wood in heaven I'll tell her what you did here today, which made the man get up in a hurry and leave him there, holding the phone. That was the last time anybody had come to see Carter at Terrell, two years ago at least.

The thing was, the woman, Mrs Wood, had always been nice to him, giving him an extra five or ten, and coming out with the iced tea on the hot days, always on a little tray, like folks did in restaurants, and the thing that had happened between them was confusing; Carter was sorry about it, sorry right down to his bones, but it still didn't make sense in his head, no matter how he turned it around. He'd never said he hadn't done it, but it didn't seem right to him to die on account of something he didn't understand, at least before he had the chance to figure it out. He went over it in his mind, but in four years it never had come any clearer to him. Maybe coming to terms, like Mr Wood had done, was the thing Carter hadn't been able to see his way to. If anything, the whole thing made less sense than ever; and with the days and weeks and months all mashed together in his brain the way they were, he wasn't even sure he was remembering the thing right to begin with.

At 6:00 a.m., when the shift changed, the guards woke everybody up again, to call out names and numbers, then moved down the hallway with the laundry bags to swap out boxers and socks. This meant today was a Friday. Carter didn't get a chance to shower but once a week or see the barber except every sixty days, so it was good to have clean clothes. The sticky feeling of his skin was worse in summer, when you sweated all day onto yourself even if you lay still as a stone, but from what his lawyer had told him in the letter he'd sent six months ago, he wouldn't have to go through another Texas summer in his life. The second of June would be the end of it.

His thoughts were broken by two hard bangs on the door. 'Carter. Anthony Carter.' The voice belonged to Pincher, head of the shift.

'Aw, come on, Pincher,' Anthony said from his bunk. 'Who'd you think was in here?'

'Present for cuffs, Tone.'

'Ain't time for rec. Ain't my day for the shower neither.'

'You think I got all morning to stand here talking about it?'

Carter eased himself off the bunk, where he'd been look-ing at the ceiling and thinking about the woman, that glass of iced tea on the tray. His body felt achy and slow, and with effort he lowered himself onto his knees with his back facing the door. He'd done this a thousand times but still didn't like

33

it. Keeping your balance was the tricky part. Once he was kneeling, he pulled his shoulder blades inward, twisted his arms around, and guided his hands, palms up, through the slot that the food came through. He felt the cold bite of the metal as Pincher cuffed his wrists. Everybody called him Pincher on account of how tight he did the cuffs.

'Stand back now, Carter.'

Carter pushed one foot forward, his left knee making a grinding sound as he shifted his center of gravity, then rose carefully to his feet, simultaneously withdrawing his cuffed hands from the slot. From the far side of the door came the clanking of Pincher's big ring of keys, and then the door opened to show him Pincher and the guard they called Dennis the Menace, on account of his hair, which looked like the kid's in the cartoon, and the fact that he liked to menace you with the stick. He had a way of finding spots on your body that you never knew could hurt so bad with just a little poke of wood.

'Seems like somebody's come to see you, Carter,' Pincher said. 'And it isn't your mother or your lawyer.' He didn't smile or anything, but Dennis looked to be enjoying himself. He gave that stick of his a twirl like a majorette.

'My mom's been with Jesus since I was ten years old,' Carter told him. 'You know that, Pincher, I told you that about a hundred times. Who is it wants me?'

'Can't say. Warden set it up. I'm just supposed to take you to the cages.'

Carter supposed this was no good. It'd been so long since the woman's husband had come to visit; maybe he'd come to say goodbye, or else to tell him I changed my mind, I don't forgive you after all, go straight to hell, Anthony Carter. Either way Carter didn't have anything else to say to the man. He'd said sorry to everyone over and over and felt done with it.

'Come on with you then,' Pincher said.

They led him down the corridor, Pincher gripping him hard by an elbow to steer him like a kid through a crowd, or a girl he was dancing with. This was how they took you anywhere, even to the shower. Part of you got used to people's hands being on you this way, and part of you didn't. Dennis led the way, opening the door that sealed administrative segregation from the rest of H-Wing and then the outer, second door that took them down the hall through general population to the cages. It'd been almost two years since Carter had been off H-Wing – H for 'hellhole,' H for 'hit my black ass with that stick some more,' H for 'Hey, Mama, I'm off to see Jesus any day now' – and walking with his eyes pointed at the ground, he still let himself peek around, if only to give his eyes something new to look at. But it was all still Terrell, a maze of concrete and steel and heavy doors, the air dank and sour with the smell of men.

At the visiting area they reported to the OD and entered an empty cage. The air inside was ten degrees warmer and smelled like bleach so strong it made Carter's eyes sting. Pincher undid the cuffs; while Dennis held the point of his stick against the soft spot under Carter's jaw, they shackled him in the front, legs too. There were signs all over the wall telling Carter what he could and couldn't do, none of which he wanted to take the trouble to read or even look at. They shuffled him over to the chair and gave him the phone, which Carter could manage to hold in place against his ear only if he bent his legs halfway up his chest – more damp crunches from his knees – pulling the chain taut across his chest like a long zipper.

'Didn't have to wear the shackles the last time,' Carter said.

Pincher barked a nasty laugh. 'I'm sorry, did we forget to ask you nicely? Fuck you, Carter. You got ten minutes.'

Then they left, and Carter waited for the door on the other side to open and show him who it was had come to see him after all this time.

Special Agent Brad Wolgast hated Texas. He hated everything about it.

He hated the weather, which was hot as an oven one

minute and freezing the next, the air so damp it felt like a wet towel over your head. He hated the look of the place, beginning with the trees, which were scrawny and pathetic, their limbs all gnarled up like something out of Dr Seuss, and the flat, windblown nothingness of it. He hated the billboards and the freeways and faceless subdivisions and the Texas flag, which flew over everything, always big as a circus tent; he hated the giant pickup trucks everybody drove, no matter that gas was thirteen bucks a gallon and the world was slowly steaming itself to death like a package of peas in a microwave. He hated the boots and the belt buckles and the way people talked, *y'all this* and *y'all that*, as if they spent the day ropin' and ridin', not cleaning teeth and selling insurance and doing the books, like people did everywhere.

Most of all, he hated it because his parents had made him live here, back in junior high. Wolgast was forty-four, still in decent shape but with the miscellaneous aches and thinning hair to show for it; sixth grade was long ago, nothing to regret, but still, driving with Doyle up Highway 59 north from Houston, springtime Texas spread all around, the wound felt fresh to him. Texas, state-sized porkchop of misery: one minute he'd been a perfectly happy kid in Oregon, fishing off the pier at the mouth of the Coos River and playing with his friends in the woods behind their house for endless, idle hours; the next he was stuck in the urban swamp of Houston, living in a crappy ranch house without a scrap of shade, walking to school in one-hundred-degree heat that felt like a big shoe coming down on his head. The end of the world, he'd thought. That's where he was. The end of the world was Houston, Texas. On his first day of sixth grade, the teacher had made him stand up to recite the Texas Pledge of Allegiance, as if he'd signed up to live in a whole different country. Three miserable years; he'd never been so glad to leave a place, even the way it happened. His father was a mechanical engineer; his parents had met when his father had taken a job the year after college as a math teacher on the reservation in Grande Ronde, where his mother, who was

36

half Chinook – her mother's family name was Po-Bear – was working as a nurse's aide. They'd gone to Texas for the money, but then his father was laid off when the oil bust hit in '86; they tried to sell the house but couldn't, and in the end, his father had simply dropped the keys off at the bank. They moved to Michigan, then Ohio, then upstate New York, chasing little bits of work, but his father had never righted himself after that. When he'd died of pancreatic cancer two months before Wolgast graduated from high school – his third in as many years – it was easy to think that Texas had somehow done it. His mother had moved back to Oregon, but now she was gone too.

Everyone was gone.

He'd gotten the first man, Babcock, from Nevada. Others came from Arizona and Louisiana and Kentucky and Wyoming and Florida and Indiana and Delaware. Wolgast didn't care much for those places, either. But anything was better than Texas.

Wolgast and Doyle had flown into Houston from Denver the night before. They'd stayed the night at a Radisson near the airport (he'd considered a brief side trip into the city, maybe tracking down his old house, but then wondered what in hell he'd want to do a thing like that for), picked up the rental car in the morning, a Chrysler Victory so new it smelled like the ink on a dollar bill, and headed north. The day was clear with a high, blue sky the color of cornflowers; Wolgast drove while Doyle sipped his latte and read the file, a mass of paper resting on his lap.

'Meet Anthony Carter,' Doyle said, and held up the photo. 'Subject Number Twelve.'

Wolgast didn't want to look. He knew just what he'd see: one more slack face, one more pair of eyes that had barely ever learned to read, one more soul that had stared into itself too long. These men were black or white, fat or thin, old or young, but the eyes were always the same: empty, like drains that could suck the whole world down into them. It was easy to sympathize with them in the abstract, but only in the abstract.

'Don't you want to know what he did?'

Wolgast shrugged. He was in no hurry, but now was as good a time as any.

Doyle slurped his latte and read: 'Anthony Lloyd Carter. African American, five foot four, a hundred and twenty pounds.' Doyle looked up. 'That explains the nickname. Take a guess.'

Already Wolgast felt tired. 'You've got me. Little Anthony?'

'You're showing your age, boss. It's T-Tone. T for "Tiny," I'm thinking, though you never know. Mother deceased, no dad in the picture from day one, a series of foster homes care of the county. Bad beginnings all around. A list of priors but mostly petty stuff, panhandling, public nuisance, that kind of thing. So, the story. Our man Anthony cuts this lady's lawn every week. Her name is Rachel Wood, she lives in River Oaks, two little girls, husband's some big lawyer. All the charity balls, the benefits, the country clubs. Anthony Carter is her *project*. Starts cutting her lawn one day when she sees him standing under an overpass with a sign that says, HUNGRY, PLEASE HELP. Words along those lines. Anyway, she takes him home, makes him a sandwich, puts in some calls and finds him a place, some kind of group home she raises money for. Then she calls all her friends in River Oaks and says, Let's help this guy, what do you need done around the place? All of a sudden she's a regular Girl Scout, rallying the troops. So the guy starts cutting all their lawns, pruning the hedges, you know, all the things they need around the big houses. This goes on about two years. Everything's hunky-dory until one day, our man Anthony comes over to cut the lawn, and one of the little girls is home sick from school. She's five. Mom's on the phone or doing something, the little girl goes out into the yard, sees Anthony. She knows who he is, she's seen him plenty of times, but this time something goes wrong. He frightens her. There's some stuff here about maybe he touched her, but the court psychiatrist is iffy on

38

that. Anyway, the girl starts screaming, Mom comes tearing out of the house, she's screaming, everybody's screaming, all of a sudden it's like a screaming contest, the goddamn screaming Olympics. One minute he's the nice man who shows up on time to cut the lawn, next thing you know, he's just a black guy with your kid, and all the Mother Teresa shit goes out the window. It gets physical. There's a struggle. Mom somehow falls or gets pushed into the pool. Anthony goes in after her, maybe to help her, but she's still screaming at him, fights him off. So now everybody's wet and yelling and thrashing around.' Doyle looked at him quizzically. 'Know how it ends?'

'He drowns her?'

'Bingo. Right there, right in front of the little girl. A neighbor heard it all and called the cops, so when they get there, he's still sitting on the edge of the pool, the lady floating in it.' He shook his head. 'Not a pretty picture.'

Sometimes it was troubling to Wolgast, how much energy Doyle put into these stories. 'Any chance it was an accident?'

'As it happens, the victim was on the varsity swim team at SMU. Still did fifty laps every morning. The prosecution made a lot of hay with that little detail. That and the fact that Carter pretty much admitted to killing her.'

'What did he say when they arrested him?'

Doyle shrugged. 'He only wanted her to stop screaming. Then he asked for a glass of iced tea.'

Wolgast shook his head. The stories were always bad, but it was the little details that got to him. A glass of iced tea. Sweet Jesus. 'How old did you say he was?'

Doyle flipped back a couple of pages. 'I didn't. Thirty-two. Twenty-eight at the time he went into custody. And here's the thing. No relatives at all. Last time anybody came to see him in Polunsky was the victim's husband, a little over two years ago. His lawyer left the state, too, after the appeal was turned down. Carter's been reassigned to somebody else in the Harris County PD office, but they haven't even opened the paperwork. Ipso facto, nobody's watching the store.

Anthony Carter goes to the needle on June second for murder one with depraved indifference, and not one soul on earth is paying attention. The guy's a ghost *already*.'

The drive to Livingston took ninety minutes, the last fifteen minutes on a farm-to-market road that carried them through the intermittent shade of piney woods and open fields of prairie grass spangled with bluebonnets. It was just noon; with luck, Wolgast thought, they could be done by dinner, enough time to drive back to Houston and dump the rental and get on a plane to Colorado. It was better when these trips were quick like that; when he lingered too long, if the guy was hemming and hawing and drawing it out – never mind that they always took the deal eventually – he'd start to get a queasy feeling in his stomach about the whole thing. It always made him think of a play he'd read in high school, *The Devil and Daniel Webster,* and how he, Wolgast, was the devil in this deal. Doyle was different; he was younger, for starters, not even thirty, a cherry-cheeked farmboy from Indiana who was glad to play Robin to Wolgast's Batman, calling him 'chief' and 'boss,' with a streak of old-fashioned midwestern patriotism so unalloyed that Wolgast had actually seen him tear up at the national anthem at the start of a Rockies game – a game on TV. Wolgast hadn't known they still *made* people like Phil Doyle. And there was no question Doyle was smart, with a good future ahead of him. Fresh out of Purdue, his law school applications already in the works, Doyle had joined the Bureau right after the Mall of America Massacre – three hundred holiday shoppers gunned down by Iranian jihadists, all the horror captured by security cameras to be replayed in painstakingly gruesome detail on CNN; it seemed like half the country was ready to sign on to something, anything that day – and after finishing his training at Quantico, he had been posted to the Denver field office, assigned to counterterrorism. When the Army had come looking for two field agents, Doyle had been the first in line to volunteer. Wolgast couldn't quite figure that; on paper, what they were calling 'Project NOAH' had looked like a dead end, and Wolgast had taken the assignment for just that reason. His divorce had just come through – his marriage to Lila hadn't ended so much as evaporated, so it had taken him by surprise, how blue the actual decree had made him – and a few months of travel seemed like just the thing to clear his mind. He'd gotten a small settlement in the divorce – his share of the equity in their house in Cherry Creek, plus a piece of Lila's retirement account from the hospital – and he'd actually thought about quitting the Bureau entirely, going back to Oregon and using the money to open up a small business of some kind: hardware, maybe, or sporting goods, not that he knew anything about either one. Guys who quit the Bureau always ended up in security, but to Wolgast the idea of a small store, something simple and clean, the shelves stocked with baseball gloves or hammers, objects with a purpose you could identify just by looking at them, was far more appealing. And the NOAH thing had seemed like a cakewalk, not a bad way to spend his last year in the Bureau if it came to that.

Of course, it had turned out to be more than paperwork and babysitting, a lot more, and he wondered if Doyle had somehow known this.

At Polunsky they were ID'd and asked to check their weapons, then went to the warden's office. Polunsky was a grim place, but they all were. While they waited, Wolgast used his handheld to check for evening flights out of Houston – there was one at 8:30, so if they hustled they could make it. Doyle said nothing, just flipped through a copy of *Sports Illustrated,* like he was waiting at the dentist. It was just after one when the secretary led them in.

The warden was a black man, about fifty, with salt-and-pepper hair and the chest of a weight lifter compressed under his suit vest. He neither rose nor offered to shake their hands as they entered. Wolgast gave him the documents to look over.

He finished reading and looked up. 'Agent, this is the

goddamnedest thing I've ever seen. What in the hell would you want Anthony Carter for?'

'I'm afraid I can't tell you that. We're just here to make the transfer.'

The warden put the papers aside and folded his hands on his desk. 'I see. And what if I said no?'

'Then I would give you a number to call, and the person on the other end of the line would do his best to explain that this is a matter of national security.'

'A number.'

'That's correct.'

The warden sighed irritably, spun in his chair, and gestured out the wide windows behind him. 'Gentlemen, do you know what that is out there?'

'I'm not following you.'

He turned to face them again. He didn't seem angry, Wolgast thought. Just a man accustomed to having his way. 'It's Texas. Two hundred sixty seven thousand square miles of Texas, to be precise. And the last time I checked, Agent, that's who I work for. Not for anybody in Washington, or Langley, or whoever the hell is on the other end of that number. Anthony Carter is an inmate in my care, and I'm charged by the citizens of this state to carry out his sentence. Short of a phone call from the governor, I'm going to do exactly that.'

Goddamn Texas, Wolgast thought. This was going to take all day. 'That can be arranged, Warden.'

He held up the papers for Wolgast to take. 'Well then, Agent. You better arrange it.'

At the visitors' entrance they collected their weapons and returned to the car. Wolgast got on the phone to Denver, which patched him through to Colonel Sykes on an encrypted line. Wolgast told him what had happened; Sykes was irritated but said he'd make the arrangements. A day at the most, he said. Just hang around and wait for the call, then get Anthony Carter to sign the papers.

'Just so you know, there may be a change in protocol coming your way,' Sykes told him.

'What sort of change?'

Sykes hesitated. 'I'll let you know. Just get Carter to sign.'

They drove to Huntsville and checked into a motel. The warden's stonewalling was nothing new – it had happened before. The delay was aggravating, but that was all it was. A few days from now, a week at most, Carter would be in the system, and all evidence that he'd ever existed would be wiped from the face of the earth. Even the warden would swear he'd never heard of the guy. Somebody would have to talk to the deceased's husband, of course, the River Oaks lawyer with the two little girls he now had to raise himself, but that wasn't Wolgast's job. There would be a death certificate involved, and probably a story about a heart attack and a quick cremation, and how justice had, in the end, been served. It didn't matter; the job would get done.

By five they hadn't heard anything, so they changed out of their suits into jeans and walked up the street to find a place for dinner, choosing a steak joint on a commercial strip between a Costco and a Best Buy. It was part of a chain, which was good – they were supposed to travel lightly, to leave as little an impression on the world around them as possible. The delay had made Wolgast antsy, but Doyle seemed not to mind. A good meal and a little time off in a strange town, courtesy of the federal government – why complain? Doyle sawed his way through a huge porterhouse, thick as a two-by-four, while Wolgast picked at a plate of ribs, and when they'd paid the check – in cash, pulled off a wad of fresh bills Wolgast kept in his pocket – they took a pair of stools at the bar.

'Think he'll sign?' Doyle asked.

Wolgast rattled the ice in his Scotch. 'They always do.'

'I suppose it's not much of a choice.' Doyle frowned into his glass. 'The needle, or whatever's behind curtain number two. But even so.'

Wolgast knew what Doyle was thinking: whatever was

behind the curtain, it was nothing good. Why else would they need death row inmates, men with nothing to lose?

'Even so,' he agreed.

A basketball game was playing on the television above the bar, the Rockets and Golden State, and for a while they watched in silence. It was early in the game, and both teams seemed sluggish, moving the ball around without doing much of anything with it.

'You hear anything from Lila?' Doyle said.

'Actually, yeah.' Wolgast paused. 'She's getting married.'

Doyle's eyes widened. 'That guy? The doctor?'

Wolgast nodded.

'That was fast. Why didn't you say something? Jesus, what'd she do, invite you to the wedding?'

'Not exactly. She sent me an email, thought I should know about it.'

'What did you say?'

Wolgast shrugged. 'I didn't.'

'You didn't say anything?'

There was more to it, but Wolgast didn't want to go into it. *Dear Brad,* Lila had written, *I thought you should know that David and I are expecting a child. We're getting married next week. I hope you can be happy for us.* He'd sat at the computer staring at the message on the screen for a good ten minutes.

'There was nothing to say. We're divorced, she can do what she wants.' He drained his Scotch and peeled off more bills to pay. 'You coming?'

Doyle passed his eyes over the room. When they'd first sat at the bar, the place was nearly empty, but more people had come in, including a group of young women who had pushed together three tall tables and were drinking pitchers of margaritas and talking loudly. There was a college nearby, Sam Houston State, and Wolgast supposed they were students, or else they worked together somewhere. The world could be going straight to hell in a handbasket, but happy hour was happy hour, and pretty girls would still fill the bars in Huntsville, Texas. They were wearing clingy shirts and low-cut jeans with fashionable tears at the knees, their faces and hair done for a night on the town, and they were drinking furiously. One of the girls, a little heavy, sitting with her back to them, wore her pants so low on her spine that Wolgast could see the little hearts on her underwear. He didn't know if he wanted to get a closer look or throw a blanket over her.

'Maybe I'll stay awhile,' Doyle said, and raised his glass in a little toast. 'Watch the game.'

Wolgast nodded. Doyle wasn't married, didn't even have a steady girlfriend. They were supposed to keep their interactions to a minimum, but he didn't see how it was any of his business how Doyle spent his evening. He felt a flicker of envy, then put the thought aside.

'Okay. Just remember—'

'Right,' Doyle said. 'Like Smokey Bear says, take only pictures, leave only footprints. As of this moment, I'm a fiber-optic sales rep from Indianapolis.'

Behind them, the girls broke into laughter; Wolgast could hear the tequila in their voices.

'Nice town, Indianapolis,' Wolgast said. 'Better than this one, anyway.'

'Oh, I wouldn't say that,' Doyle replied, and grinned mischievously. 'I think I'm going to like it here just fine.'

Wolgast left the restaurant and walked up the highway. He'd left his handheld behind at the motel, thinking they might get a call during dinner and have to leave; but when he checked it now, he found no messages. After the noise and activity of the restaurant, the quiet of the room was unsettling, and he began to wish he'd maybe stayed with Doyle, though he knew he wasn't very good company these days. He removed his shoes and lay on his bed in his clothes to watch the rest of the game, not really caring one way or the other about it, but it gave his mind something to focus on. Finally, a little past midnight – eleven in Denver, a little too late, but what the hell – he did what he'd told himself he wouldn't do and dialed Lila's number. A man's voice answered.

'David, it's Brad.'

For a moment David didn't say anything. 'It's late, Brad. What do you want?'

'Is Lila there?'

'She's had a long day,' David said firmly. 'She's tired.'

I know she's tired, Brad thought. *I slept in the same bed with her for six years.* 'Just put her on, will you?'

David sighed and put the phone down with a thump. Wolgast heard the rustling of sheets and then David's voice, saying to Lila, *It's Brad, for Pete's sake, tell him to call at a decent hour next time.*

'Brad?'

'I'm sorry to call so late. I didn't realize what time it was.'

'I don't believe that for a second. What's on your mind?'

'I'm in Texas. A motel, actually. I can't tell you where exactly.'

'Texas.' She paused. 'You hate Texas. I don't think you called to tell me you're in Texas, did you?'

'I'm sorry, I shouldn't have woken you. I don't think David's too happy.'

Lila sighed into the phone. 'Oh, it's all right. We're still friends, right? David's a big boy. He can handle it.'

'I got your email.'

'Well.' He heard her breathe. 'I kind of figured. I supposed that was why you called. I thought I'd hear from you at some point.'

'Did you do it? Get married.'

'Yes. Last weekend, here at the house. Just a few friends. My parents. They asked for you, actually, wanted to know how you were doing. They always really liked you. You should call them, if you want. I think my dad misses you more than anyone.'

He let the remark pass – more than anyone? More than you, Lila? He waited for her to say something else, but she didn't, and the silence was taken up by a picture that formed in his mind, a picture that was actually a memory: Lila in bed, in an old T-shirt and the socks she always wore because her feet got cold no matter the time of year, a pillow wedged between her knees to straighten her spine because of the baby. Their baby. Eva.

'I just wanted to tell you I was.'

Lila's voice was quiet. 'Was what, Brad?'

'That I was . . . happy for you. Like you asked. I was thinking that you should, you know, quit your job this time. Take some time off, take better care of yourself. I always wondered, you know, if—'

'I will,' Lila cut in. 'Don't worry. Everything is fine, everything is normal.'

Normal. Normal, he thought, was what everything was not. 'I just—'

'Please.' She took a deep breath. 'You're making me sad. I have to get up in the morning.'

'Lila—'

'I said I have to go.'

He knew she was crying. She didn't make a sound to tell him so, but he knew. They were both thinking about Eva, and thinking about Eva would make her cry, which was why they weren't together anymore, and couldn't be. How many hours of his life had he held her as she cried? And that was the thing; he'd never known what to say when Lila cried. It was only later – too late – that he'd realized he wasn't supposed to say anything at all.

'Damn it, Brad. I didn't want to do this, not now.'

'I'm sorry, Lila. I was just . . . thinking about her.'

'I know you were. Goddamnit. God*damn*it. Don't do this, *don't*.'

He heard her sob, and then David's voice came on the line. 'Don't call back, Brad. I mean it. Understand what I'm saying to you.'

'Fuck you,' Wolgast said.

'Whatever you say. Just don't bother her anymore. Leave us alone.' And he hung up the phone.

Wolgast looked at his handheld once before hurling it across the room. It made a handsome arc, spinning like a Frisbee, before slapping the wall above the television with the crunch of breaking plastic. He instantly felt sorry. But when he knelt and picked it up, he found that all that had happened was the battery case had popped open, and the thing was perfectly fine.

Wolgast had been to the compound only once, the previous summer, to meet with Colonel Sykes. Not a job interview, exactly; it had been made clear to Wolgast that the NOAH assignment was his if he wanted it. A pair of soldiers drove him in a van with blacked-out windows, but Wolgast could tell they were taking him west from Denver, into the mountains. The drive took six hours, and by the time they pulled into the compound, he'd actually managed to fall asleep. He stepped from the van into the bright sunshine of a summer afternoon. He stretched and looked around. From the topography, he'd have guessed he was somewhere around Ouray. It could have been farther north. The air felt thin and clean in his lungs; he felt the dull throb of a high-altitude headache at the top of his skull.

He was met in the parking lot by a civilian, a compact man dressed in jeans and a khaki shirt rolled at the sleeves, a pair of old-fashioned aviators perched on his wide, faintly bulbous nose. This was Richards.

'Hope the ride wasn't too bad,' Richards said as they shook hands. Up close Wolgast saw that Richards's cheeks were pockmarked with old acne scars. 'We're pretty high up here. If you're not used to it, you'll want to take it easy.'

Richards escorted Wolgast across the parking area to a building he called the Chalet, which was exactly what it sounded like: a large Tudor structure, three stories tall, with the exposed timbers of an old-fashioned sportsmen's lodge. The mountains had once been full of these places, Wolgast knew, hulking relics from an era before time-share condos and modern resorts. The building faced an open lawn and beyond, at a hundred yards or so, a cluster of more workaday structures: cinder-block barracks, a half dozen military inflatables, a low-slung building that resembled a roadside motel. Military vehicles, Humvees and smaller jeeps and five-ton trucks, were moving up and down the drive; in the center of the lawn, a group of men with broad chests and trim haircuts, naked to the waist, were sunning themselves on lawn chairs.

Stepping into the Chalet, Wolgast had the disorienting sensation of peeking behind a movie set; the place appeared to have been gutted to the studs, its original architecture replaced by the neutral textures of a modern office building: gray carpeting, institutional lighting, acoustic-tile drop ceilings. He might have been in a dentist's office or the high-rise off the freeway where he met his accountant once a year to do his taxes. They stopped at the front desk, where Richards asked him to turn over his handheld and his weapon, which he passed to the guard, a kid in camos, who tagged them. There was an elevator, but Richards walked past it and led Wolgast down a narrow hallway to a heavy metal door that opened on a flight of stairs. They ascended to the second floor and made their way down another nondescript hallway to Sykes's office.

Sykes rose from behind his desk as they entered: a tall, well-built man in uniform, his chest spangled with the various bars and little bits of color that Wolgast had never understood. His office was neat as a pin, its arrangement of objects, right down to the framed photos on his desk, giving the impression of having been placed for maximum efficiency. Resting in the center of the desk was a single manila folder, fat with paper. Wolgast knew it was almost certainly his personnel file, or some version of it.

They shook hands and Sykes offered him coffee, which Wolgast accepted. He wasn't drowsy but the caffeine, he knew, would help the headache.

'Sorry about the bullshit with the van,' Sykes said, and waved him to a chair. 'That's just how we do things.'

A soldier brought in the coffee, a plastic carafe and two china cups on a tray. Richards remained standing behind Sykes's desk, his back to the broad windows that looked out on the woodlands that ringed the compound. Sykes explained what he wanted Wolgast to do. It was all quite straightforward, he said, and by now Wolgast knew the basics. The Army needed between ten and twenty death row inmates to serve in the third-stage trials of an experimental drug therapy, code-named 'Project NOAH.' In exchange for their consent, the inmates would have their sentences commuted to life without parole. It would be Wolgast's job to obtain the signatures of these men, nothing more. Everything had been legally vetted, but because the project was a matter of national security, all of these men would be declared legally dead. Thereafter, they would spend the rest of their lives in the care of the federal penal system in a white-collar prison camp, under assumed identities. The men would be chosen based upon a number of factors, but all would be men between the ages of twenty and thirty-five with no living first-degree relatives. Wolgast would report directly to Sykes; he'd have no other contact, though he'd remain, technically, in the employment of the Bureau.

'Do I have to pick them?' Wolgast asked.

Sykes shook his head. 'That's our job. You'll receive your orders from me. All you have to do is get their consent. Once they're signed on, the Army will take it from there. They'll be moved to the nearest federal lockup, then we'll transport them here.'

Wolgast thought a moment. 'Colonel, I have to ask—'

'What we're doing?' He seemed, at that moment, to permit himself an almost human-looking smile.

Wolgast nodded. 'I understand I can't be very specific. But I'm going to be asking them to sign over their whole lives. I have to tell them something.'

Sykes exchanged a look with Richards, who shrugged. 'I'll leave you now,' Richards said, and nodded at Wolgast. 'Agent.'

When Richards had left, Sykes leaned back in his chair. 'I'm not a biochemist, Agent. You'll have to be satisfied with the layman's version. Here's the background, at least the part I can tell you. About ten years ago, the CDC got a call from a doctor in La Paz. He had four patients, all Americans, who had come down with what looked like hantavirus – high fever, vomiting, muscle pain, headache, hypoxemia. The four of them had been part of an ecotour, deep in the jungle. They claimed that they were part of a group of four-teen but had gotten separated from the others and had been wandering in the jungle for weeks. It was sheer luck that they'd stumbled onto a remote trading post run by a bunch of Franciscan friars, who'd arranged their transport to La Paz. Now, hanta isn't the common cold, but it's not exactly rare, either, so none of this would have been more than a blip on the CDC's radar if not for one thing: all of them were terminal cancer patients. The tour was organized by an outfit called Last Wish. You've heard of them?'

Wolgast nodded. 'I thought they just took people sky-diving, things like that.'

'That's what I thought, too. But apparently not. Of the four, one had an inoperable brain tumor, two had acute lymphocytic leukemia, and the fourth had ovarian cancer. And every single one of them became well. Not just the hanta, or whatever it was. No cancer. Not a trace.'

Wolgast felt lost. 'I don't get it.'

Sykes sipped his coffee. 'Well, neither did anyone at the CDC. But something had happened, some interaction between their immune systems and something, most likely viral, that they'd been exposed to in the jungle. Something they ate? The water they drank? No one could figure it out. They couldn't even say exactly where they'd been.' He leaned forward over his desk. 'Do you know what the thymus gland is?'

Wolgast shook his head.

Sykes pointed at his chest, just above the breastbone. 'Little thing in here, between the sternum and the trachea, about the size of an acorn. In most people, it's atrophied completely by puberty, and you could go your whole life not knowing you had one, unless it was diseased. Nobody really knows what it does, or at least they didn't, until they ran scans on these four patients. The thymus had somehow turned itself back on. More than back on: it had enlarged to three times its usual size. It looked like a malignancy but it wasn't. And their immune systems had gone into overdrive. A hugely accelerated rate of cellular regeneration. And there were other benefits. Remember these were cancer patients, all over fifty. It was like they were teenagers again: smell, hearing, vision, skin tone, lung volume, physical strength and endurance, even sexual function. One of the men actually grew back a full head of hair.'

'A virus did this?'

Sykes nodded. 'Like I said, this is the layman's version. But I've got people downstairs who think that's exactly what happened. Some of them have degrees in subjects I can't even spell. They talk to me like I'm a child, and they're not wrong.'

'What happened to them? The four patients.'

Sykes leaned back in his chair, his face darkening a little. 'Well, this isn't the happiest part of the story, I'm afraid. They're all dead. The longest any of them survived was eighty-six days. Cerebral aneurysm, heart attack, stroke. Their bodies just kind of blew a fuse.'

'What about the others?'

'No one knows. Disappeared without a trace, including the tour operator, who turned out to be a pretty shady character. It's likely he was actually working as a drug mule, using these tours as a cover.' Sykes gave a shrug. 'I've probably said too much. But I think this will help you put things in perspective. We're not talking about curing one disease, Agent. We're talking about curing *everything*. How long would a human being live if there were no cancer, no heart disease, no diabetes, no Alzheimer's? And we've reached the point where we need, absolutely require, human test subjects. Not a nice term, but there really is no other. And that's where you come in. I need you to get me these men.'

'Why not the marshals? Isn't this more up their alley?'

Sykes shook his head dismissively. 'Glorified corrections officers, if you'll excuse my saying so. Believe me, we started there. If I had a sofa I needed carried up the stairs, they'd be the first guys I'd call. But for this, no.'

Sykes opened the file on his desk and began to read. 'Bradford Joseph Wolgast, born Ashland, Oregon, September 29, 1974. BS in criminal justice 1996, SUNY Buffalo, high honors, recruited by the Bureau but declines, accepts a graduate fellowship at Stony Brook for a PhD in political science but leaves after two years to join the Bureau. After training at Quantico sent to—' He raised his eyebrows at Wolgast. '—Dayton?'

Wolgast shrugged. 'It wasn't very exciting.'

'Well, we all do our time. Two years in the sticks, a little of this, a little of that, mostly piddly shit but good ratings all around. After 9/11 asks to transfer to counterterrorism, back to Quantico for eighteen months, assigned to the Denver field office September '04 as liaison to the Treasury, tracking funds moved through US banks by Russian nationals, i.e., the Russian Mafia, though we don't call them that. On the personal side: no political affiliations, no memberships, doesn't even subscribe to the newspaper. Parents deceased. Dates a little but no steady girlfriends. Marries Lila Kyle, an orthopedic surgeon. Divorced four years later.' He closed the file and lifted his eyes to Wolgast. 'What we need, Agent, is somebody who, to be perfectly candid, has a certain polish. Good negotiation skills, not just with the prisoners but with the prison authorities. Somebody who knows how to tread lightly, won't leave a large impression. What we're doing here is perfectly legal – hell, it may be the most important piece of medical research in the history of mankind. But it could be easily misunderstood. I'm telling you as much as I am because I think it will help if you understand the stakes, how high they are.'

53

Wolgast guessed Sykes was telling him maybe ten percent of the story – a persuasive ten percent, but even so. 'Is it safe?'

Sykes shrugged. 'There's safe and then there's safe. I won't lie to you. There are risks. But we'll do everything we can to minimize them. A bad outcome isn't in anybody's interest here. And I remind you that these are death row inmates. Not the nicest men you'd ever care to meet, and they don't exactly have a lot of options. We're giving them a chance to live out their lives, and maybe make a significant contribution to medical science at the same time. It's not a bad deal, not by a long shot. Everybody's on the side of the angels here.'

Wolgast took a last moment to think. It was all a little hard to take in. 'I guess I don't see why the military is involved.'

At this, Sykes stiffened; he seemed almost offended. 'Don't you? Think about it, Agent. Let's say a soldier on the ground in Khorramabad or Grozny takes a piece of shrapnel. A roadside bomb, say, a bunch of C-4 in a lead pipe full of deck screws. Maybe it's a piece of black-market Russian ordnance. Believe me, I've seen firsthand what these things can do. We have to dust him out of there, maybe en route he bleeds to death, but if he's lucky he gets to the field hospital, where a trauma surgeon, two medics, and three nurses patch him up as best they can before evacuating him to Germany or Saud. It's painful, it's awful, it's his rotten luck, and he's probably out of the war. He's a broken asset. All the money we've spent on his training is a total loss. And it gets worse. He comes home depressed, angry, maybe missing a limb or something worse, with nothing good to say about anyone or anything. Down at the corner tavern he tells his buddies, I lost my leg, I'm pissing into a bag for the rest of my life, and for what?' Sykes leaned back in his chair, letting the story sink in. 'We've been at war for fifteen years, Agent. By the looks of things, we'll be in it for fifteen more if we're *lucky*. I won't kid you. The single biggest challenge the military faces, has always faced, is keeping soldiers on the field. So, let's say the same GI takes the same piece of shrapnel but within half a day his body's healed itself and he's back in his unit, fighting for God and country. You think the military wouldn't be interested in something like that?'

Wolgast felt chastened. 'I see your point.'

'Good, because you should.' Sykes's expression softened; the lecture was over. 'So maybe it's the military who's picking up the check. I say let them, because frankly, what we've spent so far would make your eyes pop out. I don't know about you, but I'd like to live to meet my great-great-great-grandchildren. Hell, I'd like to hit a golf ball three hundred yards on my hundredth birthday and then go home to make love to my wife until she walks funny for a week. Who wouldn't?' He looked at Wolgast searchingly. 'The side of the angels, Agent. Nothing more or less. Do we have a deal?'

They shook, and Sykes walked him to the door. Richards was waiting to take him back to the van. 'One last question,' Wolgast asked. 'Why "Noah"? What's it stand for?'

Sykes glanced quickly at Richards. In that moment, Wolgast felt the balance of power shifting in the room; Sykes might have been technically in charge, but in some way, Wolgast felt certain, he also reported to Richards, who was probably the link between the military and whoever was really running the show: USAMRIID, Homeland, maybe NSA.

Sykes turned back to Wolgast. 'It doesn't stand for anything. Let's put it this way. You ever read the Bible?'

'Some.' Wolgast looked at the both of them. 'When I was a kid. My mother was a Methodist.'

Sykes allowed himself a second, final smile. 'Go look it up. The story of Noah and the ark. See how long he lived. That's all I'll say.'

That night, back in his Denver apartment, Wolgast did as Sykes had said. He didn't own a Bible, probably hadn't laid eyes on one since his wedding day. But he found a concordance online.

And all the days of Noah were nine hundred and fifty years; and he died.

It was then that he realized what the missing piece was,

the thing Sykes hadn't said. It would be in his file, of course. It was the reason, of all the federal agents they might have chosen, that they'd picked him.

They'd chosen him because of Eva, because he'd had to watch his daughter die.

In the morning, he awoke to the chirp of his handheld; he was dreaming, and in the dream it was Lila, calling him back to tell him the baby had been born – not hers and David's baby, but their own. For a moment Wolgast felt happy, but then his mind cleared and he realized where he was – Huntsville, the motel – and his hand found the phone on the nightstand and punched the Receive button without his even looking at the screen to see who it was. He heard the static of the encryption and then the opening line.

'All set,' Sykes told him. 'Everything should be in hand. Just get Carter to sign. And don't pack your bags quite yet. We may have another errand for you to run.'

He looked at the clock: 6:58. Doyle was in the shower. Wolgast heard the faucet shut off with a groan, then the blast of a hair dryer. He had a vague memory of hearing Doyle returning from the bar – a rush of street noise from the open door, a muttered apology, and then the sound of water running – and looking at the clock and seeing it was a little after two a.m.

Doyle stepped into the room, a towel wrapped at his waist. Steam moistened the air around him. 'Good, you're up.' His eyes were bright, his skin flushed from the heat of the shower. How the guy could stay out half the night drinking and still look like he was ready to run a marathon was beyond Wolgast's comprehension.

Wolgast cleared his throat. 'How's the fiber-optic business?'

Doyle dropped onto the opposite bed and ran a hand through his damp hair. 'You'd be surprised, how interesting a business that is. People underestimate it, I think.'

'Let me guess. The one with the pants?'

Doyle grinned, giving his eyebrows a playful wag. 'They all had pants, boss.' He tipped his head at Wolgast. 'What happened to you? You look like you got dragged from a car.'

Wolgast looked down at himself to discover he'd slept the night in his clothes. This was becoming something of a habit; ever since he'd gotten the email from Lila, he'd spent most nights on the sofa of his apartment, watching television until he fell asleep, as if going to bed like a normal person was something he was no longer qualified to do.

'Forget about it,' he said. 'Must have been a boring game.' He rose and stretched. 'We heard from Sykes. Let's get this over with.'

They ate breakfast at a Denny's and drove back to Polunsky. The warden was waiting for them in his office. Was it just the mood of the morning, Wolgast thought, or did he look like he hadn't slept very well, either?

'Don't bother to sit,' the warden said, and handed them an envelope.

Wolgast examined the contents. It was all pretty much as he expected: a writ of commutation from the governor's office and a court order transferring Carter to their custody as a federal prisoner. Assuming Carter signed, they could have him in transit to the federal lockup at El Reno by dinner. From there, he'd be moved to three other federal facilities, his trail growing fainter each time, until somewhere around two weeks or three or a month at most, a black van would pull into the compound, and a man now known simply as Number Twelve would step out, blinking at the Colorado sunshine.

The last items in the envelope were Carter's death certificate and a medical examiner's report, both dated March 23. On the morning of the twenty-third, three days hence, Anthony Lloyd Carter would die in his cell from a cerebral aneurysm.

Wolgast returned the documents to the envelope and put it in his pocket, a chill snaking through him. How easy it was to make a human being disappear, just like that. 'Thank you, Warden. We appreciate your cooperation.'

The warden looked at each of them in turn, his jaw set. 'I'm also instructed to say I never heard of you guys.'

Wolgast did his best to smile. 'Is there a problem with that?'

'I'm supposing if there were, one of those ME reports would show up with my name on it. I've got *kids,* Agent.' He picked up his phone and punched a number. 'Have two COs bring Anthony Carter to the cages, then come to my office.' He hung up and looked at Wolgast. 'If you don't mind, I'd like you to wait outside. I look at you any longer, I'm going to have a hard time forgetting about all this. Good day, gentlemen.'

Ten minutes later, a pair of guards stepped into the outer office. The older one had the benevolent, overfed look of a shopping mall Santa, but the other guard, who couldn't have been more than twenty, was wearing a snarl on his face that Wolgast didn't like. There was always one guard who liked the job for the wrong reasons, and this was the one.

'You the guys looking for Carter?'

Wolgast nodded and showed his credentials. 'That's right. Special Agents Wolgast and Doyle.'

'Don't matter who you are,' the heavy one said. 'The warden says to take you, we'll take you.'

They led Wolgast and Doyle down to the visiting area. Carter was sitting on the other side of the glass, the phone wedged between his ear and shoulder. He was small, just as Doyle had said, and his jumpsuit fit him loosely, like the clothing on a Ken doll. There were many ways to look condemned, Wolgast had learned, and Carter's look wasn't scared or angry but simply resigned, like the world had been taking slow bites of him his whole life.

Wolgast gestured at the shackles, turning toward the two COs. 'Take those off, please.'

The older one shook his head. 'That's standard.'

'I don't care what it is. Take them off.' Wolgast lifted the phone from its cradle on the wall. 'Anthony Carter? I'm Special Agent Wolgast. This is Special Agent Doyle. We're from the FBI. These men are going to come around and remove those shackles. I asked them to do that. You'll co-operate with them, won't you?'

Carter gave a tight nod. His voice on the other end of the phone was quiet. 'Yessir.'

'Anything else you need to make you comfortable?'

Carter looked at him quizzically. How long since anybody had asked him a question like that?

'I's all right,' he said.

Wolgast turned to face the guards. 'Well? How about it? Am I talking to myself here, or am I going to have to call the warden?'

A moment passed as the guards looked at each other, deciding what to do. Then the one named Dennis stepped from the room and reappeared a moment later on the far side of the glass. Wolgast stood and watched, keeping his eyes fixed on the guard while he removed the shackles.

'That it?' said the heavy guard.

'That's it. We'll want to be left alone for a while. We'll tell the OD when we're done.'

'Suit yourself,' the guard said and walked out, closing the door behind him.

There was only one chair in the room, a folding metal seat, like something from a high school auditorium. Wolgast took it and positioned himself squarely to the glass, while Doyle remained standing behind him. The talking was Wolgast's to do. He picked up the phone again.

'Better?'

Carter hesitated a moment, appraising him, then nodded. 'Yessir. Thank you. Pincher always does 'em too tight.'

Pincher. Wolgast made a mental note of this. 'You hungry? They give you breakfast in there?'

'Pancakes.' Carter shrugged. 'That was five hours ago, though.'

Wolgast swiveled to look at Doyle, raising his eyebrows.

Doyle nodded and left the room. For a few minutes, Wolgast just waited. Despite the large No Smoking sign, the edge of the counter was rutted with brown burn marks.

'You said you from the FBI?'

'That's right, Anthony.'

A trace of a smile flicked across Carter's face. 'Like on that show?'

Wolgast didn't know what Carter was talking about, but that was fine; it would give Carter something to explain.

'What show's that, Anthony?'

'The one with the woman. The one with the aliens.'

Wolgast thought a moment, then remembered. Of course: *The X-Files*. It had been off the air for what, twenty years? Carter had probably seen it as a kid, in reruns. Wolgast couldn't remember very much about it, just the idea of it – alien abductions, some kind of conspiracy to hush the thing up. That was Carter's impression of the FBI.

'I liked that show too. You getting on in here all right?'

Carter squared his shoulders. 'You came here to ask me that?'

'You're a smart guy, Anthony. No, that's not the reason.'

'What the reason then?'

Wolgast leaned closer to the glass; he found Carter's eyes and held them with his own.

'I know about this place, Anthony. Terrell Unit. I know what goes on in here. I'm just making sure you're being treated properly.'

Carter eyed him skeptically. 'Does tolerable, I guess.'

'The guards okay with you?'

'Pincher's tight with the cuffs, but he's all right most of the time.' Carter lifted his bony shoulders in a shrug. 'Dennis ain't no friend of mine. Some of the others, too.'

The door opened behind Carter and Doyle entered, bearing a yellow tray from the commissary. He placed the tray on the counter in front of Carter: a cheeseburger and fries, gleaming with grease, resting on waxed paper in a little plastic basket. Beside it sat a carton of chocolate milk.

'Go on, Anthony,' Wolgast said, and gestured toward the tray. 'We can talk when you're done.'

Carter placed the receiver on the counter and lifted the cheeseburger to his mouth. Three bites and the thing was half gone. Carter wiped his mouth with the back of his hand and got to work on the fries while Wolgast watched. Carter's concentration was total. It was like watching a dog eat, Wolgast thought.

Doyle had returned to Wolgast's side of the glass. 'Damn,' he said quietly, 'that guy sure was hungry.'

'They got anything for dessert down there?'

'Bunch of dried-up looking pies. Some éclairs looked like dog turds.'

Wolgast thought a moment. 'On second thought, skip dessert. Get him a glass of iced tea. Make it nice, too, if you can. Dress it up a little.'

Doyle frowned. 'He's got the milk. I don't know if they even *have* iced tea down there. It's like a barnyard.'

'This is Texas, Phil.' Wolgast suppressed the impatience in his voice. 'Trust me, they have tea. Just go find it.'

Doyle shrugged and left again. When Carter had finished his meal, he licked the salt off his fingers, one by one, and sighed deeply. When he picked up the receiver, Wolgast did the same.

'How's that, Anthony? Feeling better?'

Through the receiver, Wolgast could hear the watery heaviness of Carter's breathing; his eyes were slack and glazed with pleasure. All those calories, all those protein molecules, all those complex carbohydrates hitting his system like a hammer. Wolgast might just as well have given him a fifth of whiskey.

'Yessir. Thank you.'

'A man's got to eat. A man can't live on pancakes.'

A silent moment passed. Carter licked his lips with a slow tongue. His voice, when he spoke, was almost a whisper. 'What you want from me?'

'You've got it backward, Anthony,' Wolgast said, nodding. 'It's me who's here to find out what *I* can do for *you*.'

Carter dropped his eyes to the counter, the grease-stained wreckage of his meal. 'He sent you, didn't he?'

'Who's that, Anthony?'

'Woman's husband.' Carter frowned at the memory. 'Mr Wood. He come here once. Told me he found Jesus.'

Wolgast remembered what Doyle had told him in the car. Two years ago, and it was still on Carter's mind.

'No, he didn't send me, Anthony. You have my word.'

'Told him I was sorry,' Carter insisted, his voice cracking. 'Told everybody. Ain't gonna say it no more.'

'No one's saying you have to, Anthony. I know you're sorry. That's why I came all this way to see you.'

'All what way?'

'A long way, Anthony.' Wolgast nodded slowly. 'A very, very long way.'

Wolgast paused, searching Carter's face. There was something about him, different from the others. He felt the moment opening, like a door.

'Anthony, what would you say if I told you I could get you out of this place?'

Behind the glass, Carter eyed him cautiously. 'How you mean?'

'Just like I said. Right now. Today. You could leave Terrell and never come back.'

Carter's eyes floated with incomprehension; the idea was too much to process. 'I'd say now I know you's fooling with me.'

'No lie, Anthony. That's why we came all this way. You may not know it, but you're a special man. You could say you're one of a kind.'

'You talk about me leaving here?' Carter frowned bitterly. 'Ain't make no sense. Not after all this time. Ain't got no appeal. Lawyer said so in a letter.'

'Not an appeal, Anthony. Better than that. Just you, getting out of here. How does that sound to you?'

'It *sound* great.' Carter sat back and crossed his arms over his chest with a defiant laugh. 'It *sound* too good to be true. This *Terrell*.'

It always amazed Wolgast how much accepting the idea of commutation resembled the five stages of grief. Right now, Carter was in denial. The idea was just too much to take in.

'I know where you are. I know this place. It's the death house, Anthony. It's not the place where you belong. That's why I'm here. And not for just anyone. Not these other men. For you, Anthony.'

Carter's posture relaxed. 'I ain't nobody special. I knows that.'

'But you are. You may not know it, but you are. You see, I need a favor from you, Anthony. This deal's a two-way street. I can get you out of here, but there's something I need for you to do for me in return.'

'A favor?'

'The people I work for, Anthony, they saw what was going to happen to you in here. They know what's going to happen in June, and they don't think it's right. They don't think it's right the way you've been treated, that your lawyer has up and left you here like this. And they realized they could do something about it, and that they had a job they needed you to do instead.'

Carter frowned in confusion. 'Cuttin', you mean? Like that lady's lawn?'

Jesus, Wolgast thought. He actually thought he wanted him to cut the grass. 'No, Anthony. Nothing like that. Something much more important.' Wolgast lowered his voice again. 'You see, that's the thing. What I need you to do is so important, I can't tell you what it is. Because I don't even know myself.'

'How you know it's so important you don't know what it is?'

'You're a smart man, Anthony, and you're right to ask that. But you're going to have to trust me. I can get you out of here, right now. All you have to do is say you want to.'

63

That was when Wolgast pulled the warden's envelope from his pocket and opened it. He always felt like a magician at this moment, lifting his hat to show a rabbit. With his free hand, he flattened the document against the glass for Carter to see.

'Do you know what this is? This is a writ of commutation, Anthony, signed by Governor Jenna Bush. It's dated today, right there at the bottom. You know what that means, a commutation?'

Carter was squinting at the paper. 'I don't go to the needle?'

'That's right, Anthony. Not in June, not ever.'

Wolgast returned the paper to his jacket pocket. Now it was bait, something to want. The other document, the one Carter would have to sign – which he *would* sign, Wolgast felt certain, when all the hemming and hawing was over; the one in which Anthony Lloyd Carter, Texas inmate 999642, handed one hundred percent of his earthly person, past, present, and future, to Project NOAH – was tucked against it. By the time this second piece of paper saw daylight, the whole point was not to read it.

Carter gave a slow nod. 'Always liked her. Liked her when she was first lady.'

Wolgast let the error pass. 'She's just one of the people I work for, Anthony. There are others. You might recognize some of the names if I told you, but I can't. And they asked me to come and see you, and tell you how much they need you.'

'So I do this thing for you, and you get me out? But you can't tell me what it is?'

'That's pretty much the deal, Anthony. Say no, and I'll move on. Say yes, and you can leave Terrell tonight. It's that simple.'

The door into the cage opened once more; Doyle stepped through, holding the tea. He'd done as Wolgast had asked, balancing the glass on a saucer with a long spoon beside it and a wedge of lemon and packets of sugar. He placed it all on the counter in front of Carter. Carter looked at the glass, his face gone slack. That was when Wolgast thought it. Anthony Carter wasn't guilty, at least not in the way the court had spun it. With the others, it was always clear right off what Wolgast was dealing with, that the story was the story. But not in this case. Something had happened that day in the yard; the woman had died. But there was more to it, maybe a lot more. Looking at Carter, this was the space into which Wolgast felt his mind moving, like a dark room with no windows and one locked door. This, he knew, was the place where he would find Anthony Carter – he'd find him in the dark – and when he did, Carter would show him the key that would open the door.

He spoke with his eyes locked on the glass. 'I jes' want . . .' he began.

Wolgast waited for him to finish. When he didn't, Wolgast spoke again. 'What do you want, Anthony? Tell me.'

Carter lifted his free hand to the side of the glass and brushed the tips of his fingers against it. The glass was cool, and sweating with moisture; Carter drew his hand away and rubbed the beads of water between his thumb and fingers, slowly, his eyes focused on this gesture with complete attention. So intense was his concentration that Wolgast could feel the man's whole mind opening up to it, taking it in. It was as if the sensation of cool water on his fingertips was the key to every mystery of his life. He raised his eyes to Wolgast's.

'I need the time . . . to figure it,' he said softly. 'The thing that happened. With the lady.'

And all the days of Noah were nine hundred and fifty years . . .

'I can give you that time, Anthony,' Wolgast said. 'All the time in the world. An ocean of time.'

Another moment passed. Then Carter nodded.

'What I got to do?'

Wolgast and Doyle got to George Bush Intercontinental a little after seven; the traffic was murderous, but they still arrived with ninety minutes to spare. They dumped the rental and rode the shuttle to the Continental terminal, showed their credentials to bypass security, and made their way through the crowds to the gate at the far end of the concourse.

Doyle excused himself to find something to eat; Wolgast wasn't hungry, though he knew he'd probably regret this decision later on, especially if their flight got hung up. He checked his handheld. Still nothing from Sykes. He was glad. All he wanted to do was get the hell out of Texas. Just a few other passengers were waiting at the gate; a couple of families, some students plugged into Blu-rays or iPods, a handful of men in suits talking on cell phones or tapping on laptops. Wolgast checked his watch: seven twenty-five. By now, he thought, Anthony Carter would be in the back of a van well on his way to El Reno, leaving in his wake a flurry of shredded records and a fading memory that he had ever existed at all. By the end of the day, even his federal ID number would be purged; the man named Anthony Carter would be nothing but a rumor, a vague disturbance no bigger than a ripple on the surface of the world.

Wolgast leaned back in his chair and realized how exhausted he was. It always came upon him like this, like the sudden unclenching of a fist. These trips left him physically and emotionally hollowed out, and with a nagging conscience he always had to apply some effort to squash. He was just too damn good at this, too good at finding the one gesture, the one right thing to say. A man sat in a concrete box long enough, thinking about his own death, and he boiled down to milky dust like water in a teapot forgotten on a stove; to understand him, you had to figure out what that dust was made of, what was left of him after the rest of his life, past and future, had turned to vapor. Usually it was something simple – anger or sadness or shame, or simply the need for forgiveness. A few wanted nothing at all; all that remained was a dumb animal rage at the world and all its systems. Anthony was different: it had taken Wolgast a while to figure this out. Anthony was like a human question mark, a living, breathing expression of pure puzzlement. He actually didn't know *why* he was in Terrell. Not that he didn't understand his sentence; that was clear, and he had accepted it – as nearly all of them did, because they had to. All you had to do was read the last words of condemned men to know that. 'Tell everyone I love them. I'm sorry. Okay, Warden, let's do this.' Always words to that effect, and chilling to read, as Wolgast had done by the pageful. But some piece of the puzzle was still missing for Anthony Carter. Wolgast had seen it when Carter touched the side of the glass – before then, even, when he'd asked about Rachel Wood's husband and said he was sorry without saying it. Whether Carter couldn't remember what had happened that day in the Woods' yard or couldn't make his actions add up to the man he thought he was, Wolgast couldn't be certain. Either way, Anthony Carter needed to find this piece of himself before he died.

From his seat, Wolgast had a good view of the airfield through the terminal windows; the sun was going down, its last rays angling sharply off the fuselages of parked aircraft. The flight home always did him good; a few hours in the air, chasing the sunset, and he'd feel like himself again. He never drank or read or slept, just sat perfectly still, breathing the plane's bottled air and fixing his eyes out the window as the ground below him slipped into darkness. Once, on a flight back from Tallahassee, Wolgast's plane had flown around a storm front so huge it looked like an airborne mountain range, its roiling interior lit like a crèche with jags of lightning. A night in September: they were somewhere over Oklahoma, he thought, or Kansas, someplace flat and empty. It could have been farther west. The cabin was dark; nearly everyone on the plane was sleeping, including Doyle, seated beside him with a pillow tucked against his stubbled cheek. For twenty full minutes the plane had ridden the edge of the storm without so much as a jostle. In all his life, Wolgast had never seen anything like it, had never felt

67

himself so completely in the presence of nature's immensity, its planet-sized power. The air inside the storm was a cataclysm of pure atmospheric voltage, yet here he was, sealed in silence, hurtling along with nothing but thirty thousand feet of empty air below him, watching it all as if it were a movie on a screen, a movie without sound. He waited for the pilot's drawling voice to crackle over the intercom and say something about the weather, to let the other passengers in on the show, but this never happened, and when they landed in Denver, forty minutes late, Wolgast never mentioned it, not even to Doyle.

He thought, now, that he'd like to call Lila and tell her about it. The feeling was so strong, so clear in his mind, that it took a moment for him to realize how crazy this was, that it was just the time machine talking. The time machine: that's the name the counselor had given it. She was a friend of Lila's from the hospital whom they had visited just a couple of times, a woman in her thirties with long hair, prematurely gray, and large eyes, permanently damp with sympathy. She liked to take her shoes off at the start of each visit and sit with her legs folded under her, like a camp counselor about to lead them in song, and she spoke so quietly that Wolgast had to lean forward from the sofa to hear her. From time to time, she explained in her tiny voice, their minds would play tricks on them. It wasn't a warning, the way she said it; she was simply stating a fact. He and Lila might do something or see something and have a strong feeling from the past. They might, for instance, find themselves standing in the checkout line of the grocery with a packet of diapers in their cart, or tiptoeing past Eva's room, as if she were asleep. Those would be the hardest moments, the woman explained, because they'd have to relive their loss all over again; but as the months passed, she assured them, this would happen less and less.

The thing was, these moments weren't hard for Wolgast. They still happened to him every now and then, even three years after the fact, and when they did, he didn't mind at all:

far from it. They were unexpected presents his mind could give him. But it was different for Lila, he knew.

'Agent Wolgast?'

He turned in his chair. The simple gray suit, the inexpensive but comfortable oxford shoes, the blandly forgettable tie: Wolgast might have been looking in a mirror. But the face was new to him.

He rose and reached into his pocket to show his ID. 'That's me.'

'Special Agent Williams, Houston field office.' They shook. 'I'm afraid you won't be taking this flight after all. I've got a car outside for you.'

'Is there a message?'

Williams drew an envelope from his pocket. 'I think this is probably what you're looking for.'

Wolgast accepted the envelope. Inside was a fax. He sat and read, then read it again. He was still reading when Doyle returned, sipping from a straw and carrying a bag from Taco Bell.

Wolgast lifted his gaze to Williams. 'Give us a second, will you?'

Williams moved off down the concourse.

'What is it?' Doyle said quietly. 'What's wrong?'

Wolgast shook his head. He passed the fax to Doyle.

'Sweet Jesus, Phil. It's a civilian.'

FOUR

Sister Lacey Antoinette Kudoto didn't know what God wanted. But she knew He wanted something.

As long as she could remember, the world had spoken to her like this, in whispers and murmurs: in the rustling of the palm fronds moving in the ocean wind above the village where she was raised; in the sound of cool water running over rocks in the stream behind her house; even in the busy sounds men made, in the engines and machines and voices of the human world. She was just a little girl, not more than six or seven, when she'd asked Sister Margaret, who ran the convent school in Port Loko, what she was hearing, and Sister laughed. *Lacey Antoinette*, she said. *How you surprise me. Don't you know?* She lowered her voice, putting her face close to Lacey's. *That's nothing less than the voice of God.*

But she did know; she understood, as soon as Sister said it, that she'd always known. She never told anyone else about the voice, the way Sister had spoken to her, as if it was something only the two of them knew, told her that what she heard in the wind and leaves, in the very thread of existence itself, was a private thing between them. There were times, sometimes for weeks or even a month, when the feeling receded and the world became an ordinary place again, made of ordinary things. She believed that this was how the world felt to most people, even those closest to her, her parents and sisters and friends at school; they lived their whole lives in a prison of drab silence, a world without a voice. Knowing this made her so sad that sometimes she couldn't stop crying for days at a time, and her parents would take her to the doctor, a Frenchman with long sideburns who sucked on candies that smelled like camphor, who poked and peeked and touched her up and down with the ice-cold disk of his stethoscope but never found anything wrong. *How terrible*, she thought, *how terrible to live like this, all alone forever.* But then one day she'd be walking to school through the cocoa fields, or eating dinner with her sisters, or doing nothing at all, just looking at a stone on the ground or lying awake in bed, and she'd hear it again: the voice that wasn't a voice exactly, that came from inside her and also from everywhere around, a hushed whisper that seemed not made of sound but light itself, that moved through as gently as a breeze on water. By the time she was eighteen and entered the Sisters, she knew what it was, that it was calling her name.

70

Lacey, the world said to her. *Lacey. Listen.*

She heard it now, all these years later and an ocean away, sitting in the kitchen of the Convent of the Sisters of Mercy in Memphis, Tennessee.

She'd found the note in the girl's backpack not long after her mother had left. Something about the circumstances had made Lacey uneasy, and looking at the girl, she realized what it was: the woman had never told her the girl's name. The girl was obviously her daughter – the same dark hair, the same pale skin and long lashes that curled upward at the ends, as if lifted by a tiny breeze. She was pretty, but her hair needed combing – there were mats in it thick as a dog's – and she had kept her jacket on the table, as if she were used to leaving places in a hurry. She seemed healthy, if a little thin. Her pants were too short and stiff with dirt. When the little girl had finished her snack, every bite, Lacey took the chair beside her. She asked her if she had anything in the bag she wanted to play with, or a book they could read together, but the little girl, who hadn't spoken a word, just nodded and passed it from her lap. Lacey examined the bag, pink with some kind of cartoon characters glued on – their huge black eyes reminded her of the girl's – and remembered what the woman had told her, that she was taking her daughter to school.

She unzipped the bag and inside found the stuffed rabbit, and the pairs of rolled-up underpants and socks and a toothbrush in a case, and a box of strawberry cereal bars, half empty. There was nothing else in the bag, but then she noticed the little zippered pouch on the outside. It was too late for school, Lacey realized; the girl had no lunch, no books. She held her breath and unzipped the pouch. There she found the piece of notebook paper, folded up.

I'm sorry. Her name is Amy. She's six years old.

Lacey looked at it for a long time. Not the words themselves, which were plain enough in their meaning. What she looked at was the space around the words, a whole page of nothing at all. Three tiny sentences were all this girl had in the world to explain who she was, just three sentences and the few little things in the bag. It was nearly the saddest thing Lacey Antoinette Kudoto had ever seen in her life, so sad she couldn't even cry.

There was no point in going after the woman. She'd be long gone by now. And what would Lacey do if she found her? What could she say? *I think you forgot something. I think you've made some mistake.* But there was no mistake. The woman, Lacey understood, had done exactly what she'd set out to do.

She folded the note and put it in the deep pocket of her skirt. 'Amy,' she said, and as Sister Margaret had done all those years ago in the yard at the school in Port Loko, she positioned her face close to the girl's. She smiled. 'Is that your name, Amy? That's a beautiful name.'

The girl looked around the room, quickly, almost furtively. 'Can I have Peter?'

Lacey thought a moment. A brother? The little girl's father? 'Of course,' she said. 'Who is Peter, Amy?'

'He's in the bag,' the girl stated.

Lacey was relieved – the girl's first request of her was something simple that she could easily provide. She removed the rabbit from the bag. It was velveteen plush, worn smooth in shiny patches, a little boy rabbit with beady black eyes and ears stiffened by wire. Lacey passed it to Amy, who placed it roughly on her lap.

'Amy,' she began again, 'where did your mother go?'

'I don't know,' she said.

'How about Peter?' Lacey asked. 'Does Peter know? Could Peter tell me?'

'He doesn't know anything,' Amy said. 'He's stuffed.' The little girl frowned sharply. 'I want to go back to the motel.'

'Tell me,' Lacey said. 'Where is the motel, Amy?'

'I'm not supposed to say.'

'Is it a secret?'

The girl nodded, her eyes fixed on the surface of the table.

A secret so deep she couldn't even say it was a secret, Lacey thought.

'I can't take you there if I don't know where it is, Amy. Is that what you want? To go to the motel?'

'It's on the busy road,' the girl explained, tugging at her sleeve.

'You live there with your mother?'

Amy said nothing. She had a way of neither looking nor speaking, of being alone with herself even in the presence of another person, that Lacey had never encountered. There was something even a little frightening about it. When the girl did this, it was as if she, Lacey, were the one who had vanished.

'I have an idea,' Lacey declared. 'Would you like to play a game, Amy?'

The girl eyed her skeptically. 'What kind?'

'I call it secrets. It's easy to play. I tell you a secret, and then you tell me one. Do you see? A *trade,* my secret for your secret. How does that sound?'

The girl shrugged. 'Okay.'

'All right then. I'll start. Here is my secret. One time, when I was very young, like you, I ran away from home. This was in Sierra Leone, where I come from. I was very cross at my mother, because she wouldn't let me go to see a carnival without doing my lessons first. I was very excited about this carnival, because I had heard they did tricks with horses, and I was crazy about horses. I bet you like horses too, don't you, Amy?'

The girl nodded. 'I guess.'

'Every girl likes horses. But me – I was in love with them! To show her how mad I was, I refused to do my lessons, and she sent me to my room for the night. Oh, I was so angry! I stamped around the room like a crazy person. Then I thought, If I run away, she'll be sorry she has treated me this way. She'll let me do what I like from now on. I was very foolish, but that is what I believed. So that night, after my parents and my sisters were asleep, I left the house. I didn't

73

know where to go, so I hid in the fields behind our yard. It was cold and very dark. I wanted to stay there all night, and then in the morning I would be able to hear my mother crying my name when she woke up and found I wasn't there. But I couldn't do this. I stayed in the field a little while, but eventually I was too cold and frightened. I went back home and got into bed, and nobody ever knew I was gone.' She looked at the girl, who was watching her closely, and did her best to smile. 'There – I've never told anyone that story, not until now. You are the first person I've told in my life. What do you think of that?'

The girl was watching Lacey attentively now. 'You just . . . went home?'

Lacey nodded. 'You see, I wasn't so angry anymore. And in the morning, it all seemed like a dream I'd had. I wasn't even sure it had actually happened, though now, many years later, I know that it did.' She patted Amy's hand encouragingly. 'Now it is your turn. Do you have a secret to tell me, Amy?'

The girl lowered her face and said nothing.

'Even a little one?'

'I don't think she's coming back,' said Amy.

The police officers who took the call, a man and a woman, got nowhere either. The female officer, a heavyset white woman with a cropped haircut like a man's, spoke to the girl in the kitchen, while the other officer, a handsome black man with a smooth, narrow face, took a description of the mother from Lacey. Did she seem nervous? he asked her. Was she drunk, on drugs? What was she wearing? Did Lacey see the car? On and on he went, but Lacey could tell he was asking only because he had to; he didn't think the girl's mother would turn up, either. He recorded her answers with a tiny pencil on a pad of paper that, as soon as she'd finished, he returned to the breast pocket of his uniform. In the kitchen, a flash of light: the woman officer had taken Amy's picture.

'Do you want to call Child Protection, or should we do it?'

the policeman asked Lacey. 'Because, seeing as how you are who you are, it might make sense if we waited. No use putting her into the system right away, especially over the weekend, if you don't mind keeping her here. We can put out a description of the woman and see if we get anywhere. We'll also put the girl in the missing child database. The mother might come back, too, though if she does, you should keep the girl here and call us.'

It was a little past noon; the other sisters were all due back at one o'clock from the Community Pantry, where they'd passed the morning stocking shelves and dispensing boxes of canned goods and cereal, spaghetti sauce, and diapers. They did this every Tuesday and Friday. But Lacey had been nursing a head cold all week – even after three years in Memphis, she still hadn't adapted to the damp winters – and Sister Arnette had told Lacey to stay home, no use making herself sicker. It was like Sister Arnette to make a decision like this, even though Lacey had woken up feeling perfectly well.

Looking at the officer, she made a quick decision. 'I will do it,' she said.

Which was how, when the sisters returned, it happened that Lacey failed to tell them the truth about the girl. *This is Amy*, she told them, as they were taking off their coats and scarves in the hall. *Her mother is a friend, and she was called away to visit a sick relative, and Amy will be spending the weekend with us.* It surprised her, how easily the lie came; she had no practice with deceit, and yet the words had assembled themselves quickly in her mind and found their way to her lips without effort. As she spoke she glanced at Amy, wondering if she would expose her, and she saw a flicker of agreement in the girl's eyes. She was, Lacey understood then, a girl used to keeping secrets.

'Sister,' said Sister Arnette, speaking with her old woman's air of perpetual disapproval, 'I'm glad to see that you are offering our help to this girl and her mother. But it is also true that this is something you should have asked me about.'

'I'm very sorry,' Lacey said. 'It was an emergency. It will only be until Monday.'

Sister Arnette looked appraisingly at Lacey, then down at Amy, who was standing with her back pressed to the pleats of Lacey's skirt. While she did this, Sister Arnette removed her gloves, one finger at a time. Cold air from outside still swirled in the close space of the hallway.

'This is a convent, not an orphanage. This isn't a place for children.'

'I understand, Sister. And I am very sorry. It simply couldn't be helped.'

Another moment passed. *Dear Lord*, Lacey thought, *help me to like this person more than I do, Sister Arnette, who is imperious and thinks much of herself, but is Your servant, as I am.*

'All right,' Sister Arnette said at last, and sighed irritably. 'Until Monday. She can use the spare room.'

It was then that Sister Lacey wondered why: why she had lied, and why the lie had come so easily, as if it weren't a lie in the larger sense of things-true and things-untrue. Her story was also full of holes. What would happen if the police returned, or telephoned, and Sister Arnette discovered what she'd done? What would happen Monday, when she had to call the county? And yet she felt no fear about these matters. The girl was a mystery, sent to them by God – and not even to *them*, but to *her*. To Lacey. It was her job to figure out what the answer to this mystery was, and by lying to Sister Arnette – not necessarily a lie, she told herself; who was to say the mother hadn't gone to visit a sick relative after all? – she had given herself the time required to unravel it. So perhaps that was why the lie had come so easily; the Holy Spirit had spoken through her, inspired her with the flame of a different, deeper sort of truth, and what it had said was that the girl was in trouble and needed Lacey to help her.

The other sisters were pleased; they never had visitors, or at least very rarely, and these were always religious – priests, other sisters. But a little girl: this was something new. The minute Sister Arnette had climbed the stairs to her room, they all began to talk. How did Sister Lacey know the girl's mother? How old was Amy? What did she like to do? To eat? To watch? To wear? They were so excited they scarcely noticed how seldom Amy spoke, that in fact she said nothing at all; Lacey did the talking. For dinner, Amy would like hamburgers and hot dogs – these were her favorites – with potato chips, and chocolate-chip ice cream. She enjoyed coloring and crafts, and liked to watch movies with princesses in them, and rabbits if they had anything like that at the store. She would need clothes; her mother, in her haste, had forgotten the little girl's suitcase, she was so frazzled by her own mission of mercy (to Arkansas, near Little Rock; the little girl's grandmother was diabetic, with heart trouble), and when she'd said she would go home for it, Lacey had insisted no, she could easily manage. The lies poured forth so gracefully upon ears so willing to believe that, within the hour, all the sisters seemed to have a slightly different version of the same story. Sister Louisa and Sister Claire took the van to Piggly Wiggly for the hamburgers and hot dogs and chips, then to Walmart, for clothing and movies and toys; in the kitchen, Sister Tracy set about planning the evening meal, announcing that not only could they expect the promised hamburgers and hot dogs and ice cream, but to go with the ice cream, a three-tier chocolate cake. (They always looked forward to Fridays, Sister Tracy's night to cook. Her parents owned a restaurant in Chicago; before she'd entered the Sisters, she had trained at Cordon Bleu.) Even Sister Arnette seemed to catch the spirit, sitting with Amy and the other sisters in the den to watch *The Princess Bride* while dinner was prepared.

Through it all, Sister Lacey set her mind on God. When the movie, which everyone agreed was wonderful, ended, and Sister Louise and Sister Claire took Amy to the kitchen to show her some of the toys they'd bought at Walmart – coloring books, crayons and paste and construction paper, a Barbie Pet Shop Kit that had taken Sister Louise fifteen minutes to free from the prison of its plastic package with all of its little parts, the combs and brushes for the dogs and the tiny dishes and the rest – Lacey climbed the stairs. In the silence of her room she prayed on this mystery, the mystery of Amy, listening for the voice that would sweep through her, filling her with the knowledge of His will; but as she lifted her mind to God, all that came to her was the feeling of a question with no certain answer. This, she knew, was another way God could speak to a person. His will was elusive most of the time, and although this was frustrating, and it would be nice if, from time to time, He chose to make His intentions more explicit, this wasn't how things worked. Though most of the sisters prayed in the little chapel behind the kitchen, and Lacey did this too, she reserved her most earnest, searching prayers for this time alone in her room, not even kneeling but sitting at her desk or on the corner of her narrow bed. She'd put her hands in her lap, close her eyes, and send her mind out as far as she could – since childhood, she had imagined it as a kite on a string, lifting higher as she let the line out – and wait to see what happened. Now, sitting on the bed, she sent the kite as high as she dared, the imaginary ball of string growing smaller in her hand, the kite itself just a speck of color far above her head, but all she felt was the wind of heaven pushing upon it, a force of great power against a thing so small.

After dinner, the sisters returned to the living room to watch a program on TV, a hospital show they had been following all year, and Sister Lacey took Amy upstairs to prepare for bed. It was eight o'clock; usually all the sisters were in bed by nine, to rise at five for morning devotions, and it seemed to Lacey that these were the kind of hours a girl of Amy's age could also keep. She gave Amy a bath, scrubbing her hair with raspberry shampoo and working in a dollop of conditioner for the tangles, then combing it all out so it was straight and glossy, its rich black hue deepening with each pull of the comb, before taking her old clothing downstairs to the laundry. By the time she returned Amy had put on the pajamas Sister Claire had bought that afternoon at Walmart.

They were pink, with a pattern of stars and moons with smiling faces, and made of a material that rustled and shone like silk. When Lacey entered the room, she saw that Amy was looking at the sleeves with a bewildered expression; they were too long, flopping clownishly over her hands and feet. Lacey rolled them up; while she watched, Amy brushed her teeth and put her toothbrush back in its case and then turned from the mirror to face her.

'Do I sleep in here?'

So many hours had passed since she'd heard the girl's voice that Lacey wasn't sure she'd heard the question correctly. She searched the little girl's face. The question, strange as it was, made sense to her.

'Why would you sleep in the bathroom, Amy?'

She looked at the floor. 'Mama says I have to be quiet.'

Lacey didn't know what to make of this. 'No, of course not. You'll sleep in your room. It's right next to mine, I'll show you.'

The room was clean and spare, bare-walled with just a bed and a bureau and a small writing table, not even a rug on the floor to warm it, and Lacey wished she had something to make it nice for a little girl. She thought that, tomorrow, she would ask Sister Arnette if she could buy a small rug to put by the bed, so Amy's feet wouldn't have to touch the cold floorboards in the mornings. She tucked Amy under the blankets and sat on the edge of the mattress. Through the floor she could hear the faint rumble of the television downstairs, and the tick of pipes expanding behind the walls, and outside, the wind fingering the March leaves of the oaks and maples and the soft hum of evening traffic on Poplar Avenue. The zoo was two blocks behind the convent, at the far end of the park; on summer nights when the windows were open, they could sometimes hear the colobus monkeys, whooping and screeching in their cages. This was a strange and wonderful thing for Lacey to hear, so many thousands of miles from home, but when she had visited the zoo she'd discovered it was an awful place, like a jail; the pens were small, the cats were kept in barren cages behind walls of Plexiglas, the elephants and giraffes wore chains on their legs. All the animals looked depressed. Most could barely be bothered to move at all, and the people who came to see them were loud and boorish and let their children throw popcorn through the bars to make the animals notice them. It was more than Lacey could bear, and she had left quickly, close to tears. It broke her heart to see God's creatures treated so cruelly, with such coldhearted indifference, for no purpose.

But now, sitting on the edge of the bed, she thought that it might be something Amy would like. Perhaps she'd never been to a zoo at all. As long as there was nothing Lacey could do to ease the animals' suffering, it didn't seem sinful, a second wrong piled on top of the first, to bring a little girl who had so little happiness in her life to see them. She would ask Sister Arnette in the morning about this, when she asked about the rug.

'There now,' she said, and adjusted Amy's blanket. The girl was lying very still, almost as if she were afraid to move. 'All safe and sound. And I'm just next door if you need anything. Tomorrow we'll do something fun, you'll see. The two of us.'

'Can you leave the light on?'

Lacey told her she would. Then she leaned over and kissed her on the forehead. The air around her smelled like jam, from the shampoo.

'I like your sisters,' Amy said.

Lacey felt herself smiling; with everything that had happened, she had somehow failed to anticipate this misunderstanding. 'Yes. Well. It's difficult to explain. You see, we're not *actual* sisters, not how you mean. We do not have the same parents. But we are sisters nonetheless.'

'But how can you be?'

'Oh, there are other ways to be sisters. We are sisters in spirit. We are sisters in the eyes of God.' She jostled Amy's hand. 'Even Sister Arnette.'

Amy frowned. 'She's cranky.'

'So she is. But it's just her way. And she's glad you're here.

80

Everyone is. I don't think we even realized how much we were missing, until you came here.' She touched Amy's hand again and rose. 'Now, enough talk. You need your sleep.'

'I promise I'll be quiet.'

At the doorway, Lacey stopped. 'You do not have to be,' she said.

That night Lacey dreamed; in the dream she was a little girl again, in the fields behind her house. She was huddled under a low palm bush, its long fronds like a tent around her, licking the skin of her arms and face, and her sisters were there, too, though not exactly; her sisters were running away. Behind them she heard men or, rather, she felt them, their dark presences; she heard the pop of gunfire and her mother's voice, yelling, screaming, telling them, Run away, children, run as fast as you can, though she, Lacey, was frozen in place with fear; she seemed to have turned into some new substance, a kind of living wood, and couldn't move a muscle. She heard more popping, and with the pops came flashes of light, severing the darkness like a blade. At those instants she could see everything around her: her house and the fields and the men moving through them, men who sounded like soldiers but weren't dressed like soldiers, who swept the ground before them with the barrels of their rifles. The world appeared to her this way, in a series of still pictures; she was afraid but could not look away. Her legs and feet were wet, not cold but curiously warm; she realized she had urinated on herself, though she did not remember doing this. In her nose and mouth she tasted bitter smoke, and sweat, and something else, which she knew but could not name. It was the taste of blood.

Then she felt it: someone was near. It was one of the men. She could hear the rattle of his breaths in his chest, his searching footsteps; she could smell the fear and anger wicking off his body like a glowing vapor. *Don't move, Lacey*, said the voice, fierce and burning. *Don't move.* She closed her eyes, not even daring to breathe; her heart was beating so hard inside her, it was as if that's all she was now, a beating heart. His shadow fell upon her, passing over her face and body like a great black wing. When she opened her eyes again he was gone; the fields were empty, and she was alone.

She awoke with a start, terror coursing through her. But even as she realized where she was, she felt the dream breaking up inside her; it turned a corner and darted out of sight. The touch of leaves on her skin. A voice, whispering. A smell, like blood. But now even that was gone.

Then she felt it. Someone was in the room with her.

She sat up abruptly and saw Amy standing in the doorway. Lacey glanced at the clock. It was just midnight; she had slept only a couple of hours.

'What is it, child?' she said softly. 'Are you all right?'

The little girl stepped into the room. Her pajamas shimmered in the light of the streetlamp outside Lacey's window, so that her body seemed draped with stars and moons. Lacey wondered for a moment if the girl was sleepwalking.

'Amy, did you have a bad dream?'

But Amy said nothing. In the darkness, Lacey couldn't see the child's face. Was she crying? She pulled the bedcovers aside to make room for her.

'It's all right, come here,' Lacey said.

Without a word, Amy climbed into the narrow bed beside her. Her body was giving off waves of heat – not a fever, but nothing ordinary, either. She was glowing like a coal.

'You don't have to be afraid,' Lacey said. 'You're safe here.'

'I want to stay,' the girl said.

Lacey realized she didn't mean the room, or Lacey's bed. She meant permanently, to live. Lacey didn't know how to respond. By Monday she would have to tell the truth to Sister Arnette; there was simply no avoiding it. What would happen after that – to both of them – she didn't know. But she saw it now, clearly: by lying about Amy, she had wrapped their fates together.

'We'll see.'

'I won't tell anyone. Don't let them take me away.'

Lacey felt a shiver of fear. 'Who, Amy? Who will take you away?'

Amy said nothing.

'Try not to worry,' Lacey said. She put her arm around Amy and pulled her close. 'Now sleep. We need our rest.'

But in the dark, for hours and hours, Lacey lay awake, her eyes wide open.

It was a little after three a.m. when Wolgast and Doyle reached Baton Rouge, where they turned north, toward the Mississippi border. Doyle had driven the first shift, taking the wheel from Houston to a little east of Lafayette, while Wolgast tried to sleep; shortly after two they'd stopped at a Waffle House off the highway to change places, and since then, Doyle had barely stirred. A light rain was falling, just enough to mist the windshield.

To the south lay the Federal Industrial District of New Orleans, which Wolgast was glad to avoid. Just the thought of it depressed him. He had visited Old New Orleans once before, on a trip to Mardi Gras with friends from college, and been instantly taken by the city's wild energy – its pulsing permissiveness, its vivid sense of life. For three days he'd barely slept, or felt the need to. One early morning he found himself in Preservation Hall – which was, despite its name, little more than a shack, hotter than the mouth of hell – listening to a jazz sextet playing 'St. Louis Blues' and realized he'd been up for almost forty-eight hours straight. The air of the room was as tumescent as a greenhouse; everyone was dancing and shuffling and clapping along, a crowd of people of all ages and colors. Where else could you find yourself listening to six old black men, none of them a day under eighty, playing jazz at five o'clock in the morning? But then Katrina hit the city in '05, and Vanessa a few years later – a full-blown Category 5 that roared ashore on 180-mile-per-hour winds, pushing a storm surge thirty feet tall – and that was the end of that. Now the place was little more than a giant petrochemical refinery, ringed by flooded lowlands so polluted that the water of its fouled lagoons could melt the skin right off your hand. Nobody lived inside the city proper anymore; even the sky above it was off-limits, patrolled by a squadron of fighter jets out of Kessler AFB. The whole place was ringed by fencing and patrolled by Homeland Security forces in full battle dress; beyond the perimeter, radiating outward for ten miles in all directions, was the N.O. Housing District, a sea of trailers once used for evacuees but now serving as a gigantic human storage facility for the thousands of workers who made the city's industrial complex hum day and night. It was little more than a giant outdoor slum, a cross between a refugee camp and some frontier outpost from the Wild West; among law enforcement, it was generally known that the murder rate inside the N.O. was completely off the charts, though because it wasn't officially a city of any kind, not even part of any state, this fact went mostly unreported.

Now, not long before sunup, the Mississippi Border Checkpoint appeared ahead of them, a twinkling village of lights in the predawn darkness. Even at this hour, the lines were long, mostly tanker trucks headed north to St. Louis or Chicago. Guards with dogs and Geiger counters and long mirrors on poles moved up and down the lines. Wolgast pulled in behind a semi with Yosemite Sam mud flaps and a bumper sticker that read: I MISS MY EX-WIFE, BUT MY AIM IS IMPROVING.

Beside him, Doyle stirred, rubbing his eyes. He sat up in his seat and looked around. 'Are we there yet, Dad?'

'It's just a checkpoint. Go back to sleep.'

Wolgast pulled the car out of line and drew up to the nearest uniform. He rolled down the window and held up his credentials.

'Federal agents. Any way you can wave us through?'

The guard was just a kid, his face soft and spotted with pimples. The body armor bulked him up, but Wolgast could tell he was probably no more than a welterweight. He should be back at home, Wolgast thought, wherever that was, snug in bed and dreaming of some girl in his algebra class, not standing on a highway in Mississippi wearing thirty pounds of Kevlar, holding an assault rifle over his chest.

He eyed Wolgast's credentials with only vague interest, then tipped his head toward a concrete building sitting off the highway.

'You'll have to pull over to the station, sir.'

Wolgast sighed with irritation. 'Son, I don't have time for this.'

'You want to skip the lines, you do.'

At that moment, a second guard stepped into their headlights. He turned his hips to their vehicle and unslung his weapon. *What the fuck*, Wolgast thought.

'For Pete's sake. Is that really necessary?'

'Hands where we can see them, sir!' the second man barked.

'For crying out loud,' Doyle said.

The first guard turned toward the man in the headlights. He waved his hand to tell him to lower his weapon. 'Cool it, Duane. They're feds.' The second man hesitated, then shrugged and walked away.

'Sorry about that. Just pull around. They'll have you out fast.'

'They better,' Wolgast said.

In the station, the OD took their credentials and asked them to wait while he phoned in their ID numbers. FBI, Homeland Security, even state and local cops; everybody was on a centralized system now, their movements tracked. Wolgast poured himself a cup of sludgy coffee from the urn, took a few halfhearted sips, and tossed it in the trash. There was a No Smoking sign, but the room reeked like an old ashtray. The clock on the wall said it was just past six; in about an hour the sun would be coming up.

The OD stepped back to the counter with their credentials. He was a trim man, nondescript, wearing the ash gray uniform of Homeland Security. 'Okay, gentlemen. Let's get you on your merry way. Just one thing: the system says you were booked to fly to Denver tonight. Probably just an error, but I need to log it.'

Wolgast had his answer ready. 'We were. We were redirected to Nashville to pick up a federal witness.'

The duty officer considered this a minute, then nodded. He typed the information into his computer. 'Fair enough. Raw deal, they didn't fly you. That must be a thousand miles.'

'Tell me about it. I just go where I'm told.'

'Amen, brother.'

They returned to their car, and a guard waved them to the exit. Moments later they were back on the highway.

'Nashville?' Doyle asked.

Wolgast nodded, fixing his eyes on the road ahead. 'Think about it. I-55 has checkpoints in Arkansas and Illinois, one just south of St. Louis and one about halfway between Normal and Chicago. But you take 40 east across Tennessee, the first checkpoint is all the way across the state, at the I-40 and 75 interchange. Ergo, this is the last checkpoint between here and Nashville, so the system won't know we *never* went there. We can make the pickup in Memphis, cross into Arkansas, bypass the Oklahoma checkpoint by driving the long way around Tulsa, pick up 70 north of Wichita, and meet Richards at the Colorado border. One checkpoint between here and Telluride, and Sykes can handle that. And nowhere does it say we went to Memphis.'

Doyle frowned. 'What about the bridge on 40?'

'We'll have to avoid it, but there's a pretty easy detour. About fifty miles south of Memphis there's an older bridge across the river, connects to a state highway on the Arkansas side. The bridge isn't rated for the big tankers coming up from the N.O., so it's passenger cars only and mostly automated. The bar-code scanner will pick us up, and so will the cameras. But that's easy to take care of later if we have to. Then we just work our way north and pick up I-40 south of Little Rock.'

They drove on. Wolgast thought about turning on the

radio, maybe getting a weather report, but decided against it; he was still alert, despite the hour, and needed to keep his mind focused. When the sky paled to gray, they were a little north of Jackson, making good time. The rain stopped, then started again. Around them the land rose in gentle swells like waves far out to sea. Though it seemed like days ago, Wolgast was still thinking about the message from Sykes.

Caucasian female. Amy NLN. Zero footprint. 20323 Poplar Ave., Memphis, TN. Make pickup by Saturday noon latest. No contact. TUR. Sykes.

TUR: travel under radar.

Don't just catch a ghost, Agent Wolgast; *be* a ghost.

'Do you want me to drive?' Doyle asked, cutting the silence, and Wolgast could tell from his voice that he'd been thinking the same thing. Amy NLN. Who was Amy NLN?

He shook his head. Around them, the day's first light spread over the Mississippi Delta like a sodden blanket. He tapped the wipers to clear the mist away.

'No,' he said. 'I'm good.'

FIVE

Something was wrong with Subject Zero.

For six days straight he hadn't come out of the corner, not even to feed. He just kind of hung there, like some kind of giant insect. Grey could see him on the infrared, a glowing blob in the shadows. From time to time he'd change positions, a few feet to the left or right, but that was it, and Grey had never seen him actually do this. Grey would just lift his face from the monitor, or leave containment to get a cup of coffee or sneak a smoke in the break room, and by the time he looked again, he'd find Zero hanging someplace else.

Hanging? Sticking? Hell, *levitating*?

No one had explained a goddamn thing to Grey. Not one

word. Like, for starters, what Zero actually *was*. There were things about him that Grey would say were sort of human. Such as, he had two arms and two legs. There was a head where a head should be, and ears and eyes and a mouth. He even had something like a johnson dangling down south, a curled-up little seahorse of a thing. But that's where the similarities stopped.

For instance: Subject Zero glowed. In the infrared, any heat source would do that. But the image of Subject Zero flared on the screen like a lit match, almost too bright to look at. Even his *crap* glowed. His hairless body, smooth and shiny as glass, looked coiled – that was the word Grey thought of, like the skin was stretched over lengths of coiled rope – and his eyes were the orange of highway cones. But the teeth were the worst. Every once in a while Grey would hear a little tinkling sound on the audio, and know it was the sound of one more tooth dropped from Zero's mouth to the cement. They rained down at the rate of half a dozen a day. These went into the incinerator, like everything else; it was one of Grey's jobs to sweep them up, and it gave him the shivers to see them, long as the little swords you'd get in a fancy drink. Just the thing if, say, you wanted to unzip a rabbit and empty it out in two seconds flat.

There was something about him that was different than the others, too. Not that he *looked* all that different. The glowsticks were all a bunch of ugly bastards, and over the six months Grey had been working on Level 4, he'd gotten used to their appearance. There were little differences, of course, that you could pick up if you looked hard. Number Six was a little shorter than the others, Number Nine a little more active, Number Seven liked to eat hanging upside down and made a goddamn mess, Number One was always chatting away, that weird sound they made, a wet clicking from deep in their throats that reminded Grey of nothing.

No, it wasn't something physical that made Zero stand out; it was how he made you *feel*. That was the best way Grey could explain it. The others seemed about as interested in the people behind the glass as a bunch of chimps at the zoo. But not Zero: Zero was paying attention. Whenever they dropped the bars, sealing Zero on the back side of the room, and Grey squeezed into his biohazard suit and went in through the air lock to clean up or bring in the rabbits – *rabbits,* for Christsakes; why did it have to be rabbits? – a kind of prickling climbed up his neck, like his skin was crawling with ants. He'd go about his work quickly, not even really looking up from the floor, and by the time he got out of there and into decon, he'd be glazed with sweat and breathing hard. Even now, a wall of glass two inches thick between them and Zero hanging so that all Grey could see was his big glowing backside and spreading, clawlike feet – Grey could still feel Zero's mind roving around the dark room, trolling like an invisible net.

Still, Grey had to say it wasn't a bad job on the whole. He'd certainly had worse in his life. Most of the time all he did was just sit there through an eight-hour shift, penning his way through a crossword and checking the monitor and logging in his reports, what Zero ate and didn't eat and how much of his piss and shit went down the drain, and backing up the hard drives when they maxed out with a hundred hours of video footage of Zero doing nothing.

He wondered if the others weren't eating, either. He thought he'd ask one of the techs about that. Maybe they'd all gone on some kind of hunger strike; maybe they were just tired of rabbits and wanted squirrel instead, or possum, or kangaroo. It was funny to think it, given the way the glowsticks ate – Grey had let himself watch this only once, and that was one time too many; it had practically turned him into a vegetarian – but he had to say there was something fussy about them, like they had rules about eating, starting with the whole business with the tenth rabbit. Who knew what that was about? You gave them ten rabbits, they'd eat only nine, leave the tenth just where it was, like they were saving it for later. Grey had owned a dog once who was like that. He'd called him Brownbear, for no particular reason; he didn't look especially bearish, and he wasn't even really brown but kind of a mellow tan color, with flecks of white on his muzzle and chest. Brownbear would eat exactly half his bowl each morning, then finish it at night. Grey was usually asleep when this happened; he'd wake up at two or three a.m. to the sound of the dog in the kitchen, cracking the kibble on his molars, and in the morning, the dish would be sitting empty in its spot by the stove. Brownbear was a good dog, the best he'd ever had. But that was years ago; he'd had to give him up, and Brownbear would be long dead by now.

All the civilian workers, the sweeps and some of the technicals, were housed together in the barracks at the south end of the compound. The rooms weren't bad, with cable and a hot shower, and no bills to pay. Nobody was going anywhere for a while, that was part of the deal, but Grey didn't mind; everything he needed he had right here, and the pay was good, right up there with oil-rig money, all piling up in an offshore account with his name on it. They weren't even taking out any taxes, some kind of special arrangement for civilians employed under the Federal Emergency Homeland Protection Act. A year or two of this, Grey figured, and as long as he didn't piss away too much at the commissary on smokes and snacks, he'd have enough socked away to put some serious mileage between himself and Zero and all the rest of them. The other sweeps were an okay bunch, but he preferred to keep to himself. In his room at night, he liked to watch the Travel Channel or National Geographic, picking places he'd go when this was all over. For a while he'd been thinking Mexico; Grey figured there'd be plenty of room, since about half the country seemed to have emptied out and was now standing around the parking lot of the Home Depot. But then last week he'd seen a program on French Polynesia – the water blue like he'd never seen blue before, and little houses on stilts sitting right out over it – and now was giving that some serious consideration. Grey was forty-six years old and smoked like a fiend, so he figured he had only about ten good years left to enjoy himself. His old man, who'd smoked like he did, had spent the last five years of his life in a little cart sucking on a tank, until he'd done the big face-plant just a month before his sixtieth birthday.

Still, it would have been nice to get off the grounds every now and then, even just to have a look around. He knew they were in Colorado someplace, from the license plates on some of the cars, and every now and again somebody, probably one of the officers or else the scientific staff, who came and went as they chose, would leave a copy of *The Denver Post* lying around; so it was no big secret, really, where they were, no matter what Richards said. One day after a heavy snowfall, Grey and some of the other sweeps had gone up to the roof of the barracks to shovel it off, and Grey could see, rising above the line of snowy trees, what looked like some kind of ski resort, with a gondola inching up the hillside and a slope with tiny figures carving down it. It couldn't have been more than five miles from where he stood. Funny, with a war on and the world the way it was, everything in such a mess, to see a thing like that. Grey had never skied in his life, but he knew there'd be bars and restaurants too, out there beyond the wall of trees, and things like hot tubs and saunas, and people sitting around talking and sipping glasses of wine in the steam. He'd seen that on the Travel Channel, too.

It was March, still winter, and there was plenty of snow on the ground, which meant that once the sun went down the temperature fell like a rock. Tonight a nasty wind was blowing too, and trudging back to the barracks with his hands stuffed in his pockets and his chin tucked into the neck of his parka, Grey felt like his face was getting slapped a hundred times over. All of which made him think some more about Bora-Bora, and those little houses on stilts. Never mind Zero, who apparently had lost his taste for fresh Easter Bunny; what Zero ate and did not eat was none of Grey's business. If they told him to serve eggs Benedict on toast points from now on, he'd do it with a smile. He wondered what a house like that would cost. With a house like that, you wouldn't even need plumbing; you could just step to the rail and do your business, any time of the day or night. When Grey had worked rigs in the Gulf, he'd liked to do that, in the early morning or late at night when no one was around; you had to mind the wind, of course, but with a breeze pushing at your back, few pleasures in life compared to taking a leak off a platform two hundred feet over the Gulf and watching it arc into the air before raining down twenty stories into the blue. It made you feel small and big at the same time.

Now the whole oil industry was under federal protection, and it seemed like practically everybody he knew from the old days had disappeared. After that Minneapolis thing, the bombing at the gas depot in Secaucus, the subway attack in LA and all the rest, and, of course, what happened in Iran or Iraq or whichever it was, the whole economy had locked up like a bad transmission. With his knees and the smoking and the thing on his record, no goddamn way they were taking Grey in Homeland, or anywhere else. He'd been out of work most of a year when he'd gotten the call. He'd thought for sure it was more rig work, maybe for some foreign supplier. They'd somehow made it sound that way without actually saying it, and he was surprised when he'd driven to the address and found it was just an empty storefront in an abandoned strip mall near the Dallas fairgrounds, with white soap smeared on the windows. The place had once housed a video store; Grey could still make out the name, Movie World West, in a ghostly formation of missing letters on the grimy stucco over the door. The place next to it had been a Chinese restaurant; another, a dry cleaner's; the rest, you couldn't say. He'd driven up and down in front a couple of times, thinking he must have had the address wrong and reluctant to climb from the air-conditioned cab of his truck for some pointless goose chase, before he'd stopped. It was about a hundred degrees out, typical for August in north Texas but still nothing you could ever get used to, the air thick and dirty-smelling, the sun gleaming like the head of a hammer coming down. The door was locked but there was a buzzer; he rang and waited a minute as the sweat started to pool under his shirt, then heard a big ring of keys jangling on the other side and the clunk of the unlocking door.

They'd set up a little desk and a couple of file cabinets in the back; the room was still full of empty racks that had once held DVDs, and a lot of tangled wires and other junk was hanging from open spaces in the drop-panel ceiling. Leaned against the rear wall of the store was a life-size cardboard figure, coated with a film of dust, of some movie star Grey couldn't place, a bald black dude in wraparounds, with biceps that bulged under his T-shirt like a couple of canned hams he was trying to smuggle out of a supermarket. The movie was nothing Grey remembered, either. Grey filled out the form but the people there, a man and a woman, barely seemed to look at it. While they typed into the computer they asked him to pee in a cup and then gave him a polygraph, but that was standard stuff. He did his best not to feel like he was lying even when he was telling the truth, and when they asked him about the time he'd done at Beeville, as he knew they would, he told them the story straight out: no way to hide it with the wires, and it was a matter of record besides, especially in Texas, with the website you could go to and see everybody's faces and all the rest. But even this seemed not to be a problem. They seemed to know a lot about him already, and most of their questions had to do with his personal life, the stuff you couldn't learn except by asking. Did he have friends? (Not really.) Did he live alone? (When hadn't he?) Did he have any living family? (Just an aunt in Odessa he hadn't seen in about twenty years and a couple of cousins he wasn't even sure he knew the names of.) The trailer park where he was living, up in Allen – who were his neighbors? (Neighbors?) And so on, in that vein. Everything he told them seemed to make them happier and happier. They were trying to hide it, but you could see it on their faces, plain as the words in a book. When he decided they weren't police, he realized he'd been thinking maybe they were.

Two days later – by which time he realized he'd never

learned the names of the man and the woman, couldn't even have said what they looked like – he was on the plane to Cheyenne. They'd explained the money and the part about not being able to leave for a year, which was all right by him, and made it clear that he shouldn't tell anybody where he was going, which, in fact, he couldn't; he didn't know. At the airport in Cheyenne he was met by a man in a black tracksuit, whom he'd later come to know as Richards – a wiry guy no more than five foot six with a permanent scowl on his face. Richards walked him to the curb; two other men, who must have come in on different flights, were standing by a van. Richards opened the driver's door and returned with a cloth bag the size of a pillowcase. He held it open like a mouth.

'Wallets, cell phones, any personal stuff, photographs, anything with writing on it, right down to the pen you got at the bank,' he told them. 'I don't care if it's a fucking fortune cookie. In it goes.'

They emptied their pockets, hoisted their duffels into the luggage rack, and climbed in through the side. It was only when Richards closed the door behind them that Grey realized the windows were blacked out. From the outside the vehicle looked like an ordinary van, but inside it was a different story: the driver's compartment was sealed off, the passenger compartment nothing but a metal box with vinyl bench seats bolted to the floor. Richards had said they were allowed to trade first names but that was all. The other two men were Jack and Sam. They looked so much like Grey he might have been staring into a mirror: middle-aged white guys with buzz cuts and puffed red hands and workingman's tans that stopped at the wrists and collar. Grey's first name was Lawrence, but he'd barely ever used it. It sounded odd coming from his mouth. As soon as he said it, shaking hands with the one named Sam, he felt like somebody different, like he'd boarded the plane in Dallas as one person and landed in Cheyenne as another.

In the dark van, it was impossible to tell where they were going, and a little nauseating. For all Grey knew, they were just circling the airport. With nothing to do or see, they all fell asleep soon enough. When Grey woke up he had no sense of the hour. He also had to pee like a jackrabbit. That was the Depo. He rose from his seat and rapped his knuckles on the sliding panel at the front of the compartment.

'Yo, I gotta stop,' he said.

Richards slid the window open, affording Grey a view through the van's windshield. The sun had set; the road ahead, a two-lane blacktop, was dark and empty. In the distance he glimpsed a purple line of light where the sky met a mountain ridge.

'I need to take a leak,' Grey explained. 'Sorry.'

In the passenger compartment behind him, the other men were rousing. Richards reached onto the floor and passed Grey a clear plastic bottle with a wide mouth.

'I gotta pee in this?'

'That's the idea.'

Richards closed the window without another word. Grey sat back down on the bench and examined the bottle in his hand. He figured it was big enough. But the thought of taking his equipment out in the van, right in front of the other men, like this was no big deal, made all the muscles around his bladder clamp like a slipknot.

'No way I'm using that,' the one named Sam said. His eyes were closed; he was sitting with his hands folded at his lap. His face wore a look of intense concentration. 'I'm just holding it.'

They rode a little farther. Grey tried to think of something that could keep his mind off his bursting bladder, but this only made matters worse. It felt like an ocean sloshing around inside him. They hit a pothole and the ocean crashed against the shoreline. He heard himself groan.

'Hey!' he said, banging on the window again. 'Hey in there! I've got an emergency!'

Richards opened the panel. 'What is it now?'

'Listen,' Grey said, and pushed his head through the narrow space. He lowered his voice so the others wouldn't hear. 'I can't. Seriously. I can't use the bottle. You've got to pull over.'

'Just hold it, for fucksake.'

'I'm serious. I'm begging you. I can't . . . I can't *go* like this. I have a medical condition.'

Richards sighed with irritation. Their eyes met quickly in the rearview, and Grey wondered if he knew. 'Stay where I can see you and no looking around. I fucking mean it.'

He pulled the vehicle to the side of the road. Grey was muttering under his breath, 'C'mon, c'mon . . .' Then the door opened and he was out, sprinting away from the rumbling light of the van. He stumbled down the embankment, each second ticking off like a bomb between his thighs. Grey was in some kind of pasture. A sliver of moon was up, wicking the tips of the grass with an icy glow. He had to get at least fifty feet away, he figured, maybe more, to do the thing right. He came to a fence line and despite his knees and the pressure of his bladder he was up and over it like a shot. He heard Richards's voice behind him yelling for him to stop, *fucking stop right now, goddammit,* and then he heard Richards yelling at the other men to do the same. Dewy grass swished against Grey's pant legs, drenched the toes of his boots. A dot of red light was skipping across the field in front of him, but who knew what that was. He could smell cows, feel their presence around him, somewhere in the field. A fresh surge of panic pressed upon him: what if they were watching?

But it was too late, he simply had to go, there was no way he could wait another second. He stopped where he was and unzipped his fly and peed so hard into the darkness he moaned with relief. No tepid arc of gold: the water shot out of him like the contents of a busted hydrant. He peed and peed and peed some more. God almighty, it was the most wonderful feeling in the world, peeing like this, like a great plug had been pulled out of him. He was almost glad he'd waited so long.

Then it was over. His tank was dry. He stood a moment, feeling the cool night air on his exposed flesh. An immense calm filled him, an almost heavenly well-being. The field stretched around him like a vast carpet, creaking with the sound of crickets. He lit a Parliament from the pack in his shirt pocket, and as the smoke hit his lungs he tipped his face to the horizon. He'd barely noticed the moon before, a rind of light, like a fingernail trimming, suspended over the mountains. The sky was full of stars.

He turned to look in the direction he'd come. He could see the headlights of the van where it was parked by the side of the road, and Richards waiting there in his tracksuit, something bright and shiny in his hand. Grey climbed the fence in time to see Jack emerging from the field as well, then spied Sam crossing the roadway from the far side. They all converged on the van at the same instant.

Richards was standing in the conical glare of the headlights, his hands on his hips. Whatever he had been holding was gone from sight.

'Thanks,' Grey said over the sound of the idling engine. He finished the last of his cigarette and tossed it on the pavement. 'I really had to go.'

'Fuck you,' Richards said. 'You have no idea.' Jack and Sam were looking at the ground. Richards tipped his head at the open door of the van. 'All of you, in. And not one more fucking word.'

They took their seats in chastened silence; Richards started the engine and pulled back onto the roadway. That was when Grey realized it. He didn't have to look at them to know. The other two, Jack and Sam: they were just like him. And something else. The thing Richards had been holding, which Grey guessed was now tucked away inside the waistband of his tracksuit or stashed in the glove compartment; that little dancing light in the grass, like a single dot of blood.

One more step, Grey knew, and Richards would have shot him.

Once a month, Grey took a shot of Depo-Povera, and every morning a little dot of a pill, star-shaped, of spironolactone.

Grey had been following this regimen for a little over six years; it was a condition of his release.

And the truth was, he didn't mind. He didn't have to shave as much, there was that. The spironolactone, an anti-androgen, decreased the size of the testicles; since he'd begun taking it, he could shave every second or third day, and his hair was finer and less coarse, like when he was a boy. His skin was clearer and softer, even with the smoking. And of course there were the 'psychological benefits,' as the prison shrink had called them. Things didn't get to him the way they had, the way a feeling could twist inside him for days at a time, like a piece of glass he'd swallowed. He slept like a rock and never remembered his dreams. Whatever it was that made him pull over the truck that day, fifteen years ago – the day that started the whole thing – was long gone. Whenever he sent his mind back there, to that period of his life and all that came after, he still felt bad about it. But even this feeling was indistinct, a picture out of focus. It was like feeling bad about a rainy day, something no one could have helped.

The Depo, though, played hell with his bladder, because it was a steroid. As for not wanting anybody to see him, he guessed that was just part of the way his mind worked now. The shrink told him about this, and like everything else, it had come to pass exactly as he'd said. The inconveniences were slight, but Grey spent a certain amount of time looking away from things. Kids, for one, which was why he'd taken so well to rig work. Pregnant women. Highway rest stops. Most of what was on television – programs he'd watched before without a second thought, not just sexy things but things like boxing or even the news. He wasn't allowed within two hundred yards of a school or day-care center, which was fine by him – he never drove if he could help it between the hours of three and four and would go blocks out of his way just to avoid a school bus. He didn't even like the *color* yellow. It was all a little weird, and certainly nothing he could explain to anyone, but it sure beat the hell out of prison. More than that: it beat the way he lived before, always feeling like he was a bomb that was about to go off.

If his old man could see him now, he thought. With the way he felt on the meds, Grey might even have been able to see his way to forgiving him for the things he'd done. The prison shrink, Dr Wilder, had spoken a lot about forgiveness. *Forgiveness* was just about his all-time, number one favorite word. Forgiveness, Wilder explained, was the first step on a long road, the long road of recovery. It was a road, but sometimes it was a door; and only by going through this door could you make peace with your past, and face the inner demon, the 'bad you' inside the 'good you.' Wilder used his fingers a lot while he was talking, making little quotation marks in the air. Grey thought Wilder was basically full of shit. Probably he said the same crap to everybody. But Grey had to admit Wilder had a point with the 'bad you' stuff. The bad Grey was real enough, and for a time, most of his life in fact, the bad Grey was really the only Grey there was. So that was the best thing about the meds, and why he planned to go on taking them the rest of his life, even after the court-ordered ten years were over: the bad Grey was nobody he ever wanted to meet again.

Grey trudged to the barracks through the snow and ate a plate of tacos in the commissary before returning to his room. Tuesday was Bingo Night, but Grey couldn't work up a head of steam over that; he'd played a couple of times and come up at least twenty dollars down, and the soldiers always won, which made him think it was rigged. It was a stupid game anyway, really just an excuse to smoke, which he could do for free in his room. He lay on his bed, propped a couple of pillows behind his head and an ashtray on his stomach, and flipped on the television. A lot of the stations were blacked out; no CNN, no MSNBC, no GOVTV or MTV or E! – not that he ever looked at those stations anymore – and where commercials would have been the screen went blue for a minute or two until the program came back on. He surfed through the channels until he came to something interesting, a show on the War Network about the Allied invasion of France. Grey had always liked history, had even done pretty well in it back in school. He was good with dates and names, and it seemed that if you kept these straight in your head, the rest was just fill-in-the-blank. Stretched out on his bed, still wearing his coveralls, Grey watched and smoked. On the screen, GIs were tumbling onto the beaches by the boatload, blasting away and dodging shells and hurling their grenades. Behind them, out to sea, huge guns poured fire and thunder onto the cliff sides of Nazi-occupied France. Now that, Grey thought, was a war. The footage was jittery and out of focus half the time, but in one shot Grey could clearly see an arm – a Nazi arm – reaching out from the slotted window of a pillbox that some nice American kid had just used a flame-thrower on. The arm was all burned up and smoking like a chicken wing left on a barbecue grill. Grey's old man had done two tours as a medic in Vietnam, and he wondered what he would have said about a thing like that. Grey some-times forgot that his father was a medic; when Grey was a kid, the guy hadn't so much as put a Band-Aid on his knee, not once.

He smoked a last Parliament and turned off the television. Two days ago, the one named Jack and the one named Sam had up and left, not a word to anyone, so Grey had agreed to take a double shift. This would put him back on Level 4 by 06:00. It was a shame, those guys leaving like they had; unless you worked the full year, you forfeited the money. Richards had let it be known in no uncertain terms that this development did not make him one goddamn bit happy, and if anybody else was thinking of skipping, they had better think about this long and hard – *very* long and hard, he had said, giving the room a long, slow scan, like a pissed-off gym teacher. He gave this little speech in the dining hall during breakfast, and Grey locked his eyes on his scrambled eggs the whole time. He figured what happened to Sam and Jack was none of his business, and in any event the warning didn't apply to him: he, for one, wasn't going anywhere, and it wasn't like he'd been friends with those guys, not really. They'd talked a bit about this and that, but it was really just passing the time, and their leaving meant more money for Grey. An overtime shift was an extra five hundred; you pulled three in a week, they gave you an extra hundred as a bonus, too. As long as the money kept rolling in, filling up his account with all those zeros lined up like eggs in a carton, Grey would sit there on the mountaintop until the last cat was hung.

He peeled off his coveralls and doused the light. Pellets of snow were blowing against his window, a sound like sand shaking in a paper sack; every twenty seconds the blinds flared as the beacon on the west perimeter swung across the glass. Sometimes the drugs made Grey restless or he got leg cramps, but a couple of ibuprofen usually did the trick. He sometimes got up in the middle of the night to smoke or take a leak, though usually he slept straight through. He lay in the dark and tried to calm his thoughts but found himself thinking about Zero again. Maybe it was the burned-up Nazi arm; he couldn't seem to push the image of Zero from his mind. Zero was a prisoner of some kind. His table manners weren't anything to brag about, and it was nothing nice to look at, the business with the rabbits. Still, food was food and Zero wasn't having any of it. All he did was hang there like he was sleeping, though Grey didn't think he was. The chip in Zero's neck broadcast all kinds of data to the console, some of which Grey understood and some of which he didn't. But he knew what sleep looked like, that it looked different from being awake. Zero's heart rate was always the same, 102 beats per minute, give or take a beat. The technicians who came into the control room to read the data never said anything about this, just nodded and checked off the boxes on their handhelds. But 102 seemed mighty awake to Grey.

And the other thing was, Zero *felt* awake. There Grey went again, thinking about how Zero made him feel, which was nuts, but even so. Grey had never had much use for cats, but this was the same kind of thing. A cat sleeping on a step wasn't really sleeping. A cat sleeping on a step was a coiled spring waiting for a mouse to totter along. What was Zero waiting for? Maybe, Grey thought, he was just tired of rabbit. Maybe he wanted Ding Dongs, or a bologna hoagie, or turkey tetrazzini. For all Grey could tell, the guy would have eaten a piece of wood. With choppers like that, there pretty much wasn't anything he couldn't bore right through.

Ugh, Grey thought with a shudder, *the teeth*, and that was when he knew he had to do something else to make himself sleep besides just lying there, stewing in his thoughts. It was already midnight. Six a.m. would jump out at him like a jack-in-the-box before he knew it. He rose and took a couple of ibuprofen, smoked a cigarette and emptied his bladder again for good measure, then slid back between the covers. The spotlights grazed the windows once, twice, three times. He made an effort to close his eyes and imagine the escalator. This was a trick Wilder had taught him. Grey was what Wilder called 'suggestible,' meaning he was easily hypnotized, and the escalator was the thing Wilder had used to do this. You imagined being on an escalator, slowly going down. It didn't matter where the escalator was, an airport or mall or whatever, and Grey's escalator wasn't anyplace in particular. The point was, it was an escalator, and you were on it, alone, and the escalator went down and down and down, headed toward the bottom, which wasn't a bottom in the ordinary sense of being the end of something but a place of cool, blue light. Sometimes it was one escalator; sometimes it was a series of shorter escalators that descended one floor at a time with turns in between. Tonight it was just the one. The mechanism clicked a little under his feet; the rubber handrail was smooth and cool to the touch. Riding the escalator, Grey could feel the blueness waiting below him, but he didn't avert his gaze to look at it, because it wasn't a thing you saw; it came from inside you. When it filled you up and took you over, you knew you were asleep.

Grey.

The light was in him now, but it wasn't blue; that was the

funny thing. The light was a warm orange color, and throbbing like a heart. Part of his brain said, *You are asleep, Grey; you are asleep and dreaming.* But another part, the part that was actually in the dream, took no mind of this. He moved through the pulsing orange light.

Grey. I am here.

The light was different now, golden; Grey was in the barn, in the straw. A dream that was a memory, but not exactly: he had straw all over him from rolling around in it, sticking to his arms and face and hair, and the other boy was there, his cousin Roy, who wasn't his real cousin, but he called him that; and Roy was covered too, and laughing. They'd been rolling around, fighting, sort of, and then the feeling of it changed, the way a song changed. He could smell the straw, and his own sweat mixing with Roy's, all of it combining in his senses to make the smell of a summer afternoon as a boy. Roy was saying, quietly, It's okay, take off them jeans, I'll take mine off too, ain't nobody coming. Just do like I do, I'll show you how it's done, it's the best feeling in the world. Grey knelt beside him in the straw.

Grey. Grey.

And Roy was right; it *was* the best feeling. Like climbing a rope in gym class only better, like a big sneeze building inside him, starting from down low and climbing up through all the hallways and alleyways and channels inside him. He closed his eyes and let the feeling rise.

Yes. Yes. Grey, listen. I am coming.

But it wasn't just Roy with him, not anymore. Grey heard the roar and then the footsteps on the ladder, like the song changing again. He saw Roy one last time from the corner of his eye and he was all burned up and smoking. His father was using the belt, the heavy black one, he didn't need to see it to know, and he buried his face in the straw as the belt fell across his bare back, slapping and ripping, again, again; and then something else, deeper, tearing at him from the inside.

You like this, is this what you like, I'll show you, be quiet now and take it.

This man – he wasn't his father. Grey remembered now. It wasn't just the belt he was using and it wasn't his father who was using it; his father had been replaced by this man, *this man named Kurt who'll be your daddy now*, and by this feeling of being torn up inside, the way his real father had torn himself up in the front seat of his truck on the morning it had snowed. Grey couldn't have been more than six years old when it happened. He awoke one morning before anyone else was up and about, the light of his bedroom floating with a glowing weightlessness, and right away he knew what had called him out of sleep, that snow had fallen in the night. He threw the cover aside and yanked back the drapes of his window, blinking into the smooth brightness of the world. Snow! It never snowed, not in Texas. Sometimes they got ice but that wasn't the same, not like the snow he saw in books and on TV, this wonderful blanket of whiteness, the snow of sledding and skiing, of snow angels and snow forts and snowmen. His heart leapt with the wonder of it, the pure possibility and newness of it, this marvelous, impossible present waiting outside his window. He touched the glass and felt the coldness leap onto his fingertips, a sudden sharpness, like an electric current.

He hurried from the window and quickly drew on jeans, thrust his bare feet into sneakers, not even bothering to tie the laces; if there was snow outside, he had to be out there in it. He crept from his room and down the stairs to the living room. It was Saturday morning. There'd been a party the night before, folks over to the house, lots of talk and loud voices that he'd heard from his room, and the smell of cigarettes that even now clung to the air like a greasy cloud. Upstairs, his parents would sleep for hours.

He opened the front door and stepped onto the porch. The air was cool and still, and there was a smell to it, like clean laundry. He breathed it in.

Grey. Look.

That was when he saw it: his father's truck. Parked like it always was in the drive, but something was different. Grey saw a splash of dark red, like a squirt of spray paint, on the driver's window, darker and redder because of the snow. He considered what he was seeing. It seemed like it might be some kind of joke – that his father had done something to tease him, to play a game, to give him something funny and strange to see when he got up in the morning before anybody else was awake. He descended the stairs of the porch and stepped across the yard. Snow filled his sneakers but he kept his eyes locked on the truck, which gave him a worried feeling now, like it wasn't the snow that had called him out of sleep but something else. The truck was running, pushing a gray smear of exhaust onto the snowy drive; the windshield was fogged with heat and moisture. He could see a dark shape pressed against the window where the redness was. His hands were little and he had no strength but still he'd done it, he'd opened the door of the truck; and as he did, his daddy tumbled past him and onto the snow.

Grey. Look. Look at me.

The body had landed face-up. One eye was pointed up at Grey, but really at nothing; Grey could tell that right off. The other eye was gone. So was that whole side of his face, like something had turned it inside out. Grey knew what dead was. He'd seen animals – possums and coons and sometimes cats or even dogs – broken to pieces on the side of the road, and this was like that. This was over and out. The gun was still in his daddy's hand, the finger curling through the little hole the way he'd showed Grey that day on the porch. *See now, see how heavy it is? You never ever point a gun at anyone.* There was blood everywhere too, mixed in with other stuff, like bits of meat and white pieces of something smashed, all over his daddy's face and jacket and the seat of the truck and the inside of the door, and Grey smelled it, so strong it seemed to coat the insides of his mouth like a melting pill.

Grey, Grey. I am here.

The scene started changing then. Grey felt movement all around him, like the earth was stretching; something was different about the snow, the snow had started *moving*, and

when he lifted his face to look, it wasn't snow he saw anymore but rabbits: thousands and thousands of fluffy white
rabbits, all the rabbits in the world, bunched so closely together that a person could walk across the yard and never
touch the ground; the yard was full of rabbits. And they
turned their soft faces toward him, pointed their little black
eyes at him, because they knew him, knew what he had
done, not to Roy but to the other ones, the boys with their
knapsacks walking home from school, the stragglers, the
ones who were alone; and that was when Grey knew that it
wasn't his daddy anymore, lying in the blood. It was Zero,
and Zero was everywhere, Zero was inside him, ripping and
tearing, emptying him out like the rabbits, and he opened his
mouth to scream but no sound came.

Grey Grey Grey Grey Grey Grey Grey.

In his office on L2, Richards was sitting at his terminal, his
mind deep inside a game of free cell. Hand number 36,592,
he had to admit, was squarely kicking his ass. He'd played it a
dozen times already, coming close but never quite figuring
out how to build his columns, how to clear out all the aces
when he needed to, to free up the red eights. In that sense it
reminded him a little of game 14,712, which was all about
the red eights, too. It had taken him most of a day to crack
that one.

But every game was winnable. That was the beauty of free
cell. The cards were dealt, and if you looked at them right, if
you made the right moves, one after the other, sooner or later
the game was yours. One victorious click of the mouse and all
the cards sailed up the columns. Richards never got tired of
it, which was good, because he still had 91,048 games to
go, counting this one. There was a twelve-year-old kid in
Washington State who claimed to have won every hand, in
order – including 64,523, the death's head of free cell – in just
under four years. That was eighty-eight games a day, every
day, including Christmas, New Year's, and the Fourth of July,
so assuming the kid took a day off every now and again, to do

kid things or even just come down with a good case of the flu, the real number was probably more like a hundred. Richards didn't see how that was possible. Didn't he ever go to school? Didn't he have homework? When did the little bastard sleep?

Richards's office, like all the underground spaces of the compound, was little more than a fluorescent box, everything pumped in and filtered. Even the light felt recycled. It was a little after two-thirty in the morning, but Richards got by on less than four hours of sleep a night, he had for years, so he paid this no mind. On the wall above his station, three dozen time-stamped monitors displayed every nook of the compound, from the guards freezing their asses off at the front gate to the vacant mess hall with its empty tables and dozing drink dispensers, to the subject containment areas, two floors below him, with their glowing, infectious cargo, and, farther down, through another fifty feet of rock, to the nuclear cells that powered it all and would keep the lights on, the juice flowing, for a hundred years, give or take a decade. He liked having everything where he could see it at a glance, where he could read it like the cards. Sometime between five and six a.m. they'd be taking a delivery, and he figured he might as well just stay up all night for that. Subject processing took a couple of hours at the most; he could grab a few winks at his desk afterward if he had to.

Then, on the computer screen, he saw the answer. It was right there, under the six: the black queen he needed to move the jack and free up the two and so on. A couple of clicks and it was over. The cards shot up the screen like a pianist's fingers flying over the keys.

Do you want to play again?

You're goddamn right he would.

Because the game was the world's natural state. Because the game was war, it always was, and when *wasn't* there a war on, somewhere, to keep a man like Richards in good employ? The last twenty years had been kind to him, a long run at the table with nothing but good news from the cards. Sarajevo,

Albania, Chechnya. Afghanistan, Iraq, Iran. Syria, Pakistan, Sierra Leone, Chad. The Philippines and Indonesia and Nicaragua and Peru.

Richards remembered the day – that glorious and terrible day – watching the planes slam into the towers, the image repeated in endless loops. The fireballs, the bodies falling, the liquefaction of a billion tons of steel and concrete, the pillowing clouds of dust. The money shot of the new millennium, the ultimate reality show broadcast 24-7. Richards had been in Jakarta when it happened, he couldn't even remember why. He'd thought it right then; no, he'd felt it, right down to his bones. A pure, unflinching rightness. You had to give the military something to do of course, or they'd all just fucking shoot each other. But from that day forward, the old way of doing things was over. The war – the real war, the one that had been going on for a thousand years and would go on for a thousand thousand more – the war between Us and Them, between the Haves and the Have-Nots, between my gods and your gods, whoever you are – would be fought by men like Richards: men with faces you didn't notice and couldn't remember, dressed as busboys or cab drivers or mailmen, with silencers tucked up their sleeves. It would be fought by young mothers pushing ten pounds of C-4 in baby strollers and schoolgirls boarding subways with vials of sarin hidden in their Hello Kitty backpacks. It would be fought out of the beds of pickup trucks and blandly anonymous hotel rooms near airports and mountain caves near nothing at all; it would be waged on train platforms and cruise ships, in malls and movie theaters and mosques, in country and in city, in darkness and by day. It would be fought in the name of Allah or Kurdish nationalism or Jews for Jesus or the New York Yankees – the subjects hadn't changed, they never would, all coming down, after you'd boiled away the bullshit, to somebody's quarterly earnings report and who got to sit where – but now the war was everywhere, metastasizing like a million maniac cells run amok across the planet, and everyone was in it.

Which was why NOAH had made a certain sense, back when it all started. Richard had been with the project since the beginning, since his first communiqué from Cole, rest in peace, you little shit. He'd known it was something important when Cole actually came to see him in Ankara, five years ago. Richards was waiting at a table by a window when Cole strolled in, swinging a briefcase that probably had nothing in it but a cell phone and a diplomatic passport. He was also wearing a Hawaiian shirt under his khaki suit, a nice touch, like something out of Graham Greene. Richards almost laughed. They ordered a pot of coffee and Cole got started, his smooth face animated with excitement. Cole was from a little town in Georgia, but all those years at Andover and Princeton had tightened up the muscles in his jaw, making him sound like Bobby Kennedy channeling Robert E. Lee. The boy had nice-looking teeth, too, Ivy League teeth, straight as a fence and so white you could read by them in a dark room. So, Cole began, think of the A-bomb, how it changed everything just to *have* it. Until the Russians set off their own in '49, the world was ours to do as we liked; for four years it was *Pax Americana, bay-by.* Now of course everybody and his uncle was cooking one up in his basement, and at least a hundred rust-bucket Soviet-era warheads were floating around on the open market and those were just the ones we *knew* about, and of course Pakistan and India had burst the cherry with all their bullshit – thanks a bunch, fellas, you made incinerating a hundred thousand people over diddly-squat just another day at the office of the deputy under-secretary of the War on Terr-rah.

But this, Cole said, and sipped his coffee. Nobody else could do *this*. This was the new Manhattan Project. This was bigger than that. Cole couldn't go into details, not yet, but for the sake of context, think of the human form itself, weaponized. Think of the American Way as something *truly* long-term. As in *permanent.*

Which was why Cole had come to see him. He needed somebody like Richards, he explained, someone off the books, but not only that. Someone practical, with practical skills. People skills, you might say. Maybe not right away, but in the coming months, as the pieces gathered to form the whole. Security was paramount. Security was at the absolute top of Cole's list. That's why he had come all this way and put on this ridiculous luau shirt. To get the buy-in. To get this piece of the puzzle nailed down.

All well and good if things had gone according to plan, which they hadn't, not by a long shot, starting with the fact that Cole was dead. A lot of people were dead, in fact, and some – well, it was hard to say just what they were. Only three people had come out of that jungle alive, not counting Fanning, who was already well on his way to being . . . well, what? More than Cole had bargained for, that was for sure. There might have been more survivors, but the order from Special Weapons was clear: anybody who didn't make it to the dust-off was bacon with a side of toast. The missile that screamed in over the mountains had made sure of that. Richards wondered what Cole would have said if he'd known he wouldn't be one of them.

By then – by the time Fanning was safely locked away, Lear was on-site in Colorado, and everything that had happened in South America had been wiped from the system – Richards had learned what it was all about. VSA, for Very Slow Aging. Richards had to hand it to whoever had dreamed up that one. VSA: Very Silly Abbreviation. A virus or, rather, a family of viruses, hidden away in the world, in birds or monkeys or sitting on a dirty toilet seat somewhere. A virus that could, with the proper refinements, restore the thymus gland to its full and proper function. Richards had read Lear's early papers, the ones that had gotten Cole's attention, the first one in *Science* and the second in *Journal of Paleovirology*, hypothesizing the existence of 'an agent that could significantly lengthen human life span and increase physical robustness and has done so, at select moments, throughout human history.' Richards didn't need a PhD in microbiology to know that it was risky stuff: vampire stuff, though no one at Special Weapons ever used the word. If it hadn't been written by a scientist of Lear's stature, a Harvard microbiologist no less, it all would have sounded like something from the *Weekly World News*. But still, something about it hit a nerve. As a kid Richards had read his share of such stories, not just the comic books – *Tales from the Crypt* and *Dark Shadows* and all the rest – but the original Bram Stoker, and seen the movies too. A bunch of silliness and bad sex, he knew that even then, and yet wasn't there something about them that struck a deep chord of recognition, even of memory? The teeth, the blood hunger, the immortal union with darkness – what if these things weren't fantasy but recollection or even instinct, a feeling etched over eons into human DNA, of some dark power that lay within the human animal? A power that could be reactivated, refined, brought under control?

That was what Lear had believed, and Cole too. A belief that had taken them into the Bolivian jungle, looking for a bunch of dead tourists. A bunch of, as it had turned out, *un*dead tourists – Richards disliked the word but couldn't think of a better one, undeadness being, in the end, a pretty solid descriptor of the condition – who had killed – ripped apart, really – what was left of the research team, all except for Lear, Fanning, one of the soldiers, and a young graduate student named Fortes. If not for Fanning, the whole thing would have been a total loss.

Lear: you had to feel for the guy. Probably he still thought he was trying to save the world, but he'd sold that dream up the river the minute he'd gotten into bed with Cole and Special Weapons. And truth be told, it was hard to say what Lear was thinking these days; the guy never came off L4, slept down there in his lab on a sweaty little cot and took his meals off a hot plate. He probably hadn't seen the sun in a year. Back at the start, Richards had done a little extra digging, and come up with a number of interesting tidbits, Exhibit A being Lear's wife's obituary in the *Boston Globe* – dated just six months before Cole had come to see him in Ankara, a full year before the Bolivia fiasco. Elizabeth Macomb Lear, age forty-one. BA Smith, MA Berkeley, PhD Chicago. Professor of English at Boston College, associate editor of *Renaissance Quarterly*, author of *Shakespeare's Monsters: Bestial Transformation and the Early Modern Moment* (Cambridge University Press, 2009). A long battle with lymphoma, et cetera. There was a picture, too. Richards wouldn't have said Elizabeth Lear was a knockout, but she'd been pretty enough, in a slightly undernourished way. A serious woman, with serious ideas. At least there weren't any kids involved. Probably the chemo and radiation had ruled this out.

So, really, when it came down to it: how much of Project NOAH was really just one grieving man sitting in a basement, trying to undo his wife's death?

Now, five years later and who knew how many hundreds of millions down the rathole, all they had to show for their troubles were about three hundred dead monkeys, who knew how many dogs and pigs, half a dozen dead homeless guys, and eleven former death row inmates who glowed in the dark and scared the shit out of absolutely everybody. Like the monkeys, the first human subjects had all died within hours, blazing with fever, bleeding out like busted hydrants. But then the first of the inmates, Babcock, had survived – Giles Babcock, as bullshit crazy a man as ever walked the earth; everyone on L4 called him the Talker, on account of the fact that the guy couldn't shut up even for a second, not before and not after – followed by Morrison and Chávez and Baffes and the rest, each refinement making the virus progressively weaker, so the inmates' bodies could combat it. Eleven vampires – why not use the word? – who weren't much good to anyone, as far as Richards could tell. Sykes had confessed that he wasn't sure you could actually *kill* them, short of shooting an RPG down their throats. *VSA: Vampires, Say Aaaah.* The virus had turned their skin into a kind of protein-based exoskeleton, so hard it made Kevlar look like pancake batter. Only over the breastbone, a strike zone about three inches square, was this material thin enough to penetrate. But even that was just a theory.

And the sticks were just crawling with virus. Six months ago, a technician had been exposed; nobody could quite figure out how. But one minute he was fine, the next he was puking onto his faceplate and seizing on the floor of the decon chamber, and if Richards hadn't seen him twitching on the monitor and sealed the level, who knew what might have happened. As it was, all he'd had to do was purge the chamber and watch the man die, then call for cleanup. He thought the tech's name was Samuels, or Samuelson. It didn't matter. The scrubbers showed up clear of virus, and after a seventy-two-hour quarantine, Richards had unsealed the level.

He didn't wonder for a second that he'd pull the plug, if and when the time came. The Elizabeth Protocol: Richards had to hand it to whoever had come up with the name, if it was somebody's idea of a joke. Though of course there was no doubt in Richards's mind who that somebody was. The name was pure Cole – vintage Cole, you might say, since Cole was Cole no more. Beneath that smarmy country club exterior had always lain the heart of a true Machiavellian cutup. *Elizabeth*, for Christsakes. Only Cole would have actually named it for the guy's dead wife.

Richards could feel it now; the whole thing was adrift. Part of the problem was the sheer boredom of it all. You couldn't drop eighty men onto a mountainside with nothing to do but count rabbit skins and ask them to stay put and keep their mouths shut forever.

And then there were the dreams.

Richards had them, too, or thought he did. He never quite remembered. But he sometimes woke up feeling like something strange had happened in the night, as if he'd taken an unplanned trip and only just returned. That's what had happened with the two sweeps who'd gone AWOL. The castrati had been Richards's idea, and for a time it had worked out nicely; you'd never meet a more docile bunch of fellows, mellow as the Buddha every one, and when the game was finally over, nobody that anyone was ever going to miss. The two sweeps, Jack and Sam, had gotten out of the compound by stuffing themselves into a couple of garbage bins. When Richards tracked them down the next morning – holed up in a Red Roof by the interstate twenty miles away, just waiting to be caught – that's all they could talk about, the dreams. The orange light, the teeth, the voices calling their names from the wind. They were just fucking berserk with it. For a while he just sat on the edge of the bed and let them talk it out: two middle-aged sex offenders with skin soft as cashmere and testicles the size of raisins, blowing their noses on their hands, blubbering like kids. It was touching in a way, but you could listen to something like that for only so long. Time to go, boys, Richards said, it's all right, nobody's mad at you, and he drove to a place he knew, a pretty spot with a view of a river, to show them the world they'd be leaving, and shot them in the forehead.

Now Lear wanted a kid, a girl. Even Richards had to pause and think about that. A bunch of homeless drunks and death row inmates were one thing, human recyclables as far as Richards was concerned – but a kid? Sykes had explained that it had to do with the thymus gland. The younger it was, he'd told Richards, the better it could fight off the virus, to bring it to a kind of stasis. That was what Lear had been working toward – all the benefits without the unpleasant side effects. Unpleasant side effects! Richards had to allow himself a laugh at that. Never mind that in their former, human lives, the glowsticks had been men like Babcock, who'd cut their mothers' throats for bus fare. So maybe that had something to do with it, too: Lear wanted a clean slate, somebody whose brain hadn't filled up with junk yet. For all Richards knew, he'd come asking for a baby next.

And Richards had gotten the goods. A few weeks of trolling until he'd found the right one: Caucasian Jane Doe, approximately age six, dumped like a bad habit at a convent in Memphis by a mother who was probably too strung out to care. *Zero footprint*, Sykes had told him, and this girl, this Jane-Doe-approximately-age-six, wouldn't have parted a summer breeze. By Monday, though, she would be in the care of Social Services and you could just kiss her six-year-old backside goodbye. That left a forty-eight-hour window for the grab, assuming the mother didn't return to claim her, like a piece of lost luggage. As for the nuns, well, Wolgast would find a way to handle them. The guy could sell sunlamps in a cancer ward. He'd proved that well enough.

Richards turned from his screen to eyeball the monitors. All the children were snug in their beds. Babcock looked like he was jabbering away as usual, his throat bobbing like a toad's; Richards flicked on the audio and listened for a minute to the clicks and grunts, wondering, as he always did, if it added up to something: 'Let me out of here' or 'I could go for some more rabbits right about now' or 'Richards, the first thing I'm doing when I get out of here is coming for you, brother.' Richards himself spoke a dozen languages – the usual European ones, but also Turkish, Farsi, Arabic, Russian, Tagalog, Hindi, even a little Swahili – and sometimes, listening to Babcock on the monitor, he got the distinct feeling that there were words in there somewhere, chopped up and scrambled, if only he could teach his ears to hear them. But listening now, all he heard was noise.

'Couldn't sleep?'

Richards turned to find Sykes standing in the doorway, holding a cup of coffee. He was wearing his uniform but his tie was undone and the flaps of his jacket hung open. He brushed his hand through his thinning hair and spun a chair around to straddle it, facing Richards.

'Right,' Sykes said. 'Me neither.'

Richards thought to ask him about his dreams but decided against it: the question was moot. He could read the answer in Sykes's face.

'I don't sleep,' Richard said. 'Not much, anyway.'

'Yeah, well.' Sykes shrugged. 'Of course you don't.' When

115

Richards didn't say anything, he tipped his head toward the monitors. 'Everything quiet downstairs?'

Richards nodded.

'Anyone else going out for a walk in the moonlight?'

He meant Jack and Sam, the sweeps. It wasn't Sykes's style to be sarcastic, but he had a right to be steamed. Garbage bins, for Christsakes. The sentries were supposed to inspect everything coming in or out, but they were just kids, really, ordinary enlisted. They acted like they were still in high school because that's pretty much all they knew. You had to keep riding them, and Richards had let things slide.

'I've spoken to the OD. It's not a conversation he's going to forget.'

'You wouldn't by any chance want to tell me what happened to those guys?'

Richards had nothing to say about that. Sykes needed him, but there was no way he'd ever bring himself to like him or, for that matter, approve of him.

Sykes stood and stepped past Richards to the monitors. He adjusted the gain and zoomed in on the one showing Zero.

'They used to be friends, you know,' he said. 'Lear and Fanning.'

Richards nodded. 'So I've heard.'

'Yeah. Well.' Sykes took in a deep breath, his eyes still locked on Zero. 'Hell of a way to treat your friends.'

Sykes turned to point his eyes at Richards, still sitting at his terminal. Sykes looked like he hadn't shaved in a couple of days, and his eyes, squinting in the fluorescent light, were cloudy. He appeared, for a moment, like a man who had forgotten where he was.

'What about us?' he asked Richards. 'Are we friends?'

Now, that was a new one on Richards. Sykes's dreams had to be worse than he'd thought. Friends! Who cared?

'Sure,' Richards said, and allowed himself a smile. 'We're friends.'

Sykes regarded him for another moment. 'On second

116

thought,' he said, 'maybe that's not such a hot idea.' He waved the idea away. 'Thanks anyway.'

Richards knew what was bothering Sykes: the girl. Sykes had a couple kids of his own – two grown boys, both West Point like the old man, one at the Pentagon doing something with intelligence, another with a desert tank unit stationed in Saud – and Richards thought maybe there were grandkids somewhere in the mix, too; Sykes had probably mentioned this in passing, but it wasn't the sort of thing they usually talked about. Either way, this thing with the girl wasn't going to sit well with him. Truthfully, Richards didn't really give a damn what Lear wanted, one way or the other.

'You really should get some shut-eye,' Richards said. 'We've got intake in' – he checked his watch – 'three hours.'

'Might as well just stay up.' Sykes moved to the door, where he turned and gave his weary gaze to Richards again. 'Just between us, and if you don't mind my asking, how'd you get him here so fast?'

'It wasn't hard.' Richards shrugged. 'I got him on a troop transport out of Waco. Bunch of reservists, but it counts as a federal corridor. They landed in Denver a little after midnight.'

Sykes furrowed his brow. 'Federal corridor or not, it's too quick. Any idea what the rush is all about?'

Richards couldn't say for sure; the order had come from the liaison at Special Weapons. But if he had to guess, he would have bet it had something to do with the sweaty cot and soup-encrusted hot plate and a year without sunshine or fresh air, with the bad dreams and the Red Roof and all the rest of it. Hell, if you looked at the situation carefully – something he'd long since stopped bothering to do – it probably all went back to the bookishly pretty Elizabeth Macomb Lear, long battle with cancer, et cetera, et cetera.

'I called in a favor and had the purge done from Langley. Systemwide, soup to nuts. From a big-box perspective, Carter is already nobody. He couldn't buy a pack of gum.'

Sykes frowned. 'Nobody's nobody. There's always someone who's interested.'

'Maybe so. But this guy comes close.'

Sykes lingered another moment at the doorway, saying nothing, both of them knowing what the silence was about. 'Well,' he concluded, 'I still don't like it. We have a protocol for a reason. Three prisons, thirty days, then we bring him in.'

'Is that an order?' A joke; Sykes couldn't give him an order, not really. That he could was a pretense Richards only indulged.

'No, forget it,' Sykes said, and yawned into the back of his hand. 'What would we do, return him?' He rapped the side of the door with his hand. 'Call me when the van gets here. I'll be upstairs, not sleeping.'

Funny thing: when Sykes was gone, Richards found himself wishing he'd hung around. Maybe they were friends, in a sense. Richards had been on bad jobs before; he knew there was a moment when the tone changed, like a quart of milk left out on the counter too long. You found yourself talking as if nothing mattered, like the whole thing was already over. That was when you got to actually liking people, which was a problem. Things fell apart fast after that.

Carter was nobody unusual, just another con with nothing but his life to trade away. But the girl: what could Lear want with a six-year-old girl?

Richards returned his attention to the monitors and picked up the earphones. Babcock was back in the corner, chattering away. It was funny: something about Babcock always gnawed at him. It was as if Richards was *his*, like Babcock owned a piece of him. He couldn't shake the feeling. Richards could sit and listen to the guy for hours. Sometimes he'd fall asleep at the monitors, still wearing the earphones.

He checked his watch again, knowing that he shouldn't but unable to stop himself. It was just past three. He wasn't in the mood for another hand of cards, never mind that little bastard in Seattle, and the hours of waiting for the van to pull into the compound suddenly opened before him like a mouth that could swallow him whole.

There was no fighting it. He adjusted the volume and settled back to listen, wondering what the sounds he heard were trying to tell him.

SIX

Lacey awoke to the sound of rain, fanning into the leaves outside her window.

Amy.

Where was Amy?

She rose quickly, threw on her robe, and hurried down the stairs. But by the time she reached the bottom, her panic had eased; surely the child had simply gotten out of bed in search of breakfast, or to watch TV, or simply to have a look around. In the kitchen Lacey found the girl sitting at the table, still in her pajamas, forking bites of toaster waffle into her mouth. Sister Claire was sitting at the head of the broad table, dressed in sweats from her morning jog through Overton Park, holding a steaming mug of coffee and reading the *Commercial Appeal*. Sister Claire wasn't actually a sister yet, just a novitiate. The shoulders of her sweatshirt were dappled with rain; her face was moist and flushed.

She put the paper down and smiled at Lacey. 'Good, you're up. We've already had our breakfast, right, Amy?'

The little girl nodded, chewing. Before she'd joined the order, Sister Claire had sold houses in Seattle, and as Lacey took a place at the table, she saw what the sister had been reading: the real estate section. If Sister Arnette had seen this, she would have been annoyed, might even have given one of her impromptu speeches about the distractions of material life. But the clock on the stove said it was a little after eight;

the other sisters would be next door at Mass. Lacey felt a stab of embarrassment. How could she have slept so late?

'I went to early services,' Claire said, as if answering her thoughts. Sister Claire often went to the 6:00 a.m. before her daily jog, which she referred to as a visit to 'Our Lady of Endorphins.' Unlike the rest of the sisters, who had never been anything else, Claire had lived a whole life outside the order: been married, made money, owned things, like a condo and nice shoes and a Honda Accord. She hadn't felt the call until she was in her late thirties and divorced from the man she once referred to as 'the worst husband in the world.' Nobody knew the details except perhaps Sister Arnette, but Claire's life was a source of wonder to Lacey. How was it possible for a person to have two lives, so very different from each other? Sometimes Claire would say something like 'Those are cute shoes' or 'The only real good hotel in Seattle is the Vintage Park,' and for a moment all the sisters would be stunned into a silence that was one part disapproval, one part envy. It was Claire who had gone to shop for Amy, the unstated implication being that she was the only one of them who really knew how to do this.

'If you hurry you can still make it to the eight o'clock,' Claire offered. Though of course it was too late; Claire's real meaning, Lacey understood, was something else. 'I can watch Amy.'

Lacey looked at the girl. Her hair was disordered from sleep, but her skin and eyes were bright, rested. Lacey ran the tips of her fingers through the girl's bangs. 'That's very kind of you,' Lacey said. 'Perhaps, today, just this once, because Amy is here—'

'Say no more,' Sister Claire said and, laughing, halted Lacey's words with a hand. 'I'll cover for you.'

The looming day assembled in Lacey's mind. Sitting at the table, she remembered her plan for the zoo. When did it open? What about the rain? It would be best, she thought, to be out of the house before the other sisters returned. Not only because they would wonder why she hadn't come to

Mass; they might also start to ask questions about Amy. The lie had worked so far, but Lacey felt its softness, like a floor of rotten boards beneath her feet.

When Amy had finished her waffles and a tall glass of milk, Lacey led her back upstairs and got her quickly into her clothes: a fresh pair of jeans, stiff with newness, and a T-shirt with the word SASSY stenciled on it, the letters outlined with sequins. Only Sister Claire would have possessed the courage to choose something like that. Sister Arnette wouldn't like the shirt, not at all – if she saw it she'd probably sigh and shake her head as she always did, souring the air of the room – but Lacey knew the shirt was perfect, just the sort of thing a little girl would want to wear. The sequins made the shirt special, and surely that's what God would want for a child like Amy: some happiness, however small. In the bathroom she wiped the syrup off Amy's cheeks and brushed out her hair, and when this was done she dressed herself, in her usual pleated gray skirt and white shirt and veil. Outside, the rain had stopped; a warm, unhurried sun was gathering in the yard outside. The day would be hot, Lacey guessed, a blast of warmth sailing in from the south behind the cold front that had pushed rain over the house all night.

She had a little cash, enough for tickets and a treat, and the zoo, of course, was something they could walk to. They stepped outside, into air that had begun to swell with heat and the sweetness of wet grass. The bells of the church had begun to bong out the hour; Mass would be ending at any moment. She led Amy quickly through the garden gate, through the tart aroma of herbs, the rosemary and tarragon and basil that Sister Louise tended so carefully, into the park, where people were already gathering for the first warm day of spring, to taste the sun and feel it on their skin: young people with dogs and Frisbees, joggers plodding along the paths, families staking out shady tables and barbecue pits. The zoo stood at the north end of the park, flanked by a broad avenue that cleaved the neighborhood like a blade. On the far side, the big houses and wide, princely lawns of old Midtown were forgotten, replaced by shotgun shacks with broken-down porches and half-assembled cars melting into the packed-dirt yards. Young men floated up and down the streets like pigeons, roosting on this corner or that and then moving on, all of it benumbed with idleness and vaguely ominous. Lacey should have felt better about this neighborhood than she did, but the blacks who lived there were different from Lacey, who had never been poor, at least not in the same way. In Sierra Leone her father had worked for the ministry; her mother kept a car and driver for shopping trips to Freetown and the polo matches at the fairgrounds; one time they'd attended a party where the president himself had danced a waltz with her.

At the edge of the zoo the air changed, smelling of peanuts and animals. A line had already formed at the entrance. Lacey purchased their tickets, counting out her change to the penny, then took Amy's hand again and led her through the turnstile. The little girl was wearing her backpack with Peter Rabbit inside; when Lacey had suggested that it could remain at the house, she had seen, quickly, in the flash of the girl's eyes, that this wasn't even a question. The bag was nothing she could leave.

'What do you want to see?' she asked. Twenty feet from the entrance, they found a kiosk with a large map, blocked out in colors for different habitats and species. A white couple was examining it, the man with a camera swinging from a lanyard around his neck, the woman gently pushing a stroller back and forth; the baby, buried in a mound of pink fabric, was asleep. The woman glanced at Lacey and regarded her, momentarily, with suspicion: what was a black nun doing with a little white girl? But then she smiled, a little too forcibly – a smile of apology, of retraction – and the couple moved away down the path.

Amy peered at the map. Lacey didn't know if she could read, but there were pictures beside the words.

'I don't know,' she said. 'Bears?'

'What kind?'

The girl thought a moment, scanning the images. 'Polar bears.' Her eyes warmed with anticipation as she spoke; the idea of the zoo, of seeing the animals, was something the two of them now shared. It was just as Lacey had hoped. As they'd stood there, more people had come through the gate; suddenly the zoo was humming with visitors. 'Also zebras and elephants and monkeys.'

'Wonderful,' Lacey said, and smiled. 'We will see them all.'

At a snack stand they bought a bag of peanuts and made their way into the zoo's interior, its rich zone of sounds and smells. As they approached the polar bear tank they heard laughter and splashing and shouts of hilarious terror, a mixture of voices both young and old. Amy, who had been holding Lacey's hand, released it suddenly and dashed ahead.

Lacey made her way between the shoulders of the people who had gathered at the bear tank. She found Amy standing with her face just inches from the glass that gave an underwater view of the bears' habitat – a curious sight in the Memphis heat, with rocks painted to look like ice floes and a deep pool of Arctic blueness. Three bears were basking in the sun, lounging like gigantic rugs by a fire; a fourth was paddling in the water. While Amy and Lacey watched he swam right up to them and, fully submerged, bumped his nose on the glass. The people around her gasped; a jolt of pleasurable fear shot down Lacey's spine, into her feet and fingertips. Amy reached out and touched the sweating glass, inches from the bear's face. The bear opened his mouth, showing his pink tongue.

'Careful there,' a man behind them warned. 'They may look cute, but to them you're just lunch, little girl.'

Startled, Lacey turned her head, searching for the source of the voice. Who was this man, to try to scare a child like that? But none of the faces behind her returned her look; everyone was smiling and watching the bears.

'Amy,' she said softly, and put her hand on the girl's shoulder. 'Perhaps it's best not to tease them.'

Amy seemed not to hear her. She leaned her face closer to the glass. 'What's your name?' she asked the bear.

'There now, Amy,' Lacey said. 'Not so close.'

Amy stroked the glass. 'He has a bear name. It's something I can't pronounce.'

Lacey hesitated. Was it a game? 'The bear has a name?'

The girl looked up, squinting. A knowing light was in her face. 'Of course he does.'

'He told you this.'

The pool erupted with a tremendous splash. The crowd drew a sharp intake of breath. A second bear had leapt into the water. He – she? – paddled through the blue toward Amy. So now there were two, bumping the glass just inches from her face, their bodies big as automobiles, their white fur rippling in the underwater currents.

'Will you look at that,' someone said. It was the woman Lacey had seen at the kiosk. She was standing beside them, holding her infant up to the glass by the armpits, like a doll. The woman, whose long hair was stretched away from her face by a tight ponytail, was wearing shorts and a T-shirt and flip-flops. Lacey could discern, through the folds of her shirt, the still-loose belly of her pregnancy. The husband was behind them, guarding the empty stroller and holding the camera.

'I think they like you,' the woman said to Amy. 'Look, sweetie,' she sang, and jiggled the infant, making her arms flap like a bird's. 'See the bears. See the bears, sweetie. Honey, take the picture. Take . . . the . . . picture.'

'I can't,' said the man. 'You're not looking the right way. Turn her around.'

The woman sighed irritably. 'Come on, just take it while she's smiling, is that so hard?'

Lacey was watching this when it happened: a second splash, and then, before she could turn her head, a third. She felt the glass bulge beside her. A ridge of water crested the lip and began to fall, everyone aware of what was happening but powerless to act.

124

'Look out!'

The icy water hit Lacey like a slap, filling her nose and mouth and eyes with the taste of salt, hurling her back from the glass. A chorus of screams erupted all around. She heard the baby's cry, and then the mother yelling, *Get away, get away!* Bodies banged against her; Lacey realized she'd closed her eyes, against the stinging salt. She tumbled backward, her feet catching and tripping, and fell onto a pile of people. She waited for the sound of the glass breaking, the slam of the tank's unleashed water.

'Amy!'

She opened her eyes to find a man looking at her, his face inches from her own. It was the man with the camera. Around her the crowd had fallen silent. The glass had held after all.

'Sorry,' the man said. 'Are you all right, Sister? I must have tripped.'

'Goddamnit!' The woman was standing over them, her clothing and hair soaked through. The baby was screaming against her shoulder. Her face was furious. 'What did your kid do?'

Lacey realized she was talking to *her.*

'I'm sorry—' she began. 'I don't—'

'Look at her!'

The crowds had backed away from the tank, all eyes locked on the little girl with the backpack who was kneeling before it, her hands on the glass, and the four bear faces crowded against it.

Lacey climbed to her feet and moved quickly. The little girl's head was bowed, water still raining from her drenched hair onto her knees. Lacey saw that her lips were moving, as if in prayer.

'Amy, what is it?'

'That girl's talking to the bears!' a voice cried, and a buzz of wonder went up from the crowd. 'Look at that!'

Cameras began to click. Lacey crouched beside Amy. With her fingers she pulled the dark strands of the girl's hair away from her face. Her cheeks were streaked with tears, mixed in with all the water from the tank.

'Tell me, child.'

'They know,' Amy said, her hands still pressed to the glass.

'What do the bears know?'

The girl raised her face. Lacey was stunned; never had she seen such sadness in a child's expression, such knowing grief. And yet, as she searched Amy's eyes, she saw no fear. Whatever Amy had learned, she had accepted it.

'What I am,' she said.

Sister Arnette, sitting in the kitchen of the Convent of the Sisters of Mercy, had decided to do something.

It was 9:00, it was 9:30, it was 10:00; Lacey and the girl, Amy, had not returned from wherever they had gone. Eventually Sister Claire had surrendered the story: that Lacey had skipped Mass, and that the two of them had left shortly thereafter, the girl with her backpack; Claire had heard them leave and then watched from the window as they made their way through the back gate, to the park.

Lacey was up to something. Arnette should have known.

The story about the girl didn't wash, she'd known that right away; or, if not known exactly, then certainly she had felt it, a kernel of suspicion that had grown overnight into the certainty that something was not right. Like Miss Clavel, in the Madeline books, Sister Arnette *knew*.

And now, just like in the story: one of the little girls was gone.

None of the other sisters knew the truth about Lacey. Even Arnette hadn't learned the full story until the office of the superior general had forwarded the psychiatric report. Arnette remembered hearing something about it on the news, all those years ago, but wasn't something like that always happening somewhere, especially in Africa? Those awful little countries where life seemed to mean nothing, where His will was the strangest and most unknowable of all? It was heartbreaking, horrifying, but the mind could take in only so much, so many stories of this kind, and Arnette had forgotten all about it; and now here was Lacey, under her care, no one else knowing the truth; Lacey, who, she had to admit, was in nearly every way a model sister, if a little self-contained, perhaps a little too mystical in her devotions. Lacey said, and no doubt believed, too, that her father and mother and sisters were still in Sierra Leone, going to palace balls and riding their polo ponies; since the day she'd been found hiding in a field by the UN peacekeepers who had turned her over to the sisters, Lacey had never said otherwise. It was a mercy, of course; it was God's own mercy, protecting Lacey from the memory of what had happened. Because after the soldiers had killed her family, they hadn't simply gone away; they'd stayed with Lacey in the field, for hours and hours, and the little girl they'd left for dead might just as well have *been* dead, if God hadn't protected her by washing her mind of these events. That He had chosen not to take her at that instant was simply an expression of His will, and nothing for Arnette to question. It was a burden, this knowledge, and the worry that came with it, for Arnette to bear in silence.

But now there was the girl. This Amy. Polite to a fault, quiet as a ghost, but wasn't there something rather obviously wrong with the whole situation? Something completely unbelievable? Now that she thought about it, Lacey's explanation made less than no sense. She was friends with her mother? Impossible. Except for daily Mass, Lacey barely set foot outside the house; how she would have come into contact with such a woman, let alone a woman who would trust her with her daughter, Arnette could not explain. Because there was no explanation; the story was a lie. And now the two of them were gone.

Sitting in the kitchen at 10:30, Sister Arnette knew what she had to do.

But what would she say? Where would she start? With Amy? None of the other sisters seemed to know anything. The girl had arrived when Lacey was alone in the house, as she often was; Arnette had tried many times to coax her out, for their days at the Pantry and also on small trips, to the store and what-have-you, but always Lacey declined, her face at such instances radiating a kind of cheerful blankness that put the question instantly to rest. *No thank you, Sister. Perhaps another day.* Three, four years of this, and now the girl had appeared out of nowhere, Lacey claiming to know her. So if she called the police, the story would have to start there, she understood, with Lacey, and the story of the field.

Arnette picked up the phone.

'Sister?'

She turned: Sister Claire. Claire, who had just come into the kitchen, still in her sweat suit, when she should have changed for the day by now; Claire, who had sold real estate, who'd been not only married but also *divorced*; who still kept a pair of high-heeled shoes and a black cocktail dress hanging in her closet. But that was an altogether different problem, not the one she was thinking about now.

'Sister,' Claire said, her voice concerned, 'there's a car in the driveway.'

Arnette hung up the phone. 'Who is it?'

Claire hesitated. 'They look . . . like police.'

Arnette reached the front door just as the bell was ringing. She drew back the curtain of the side window to look. Two men, one maybe in his twenties, the other older but still somebody she thought of as a young man, the pair of them looking like funeral directors in dark suits and ties. Police, but not exactly. Something serious, official. They were standing in the sunshine at the bottom of the steps, away from the door. The older one saw her and smiled in a friendly way but didn't say anything. He was nice-looking but unremarkable, with a trim physique and a pleasant, well-shaped face. A bit of gray fanned away at the temples, which shimmered faintly with perspiration in the sun.

'Should we open it?' Claire asked, standing behind her. Sister Louise had heard the bell and come downstairs as well.

128

Arnette took a deep breath to calm herself. 'Of course, Sisters.'

She opened the door but left the screen closed and latched. The two men stepped forward.

'May I help you gentlemen?'

The older one reached into his breast pocket and produced a small billfold. He opened it and in a flash she saw the initials: FBI.

'Ma'am, I'm Special Agent Wolgast. This is Special Agent Doyle.' Just like that, the billfold was gone, returned to the insides of his suit coat. She saw a scrape on his chin; he had cut himself shaving. 'Sorry to disturb you like this on a Saturday morning—'

'It's about Amy,' Arnette said. She couldn't explain it: she'd just blurted it out, like he'd somehow made her do this. When he didn't reply, she continued, 'It is, isn't it? It's about Amy.'

The older agent – his name had already slipped her mind – glanced past Arnette at Sister Louise, sending her a quick, reassuring smile before returning his eyes to Arnette.

'Yes, ma'am. That's correct. It's about Amy. Would it be all right if we came in? To ask you and the other ladies a couple of questions?'

Which was how they came to be standing in the living room of the Convent of the Sisters of Mercy: two large men in dark suits, smelling of masculine sweat. Their hulking presence seemed to change the room, make it smaller. Except for the occasional repairman or a visit from Father Fagan from the rectory, no other men ever came into the house.

'I'm sorry, Officers,' Arnette said, 'could you tell me your names again?'

'Of course.' That smile again: confident, ingratiating. So far, the young one hadn't said a single word. 'I'm Agent Wolgast, this is Agent Doyle.' He glanced around. 'So, is Amy here?'

Sister Claire cut in. 'Why do you want her?'

'I'm afraid I can't tell you ladies everything. But you should know, for your own safety, that Amy is a federal witness. We're here to place her under protection.'

Federal protection! Arnette's chest tightened with panic. It was worse than she had thought. Federal protection! Like something on TV, on those police shows she didn't want to watch but sometimes did, because the other sisters wanted to.

'What did Lacey do?'

The agent's eyebrows lifted with interest. 'Lacey?'

He was trying to pretend that he knew, to open a space for her to talk so he could draw information out of her; Arnette could see this clearly. But of course that's just what she'd done; she'd given them Lacey's name. No one had said anything about Lacey except Arnette. Behind her, she could feel the other sisters' silence pressing upon her.

'Sister Lacey,' she explained. 'She told us Amy's mother was a friend.'

'I see.' He glanced at the other agent. 'Well, perhaps we'd better talk to her as well.'

'Are we in any danger?' Sister Louise said.

Sister Arnette turned to her with a silencing scowl. 'Sister, I know you mean well. But let me handle this, please.'

'I wouldn't say danger, not exactly,' the agent explained. 'But I think it would be best if we could speak to her. Is she in the house now?'

'No.' This was Sister Claire. She was standing defiantly, her arms crossed over her chest. 'They left. At least an hour ago.'

'Do you know where they went?'

For a moment, no one said anything. Then, within the house, the telephone rang.

'Please excuse me, gentlemen,' Arnette said.

She retreated to the kitchen. Her heart was pounding. She was grateful for the interruption, as it could give her a chance to think. But when she answered the phone, the voice on the other end was no one she recognized.

'Is this the convent? I know I've seen you ladies over there. You'll have to pardon my calling like this.'

'Who is this?'

'Sorry.' He was speaking in a rush, his voice distracted. 'The name's Joe Murphy. I'm head of security at the Memphis Zoo.'

There was some kind of commotion in the background. For a moment he spoke to someone else: *Just open the gate*, he said. *Just do it, now.*

Then he was back on the line. 'Do you know anything about a nun who might be over here with a little girl? A black lady, dressed like you all do.'

A buzzing weightlessness, like a swarm of bees, filled Sister Arnette. On a perfectly pleasant morning, something had happened, something terrible. The door to the kitchen swung open; the agents stepped into the room, trailed by Sister Claire and Sister Louise. Everyone was staring at her.

'Yes, yes, I know her.' Arnette was trying to keep her voice low but knew this was pointless. 'What is it? What's going on?'

For a moment the line was muffled; the man at the zoo had placed his hand over the receiver. When he lifted his hand she heard yelling, and crying children, and behind it, something else: the sound of animals. Monkeys and lions and elephants and birds, screeching and roaring. It took Arnette a moment to realize that she wasn't just hearing these sounds over the phone; they were coming through the open window, too, traveling clear across the park into the kitchen.

'What's going on?' she pleaded.

'You better get over here, Sister,' the man said. 'This is the goddamnedest thing I've ever seen.'

Lacey, breathless and running, soaked to the bone: she was carrying Amy now, clutching the little girl to her chest, the girl's legs clamped tightly around her waist, the two of them lost in the zoo, its maze of pathways. Amy was crying, sobbing into Lacey's blouse – *what I am, what I am* – and other people were running, too. It had started with the bears, whose movements had grown more and more frantic until Lacey had pulled Amy away from the glass, and then, behind them, the sea lions, who began to hurl themselves in and out of the water with manic fury; and as they turned and dashed back toward the zoo's center, the grassland animals, the gazelles and zebras and okapis and giraffes, who broke into wild circles, running and charging the fences. It was Amy who was doing it, Lacey knew – something about Amy. Whatever had happened to the polar bears was happening to everything now, not just the animals but the people too, a ring of chaos widening over the entire zoo. They passed by the elephants and at once she felt their size and force; they stomped the ground with their immense feet and lifted their trunks to trumpet into the Memphis heat. A rhino charged the fence, a huge noise like a car crashing, and began, furiously, to bang it with his massive horn. The air was suddenly swollen with these sounds, great and terrible and full of pain, and people were tearing about and calling out to their children, pushing and shoving and pulling, the crowds parting for Lacey as she raced ahead.

'That's her!' a voice rang out, and the words struck Lacey from behind – hit her like an arrow. Lacey spun to see the man with the camera, pointing a long finger right at her. He was standing beside a security guard in a pastel yellow jersey. 'That's the kid!'

Still clutching Amy, Lacey turned and ran, past cages of shrieking monkeys, a lagoon where swans were honking and flapping their huge, useless wings, tall cages erupting with the cries of jungle birds. Terrified crowds were pouring out of the reptile house. A group of panicked schoolchildren in matching red T-shirts stepped into Lacey's path and she twisted around them, nearly falling but somehow staying upright. The ground before her was littered with the debris of flight, brochures and small articles of clothing and blobs of melting ice cream stuck to paper. A group of men tore past, breathing hard; one was carrying a rifle. From somewhere, a voice was saying, with robotic calm, 'The zoo is now closed. Please move quickly to the nearest exit. The zoo is now closed . . .'

Lacey was going in circles now, looking for a way out, finding none. Lions were roaring, baboons, meerkats, the monkeys she'd listened to from her bedroom window on summer nights. The sounds came from everywhere, filled up her mind like a chorus, ricocheting like the sound of gunfire, like the gunfire in the field, like her mother's voice crying from the doorway: *Run away, run away as fast as you can.*

She stopped. And that was when she felt it. Felt *him.* The shadow. The man who wasn't there but also was. He was coming for Amy, Lacey knew that now. That's what the animals were telling her. The dark man would take Amy to the field where the branches were, the ones Lacey had watched for hours and hours as she lay and looked at the sky as it paled from night to morning, hearing the sounds of what was happening to her and the cries coming from her mouth; but she had sent her mind away from her body, up and up through the branches to heaven, where God was, and the girl in the field was someone else, nobody she remembered, and the world was wrapped in a warm light that would keep her safe forever.

The stinging taste of salt was in her mouth, but it wasn't just the water from the tank. She was weeping now, too, watching the path through the shimmering curtain of her tears, holding Amy fiercely as she ran. Then she saw it: the snack stand. It appeared before her like a beacon, the snack stand with the big umbrella where she had bought the peanuts, and beyond it, standing open like a mouth, the wide gate of the exit. Guards in their yellow jerseys were barking into their walkie-talkies and waving people frantically through. Lacey took a deep breath and moved into the crowd, holding Amy to her chest.

She was just a few feet from the exit when a hand gripped her arm. She turned sharply: one of the guards. With his free hand he gestured over her head to someone else, his grip tightening.

Lacey. Lacey.

'Ma'am, please come with me—'

She didn't wait. With a shove she pushed forward with all the strength she had left, felt the crowd bending. Behind her she heard the grunts and cries of people falling as she broke free, and the guard calling out for her to stop; but they were through the gate now, Lacey tearing down the pathway into the parking lot and the sound of sirens drawing near. She was sweating and breathing hard and knew that at any moment she could fall. She didn't know where she was going but it didn't matter. *Away,* she thought, *away. Run as fast as you can, children. Away with Amy, away.*

Then, from behind her, somewhere in the zoo, she heard a rifle shot. The sound cleaved the air, freezing Lacey in her tracks. In the sudden silence of its aftermath a van pulled up, skidding to a stop in front of her. Amy had gone limp against her chest. It was their van, Lacey saw, the one the sisters used, the big blue van they drove to the Pantry and to run errands. Sister Claire was driving, still in her sweats. A second vehicle, a black sedan, pulled in behind them as Sister Arnette burst from the van's passenger seat. Around them the crowds were streaming past, cars were zooming out of the lot.

'Lacey, what in the world—'

Two men emerged from the second vehicle. Darkness poured off them. Lacey's heart clenched, her voice stopped in her throat like a cork. She didn't have to look to know what they were. *Too late! All lost!*

'No!' She was backing away. 'No!'

Arnette gripped her by the arm. 'Sister, get ahold of yourself!'

People were pulling at her. Hands were trying to wriggle the child free. With every ounce of strength Lacey held fast, squeezing the child to her chest. 'Don't let them!' she cried. 'Help me!'

'Sister Lacey, these men are from the FBI! Please, do as they ask!'

'Don't take her!' Lacey was on the ground now. 'Don't take her! Don't take her!'

It was Arnette, after all; it was Sister Arnette who was taking Amy from her. As it had been in the field, Lacey kicking and fighting and screaming.

'Amy, Amy!'

She shook with a huge sob then, the last of her strength leaving her body in a rush; a space opened around her as she felt Amy lifted away. She heard the girl's small voice crying out to her, *Lacey, Lacey, Lacey*, and then the muffling clap of the car's doors as Amy was sealed away inside. She heard the sound of an engine, wheels turning, a car pulling away at high speed. Her face was in her hands.

'Don't take me, don't take me,' she was sobbing. 'Don't take me, don't take me, don't take me.'

Claire was beside her now. She put an arm around Lacey's shaking shoulders. 'Sister, it's all right,' she said, and Lacey could tell she was crying, too. 'It's all right. You're safe now.'

But it wasn't; *she* wasn't. No one was safe, not Lacey or Claire or Arnette or the woman with the baby or the guard in his yellow shirt. Lacey knew that now. How could Claire tell her everything was all right? Because it wasn't all right. That was what the voices had been saying to her all these years, since that night in the field when she was just a girl.

Lacey Antoinette Kudoto. Listen. Look.

In her mind's eye she saw it, saw it all at last: the rolling armies and the flames of battle; the graves and pits and dying cries of a hundred million souls; the spreading darkness, like a black wing stretching over the earth; the last, bitter hours of cruelty and sorrow, and terrible, final flights; death's great dominion over all, and, at the last, the empty cities, becalmed by the silence of a hundred years. Already these things were coming to pass. Lacey wept, and wept some more. Because, sitting on the curb in Memphis, Tennessee, she saw Amy too; her Amy, whom Lacey could not save, as she could not save herself. Amy, time-stilled and nameless, wandering the forgotten, lightless world forever, alone and voiceless, but for this:

What I am, what I am, what I am.

SEVEN

Carter was someplace cold; that was the first thing he could tell. They took him off the plane first – Carter had never been on a plane in his life and would have liked to have had a window seat, but they'd stuffed him in the back with all the rucksacks, his left wrist chained to a pipe and two soldiers to watch him – and as he stepped onto the stairs leading down to the tarmac, the cold hit his lungs like a slap. Carter had been cold before, you couldn't sleep under a Houston freeway in January and not know what cold was, but the cold here was different, so dry he could feel his lips puckering. His ears had clogged up, too. It was late, who knew how late exactly, but the airfield was lit like a jailyard; from the top of the stairs, Carter counted a dozen aircraft, big fat ones with huge doors dropped open at the back like a kid's pajamas, and forklifts moving to and fro along the tarmac, loading pallets draped with camo. He wondered if maybe they were going to make some kind of soldier out of him, if that's what he'd traded his life for.

Wolgast: he remembered the name. It was funny how he'd found himself trusting the man. Carter hadn't trusted anyone in a long, long time. But there was something about Wolgast that made him think the man knew the place he was in.

Carter's wrists and feet were shackled, and he made his way gingerly down the stairs, minding his balance, one soldier ahead of him, one behind. Neither had spoken a word to him or even to each other that Carter could tell. He was wearing a parka over his jumpsuit, but it was unzipped for the chains, and the wind cut through him easily. They led him across the field toward a brightly lit hangar where a van was idling. The door slid open as they approached.

The first soldier poked him with his rifle. 'In you go.'

Carter did as he said, then heard a small motor whir and the door closed behind him. At least the seats were comfortable, not like the hard bench on the plane. The only light was from a little bulb in the ceiling. He heard two thumps on the door and the van pulled away.

He'd dozed on the plane and wasn't tired enough to sleep more. With no windows and no way to tell the time, he had no sense of distance or direction. But he'd sat still for whole months of his life; a few hours more wasn't anything he couldn't do. He let his mind go blank for a while. Time passed, and then he felt the van slowing. From the other side of the wall that sealed him from the driver's compartment came the muffled sound of voices, but Carter didn't know what it was all about. The van lurched forward and stopped again.

The door slid open to show two soldiers stamping their feet in the cold, white boys wearing parkas over their fatigues. Behind the soldiers, the brightly lit oasis of a McDonald's throbbed in the gloom. Carter heard the rush of traffic and figured they were by a highway somewhere. Though it was still dark, something about the sky felt like morning. His legs and arms were stiff from sitting.

'Here,' one of the guards said and tossed him a bag. He noticed then that the other guard was biting into the last of a sandwich. 'Breakfast.'

Carter opened the bag, which contained an Egg McMuffin and a disk of hash browns wrapped in paper and a plastic cup of juice. His throat was bone dry from the cold, and he wished there was more of the juice, or even just water to drink. He drained it quickly. It was so sugary it made his teeth tingle.

'Thank you.'

The soldier yawned into his hand. Carter wondered why they were being so nice. They didn't seem at all like Pincher and the rest of them. They were wearing sidearms but didn't act like this was anything.

'We've got a couple of hours yet,' the soldier said as Carter finished eating. 'You need to make a pit stop?'

Carter hadn't peed since the plane, but he was so dried out he didn't figure there was much in him to go with. He'd always been like that, could hold it for hours and hours. But he thought about the McDonald's, the people inside, the smell of food and the bright lights, and knew he wanted to see it.

'I reckon so.'

The soldier climbed into the van, his heavy boots clanging on the metal floor. Crouching in the tiny space, he removed a shiny key from a pouch on his belt and unlocked the shackles. Anthony could see his face up close. He had red hair and wasn't no more than twenty, give or take.

'No funny stuff, understand?' he told Anthony. 'We're not really supposed to do this.'

'No sir.'

'Here, zip up your coat. It's fucking freezing out here.'

They led him across the parking lot, one on either side but not touching him. Carter couldn't remember when he'd gone anywhere without somebody else's hand on him someplace. Most of the cars in the lot had Colorado plates. The air smelled clean, like Pine-Sol, and he felt the presence of mountains around him, pressing down. There was snow on the ground, too, piled high against the edges of the lot and crusted with ice. He'd only seen snow once or twice in his life.

The soldiers knocked on the bathroom door, and when nobody answered, they let Carter inside. One came in while the other watched the door. There were two urinals, and Carter took one. The soldier who was with him took the other.

'Hands where I can see 'em,' the soldier said, and laughed. 'Just kidding.'

Carter finished up and stepped to the sink to wash. The McDonald's he remembered from Houston were pretty dirty, especially the restrooms. When he was living on the street, he used to use one up in Montrose to wash up once in a while, until the manager caught on and chased him away. But this one was nice and clean, with flowery-smelling soap and a little potted plant sitting beside the sink. He washed his hands, taking his time, letting the warm water flow over his skin.

'They got plants in McDonald's now?' he asked the soldier.

The soldier gave him a puzzled look, then burst into laughter. 'How long you been away?'

Carter didn't know what was so funny. 'Most my life,' he said.

When they exited the bathroom, the first soldier was standing in line, so the three of them waited together. Neither had so much as laid a hand on him. Carter took a slow look around the room: a couple of men sitting alone, a family or two, a woman with a teenage boy who was playing a handheld video game. Everyone was white.

They got to the counter and the soldier ordered coffee.

'You need anything else?' he asked Carter.

Carter thought a moment. 'They got iced tea here?'

'You got iced tea?' the soldier asked the girl behind the counter.

She shrugged. She was loudly chewing gum. 'Hot tea.'

The soldier looked at Carter, who shook his head.

'Just the coffee.'

The soldiers were Paulson and Davis. They introduced themselves when they got back to the van. One was from Connecticut, the other one from New Mexico, though Carter got them confused, and he didn't figure it made much difference, since he'd never been to either place. Davis was the one with the red hair. For the rest of the drive they left open the little window that connected the two compartments in the van; they left the shackles off, too. They were in Colorado, like he'd guessed, but whenever they came to a road sign the soldiers told him to cover his eyes, laughing like this was a big joke.

After a time they got off the interstate and took a rural highway that wound tight against the mountains. Sitting on the front bench of the passenger compartment, Carter could view a bit of the passing world through the windshield. Snow was piled steeply against the roadsides. There were no towns at all that Carter could see; only once in a while did a car approach them from the other direction, a blaze of light followed by the splash of melted snow as it passed. He'd never been anyplace like this, that had so few people in it. The clock on the dash said it was a little after six a.m.

'Cold up here,' Carter said.

Paulson was driving; the other one, Davis, was reading a comic book.

'You got that right,' said Paulson. 'Colder'n Beth Pope's back brace.'

'Who Beth Pope?'

Paulson shrugged, peering over the wheel. 'Girl I knew in high school. She had, what's that thing, scoliosis.'

Carter didn't know what that was, either. But Paulson and Davis thought it was funny enough. If the job Wolgast had for him meant working with these two, he'd be glad to do it.

'That Aquaman?' Carter asked Davis.

Davis passed him a couple of comic books from the pile, a League of Vengeance and an X-Men. It was too dark to read the words, but Carter liked looking at the pictures, which told the story anyway. That Wolverine was a badass; Carter had always liked him, though he always felt sorry for him, too. It couldn't be no fun having all that metal in your bones, and somebody he cared about was always dying or getting killed.

After another hour or so Paulson pulled the van over. 'Sorry, dude,' he told Carter. 'We've got to lock you up again.'

''Sall right,' Carter said, and nodded. 'I appreciate the time.'

Davis climbed out of the passenger seat and came around back. The door opened to a blast of cold air. Davis redid the shackles and pocketed the key.

'Comfortable?'

Carter nodded. 'How much longer we got to go?'

'Not much,' he said.

They drove on. Carter could tell they were climbing now. He couldn't see the sky but guessed it would be light soon. As they slowed to cross a long bridge, wind buffeted the van.

They had reached the other side when Paulson met his eyes through the rearview. 'You know, you don't seem like the others,' he said. 'What you do, anyway? You don't mind my asking.'

'Who the others?'

'You know. Other guys like you. Cons.' He swiveled his head to Davis. 'Remember that guy, Babcock?' He shook his head and laughed. 'Christ on a stick, what a whack job.' He looked at Carter again. 'He wasn't like you, that guy. I can tell you're different.'

'I ain't crazy,' Carter said. 'Judge said I wasn't.'

'But you did somebody, right? Else you wouldn't be here now.'

Carter wondered if talking like this was something he had to do, if it was part of the deal. 'They said I killed a lady. But I didn't mean to.'

'Who was she? Wife, girlfriend, something like that?' Paulson was still grinning at him in the rearview, his eyes flashing with interest.

'No.' Carter swallowed. 'I cut the lady's lawn.'

Paulson laughed and glanced at Davis again. 'Listen to this. He cut the lady's lawn.' He looked at Carter through the mirror again. 'Little guy like you, how'd you do it?'

Carter didn't know what to say. He had a bad feeling now, like maybe they'd been nice to him just to mess with his head.

141

'Come on, Anthony. We got you a McMuffin, right? Took you to the bathroom? You can tell us.'

'For fucksakes,' Davis said to Paulson. 'Just shut up. We're almost there, what's the point?'

'The point is,' Paulson said, and drew in a breath, 'I want to know what this guy *did*. They all did *something*. Come on, Anthony, what's your story? You rape her before you did her? Was that it?'

Carter felt his face go hot with shame. 'I wouldn't never do that,' he managed.

Davis turned to Carter. 'Don't listen to this douche bag. You don't have to say anything.'

'Come on, the dude's *retarded*. Can't you see that?' Paulson eyed Carter eagerly through the mirror again. 'I bet that's what happened, isn't it? I bet you fucked the nice white lady whose lawn you were cutting, didn't you, Anthony?'

Carter felt the air stick in his throat. 'I ain't . . . sayin' . . . no more.'

'You know what they're going to do with you?' Paulson asked. 'You thought maybe this was all a free ride?'

'Goddamnit. Zip your mouth,' Davis said. 'Richards will have both our asses for this.'

'Yeah, fuck him too,' Paulson said.

'Man . . . said I got a job,' Anthony managed. 'Said it was important. Said . . . I special.'

'Special.' Paulson snickered over the word. 'You're special, all right.'

They drove on in silence. Carter looked at the floor of the van, feeling dizzy and sick to his stomach. He wished now he'd never eaten the McMuffin. He'd begun to cry. Didn't know when he'd done that last. Nobody had ever said anything about raping the woman, not that he recalled. They'd asked about the girl but he'd always said no, which was the God's truth, he swore it. The little thing weren't no more than five year old. He'd just been trying to show her a toad he found in the grass. He thought she'd like to see something like that, something tiny, like she was. That's all he'd meant to do, nice. Ain't nobody ever done things like that for him when he was a boy. *C'mere honey, I got something to show you. Just a little bit of a thing, like you.*

At least he'd known what Terrell was, what was going to happen to him there. Nobody'd said nothing about raping the lady, Mrs Wood. That day in the yard, she'd gone just flat-out crazy on him, screaming and hitting, telling the little girl to run, and it wasn't his fault she'd fallen in, he'd just been trying to make her calm down, tell her nothing had happened, he'd go away and never come back if that's what she wanted. He'd been okay with that, and okay with the rest too, when it came down to it. But then Wolgast had showed up and told him he didn't have to go to the needle after all, turning Carter's mind in another direction, and now look where he was. There weren't no sense in any of it. It made him sick and shaky to his bones.

He lifted his head to find Paulson grinning at him. The whites of his eyes widened.

'Boo!' Paulson slapped the wheel and burst into laughter, like he'd just told the best joke of his life. Then he slammed the window shut.

Wolgast and Doyle were somewhere in South Memphis now, working their way out of the city's suburban ring through a warren of residential streets. The whole thing had gone bad from the start. Wolgast had no idea what in the hell had been going on at the zoo, the whole place was going berserk, and then the woman, the old nun, Arnette, had just about tackled the other one, Lacey, to get the girl out of her hands.

The girl. Amy NLN. She couldn't have been more than six years old.

Wolgast had been ready to pull the plug but then she'd let the girl go, and the old one handed her off to Doyle, who carried her to the car before Wolgast could get in another word. After that, there was nothing to do but get out of there as fast as they could before the locals showed up and started asking questions. Who knew how many witnesses there'd been; it had all happened too fast.

He had to dump the car. He had to call Sykes. He had to get them out of Tennessee, all in that order, and he had to do it now. Amy was lying across the backseat, facing away, clutching the stuffed rabbit she'd gotten out of her backpack. Sweet Jesus, what had he done? A six-year-old girl!

In a dreary neighborhood of apartments and strip malls, Wolgast pulled into a gas station and shut off the engine. He turned to Doyle. The two of them hadn't spoken since the zoo.

'What the hell is wrong with you?'

'Brad, listen—'

'Are you crazy? Look at her. She's a kid.'

'It just kind of happened.' Doyle shook his head. 'Everything was so crazy. Okay, maybe I fucked up, I admit that. But what was I supposed to do?'

Wolgast breathed deeply, trying to calm himself. 'Wait here.'

He stepped from the car and punched in the code for Sykes's secure line. 'We've got a problem.'

'You have her?'

'Yes, we have her. She's a *child.* What the fuck.'

'Agent, I know you're angry—'

'You're goddamn right I'm angry. And we had about fifty witnesses, starting with the nuns. I feel like dropping her off at the nearest cop shop.'

Sykes was silent a moment. 'I need you to focus, Agent. Let's just get you out of state. Then we'll figure out what happens next.'

'Nothing's going to happen next. This is not what I signed on for.'

'I can hear you're upset. You have a right to be. Where are you?'

Wolgast took a deep breath, bringing his anger under control. 'At a gas station. South Memphis.'

'Is she all right?'

'Physically.'

'Don't do anything stupid.'

'Are you threatening me?' But even as he said the words, Wolgast knew, with a sudden, icy clarity, what the situation was. The moment to break ranks had passed, at the zoo. They were all fugitives now.

'I don't have to,' Sykes said. 'Wait for my call.'

Wolgast clicked off the phone and stepped into the station. The attendant, a trim Indian man in a turban, was sitting behind the bulletproof glass, watching a church show on TV. The girl was probably hungry; Wolgast got some peanut butter crackers and some chocolate milk and took it to the counter. He was looking up, noticing the cameras, when his handheld buzzed at his waist. He paid quickly and stepped outside.

'I can get you a car out of Little Rock,' Sykes said. 'Somebody from the field office can meet you if you give me an address.'

Little Rock was at least two hours. Too long. Two men in suits, a little girl, a black sedan so plain it couldn't have been more obvious. The nuns had probably given the plate number, too. There was no way they could go through the scanner on the bridge; if the girl had been reported as a kidnap victim, the Amber Alert system would be activated.

Wolgast looked around. Across the avenue he saw a used-car lot, strings of multicolored banners fluttering above it. Most of the cars were junk, old gas guzzlers nobody could afford to fill anymore. An old-style Chevy Tahoe, ten years if it was a day, was parked to face the street. The words EASY FINANCING were stenciled on the windshield.

Wolgast told Sykes what he wanted to do. At the car he gave Doyle the milk and crackers for Amy and jogged across the avenue. A man with huge eyeglasses and a flapping comb-over stepped from the trailer as Wolgast approached the Tahoe.

'A beaut, isn't she?'

He got the man down to six grand, which was nearly all

the cash he had left. Sykes would have to see to the money question, too. Because today was a Saturday, the paperwork on the Tahoe wouldn't hit the DMV computers until Monday morning. By then, they'd be long gone.

Doyle followed him to an apartment complex about a mile away. Doyle parked the car in back, away from the road, and carried Amy to the Tahoe. Not perfect, but as long as Sykes got somebody to ghost the car by the end of the day, they'd be untraceable. The inside of the Tahoe smelled too strongly of lemon air freshener, but it was otherwise clean and comfortable, and the mileage on the odometer wasn't bad, a little over ninety thousand.

'How much cash do you have?' he asked Doyle.

They put their money together: they had a little over three hundred dollars left. It would cost at least two hundred bucks to fill the tank, but that would get them to western Arkansas, maybe as far as Oklahoma. Somebody could meet them with cash, and a new vehicle too.

They crossed back into Mississippi and turned west toward the river. The day was clear, just a few clouds ribboning the sky. In the backseat, Amy was motionless as a stone. She hadn't touched the food. She was just a little bit of a thing, a baby. The whole thing gave Wolgast a sick feeling in his stomach – the Tahoe was a rolling crime scene. But for now he had to get them out of the state. Beyond that, Wolgast didn't know.

By the time they were approaching the bridge it was nearly one o'clock.

'You think we're okay?' Doyle asked.

Wolgast kept his eyes straight ahead. 'We'll find out.'

The gates were open, the guardhouse unmanned. They sailed through easily, across the wide girth of the muddy river, swollen with spring runoff. Below them, a long line of barges pushed obliviously northward against the foaming current. The scanner would log their vehicle signature, but the car would still be registered to the dealer. It would take days to sort it all out, to check the video stream and connect them to the girl and the car. On the far side, the road reclined to the open fields of the western floodplain, sodden with moisture. Wolgast had thought about the route carefully; they wouldn't hit a good-sized town until they were nearly to Little Rock. He set the cruise control for fifty-five, the posted limit, and headed north again, wondering how it was that Sykes had known just what he'd do.

By the time the van bringing Anthony Carter pulled into the compound, Richards was asleep in his office, his head on his desk. His com buzzed to wake him; it was the guardhouse, telling him Paulson and Davis were outside.

He rubbed his eyes, brought his mind into focus. 'Bring him straight in.'

He decided to let Sykes sleep. He stood and stretched, called for a member of the medical staff and a security detail to meet him, then put on his jacket and took the stairs up to ground level. The loading dock stood at the rear of the building, on the south side, facing the woods and, beyond that, the river gorge. The compound had once been some kind of institute, a retreat for corporate executives and government officials. Richards was a little vague on the history. The place had been closed up for at least ten years before Special Weapons had taken it over. Cole had ordered the Chalet dismantled piece by piece to excavate the lower levels and build the power plant; they'd then rebuilt the exterior almost exactly as it had been.

Richards stepped into the gloom and cold. A wide roof was suspended over the concrete dock, keeping the surface clear of snow and obstructing the view from the rest of the compound. He checked his watch: 07:12. By now, he figured, Anthony Carter would be a psychological wreck. With the other subjects, there had been time for adjustment. But Carter had been plucked straight off death row and landed here in less than a day; his mind would be tumbling like a dryer. The important thing in the next two hours was to keep him calm.

147

The space swelled with the headlights of the approaching van. Richards descended the steps as the security detail, two soldiers wearing sidearms, jogged in out of the snow. Richards told them to keep their distance and leave their weapons holstered. He'd read Carter's file and doubted he'd be violent; the guy was basically as gentle as a lamb.

Paulson killed the engine and climbed from the van. There was a keypad on the van's sliding door; he punched in the numbers and Richards watched it draw slowly open.

Carter was sitting on the front bench. His head was tipped forward, but Richards could see that his eyes were open. His hands, shackled, lay folded in his lap. Richards saw a crumpled McDonald's bag on the floor at his feet. At least they'd fed him. The window between the compartments was closed.

'Anthony Carter?'

No response. Richards called his name again. Nothing, not a twitch. Carter seemed completely catatonic.

Richards stepped back from the door and pulled Paulson aside. 'Okay, you tell me,' he said. 'What's the story?'

Paulson gave a stagy, 'who me?' shrug. 'Beats me. Dude's just fucked up or something.'

'Don't bullshit me, son.' Richards turned his attention to the other one, with the red hair: Davis. He was holding a sheaf of comic books in his hand. Comic books, for the love of God. For the thousandth time, Richards thought it: these were *kids*.

'What about you, soldier?' he asked Davis.

'Sir?'

'Don't play stupid. You got anything to say for yourself?'

Davis's eyes darted toward Paulson, then back to Richards. 'No, sir.'

He'd deal with these two later. Richards stepped back toward the van. Carter hadn't moved a muscle. Richards could see that his nose was running; his cheeks were streaked with tears.

'Anthony, my name is Richards. I'm the head of security at

148

this facility. These two boys aren't going to bother you any-more, you hear me?'

'We didn't *do* anything,' Paulson pleaded. 'It was just a joke. Hey, Anthony, can't you take a joke?'

Richards turned sharply to face them again. 'That little voice in your head, telling you to shut the fuck up? That's the voice you should be listening to right about now.'

'Aw, come on,' Paulson whined. 'The dude's mental or something. Anyone can see that.'

Richards felt the last of his patience run out of him like the last drops of water from a leaky bucket. The hell with it. Without speaking he withdrew his weapon from its spot at the base of his spine. A long-slide Springfield .45 that he used mostly for show: a huge gun, a hilarious gun. But despite its bulk, it rode comfortably, and in the predawn light of the loading area, its titanium casing radiated with the menace of its perfect mechanical efficiency. In a single motion Richards popped the safety with his thumb and chambered a round, grasping Paulson by the belt buckle to pull him close, then shoved the muzzle into the soft V of flesh below his chin.

'Don't you understand,' Richards said quietly, 'that I'd shoot you right here just to put a smile on this man's face?'

Paulson's body had gone rigid. He was trying to cast his eyes toward Davis, or maybe the security detail, but was facing the wrong way. 'What the *fuck*?' he sputtered against the clenching muscles of his throat. He swallowed hard, his Adam's apple bobbing up against the muzzle of the gun. 'I'm cool, I'm cool.'

'Anthony,' Richards said, his eyes still fixed on Paulson's, 'it's your call, my friend. You tell me. Is he cool?'

From the van, a long silence. Then, quietly: ' 'Sall right. He cool.'

'You're sure now? Because if he isn't, I want you to tell me. You get the last word on this.'

Another pause. 'He cool.'

'You hear that?' Richards said to Paulson. He released the

149

soldier's belt and pulled his weapon away. 'The man says you're cool.'

Paulson looked like he was about to cry for his mama. On the loading dock, the security detail burst out laughing.

'The key,' Richards said.

Paulson reached into his belt and passed it to Richards. His hands were trembling; his breath smelled like vomit.

'Go on now,' Richards said. He shot a look at Davis, holding his pile of comic books. 'You too, junior. The both of you, get the fuck out of here.'

They scrambled off into the snow. In the few minutes since the van had pulled up, the sun had lifted from behind the mountains, giving the air a pale glow. Richards bent into the van and undid Carter's shackles.

'You okay? Those boys hurt you anywhere?'

Carter rubbed his damp face. 'They didn't mean nothing.' He swung his feet from the bench and lowered himself stiffly onto the ground. He blinked and looked around. 'They gone?'

Richards said they were.

'What this place?'

'Fair question.' Richards nodded. 'All in time. You hungry, Anthony?'

'They fed me. McDonald's.' Carter's eyes found the security detail, standing on the dock above them. His expression told Richards nothing. 'What about them?' he asked.

'They're here for you. You're the guest of honor, Anthony.'

Carter narrowed his eyes at Richards. 'You really shoot that guy if I'd said to?'

Something about Carter made him think of Sykes, standing in his office with that lost look on his face, asking him if they were friends.

'What do you think? You think I would have?'

'I wouldn't know *what* to think.'

'Well, just between us, no. I wouldn't have. I was just fooling with him.'

'I *thought* you was.' Carter's face broke into a grin. 'Thought

150

it was funny, though. You doing him like you did.' He shook his head, laughing a little, and looked around again. 'What happen now?'

'What happens now,' Richards said, 'is we get you inside, where it's warm.'

EIGHT

By nightfall they were fifty miles past Oklahoma City, hurtling west across the open prairie toward a wall of spring thunderheads ascending from the horizon like a bank of blooming flowers in a time-lapse video. Doyle was fast asleep in the Tahoe's passenger seat, his head wedged into the space between the headrest and the window, cushioned against the bumps in the road by a folded jacket. At times like this, Wolgast found himself envying Doyle, his powers of oblivion. He could turn his own lights off like a ten-year-old, put his head down and sleep virtually anywhere. Wolgast's fatigue was deep; he knew the smart thing would have been to pull off and change places, catch a few winks himself. But he had driven the whole distance from Memphis, and the feel of the wheel in his hands was the only thing that made him think he still had a card to play.

Since his call to Sykes, their only contact had taken place in a truck-stop parking lot outside Little Rock, where a field agent had met them with an envelope of cash – three thousand dollars, all in twenties and fifties – and a fresh vehicle, a plain-wrapper Bureau sedan. But by then Wolgast had decided he liked the Tahoe and wanted to keep it. He liked its big, muscular eight-cylinder engine and swishy steering and bouncy suspension. He hadn't driven anything like it in years. It seemed a pity to send a vehicle like that into the crusher, and when the agent offered him the keys to the sedan, he waved them off imperiously, without a second thought.

'Is there anything on the wires about us?' he'd asked the agent – a fresh recruit with a face pink as a slice of ham.

The agent frowned with confusion. 'I don't know anything about it.'

Wolgast considered this. 'Good,' he said finally. 'You'll want to keep it that way.'

The agent had then taken him around to the sedan's trunk, which sprang open to meet them. Inside was the black nylon duffel bag he hadn't asked for but still expected.

'Keep it,' he said.

'You sure? I'm supposed to give it to you.'

Wolgast shifted his gaze toward the Tahoe, parked at the edge of the lot between two dozing semis. Through the rear window, he could see Doyle but not the girl, who was lying down on the backseat. He really wanted to get moving; whatever else was true, sitting still was not an option. As for the bag, maybe he needed it and maybe he didn't. But the decision to leave it behind felt right.

'Tell the office anything you want,' he said. 'What I could really use is some coloring books.'

'I'm sorry?'

Wolgast would have laughed if he were in the mood. He put his palm on the lid of the trunk and pushed it closed. 'Never mind,' he said.

The bag held guns, of course, and ammunition, and maybe a couple of armored vests. Probably there'd be one in there for the girl, too; there was a company in Ohio that was making them for kids now, since that thing in Minneapolis. Wolgast had caught a segment about it on the *Today* show. They were actually making a Zylon snapsuit for infants. What a world, he thought.

Now, Little Rock six hours behind them, he was still glad he'd declined the bag. Whatever happened, happened; part of him wanted to be stopped. Outside Little Rock, he'd actually let the speedometer drift up to eighty, only dimly aware of what he was doing – that he was daring some state trooper or even a local cop sitting behind a billboard to call the whole thing off. But then Doyle had told him to slow down – *Yo, chief, shouldn't you ease off the pedal a bit?* – and his mind had snapped back into focus. He'd actually been playing out the scene in his mind: the flashing lights and a single, tart bleep of the siren; pulling the truck over to the side and placing his open hands on the wheel, lifting his eyes to the rearview to watch the officer calling in the plate number on his radio. Two grown men and a minor in a vehicle with temporary Tennessee tags: it wouldn't take long to put the whole thing together, to connect them to the nun and the zoo. Whenever he imagined the scene, he couldn't see beyond that moment, the cop with one hand on his mike, the other resting on the butt of his weapon. What would Sykes do? Would he say he'd never even heard of them? No, he and Doyle would go into the shredder, just like Anthony Carter.

As for the girl: he didn't know.

They'd skirted the Oklahoma City limits to the northeast, dodging the Interstate 40 checkpoint and bisecting I-35 on an anonymous rural blacktop, far from any cameras. The Tahoe lacked a GPS, but Wolgast had one on his handheld. Guiding the steering wheel with one hand, nimbly thumbing away on the handheld's tiny keys with the other, he let their route evolve as they went, a patchwork of county and state roads, some gravel or even just hard-packed dirt, to carry them gradually north and west. Now, all that lay between them and the Colorado border were a few small towns – towns with names like Virgil and Ricochet and Buckrack – half-abandoned oases in a sea of tallgrass prairie with little to show for themselves but a mini-mart, a couple of churches, a grain elevator and, between them, the miles of open plain. Flyover country: the word it made him think of was *eternal*. He guessed it looked much the same as it always had, the way it would go on looking just about forever. A man could

153

disappear into a place like this without hardly trying, live his life without one soul to notice.

Maybe, Wolgast thought, when this was all over, he'd come back. He might need a place like that.

Amy was so quiet in the backseat it might have been possible to forget she was there at all, if not for the fact that everything about her being there was wrong. A six-year-old girl. Goddamn Sykes, Wolgast thought. Goddamn the Bureau, goddamn Doyle, and goddamn himself while he was at it. Lying across the wide backseat with her hair spilled over her cheek, Amy looked as if she were sleeping, but Wolgast didn't think she was; she was pretending, watching him like a cat. Whatever had happened in her life so far, it had taught her how to wait. Whenever Wolgast had asked her if she needed to stop to use the bathroom or get something to eat – she hadn't touched the crackers and milk, warm and spoiled by now – the lids of her eyes had lifted with a feline quickness at the sound of her name, meeting his gaze in the mirror for a single second that went through him like a three-foot icicle. Then she'd shut them again. He hadn't heard her voice since the zoo, more than eight hours ago.

Lacey. That was the nun's name. Who'd held on to Amy like death itself. When Wolgast thought about that awful human tug-of-war in the parking lot, everyone yelling and screaming, the memory twisted in his gut with an actual physical pain. *Hey, Lila, guess what? I stole a kid today. So now we'll each have one, how about that?*

Doyle was rousing in the passenger seat. He sat up and rubbed his eyes, his expression blank and focusless. His mind, Wolgast knew, was reassembling his awareness of where he was. He looked back at Amy quickly, then turned to face forward again.

'Looks like some weather ahead,' he said.

The thunderheads had risen to a boil, blocking the sunset and sinking them into a premature darkness. At the horizon, beneath a shelf of clouds, a haze of rain was falling through a band of golden sunlight onto the fields.

Doyle leaned forward to examine the sky through the windshield. His voice was quiet. 'How far away you think that is?'

'I guess about five miles.'

'Maybe we should get off the road.' Doyle checked his watch. 'Or turn south for a while.'

Two miles later, they passed an unmarked dirt road, its edges lined with barbed-wire fencing. Wolgast stopped the car and backed up. The road crested a gentle rise and vanished into a line of cottonwoods; probably there was a river on the other side of the hill, or at least a gully. Wolgast checked the GPS; the road wasn't on it.

'I don't know,' Doyle said, when Wolgast showed him. 'Maybe we should look for something else.'

Wolgast turned the wheel of the Tahoe and headed south. He didn't think the road was a dead end; there would have been postal boxes at the intersection if it were. Three hundred yards later, the road narrowed to a single lane of rutted dirt. Beyond the tree line they crossed an old wooden bridge that spanned the creek Wolgast had foreseen. The evening light had gone a sallow green. He could see the storm rising above the horizon in his rearview mirror; he knew, from the blowing tips of the ditch grass on either side, that it was following them.

They had traveled another ten miles when the rain started to fall. They'd passed no houses or farms; they were in the middle of nowhere, with no cover. First just a few drops, but then, within seconds, a downpour of such force that Wolgast couldn't see a thing. The wipers were useless. He pulled to the edge of the ditch as a huge gust of wind buffeted the car.

'What now, chief?' Doyle asked over the racket.

Wolgast looked at Amy, still pretending to sleep in the backseat. Thunder roiled overhead; she didn't flinch. 'Wait, I guess. I'm going to rest a minute.'

Wolgast closed his eyes, listening to the rain on the roof of the Tahoe. He let the sound wash through him. He'd learned to do this during those months with Eva, to rest without quite giving himself over to sleep, so that he could rise quickly and go to her crib if she awakened. Scattered memories began to gather in his mind, pictures and sensations from other times in his life: Lila in the kitchen of the house in Cherry Creek, on a morning not long after they'd bought the place, pouring milk into a bowl of cereal; the cold dousing of water as he dove from the pier in Coos Bay, the sounds of his friends' voices above him, laughing and urging him on; the feeling of being very small himself, no more than a baby, and the noises and lights of the world around him, all of it letting him know he was safe. He had entered sleep's antechamber, the place where dreams and memories mingled, telling their strange stories; yet part of him was still in the car, listening to the rain.

'I have to go.'

His eyes snapped open; the rain had stopped. How long had he slept? The car was dark; the sun had set. Doyle was twisted at the waist, turned to face the backseat.

'What did you say?' Doyle asked.

'I have to go,' the little girl stated. Her voice, after hours of silence, was startling: clear and forceful. 'To the bathroom.'

Doyle looked at Wolgast nervously. 'Want me to take her?' he said, though Wolgast knew he didn't want to.

'Not *you*,' Amy said. She was sitting up now, holding her rabbit. It was a floppy thing, filthy with wear. She eyed Wolgast in the mirror, lifted her hand and pointed. 'Him.'

Wolgast undid his seat belt and stepped from the Tahoe. The air was cool and still; he could see, to the southeast, the last of the storm receding, leaving in its wake a dry sky the color of ink, a deep blue-black. He hit the key fob to unlock the passenger door and Amy climbed out. She had zipped the front of her sweatshirt and pulled the hood up over her head.

'Okay?' he asked.

'I'm not doing it *here*.'

Wolgast didn't say anything about not wandering off; there seemed no point. Where would she go? He led her fifty feet down the roadway, away from the lights of the Tahoe.

Wolgast looked away while she stood at the edge of the ditch and pulled down her jeans.

'I need help.'

Wolgast turned. She was facing him, her jeans and underpants bunched around her ankles. He felt his face warm with embarrassment.

'What do you need me to do?'

She held out both her hands. Her fingers felt tiny in his own; her palms were moist with childlike heat. He had to hold tightly as she leaned back, giving him nearly all her weight, to position herself in a crouch, suspending her body out over the ditch like a piano swinging from a crane. Where had she learned to do this? Who else had held her hands this way?

When she was done he turned around so she could pull her pants back up.

'You don't have to be afraid, honey.'

Amy said nothing; she made no motion to return to the Tahoe. Around them, the fields were empty, the air absolutely still, as if caught between breaths. Wolgast could feel it, the emptiness of the fields, the thousands of miles they spread in every direction. He heard the front door of the Tahoe open and slam closed; Doyle, going off to take a leak himself. Far off to the south, he heard a distant echo of thunder rolling away and, in the clear aural space behind it, a new sound – a kind of tinkling, like bells.

'We can be friends if you want,' he ventured. 'Would that be okay?'

She was a strange girl, he thought again; why hadn't she cried? Because she hadn't, not since the zoo, and she'd never asked for her mother, or said she wanted to go home, or even back to the convent. Where was home for her? Memphis, maybe, but he had the feeling it wasn't. No place was. Whatever had happened to the girl had taken the idea of home away.

Then, 'I'm not afraid. We can go back to the car if you want.'

For a moment she just looked at him, in that evaluating way of hers. His ears had adjusted to the silence, and he was certain now that it was music he was hearing, the sound distorted by distance. Somewhere, down the road they were driving on, somebody was playing music.

'I'm Brad.' The name felt bland and heavy in his mouth.

She nodded.

'The other man? He's Phil.'

'I know who you are. I heard you talking.' She shifted her weight. 'You thought I wasn't listening, but I was.'

A spooky kid. And smart, too. He could hear it in her voice, see it in the way she was sizing him up with her eyes, using the silence to appraise him, to draw him out. He felt as if he were speaking with somebody much older, though not exactly. He couldn't put his finger on what the difference was.

'What's in Colorado? That's where we're going, I heard you say it.'

Wolgast wasn't sure how much to say. 'Well, there's a doctor there. He's going to look at you. Like a checkup.'

'I'm not sick.'

'That's why, I think. I don't . . . well, I don't really know.' He winced inwardly at the lie. 'You don't have to be afraid.'

'Don't keep saying that.'

He was so taken aback by her directness that for a moment he said nothing. 'Okay. That's good. I'm glad you're not.'

'Because I'm not afraid,' Amy declared, and began walking toward the lights of the Tahoe. 'You are.'

A few miles later, they saw it up ahead: a domelike zone of thrumming light that sorted, as they approached, into discrete, orbiting points, like a family of constellations spinning low against the horizon. Just as Wolgast figured out what he was seeing, the road ended at an intersection. He turned on the overhead light and checked the GPS. A line of cars and pickup trucks, more than they had seen in hours, was passing on the highway, all headed in the same direction. He opened his window to the night air; the sound of music was unmistakable now.

'What *is* that?' Doyle asked.

Wolgast said nothing. He turned west, threading into the line of traffic. In the bed of the pickup ahead of them, a group of teenagers, about a half dozen, were sitting on bales of hay. They passed a sign that read, HOMER, OKLAHOMA, POP. 1,232.

'Not so close,' Doyle said, referring to the pickup. 'I don't like the looks of this.'

Wolgast ignored him. A girl, spotting Wolgast's face through the windshield, waved at him, the wind blowing her hair around her face. The lights of the fair were growing clearer now, as were the signs of civilization: a water tank on stilts, a darkened farm-implements store, a low-slung modern building that was probably a retirement community or health clinic, set back from the highway. The pickup pulled off into a Casey's General Store, its lot bustling with cars and people; the kids were up and out of the bed before the vehicle had even stopped, rushing to meet their friends. Traffic on the roadway slowed as they entered the little town. In the backseat, Amy was sitting up, looking through the windows at the busy scene.

Doyle turned around. 'Lie down, Amy.'

'It's all right, let her look.' Wolgast raised his voice so Amy could hear. 'Don't listen to Phil. You look all you want, honey.'

Doyle leaned his head toward Wolgast's. 'What are you . . . doing?'

Wolgast kept his eyes ahead. 'Relax.'

Honey. Where had that come from? The streets teemed with people, all walking in the same direction, carrying blankets and plastic coolers and lawn chairs. Many were holding small children by the hand or pushing strollers: farm people, ranch people, dressed in jeans and overalls, everyone in boots, some of the men wearing Stetson hats. Here and there Wolgast saw wide puddles of standing water, but the night sky was crisp and dry. The rain had pushed through; the fair was on.

Wolgast flowed with the traffic to the high school, where a marquee-style sign read, BRANCH COUNTY CONSOLIDATED HS: GO WILDCATS! SPRING FLING, MARCH 20–22. A man in a reflective orange vest waved them into the lot, where a second man directed them to extra parking in a muddy field. Wolgast shut off the engine and glanced at Amy through the rearview; her attention was directed out the window, toward the lights and sounds of the fair.

Doyle cleared his throat. 'You're kidding, right?'

Wolgast twisted in his seat. 'Amy, Phil and I are going to step outside for a second to talk. Okay?'

The little girl nodded; suddenly, the two of them had an understanding, one Doyle wasn't part of.

'We'll be right back,' said Wolgast.

Outside, Doyle met him at the back of the Tahoe. 'We're *not* doing this,' he said.

'What's the harm?'

Doyle lowered his voice. 'We're lucky we haven't seen a local yet. Think about it. Two men in suits and a little girl – you think we won't stand out?'

'We'll separate. I'll take Amy. We can change in the car. Go get yourself a beer, have some fun.'

'You're not thinking clearly, boss. She's a prisoner.'

'No, she's not.'

Doyle sighed. 'You know what I mean.'

'Do I? She's a kid, Phil. A little girl.'

They were standing very close; Wolgast could smell the staleness on Doyle, after hours in the Tahoe. A group of teenagers walked past, and for a moment they fell silent. The parking lot was filling up.

'Look, I'm not made of stone,' Doyle said quietly. 'You think I don't know how fucked up this is? It's all I can do not to throw up out the window.'

'You seem pretty relaxed, actually. You slept like a baby the whole way from Little Rock.'

Doyle frowned defensively. 'Fine, shoot me. I was *tired*. But we are not taking her on a bunch of kiddie rides. Kiddie rides are not part of the plan.'

'One hour,' Wolgast said. 'You can't leave her cooped up in a car all day without a break. Let her have a little fun, blow off some steam. Sykes doesn't have to know a thing about it. Then we'll get back on the road. She'll probably sleep the rest of the way.'

'And what if she takes off?'

'She won't.'

'I don't know how you can be so sure.'

'You can shadow us. If anything happens, there's two of us.'

Doyle frowned skeptically. 'Look, you're in charge. It's your call. But I still don't like it.'

'Sixty minutes,' Wolgast said. 'Then we're gone.'

In the front seat of the Tahoe, they wriggled into sport shirts and jeans while Amy waited. Then Wolgast explained to Amy what they were going to do.

'You have to stay close,' he said. 'Don't talk to anyone. Do you promise?'

'Why can't I talk to anyone?'

'It's just a rule. If you don't promise, we can't go.'

The girl thought a moment, then nodded. 'I promise,' she said.

Doyle hung back as they made their way to the entrance of the fairgrounds. The air was sweet with the smell of frying grease. Over the PA system a man's voice, flat as the Oklahoma plain, was calling out numbers for bingo. *B . . . seven. G . . . thirty. Q . . . sixteen.*

'Listen,' Wolgast said to Amy, when he was sure Doyle was out of earshot. 'I know it might seem strange, but I want you to pretend something. Can you do that for me?'

They stopped on the path. Wolgast saw that the girl's hair was a mess. He crouched to face her and did his best to smooth it out with his fingers, pushing it away from her face. Her shirt had the word SASSY on it, outlined with some kind of glittery flakes. He zipped up her sweatshirt against the evening's chill.

'Pretend I'm your daddy. Not your real daddy, just a pretend daddy. If anyone asks, that's who I am, okay?'

'But I'm not supposed to talk to anyone. You said.'

'Yes, but if we do. That's what you should say.' Wolgast looked over her shoulder to where Doyle was waiting, his hands in his pockets. He was wearing a windbreaker over his polo shirt, zipped to the chin; Wolgast knew he was still armed, that his weapon lay snug in its holster under his arm. Wolgast had left his weapon in the glove compartment.

'So, let's try it. Who's the nice man you're with, little girl?'

'My daddy?' the girl ventured.

'Like you mean it. Pretend.'

'My . . . daddy.'

A solid performance, Wolgast thought. The kid should act. 'Attagirl.'

'Can we ride on the twirly?'

'The twirly. Which one's the twirly, sweetheart?' *Honey, sweetheart.* He couldn't seem to stop himself; the words just popped out.

'That.'

Wolgast looked where Amy was pointing. In the air beyond the ticket booth he saw a huge contraption with rotating disks at the end of each arm, spinning out its riders in brightly colored carts. The Octopus.

'Of course we can,' he said, and felt himself smile. 'We can do whatever you want.'

At the entrance he paid for their admission and moved down the line to a second booth to buy tickets for the rides. He thought she might want to eat, but decided to wait; it might, he reasoned, make her feel sick on the rides. He realized he liked thinking this way, imagining her experience, the things that would make her happy. Even he could feel it, the excitement of the fair. A bunch of broken-down rides, most of them probably dangerous as hell, but wasn't that the point? Why had he said only an hour?

'Ready?'

The line for the Octopus was long but moved quickly. When their turn to board came, the operator stopped them with a raised hand.

'How old is she?'

The man squinted skeptically over his cigarette. Purple tattoos snaked along his bare forearms. Before Wolgast could open his mouth to answer, Amy stepped forward. 'I'm eight.'

Just then Wolgast saw the sign, propped on a folding chair: NO RIDERS UNDER SEVEN YEARS OF AGE.

'She don't look eight,' the man said.

'Well, she is,' Wolgast said. 'She's with me.'

The operator looked Amy up and down, then shrugged. 'It's your lunch,' he said.

They climbed into the wobbling car; the tattooed man pushed the safety bar against their waists. With a lurch the car rose into the air and abruptly halted so other riders could board behind them.

'Scared?'

Amy was pressed against him, her sweatshirt drawn up around her face in the cold, both hands clutching the bar. Her eyes were very wide. She shook her head emphatically. 'Uh-uh.'

Four more times the car lifted and stopped. At its apex, the view took in the whole fairgrounds, the high school and its parking lots, the little town of Homer beyond, with its grid of lighted streets. Traffic was still streaming in from the county road. From so far up, the cars seemed to move with the sluggishness of targets in a shooting gallery. Wolgast was scanning the ground below for Doyle when he felt the car lurch again.

'Hold on!'

They descended in a spinning, plunging rush, their bodies pressing upward against the bar. Screams of pleasure filled the air. Wolgast closed his eyes against the force of their descent. He hadn't been on a carnival ride in years and years; the violence of it was astonishing. He felt Amy's weight against his body, pushed toward him by the car's momentum as they spun and fell. When he looked again, they were dipping close to the ground, skating just inches above the hard-packed field, the lights of the fair whirling around them like a rain of shooting stars; then they were vaulted skyward once more. Six, seven, eight times around, each rotation rising and falling in a wave. It took forever and was over in an instant.

As they began their jerking descent to disembark, Wolgast looked down at Amy's face; still that neutral, appraising gaze, yet he detected, behind the darkness of her eyes, a warm light of happiness. A new feeling opened inside him: no one had ever given her such a present.

'So how was that?' he asked, grinning at her.

'That was *cool*.' Amy lifted her face quickly. 'I want to go again.'

The operator freed them from the bar; they returned to the back of the line. Ahead of them stood a large woman in a flowered housedress and her husband, a weather-beaten man in jeans and a tight western shirt, a fat plug of tobacco pouched under his lip.

'Aren't you the cutest,' she proclaimed, and looked warmly at Wolgast. 'How old is she?'

'I'm eight,' Amy said, and slipped her hand into Wolgast's. 'This is my daddy.'

The woman laughed, her eyebrows lifting like parachutes catching the air. Her cheeks were clumsily rouged. 'Of course he's your daddy, honey. Anyone can see that. It's just as plain as the nose on your face.' She poked her husband in the ribs. 'Isn't she the cutest, Earl?'

The man nodded. 'You bet.'

'What's your name, honey?' the woman asked.

'Amy.'

The woman shifted her eyes to Wolgast again. 'I've got a niece just about her age, doesn't speak half so well. You must be so proud.'

Wolgast was too amazed to respond. He felt as if he were

164

still on the ride, his mind and body caught in some tremendous gravitational force. He thought of Doyle, wondering if he was watching the scene unfold from somewhere in the crowds. But then he knew he didn't care; let Doyle watch.

'We're driving to Colorado,' Amy added, and squeezed Wolgast's hand conspiratorially. 'To visit my grandmother.'

'Is that so? Well, your grandmother's very lucky, to have a girl like you come to visit.'

'She's sick. We have to take her to the doctor.'

The woman's face fell with sympathy. 'I'm sorry to hear it.' She spoke with quiet earnestness to Wolgast. 'I hope everything's all right. We'll keep you in our prayers.'

'Thank you,' he managed.

They rode the Octopus three more times. As they moved into the fairgrounds in search of dinner, Wolgast couldn't spot Doyle anywhere; either he was shadowing them like a pro or he had decided to leave them alone. There were a lot of pretty women around. Maybe, Wolgast thought, he'd gotten distracted.

Wolgast bought Amy a hot dog and they sat together at a picnic table. He watched her eat: three bites, four bites, then it was gone. He got her a second and, when that was gone, a funnel cake, dusted with powdered sugar, and a carton of milk. Not the most nutritious meal, but at least she had the milk.

'What's next?' he asked her.

Amy's cheeks were spattered with sugar and grease. She reached up to wipe them with the back of her hand, but Wolgast stopped her. 'Use a napkin,' he said, and handed one to her.

'The carousel,' she said.

'Really? Seems pretty tame after the Octopus.'

'They got one?'

'I'm sure they do.'

The carousel, Wolgast thought. Of course. The Octopus was for one part of her, the grown-up part, the part that could watch and wait and lie with confident charm to the woman in the line; the carousel was for the other Amy, for the little girl she really was. Under the spell of the evening, its lights and sounds and the still-churning part of him that had ridden the Octopus four times in a row, he wanted to ask her things: who she really was; about her mother, her father if she had one, and where she was from; about the nun, Lacey, and what had happened at the zoo, the craziness in the parking lot. Who are you, Amy? What brought you here, what brought you to me? And how do you know I'm afraid, that I'm afraid all the time? She took his hand again as they walked; the feel of her palm against his own was almost electrical, the source of a warm current that seemed to spread through his body as they walked. When she saw the carousel with its glowing deck of painted horses, he felt her pleasure actually pass from her body into his.

Lila, he thought. *Lila, this was what I wanted. Did you know? It's all I ever wanted.*

He handed the operator their tickets. Amy picked a horse on the outer rim, a white Lipizzaner stallion frozen in mid-prance, grinning a bright row of ceramic teeth. The ride was almost empty; it was past nine o'clock, and the youngest children had gone home.

'Stand next to me,' Amy commanded.

He did; he placed one hand on the pole, another on the horse's bridle, as if he were leading her. Her legs were too short to reach the stirrups, which dangled freely; he told her to hold tight.

That was when he saw Doyle, standing not a hundred feet away, beyond a row of hay bales that marked the edge of the beer tent, talking energetically to a young woman with great handfuls of red hair. He was telling a story, Wolgast could see, gesturing with his cup to make some point or pace a punch line, inhabiting the role of the handsome fiber-optic salesman from Indianapolis – just as Amy had done with the woman in line, spinning out the detail of the sick grand-mother in Colorado. It was what you did, Wolgast under-stood; you started to tell a story about who you were, and soon enough the lies were all you had and you became that person. Beneath his feet, the carousel's wooden decking shuddered as its gears engaged; with a burp of music from speakers overhead, the carousel began to move as the woman, in a gesture of practiced flirtatiousness, tossed back her head to laugh, while at the same time reaching out to touch Doyle, quickly, on the shoulder. Then the deck of the carousel turned and the two of them were gone from sight.

Wolgast thought it then. The sentences were as clear in his mind as if written there.

Just go. Take Amy and go.

Doyle's lost track of time. He's distracted. Do it.

Save her.

Around and around they went. Amy's horse bobbed up and down like a piston. In just these few minutes, Wolgast felt his thoughts gather into a plan. When the ride was over, he would take her, glide into the darkness, the crowds, away from the beer tent and out the gate; by the time Doyle realized what had happened, they'd be nothing but an empty space in the lot. A thousand miles in every direction; they'd be swallowed whole into it. He was good, he knew what he was doing. He'd kept the Tahoe, he saw, for just this reason; even back then, standing in the parking lot in Little Rock, the germ of the idea had lain inside him, like a seed about to break open. He didn't know what he'd do about finding the girl's mother, but he'd figure that out later. He'd never felt anything like it, this blast of clarity. All his life seemed to gather behind this one thing, this singular purpose. The rest – the Bureau, Sykes, Carter, and the others, even Doyle – was a lie, a veil his true self had lived behind, waiting to step into the light. The moment had come; all he had to do was follow his instincts.

The ride began to slow. He didn't even look in Doyle's direction, not wanting to jinx this new feeling, to scare it away. When they reached a complete stop, he lifted Amy from her horse and knelt so they were eye to eye.

'Amy, I want you to do something for me. I need you to pay attention to what I'm saying.'

The girl nodded.

'We're leaving now. Just the two of us. Stay close, don't say a word. We're going to be moving quickly, but don't run. Do just as I say and everything will be fine.' He searched her face for comprehension. 'Do you understand?'

'I shouldn't run.'

'Exactly. Now let's go.'

They stepped from the deck; they'd come to rest on the far side, away from the beer tent. Wolgast hoisted her quickly over the fence that surrounded the ride, then, bracing his hand on a metal post, vaulted over himself. No one seemed to notice – or maybe they did, but he didn't look back. With Amy's hand in his he strode briskly toward the rear of the fairgrounds, away from the lights. His plan was to circle around to the main gate or else find another exit. If they moved quickly, Doyle would never notice until it was too late.

They came to a tall chain-link fence; beyond it stood a dark line of trees and, farther still, the lights of a highway, hemming the high school's playing fields to the south. There was no way through; the only route was around the perimeter, following the fence back to the main entrance. They were moving through unmown grass, still wet from the storm, soaking their shoes and pants. They reemerged back near the food stands and the picnic table where they had eaten. From there, Wolgast could see the exit, just a hundred feet away. His heart was thumping in his chest. He paused to quickly scan the scene; Doyle was nowhere.

'Straight out the exit,' he told Amy. 'Don't even look up.'

'Yo, chief!'

Wolgast froze. Doyle came jogging up behind them, pointing at his watch. 'I thought we said an hour, boss.'

Wolgast looked at him, his bland midwestern face. 'Thought we'd lost you,' he said. 'We were just coming to look for you.'

Doyle glanced quickly over his shoulder toward the beer tent. 'Well, you know,' he said. 'Got caught up in a little conversation.' He smiled, a little guiltily. 'Nice folks around here. Real talkers.' He gestured at Wolgast's water-stained slacks. 'What happened to you? You're all wet.'

For a moment, Wolgast said nothing. 'Puddles.' He did his best not to look away, to hold Doyle in his gaze. 'The rain.' There was one other chance, maybe, if he could somehow distract Doyle on the way to the Tahoe. But Doyle was younger and stronger, and Wolgast had left his weapon back in the car.

'The rain,' Doyle repeated. He nodded, and Wolgast saw it in the younger man's face: he knew. He'd known all along. The beer tent was a test, a trap. He and Amy had never been out of sight, not for a second. 'I see. Well, we have a job to do. Right, chief?'

'Phil—'

'Don't.' His voice was quiet – not menacing, merely stating the facts. 'Don't even say the words. We're partners, Brad. It's time to go.'

All Wolgast's hopefulness collapsed inside him. Amy's hand was still in his; he couldn't bear even to look at her. *I'm sorry*, he thought, sending her this message through his hand. *I'm sorry*. And together, Doyle following five paces behind them, they moved through the exit toward the parking lot.

Neither of them noticed the man – the off-duty Oklahoma state trooper who, two hours before, had seen the wire report on a girl kidnapped by two Caucasian males at the Memphis Zoo, before clocking out and heading off to the high school to meet his wife and watch his kids ride the bumper cars – following them with his eyes.

NINE

I was called . . . Fanning.

All that day the words sat on his lips: when he awoke at eight, as he bathed and dressed and ate his breakfast and sat on the bed in his room, flipping through the channels and smoking Parliaments, waiting for the night to come. All day long, this was what he heard:

Fanning. I was called Fanning.

The words meant nothing to Grey. The name wasn't one he knew. He'd never met anybody named Fanning, or anything *like* Fanning, not that he could remember. Yet somehow, while he'd slept, the name had taken up residence in his head, as if he'd gone to sleep listening to a song played over and over, the lyrics digging a rut into his brain like a plow, and now part of his mind was still in that rut and couldn't get out. Fanning? What the hell? It made him think of the prison shrink, Dr Wilder, and the way he'd led Grey down into a state deeper than sleep, the room he called forgiveness, with the slow *tap-tap-tap* of his pen on the table, the sound snaking inside him. Now Grey couldn't pick up the channel changer or scratch his head or light a smoke without hearing the words, their syncopating rhythm building a backbeat to every little thing he did.

I(flick) . . . *was*(light) . . . *called*(draw) . . . *Fanning*(exhale).

He sat and smoked and waited and smoked some more. What the hell was wrong with him? He felt different, and the change was no good. Antsy, out of sync with himself. Usually he could just sit still and do virtually nothing while he let the hours pass – he'd learned to do that well enough in Beeville, letting whole days slip by in a kind of thoughtless trance – but not today. Today he was jumpy as a bug in a pan. He tried to watch TV, but the words and the images didn't even seem related to each other. Outside, beyond the windows of the barracks, the afternoon sky looked like old plastic, a

170

washed-out gray. Gray like Grey. A perfect day to snooze away the hours. Yet here he was, sitting on the edge of his unmade bed, waiting for the afternoon to be over, his insides buzzing like a paper harmonica.

He felt like he hadn't slept a wink, too, though he'd somehow snoozed straight through his alarm at 05:00 and missed his morning shift. It was OT, so he could make up some excuse – that it was all a mix-up or he'd simply forgotten – but he was going to hear about it either way. He was on again at 22:00. He really needed to nap, to store up some shut-eye for another eight hours of watching Zero watching him.

At 18:00 he pulled on his parka to walk across the compound to the commissary. Sunset was an hour off but the clouds were hanging low, sponging up the last of the light. A damp wind cut through him as he trudged across the open field between the barracks and the dining hall, a cinder-block building that looked like it had been built in a hurry. He couldn't see the mountains at all, and on days like this it sometimes felt to Grey as if the compound were actually an island – that the world came to a stop, tipping into a black sea of nothingness, somewhere beyond the end of the long drive. Vehicles came and went, delivery trucks and step vans and Army five-tons loaded with supplies, but the place they came from and then went back to, wherever that was, might have been the moon for all Grey knew. Even his memory of the world was beginning to fade. He hadn't been past the fence line in six months.

The commissary should have been busy at this hour, fifty or more bodies filling the room with heat and noise, but as he stepped through the door, unzipping his parka and stamping the snow off the soles of his shoes, Grey surveyed the space and saw just a few people scattered at the tables, alone and in small groups, not more than a dozen all told. You could tell who did what by what they wore – the med staff in their scrubs and rubber clogs; the soldiers in their winter camos, hunched over their trays and scooping the food into their mouths like farmhands; the sweeps in their UPS-brown jumpsuits. Behind the dining hall there was a lounge with a ping-pong table and air hockey, but nobody was playing or watching the big-screen television either, and the room was quiet, just a few murmuring voices and the clink of glass and flatware. For a while the lounge had held some tables with computers, sleek new vMacs for email and whatnot, but one morning in the summer, a tech crew had wheeled them all out on a dolly, right in the middle of breakfast. Some of the soldiers had complained, but it hadn't done any good; the computers never returned, and all that remained to say they'd been there were a bunch of wires dangling from the wall. Taking them away had been some kind of a punishment, Grey figured, but he didn't know what for. He'd never bothered with the computers himself.

Despite the nervous feeling in his body, the smell of warm food made him hungry – the Depo gave him such a voracious appetite it was a wonder he wasn't heavier than he was – and he filled his tray as he moved down the line, his mind savoring the thought of the meal to come: a bowl of minestrone, salad with croutons and cheese, mashies and pickled beets, a slab of ham with a ring of dried-out pineapple sitting on it like a citrus tiara. He topped it all off with a wedge of lemon pie and a tall glass of ice water and carried everything back to the corner to an empty table. Most of the sweeps ate alone like he did; there wasn't much you were allowed to actually talk about. Sometimes a whole week would pass without Grey saying so much as boo to anyone except the sentry on L3 who clocked him in and out of Containment. There had been a time, not that many months ago in fact, when the techs and medical staff would ask him questions, things about Zero and the rabbits and the teeth. They'd listen to his answers, nodding, maybe jot something down on their handhelds. But now they just picked up the reports without a word, as if the whole matter of Zero had been settled and there was nothing new to learn.

Grey moved through his meal methodically, course by course. The Fanning thing was still running through his mind like a news crawl, but eating seemed to calm it some; for a few minutes he almost forgot it was there. He was finishing the last of the pie when someone stepped up to his table: one of the soldiers. Grey thought his name was Paulson. Grey had seen him around, though the soldiers had a way of all looking the same in their camos and T-shirts and shiny boots, their hair so short their ears stuck out like somebody had pasted them to the sides of their heads as a joke. Paulson's cut was so tight Grey couldn't have said what color his hair really was. He took a chair at right angles to Grey and spun it around to straddle it, smiling at him in a way that Grey wouldn't have described as friendly.

'You fellows sure like to eat, don'tcha?'

Grey shrugged.

'You're Grey, right?' The soldier narrowed his eyes. 'I've seen you.'

Grey put down his fork and swallowed a bite of pie. 'Yeah.'

Paulson nodded thoughtfully, like he was deciding if this was a good name or not. His face wore an outward expression of calm, but there was something effortful about this. For a moment his eyes darted to the security camera hanging in the corner over their heads, then found Grey's face again.

'You know, you fellas don't say much,' Paulson said. 'It's a little spooky, you don't mind my saying so.'

Spooky. Paulson didn't know the half of it. Grey said nothing.

'Mind if I ask you a question?' Paulson lifted his chin toward Grey's plate. 'Don't let me interrupt. You can go on and finish while we talk.'

'I'm done,' Grey said. 'I have to go to work.'

'How's the pie?'

'You want to ask me about the pie?'

'The pie? No.' Paulson shook his head. 'I was just being polite. That would be an example of what's called small talk.'

Grey wondered what he wanted. The soldiers never said one word to him, and here was this guy, Paulson, giving him etiquette lessons like the cameras weren't looking straight at them.

'It's good,' Grey managed. 'I like the lemon.'

'Enough with the pie. I couldn't give two shits about the pie.'

Grey gripped the sides of his tray. 'I gotta go,' he said, but as he started to rise, Paulson dropped a hand on his wrist. Grey could feel, in just that one touch, how strong the man was, as if the muscles of his arms were hung on bars of iron.

'Sit. The fuck. Down.'

Grey sat. The room suddenly felt empty to him. He glanced past Paulson and saw that this was so, or nearly: most of the tables were empty. Just a couple of techs on the far side of the room, sipping coffee from throwaway cups. Where had everybody gone?

'You see, we know who you fellas *are*, Grey,' Paulson said with a quiet firmness. He was leaning over the table, his hand still on Grey's wrist. 'We *know* what you all did, is what I'm saying. Little boys, or whatever. I say God bless, each to his own gifts. What's good for the goose is good for the gander. You follow me?'

Grey said nothing.

'Not everybody feels the way I do, but that's my *opinion*. Last time I checked it was still a free country.' He shifted in his chair, bringing his face even closer. 'I knew a guy, in high school? Used to put cookie dough on his joint and let the *dog* lick it off. So you want to nail some little kid, you go right ahead. Personally I don't get it, but your business is your business.'

Grey felt ill. 'I'm sorry,' he managed. 'I really gotta go.'

'Where do you have to go, Grey?'

'Where?' He tried to swallow. 'To work. I have to go to work.'

'No you don't.' Finally releasing Grey's wrist, Paulson took a spoon from Grey's tray and began to twirl it on the tabletop with the point of his index finger. 'You've got three hours

174

till your shift. I can tell time, Grey. We're *chatting* here, goddamnit.'

Grey watched the spoon, waiting for Paulson to say something else. He suddenly needed a smoke with every molecule of his body, a force like possession. 'What do you want from me?'

Paulson gave the spoon a final spin. 'What do I want, Grey? That's the question, isn't it? I do want something, you're right about that.' He leaned toward Grey, making a 'come closer' gesture with his index finger. His voice, when he spoke, was just above a whisper. 'What I want is for you to tell me about Level Four.'

Grey felt his insides drop, like he'd placed a foot on a step that wasn't there.

'I just clean. I'm a janitor.'

'Pardon me,' Paulson said. 'But no. I don't buy that for a second.'

Grey thought again of the cameras. 'Richards—'

Paulson snorted. 'Oh, *fuck* him.' He looked up at the camera, gave a little wave, then slowly rotated his hand, clenching all but his middle finger. He held it that way for a few seconds.

'You think anybody's actually watching those things? All day, every day, listening to us, watching what we do?'

'There's nothing down there. I swear.'

Paulson shook his head slowly; Grey saw that wild look in his eyes again. 'We both know that's bullshit, so can we please? Let's be honest with each other.'

'I just clean,' Grey said weakly. 'I'm just here to work.'

Paulson said nothing. The room was so quiet Grey thought he could hear his own heart beating.

'Tell me something. You sleep okay, Grey?'

'What?'

Paulson's eyes narrowed with menace. 'I'm asking, do . . . you . . . sleep . . . okay?'

'I guess,' he managed. 'Sure, I sleep.'

Paulson gave a little fatalistic laugh. He leaned back and rocked his eyes toward the ceiling. 'You guess. You *guess*.'

'I don't know why you're asking me this stuff.'

Paulson exhaled sharply. '*Dreams*, Grey.' He pushed his face close to Grey's. 'I'm talking about *dreams*. You fellas do dream, don't you? Well, I sure as hell dream. All goddamn night long. One after the other. I am dreaming some crazy shit.'

Crazy, Grey thought; that just about summed the situation up, right there. Paulson was crazy. The wheels weren't on the road anymore, the oars were out of the water. Too many months on the mountain, maybe, too many days of cold and snow. Grey had known guys like that in Beeville, fine when they got there but who, before even a few months had gone by, couldn't string two sentences together that made a lick of sense.

'Want to know what I dream about, Grey? Go on. Take a guess.'

'I don't want to.'

'*Take a fucking guess.*'

Grey looked down at the table. He could feel the cameras watching – could feel Richards, somewhere, taking all of this in. He thought: Please. For godsakes. No more questions.

'I don't . . . know.'

'You don't.'

He shook his head, his eyes still averted. 'No.'

'Then I'll tell you,' Paulson said quietly. 'I dream about *you*.'

For a moment neither spoke. Paulson was crazy, Grey thought. Crazy crazy crazy.

'I'm sorry,' he stammered. 'There's really nothing down there.'

He made to leave again, waiting to feel Paulson's hand on his elbow, stopping him.

'Fine,' Paulson said, and gave a little wave. 'I'm done for now. Get out of here.' He twisted in his chair to look up at

Grey, standing with his tray. 'I'll tell you a secret, though. You want to hear it?'

Grey shook his head.

'You know those two sweeps who left?'

'Who?'

'You know those guys.' Paulson frowned. 'The fat ones. Dumbshit and his friend.'

'Jack and Sam.'

'Right.' Paulson's eyes drifted. 'I never did get the names. I guess you could say the names didn't come with the deal.'

Grey waited for Paulson to say something else. 'What about them?'

'Well, I hope they weren't friends of yours. Because here's a little bulletin. They're dead.' Paulson rose; he didn't look at Grey as he spoke. 'We're all dead.'

It was dark, and Carter was afraid.

He was somewhere down below, way down; he'd seen four buttons on the elevator, the numbers running backward, like the buttons in an underground garage. By the time they'd put him in there on the gurney, he was woozy and feeling no pain – they'd given him something, some kind of shot that made him sleepy but not actually asleep, so he'd felt it a little, what they were doing to the back of his neck. Cutting there, putting something in. Restraints on his wrists and feet – to make him comfortable, they said. Then they'd wheeled him to the elevator and that was the last thing he remembered, the buttons, and somebody's finger pushing the one that said L4. The guy with the gun, Richards, had never come back like he'd promised.

Now he was awake, and though he couldn't say for sure, he felt like he was down, way down in the hole; he was still bound at the wrists and ankles and probably his waist, too. The room was cold and dark, but he could see lights blinking somewhere, he couldn't tell how far, and hear the sound of a fan blowing air. He couldn't remember much of the conversation he'd had with the men before they'd brought him down. They'd weighed him, Carter remembered that, and done other things like any doctor would do, taking his blood pressure and asking him to pee in a cup and tapping his knees with the hammer and peering inside his nose and mouth. Then they'd put the tube in the back of his hand – that hurt, that hurt like hell, he remembered saying so, *Goddamn* – and hooked the tube up to the bag on the hanger, and the rest was all a blur. He recalled a funny light, glowing bright red on the tip of a pen, and all the faces around him suddenly wearing masks, one of them saying, though he couldn't tell which one, 'This is just the laser, Mr Carter. You may feel a little pressure.' Now, in the dark, he remembered thinking, before his brain had gone all watery and far away, that God had played one last joke on him and maybe this was his ride to the needle after all. He'd wondered if he'd be seeing Jesus soon or Mrs Wood or the Devil his own self.

But he hadn't died, all he'd done was sleep, though he didn't know how long. His mind had drifted for a while, out of one kind of darkness and into another, like he was walking through a house without lights; and with nothing to look at now, he had no way to get his bearings. He couldn't tell up from down. He hurt all over and his tongue felt like a balled-up sock in his mouth, or some strange furry animal, burrowing there. The back of his neck, where it met his shoulder blades, was humming with pain. He lifted his head to look around, but all he could see were some little points of light – red lights, like the one on the pen. He couldn't tell how far away they were or how big. They could have been the lights of a distant city for all he knew.

Wolgast: the name floated up to his mind out of the darkness. Something about Wolgast, that thing he'd said, about time being like an ocean and his to give. *I can give you all the time in the world, Anthony. An ocean of time.* Like he knew what was in the deepest place of Carter's heart, like they hadn't just met but had known each other for years. Nobody had talked to Anthony like that for as long as he could remember.

It made him think of the day that had started it all, like the two were of a piece. June: it was June; he remembered that. June, the air under the freeway sizzling hot, and Carter, standing in a wedge of dirty shade and holding his cardboard sign over his chest – HUNGRY, ANYTHING WILL HELP, GOD BLESS YOU – had watched as the car, a black Denali, drew up to the curb. The passenger window opened: not just the usual crack, so whoever was inside could pass him a few coins or a folded bill without their fingers even touching his, but gliding all the way down in a single, liquid motion, so that Carter's reflection in the window's dark tint fell like a curtain in reverse – like a hole had opened in the world, revealing a secret room within. The hour was just noon, the lunchtime traffic building on the surface roads and on the West Loop, which banged in a tight rhythm over his head, like a long clicking line of freight cars.

'Hello?' the driver was calling. A woman's voice, straining over the roar of cars and the echoing acoustics under the freeway. 'Hello there? Sir! Excuse me, sir!'

As he stepped forward to the open window, Carter could feel the cool air of the inside of the car on his face; could smell the sweet smokiness of new leather and then, closer still, the scent of the woman's perfume. She was leaning toward the passenger window, her body straining against her seat belt, sunglasses perched on top of her head. A white woman, of course. He'd known that even before he looked. The black Denali with its shining paint job and huge gleaming grille. The eastbound lane on San Felipe, connecting the Galleria with River Oaks, where the big houses were. The woman was young, though, younger than he would have thought for a car like that, thirty at the most, and wearing what looked like tennis clothes, a white skirt and top that matched, her skin moist and shining. Her arms were lean and strong and coppered by the sun. Straight hair, blond with streaks of a darker color, pulled back from the planes of her face, her delicate nose and well-cut cheekbones. No jewelry he could see except a ring, a diamond fat as a tooth. He knew he shouldn't look any closer, but he couldn't stop himself; he let his eyes skim through the back of the car. He saw a baby seat, empty, with brightly colored plush toys hanging over it and beside it a large shopping bag that was made of paper but looked like metal. The name of the store, Nordstrom, was written on the bag.

'Whatever you can give,' Carter muttered. 'God bless you.'

Her purse, a fat leather satchel, was resting on her lap. She began tossing the contents out onto the seat: a tube of lipstick, an address book, a tiny, jewel-like phone. 'I want to give you something,' she was saying. 'Would a twenty be enough? Is that what people do? I don't know.'

'God bless you now.' The light, Carter knew, was about to change. 'Whatever you can do.'

She withdrew her wallet just as, behind them, they heard the first impatient honk. The woman turned her head quickly at the sound, then looked up at the traffic signal, now green. 'Oh, damnit, damnit.' She was frantically riffling through the wallet, a huge thing the size of a book, with snaps and zippers and compartments crammed with slips of paper. 'I don't know,' she was saying, 'I don't know.'

More honking, and then, with a roar, the vehicle behind her, a red Mercedes, accelerated to jam itself across the middle lane, cutting off an SUV. The driver of the SUV slammed on his brakes and leaned on his horn.

'I'm sorry, I'm sorry,' the woman kept saying. She was looking at the wallet like it was a locked door she couldn't find the key to open. 'It's all *plastic* in here, I thought I had a *twenty*, maybe it was a ten, oh goddamnit, *goddamnit* . . .'

'Hey, asshole!' A man leaned his head from the window of a big pickup, two cars back. 'Can't you see the light? Get out of the road!'

' 'Sall right,' Anthony said, backing away. 'You should go.'

'You heard me?' the man cried. More long blasts of the horn. He waved a bare arm out the window. 'Get outta the fucking way!'

The woman arched her back to look into the rearview. Her

eyes grew very wide. 'Shut up!' she cried bitterly. She hit the steering wheel with her fists. 'Jesus, just shut up!'

'Lady, move your fucking car!'

'I wanted to give you something. That's all I wanted. Why should it be so *hard*, just to do this *one thing*, I wanted to *help* . . .'

Carter knew it was time to run. He could see how the rest was going to unfold: the car door flying open; the furious footsteps coming toward him; a man's face pressed close to Carter's, sneering – *You bothering this lady? What you think you're doing, fella?* – and then more men, who knew how many, there were always plenty of men when the time came, and no matter what the woman said, she wouldn't be able to help him, they'd see what they wanted to see: a black man and a white woman with a baby seat and shopping bags, her wallet open in her lap.

'Please,' he said. 'Lady, you *got* to go.'

The door of the pickup swung open, disgorging a huge red-faced man in jeans and a T-shirt, with hands big as catcher's mitts. He'd crush Carter like a bug.

'Hey!' he yelled, pointing. His big round belt buckle gleamed in the sunshine. 'You there!'

The woman lifted her eyes to the mirror and saw what Carter did: the man was holding a gun. 'Oh my God, oh my God!' she cried.

'He's carjacking her! That little nigger's stealing her car!'

Carter was frozen. It was all bearing down on him, a furious roar, the whole world honking and shouting and coming to get him, coming to get him at last. The woman reached quickly across the passenger seat and opened the door.

'Get in!'

Still he couldn't move.

'Do it!' she shouted. 'Get in the car!'

And for some reason, he did. He dropped his sign and got in fast and slammed the door behind him. The woman hit the gas, jumping the light, which had turned from green to red again. Cars swerved all around them as they rocketed through the intersection. For a second Carter thought they were going to crash for sure and closed his eyes tight, bracing himself for the impact. But nothing happened; everybody missed.

It was, he thought, the damnedest thing. They shot out from under the freeway into sunshine again, the woman driving so fast, it was like she'd forgotten he was there. They hit some railroad tracks and the Denali bounced so high he felt his head actually touch the ceiling. It seemed to jar her, too; she hit the brakes, too hard, sending him pitching forward against the dash, then turned the wheel and pulled into a parking lot with a dry cleaner's and a Shipley Do-Nuts. And without looking at Anthony or saying a word to him, she dropped her head onto the steering wheel and began to cry.

He'd never seen a white woman cry before, not up close, just movies and TV. In the sealed cabin of the Denali, he could smell her tears, like melting wax, and the clean smell of her hair. Then he realized he could smell himself, too, which he hadn't done in a long time, and the smell was nothing good. It was bad, really bad, like spoiled meat and sour milk, and he looked down at his body, his dirty hands and arms and the same T-shirt and jeans he'd worn for days and days, and felt ashamed.

After some time she lifted her face off the wheel and wiped her nose with the back of her hand. 'What's your name?'

'Anthony.'

For a moment, Carter wondered if maybe she was going to drive him straight to the police. The car was so clean and new he felt like a big dirty stain sitting there. But if she could smell him, she didn't show it any.

'I can get out here,' Carter said. 'I'm sorry to have caused you trouble like I did.'

'You? What did *you* do? You didn't do anything.' She took in a long breath, tilted her head back against the headrest, and closed her eyes. 'Jesus, my husband's going to *kill* me. Jesus, Jesus, Jesus. Rachel, what were you *thinking*?'

She seemed angry, and Carter guessed she was waiting for

him to just get out on his own. They were a few blocks north of Richmond; from there he could catch a bus back to the place he'd been sleeping, a vacant lot down on Westpark beside the recycling center. It was a good spot, he'd had no trouble there, and if it rained the people at the center let him sleep in one of the empty garages. He had a little over ten dollars on him, some bills and change from his morning under the 610 – enough to get home with, and buy something to eat.

He put his hand on the door.

'No,' she said quickly. 'Don't go.' She turned toward him. Her eyes, puffy from crying, searched his face. 'You have to tell me if you meant it.'

Carter drew a blank. 'Ma'am?'

'What you wrote on the sign. What you said. "God bless you." I heard you say it. Because the thing is,' the woman said, not waiting for his answer, 'I don't feel blessed, Anthony.' She gave a haunted laugh, showing a row of tiny, pearl-like teeth. 'Isn't that strange? I should, but I just don't. I feel awful. I feel awful all the time.'

Carter didn't know what to say. How could a white lady like her feel awful? In the corner of his eye, he could see the empty baby seat in back, with its bright array of toys, and he wondered where the child was now. Maybe he should say something about her having a baby, how nice that must be for her. Folks liked having babies in his experience, women especially.

'It doesn't matter,' the woman said. She was staring vacantly out the windshield toward the doughnut shop. 'I know what you're thinking. You don't have to say anything. I probably just seem like some crazy woman.'

'You seems all right to me.'

She laughed again, bitterly. 'Well that's just it, isn't it? That's the thing. I *seem* all right. You can ask anybody. Rachel Wood has everything a person could want. Rachel Wood *seems* perfectly all right . . .'

For a minute they just sat there, the woman quietly crying

183

and staring woefully into space, Carter still wondering if he should get out of the car or not. But the lady was upset, and it felt wrong to leave her like that. He wondered if she wanted him to feel sorry for her. Rachel Wood: he guessed that was her name, that she was talking about herself. But he couldn't say for sure. Maybe Rachel Wood was a friend of hers, or somebody who was looking after the baby. He knew he'd have to go sooner or later. Whatever mood had taken her would pass, and she'd figure out she'd just about gotten herself shot for this smelly nigger who was sitting in her car. But for the moment, the feel of cool air on his face from the dashboard vents and the woman's strange, sad silence were enough to keep him where he was.

'What's your last name, Anthony?'

The question wasn't one he could remember anybody asking him. 'Carter,' he said.

What she did next surprised him more than anything that had happened so far. She turned in her seat and, looking right at him with a clear gaze, offered him her hand to shake.

'Well,' she said, her voice still etched with sadness, 'how do you do, Mr Carter. I'm Rachel Wood.'

Mr Carter: he liked that. Her hand was small but she shook like a man, her grip strong. He felt – but he couldn't think of the words for it. He watched to see if she'd wipe her hand off, but she made no move to do this.

'Oh my *God*!' Her eyes widened with amazement. 'My husband's going to have a heart attack. You can't tell him about what happened back there. I mean it. You *absolutely* can't.'

Carter shook his head.

'I mean, it's not his fault he's such a complete and total asshole. He just wouldn't see it the way we do. You have to promise, Mr Carter.'

'I won't say nothing.'

'Good.' She nodded briskly, satisfied, and pointed her eyes out the windshield again, her smooth brow furrowing thoughtfully. 'Doughnuts. Now, I don't know why I stopped here of all places. You probably don't want doughnuts, do you?'

Just the word made a blast of saliva wash down the insides of his mouth. He felt his stomach growl. 'Doughnuts is all right,' Carter said. 'The coffee's good.'

'But they're not a real meal, are they?' Her voice was firm; she'd decided something. 'A real meal is what you need.'

That was when Carter realized what the feeling was. He felt *seen*. Like all along he'd been a ghost without knowing it. It came to him all of a sudden that she meant to take him with her, take him home. He'd heard about folks like her but never believed it.

'You know, Mr Carter, I think God put you under that freeway today for a reason. I think he was trying to tell me something.' She put the Denali in gear. 'You and I are going to be friends. I can just feel it.'

And they *were* friends, just like she'd said. That was the funny thing. He and this white lady, Mrs Wood, with her husband – old enough to be her father, though Carter almost never saw him – and her big house under the live oaks with its thick lawn and hedges, and her two little girls – not just the baby but the older one too, cute as a bug like her sister was, the two of them like something in a picture. He felt it right down to the marrow, the deepest part of him. They were friends. She'd done things for him that no one ever had; it was as if she'd opened the door to her car and inside was a whole big room, and in that room were people, and voices saying his name and food to eat and a bed to sleep on and all the rest. She'd gotten him work, not just her yard but other houses, too; and wherever he went, people called him Mr Carter, asking him if maybe he could do something a little extra today, because they were having folks over: blowing leaves off the patio or painting a set of chairs or pulling leaves from the gutters, or even walking a dog every now and again. *Mr Carter, I know you must be busy, but if it's not too much trouble, could you . . . ?* And always he said yes, and in the envelope under the mat or the flowerpot they'd leave an extra ten or twenty, without his having to ask. He liked these other folks, but the truth was they didn't matter to him; he did it all for her. Wednesdays, the best day of the week – her day – she'd wave to him from a window as he wheeled the mower from the garage, and sometimes, lots of times, come out of the house when he was done and cleaning up – she didn't leave the money under the mat like the others, but put it in his hand – and maybe sit for a spell with cold glasses of tea on the patio, telling him things about her life, but asking him about his, too. They'd talk like real people, sitting in the shade. *Mr Carter*, she'd tell him, *you're a godsend. Mr Carter, I don't know how I ever got one thing done without you. You're the piece of the puzzle that was missing.*

He loved her. It was true. That was the mystery, the sad and sorrowful mystery of it all. As he lay now in the dark and cold, he felt the tears coming, rising all the way from his gut. How could anybody ever say he'd done anything to Mrs Wood when he'd loved her like he did? Because he knew. Knew that even though she smiled and laughed and went about her business, shopping and playing her tennis and taking trips to the salon, inside of her was an empty place, he'd seen it that first day in the car, and his heart went out to this, like he could fill it for her just by wanting to. The days when she didn't come out to the yard, more and more as time went by, he'd catch sight of her, sometimes, sitting on the sofa for hours, letting the baby just cry and cry because she was wet or hungry, but not moving a muscle: it was like all the air had gone out of her. Some days he didn't see her at all, and he guessed she was deep in the house somewhere, being sad. He'd do extra things on those days, trimming the hedges just so, or picking weeds out of the walk, hoping if he waited long enough she'd come out with the tea. The tea meant she was all right, that she'd gotten through another day of feeling awful like she did.

And then that afternoon in the yard – that terrible afternoon – he found the older girl, Haley, alone. It was December, the air raw with dampness, the pool full of winter leaves;

the little girl, who was in kindergarten, was wearing her blue school shorts and a collared blouse but nothing else, not even shoes, and sitting on the patio. She was holding a doll, a Barbie. Didn't she have school today? Carter asked, and she shook her head, not looking at him. Was her mama around? Daddy's in Mexico, the girl stated, and shivered in the cold. With his girlfriend. Her mama wouldn't get out of bed.

He tried the door but it was locked, and rang the bell and then he called up to the windows, but no one answered. He didn't know what to make of the little girl, outside alone like that, but there was lots he didn't know about people like the Woods, not everything they did made sense to him. All he had was his dirty old sweater to give the girl, but she took it, wrapping it around herself like a blanket. He got to work on the lawn, thinking maybe the noise of the mower would wake up Mrs Wood and she'd remember her little girl was outside alone by the pool, that she'd accidentally locked the door somehow. *Mr Carter, I don't know how it happened, I fell asleep somehow, thank God you were here.*

He finished the lawn, the girl watching him silently with her doll, and got the skimmer from the garage to clean the pool. That was when he found it, along the edge of the path: a baby toad. Weren't no bigger than a penny. He was lucky he'd missed it with the mower. He bent to pick it up; it weighed nothing in his hand. If he hadn't been looking at it with his own eyes he'd have said his hand was empty, that's how light it was. Maybe it was the girl watching him from the patio, or else Mrs Wood sleeping behind him in the house; but it seemed, right then, like the toad could set things right somehow, this tiny thing in the grass.

—C'mere, he said to the girl. C'mere, I've got something to show you. Just a little baby of a thing, Miss Haley. A little baby thing like you.

He turned then to find Mrs Wood, standing in the yard behind him, not ten feet away; she must have come out the front, because he hadn't heard a sound. She was wearing a big T-shirt, like a nightgown, her hair all whichaway around her face.

—Mrs Wood, he said, why there you are, glad to see you're up now. I was just about to show Haley here—

Get away from her!

But it wasn't Mrs Wood, not the one he knew. Her eyes were gone all wild and crazy. She looked like she didn't know who he was.

—Mrs Wood, I just meant to show her something nice—

Get away! Get away! Run, Haley, run!

And before he could say another word she'd shoved him, hard, with all her strength; he tumbled backward, his foot tangled on the skimmer where he'd left it on the pool deck. He reached out, a reflex, his fingertips catching and holding the front of her shirt; he felt his weight taking her with him, nothing he could do to stop it, and that was when they fell into the water.

The water. It hit him like a fist, his nose and eyes and mouth filling with it, with its awful chemical taste, like demon's breath. She was under and over and all around him as they sank, their arms and legs twisted around each other's like a net; he tried to free himself but she held fast, dragging him down and down. He couldn't swim, not a stroke, he could sort of bob along if he had to but even that scared him, and he had no strength to stop her. He craned his head to find the shining surface of the water where it met the air, but it could have been a mile away. She was pulling him down, into a world of silence, as if the pool were an inverted piece of sky, and that was when he figured it: that was where she wanted to go. That's where she'd been headed, all along, since that day under the freeway when she had stopped her car and said his name. Whatever had kept her in that other world, the one above the water, had finally snapped, like the string of a kite, but the world was upside down, and now the kite was falling. She pulled him into a hug, her chin against his shoulder, and for an instant he glimpsed her eyes through the swirling water and saw they were full of a terrible, final darkness. Oh please, he thought, let me. I'll die if you want me to, I would die for you if you asked, let me be the one to die instead. All he had to do was breathe. He knew that as clear as he knew his own name, but try as he might he couldn't make himself do this; he had lived his life too long to give it up by will alone. They hit the bottom with a soft thump, Mrs Wood still holding him, and he felt her shoulders twitch when she took the first breath. She took another, and then a third, the bubbles of the last air in her lungs rising beside his ear like a whispered secret – *God bless you, Mr Carter* – and then she let him go.

He didn't remember getting out of the pool, or what he'd said to the little girl. She was crying loudly and then stopped. Mrs Wood was dead, her soul was nowhere around anymore, but her empty body slowly made its way to the surface, taking its place among the floating leaves he'd meant to clean. There was a kind of peacefulness to everything, a terrible brokenhearted peacefulness, like something that had gone on too long had finally found a way to finish. Like he'd begun to disappear again. It might have been hours or minutes before the neighbor lady came, and then the police, but by that time he knew he wouldn't tell a soul what had happened, the things he'd seen and heard. It was a secret she had given him, the final secret of who she was, and he was meant to keep it.

Carter decided it was all right, what was going to happen to him now. It felt inevitable. Maybe Wolgast had lied, or maybe he hadn't, but the work of Carter's life was over; he knew that now. Nobody was going to ask him again about Mrs Wood. She was just a thing in his mind, like some part of her had passed straight into him, and he wouldn't have to tell nobody about it.

The air around him broke with a hissing sound, like air leaking from a tire, and a single green light appeared on the far wall where a red one used to be; a door swung open, bathing the room in a pale blue light. Carter saw he was lying on a gurney, wearing a gown. The tube was still threaded into his hand, and looking at the place where it pulled at his skin under the tape made it hurt fiercely again. The room was larger than he'd guessed, nothing but pure white surfaces except for the place where the door had opened and a few machines on the far wall that looked like nothing he knew.

A figure was standing in the doorway.

He closed his eyes and leaned back, thinking, All right now. All right. I'm ready. Let them come.

'We have a situation.'

It was just past ten p.m. Sykes had appeared at the door of Richards's office.

'I know,' Richards said. 'I'm on it.'

The situation was the girl, the Jane Doe. She wasn't a Jane Doe anymore. Richards had gotten the news off the law enforcement general feed a little after nine. The girl's mother was a suspect in a shooting, something at a fraternity house; the boy she'd shot was the son of a federal circuit judge. The gun, which she'd left at the scene, had led local police to a motel near Graceland, where the manager – a list of priors that filled two pages – had ID'd the girl from the photograph the cops had taken of her on Friday, at the convent where the mother had dumped her. The nuns had spilled their story, and something else that Richards didn't know what to make of – some kind of disturbance at the Memphis Zoo – before one of them had picked out Doyle and Wolgast from a surveillance video taken the night before at the I-55 checkpoint north of Baton Rouge. Local TV had gotten the story in time for the evening news, when the Amber Alert had gone out.

Just like that, the whole world was looking for two federal agents and a little girl named Amy Bellafonte.

'Where are they now?' Sykes asked.

On his terminal, Richards called up the satellite feed and pointed his viewer at the states between Tennessee and Colorado. The transmitter was in Wolgast's handheld. Richards counted eighteen hot points in the region, then found the one that matched the number of Wolgast's tracking tag.

'Western Oklahoma.'

Sykes was standing behind him, looking over his shoulder. 'Do you think he knows yet?'

Richards recalibrated the viewer, zooming in.

'I'd say so,' he said, and showed Sykes the data stream.

Target velocity, 120 kph.

Then, a moment later:

Target velocity, 133 kph.

They were on the run now. Richards would have to go get them. Locals were involved, maybe state cops. It was going to be ugly, assuming he could even reach them in time. The chopper was already inbound from Fort Carson; Sykes had made the call.

They took the rear stairs to L1 and stepped outside to wait. The temperature had risen since sunset. A thick fog was ascending in loose coils under the lights of the parking circle, like dry ice at a rock concert. They stood together without talking; there was nothing to say. The situation was more or less a complete and total screwup. Richards thought of the photograph, the one that was all over the wires. Amy Bellafonte: *beautiful fountain*. Black hair falling straight to her shoulders – it looked damp, like she'd been walking in the rain – and a smooth, young face, still with some baby fat fluffing her cheeks; but beneath her brow, dark eyes with a knowing depth. She was wearing jeans and a sweatshirt zipped to her throat. In one hand she was clutching some kind of toy, a stuffed animal. It might have been a dog. But the eyes: the eyes were what Richards kept coming back to. She was looking straight at the camera as if to say, *See? What did you* think *I was, Richards? You think nobody in the world loves me?*

For a second, just one, he thought it. It brushed him like a wing: the wish that he were a different kind of person, that the look in a child's eyes meant something to him.

Five minutes later they heard the chopper, a pulsing

presence coasting in low over the wall of trees to the south-east. It made a single, searching turn, dragging a cone of light, then dropped toward the parking lot with balletic precision, shoving a wave of shuddering air under its blades. A UH-60 Blackhawk with a full armament rack, rigged for night reconnaissance. It seemed like a lot, for one little girl. But that was the situation in which they now found themselves. They held their hands over their brows against the wind and noise and swirling snow.

As the chopper touched down, Sykes seized Richards's elbow.

'She's a kid!' he said over the din. 'Do this right!'

Whatever that meant, Richards thought, and stepped briskly away, toward the opening door.

TEN

They were moving quickly now, Wolgast at the wheel, Doyle beside him, thumbing away furiously on his handheld. Calling in to let Sykes know who was in charge.

'No goddamn signal.' Doyle tossed his handheld onto the dash. They were fifteen miles outside of Homer, headed due west; the open fields slid endlessly away under a sky thick with stars.

'I could have told you that,' Wolgast said. 'It's the back side of the moon out here. And why don't you watch your language?'

Doyle ignored him. Wolgast lifted his eyes quickly to the rearview to find Amy looking back at him. He knew she felt it too: they were joined together now. From the moment they'd stepped off the carousel, he'd cast his lot with her.

'How much do you know?' Wolgast asked. 'I don't suppose it matters now if you tell me.'

'As much as you do.' Doyle shrugged. 'Maybe more. Richards thought you might have problems with this.'

When had they spoken? Wolgast wondered. While he and Amy were on the rides? That night in Huntsville, when Wolgast had gone back to the motel to call Lila? Or was it before?

'You should be careful. I mean it, Phil. A guy like that. Private security contractor. He's little more than a mercenary.'

Doyle sighed irritably. 'You know what your problem is, Brad? You don't know who's on your side here. I gave you the benefit of the doubt back there. All you had to do was bring her back to the car when you said you would. You're not seeing the whole picture.'

'I've seen enough.'

A filling station appeared ahead of them, a glowing oasis in the gloom. As they approached, Wolgast eased off the gas.

'Christ. Don't stop,' Doyle said. 'Just drive.'

'We're not going to get very far without gas. We're down to a quarter tank. This could be the last station for a while.'

If Doyle wanted to be in charge, Wolgast thought, at least he would have to act like it.

'Fine. But just the gas. And both of you stay in the car.'

They pulled up to the pump. After Wolgast shut off the engine, Doyle reached across and withdrew the keys from the ignition. Then he opened the glove box and removed Wolgast's weapon. He released the clip, buried it in the pocket of his jacket, and returned the empty gun to the glove box.

'Stay put.'

'You might want to check the oil too.'

Doyle exhaled sharply. 'Jesus, anything else, Brad?'

'I'm just saying. We don't want to break down.'

'Fine. I'll check it. Just stay in the car.'

Doyle stepped around the back of the Tahoe and began to fill the tank. With Doyle out of the car, Wolgast had a moment to think, but unarmed and without the keys, there

193

wasn't much he could do. Part of him had decided not to take Doyle completely seriously, but for the moment, the situation was what it was. He pulled the lever under the dash; Doyle moved to the front of the Tahoe and lifted the hood, momentarily shielding the cabin from view.

Wolgast twisted around to face Amy.

'Are you okay?'

The girl nodded. She was holding her knapsack in her lap; the well-stroked ear of her stuffed rabbit was peeking through the opening. In the light of the filling area, Wolgast could see a bit of powdered sugar still on her cheeks, like flecks of snow.

'Are we still going to the doctor?'

'I don't know. We'll see.'

'He has a gun.'

'I know, honey. It's all right.'

'My mother had a gun.'

Before Wolgast could assemble a response, the hood of the Tahoe slammed closed. Startled, he turned sharply in time to see three state police cruisers, lights on, tearing past the filling station in the opposite direction.

The passenger door of the Tahoe opened to a gust of damp air. 'Shit.' Doyle handed Wolgast the keys and swiveled in his seat to look at the cruisers as they passed. 'You think that's about us?'

Wolgast angled his head to watch the cruisers through the side-view mirror. They were doing at least eighty, maybe more. It could have been something ordinary, a wreck or a fire. But his gut told him it wasn't. He counted off the seconds, watching the lights recede into the distance. He had reached twenty by the time he was certain they were turning around.

He turned the key, felt the engine roar to life.

'That's us all right.'

Ten o'clock, and Sister Arnette couldn't sleep. She couldn't even close her eyes.

Oh, it was awful, just awful, everything that had happened

– first the men coming for Amy, how they had deceived her, deceived everyone, though Sister Arnette still didn't understand how they could be both FBI and also kidnappers; and then that terrible thing at the zoo, the shouts and screams and everyone running, and Lacey holding on to Amy the way she had, refusing to let go; and the hours they'd spent at the police station, the whole rest of the day, not treated like criminals exactly but certainly not spoken to in a way that Sister Arnette was accustomed to, all of it vaguely accusing, the detective asking them the same questions over and over again; and then the reporters and camera trucks lined up on the street outside the house, huge spotlights filling the front windows as the evening wore on, the phone ringing nonstop until finally Sister Claire had thought to unplug it.

The girl's mother had killed someone, a boy. That's what the detective had told her. The detective's name was Dupree, a young fellow with a prickly little beard, and he spoke to her courteously, a bit of old New Orleans in his voice, which meant he was probably Catholic, calling her *dawlin'* and *cher*; but wasn't that what Sister Arnette had thought of the other two when they'd appeared at the door? Wolgast and the younger, good-looking one? Whose faces she had seen again on the grainy video Dupree showed her, from someplace in Mississippi, taken when – she guessed – they thought no one was looking? That they were nice men because they looked nice? And the mother, Detective Dupree told her, the mother was a *prostitute*. 'A prostitute is a deep pit; she hides and waits like a robber, looking for another victim who will be unfaithful to his wife.' Proverbs, chapter 23. 'For the lips of an immoral woman drip honey, and her mouth is smoother than oil; but in the end she is bitter as wormwood, sharp as a two-edged sword. Her feet go down to death, her steps lay hold of hell.'

Hold of hell. The very words made Sister Arnette shudder in her bed. Because hell was real, that was a fact; it was a real place, where souls in torment writhed in agony forever and ever. That's the kind of woman Lacey had let into their kitchen, who had stood in their very house not more than thirty-six hours ago: a woman who had *hold of hell*. The woman had ensnared this boy somehow – Arnette didn't want to imagine that part – and then shot him, shot him with a *gun* in the *head*, and then given her girl to Lacey while she made her escape, a girl who had who-knew-what inside her. For it was true: there had been something . . . unearthly about her. It wasn't nice to think it, but there it was. How else to explain what had happened at the zoo, all the animals running and making a ruckus?

The whole situation was awful. Awful awful awful.

Arnette tried to make herself sleep, but this accomplished nothing. She could still hear the thrum of the vans' generators, could see, through the veil of her closed eyes, the ravenous glow of their spotlights. If she turned on the TV she knew what she'd find: reporters with their microphones, speaking in earnest tones and gesturing behind them toward the house where Arnette and the other sisters now attempted to sleep. The scene of the crime, they'd call it, of the latest development in this breaking story of murder and kidnapping, and federal agents somehow involved – though Dupree had forbidden, absolutely forbidden the sisters from talking about this part to anyone. When the sisters had returned home in the police van that had carried them back from the station, all of them wordless with exhaustion, to find the TV trucks, at least a dozen, lined up at the curb in front of the house like a circus train, it was Sister Claire who'd noticed that they weren't just the local Memphis network affiliates but came from as far away as Nashville and Paducah and Little Rock, even St. Louis. As soon as they'd turned into the driveway the reporters had swarmed the van, pointing their lights and cameras and microphones and barking their furious, incomprehensible questions. These people had no decency. Sister Arnette was so frightened she began to shake. It had taken two police officers to move the reporters off the property – *Can't you see they're nuns? Whaddaya wanna go*

bothering a buncha nuns for? All of you just back it up, right now –
so the sisters could walk safely into the house.

Yes, hell was real, and Arnette knew where it was. She was in it, right now.

After that they'd sat together in the kitchen, none of them hungry but still needing to be somewhere – everyone except Lacey, whom Claire had taken straight upstairs to her room to rest. It was odd: of all of them, Lacey seemed the least shaken by the events of the afternoon. She'd barely uttered a word for hours, not to the sisters and not to Dupree, either, just sat with her hands in her lap, tears rolling down her cheeks. But then a funny thing had happened; the officers showed them the videotape from Mississippi, and when Dupree froze the image on the two men, Lacey stepped forward and looked, hard, at the monitor. Arnette had already told Dupree that that was them, she'd had a good look and there wasn't a single doubt in her mind that the men on the screen were the same two who had come to the house and taken the girl; but the expression on Lacey's face, which was something like surprise but not exactly – the word Arnette thought of was *astonishment* – made them all wait.

'I was wrong,' Lacey said finally. 'It isn't . . . him. He is not the one.'

'Which him, Sister?' Dupree asked gently.

She lifted a finger to the older of the two agents, the one who'd done all the talking – though it was the younger one, Arnette recalled, who'd actually taken Amy and put her in the car. In the image, he was looking straight up at the camera, holding a disposable cup in his hand. The time signature on the bottom right corner of the screen said that it was 06:01 on the same morning the two of them had come to the convent.

'Him,' Lacey said, and touched the glass.

'He didn't take the girl?'

'He most assuredly did, Detective,' Arnette declared. She turned and looked at Sister Louise and Sister Claire, who nodded their assent. 'We're all agreed to that. Sister is just upset.'

But Dupree was not deterred. 'Sister Lacey? What do you mean he's not the one?'

Her face was shining with conviction. 'That man,' she said. 'Do you see?' She turned and looked at all of them. She actually smiled. 'Do you see? He loves her.'

He loves her. What to make of that? But these were the only words Lacey had offered on the matter, as far as Arnette was aware. Did she mean to imply that Wolgast actually knew the girl? Could he have been Amy's father? Was that what all this was about? But it didn't explain what had occurred at the zoo, a terrible thing – a child had actually been trampled in the chaos and was in the hospital; two of the animals, a cat of some kind and one of the apes, had been shot – or the dead boy at the college, or any of the rest of it. And yet for the remainder of the afternoon at the station, in and out of various offices, telling their story, Lacey had sat quietly, smiling that strange smile, as if she knew something no one else did.

It all went back, Arnette believed, to what had happened to Lacey so long ago, as a little girl in Africa. Arnette had confessed the whole thing to the sisters, as they sat in the kitchen waiting for the hour when they could go to bed. She probably shouldn't have, but she'd had to tell Dupree; once they were back at the house, it had all just kind of come out. An experience like that didn't ever leave a person, the sisters agreed; it went inside them and stayed forever. Sister Claire – of course it was Sister Claire, who had gone to college and kept a nice dress and good shoes in her closet as if at any moment she'd get an invitation to a fancy party – knew a name for it: post-traumatic stress disorder. It made sense, Sister Claire said; it added up. It explained Lacey's protective feelings for the girl, and why she never went out of the house, and the way she seemed separate from all of them, living among them but also not, as if a part of her were always elsewhere. Poor Lacey, to carry such a memory inside her.

Arnette checked the clock: 12:05. Outside, the roar of the generators had ceased at last; the camera crews had all gone home. She drew back the covers and breathed a worried sigh. There was no denying it. All of this was Lacey's fault. Arnette would never have given the girl to those men if Lacey hadn't lied to them all in the first place, and yet now it was Lacey who was fast asleep, while she, Arnette, was lying in bed awake. The other sisters, couldn't they see that? But probably they were all sleeping, too. It was only she, Arnette, who was sentenced to a night of pacing the halls of her mind.

Because she was worried. Deeply worried. Something didn't add up, no matter what Sister Claire said. *He's not the one. He loves her.* That strange, knowing smile on Lacey's lips. Dupree had questioned Lacey closely, asking her what this meant, but all Lacey had done was smile and say these words again, as if they explained everything. And it flew straight in the face of the facts. Wolgast *was* the one: everyone was agreed on that point. Wolgast and the other man, the one who had taken the girl, whose name Arnette remembered now was Doyle, Phil Doyle. Where they had taken the girl and why – well, no one had told Arnette anything. She sensed Dupree was puzzled too, the way he kept posing the same questions over and over, clicking his pen, frowning incredulously and shaking his head, making phone calls, drinking cup after cup of coffee.

And then, despite all these concerns, Arnette felt her mind begin to loosen, the images of the day unwinding inside her like a spool of thread, pulling her down into sleep. *Tell us again about the parking lot, Sister.* Arnette in the little room with the mirror that wasn't a mirror – she knew that. *Tell us about the men. Tell us about Lacey.* Arnette was facing the glass; over Dupree's shoulder she could see her face reflected there, an old face, lined by time and exhaustion, its edges wrapped by the gray cloth of her veil so that it seemed disembodied somehow, floating in space; and behind it, on the other side of the glass, above and around her, she detected the presence of a dark form, watching her. Who was behind her face? She could hear Lacey's voice now, too, Lacey in the parking lot, crazy Lacey who seemed apart from all of them, sitting on the ground and clutching the girl fiercely; Arnette was standing above her, and Lacey and the girl were crying. *Don't take her.* Her mind followed the sound of Lacey's voice, down into a dark place.

Don't take me, don't take me, don't take me . . .

A bolt of anxiety hit her chest; she sat upright, too fast. The air of the room seemed lighter, as if all the oxygen had leaked away. Her heart was hammering. Had she fallen asleep? Was she dreaming? What in the world?

And then she knew, knew it for a fact. They were in danger, terrible danger. Something was coming. She didn't know what. Some dark force had come loose in the world, and it was sweeping toward them, coming for them all.

But Lacey knew. Lacey, who'd lain in the field for hours, knew what evil was.

Arnette tore from the room, into the hall. To be sixty-eight, and consumed by such terror! To give your life to God, to His loving peace, and come to such a moment! To lie with it in the dark all alone! A dozen steps to Lacey's door: Arnette tried the handle but the door refused her; it was locked from the inside. She pounded the door with her fists.

'Sister Lacey! Sister Lacey, open this door!'

Then Claire was at her side. She was wearing a T-shirt that seemed to glow in the dark hall; her face was smeared with a penumbra of bluish cream. 'What is it? What's wrong?'

'Sister Lacey, open this door this instant!' Silence, still, from the far side. Arnette seized the handle and shook it like a dog with a rag in his teeth. She pounded and pounded. 'Do as I say right now!'

Lights coming on, the sounds of doors and voices, a great commotion all around her. The other sisters were in the hallway now too, their eyes wide with alarm, everyone talking at once.

'What's going on?'

'I don't know, I don't know—'

'Is Lacey all right?'

'Somebody call 911!'

'Lacey,' Arnette was yelling, 'open this door!'

A huge force gripped her, pulling her away. Sister Claire: it was Sister Claire who had grabbed Arnette from behind, seizing her by her arms. She felt her diminishment, how her strength, against Sister Claire's, was nothing.

'Look – Sister's hurt herself—'

'Dear Lord in heaven!'

'Look at her hands!'

'Please,' Arnette sobbed. 'Help me.'

Sister Claire released her. A reverent hush had fallen over them all. Crimson ribbons were running down Arnette's wrists. Claire took one of Arnette's fists and gently unclenched it. The palm was filled with blood.

'Look, it's just her fingernails,' Claire said, and showed them. 'She dug into her palms with her fingernails.'

'Please,' Arnette begged, tears rolling down her cheeks. 'Just open the door and see.'

No one knew where the key was. It was Sister Tracy who thought to get the screwdriver from the toolbox under the kitchen sink and wedge it into the lock. But by the time this happened, Sister Arnette had already figured out what they'd find.

The bed that had never been slept in. The curtains of the open window shifting in the evening air.

The door swung open on an empty room. Sister Lacey Antoinette Kudoto was gone.

Two a.m. The night was moving at a crawl.

Not that it had begun well for Grey. After his run-in with Paulson in the commissary, Grey had returned to his room in the barracks. He still had two hours to kill until his shift, more than enough time to think about what Paulson had said about Jack and Sam. The only upside was that it sort of took his mind off the other thing, that funny echo in his head, but still it was no good, just sitting around feeling worried, and at a quarter to ten, just about ready to jump out of his skin, he put on his parka and crossed the compound to the Chalet. Under the lights of the parking area he treated himself to one last Parliament, gulping down the smoke, while a couple of doctors and lab techs, wearing heavy winter coats over their scrubs, exited the building and got into their cars and drove away. Nobody so much as waved at him.

The floor by the front door was slick with melted snow. Grey banged his boots clean and stepped to the desk, where the sentry took his badge and ran it through the scanner and waved him to the elevator. Inside, he pushed the button for Level 3.

'Hold the elevator.'

Grey's insides jumped: Richards. An instant later he stepped briskly into the car, a cloud of cold air from outside still clinging to his nylon jacket.

'Grey.' He pushed the button for L2 and quickly checked his watch. 'Where the fuck were you this morning?'

'I overslept.'

The doors slid closed and the car began its slow descent.

'You think this is a vacation? You think you can just show up when you feel like it?'

Grey shook his head, his eyes cast down at the floor. Just the sound of the man's voice could make his backside clench like a fist. No way Grey was going to look at him.

'Uh-uh.'

'That's all you have to say?'

Grey could smell the nervous sweat coming off himself, a rancid stink, like onions left too long in a crisper drawer. Probably Richards could smell it too.

'I guess.'

Richards sniffed and said nothing. Grey knew he was deciding what to do.

'I'm docking you for two shifts,' Richards said finally, keeping his eyes forward. 'Twelve hundred bucks.'

The doors slid open on L2.

'Don't let it happen again,' Richards warned.

He exited the elevator and strode away. As the doors closed behind him, Grey released the breath he realized he'd been holding in his chest. Twelve hundred bucks – that hurt. But Richards. He made Grey more than a little jumpy. Especially now, after the little speech Paulson had given in the mess. Grey had begun to think maybe something *had* happened to Jack and Sam, that they hadn't just flown the coop. Grey remembered that dancing red light in the field. It had to be true: something had happened, and Richards had put that light on Jack and Sam.

The doors opened on L3, giving a view of the security detail, two soldiers wearing the orange armband of the watch. He was well below ground now, which always made him feel a little claustrophobic at first. Above the desk was a big sign: AUTHORIZED PERSONNEL ONLY. BIOLOGICAL AND NUCLEAR HAZARDS PRESENT. NO EATING, DRINKING, SMOKING. REPORT ANY OF THE FOLLOWING SYMPTOMS TO THE OD. This was followed by a list of what sounded like a bad case of stomach flu, only worse: fever, vomiting, disorientation, seizures.

He gave his badge to the one he knew as Davis.

'Hey, Grey.' Davis took his badge and ran it under the scanner without even looking at the screen. 'I got a joke for you. How many kids with ADD does it take to screw in a lightbulb?'

'I don't know.'

'*Hey, you wanna go ride bikes?*' Davis laughed and slapped his knee. The other soldier frowned; Grey didn't think he understood the joke, either. 'Don't you get it?'

' 'Cause he likes to ride bikes?'

'Yeah, 'cause he likes to ride bikes. He's got ADD. It means he can't pay attention.'

'Oh. I get it now.'

'It's a *joke*, Grey. You're supposed to laugh.'

'It's funny,' Grey managed. 'But I gotta get to work.'

Davis sighed heavily. 'Okay, hold your horses.'

Grey stepped back into the elevator with Davis. From around his neck Davis took a long, silver key and placed it in a slot beside the button for L4.

'Have fun down there,' Davis said.

'I just clean,' Grey said nervously.

Davis frowned and shook his head. 'I don't want to know anything about it.'

In the locker room on L4, Grey switched out his jumpsuit for scrubs. Two other men were there, sweeps like him, one named Jude and one named Ignacio. On the wall, a large whiteboard listed the duties of each worker for the shift. They dressed together without speaking and exited the room.

Grey had drawn the lucky straw: all he had to do was mop the halls and empty the trash, then babysit Zero for the rest of the shift, to see if he ate anything. From the storage closet he fetched his mop and supplies and got to work; by midnight he was done. Then he went to the door at the end of the first corridor, ran his card through the scanner, and stepped inside.

The room, about twenty feet square, was empty. On the left side, a two-stage air lock led into the containment chamber. Going through took at least ten minutes, more on the return trip, when you had to shower. To the right of the air lock was the control panel. It was all a bunch of lights and buttons and switches, most of which Grey didn't understand and wasn't supposed to touch. Above it was a wall of reinforced glass, dark, which looked out on the chamber.

Grey took a seat at the panel and examined the infrared. Zero was kind of huddled in the corner, away from the gates, which had been left open when the last shift had brought in the rabbits. The galvanized cart was still there, sitting in the middle of the room, with its ten open cages. Three of the rabbits were still inside. Grey looked around the room. The others were all scattered about, untouched.

At a little after one a.m. the door to the corridor opened, and one of the techs stepped in, a large Hispanic man named Pujol. He nodded at Grey and looked at the monitor.

'Still not eating?'

'Uh-uh.'

Pujol made a mark on the screen of his handheld. He had one of those complexions that made it look as if he hadn't shaved even when he had.

'I was wondering something,' Grey said. 'How come they don't eat the tenth one?'

Pujol shrugged. 'How should I know? Maybe they're just saving it for later.'

'I had a dog who did that,' Grey volunteered.

Pujol made more marks on his handheld. 'Yeah, well.' He lifted one broad shoulder in a shrug; the information meant nothing to him. 'Call the lab if he decides to eat.'

After Pujol left, Grey wished he'd thought to ask him some of the other questions on his mind. Like, why rabbits at all, or how Zero stuck to the ceiling like he sometimes did, or why just sitting there had begun to make Grey's skin crawl. Because that was the thing with Zero, more even than with the rest of them; being with Zero felt like being with an actual person in the room. Zero had a mind, and you could feel that mind working. Five more hours: Zero hadn't moved an inch since Grey had gotten there. But the readout below the infrared still gave his heartrate at 102 bpm, same as when he was moving about. Grey wished he'd thought to bring a magazine to read or maybe a crossword book, to help him stay alert, but Paulson had rattled him so bad he'd forgotten. He also wanted a smoke. A lot of guys snuck them in the john, not just the sweeps but also the techs and even a doctor or two. It was generally understood that you could smoke there if you had to and weren't gone more than five minutes, but Grey didn't want to push his luck with Richards, not after their run-in in the elevator.

He leaned back in the chair. Five more hours. He closed his eyes.

Grey.

Grey's eyes flew open; he sat upright.

Grey. Look at me.

It wasn't a voice he was hearing, not exactly. The words were in his head, almost like something he was reading; the words were someone else's, but the voice was his own.

'Who's that?'

On the monitor, the glowing shape of Zero.

I was called Fanning.

Grey saw it then, like somebody had opened a door in his head. A city. A great city thrumming with light, so many lights it was as if the night sky had fallen to earth and wrapped itself around all the buildings and bridges and streets. Then he was stepping through the door and he felt and smelled where he was, the hardness of cold pavement under his feet, the dirt of exhaust and the smell of stone, the way the winter air moved in channels around the buildings so there was always a breeze on your face. But it wasn't Dallas, or any other city he'd ever been to; it was someplace old, and it was winter. Part of him was sitting at the panel on L4 and another part was in this other place. He knew his eyes had closed.

I want to go home. Take me home, Grey.

A college, he knew, though why would he think such a thing, that this was a college he was seeing? And how would he know this was New York City, where he'd never been in his life, had seen only in pictures, and that the buildings around him were the buildings of a campus: offices and lecture halls and dormitories and labs. He was walking along a path, not really walking but somehow moving down it, and people were flowing past him.

See them.

They were women. Young women, bundled in heavy woolen coats and scarves tucked up tight to their throats, some with hats pulled down over their heads, rich handfuls of young hair flowing like shawls of silk from under these compressive domes onto their smoothly rounded shoulders, into the cold air of New York City in winter. Their eyes were bright with life. They were laughing, books tucked under their arms or pressed to their slender chests, talking in animated voices to one another, though the words were nothing he could hear.

They're beautiful. Aren't they beautiful, Grey?

And they were. They were beautiful. Why had Grey never known this?

Can't you feel them, walking past, can't you smell them? I never get tired of smelling them. How the air behind them sweetens as they pass. I used to just stand and breathe it in. You smell them too, don't you, Grey? Like the boys.

—The boys.

You remember the boys, don't you, Grey?

He did. He remembered the boys. The ones walking home from school, sweating in the heat, bookbags sagging from their shoulders, their damp shirts clinging to them; he remembered the smell of sweat and soap of their hair and skin, and the damp crescent on their backs where their bookbags had pressed against their shirts. And the one boy, the boy trailing behind, now taking the shortcut down the alley, the quickest way home from school: that boy, his skin bronzed from the sun, his black hair pressed to the back of his neck, his eyes cast down at the sidewalk, playing some game with the cracks so that he didn't notice Grey at first, the pickup moving slowly behind him, then stopping. How alone he seemed—

You wanted to love him, didn't you, Grey. To make him feel that love?

He felt a great, sleeping thing lumbering to life inside him. The old Grey. Panic swelled his throat.

—I don't remember.

Yes you do. But they've done something to you, Grey. They've taken that part of you away, the part that felt love.

—I don't . . . I can't . . .

It's still there, Grey. It's just hidden from you. I know, because that part was hidden in me, too. Before I became what I am.

207

—What you are.

—You and I, we're the same. We know what we want, Grey. To give love, to feel love. Girls, boys, it's all the same. We want to love them, as they need to be loved. Do you want it, Grey? Do you want to feel that again?

He did. He knew it then.

—Yes. That's what I want.

I need to go home, Grey. I want to take you with me, to show you.

Grey saw it again, in his mind's eye, rising up around him: the great city, New York. All around him, humming, buzzing, its energies passing through each stone and brick, following unseen lines of connectedness into the soles of his feet. It was dark, and he felt the darkness as something wonderful, something he belonged to. It flowed into him, down his throat and into his lungs, a great, easeful drowning. He was everywhere and nowhere all at once, moving not over the landscape but through it, into and out of it, breathing the dark city that was also breathing him.

Then he saw her. There she was. A girl. She was alone, walking the path between the school buildings – a dormitory of laughing students; a library of quiet hallways, its wide windows fogged by frost; an empty office where a lone cleaning woman, listening to Motown on headphones, bent to rinse her mop in a wheeled bucket. He knew it all, he could hear the laughter and the sounds of quiet studying and count the books on the shelves, he could hear the words of the song as the woman with the bucket hummed along, *whenever you're near . . . uh-uh . . . I hear a symphony* – and the girl, ahead on the pathway, her solitary figure shimmering, pulsing with life. She was walking straight toward him, her head tipped against the wind, her shoulders lifted in a delicate hunch beneath her heavy coat to tell him she was holding something in her arms. The girl, hurrying home. So alone. She had stayed out late, studying the words of the book she held to her chest, and now she was afraid. Grey knew he had something to tell her, before she slipped away. *You like this, is that what you like, I'll show you.* He was lifting, he was rising up, he was falling down upon her—

Love her, Grey. Take her.

Then he was ill. He rocked forward in his chair and in a single spasm released the contents of his stomach onto the floor: the soup and salad, the pickled beets, the mashies and the ham. His head was between his knees; a long string of spittle was swinging from his lips.

What the hell. What the goddamn.

He eased himself upright. His mind began to clear. L4. He was on L4. Something had happened. He couldn't remember what. An awful dream of flying. He'd been eating something in the dream; the taste was still in his mouth. A taste like blood. And then he'd puked just like that.

Puking, he thought, and he felt his stomach drop – that was bad. Very very bad. He knew what he was supposed to watch for. Vomiting, fever, seizures. Even a hard sneeze out of nowhere. The signs were everywhere, not just in the Chalet but the barracks, the dining hall, even in the johns: 'Any of the following symptoms, report *immediately* to the duty officer . . .'

He thought of Richards. Richards, with his little dancing light, and the ones named Jack and Sam.

Oh crap. Oh crap oh crap oh crap.

He had to move fast. No one could find it, the big puddle of puke on the floor. He told himself to calm down. Steady, Grey, steady. He checked his watch: 02:31. No way he was waiting another three and a half hours. He got to his feet, stepping around the mess, and quietly opened the door. A quick peek down the hall: not a soul in sight. Speed, that was the thing; get it done fast and then get the hell out. Never mind the cameras; Paulson probably had that right – how could somebody be watching every minute of the day and night? In the supply closet he got a mop and began to fill a bucket in the sink and poured in a cup of bleach. If anybody saw him he could say he'd spilled something, a Dr Pepper or a cup of coffee, which he wasn't supposed to have, though

209

people did. He'd spilled a Dr Pepper. Couldn't be sorrier. That was what he'd say.

He also wasn't really sick, he could tell, not the way the signs made it sound. He was sweating under his shirt, but that was just the panic. As he watched the bucket fill and then hoisted it, reeking of chlorine, from the deep well of the sink, his body was telling him so in no uncertain terms. Something else had made him toss, something in the dream. The sensation was still in his mouth, not just the taste – a too warm, sticky sweetness that seemed to coat his tongue and throat and teeth – but the feel of soft meat yielding under his jaws, exploding with juice. Like he'd bitten into a rotten piece of fruit.

He yanked a few yards of paper towel off the dispenser, got a hazard bag and gloves from the cabinet, and carted it all back to the room. The mess was too big just to mop it, so he got on his knees and did his best to soak it up with the towels, pushing the bigger pieces into clumps he could pick up with his fingers. He put it all into the bag and cinched it tight, then spread water and bleach over the floor, working in circles. There were some chunks of something on his slippers and he wiped those off, too. The taste in his mouth was different now, like something spoiled, and it made him think of Brownbear, whose breath got like that sometimes; it was the only thing bad about him, how he'd come back to the trailer reeking of week-old roadkill and stick his face right up close to Grey's, smiling that dog smile he had, his gums pulled back at his molars. Grey couldn't hold it against him, Brownbear being just a dog, though he didn't like that smell one bit, and not in his own mouth like it was now.

In the locker room he changed quickly, shoved his scrubs in the laundry bin, and rode the elevator up to L3. Davis was still there, leaning back in his chair with his feet propped up on the desk, reading a magazine, his boots bobbing to some song playing on little earphones tucked in the sides of his head.

'You know, I don't know why I even look at this stuff

anymore,' Davis said loudly over the music. 'What's the point? I'm never getting off this iceball.'

Davis dropped his feet to the floor and held up the cover of the magazine for Grey to see: two naked women in a winding embrace, their mouths open and the tips of their tongues just touching. The magazine was called *Hoteez*. Their tongues looked to Grey like slabs of muscle, something you'd put on ice in a deli case. The sight sent a fresh current of nausea churning through him.

'Oh, that's right,' Davis said when he saw Grey's expression. He plucked the buds from his ears. 'You guys don't like this stuff. Sorry.' Davis sat forward and wrinkled his nose. 'Man, you stink. What *is* that?'

'I think I ate something bad,' Grey said cautiously. 'I gotta go lie down for a while.'

Davis flinched with alarm; he pushed away from the desk, widening the gap between them. 'Don't fucking say that.'

'I swear that's all it is.'

'Jesus Christ, Grey.' The soldier's eyes were wide with panic. 'What are you trying to do to me? You got a fever or anything?'

'I just tossed is all. In the can. I think maybe I ate too much. I just need to get off my feet for a bit.'

Davis took a second to think, eyeing Grey nervously. 'Well, I've seen you eat, Grey. All you guys. You shouldn't shovel it in like that. And you don't look so hot, I'll say that. No offense, but you look like crap. I really should call this in.'

They'd have to seal the level, Grey knew. That meant Davis would be stuck down here, too. As for what would happen to him, he didn't know. He didn't want to think about it. He wasn't really sick, he knew that much. But there was something wrong with him. He'd had bad dreams before, but nothing that ever made him puke.

'You're *sure*?' Davis pressed. 'I mean, you'd tell me if there was something really wrong with you?'

Grey nodded. A drop of sweat slithered the length of his torso.

211

'Man, what a fucking day.' Davis sighed resignedly. 'All right, hang on.' He tossed Grey the elevator key and freed his com from his belt. 'Don't say I never did anything for you, okay?' He spoke into the mouthpiece. 'This is the sentry on three? We need a relief worker—'

But Grey didn't stay to listen. He was already in the elevator, gone.

ELEVEN

Somewhere west of the town of Randall, Oklahoma, a few miles south of the Kansas border, Wolgast decided to surrender.

They were parked inside a car wash, off a rural blacktop the number of which he'd long forgotten. It was almost dawn; Amy was fast asleep, curled like a cub on the backseat of the Tahoe. Three hours of driving hard and fast, Doyle calling out a route he quickly assembled off the GPS, a line of lights flashing in the distance behind them, sometimes fading when they made a turn but always reassembling, picking up their trail. It was just after two a.m. when Wolgast had seen the car wash. He took a chance and pulled in. They'd sat in the dark and listened to the cruisers fly past.

'How long do you think we should wait?' Doyle asked. All his bluster had left him.

'A while,' Wolgast said. 'Let them put some distance between us.'

'That'll just give them time to set up roadblocks at the state line. Or double back when they realize they've lost us.'

'You have a better idea I'd like to hear it,' Wolgast said.

Doyle thought a moment. The big scrub brushes hanging over the windshield made the space in the car seem closer. 'Not really, no.'

So they'd sat. At any second Wolgast expected the car

wash to blaze with light, to hear the amplified voice of a state cop telling them to come out with their hands up. But this hadn't happened. They had a signal now, but it was analog and wouldn't encrypt, so there was no way to tell anyone where they were.

'Listen,' Doyle said. 'I'm sorry about what happened back there.'

Wolgast was too tired to engage. The fair seemed like days ago. 'Forget about it.'

'You know, the thing is, I really liked my job. The Bureau, all of it. It's all I ever wanted to do.' Doyle took a deep breath and fingered a bead of condensation on the passenger window. 'What do you think's going to happen?'

'I don't know.'

Doyle frowned acidly. 'Yeah you do. That guy, Richards. You were right about him.'

The windows of the car wash had begun to pale. Wolgast checked his watch; it was a little before six. They'd waited as long as they could. He turned the key to the Tahoe and backed out of the car wash.

Amy awoke then. She sat upright and rubbed her eyes, looking about. 'I'm hungry,' she announced.

Wolgast turned to Doyle. 'How about it?'

Doyle hesitated; Wolgast could see the idea taking shape in his mind. He knew what he was really saying: it's over.

'Might as well.'

Wolgast turned the Tahoe around and headed back in the direction they'd come, into the town of Randall. The main thoroughfare didn't amount to much, not more than a half dozen blocks long. An air of abandonment hung over the street; most of the windows were papered over or smeared with soap. Probably there was a Walmart not far away, Wolgast thought, or some other big store like that, the kind that wiped little towns like Randall right off the map. At the end of the block, a square of light spilled onto the sidewalk; a half dozen pickups were angled at the curb.

'Breakfast,' he declared.

213

The restaurant was a single, narrow room with a drop ceiling stained by years of cigarette smoke and airborne grease. A long counter stood to one side, facing a line of padded, high-backed booths. The air smelled of boiled coffee and fried butter. A few men in jeans and workshirts were seated at the counter, their broad backs hunched over plates of eggs and cups of coffee. The three of them took a booth in the back. The waitress, a middle-aged woman, broad across the middle and with clear gray eyes, brought over coffee and menus.

'What can I get for you gentlemen?'

Doyle said he wasn't hungry and would stick to coffee. Wolgast looked up at the woman, who was wearing a name tag: LUANNE. 'What's good, Luanne?'

'It's all good if you're hungry.' She smiled noncommittally. 'The grits aren't bad.'

Wolgast nodded and passed his menu to her. 'Sounds fine.'

The woman looked at Amy. 'For the little one? Whatcha want, honey?'

Amy lifted her eyes from the menu. 'Pancakes?'

'And a glass of milk,' Wolgast added.

'Coming right up,' the woman said. 'You'll like 'em, honey. Cook does them up special.'

Amy had brought her backpack into the restaurant. Wolgast walked her back to the ladies' room to clean up. 'You need me to come in with you?'

Amy shook her head.

'Wash your face and brush your teeth,' he said. 'And comb your hair, too.'

'Are we still going to the doctor?'

'I don't think so. We'll see.'

Wolgast returned to the table. 'Listen,' he said quietly to Doyle. 'I don't want to drive into a roadblock. Something could go wrong.'

Doyle nodded. The meaning was plain. All that firepower,

anything could happen. Next thing you knew, the Tahoe was riddled with rounds and everyone was dead.

'What about the district office in Wichita?'

'Too far. I don't see how we could get there. And at this point, I'm thinking no one's going to say they ever heard of us. This is all off the books.'

Doyle gazed down into his coffee cup. His face was drawn, defeated, and Wolgast experienced a blast of sympathy for him. None of this was what he'd bargained for.

'She's a good kid,' Doyle said. He sighed hard through his nose. 'Fuck.'

'This will go better with the locals, I think. You decide what you want to do. I'll give you the keys if you want. I'm going to tell them everything I know. It's our best chance, I think.'

'*Her* best chance, you mean.' Doyle didn't say this accusingly; he was merely stating a fact.

'Yes. Her best chance.'

Their food arrived as Amy returned from the restroom. The cook had done the pancakes up to look like a clown face, with whipped cream from a can and blueberries for the eyes and mouth. Amy poured syrup over all of it and dug in, alternating huge bites with gulps of milk. It was good to watch her eat.

Wolgast left the table when they were done and went back to the little hall off the restrooms. He didn't want to use his handheld, and it was back in the Tahoe in any event; he'd seen a pay phone back there, a relic. He dialed Lila's number in Denver, but the phone just rang and rang, and when it went to voice mail he couldn't think of what to say and hung up. If David got the message, he'd just erase it anyway.

When he returned to the table, the waitress was clearing away their plates. He took the check and stepped to the register to pay. 'Is there a police station anywhere around here?' he asked the woman as he handed her the money. 'Sheriff's office, something like that?'

'Three blocks down the way,' she said, sliding his money

into the register. 'But you don't have to go that far.' She slammed the drawer with a *ka-ching*. 'Kirk over there's a sheriff's deputy. Ain't that right, Kirk?'

'Aw, leave off, Luanne. I'm eating.'

Wolgast looked down the length of the counter. The man, Kirk, was poised over a plate of French toast. He had a jowly face and thick, weather-beaten hands and was dressed as a civilian, in snug Wranglers wedged under his belly and a grease-stained Carhartt jacket the color of burnt toast. A little town like this, probably he worked about three different jobs.

Wolgast stepped over to him. 'I need to report a kidnapping,' Wolgast said.

The man turned on his stool. He wiped his mouth on a napkin and looked at Wolgast incredulously. 'What are you talking about?' His face was unshaven; his breath smelled of beer.

'See that girl over there? She's the one everyone is looking for. I'm guessing you saw something about it on the wire.'

The man glanced over at Amy, then back at Wolgast. His eyes widened. 'Shit. You're kidding. The one from over in Homer?'

'He's right,' Luanne said brightly. She was pointing at Amy. 'I saw it on the news. That's the girl. You're the one, ain't you, sweetheart?'

'I'll be damned.' Kirk hoisted himself off his stool. The room had grown quiet; everyone was watching now. 'Staties are looking for her all over. Where'd you find her?'

'We're the ones who took her, actually,' Wolgast explained. 'We're the kidnappers. I'm Special Agent Wolgast, that's Special Agent Doyle. Say hi, Phil.'

Doyle waved listlessly from the booth. 'Howdy.'

'Special agents? You mean FBI?'

Wolgast withdrew his credentials and put them on the counter for Kirk to see. 'It's hard to explain.'

'And *you* took the girl.'

Wolgast said so again. 'We'd like to surrender to you, Deputy. As long as you're done with your breakfast.'

Somebody, one of the other men at the counter, snickered.

'Oh, I'm done all right,' Kirk said. He was still holding Wolgast's credentials, studying them like he couldn't believe what he was seeing. 'I'll be dipped. Holy goddamn.'

'Go on, Kirk,' the other man said, and laughed. 'Arrest them if that's what they want. You do remember how to do that, don't you?'

'Just hold the phone, Frank. I'm thinking.' Kirk looked sheepishly at Wolgast. 'Sorry, it's been a while. I mostly dig wells. Not much goes on around here, except a little drunk and disorderly, and half the time that's me. I don't even have handcuffs or nothing.'

'That's all right,' Wolgast said. 'We can loan you some.'

Wolgast told him to impound the Tahoe, but Kirk said he'd have to come back for it later. They surrendered their weapons and all piled into the cab of Kirk's pickup to drive the three blocks to town hall, a two-story brick building with a date, 1854, in large block letters set over the front door. The sun was up now, washing the town in a flat, muted light. As they stepped from the truck, Wolgast could hear birds singing from a stand of poplars that were just budding out. He felt a kind of airy happiness that he recognized as relief. On the drive over, pressed into the truck's cab, he'd held Amy on his lap. He knelt by her now and put his hands on her shoulders.

'Whatever this man tells you to do, I want you to do it, all right? He's going to put me in a cell, and probably I won't see you for a while.'

'I want to stay with you,' she said.

He saw her eyes had filmed with tears, and Wolgast felt a lump lodge in his throat. But he knew he was doing the right thing. The Oklahoma state police would swarm down on the place pretty fast once Kirk called in the collar, and Amy would be safe.

'I know,' he said, and did his best to smile. 'Everything's going to be okay now. I promise.'

The sheriff's office was located in the basement. Kirk hadn't handcuffed them after all, seeing how cooperative they were being, and he walked them around the side of the building and led them down the steps into a low-ceilinged room with a couple of metal desks, a gun case full of shotguns, and banks of file cabinets pushed against the walls. The only illumination came from a couple of high windows, welled from the outside and clotted with old leaves. The office was empty; the woman who manned the phones didn't come in until eight o'clock, Kirk explained, turning on the lights. As for the sheriff, who knew where he was. Probably out driving around someplace.

'To tell you the truth,' Kirk said, 'I'm not even sure I'd book you right. I better try to get him on the radio.'

He asked Wolgast and Doyle if they'd mind waiting in a cell. They had only the one, and it was mostly full of cardboard boxes, but there was room enough for the two of them. Wolgast said that would be fine. Kirk took them back to the cell, unlocked the door, and Wolgast and Doyle stepped inside.

'I want to go into the cell too,' Amy said.

Kirk frowned in disbelief. 'This is the strangest kidnapping I ever heard of.'

'It's fine,' Wolgast said. 'She can wait with me.'

Kirk considered this a moment. 'Okay, I guess. At least until my brother-in-law gets here.'

'Who's your brother-in-law?'

'John Price,' he said. 'He's the sheriff.'

Kirk got on the radio, and ten minutes later a man in a tight-fitting khaki uniform came striding through the door to the office and marched straight back to the cell. He was small, with a boy's slenderly muscled frame, and he stood not more than five foot four, even on the heels of his cowboy boots, which looked to Wolgast like they were something fancy – lizard maybe, or ostrich. He probably wore the boots to give him a little extra height.

'Well, holy crap,' he said in a surprisingly deep voice. He

218

was looking them over with his hands on his hips. There was a little bit of paper on his chin where he'd cut himself, shaving in a hurry. 'You guys are feds?'

'That's right.'

'Ain't this a can of peas.' He turned to Kirk. 'Whatcha got the girl in the cell for?'

'She said she wanted to.'

'Jesus, Kirk. You can't put a little kid in there. Did you book the other two?'

'I wanted to wait for you to get here.'

Price sighed with exasperation. 'You know,' he said, and rolled his eyes, 'you really got to work on your confidence, Kirk. We've talked about this. You let Luanne and all them others bust on you too much.' When Kirk said nothing, he continued. 'Well, might as well get on the horn. I know they're looking all over hell and earth for this one.' He looked at Amy. 'You okay, girl?'

Amy, who was sitting on the concrete bench next to Wolgast, gave a little nod.

'She said she wanted to,' Kirk repeated.

'I don't care what she *said*.' Price took a key from a compartment on his belt and unlocked the cell. 'Come on, girly,' he said, and extended a hand. 'Jail cell's no place for you. Let's get you a pop or something. And Kirk, get Mavis on the phone, will you? Tell her we need her over here pronto.'

When they were alone again, Doyle, who was slouched on the concrete bench, tipped his head back, closing his eyes. 'For Christsakes,' he moaned. 'It's like an episode of *Green Acres*.'

About half an hour passed; Wolgast could hear Kirk and Price talking in the other room, deciding what to do, whom to call first. The state police? The DA's office? So far, they hadn't even booked them yet. But it was all right; this would happen in due course. Wolgast heard the door open and then a woman's voice, talking to Amy, telling her what a pretty girl she was and asking her what her rabbit's name was, and would she maybe like an ice cream, the store around the corner was opening in just a few minutes, she'd be glad to go and get her one. All of it just as Wolgast had foreseen when, sitting in the Tahoe in the darkened car wash, he'd decided to turn himself in. He was glad he'd done it, so glad it surprised him, and the cell, which he guessed was the first of many in his life, didn't seem so bad. He wondered if that was how Anthony Carter had felt, if he had said to himself, *This is my life from now on.*

Price stepped up to the cell, holding the key. 'Staties on the way,' he said, rocking on his heels. 'You all must have stirred up some real hornets' nest from the sound of it.' He tossed a pair of cuffs through the bars. 'I'm thinking you all know how to use these.'

Doyle and Wolgast cuffed themselves; Price opened the cell and led them back to the office. Amy was sitting in a folding metal chair by the reception desk, her backpack on her lap, eating an ice cream sandwich. A grandmotherly woman in a green pantsuit was sitting beside her, showing her a coloring book.

'He's my daddy,' Amy told the woman.

'This one here?' the woman said, turning her head. She had dark, drawn-on eyebrows and a rigid helmet of raven-black hair – a wig. She looked at Wolgast quizzically, then back at Amy. 'This man here's your daddy?'

'It's all right,' Wolgast said.

'That's my daddy,' Amy repeated. Her voice was stern, correcting. 'Daddy, we have to go *right now.*'

Price had taken out a fingerprinting kit; behind them, Kirk was setting up a screen and camera, to take their mug shots.

'What's that about?' Price asked him.

'It's a long story,' Wolgast managed.

'Daddy, *now.*'

Wolgast heard the door to the office open behind him. The woman lifted her face. 'Help you?'

'Hey, good morning,' said a man's voice. There was something familiar about it. Price was holding Wolgast's right hand by the wrist, to roll his fingers in the ink. Then Wolgast saw the expression on Doyle's face, and he knew.

'This the sheriff's office?' Richards was saying. 'Hey, everyone. Whoa, are those things real? That's a lot of guns. Here, I've got something to show you.'

Wolgast swiveled in time to see Richards shoot the woman in the forehead. One shot, close range, muffled to a clap by the long bore of the suppressor. She rocked back in her chair, her eyes startled open, her wig askew on her head. A delicate frond of blood wet the floor behind her. Her arms lifted and then fell again, into stillness.

'Sorry,' Richards said, wincing a little. He stepped around the desk. The room was filled with the acrid odor of gunpowder smoke. Price and Kirk were frozen with fear where they stood, their jaws hanging open. Or perhaps it wasn't fear they were feeling, but mute incomprehension. As if they'd stepped into a movie, a movie that made no sense.

'Hey,' Richards said, taking aim, 'stand still. Just like that. Super-duper.' And Richards shot them too.

No one moved. It had all happened with a curious, dreamlike slowness but was over in an instant. Wolgast looked at the woman, then at the two bodies on the floor, Kirk and Price. How surprising death was, how irrevocable and complete, how much itself. At the reception desk, Amy's eyes were locked on the dead woman's face. The girl had been sitting just a few feet away when Richards had shot her. Her mouth was open, as if she were about to speak; blood was running down her forehead, seeking out the deep creases of her face, fanning across it like a river delta. Clutched in Amy's hand were the melting remains of her half-eaten ice cream sandwich; probably some of it was actually in her mouth at that moment, coating her tongue with its sweetness. A strange thing, but Wolgast thought it: for the rest of her life, the taste of ice cream would recall this image.

'What the fuck!' Doyle said. 'You fucking shot them!'

Price had hit the floor face-down behind his desk. Richards knelt by his body and patted his pockets until he found the key to the handcuffs, which he tossed to Wolgast. He waved his gun listlessly at Doyle, who was eyeing the glass case of shotguns.

'I wouldn't,' Richards cautioned, and Doyle sat down.

'You're not going to shoot us,' Wolgast said, freeing his hands.

'Not just now,' Richards said.

Amy had begun to cry, her breath hiccuping in her chest. Wolgast gave the key to Doyle and picked her up and held her tightly to his chest. Her body went limp against his own. 'I'm sorry, I'm sorry.' It was all he could think to say.

'This is very touching,' Richards said, handing Doyle the little backpack of Amy's belongings, 'but if we don't leave now, I'm going to be shooting a lot more people, and I feel like I've had a very full morning already.'

Wolgast thought of the coffee shop. It was possible everybody there was dead too. Amy hiccuped against his chest; he could feel her tears soaking his shirt. 'Goddamnit, she's a *kid*.'

Richards frowned. 'Why does everybody keep saying that?' He motioned with his weapon toward the door. 'Let's go.'

The Tahoe was waiting outside in the morning light, parked beside Price's cruiser. Richards told Doyle to drive and sat in the backseat with Amy. Wolgast felt completely helpless; after all he'd done, the hundreds of decisions he'd made, there was nothing left to do but obey. Richards directed them out of town, to an open field where an unmarked helicopter with a lean black body was waiting. At their approach its wide blades began to turn. Wolgast heard the wail of sirens in the distance, coming closer.

'Let's be quick now,' Richards said, motioning with his weapon.

They climbed into the helicopter and were airborne almost instantly. Wolgast held Amy tight. He felt as if he were in a trance, a dream – a terrible, unspeakable dream in which everything he'd ever wanted in his life was being taken away from him, while all he could do was watch. He'd had this dream before; it was a dream in which he wanted to die but couldn't. The copter banked steeply, opening a view of the sodden field and beyond, at its edge, a line of police cars, moving fast. Wolgast counted nine. In the cockpit Richards pointed out the windshield and said something to the pilot that made him bank the other way, then guide the chopper into a hovering position. The cruisers were coming closer now, within just a few hundred yards of the Tahoe. Richards motioned for Wolgast to pick up a headset.

'Watch this,' he told him.

Before Wolgast could answer there was a blinding flash of light, like a gigantic camera going off; a concussive thump rocked the chopper. Wolgast gripped Amy by the waist and held on. When he looked out the window again, all that remained of the Tahoe was a smoking hole in the earth, big enough to fit a house in. He heard Richards laughing through the headset. Then the helicopter banked once more, the force of its acceleration pressing them into their seats, and took them all away.

TWELVE

That he was dead was a fact. Wolgast accepted it, as he accepted any fact of nature. When everything was over – in whatever manner this occurred – Richards would take him to a room somewhere, give him the same cool, final look he'd given Price and Kirk – like a man performing some simple test of accuracy, lining up a cue ball or tossing a piece of wadded paper into the trash – and that would be the end of it.

It was possible Richards would take him outside to do it. Wolgast hoped he would, someplace he could see trees and feel the touch of sunlight on his skin, before Richards put a bullet in his head. Maybe he'd even ask. Would you mind? he'd say. If it's not too much trouble. I'd like to be looking at the trees.

He'd been at the compound for twenty-seven days. By his count it was the third week of April. He didn't know where Amy was, or Doyle. They'd been separated the minute they landed, Amy hustled away by Richards and a group of armed soldiers, Wolgast and Doyle with a coterie of their own – but then they'd been split up, too. Nobody had debriefed him, which at first struck him as strange, but when enough time had passed, Wolgast understood the reason. None of it had officially happened. Nobody was going to debrief him because his story was just that, a story. The only remaining question for him to puzzle over was why Richards hadn't just shot him in the first place.

The room they'd locked him in was like something in a cheap motel, though plainer: no carpet on the floor, no drapes on the lone window, heavy institutional furniture, bolted down. A tiny closet of a bathroom with a floor as cold as ice. A tangle of wires on the wall where a TV had once been. The door to the hall was thick and opened with a buzz from the outside. His only visitors were the men who brought him his meals: silent, hulking figures wearing unmarked brown jumpsuits who left his trays of food on the small table where Wolgast passed most of each day, sitting and waiting. Probably Doyle was doing the same thing, assuming Richards hadn't shot him already.

The view wasn't anything, just empty pine forest, but sometimes Wolgast would stand and look out there for hours, too. Spring was coming. The woods were sodden with melting snow, and from everywhere came the sound of running water – dripping from the roofs and branches, running down the gutters. If he stood on his toes, Wolgast could just make out a fence line through the trees, and figures moving along it. One night at the beginning of the fourth week of his imprisonment, a heavy rainstorm blew through. The force of it was practically biblical; thunder rocked over the mountains all night long, and in the morning he looked out his window and saw that winter was over, rinsed away by the rain.

For a while he'd tried to talk to the men who brought him his meals and, every other day, a clean set of surgical scrubs and slippers for him to wear, even just to ask them their names. But none had offered so much as one word in reply. They moved heavily, their movements clumsy and imprecise, their expressions benumbed and incurious, like the living dead in some old movie. Corpses gathering outside a farmhouse, moaning and tripping over their feet, wearing the tattered uniforms of their forgotten lives: he'd loved such films when he was a boy, not understanding how true they really were. What were the living dead, Wolgast thought, but a metaphor for the misbegotten march of middle age?

It was possible, he understood, for a person's life to become just a long series of mistakes, and that the end, when it came, was just one more instance in a chain of bad choices. The thing was, most of these mistakes were actually borrowed from other people. You took their bad ideas and, for whatever reason, made them your own. That was the truth he'd learned on the carousel with Amy, though the thought had been building in him for a while, most of a year, in fact. Wolgast had more than enough time now to think this over. You couldn't look into the eyes of a man like Anthony Carter and fail to see how this worked. It was as if, that night in Oklahoma, he'd had his first real idea in years. His first since Lila, since Eva. But Eva had died, three weeks short of her first birthday, and since that day he'd walked the earth like the living dead, or a man holding a ghost, the empty space in his arms where Eva had been. That's why he'd been so good with Carter and the others: he was just like them.

He wondered where Amy was, what was happening to her. He hoped she wasn't lonely and afraid. More than hoped: he held the idea with the fierceness of a prayer, trying to make it so with his mind. He wondered if he'd ever see her again, and the thought made him rise from his chair and go to the window, as if he might find her out there, in the shifting shadows of the trees. And more hours would somehow go by, the passage of time marked only by the changing light from the window and the comings and goings of the men with his meals, most of which he barely touched. All night long he slept a dreamless sleep that left him dazed in the morning, his arms and legs heavy as iron. He wondered how much longer he had.

Then, on the morning of the thirty-fourth day, someone came to see him. It was Sykes, but he was different. The man he'd met a year ago was all spit and polish. This man, though he was wearing the same uniform, looked like he'd slept under a highway overpass. His uniform was wrinkled and stained; his cheeks and chin were glazed with gray stubble; his eyes were as bloodshot as a boxer's after a few rounds of a badly mismatched fight. He sat heavily at the table where Wolgast was. He folded his hands, cleared his throat, and spoke.

'I'm here to ask a favor.'

Wolgast hadn't uttered a word in days. When he tried to answer, his windpipe felt half-closed, thickened from disuse; his voice emerged as a croak.

'I'm done with favors.'

Sykes drew in a long breath. A stale smell was rising off him, dried sweat and old polyester. For a moment he let his eyes drift around the tiny room.

'Probably this all seems a little . . . ungrateful. I admit that.'

'Fuck yourself.' It pleased Wolgast enormously to say this.

'I'm here about the girl, Agent.'

'Her name,' Wolgast said, 'is Amy.'

'I know her name. I know a great deal about her.'

'She's six. She likes pancakes and carnival rides. She has a toy rabbit named Peter. You're a heartless prick, you know that, Sykes?'

Sykes withdrew an envelope from the pocket of his coat and placed it on the table. Inside were two photographs. One was a picture of Amy, taken, Wolgast guessed, at the convent. Probably it was the same one that had gone out with the

Amber Alert. The second was a high school yearbook photo. The woman in the picture was obviously Amy's mother. The same dark hair, the same delicate arrangement of the facial bones, the same deep-set, melancholy eyes, though suffused, at the instant that the shutter opened, with a warm, expectant light. Who was this girl? Did she have friends, family, a boyfriend? A favorite subject in school? A sport she loved and was good at? Did she have secrets, a story of herself that no one knew? What did she hope her life would become? She was positioned at a three-quarter angle to the camera, looking over her right shoulder, wearing what looked like a prom dress, pale blue; her shoulders were bare. At the bottom of the photo was a caption: 'Mason Consolidated High School, Mason, IA.'

'Her mother was a prostitute. The night before she left Amy at the convent, she shot a trick on the front lawn of a frat house. For the record.'

Wolgast wanted to say, *So?* How was any of that Amy's fault? But the image of the woman in the photograph – not even really a woman, just a girl herself – belayed his anger. Maybe Sykes wasn't even telling the truth. He put the photo down. 'What happened to her?'

Sykes lifted his shoulder in a shrug. 'No one knows. Gone.'

'And the nuns?'

A shadow skittered across Sykes's face. Wolgast could tell that he'd hit the mark without even meaning to. Jesus, he thought. The nuns, too? Had it been Richards or somebody else?

'I don't know,' Sykes answered.

'Look at you,' Wolgast said. 'Yes, you do.'

Sykes said nothing more about it, his silence telling Wolgast, *This line of conversation is over.* He rubbed his eyes and returned the photos to their envelope and put it away.

'Where is she?'

'Agent, the thing is—'

'*Where's Amy?*'

Sykes cleared his throat again. 'That's the reason I'm here, you see,' he said. 'The favor. We think Amy may be dying.'

Wolgast wasn't allowed to ask any questions. He wasn't allowed to speak to anyone, or look around, or step from Sykes's line of vision. A detail of two soldiers led him across the compound, through the damp morning light. The air felt and smelled like spring. After almost five weeks in his room, Wolgast found himself taking deep, hungry breaths. The sun was painful to his eyes.

Once they were in the Chalet, Sykes took him down an elevator, four floors. They exited onto an empty hallway, Spartan and white, like a hospital. Wolgast guessed they were fifty feet belowground, maybe more. Whatever Sykes's people kept down here, they wanted at least that much dirt separating it from the world above. They came to a door marked MAIN LAB, but Sykes passed it without slowing his stride. More doors, and then they came to the one Sykes wanted. He slid a card through the reader and opened it.

Wolgast found himself in some kind of observation room. On the other side of the broad window, in dim, blue light, Amy's small form lay on a hospital bed, alone. She was connected to an IV, but that was all. Beside her bed was a plastic chair, empty. From tracks on the ceiling hung a group of color-coded hoses, coiled like the pneumatic hoses at a garage. Otherwise the room was bare.

'This is him?'

Wolgast turned to see a man he hadn't noticed before. He was wearing a lab coat and green scrubs, like Wolgast's.

'Agent Wolgast, this is Dr Fortes.'

They nodded without shaking hands. Fortes was young, not even thirty. Wolgast wondered if he was an MD or something else. Like Sykes, Fortes appeared exhausted, physically spent. His skin was oily, and he needed a haircut and a shave. His glasses looked like they hadn't been cleaned in a month.

'She has an embedded chip. It transmits vitals to the

panel here.' Fortes showed him: heart rate, respiration, blood pressure, temperature. Amy's was 102.6.

'Where?'

'Where what?' The doctor's eyes floated with incomprehension.

'Where's the chip?'

'Oh.' Fortes looked at Sykes, who nodded. Fortes pointed at the back of his own neck. 'Subcutaneous, between the third and fourth cervical vertebrae. The power source is pretty nifty, actually, a tiny nuclear cell. Like the kind on satellites, only much smaller.'

Nifty. Wolgast shuddered. A nifty nuclear power source in Amy's neck. He turned to Sykes, who was watching with a look of caution.

'Is this what happened to the others? Carter and the rest.'

'They were . . . preliminary,' Sykes said.

'Preliminary to what?'

He paused. 'To Amy.'

Fortes explained the situation: Amy was in a coma. No one had expected this, and her fever was too high and had gone on too long. Her kidney and liver values were depressed.

'We were hoping you could talk to her,' Sykes said. 'This sometimes helps with patients in a prolonged state of unconsciousness. Doyle tells us that she's pretty . . . bonded with you.'

A two-stage air lock connected them to Amy's room. Sykes and Fortes led him into the first chamber. An orange biosuit was hanging on the wall, the empty helmet tipped forward, like a man with a broken neck. Sykes explained how it worked.

'You'll need to put this on, then wrap all seams with duct tape. The valves at the base of the helmet connect to the hoses in the ceiling. They're color-coded, so that should be obvious. When you come back through, you need to shower in the suit, then shower again without it. There are instructions on the wall.'

Wolgast sat on the bench to remove his slippers. Then he stopped.

'No,' he said.

Sykes looked at him and frowned. 'No what?'

'No, I'm not wearing it.' He turned and faced Sykes squarely. 'It's not going to help if she wakes up and sees me in a space suit. You want me to go in there, I go as I am.'

'That's not a good idea, Agent,' Sykes warned.

His mind was made up. 'No suit or no deal.'

Sykes glanced at Fortes, who shrugged. 'It could be . . . interesting. In theory, the virus should be inert by now. On the other hand, it might not be.'

'The virus?'

'I guess you'll find out,' Sykes said. 'Let him in on my authority. And, Agent, once you're in, you're in. I can't guarantee anything beyond that. Is that clear?'

Wolgast said it was; Sykes and Fortes stepped from the air lock. Wolgast realized he hadn't expected them to say yes. At the last instant Wolgast called back to them. 'Where's her backpack?'

Fortes and Sykes exchanged another private look. 'Wait here,' Sykes said.

He returned a few minutes later with Amy's knapsack. The Powerpuff Girls: Wolgast had never really looked at it, not closely. Three of them, their images made of a rubbery plastic glued onto the rough canvas of the pack, fists raised and flying. Wolgast unzipped it; some of Amy's things were missing, such as her hairbrush, but Peter was still inside.

He fixed his gaze on Fortes. 'How will I know if it's not . . . inert?'

'Oh, you'll know,' Fortes said.

They sealed the door behind him. Wolgast felt the pressure drop. Above the second door, the light switched from red to green. Wolgast turned the handle and stepped inside.

A second room, longer than the first, with a fat drain in the floor and a sunflower-head shower, activated by a metal chain. The light in here was different; it had a bluish cast, like autumn twilight. A sign on the wall bore the instructions Sykes had indicated: a long list of steps that ended in nakedness, standing above the drain, rinsing the mouth and eyes and then clearing the throat and spitting. A camera peered down at him from a corner of the ceiling.

He paused at the second door. The light above it was red. A keypad was affixed to the wall. How would he go through? Then the light switched from red to green, as the first had done – Sykes, from outside, overriding the system.

He paused before opening the door. It looked heavy, made of gleaming steel. Like a bank vault, or something on a submarine. He couldn't say exactly why he'd insisted on not wearing the biosuit, a decision that now seemed rash. For Amy, as he'd said? Or to tease out some information, however meager, from Sykes? Either way, the decision had felt right to him.

He turned the handle, felt his ears pop as the pressure dropped again. He drew in a lungful of air, holding it in his chest, and stepped through.

Grey had no idea what was happening. Days and days of this: he'd report for his shift, ride the elevator down to L4 – nothing had happened after that first night; Davis had covered for him – change in the locker room and do his work, cleaning the halls and bathrooms, then step into Containment, and step out six hours later.

All perfectly normal, except that those six hours were a blank, like an empty drawer in his brain. He'd obviously done the things he was supposed to, filed his reports and backed up the drives, moved the rabbit cages in and out, even exchanged a few words with Pujol or the other techs who came in. And yet he couldn't remember any of it. He'd slide his card to enter the observation room and the next thing he knew his shift was over and he was coming out the other side.

Except for little things: fleeting things, small but bright somehow, little bits of recorded data that seemed to catch the light like confetti as they fluttered down through his mind throughout the day. They weren't pictures, nothing as clear and straightforward as that, and nothing he could hold on to. But he'd be sitting in the commissary, or back in his room, or crossing the yard to the Chalet, and a taste would bubble from the back of his throat, and a queer juicy feeling in his teeth. Sometimes it struck him so hard it actually made him freeze in his tracks. And when this happened, he'd think of funny things, unrelated, a lot of which had to do with Brownbear. Like the taste in his mouth would push a button that would start him up thinking about his old dog, who, truth be told, he hadn't really thought about much at all until recently, not for years and years, until that night he'd had that dream in Containment and tossed all over the floor.

Brownbear and his reeking breath. Brownbear dragging something dead, a possum or raccoon, up the front steps. That time he got into a nest of bunnies under the trailer, tiny little balls of peach-colored skin, not even covered with fur yet, and crunched them one by one, their little skulls popping between his molars, like a kid sitting in the movies with a box of Whoppers.

Funny thing: he couldn't say for sure Brownbear had actually *done* that.

He wondered if he was sick. The sign over the sentry station on L3 made him nervous, in a way it hadn't before. It seemed to be talking right to him. ANY OF THE FOLLOWING SYMPTOMS . . . One morning, returning from breakfast, he'd felt a tickle in this throat, like maybe he was getting a cold; before he knew it he'd sneezed hard into his hand. His nose had been running a little ever since. Then again, it was spring now, still cold at night but rising into the fifties or even sixties during the afternoon, and all the trees were budding out, a faint haze of green, like a spatter of paint over the mountains. He'd always been allergic.

And then there was the quiet. It took Grey a while to notice what this was. Nobody was saying anything – not just the sweeps, who never spoke much to begin with, but the

232

techs and soldiers and doctors, too. It wasn't like it happened all at once, in a day or even a week. But slowly, over time, a hush had settled over the place, sealing down on it like a lid. Grey had always been more of a listener himself – that's what Wilder, the prison shrink, had said about him: 'You're a good listener, Grey.' He'd meant it as a compliment, but mostly Wilder was just in love with the sound of his own voice and happy to have an audience. Still, Grey missed the sound of human voices. One night in the commissary he counted thirty men hunched over their trays, and not one of them was saying a word. Some weren't even eating, just sitting in their chairs, maybe nursing a cup of coffee or tea and staring into space. Like they were half asleep.

One thing: Grey was fine in the shut-eye department. He slept and slept and slept, and when his alarm went off at 05:00, or noon if, as likely as not, he'd been on the late shift, he'd roll over in bed, light a smoke from the pack on the nightstand, and stay still for a few minutes, trying to decide if he'd dreamed or not. He didn't think he had.

Then one morning he sat down at a table in the commissary to eat – French toast stamped with butter, a couple of eggs, three sausages, and a bowl of grits on the side; if he was sick it sure hadn't killed his appetite any – and when he lifted his face to take his first bite, a dripping slab of toast just inches from his lips, he saw Paulson. Sitting there, right across from him, two tables away. Grey had caught sight of him once or twice since their conversation, but not up close, not like this. Paulson was sitting over a plate of eggs he hadn't touched. He looked like shit, his skin stretched so tight over his face you could see the edges of his bones. For an instant, just one, their eyes met.

Paulson looked away.

That night, checking in for his shift, Grey asked Davis, 'You know that guy Paulson?'

Davis wasn't his usual cheerful self these days. Gone were the jokes and the dirty magazines and the headphones with their buzz saws of leaking music. Grey wondered what in hell

Davis did all night at the desk; though it was also true that Grey didn't know what he himself was doing all night, either.

'What about him?'

But Grey's question stopped right there; he couldn't think what else to ask.

'Nothing. Just wondering if you knew him was all.'

'Do yourself a favor. Stay away from that asshole.'

Grey went downstairs and got to work. It wasn't until later, running a scrub brush around a toilet bowl on L4, that he thought of the question he'd meant to ask.

What is he so afraid of?

What is everyone so afraid of?

They were calling him Number Twelve. Not Carter or Anthony or Tone, though he was so sick now, lying alone in the dark, that those names and the person they referred to seemed like somebody else, not him. A person who had died, leaving only this sick, writhing form in his place.

The sickness felt like forever. That's the word it made him think of. Not that it would last forever; more that he was sick with time itself. Like the idea of time was inside him, in each cell of his body, and time wasn't an ocean, like somebody had told him once, but a million tiny wicks of flame that would never be extinguished. The worst feeling in the world. Someone had told him he'd be feeling better soon, much better. He'd held on to those words for a while. But now he knew they were a lie.

He was aware, dimly, of movements around him, the comings and goings, the pokings and prickings of the men in the space suits. He wanted water, just a sip of water, to slake his thirst, but when he asked for this, he heard no sound from his lips, nothing except the roaring and ringing in his ears. They'd taken a lot of his blood. It felt like whole gallons of it. The man named Anthony had sold his blood from time to time; he'd squeeze the ball and watch the bag fill up with it, amazed at its density, its rich red color, how alive it looked. Never more than a pint before they gave him the cookies and the folded bills and sent him on his way. But now the men in the suits filled bag after bag, and the blood was different, though he couldn't say just how. The blood in his body was alive but he didn't think it was only his own anymore; it belonged to someone, something, else.

It would have been good to die about now.

Mrs Wood, she'd known that. And not just about herself but about Anthony too, and when he thought this, for a second he *was* Anthony again. It was good to die. There was a lightness in it, a letting go, like love.

He tried to hold on to this thought, the thought that made him still Anthony, but bit by bit it slipped away, a rope pulled slowly through his hands. How many days had passed he couldn't tell; something was happening to him, but it wasn't happening quick enough for the men in the suits. They were talking and talking about it, poking and prodding and taking more of his blood. And he was hearing something else now, too: a soft murmur, like voices, but it wasn't coming from the men in the suits. The sounds seemed to come from far away and from inside him all at once. Not words he knew but words nonetheless; it was a language he was hearing, it had order and sense and a mind, and not just one mind: twelve. Yet one was more than the others, not louder but *more*. The one voice and then behind it the others, twelve in sum. And they were speaking to him, calling to him; they knew he was there. They were in his blood and they were forever, too.

He wanted to say something back.

He opened his eyes.

'Drop the gate!' a voice cried out. 'He's flipping!'

The restraints were nothing, like paper. The rivets popped from the table and shot across the room. First his arms and then his legs. The room was dark but hid nothing from his eyes, because the darkness was part of him now. And inside him, far down, a great, devouring hunger uncoiled itself. To eat the very world. To take it all inside him and be filled by it, made whole. To make the world eternal, as he was.

A man was running for the door.

235

Anthony fell on him swiftly, from above. A scream and then the man was silent in wet pieces on the floor. The beautiful warmth of blood! He drank and drank.

The one who'd told him he'd be feeling better soon: he wasn't wrong, after all.

Anthony Carter had never felt better in his life.

Pujol, that dumb fuck, was dead.

Thirty-six days: that was how long it had taken Carter to flip, the longest since they'd begun. But Carter was supposed to be the meanest of the lot, the last stage before the virus reached its final form. The one the girl had gotten.

Richards personally didn't care one way or another about the girl. She would survive or she wouldn't. She would live forever or die in the next five minutes. Somewhere along the way, the girl had become beside the point, as far as Special Weapons was concerned. They had Wolgast in there with her now, talking to her, trying to bring her around. So far he was fine, but if the girl died, this wouldn't make a lick of difference.

What the hell had Pujol been thinking? They should have dropped the gate days ago. But at least now they knew what these things could do. The report from Bolivia had indicated as much, but it was another thing to see it with your own eyes, to watch the video feed of Carter, this little twig of a man with an IQ not much more than 80 on a good day and scared of his own shadow, launch himself twenty feet through the air, so fast it was as if he were moving not through space but around it, and rip a man from crotch to jowls like a letter he couldn't wait to open. By the time it was all over – about two seconds – they'd had to blast Carter with the lights, to push him back to the corner so they could drop the gate.

They had the twelve now, thirteen counting Fanning. Richards's job was done, or nearly. The order had just come through. Project NOAH was graduating to Operation

236

Jumpstart. In a week, they'd be moving the sticks to White Sands. After that, it would be out of Richards's hands.

The ultimate bunker busters. That's what Cole had called them, way back when, when it was all just a theory – before Bolivia and Fanning and all the rest. Just imagine what one of these things could do, say, in the mountain caves of northern Pakistan, or the eastern deserts of Iran, or the shot-up buildings of the Chechen Free Zone. Think high colonic, Richards: a good cleaning out from the inside.

Maybe Cole would have wised up eventually. But in his absence, the idea had acquired a life of its own. Never mind that it violated about half a dozen international treaties that Richards could think of. Never mind that it was just about the stupidest idea he'd ever heard of in his life. A bluff, probably; but bluffs had a way of being called. And did anyone seriously think, for one goddamn second, that you could contain one of these things to the caves of northern Pakistan?

He felt bad for Sykes, and not a little worried. The guy was a wreck, had barely come out of his office since word had come down from Special Weapons. When Richards had asked him if Lear knew, Sykes had given a long, wretched-sounding laugh. *Poor guy*, he'd said. *He still thinks he's trying to save the world. Which, the way things are playing out, might need saving after all. I can't believe this is even on the table.*

Armored trucks would transport the sticks to Grand Junction; from there, they'd be moved by train to White Sands. As for Richards: once everything had been brought to its proper conclusion, he was giving serious consideration to buying property in, say, northern Canada.

The sweeps would be the first to go. The techs and most of the soldiers, too, starting with the ones who were the most screwed up, like Paulson. After that day on the loading dock, Richards had checked his file. Paulson, Derrick G. Age twenty-two. Enlisted straight out of high school in Glastonbury, Connecticut; a year in the sands, then back stateside. No record, and the guy was smart; he had an IQ of 136. No question he could have gone to college, or OCS. He'd been on-site now for twenty-three months. He'd been disciplined twice for sleeping on watch and once for unauthorized use of email, but that was all.

What bothered him was that Paulson *knew*, or believed he did; Richards had sensed it right off. Not in anything Paulson had done or said, but in the look on Carter's face when Richards had opened the van's door – like the poor guy had seen a ghost, or worse. Nobody except the scientific staff and the sweeps set foot on Level 4. With nothing else to do but stand around in the snow, a certain amount of idle conjecture among the enlisted was inevitable, loose talk around the mess table. But Richards had the feeling in his gut that whatever Paulson had said was more than just gossip.

Maybe Paulson was dreaming. Maybe they *all* were.

If Richards was dreaming these days, it was about the nuns. He hadn't cared for that part very much at all. Way back when, so long ago it seemed like a different life entirely, he'd gone to Catholic school. A bunch of withered old bitches who liked to slap and hit, but he'd respected them; they meant what they said and did it. So shooting nuns went against the grain. Most of them had just slept through it. But there was one who'd woken up. The way she opened her eyes made him think she'd been expecting him. He'd done two of them already; she was the third. She opened her eyes in bed and he saw, in the pale light coming through the window, that she wasn't some dried-up seahorse like the others but young, and not bad-looking. Then she closed her eyes and murmured something, a prayer probably, and Richards shot her through a pillow.

He'd come up one nun short. Lacey Antoinette Kudoto, the crazy one. He'd read her psych workup from the diocese. Nobody would believe her story, and even if they did, the chain was broken in western Oklahoma with a bunch of dead cops shot by rogue FBI agents and a ten-year-old Chevy Tahoe you'd need tweezers and about a thousand years to reassemble.

Still, he hadn't liked shooting that nun.

Richards was sitting in his office, watching the security monitors. The time stamp read 22:26. The sweeps were in and out of Containment with the rabbit carts, but nobody was having any of it. The fast had started with Zero but had spread to the others since Carter had shown up, maybe a couple of days after. This was a puzzler, but in any event, if Special Weapons had its way, the sticks would all be eating soon enough. By which time Richards hoped he'd be ice-fishing on Hudson Bay or digging out snow for an igloo.

He looked at the monitor for Amy's chamber. There was Wolgast, sitting at her bedside. They'd brought in a little portable toilet with a nylon curtain, and a cot where he could sleep. But he hadn't slept at all, just sat in the chair by her bed day after day, touching her hand, talking to her. What he was saying, Richards didn't care to know. And yet he'd find himself watching them for hours, almost as much as he watched Babcock.

He turned his attention to Babcock's chamber. Giles Babcock, Number One. Babcock was hanging upside down from the bars, his eyes, that weird orange color, shooting straight at the camera, his jaws quietly working, chewing the air. *I am yours and you are mine, Richards. We are all meant for someone, and I am meant for you.*

Yeah, Richards thought. Fuck you, too.

Richards's com buzzed against his waist.

'This is the front gate,' the voice on the other end said. 'We've got a woman out here.'

Richards examined the monitor that showed the guard-house. Two sentries, one holding the com to his ear, the other with his weapon unslung. The woman was standing just outside the circle of light around the hut.

'So?' he said. 'Get rid of her.'

'That's the thing, sir,' the sentry said. 'She won't go. She doesn't look like she has a car, either. I think she actually *walked.*'

Richards was looking hard at the monitor. He saw the sentry drop the com to the ground and unsling his weapon.

'Hey!' Richards heard him say. 'Get back here! Stop or I'll fire!'

Richards heard the pop of his weapon. The second soldier took off running into the dark. Two more shots, the sound muffled through the com where it lay in the mud. Ten seconds passed, twenty. Then they stepped back into the light. Richards could tell from their body language that they'd lost her.

The first sentry retrieved his com and looked up into the camera.

'Sorry. She got away somehow. You want us to go look for her?'

Jesus. This was all Richards needed. 'Who was she?'

'Black woman, some kind of accent,' the sentry explained. 'Said she was looking for someone named Wolgast.'

He didn't die. Not right away and not as the days went by. And on the third day, he told her the story.

—*There once was a little girl*, Wolgast told her. *More little even than you. Her name was Eva, and her mother and father loved her very much. The night after she was born, her father took her from her bassinet in the room at the hospital where they were all sleeping and held her, her bare skin against his own, and from that moment on she was inside him, really and truly. His girl was inside him, in his heart.*

Somebody was probably watching, listening. The camera was over his shoulder. He didn't care. Fortes came and went. He took her blood and changed her bags, and Wolgast talked, through the hours of the third day, telling it all to Amy, the story he'd told no one.

—*And then something happened. It was her heart. Her heart, you see* – he showed her the place on his chest where this was – *began to shrink. While around her, her body grew, her heart did not, and then the rest of her stopped growing too. He would have given her his heart if he could, because it was hers to begin with. It*

240

had always been, and always would be, hers. But he couldn't do this for her, he couldn't do anything, no one could, and when she died, he died with her. The man that he was, was gone. And the man and the woman couldn't love each other anymore, because their love was nothing but sadness now, and missing their little girl.

He told her the story, told it all. And when the story was ending, the day was ending with it.

—And then you came, Amy, he said. *Then I found you. Do you see? It was like she'd come back to me. Come back, Amy. Come back, come back, come back.*

He lifted his face. He opened his eyes.

And Amy opened hers, too.

THIRTEEN

Lacey in the woods: she moved at a crouch, darting tree to tree, putting distance between herself and the soldiers. The air was cold and thin, sharp in her lungs. She stood with her back against a tree and let herself breathe.

She wasn't afraid. The soldiers' bullets were nothing. She'd heard them ripping through the underbrush, but they hadn't even come close. And so small! Bullets – how could bullets hurt a person? After the long distance she'd traveled, against such odds, how could they hope to scare her away with something as meager as that?

She peeked around the barrel-like trunk. She could see, through the undergrowth, the glow of the sentry hut, hear the two men talking, their voices carrying easily across the moonless night. *Black woman, some kind of accent,* and the other one saying over and over, *Shit, he's going to have our ass for this. How the fuck did we miss her? Huh? How the fuck! You didn't even fucking aim!*

Whoever they were talking to on the phone, they were

afraid of him. But this man – Lacey knew he was nothing, no one. And the soldiers, they were like children, without minds of their own. Like the ones in the field, so long ago. She remembered how, through the long hours, they'd done and done. They'd thought they were taking something from her – she could see it in the dark smiles streaked across their mouths, taste it in their sour breath on her face – and it was true, they had. But now she'd forgiven them and taken this thing back, which was Lacey herself, and more besides. She closed her eyes. *But you are a shield around me, O LORD,* she thought:

You bestow glory on me and lift up my head.

To the LORD I cry aloud,
and he answers me from his holy hill.
Selah.

I lie down and sleep;
I wake again, because the LORD sustains me.

I will not fear the tens of thousands
drawn up against me on every side.

Arise, O LORD!
Deliver me, O my God!
Strike all my enemies on the jaw;
break the teeth of the wicked.

She was moving through the trees again. The man on the other end of the sentry's phone: he would send more soldiers to hunt her down. And yet a feeling like joy was coursing through her – a new, nimble energy, richer and deeper than anything she'd felt in her life. It had been building through the weeks as she made her way to – well, where? She didn't know what it was called. In her mind it was simply the place where Amy was.

She'd taken some buses. She'd ridden awhile in the back of someone's truck with two Labrador retrievers and a crate of baby pigs. Some days she'd awakened wherever she was and known it was a day to walk, just walk. From time to time she ate or, if it felt right, knocked on a door and asked if it would be all right if she slept in a bed. And the woman who answered the door – for it was always a woman, no matter what door Lacey knocked on – would say, Of course, come right in, and lead her to a room with a bed all made up and waiting, without saying one more word about it.

And then one day she was climbing a long mountain road, the glory of God in the sunshine all around her, and knew that she'd arrived.

Wait, the voice said. *Wait for sunset, Sister Lacey. The way will show you the way.*

And so it did: the way showed the way. More men were pursuing her now; each footfall, each snap of a twig, each breath was as a gunshot, louder than loud, telling Lacey where they were. They were spread out behind her in a wide line, six of them, pointing their guns into the darkness, at nothing, at a place where Lacey had stood but stood no longer.

She came to a break in the trees. A road. To the left, two hundred yards distant, stood the sentry hut, bathed in its halo of light. To the right the road turned into the trees and descended sharply. From somewhere far below, was the sound of the river.

Nothing about this place revealed its meaning to her; and yet she knew to wait. She dropped and pressed her belly against the forest floor. The soldiers were behind her, fifty yards, forty, thirty.

She heard the low, labored sound of a diesel engine, its pitch dropping as the driver downshifted to ascend the final rise. Slowly it pushed its light and noise toward her. She rose to a crouch as its headlights burst over the crest of the hill. Some kind of Army truck. The pitch of the engine changed as the driver shifted again and began to gather speed.

Now?

And the voice said: *Now.*

She was up and running with all her might, aiming her body at the rear of the truck. A wide bumper and, above it, an open cargo area, concealed by swaying canvas. For a moment it seemed as if she'd moved too late, that the truck would race away, but in a burst of speed she caught it. Her hands found the lip of the gate, one bare foot and then the other left the road. Lacey Antoinette Kudoto, airborne: she was up and over and she was rolling in.

Her head hit the floor of the cargo compartment with a thump.

Boxes. The truck was full of boxes.

She scrambled to the front, against the rear wall of the cab. The truck slowed again as it approached the sentry hut. Lacey held her breath. Whatever happened now would happen; there was nothing she could do.

The hiss of air brakes; the truck jerked to a halt.

'Let me see the manifest.'

The voice belonged to the first sentry, the one who'd told Lacey to stop. The man-boy with his gun. She could discern, from the angle of his voice, that he was standing on the running board. The air suddenly tanged with cigarette smoke.

'You shouldn't smoke.'

'Who are you, my mother?'

'Read your own manifest, dickhead. You're carrying enough ordnance to blow us all halfway to Mars.'

A snickering laugh from the passenger seat.

'It's your funeral. You see anyone down the road?'

'You mean, like a civilian?'

'No, I mean the abominable snowman. Yes, a civilian. A black woman, about five-six, wearing a skirt.'

'You're kidding.' A pause. 'We didn't see anyone. It's dark. I don't know.'

The sentry climbed down from the running board. 'Hang on while I check the back.'

Don't move, Lacey, the voice said. *Don't move.*

The canvas flaps opened, closed, opened again. A beam of light shot into the back of the truck.

Close your eyes, Lacey.

She did. She felt the beam of the flashlight rake her face: once, twice, three times.

You are a shield around me, O Lord—

She heard two hard pounds on the side of the truck, right beside her ear.

'Clear!'

The truck pulled away.

Richards wasn't one bit happy. The crazy nun – what the blue fuck was she doing here?

He decided not to tell Sykes. Not until he knew more about it. He'd sent six men. Six! Just fucking shoot her! But they'd come back with nothing. He'd sent them back out, around the perimeter. Just find her! Put a bullet in her! Is that so hard?

The business with Wolgast and the girl had gone on too long. And Doyle – why was *he* still alive? Richards checked his watch: 00:03. He retrieved his weapon from the bottom drawer of his desk and checked the load and tucked it against his spine. He left his office and took the back stairs to Level 1 and exited through the loading dock.

Doyle was stashed over in civilian housing; the room had belonged to one of the dead sweeps. The sentry at the door was dozing in his chair.

'Get up,' Richards said.

The soldier jerked awake. His eyes floated with incomprehension; he didn't look like he knew where he was. When he saw Richards standing above him, he rose quickly to attention. 'Sorry, sir.'

'Open the door.'

The soldier keyed in the code and stepped away.

'You can go,' Richards said.

'Sir?'

'If you're going to sleep, do it in the barracks.'

A look of relief. 'Yes, sir. Sorry, sir.'

The soldier jogged down the catwalk, away. Richards pushed the door open. Doyle was sitting on the end of the bed, his hands folded in his lap, looking at the empty square on the wall where the TV had once been. An untouched tray of food rested on the floor, exuding a faint smell of rotting fish. As Doyle lifted his face, a thin smile creased his lips.

'Richards. You fuck.'

'Let's go.'

Doyle sighed and slapped his knees. 'You know, he was right about you. Wolgast, I mean. I was just sitting here thinking, When is my old friend Richards going to pay me a visit?'

'If it was up to me, I would have come sooner.'

Doyle looked like he was about to laugh. Richards had never seen such a good mood in a man who had to know what was about to happen to him. Doyle shook his head ruefully, still smiling. 'I should have gone for those shotguns.'

Richards withdrew his weapon and thumbed the safety. 'It would have saved some time, yes.'

He led Doyle across the compound, toward the lights of the Chalet. It was possible Doyle would take off running, but how far would he get? And, Richards wondered, why hadn't he asked about Wolgast or the girl?

'Tell me one thing,' Doyle said, as they reached the parking area. A handful of cars were still there, belonging to the lab's night shift. 'Is she here yet?'

'Is who here?'

'Lacey.'

Richards stopped.

'So she is,' Doyle said, and chuckled to himself. 'Richards, you should see your face.'

'What do you know about it?'

It was strange. A cool, blue light seemed to be shining from Doyle's eyes. Even in the ambient glow of the parking lot, Richards could see it. Like looking into a camera at the moment the shutter opened.

'Funny thing, but you know?' Doyle said, and lifted his gaze toward the dark shapes of the trees. 'I could hear her coming.'

Grey.

He was on L4. On the monitor, the glowing shape of Zero.

Grey. It's time.

He remembered then, remembered all of it at last: his dreams and all those nights he'd spent in Containment, watching Zero, listening to his voice, hearing the stories he told. He remembered New York City and the girl and all the others, every night a new one, and the feel of the darkness moving through him and the soft joy in his jaw as he flew down upon them. He was Grey and not Grey, he was Zero and not Zero, he was everywhere and nowhere. He rose and faced the glass.

It's time.

It was funny, Grey thought. Not funny ha-ha but funny strange, the whole idea of *time*. He'd thought it was one thing but it was actually another. It wasn't a line but a circle, and even more; it was a circle made of circles made of circles, each lying on top of the other, so that every moment was next to every other moment, all at once. And once you knew this you couldn't unknow it. Such as now, the way he could see events as they were about to unfold, as if they'd already happened, because in a way they had.

He opened the air lock. His suit hung limply on the wall. He had to close the first door to open the second, the second to open the third, but there was nothing that said he had to put the suit on, or that he had to be alone.

The second door, Grey.

He stepped into the inner chamber. Above his head, the showerhead hung like the face of some monstrous flower. The camera was watching him, but no one was on the other side; he knew that. And he was hearing other voices now, not just Zero's, and he knew who these were, too.

The third door, Grey.

Oh, it was such happiness, he thought. Such relief. This letting go. This putting down and away. Day by day he'd felt it happening, the good Grey and the bad Grey coming together, forming something new, something inevitable. The next new Grey, the one who could forgive.

I forgive you, Grey.

He turned the wide handle. The gate was open. Zero uncurled before him in the dark. Grey felt his breath on his face, on his eyes and mouth and chin; he felt his hammering heart. Grey thought of his father, on the snow. He was weeping, weeping with happiness, weeping with terror, weeping weeping weeping, and as Zero's bite found the soft place on his neck where the blood moved, he knew at last what the tenth rabbit was.

The tenth rabbit was him.

FOURTEEN

It happened fast. Thirty-two minutes for one world to die, another to be born.

'What did you say?' Richards said, and then he heard – both of them heard – the sound of the alarm. The one that was never, ever supposed to ring, a great, atonal buzzing that ricocheted across the open compound so that it seemed to come from everywhere at once.

Security breach. Subject Containment, Level 4.

Richards turned quickly to look toward the Chalet. A quick decision: he swung around to point his gun at the spot where Doyle had stood.

Doyle was gone.

Goddamn, he thought, and then he said it: 'Goddamn!'

Now there were two of them on the loose. He quickly scanned the parking lot, hoping for a shot. Lights came on everywhere, bathing the compound in a harsh, artificial daylight; he heard shouts from the barracks, soldiers running.

No time to deal with Doyle now.

He raced up the steps of the Chalet, past the sentry who was yelling at him, something about the elevator, and took the stairs to L2, his feet barely touching the steps. The door to his office was open. He quickly scanned the monitors.

Zero's chamber was empty.

Babcock's chamber was empty.

All of the chambers were empty.

He hit the audio feed. 'Sentries, Level Four, this is Richards. Report.'

Nothing, not a word in reply.

'Main Lab, report. Somebody tell me what the fuck is going on down there.'

A terrified voice came through: Fortes? 'They let them out!'

'Who? Who let them out?'

A blast of static, and Richards heard the first screams coming over the audio, and gunshots, and more screams – the screams men made when they died.

'Holy fuck!' Another blast of static. 'They're all loose down here! The fucking sweeps let them all go!'

Quickly Richards called up the monitor for the sentry post on L3. A broad mural of blood was on the wall; the sentry, Davis, was slumped on the floor below it, his face pressed to the tiles, as if he were probing the ground for a lost contact. A second soldier stepped into view and Richards saw that it was Paulson, holding a .45. Behind him, the doors to the elevator stood open. Paulson looked straight into the camera as he holstered the gun and removed the grenade from his pocket, then two more. He pulled the pins, using his teeth, and rolled them into the elevator. Then he took one more look at Richards, who saw his empty eyes, drew the .45, raised it to the side of his head, and pulled the trigger.

Richards reached for the switch to seal the level, but it was too late. He heard the explosion, ripping through the elevator shaft, and then a second blast of sound as what was left of the car went sailing to the bottom, and all the lights went out.

At first Wolgast didn't know what he was hearing; the sound of the alarm was so sudden, so completely alien, that for a moment it obliterated all thought. He rose from his chair beside Amy's bed and tried the door, but of course it wouldn't open; they were sealed inside. The alarm rang and rang. A fire? No, he reasoned, over the din in his ears, it was something else, something worse. He looked up at the camera where it hung in the corner.

'Fortes! Sykes, goddamnit! Open this door!'

He heard the pop of automatic-weapon fire, muffled by its passage through the thick walls. For an instant he thought hopefully of rescue. But of course that was out of the question; who would rescue them?

And then, before he could generate another thought, there was a great concussive bang, and a terrible roar that ended in a second bang, louder than the first, bringing with it a deep, sonorous trembling, like an earthquake, and the room plunged into darkness.

Wolgast froze. The blackness was total, an overwhelming absence of light, completely disorienting. The alarms had stopped. He felt a blind urge to run, but there was nowhere to go. The room seemed to expand and to be closing in upon him, all at once.

'Amy, where are you? Help me find you!'

Silence. Wolgast drew a deep breath and held it. 'Amy, say something. Say anything.'

He heard, behind him, a soft moan.

'That's it.' He turned, listening hard, trying to calibrate the distance and direction. 'Do it again. I'll find you.'

His mind began to focus, his initial panic giving way to a sense of purpose, the task at hand. Cautiously Wolgast took a step forward toward her voice, then another. A second moan, barely audible. The room was small, not twenty feet square, so how could it be that Amy should seem so far away from him in the dark? He heard no more gunfire, no sounds at all from outside. Only the soft notes of Amy's breathing, summoning him.

Wolgast had reached the foot of her bed and was feeling his way along its metal rails when the emergency lights came on, two beams that shot from the corners of the ceiling over the door. Barely enough to see by, but enough. The room was the same; whatever was happening outside, it had yet to reach them. He sat by Amy's bed and felt her forehead. Still warm, but her fever was down, her skin a little damp. With the power out, her IV pump had stopped. He wondered what to do, and decided to disconnect her. Perhaps this was wrong, but he didn't think so. He had watched Fortes and the others change the drip enough times to know the ritual. He adjusted the clamp, sealing off the flow of liquid, and withdrew the long needle from the rubber stopper at the top of the tube buried in the skin of her hand. With the IV disconnected there was no reason to leave the port in place; he removed this also, pulling it gently away. The wound didn't bleed, but to be sure, he covered it with gauze and tape from the supply cart. Then he waited.

The minutes passed. Amy shifted restlessly on the bed, as if she were dreaming. Wolgast had the curious intuition that somehow, if he could see her dreams, he'd know what was happening outside. But part of him wondered if any of it mattered now. They were well belowground, sealed away. They might as well have been locked in a tomb.

Wolgast had all but resigned himself to their abandonment when he heard, behind him, a hiss of equalizing pressure. His hopes soared; someone had come after all. The door swung open to reveal a solitary figure, backlit, his face draped in shadow, wearing only street clothes. As the man stepped under the beams of the emergency lights, Wolgast saw somebody entirely new to him. The stranger had long hair, wild and unkempt, shot with streaks of gray, and a coarse beard that climbed halfway up his cheeks; his lab coat was rumpled and stained. He approached Amy's bedside with the preoccupied air of an accident victim, or the bystander to some terrible calamity. He'd done nothing so far even to acknowledge Wolgast's presence.

'She knows,' he murmured, gazing at Amy. 'How does she know?'

'Who the hell are you? What's going on out there?'

Still the man ignored him. An otherworldly feeling seemed to radiate off his entire person, an almost fatalistic calm. 'It's strange,' he said after a moment. He sighed deeply and touched his beard, sweeping his eyes over the barren room. 'All of this. Is this . . . what I wanted? I wanted there to be one, you see. Once I *saw*, once I *knew* what they were planning, how it would all end, I wanted there to be at least one.'

'What are you talking about? Where's Sykes?'

At last the stranger seemed to take notice of him. He regarded Wolgast closely, his face tightening with a sudden frown. 'Sykes? Oh, he's dead. I rather think they're all dead, don't you?'

'What do you mean *dead*?'

'Dead, gone, in pieces probably. The lucky ones, anyway.' He gave his head a slow shake of wonder. 'You should have seen it, the way they swooped down from the trees. Like the bats. We really should have seen that coming.'

Wolgast felt completely lost. 'Please. I don't know . . . what you're talking about.'

The stranger shrugged. 'Well, you will. Soon enough, I'm sorry to say.' He looked at Wolgast again. 'My manners. You'll have to excuse me, Agent Wolgast. It's been a while for me. I'm Jonas Lear.' He gave a rueful smile. 'You could say I'm the person in charge around here. Or not. Under the circumstances, I rather think nobody's in charge anymore.'

Lear. Wolgast searched his memory, but the name meant nothing. 'I heard an explosion—'

'Quite right,' Lear interrupted. 'That would have been the elevator. Now, my guess would be it was one of the soldiers. But I was locked in the freezer, so I didn't see that part.' He sighed heavily and cast his eyes around the room once more. 'Not a moment of great heroism, was it, Agent Wolgast, locking myself in the freezer? You know, I really wish there was another chair in here. I'd like to sit down. I can't tell you how long it's been since I sat down.'

Wolgast shot to his feet. 'Jesus. Take mine. Just please, tell me what's going on.'

But Lear shook his head, his greasy hair swaying. 'There's no time, I'm afraid. We have to be going. It's all over, isn't it, Amy?' He looked down at the girl's sleeping form and gently touched her hand. 'Over at last.'

Wolgast could stand it no more. *'What's over?'*

Lear lifted his face; his eyes were full of tears.

'Everything.'

Lear led them down the corridor, Wolgast carrying Amy in his arms. The air smelled burnt, like molten plastic. As they turned the corner toward the elevator, Wolgast saw the first body.

It was Fortes. There wasn't much left. His body looked smeared, like it had been hit and dragged by something huge. Pooling blood glistened under the throb of the emergency lights. Beyond Fortes was another one, or so Wolgast thought. It took him a moment to understand he was looking at more of Fortes, just a different part of him.

Amy's eyes were closed, but Wolgast did his best to cover them anyway, pressing her face to his chest. Beyond Fortes lay two more bodies, or three, he couldn't tell. The floor was slick with blood, so much blood that he felt his feet sliding on it, the grease of human remains.

The elevator was blown away, nothing more than a hole, its darkened interior lit by the dancing sparks of broken wiring. Its heavy metal doors had shot across the hallway, caving in the opposite wall. Under the angular light of the emergency beams, Wolgast could see two more dead men, soldiers, crushed by pieces of the door. A third was propped against the wall, seated like a man taking a siesta, except he was resting in a pool of his own blood. His face was drawn and desiccated; his uniform hung limply on his frame, as if it were a size too large.

Wolgast tore his gaze away. 'How do we get out of here?'

'This way,' Lear said. The fog had lifted from him; he was pure urgency and purpose now. 'Quickly.'

Down another corridor. Doors stood open all up and down its length – heavy metal doors, identical to the one that led to Amy's chamber. And on the floor of the hallway, more bodies, but Wolgast didn't – couldn't – count. The walls were riddled with bullet holes, cartridges lay all over the floor, their brass casings gleaming.

Then a man stepped through one of the doors. Not stepped: stumbled. A big soft man, like the ones who'd delivered Wolgast's meals to his room, though his face was not familiar. He was holding a hand to a deep gash on his neck, the blood flowing through and around his fingers where they pressed into his flesh. His shirt, a white hospital tunic like Wolgast's, was a glistening bib of blood.

'Hey,' he said. 'Hey.' He looked at the three of them, then up and down the hall. He seemed not to notice the blood or, if he did, not to care. 'What happened to the lights?'

Wolgast didn't know what to say. A wound like that – the man should be dead already. Wolgast couldn't believe he was even standing.

'Oooo,' the bleeding man said, wobbling on his feet. 'I gotta sit down.'

He slid heavily to the floor, his body seeming to cave in on itself, like a tent without poles. He took a long breath and looked up at Wolgast. His body shuddered with a deep twitch.

'Am I . . . asleep?'

Wolgast said nothing. The question made no sense to him.

254

Lear touched his shoulder. 'Agent, leave him. There's no time.'

The man licked his lips. He'd lost so much blood he was becoming dehydrated. His eyes had started to flutter; his hands lay loosely, like empty gloves, on the floor at his sides.

'Because I'm here to tell you, I've been having the worst goddamn dream. I said to myself, Grey, you are having the worst dream in the world.'

'I don't think it was a dream,' Wolgast said.

The man considered this and shook his head. 'I was afraid of that.'

He twitched again, a hard spasm, as if he'd been hit by a jolt of current. Lear was right – there was nothing to do for him. The blood from his neck had darkened to a deep blue-black. Wolgast had to get Amy away.

'I'm sorry,' Wolgast said. 'We have to go.'

'You think *you're* sorry,' the man said, and let his head rock back against the wall.

'Agent—'

But Grey's mind already seemed elsewhere. 'It wasn't just me,' he said, and closed his eyes. 'It was all of us.'

They hurried on, to a room with lockers and benches. A dead end, Wolgast thought, but then Lear withdrew a key from his pocket and opened a door marked MECHANICALS.

Wolgast stepped inside. Lear was on his knees, using a small knife to pry loose a metal panel. It swung free on a pair of hinges, and Wolgast bent to look inside. The opening wasn't more than a yard square.

'Straight on, about thirty feet, and you'll come to an intersection. A tube leads straight up. There's a ladder inside for maintenance. It goes all the way to the top.'

Fifty feet at least, climbing a ladder in pitch blackness holding Amy, somehow, in his arms. Wolgast didn't see how he could do it.

'There has to be another way.'

Lear shook his head. 'There isn't.'

The man held Amy while Wolgast entered the duct.

Seated, his head bent low, he'd be able to pull Amy along, holding her by the waist. He backed in until his legs were straight; Lear positioned Amy between them. She seemed to be poised on the edge of awareness now. Through her thin gown, Wolgast could still feel the warmth of her fever rising off her skin.

'Remember what I said. Ten yards.'

Wolgast nodded.

'Be careful.'

'What killed those men?'

But Lear didn't answer. 'Keep her close,' he said. 'She's everything. Now go.'

Wolgast began to scooch away, one hand clutching Amy by the waist, the other pulling them deeper into the duct. It was only when the panel sealed behind him that he realized that Lear had never meant to come with them.

The sticks were everywhere now, all over the compound. Richards could hear the screams and the gunfire. He took extra clips from his desk and ran upstairs to Sykes's office.

The room was empty. Where was Sykes?

They had to establish a perimeter. Push the sticks back inside the Chalet and throw the switch. Richards stepped from Sykes's office, his gun raised.

Something was moving down the hall.

It was Sykes. By the time Richards got to him, he had slumped to the floor, his back propped against the wall. His chest was heaving like a sprinter's, his face sheened with sweat. He was holding a wide tear on his lower arm, just above the wrist, from which blood was running freely. His gun, a .45, lay on the floor near his upturned palm.

'They're all over the place,' Sykes said, and swallowed. 'Why didn't he kill me? The son of a bitch looked right at me.'

'Which one was it?'

'What the fuck does that matter?' Sykes shrugged. 'Your pal. Babcock. What is it with you two?' A deep tremor moved through him. 'I don't feel so good,' he said, and then he vomited.

Richards jumped away, but too late. The air tanged with the stench of bile, and something else, elemental and metallic, like turned earth. Richards felt the wetness through his pants, his socks. He knew without looking that Sykes's vomitus was full of blood.

'Fuck!'

He raised his weapon at Sykes.

'Please,' Sykes said, meaning no, or maybe yes, but either way, Richards figured he was doing Sykes a favor when he pointed the barrel at the center of his chest, the sweet spot, and then he squeezed the trigger.

Lacey saw the first one come out an upper window. So quick! Like light itself! How a man would move if he were made of light! It was up and over in an instant, vaulting off the roof into space, sailing through the air above the compound, alighting in a stand of trees a hundred yards away. A man-sized flash of throbbing luminescence, like a shooting star.

She'd heard the alarm as the truck pulled into the compound. The two men in the cab had argued for a minute – should they just drive away? – and Lacey had used this moment to climb out the back and scurry into the woods. That was when she'd seen the demon flying from the window. The treetops where he landed absorbed his weight with a shudder.

Lacey saw what was about to happen.

The driver of the truck was opening the truck's rear gate. Ordnance, the sentry had said – guns? The truck was full of guns.

The treetops moved again. A streak of green fell toward him.

Oh! Lacey thought. Oh! Oh!

Then there were more of them, pouring out of the building, through its windows and doors, launching themselves into the air. Ten, eleven, twelve. And soldiers too, everywhere, running and yelling and shooting, but their bullets did nothing; the demons were too fast, or else the bullets were harmless against them; one by one the demons fell upon the soldiers and they died.

This was why she had come – to save Amy from the demons.

Quickly, Lacey. Quickly.

She stepped from the edge of the woods.

'Halt!'

Lacey froze. Should she raise her hands? The soldier appeared from the woods where he'd been hiding, too. A good boy, doing what he thought was his duty. Trying not to be afraid, though of course he was; she could feel the fear coming off him, like waves of heat. He didn't know what was about to happen to him. She felt a tender pity.

'Who are you?'

'I am no one,' Lacey said, and then the demon was upon him – before he could even point his weapon, before he could finish the word he was speaking as he died – and Lacey was running toward the building.

By the time they got to the base of the tube, Wolgast was sweating and breathing hard. A faint light was falling down upon them. Far above, he could see the twin beams of an emergency light and, farther still, the stilled blades of a giant fan. The central ventilation shaft.

'Amy, honey,' he said. 'Amy, you have to wake up.'

Her eyes fluttered open and closed again. He guided her arms around his neck and stood, felt her feet clamping around his waist. But he could tell she had no strength.

'You have to hold on, Amy. Please. You have to.'

Her body tightened in reply. But still, he'd have to use one of his arms to support her weight. This would leave only one hand free to pull them up the ladder. Jesus.

He turned and faced the ladder, set his foot onto the first rung. It was like a problem on a standardized test: *Brad Wolgast is holding a little girl. He has to climb a ladder, fifty feet, in a poorly lit ventilation shaft. The girl is semiconscious at best. How does Brad Wolgast save both their lives?*

Then he saw how he could do it. One rung at a time, he'd use his right hand to pull them up, then hook that same elbow through the ladder, balancing Amy's weight on his knee while he changed hands and moved up another rung. Then the left hand, then the right, and so on, moving Amy's weight between them, rung by rung to the top.

How much did she weigh? Fifty pounds? All suspended, at the moment he changed hands, by the strength of a single arm.

Wolgast began to climb.

Richards could tell from the shouts and the shooting that the sticks were outside now.

He'd known what was happening to Sykes. Probably it would happen to him too, since Sykes had puked his god-damn infected blood all over him, but he doubted he'd live long enough for this to matter. Hey, Cole, he thought. Hey, Cole, you weasel, you little shit. Was this what you had in mind? Is this your Pax Americana? Because there's only one outcome I can see here.

There was just one thing Richards wanted now. A clean exit, with a good showing at the last.

The front entrance of the Chalet was all broken glass and bullet holes, the doors ripped half off their hinges, hanging kitty-corner. Three soldiers lay dead on the floor; it looked as if they'd been shot by friendly fire in the chaos. Maybe they'd actually shot one another on purpose, just to hustle things along. Richards raised his hand and looked at the Springfield – why would he think this would do any good? The soldiers' rifles would be no use either. He needed something larger. The armory was across the compound, behind the barracks. He'd have to make a run for it.

He looked out the door, across the open ground of the compound. At least the lights were still on. Well, he thought.

Better now than later, since probably there would be no later. He took off at a run.

The soldiers were everywhere, scattered, running, shooting at nothing, at one another. Not even pretending to make an organized defense, let alone an assault on the Chalet. Richards ran full tilt, half-expecting to be hit.

Richards was halfway across the compound when he saw the five-ton. It was parked at the edge of the lot, at a careless angle, its doors open. He knew what was inside it.

Maybe he wouldn't have to make it across the compound after all.

'Agent Doyle.'

Doyle smiled. 'Lacey.'

They were on the first floor of the Chalet, in a small, cramped room of desks and file cabinets. Doyle had been waiting there since the shooting had started, hidden beneath a desk. Waiting for Lacey.

He stood.

'Do you know where they are?'

Lacey paused. There were scratches on her face and neck, and bits of leaves caught in her hair.

She nodded. 'Yes.'

'I . . . heard you,' Doyle said. 'All these weeks.' Something huge was breaking open inside him. His throat choked with tears. 'I don't know how I did that.'

She took his hands in hers. 'It wasn't me you heard, Agent Doyle.'

At least Wolgast couldn't look down. He was sweating hard now, his palms and fingers slick on the rungs as he pulled them farther up. His arms were trembling with exertion; the crooks of his elbows, where he held each rung when he traded hands, felt bruised to the bone. There was a moment, he knew, when the body simply reached its limits, an invisible line that, once crossed, could not be uncrossed. He pushed the thought aside and climbed.

Amy's arms, crossed behind his neck, held firm. Together they ascended, rung by rung by rung.

The fan was closer now. Wolgast could feel a thin breeze, cool and smelling of night, spilling over his face. He craned his neck to scan the sides of the tube for an opening.

He saw it, ten feet above him: beside the ladder, an open duct.

He'd have to push Amy in first. Somehow he'd have to manage his own weight on the ladder and hers as well, while he swung her out from the ladder and into the duct; then he'd climb in himself.

They reached the opening. The fan was higher than he'd thought, another thirty feet above their heads at least. He guessed they were somewhere on the first floor of the Chalet. Maybe he was supposed to go higher, find another exit. But his strength was nearly gone.

He positioned his right knee to take Amy's weight and reached his left hand out. A featureless wall of cool metal met his fingertips, smooth as glass, but then he found the edge. He drew his hand back. Three more rungs should do it. He took a deep breath and ascended, positioning the two of them just above the duct.

'Amy,' he rasped. His mouth and throat were dry as bone. 'Wake up. Do your best to wake up, honey.'

He felt her breathing change against his neck as she tried to rouse.

'Amy, I'm going to need you to let go when I say. I'll hold you. There's an opening in the wall. I need you to try to get your feet into it.'

The girl gave no reply. He hoped she had heard him. He tried to imagine how this was going to work, exactly – how he was going to get her inside the duct and then himself – and couldn't. But he was out of options. If he waited any longer, he'd have no strength for any of it.

Now.

He pushed with his knee, lifting Amy up. Her arms released his neck and with his free hand he took her by the wrist, suspending her over the tube like a pendulum, and then he saw the way: he released his other hand, let her weight pull him away and to his left, toward the hole, and then her feet were inside it, she was sliding into the tube.

He began to fall. He'd been falling all along. But as he felt his feet lose contact with the ladder, his hands madly scrabbling at the wall, his fingers found the lip of the duct, a thin metal ridge that bit into his skin.

'Whoa!' he cried, his voice ricocheting down the length of the shaft. He seemed to be clinging to the side of the shaft by will alone; his feet were dangling in space. 'Whoa now!'

How he did it he couldn't have explained. Adrenaline. Amy. That he didn't want to die, not yet. He pulled with all his might, his elbows bending slowly, drawing himself inexorably upward – first his head and then his chest and then his waist and finally the rest of him, sliding into the duct.

For a moment he lay still, gulping air into his lungs. He lifted his face then and saw a light ahead – some kind of opening in the floor. He twisted himself around and held Amy as he'd done before, scooting along on his backside, clutching her by the waist. The light grew stronger as they moved toward it. They came to a slatted grate.

It was sealed, screwed shut from the outside.

He wanted to cry. To come so close! Even if he'd been able to reach through the narrow slats, somehow, to find the screws with his fingers, he had no tools, no way to open it. And going back – impossible. He'd spent the last of his strength.

He heard movement below them.

He pulled Amy tight. He thought of the men they'd seen – Fortes, the soldier in the pool of blood, the one called Grey. It wasn't how he wanted to die. He closed his eyes and held his breath, willing the two of them into absolute silence.

Then a voice, quiet and searching: 'Chief?'

It was Doyle.

*

One of the lockers was already resting on the ground at the rear of the truck. It looked like somebody had been unloading and then, in a panic, dropped it. Richards searched quickly inside the cargo compartment and found a tire iron.

The hinge gave way with a bright snap. Inside, cradled in beds of foam, lay a pair of RPG-29s. He lifted the rack to find, beneath it, the rockets: finned cylinders, about half a meter long, tipped with tandem-charge HEATs, capable of penetrating the armor of a modern battle tank. Richards had seen what they could do.

He'd placed the requisition when the order had come through to move the sticks. Better safe than sorry, he'd thought. *Vampires, say aaah.*

He fixed the first rocket to the launcher. With a twist it issued the satisfying hum that meant the warhead was armed. Thousands of years of technical advancement, the whole history of human civilization, seemed contained within that sound, the hum of an arming HEAT. The 29 was reusable, but Richards knew he'd only get one shot. He hoisted it to his shoulder, lifted the sighting mechanism into position, and stepped away from the truck.

'Hey!' he yelled, and, at precisely that moment, the sound of his voice streaming away into the gloom, a cold shudder of nausea burbled from his gut. The ground beneath him swayed, like the deck of a boat at sea. Beads of sweat were popping out all over. He felt the urge to blink, a random current from the brain. So. It was happening quicker than he'd thought. He swallowed hard and took two more steps into the light, swinging the RPG toward the treetops.

'Here, kitty, kitty!'

An anxious minute passed as Doyle scrabbled through various drawers until he found a penknife. Standing on a chair, he used the blade to undo the screws. Wolgast lowered Amy into Doyle's arms, then dropped to the floor himself.

He didn't at first know whom he was seeing.

'Sister Lacey?'

She was holding the sleeping girl against her chest. 'Agent Wolgast.'

Wolgast looked at Doyle. 'I don't—'

'Get it?' Doyle lifted his eyebrows. He was, like Wolgast, wearing scrubs. They were too large, hanging loosely on his body. He gave a little laugh. 'Trust me, I don't get it either.'

'This place is full of dead men,' Wolgast said. 'Something . . . I don't know. There was an explosion.' He couldn't explain himself.

'We know,' Doyle said, nodding. 'It's time for us to go.'

They stepped from the room into the hall. Wolgast guessed they were somewhere near the rear of the Chalet. It was quiet, though they could hear scattered pops of gunfire from outside. Quickly, without speaking, they made their way to the front entrance. Wolgast saw the dead soldiers sprawled there.

Lacey turned to him. 'Take her,' she said. 'Take Amy.'

He did. His arms were still weak from his ascent up the ladder, but he held her hard against him. She was moaning a little, trying to wake up, fighting the force that was keeping her in twilight. She needed to be in a hospital, but even if he could get her to one, what would he say? How would he explain any of this? The air near the doors was wintry cold, and in her thin gown Amy shivered against him.

'We need a vehicle,' Wolgast said.

Doyle ducked out the door. A minute later he returned, holding a set of keys. He'd gotten a gun from somewhere, too, a .45. He took Wolgast and Lacey to the window and pointed.

'The one all the way down, at the edge of the lot. The silver Lexus. See it?'

Wolgast did. The car was a hundred yards away, at least.

'Nice ride like that,' Doyle said, 'you'd think the driver wouldn't just leave the keys under the visor.' Doyle pressed them into Wolgast's hand. 'Hold on to these. They're yours. Just in case.'

It took Wolgast a moment. Then he understood. The car was for him, for him and Amy. 'Phil—'

Doyle held up his hands. 'That's how it has to be.'

Wolgast looked at Lacey, who nodded. Then she stepped toward him. She kissed Amy, touching her hair, and then she kissed him, too, once, on the cheek. A deep calm and a feeling of certainty seemed to radiate through his entire body from the place where she had kissed him. He'd never felt anything like it.

They stepped from the door, Doyle leading them. Together they moved quickly under the cover of the building. Wolgast could barely keep up. He heard more gunfire from somewhere, but it didn't seem aimed at them. The shots seemed to be going up and away, into the trees, at the rooftops; random shots, like some kind of sinister celebration. Each time it happened he'd hear a scream, a moment of silence, and then the shooting would start up again.

They reached the corner of the building. Wolgast could see the woods beyond it. In the other direction, toward the lights of the compound, lay the parking area. The Lexus waited at the end, facing away, no other cars around it for cover.

'We'll just have to make a run for it,' Doyle said. 'Ready?'

Wolgast, panting, did his best to nod.

Then they were up and racing toward the car.

Richards felt him before he saw him. He turned, swinging the RPG like a vaulter's pole.

It wasn't Babcock.

It wasn't Zero.

It was Anthony Carter.

He was in a kind of crouch, twenty feet away. He lifted his face and twisted his head, looking at Richards appraisingly. There was something doglike about it. Blood glistened on Carter's face, his clawlike hands, his sworded teeth, row upon row. A kind of clicking sound was coming from his throat.

Slowly, in a gesture of languid pleasure, he began to rise. Richards put Carter's mouth in his sights.

'Open up,' Richards said, and fired.

He knew, even as the grenade shot from the tube, the force of its ejection pushing Richards backward, that he'd missed. The place where Carter had stood was empty. Carter was in the air. Carter was flying. Then he was falling, down upon Richards. The grenade went off, taking out the front of the Chalet, but Richards heard this only vaguely – the noise receding, fading to some impossible distance – as he experienced the sensation, utterly new to him, of being torn in half.

The explosion hit Wolgast as a white sheen, a wall of heat and light that slapped the left side of his face like a punch; he was lifted from the ground and felt Amy fall away. He hit the pavement and rolled and rolled again before coming to rest on his back.

His ears were ringing; his breath felt like it was stuck in a tube, far down in his chest. Above him he saw the deep, velvety blackness of the night sky, and stars, hundreds and hundreds of stars, and some of them were falling.

He thought: Falling stars. He thought: Amy. He thought: Keys.

He lifted his head. Amy was lying on the ground a few yards away. The air was full of smoke. In the flickering light of the burning Chalet, she looked as if she might be sleeping – a character in a fairy tale, the princess who had fallen asleep and couldn't wake. Wolgast rolled himself onto all fours and frantically patted the ground for the keys. He could tell one of his ears was messed up; it was like a curtain had fallen over the left side of his face, absorbing all sound. The keys. The keys. Then he realized they were still in his hand; he'd never let them go to begin with.

Where were Doyle and Lacey?

He went to where Amy lay. The fall didn't seem to have hurt her any, or the explosion, as far as he could tell. He put his hands under her arms and hoisted her over his shoulder, then made for the Lexus as fast as he could.

He bent to ease Amy in, laying her across the backseat. He got in himself and turned the key. The headlights blazed across the compound.

Something hit the hood.

Some kind of animal. No: some kind of monstrous thing, throbbing with a pale green light. But when he saw its eyes, and what was inside them, he knew that this strange new being on the hood was Anthony Carter.

Carter rose as Wolgast found the gearshift and plunged it into reverse and gunned the engine. Carter fell away. Wolgast could see him in the lights of the Lexus, rolling on the ground and then, in a series of movements almost too quick for the eye, launching himself into the air, gone.

What in the name of—

Wolgast stomped the brake, turning the wheel hard to the right. The car spun and spun and came to rest, pointed at the driveway. Then the passenger door opened: Lacey. She climbed in quickly, saying nothing. There were streaks of blood on her face, her shirt. She was holding a gun in her hand. She looked at it, amazed, and dropped it on the floor.

'Where's Doyle?'

'I do not know,' she said.

He put the car back into drive and hit the accelerator.

Then he saw Doyle. He was running toward the Lexus at an angle, waving the .45.

'Just go!' he was yelling. 'Go!'

A concussive thump on the roof of the car, and Wolgast knew it was Carter. Carter was on the roof of the Lexus. Wolgast hit the brakes again, sending all of them lurching forward. Carter tumbled onto the hood but held on. Wolgast heard Doyle firing, three quick shots. Wolgast saw a round actually strike Carter in the shoulder, a quick spark of impact. Carter seemed barely to notice.

'Hey!' Doyle was yelling. 'Hey!'

Carter turned his face, saw Doyle. With a compressive

twitch of his body he launched himself into the air as Doyle got off a final shot. Wolgast turned in time to see the creature that had once been Anthony Carter fall upon his partner, taking him in like a giant mouth.

It was over in an instant.

Wolgast stamped on the accelerator, hard. The car shot over a strip of grass, the wheels digging and spinning, then hit the pavement with a screech. They barreled down the long drive away from the burning Chalet, through the hall-way of the trees, everything streaming past. Fifty, sixty, seventy miles per hour.

'What the hell was that?' Wolgast said to Lacey. 'What was that!'

'Stop here, Agent.'

'What? You can't be serious.'

'They will catch us. They will follow the blood. You must stop the car now.' She put her hand on his elbow. Her grip was firm, insistent. 'Please. Do as I ask.'

Wolgast drew the Lexus to the side of the road; Lacey turned to face him. Wolgast saw the wound in her arm, a clean shot just below the deltoid.

'Sister Lacey—'

'It is nothing,' Lacey said. 'It is only flesh and blood. But I'm not to go with you. I see that now.' She touched his arm again and smiled – a final smile of benediction, sad and happy at once. A smile at the trials of a long journey, now ended.

'Take care of her. Amy is yours. You will know what to do.' Then she stepped from the car and slammed the door before Wolgast could say another word.

He lifted his eyes to the rearview and saw her running the way they'd come, waving her arms in the air. A warning? No, she was calling them down upon her. She didn't get a hundred feet before a swoop of light shot from the trees, and then another, and then a third, so many Wolgast had to look away, and he hit the accelerator and drove away as fast as he could without looking back again.

II
THE YEAR OF
ZERO

Come, let's away to prison;
We two alone will sing like birds i' the cage:
When thou dost ask me blessing, I'll kneel down
And ask of thee forgiveness.

– SHAKESPEARE,
King Lear

FIFTEEN

When all time ended, and the world had lost its memory, and the man that he was had receded from view like a ship sailing away, rounding the blade of the earth with his old life locked in its hold; and when the gyring stars gazed down upon nothing, and the moon in its arc no longer remembered his name, and all that remained was the great sea of hunger on which he floated forever – still, inside him, in the deepest place, was this: one year. The mountain and the turning seasons, and Amy. Amy and the Year of Zero.

They arrived at the camp in darkness. Wolgast drove the last mile slowly, following the beams of the headlights where they broke through the trees, braking to crawl over the worst of the potholes, the deep ruts left by winter runoff. Fingering branches, dripping with moisture, scraped the length of the roof and windows as they passed. The car was junk, an ancient Corolla with huge, gaudy rims and an ashtray full of yellowed butts; Wolgast had stolen it at a mobile home park outside Laramie, leaving the Lexus with the keys in the ignition and a note on the dash: *Keep it, it's yours.* An old mutt on a chain, too tired to bark, had watched with disinterest as Wolgast jimmied the ignition, then carried Amy from the Lexus to the Toyota, where he laid her across the backseat, cluttered with fast food wrappers and empty cigarette packs.

For a moment Wolgast had wished he could be there to see the owner's face when he awoke in the morning to find his old car replaced by an eighty-thousand-dollar sports sedan, like Cinderella's pumpkin turned into a coach. Wolgast had never driven anything like it in his life. He hoped that the new owner, whoever he was, would give himself the gift of driving the car once, before finding a way to make it quietly vanish.

271

The Lexus belonged to Fortes. *Had* belonged, Wolgast reminded himself, because Fortes was dead. Fortes, James B. Wolgast had never actually learned his first name until he read the registration card. A Maryland address, which probably meant USAMRIID, maybe NIH. Wolgast had tossed the registration out the window into a wheat field somewhere near the Colorado-Wyoming border. But he'd kept the contents of the wallet he'd found on the floor beneath the driver's seat: a little over six hundred dollars in cash and a titanium Visa.

But all that was hours ago, time's passage magnified by the distance they had traveled. Colorado, Wyoming, Idaho, the last passed entirely in darkness, viewed only through the cones of the Corolla's headlamps. They'd crossed into Oregon at sunrise on the second morning, traversed the wrinkled plateaus of the state's arid interior as the day wore away. All around them the empty fields and golden, wind-swept hills were blooming with purple sagebrush. To keep alert, Wolgast drove with the windows open, swirling the interior of the car with its sweet perfume: the smell of boyhood, of home. In midafternoon he felt the Toyota's engine straining; they'd begun, at last, to climb. As darkness was falling the Cascades rose to meet them, a brooding bulk that sawtoothed the rays of the setting sun and lit the western sky in a fiery collage of reds and purples, like a wall of stained glass. High up, their rocky tips glinted with ice.

'Amy,' he said. 'Wake up, honey. Look.'

Amy lay across the backseat, covered with a cotton blanket. She was still weak, had slept most of the last two days. But the worst seemed over. Her skin looked better, the waxy pallor of fever worn away. That morning she'd actually managed a few bites of an egg sandwich and some sips of chocolate milk that Wolgast had bought at a drive-through. One funny thing: she was acutely sensitive to sunlight. It seemed to cause her physical pain, and not just to her eyes. Her whole body recoiled from it, as if from an electric charge. At a service station he'd purchased her a pair of sunglasses –

movie-star pink, the only ones small enough to fit her face – and a foam trucker's cap with the John Deere logo, to pull down over her eyes. But even with the hat and glasses, she'd barely peeked her head from the blanket all day.

At the sound of his voice, she rose against the tidal pull of sleep and followed his gaze out the windshield. Still wearing the pink sunglasses, she squinted into the sunlight, cupping her hands around her temples. The wind of the open car tossed the long strands of hair about her face.

'It's . . . bright,' she said quietly.

'The mountains,' he explained.

He drove the final miles by instinct, following unmarked roads that took him ever deeper into the forested folds of the mountains. A hidden world: where they were going there were no towns, no houses, no people at all. At least that was how he remembered it. The air was cold and smelled of pine. The gas gauge was nearly on empty. They passed a darkened general store that Wolgast recalled vaguely, though the name was not familiar – MILTON'S DRY GOODS / HUNTING, FISHING LIC. – and began their final ascent. Three forks later he was on the verge of panic, thinking he'd gotten them lost, when a series of small details seemed to rise before him out of the past: a certain slope of the roadway, a glimpse of star-dressed sky as they rounded a bend, and then, beneath the Toyota's wheels, the expansive acoustics of open air as they crossed the river. All just as it had been when he was small, his father beside him, driving him up to camp.

Moments later they came to a break in the trees. By the side of the road stood a weathered sign reading, BEAR MOUNTAIN CAMP, and beneath that, hanging from a pair of rusted chains, FOR SALE, with the name of a real estate agency and a phone number with a Salem exchange. The sign, like many Wolgast had seen along the road, was pocked with bullet holes.

'This is the place,' he said.

The camp's driveway, a mile long, traced the crest of a high embankment above the river, then hooked right around an outcrop of boulders and took them into the trees. The place, he knew, had been closed up for years. Would the buildings even still be there? What would they find? The charred ruins of a devastating fire? Roofs rotted and collapsed under the weight of winter snow? But then, out of the trees, the camp emerged: the building the boys had called Old Lodge – because it was old even then – and behind and around it, the smaller outbuildings and cabins, about a dozen all told. Beyond lay more woods and a pathway that descended to the lake, two hundred acres of glasslike stillness held in place by an earthen dam and shaped like a kidney bean. As they approached the lodge, the Toyota's headlights flared across the front windows, momentarily creating the illusion of lights coming on inside, as if their arrival were expected – as if they had traveled not across the width of the country but back through time itself, across the gulf of thirty years to when Wolgast was a boy.

He pulled the car up to the porch and shut off the ignition. Wolgast felt, strangely, the urge to say a prayer of thanks, to acknowledge their arrival in some manner. But it had been many years since he'd done this – too many. He climbed from the car, into the stunning cold. His breath gathered in equine streams around his face. The beginning of May, and still the air seemed to hold the memory of winter. He stepped around to the trunk and keyed the lock. When he'd opened it the first time, in the parking lot of a Walmart west of Rock Springs, he'd found it full of empty paint cans. Now it held supplies – clothes for the two of them, food, toiletries, candles, batteries, a camp stove and bottles of propane, a few obvious tools, a first aid kit, a pair of down-filled sleeping bags. Sufficient to get them settled, though he would have to go down the mountain soon enough. Under the glow of the trunk's bulb, he found what he was looking for and ascended the porch.

The hasp on the front door gave way with one hard yank of the Toyota's tire iron. Wolgast turned on his flashlight and stepped inside. If Amy woke up alone, she might be frightened; but still he wanted to have a quick look around, to make sure the place was safe. He tried the light switch by the door, but nothing happened; the power was off, of course. Probably there was a backup generator somewhere, although he'd need fuel to get it going, and even then, who knew if it would work at all. He shone his beam around the room: a disorganized assemblage of wooden tables and chairs, a cast-iron woodstove, a metal office desk shoved against the wall, and above it a bulletin board, bare except for a single sheet of paper, curling with age. The windows were uncovered, but the glass had held; the space was tight and dry and, with the woodstove going, would warm up fast.

He followed his beam toward the bulletin board. WELCOME CAMPERS, SUMMER 2014, the paper read, and beneath it, filling the page, a list of names – the usual Jacobs and Joshuas and Andrews, but also a Sacha and even an Akeem – each followed by the number of the cabin to which he'd been assigned. Wolgast had been a camper for three years, the last – the summer he'd turned twelve – working as a junior counselor, sleeping in a cabin with a group of younger boys, many of them beset by a homesickness so debilitating it was like an illness. Between the ones who cried all night and the midnight antics of their tormentors, Wolgast had barely slept a wink all summer. And yet he'd never been so happy; those days were, in many ways, the best of his boyhood, a golden hour. It was, in fact, the very next autumn that his parents had taken him to Texas and all their troubles began. The camp had been owned by a man named Mr Hale – a high school biology teacher with the deep voice and barrel rib cage of a linebacker, which he once had been. He was a friend of Wolgast's father, though he'd never acknowledged this friendship through any special treatment that Wolgast could recall.

Mr Hale had lived upstairs during the summers with his wife, in some kind of apartment. That's what Wolgast was looking for now. He stepped through a swinging door off the common area and found himself in the kitchen: rustic pine cabinets, a pegboard of oxidizing pots and saucepans, a sink with an old-fashioned pump, and a stove and refrigerator with its door half open, all surrounding a wide pine-plank table. Everything was coated with a heavy scrim of dust. The stove was an old commercial unit, white steel, with a clock on the faceplate, the hands frozen at six minutes after three. He turned one of the burner dials and heard a hiss of gas.

From the kitchen, a narrow stairway ascended to the second floor, a warren of tiny rooms tucked under the eaves. Most were empty, but in two he found a couple of cots, the mattresses turned over to face the walls. And something else: in one of the rooms, on a trestle table by the window, an apparatus of dials and switches that he took to be a short-wave radio.

He returned to the car. Amy was still sleeping, curled beneath the blanket. He shook her gently awake.

She rose and rubbed her eyes. 'Where are we?'

'Home,' he told her.

He found himself, in those first days on the mountain, thinking of Lila. Strangely, his thoughts did not include a more general curiosity about the world, what was happening out there now. His days were consumed by chores, by setting the place to rights and attending to Amy; but his mind, free to go wherever it wished, chose to move over the past, hovering atop it like a bird over some immense body of water, no shoreline in sight, only the distant reflection of himself in its shining surface for company.

It was not true that he had loved Lila right away. But something had happened that felt like falling. He'd met her on a wintry Sunday when he came into the ER, suspended by the shoulders of two friends reeking of gymnasium sweat. Wolgast wasn't much of a basketball player, hadn't played at all since high school, but he had let himself be talked into playing on a team for a charity tournament – three-on-three, half-court, the stakes low as could be. Miraculously, they'd made it through two rounds before Wolgast went up for a jump shot and came down to a wet pop in his left Achilles tendon and then, as he melted to the floor – the shot bouncing sadly off the rim, adding insult, literally, to injury – an explosion of pain that brought tears to his eyes.

The ER doc who examined him declared the tendon ruptured and sent him upstairs, to an orthopedist. This was Lila. She stepped into the room, spooning the last of a cup of yogurt into her mouth, dropped it in the trash, and turned to the sink to wash her hands, all without once glancing at him.

'So.' She dried her hands and looked briskly at his chart, then at Wolgast, sitting on the table. She was not what Wolgast would have described, right off, as classically pretty, though there was something about her that caught him short, a feeling like déjà vu. Her hair, the color of cocoa, was held in a bun by some kind of stick. She was wearing a pair of black eyeglasses, very small, that rode down the slope of her narrow nose. 'I'm Dr Kyle. You hurt yourself playing basketball?'

Wolgast nodded sheepishly. 'I'm not what you'd call an athlete,' he admitted.

At that moment her handheld buzzed at her waist. She peeked at it quickly, frowning. Then, with calm precision, she placed a single outstretched finger on the soft spot behind the third toe of his left foot.

'Press here.'

He did, or tried to. The pain was so fierce he thought he might be ill.

'What kind of work do you do?'

Wolgast swallowed. 'Law enforcement,' he managed. 'Jesus, that hurt.'

She was writing something on the chart. 'Law enforcement,' she repeated. 'As in, police?'

'FBI actually.'

He looked for a flicker of interest in her eyes but saw none. On her left hand, he noted, she wore no ring. Though this didn't necessarily mean anything – maybe she removed it when she saw her patients.

'I'm sending you for a scan,' she said, 'but I'm ninety percent sure the tendon is ruptured.'

'Meaning?'

She shrugged. 'Surgery. I won't lie. It's not fun. An immobilizer for eight weeks, six months to fully recover.' She smiled ruefully. 'Your basketball days are over, I'm sorry to say.'

She gave him something for the pain that made him instantly sleepy. He barely awoke when they wheeled him in for the MRI. When he opened his eyes again, Lila was standing at the foot of his bed. Somebody had pulled a blanket over him. He checked his watch to find it was nearly nine p.m. He'd been at the hospital for almost six hours.

'Are your friends still here?'

'I doubt it.'

She had scheduled him for surgery at seven o'clock the next morning. There were forms to sign, and then he'd be taken to a room for the night. She asked him if there was anybody he needed to call.

'Not really.' His head was still woozy from the Vicodin. 'It seems a little pathetic, I guess. I don't even have a cat.'

She was regarding him expectantly, as if waiting for him to say something else. He was on the verge of asking her if they'd met before when she broke the silence with a sudden, shining smile.

'Well, good,' she said.

Their first date, two weeks after Wolgast's surgery, was dinner in the hospital cafeteria. Wolgast, on crutches, his left leg entombed in an apparatus of plastic and Velcro from knee to toe, was forced to wait at the table like an invalid while she fetched their food. She was wearing scrubs – she was on call all night, she'd explained, and would be sleeping at the hospital – but she'd put on a bit of lipstick and mascara, he saw, and brushed her hair.

Lila's family was all back east, near Boston. After med school at BU – horrible, she said, the worst four years of her life, of anyone's life, like being dragged from a car – she'd moved to Colorado for her residency in orthopedics. She thought she'd hate it, this huge, faceless city far from home, but the opposite was true: she felt nothing but relief. The heedless sprawl of Denver, its chaotic snarl of subdivisions and freeways; the openness of the high plains and the indifferent mountains; the way people talked to each other, easily, without pretense, and the fact that nearly everyone was from somewhere else: exiles, like her.

'I mean, it seemed so *normal* here.' She was spreading cream cheese onto a bagel – breakfast for her, though it was nearly eight o'clock at night. 'I guess I never even knew what normal was. It was just what an uptight Wellesley girl needed,' she explained.

Wolgast felt hopelessly outclassed, and told her so. She laughed brightly, with embarrassment, and quickly touched his hand. 'You shouldn't,' she said.

She worked long hours; seeing each other in any kind of customary way, going to restaurants or movies, was impossible. Wolgast was on disability and spent his days sitting around his apartment, feeling antsy; then he would drive to the hospital, and the two of them would eat dinner together in the cafeteria. She told him all about growing up in Boston, the daughter of college teachers, and about school, her friends and studies and a year she'd spent in France, trying to be a photographer. He got the idea she'd been waiting for somebody to come along in her life for whom all this would be new. He was wholly content to listen, to be that person.

They didn't so much as hold hands until nearly a month had passed. They had just finished their dinner when Lila removed her glasses, leaned across the table, and kissed him, long and tenderly, her breath tasting of the orange she had just eaten.

'There,' she said. 'Okay?' She looked around the room theatrically and lowered her voice. 'I mean, I am, technically, your doctor.'

'My leg feels better already,' Wolgast said.

He was thirty-five, Lila thirty-one, when they married. A day in September: the ceremony was held on Cape Cod, at a small yacht club overlooking a tranquil bay of bobbing sailboats beneath a sky of crisp, autumnal blue. Nearly everybody who came was from Lila's side of the family, which was huge, like some enormous tribe – so many aunts and uncles and cousins that Wolgast couldn't keep count, couldn't hope to keep everyone's name straight. Half the women in attendance seemed to have been Lila's roommates at one time or another, eager to tell him tales about various youthful escapades that seemed, in the end, to be all the same story. Wolgast had never been so happy. He drank too much champagne and stood on a chair to give a long, maudlin toast, utterly sincere, that ended with his singing, wincingly off-key, a verse from 'Embraceable You.' Everyone laughed and applauded before sending them off under a corny torrent of rice. If anybody knew that Lila was four months pregnant, they didn't say a word to him about it. Wolgast chalked this up to New England reserve, but then he realized that no one cared; everyone was honestly happy for them.

With Lila's money – her income made his own look laughable – they bought a house in Cherry Creek, an older neighborhood with trees and parks and good schools, and waited for the baby to come. They knew she would be a girl. Eva had been the name of Lila's grandmother, a fiery character who, according to family lore, had both sailed on the *Andrea Doria* and dated a nephew of Al Capone's. Wolgast simply liked the name, and in any event, once Lila suggested it, it stuck. The plan was for Lila to work until her due date; after Eva was born, Wolgast would stay home with her for a year, and then Lila would go down to half-time at the hospital when he returned to the Bureau. A crazy plan, full of potential problems they both foresaw but didn't dwell on. Somehow, they would make things work.

In her thirty-fourth week, Lila's blood pressure went up, and her obstetrician put her on bed rest. Lila told Wolgast not to worry – it wasn't so high that the baby was in any danger. She was a doctor, after all; if there was a real problem, she'd tell him. He worried that she'd worked too hard, spent too many hours on her feet at the hospital, and he was glad to have her home, lying about like a queen, calling down the stairs for her meals and movies and things to read.

Then one night, three weeks before her due date, he came home and found her sobbing, sitting on the edge of the bed as she held her head in agony.

'Something's wrong,' she said.

At the hospital, they told Wolgast her blood pressure was 160 over 95, a condition known as preeclampsia. That was the source of the headache. They were concerned about seizures, about Lila's kidneys, about harm to the baby. Everyone was very serious, especially Lila, whose face was gray with worry. They would have to induce, her doctor told him. A vaginal delivery was best in cases like this, but if she didn't deliver in six hours, they would have to do a section.

They hooked her up to a Pitocin drip and a second IV, of magnesium sulfate, to suppress seizures. By this time it was after midnight. The magnesium, the nurse said, with infuriating cheerfulness, would be uncomfortable. Uncomfortable how? Wolgast asked. Well, the nurse said, it was hard to explain, but she wouldn't like it. They hooked her up to a fetal monitor, and after that they waited.

It was awful. Lila, on the bed, moaned in pain. The sound was like nothing Wolgast had ever experienced; it rocked him to the core. It felt like tiny fires, Lila said, all over. Like her own body hated her. She had never felt so terrible. Whether this was the magnesium or the Pitocin, Wolgast didn't know, and nobody would answer his questions. The contractions began, hard and close, but the OB said she wasn't dilated enough, not even close. Two centimeters, tops. How long could this go on? They had been to the classes, done everything right. No one had said it would be like this, like watching a car crash in slow motion.

Finally, just before dawn, Lila said she had to push. *Had* to.

Nobody believed she was ready but the doctor checked her and found, miraculously, that she was at ten centimeters. Everybody began running around, rearranging the room with all its wheeled objects, snapping on fresh gloves, folding away a section of the bed below Lila's pelvis. Wolgast felt useless, a rudderless ship at sea. He took Lila's hand as she pushed, once, twice, three times. Then it was over.

Somebody held out a pair of angled scissors, for Wolgast to cut the cord. The nurse put Eva in a warmer and did her Apgars. Then she put a hat on the baby's tiny head and wrapped her in a blanket and handed her to Wolgast. How astonishing! Suddenly it was all behind them, all the pain and panic and worry, and here was this sparkling new being in the room. Nothing in his life had prepared him for this, the feel of a baby, his daughter, in his arms. Eva was small, just five pounds. Her skin was warm and pink – the pink of sun-ripened peaches – and, as he pressed his face close to hers, gave off a smoky smell, as if she'd been plucked from a fire. They were sewing Lila up; she was still groggy from the drugs. Wolgast was surprised to find there was blood on the floor, a wide dark slick below her; in all the confusion, he had never seen this happen. But Lila was fine, the doctor said. Wolgast showed her their baby and then held Eva a long, long time, saying her name over and over, before they took her to the nursery.

Amy grew stronger by the day, but her sensitivity to light did not abate. Wolgast found, in one of the outbuildings, stacks of plywood and a ladder, and a hammer and saw and nails. He had to measure and cut the boards by hand, then carry them up the ladder and hold them in place while he nailed, to seal the windows of the second floor. But after the long climb at the compound – a feat that, in hindsight, seemed completely incredible – this small, ordinary chore seemed like not so much.

Amy rested most of each day, awakening at dusk to eat. She asked him about where they were – Oregon, he explained, in the mountains, a place where he had gone to camp as a boy – but never why; she either knew already or didn't care. The lodge's propane tank was nearly full. He cooked small, easy meals on the stove, soups and stews from cans, crackers and cereal wetted with powdered milk. The camp's water supply was faintly sulfurous but otherwise drinkable, and poured from the kitchen pump so icy cold it made his fillings tingle. He could see right away he hadn't brought nearly enough food; he'd have to go down the mountain soon. In the basement he'd found boxes of old books – classic novels in a bound set, moldy with age and dampness – and at night under the glow of candlelight he read to her: *Treasure Island, Oliver Twist, 20,000 Leagues Under the Sea.*

Sometimes she would come out during the day, if it was cloudy, and watch him do the chores – cutting wood, fixing a hole in the roof under the eaves, trying to make heads or tails of an old gasoline generator he'd found in one of the sheds. Amy would sit on a tree stump in the shade, wearing her glasses and cap, with a long towel tucked under the head-band to cover her neck. But these visits never lasted long; an hour, and her skin would turn a ferocious pink, as if scalded by hot water, and he'd send her back upstairs again.

One evening, after they had been at the camp for nearly three weeks, he took her down the path to the lake to bathe. Apart from her brief hours outside watching him work, she hadn't ventured from the lodge, and never so far. At the base of the path was a rickety dock, extending thirty feet past the grassy shoreline. Wolgast stripped to his underclothes and told Amy to do the same. He'd brought towels, shampoo, a bar of soap.

'Do you know how to swim?'

Amy shook her head.

'All right, I'll teach you.'

He took her by the hand and led her into the lake. The water was shockingly cold. They stepped together into deeper water, until it reached Amy's chest. Wolgast picked her up then and, holding her horizontally, told her to move her arms and legs, like so.

'Let go,' she told him.

'Are you sure?'

She was breathing quickly. 'Uh-huh.'

He released her; she sank like a stone. Through the ice-clear water, Wolgast could see that she'd stopped moving; her eyes were open and looking around, like an animal examining some new habitat. Then, with a startling grace, she extended her arms and brought them around, turning her shoulders and pushing herself through the water in a deft, froglike motion. A perfect whip kick: in an instant she was gliding along the sandy bottom, gone. Wolgast was about to dive in after her when she emerged ten feet away, in water that reached well over her head, smiling with exhilaration.

'Easy,' she said, treading with her legs. 'Like flying.'

Wolgast, dumbfounded, could only laugh. 'Be careful—' he said, but before he could finish she'd filled her lungs with a gulp of air and dived down again.

He washed her hair, did his best telling her how to do the rest. By the time they were done, the sky had darkened from purple to black. Stars by the hundreds, their flickering light doubled in the lake's still surface; no sounds at all except for their own voices and the basal throb of the lake's water against the shoreline. He led them up the path with the beam of his flashlight. They ate a dinner of soup and crackers in the kitchen, and afterward, he took her upstairs to her room. He knew she would be awake for hours; the night was her domain now, as it was becoming his own as well. Sometimes he'd sit up half the night, reading to her.

'Thank you,' Amy said as he was settling down with a book: *Anne of Green Gables*.

'What for?'

'For teaching me to swim.'

'It looked like you already knew. Somebody must have showed you.'

She considered this claim with a puzzled expression. 'I don't think so,' she said.

He didn't know what to make of any of it. So much of Amy was a mystery. She seemed well – better than well, in fact. Whatever had happened to her at the compound, whatever the virus was, she appeared to have weathered it; and yet the business with the light was strange. And other things: why, for instance, did Amy's hair not seem to grow? Wolgast's hair now curled below his collar; and yet Amy, as he looked at her, appeared exactly the same. He'd never trimmed her fingernails either, nor seen her do this. And of course the deeper mysteries: What had killed Doyle and everyone else in Colorado? How could that have been both Carter and not Carter on the hood of the car? What had Lacey meant when she'd said to him that Amy was his, that he'd know what to do? It seemed so; he had known what to do. And yet he could explain none of this.

Later, when he finished reading for the night, he told her that in the morning he'd be going down the mountain. She was well enough, he thought, that she could stay in the lodge by herself. It would only be for an hour or two. He'd be back before she knew it, before she was even awake.

'I know,' she told him, and Wolgast didn't know what to make of this, either.

He left at a little after seven. After so many weeks sitting idle, collecting pollen from the trees, the Toyota put up a long, wheezing protest when he tried to start it, but eventually the engine caught and held. The morning fog off the lake was just beginning to burn away. He put it in gear and began his long creep down the drive.

The closest real town was thirty miles away, but Wolgast didn't want to go that far. If the Toyota broke down, he'd be stranded, and so would Amy. The gas gauge was close to empty in any event. He retraced the route of their arrival, pausing at each fork to double-check his memory. He saw no other vehicles, which wasn't surprising in such a remote place; and yet this absence disturbed him. The world he was returning to, however briefly, felt like a different place than the one he'd left three weeks ago.

Then he saw it: MILTON'S DRY GOODS / HUNTING, FISHING LIC. In the dark, that first night, it had seemed larger than it was; in fact it was just a small, two-story house of weathered shingles. A cottage in the woods, like something in a fairy tale. No other cars were in the lot, though an old van, mid-1990s vintage, was parked on the grass at the rear. Wolgast exited the Toyota and stepped to the front door.

On the porch were half a dozen newspaper vending boxes, all empty but one: *USA Today*. He could see the large head-line splashed across it through the dusty door, which was propped open. When he withdrew a copy, he found that the paper was just two folded sheets long. He stood on the porch and read.

CHAOS IN COLORADO
Rocky Mountain State Overrun by Killer Virus; Borders Sealed
Outbreaks Reported in Nebraska, Utah, Wyoming
President Places Military on High Alert, Asks the Nation to Remain Calm in the Face of 'Unprecedented Terroristic Threat'

WASHINGTON, May 18 – President Hughes vowed tonight to take 'all necessary measures' to contain the spread of the so-called Colorado fever virus and punish those responsible, declaring, 'The righteous anger of the United States of America will swiftly befall the haters of liberty and the outlaw governments that give them harbor.'

The president spoke from the Oval Office in his first address to the nation since the crisis began, eight days ago.

'Unmistakable evidence exists that this devastating epidemic is not an occurrence of nature but the work of anti-American extremists, operating within our own borders but supported by our enemies abroad,' Hughes

286

told an anxious nation. 'This is a crime not only against the people of the United States but against all humanity.'

His speech came after a day when the first cases of the illness were reported in neighboring states, just hours after Hughes ordered Colorado's borders closed and placed the nation's military on high alert. All domestic and international air travel was also grounded by presidential order, leaving the nation's transportation hubs in turmoil, as thousands of stranded travelers sought other means to get home.

Seeking both to reassure the country and counter growing criticism that his administration has been slow to act on the crisis, Hughes told the nation to prepare for a formidable struggle.

'I ask you tonight for your trust, your resolve, and your prayers,' the president told the country. 'We will leave no stone unturned. Justice will be swift.'

The president did not specify which groups or nations were the targets of federal scrutiny. He also declined to elaborate on the nature of any evidence the administration had uncovered to indicate the epidemic is the work of terrorists.

Presidential spokesman Tim Romer, when asked about a possible military response, told reporters, 'We're ruling nothing out at this point.'

Reports from local officials inside the state indicate that as many as fifty thousand people may have died already. It is unclear how many of the victims succumbed to the disease itself and how many were slain by violent attacks at the hands of those infected. Early signs of exposure include dizziness, vomiting, and a high fever. After a brief incubation period – as short as six hours – the illness appears, in some cases, to bring about a marked increase in physical strength and aggressiveness.

'Patients are going crazy and killing everybody,' said one Colorado health official, who asked to remain anonymous. 'The hospitals are like war zones.'

Shannon Freeman, spokesman for the Centers for Disease Control in Atlanta, downplayed these reports as 'hysteria' but conceded that communication with officials inside the quarantine zone had broken down.

'What we know is that this illness has a very high fatality rate, as high as fifty percent,' said Freeman. 'Other than that, we can't really tell what's going on in there. The best thing anyone can do for the moment is stay indoors.'

Freeman confirmed reports of outbreaks in Nebraska, Utah, and Wyoming, but declined to elaborate.

'That appears to be happening,' she said, adding, 'Anyone who thinks they have been exposed should report to the nearest law enforcement official or hospital emergency room. That's what we're telling people at this point.'

The cities of Denver, Colorado Springs, and Fort Collins, placed under martial law on Tuesday, were all but empty tonight, as residents ignored Colorado Governor Fritz Millay's orders to 'evacuate in place' and fled the cities in droves. Rumors that Homeland Security forces had been ordered to use deadly force to turn back refugees from the border were widespread but unconfirmed, as were reports that units of the Colorado National Guard had begun to evacuate the ill from hospitals and move them to an undisclosed location.

There was more; Wolgast read and read again. They were rounding up the sick and shooting them – that much seemed clear, if between the lines. May 18, Wolgast thought. The paper was three – no, four – days old. He and Amy had arrived at the camp on the morning of May 2.

Everything in the paper: it had happened in just eighteen days.

He heard movement in the store behind him – just enough to tell him he was being watched. Tucking the paper under his arm, Wolgast turned and stepped through the screen door. A small space, smelling of dust and age, crammed to

288

the rafters with every kind of merchandise: camping supplies, clothing, tools, canned goods. A large buck's head was suspended over a doorway, guarded by a beaded curtain, that led to the rear. Wolgast recalled when he'd come down here with his friends to buy candy and comic books. Back then, a spinning wire rack had stood by the front door: *Tales from the Crypt*, *Fantastic Four*, the *Dark Knight* series, Wolgast's favorite.

On a stool behind the counter sat a large man, bald, in a checked flannel shirt, his jeans held up on his wide waist by a pair of red suspenders. On his hip he wore, in a tight leather holster, a .38 revolver. They exchanged wary nods.

'Paper's two bucks,' the man said.

Wolgast took a pair of bills from his pocket and put them on the counter. 'Got anything newer than this?'

'That's the last I've seen,' the man said, tucking the bills into the register. 'Guy who delivers hasn't shown up since Tuesday.'

Which meant today was Friday. Not that it mattered.

'I need some supplies,' Wolgast said. 'Ammunition.'

The man looked him over, his heavy gray eyebrows furrowed appraisingly. 'What you got?'

'Springfield. A .45,' Wolgast said.

The man drummed his fingers on the counter. 'Well, let's have a look. I know you got it on you.'

Wolgast withdrew the gun from its place against his spine. It was the one Lacey had left on the floor of the Lexus. The clip was empty; whether she'd been the person to fire it or somebody else, Wolgast didn't know. Maybe she had said something, but he couldn't remember. In all the chaos it had been hard to tell what was what. In any event, the gun was familiar to him; Springfields were standard Bureau issue. He freed the clip and locked the slide to show the man it was empty and placed it on the counter.

The man took the weapon in his big hand and examined it. Wolgast could tell, from the way he turned it around, letting its finish hold the light, that he knew guns.

'Tungsten frame, beveled ejection port, titanium pin with the short trigger reset. Pretty fancy.' He looked at Wolgast expectantly. 'I didn't know better, I'd say you were a fed.'

Wolgast did his best to look innocent. 'You could say I used to be. In a former life.'

His man's face took up a sad smirk. He placed the gun on the counter. 'A former life,' he said with a dispirited shake of his head. 'Guess we've all got one of those. Let me take a look.'

He passed through the curtain into the back, returning a moment later with a small cardboard box.

'This is all I have in a .45 ACP. Keep some around for a fellow retired from the ATF, likes to take a twelve-pack up into the woods and shoot the cans as he empties them. Calls it his recycling day. But I haven't seen him in a while. You're the first person to come in here in most of a week. You might as well have them as anyone.' He placed the box on the counter: fifty rounds, hollow points. He tipped his head toward the counter. 'Go on, they're no good in the box. You go right ahead and load it if you want.'

Wolgast freed the clip and began thumbing rounds into place.

'Anyplace else I can get more?'

'Not unless you want to go down into Whiteriver.' The man tapped his breastbone, twice, with his index finger. 'They're saying you got to hit them right here. One shot. They go down like a hammer if you do it right. Otherwise, that's it, you're history.' He stated this fact flatly, without satisfaction or fear; he might have been telling Wolgast what the weather was. 'Doesn't matter if it used to be your sweet old grandma. She'll drink you dry before you can aim twice.'

Wolgast finished loading the clip, pulled the slide to chamber a round, and checked the safety. 'Where'd you hear that?'

'Internet. It's all over.' He shrugged. 'Conspiracy theories, government cover-ups. Vampire stuff. Most of it sounds half crazy. Hard to tell what's bullshit and what ain't.'

Wolgast returned his weapon to the hollow of his spine. He considered asking the man if he could use his computer, to see the news for himself. But he already knew more than enough. It was entirely possible, he realized, that he knew more than any person alive. He'd seen Carter and the others, what they could do.

'I'll tell you one thing. There's a guy, calls himself "Last Stand in Denver." Posting a video blog from a high-rise downtown. Says he's barricaded in there with a high-powered rifle. Got some good footage, you should see these bastards move.' The man tapped his breastbone again. 'Just remember what I told you. One shot. You don't get two. They move at night, in the trees.'

The man helped Wolgast gather up supplies and carry them to the car: canned goods, powdered milk and coffee, batteries, toilet paper, candles, fuel. A pair of fishing rods and a box of tackle. The sun was high and bright; around them, the air seemed frozen with an immense stillness, like the silence just before an orchestra began to play.

At the back of the car, the two shook hands. 'You're up at Bear Mountain, aren't you?' the man said. 'You don't mind my asking.'

There seemed no reason to hide it. 'How did you know?'

'The way you came.' The man shrugged. 'There's nothing else up there except for the camp. Don't know why they never could sell it.'

'I went there as a kid. Funny, it hasn't changed at all. I guess that's the point of places like that.'

'Well, you're smart. It's a good spot. Don't worry, I won't tell anyone.'

'You should bug out, too,' Wolgast said. 'Head higher into the mountains. Or go north.'

Wolgast could read it in the man's eyes; he was making a decision.

'Come on,' he said finally. 'I'll show you something.'

He led Wolgast back into the store and passed through the beaded curtain. Behind it lay the store's small living area. The air was stale and close, the shades drawn tight. An air conditioner hummed in the window. Wolgast paused in the doorway, letting his eyes adjust. In the center of the room was a large hospital bed on which a woman lay sleeping. The head of the bed was elevated at a forty-five-degree angle, showing her drawn face, which was tipped to the side, toward the light that pulsed in the shaded windows. Her body was covered with a blanket, but Wolgast could see how thin she was. On a small table were dozens of pill bottles, gauze and ointment, a chrome basin, syringes sealed in plastic; an oxygen tank, pale green, was parked beside the bed. A corner of the blanket had been drawn aside, exposing her naked feet. Cotton balls were tucked between her yellowed toes. A chair had been pulled up to the foot of the bed, and on it Wolgast saw a nail file and bottles of colored polish.

'She always liked to have pretty feet,' the man said quietly. 'I was doing them for her when you came in.'

They retreated from the room. Wolgast didn't know what to say. The situation was obvious; the man and his wife weren't going anywhere. The two of them stepped back into the bright sunlight of the parking area.

'She has MS,' the man explained. 'I was hoping to keep her at home as long as I could. That's what we agreed, when she started to get bad last winter. They're supposed to send a nurse, but we haven't seen one in a while now.' He shifted his feet on the gravel and wetly cleared his throat. 'My guess is, nobody's making any more house calls.'

Wolgast told him his name. The man was Carl; his wife was Martha. They had two grown sons, one in California, the other in Florida. Carl had been an electrician at Oregon State down in Corvallis, until they'd bought the store and retired up here.

'What can I do?' Wolgast asked.

They'd shaken hands before but did so again. 'Just keep yourself alive,' Carl said.

Wolgast was driving back to the camp when, suddenly, he

thought of Lila. They were memories of another time, another life. A life that was over now – over for him, over for everyone. Thinking about Lila, as he had: he was saying goodbye.

SIXTEEN

It was August, the days long and dry, when the fires came.

Wolgast smelled smoke one afternoon as he was working in the yard; by morning the air was thickened with an acrid haze. He climbed to the roof to look but saw only the trees and the lake, the mountains rolling away. He had no way of knowing how close the fires were. The wind could blow the smoke, he knew, for hundreds of miles.

He hadn't been off the mountain in over two months, not since his trip down to Milton's. They'd found a routine: Wolgast slept each day till nearly noon, worked outside till dusk; then, after dinner and a swim, the two of them stayed up half the night, reading or playing board games, like passengers on a long sea voyage. He'd found a box of games stored in one of the cabins: Monopoly, Parcheesi, checkers. For a while he let Amy win, but then found he didn't need to; she was a shrewd player, especially at Monopoly, buying up property after property and swiftly calculating the rents they'd bring in and counting her money with glee. Boardwalk, Park Place, Marvin Gardens. What did the names of these places mean to her? One night he'd settled in to read to her – *20,000 Leagues Under the Sea*, which they'd read before but she wanted to hear again – when she took the book from his hand and, in the flickering candlelight, started to read aloud to him. She didn't so much as pause over the book's difficult words, its contorted, old-fashioned syntax. When did you learn to do that? he asked her, utterly incredulous, as she paused to turn the page. Well, she explained, we read it before. I guess I just remembered.

The world off the mountain had become a memory, remoter by the day. He'd never managed to get the generator working – he'd hoped to use the shortwave – and had long since stopped trying. If what was happening was what he thought was happening, he reasoned, they were better off not knowing. What could he have done with the information? Where else could they go?

But now the woods were burning, driving a wall of choking smoke from the west. By the afternoon of the next day it was clear they had to leave; the fire was headed their way. If it jumped the river, there'd be nothing else to stop it. Wolgast loaded the Toyota and placed Amy, wrapped in a blanket, in the passenger seat. He had a soaked cloth for each of them, to hold over their mouths, their stinging eyes.

They didn't get two miles before they saw the flames. The road was blocked with smoke, the air unbreathable, a toxic wall. A hard wind was blowing, driving the fire up the mountain toward them. They would have to turn back.

He didn't know how long they would have until the fires arrived. He had no way to wet the roof of the lodge – they would simply have to wait it out. The sealed windows at least offered some protection from the smoke, but by nightfall they were both coughing and sputtering.

In one of the outbuildings was an old aluminum canoe. Wolgast dragged it to the shore, then fetched Amy from upstairs. He paddled to the middle of the lake while he watched the fires burning up the mountain toward the camp, a sight of furious beauty, as if the gates of hell had opened. Amy lay against him in the bottom of the canoe; if she was afraid, she showed no sign. There was nothing else to do. All the energy of the day left him and, despite himself, he fell asleep.

When he awoke in the morning, the camp was still standing. The fires hadn't jumped the river after all. The wind had shifted sometime in the night, pushing the flames to the south. The air was still heavy with smoke, but he could tell the danger had passed. Later that afternoon, they heard a great boom of thunder, like a huge sheet of tin shaking over their heads, and rain poured down, all through the night. He couldn't believe their luck.

In the morning he decided to use the last of his gasoline to drive down the mountain to check on Carl and Martha. He would bring Amy this time – after the fires, he intended never to let her out of his sight again. He waited until dusk and set out.

The fires had come close. Less than a mile away from the camp's entrance the forest had been reduced to smoking ruins, the ground scorched and denuded, like the aftermath of a terrible battle. From the roadway Wolgast could see the bodies of animals, not just small creatures like possums and raccoons but deer and antelope and even a bear, folded onto himself at the base of a blackened tree trunk as he'd searched the ground for a pocket of breathable air and perished.

The store was still standing, undisturbed. No lights were on, but of course the power would be out. Wolgast told Amy to wait in the car, retrieved a flashlight, and stepped onto the porch. The door was locked. He knocked, loudly, again and again, calling Carl's name, but received no reply. Finally he used the flashlight to break the window.

Carl and Martha were dead. They were spooned together in Martha's hospital bed, Carl curled against her back with one arm draped over her shoulder, as if they were napping. It could have been the smoke, but the air in the room told Wolgast they'd been dead much longer than that. On the nightstand was a half-empty bottle of Scotch and, beside it, a folded newspaper, like the first one he'd seen, disquietingly thin, with a huge, shouting headline he averted his eyes from, choosing instead to put it in his pocket to read later. He stood a moment at the foot of the bed where the bodies lay. Then he closed up the room and, for the first time, he wept.

Carl's van was still parked behind the store. Wolgast cut a

length of garden hose and drew the Toyota around to the rear, to siphon the contents of the van's tank into his car. He didn't know where they might need to go, but the fire season wasn't over. It had been a mistake, nearly fatal, to let himself be caught off guard. He'd found an empty gas can in a shed behind the house, and when the Toyota's tank was topped off, he filled this as well. Then Amy helped him go through the store to gather supplies. He took all the food and batteries and propane he thought he could fit, put it all in boxes and carried it to the car. Then he returned to the room where the bodies lay and, carefully, holding his breath, removed Carl's .38 from the holster on his waist.

In the early hours of the morning, when Amy was finally asleep, Wolgast took the paper from the pocket of his jacket. Just a single sheet this time, dated July 10 – almost a month ago. Who knew where Carl had gotten it. Probably he'd driven down into Whiteriver, and then, when he returned, and because of what he'd read and seen, put an end to things. The house was full of medicine; it would have been easy enough for him to accomplish this task. Wolgast had put the paper in his pocket out of fear, but also a fatalistic certainty about what he would find written there. Only the details would be new to him.

CHICAGO FALLS
'Vampire' Virus Reaches East Coast; Millions Dead
Quarantine Line Moves East to Central Ohio
California Secedes from Union, Vows to Defend Itself
India Rattles Missile Might, Threatens 'Limited' Nuclear Strike Against Pakistan

WASHINGTON, July 10 – President Hughes ordered US military forces to abandon the Chicago perimeter today, after a night of heavy losses when Army and National Guard units were overwhelmed by a large force of Infected Persons moving into the city.

'A great American city has been lost,' Mr Hughes said in a printed statement. 'Our prayers are with the people of Chicago and the fighting men and women who gave their lives to defend them. Their memory will sustain us in this great struggle.'

The attack came just after nightfall, when US forces positioned along the South Loop reported a force of unknown size amassing outside the city's central business district.

'This assault was clearly organized,' said General Carson White, commander of the Central Quarantine Zone, who called this 'a disturbing development.'

'A new defensive perimeter has been established on Route 75, from Toledo to Cincinnati,' White told reporters early Tuesday morning. 'That's our new Rubicon.'

When questioned about reports that large numbers of troops were abandoning their posts, White replied that he had 'heard nothing of the kind' and called such rumors 'irresponsible.'

'These are the bravest men and women I've ever had the honor to serve with,' the general said.

New outbreaks of the illness were reported in cities from Tallahassee, FL, and Charleston, SC, to Helena, MT, and Flagstaff, AZ, as well as southern Ontario and northern Mexico. Casualty estimates provided by the White House and the Centers for Disease Control now top 30 million. The Pentagon placed the number of Infected Persons at another 3 million.

Large portions of St. Louis, abandoned on Sunday, were burning tonight, as were portions of Memphis, Tulsa, and Des Moines. Observers on the ground reported seeing low-flying aircraft over the city's famous arch moments before the fires broke out and quickly engulfed the downtown area. No one in the administration has confirmed rumors that the fires are part of a federal effort to disinfect the major cities of the Central Quarantine Zone.

Gasoline was scarce or nonexistent virtually everywhere

in the country, as transportation corridors continued to be choked by people fleeing the spread of the epidemic. Food was also hard to come by, as were medical supplies from bandages to antibiotics.

Many of the nation's stranded refugees found themselves with no place to go and no way to get there.

'We're stuck, just like everybody else,' said David Callahan, outside a McDonald's east of Pittsburgh. Callahan had driven with his family, a wife and two young children, from Akron, OH – a journey that ordinarily would have taken just two hours but that night had taken twenty. Nearly out of gas, Callahan had pulled off at a comfort station in suburban Monroeville, only to find that the pumps were dry and the restaurant had run out of food two days ago.

'We were going to my mother's in Johnstown, but now I heard it's there too,' Callahan said, as an Army convoy, fifty vehicles long, passed on the empty westbound side of the roadway.

'No one knows where to go,' he said. 'These things are everywhere.'

Though the illness has yet to appear beyond the US, Canada, and Mexico, nations around the world appeared to be preparing themselves for this eventuality. In Europe, Italy, France, and Spain have closed their borders, while other nations have stockpiled medical supplies or banned intercity travel. The UN General Assembly, meeting for the first time at The Hague since vacating its New York headquarters early last week, passed a resolution of international quarantine, forbidding any shipping or aircraft from approaching within 200 miles of the North American continent.

Across the US, churches and synagogues reported record attendance, as millions of the faithful gathered in prayer. In Texas, where the virus is now widespread, Houston Mayor Barry Wooten, the bestselling author and former head of Holy Splendor Bible Church, the nation's largest, declared the city 'a Gateway to Heaven' and urged residents and refugees from elsewhere in the state to gather at Houston's Reliant Stadium to prepare for 'our ascension to the throne of the Lord, not as monsters but as men and women of God.'

In California, where the infection has yet to appear, the state legislature met in an emergency session last night and quickly passed the First California Articles of Secession, severing the state's ties to the United States and declaring it a sovereign nation. In her first action as president of the Republic of California, former governor Cindy Shaw ordered all US military and law enforcement assets within the state placed under the command of the California National Guard.

'We will defend ourselves, as any nation has the right to do,' Shaw told the legislature, to thundering applause. 'California, and all that it stands for, will endure.'

Reacting to the news from Sacramento, Hughes administration spokesman Tim Romer told reporters, 'This is absurd on its face. Now is obviously not the time for any state or local government to take the safety of the American people into its own hands. Our position remains that California is part of the United States.'

Romer also cautioned that any military or law enforcement personnel in California who interfered with federal relief efforts would face harsh sanctions.

'Make no mistake,' Romer said. 'They will be regarded as unlawful enemy combatants.'

By Wednesday, California had been recognized by the governments of Switzerland, Finland, the tiny South Pacific Republic of Palau, and the Vatican.

The government of India, apparently in response to the departure of US military forces from South Asia, yesterday repeated its earlier threats to use nuclear weapons against rebel forces in eastern Pakistan.

'Now is the time to contain the spread of Islamic extremism,' Indian Prime Minister Suresh Mitra told Parliament. 'The watchdog is sleeping.'

So there it was, Wolgast thought. There it was at last. There was a term he knew and thought of now; he had heard it used only in the context of aviation, to explain how, on an otherwise clear day, a plane could fall so quickly from the sky. OBE. Overcome by events. That was what was happening now. The world – the human race – had been overcome by events.

Take care of Amy, Lacey had said. *Amy is yours.* He thought of Doyle, placing the keys to the Lexus in his hand, Lacey's kiss on his cheek; Doyle running after them, waving them on, yelling, 'Go, go'; Lacey leaping from the car, to call the stars – for that's how Wolgast thought of them, as human stars, burning with a lethal brightness – down upon her.

The time for sleeping, for rest, was over. Wolgast would stay awake all night, watching the door with Carl's .38 in one hand and the Springfield in the other. It was a cool night, the temperature down in the fifties, and Wolgast had set the woodstove going when they'd returned from the store. He took the paper now and folded it into quarters, into eighths, and finally sixteenths, and opened the door to the woodstove. Then he placed the paper in the fire, watching with amazement at how quickly it disappeared.

SEVENTEEN

Summer ended, and fall came, and the world left them alone.

The first snows fell in the last week of October. Wolgast was chopping wood in the yard when he saw, from the corner of his eye, the first flakes falling, fat feathers light as dust. He'd stripped to his shirtsleeves to work, and when he paused to lift his face and felt the cold on his damp skin, he realized what was happening, that winter had arrived.

He sunk his axe into a log and returned to the house and called up the stairs. 'Amy!'

She appeared on the top step. Her skin saw so little sunlight that it was a rich, porcelain white.

'Have you ever seen snow?'

'I don't know. I think so?'

'Well, it's snowing now.' He laughed, and heard the pleasure in his voice. 'You don't want to miss it. Come on.'

By the time he got her dressed – in her coat and boots but also the glasses and cap, and a thick layer of sunscreen over every exposed inch of her skin – the snow had begun to fall in earnest. She stepped out into the whirling whiteness, her movements solemn, like an explorer setting foot on some new planet.

'What do you think?'

She tipped her face and stuck out her tongue, an instinctive gesture, to catch and taste the snow.

'I like it,' she declared.

They had shelter, food, heat. He'd made two more trips down to Milton's in the autumn, knowing that once winter came the road would be impassable, and had taken all the food that was left there. Rationing the canned goods, the powdered milk, the rice and dried beans, Wolgast believed he could make their stores last until spring. The lake was full of fish, and in one of the cabins he'd found an auger. A simple enough matter, then, to set up fishing lines. The propane tank was still half full. So, the winter. He welcomed it, felt his mind relax into its rhythm. No one had come after all; the world had forgotten them. They would be sealed away together, in safety.

By morning a foot of snow had piled around the cabin. The sun burst through the clouds, glaringly bright. Wolgast spent the afternoon digging out the woodpile, cutting a trail to connect it to the lodge, and then a second trail to the small cabin he planned to use as an icehouse, now that the cold weather had arrived. By now he was living an existence that was almost entirely nocturnal – it was easiest simply to adopt Amy's schedule – and the sunlight on the snow seemed blinding to him, like an explosion he was forced to stare directly into. Probably, he thought, that was how even ordinary light felt to her, all the time. When darkness fell, the two of them went back outside.

'I'll show you how to make snow angels,' he said. He lay down on his back. Above him, a sky effulgent with stars. From Milton's he'd recovered a jar of powdered cocoa, which he hadn't told Amy about, planning to save it for a special occasion. Tonight they'd dry their wet clothes on the wood-stove and sit in its glow and drink hot cocoa. 'Move your arms and legs,' he told her, 'like this.'

She got down in the snow beside him. Her tiny body was as light and agile as a gymnast's. She moved her nimble limbs back and forth.

'What's an angel?'

Wolgast thought a moment. In all their conversations, nothing of the sort had ever come up. 'Well, it's a kind of ghost, I guess.'

'A ghost. Like Jacob Marley.' They had read *A Christmas Carol* – or, rather, Amy had read it to him. Since that night in summer when he'd learned she could read – not just read but read expertly, with feeling and expression – Wolgast had merely sat and listened.

'I guess, yes. But not as scary as Jacob Marley.' They were still lying side by side in the snow. 'Angels are . . . well, I guess they're like good ghosts. Ghosts who watch over us, from heaven. Or at least some people think so.'

'Do you?'

Wolgast was taken aback. He'd never gotten completely accustomed to Amy's directness. Her lack of inhibition struck him on the one hand as quite childlike, but it was often true that the things she said and the questions she asked him possessed a bluntness that felt somehow wise.

'I don't know. My mother did. She was very religious, very devout. My father, probably not. He was a good man, but he was an engineer. He didn't think that way.'

For a moment, they were silent.

'She's dead,' Amy said quietly. 'I know that.'

Wolgast sat upright. Amy's eyes were closed.

'Who's dead, Amy?' But as soon as he asked this, he knew whom Amy meant: *My mother. My mother is dead.*

'I don't remember her,' Amy said. Her voice was impassive, as if she were telling him something he must surely know already. 'But I know she's dead.'

'How do you know?'

'I could feel it.' Amy's eyes met Wolgast's in the dark. 'I feel all of them.'

Sometimes, in the early hours just before dawn, Amy dreamed; Wolgast could hear her soft cries coming from the next room, the squeak of the springs of her cot as she moved restlessly about. Not cries exactly but murmurs, like voices working through her in sleep. Sometimes she would rise and go downstairs to the main room of the lodge, the one with the wide windows that looked out over the lake; Wolgast would watch her from the stairs. Always she would stand quietly for just a few moments in the glowing light and warmth of the woodstove, her face turned toward the windows. She was obviously still asleep, and Wolgast knew better than to wake her. Then she would turn and climb the stairs and get back into bed.

How do you feel them, Amy? he asked her. *What do you feel?* – I don't know, she'd say, I don't know. They're sad. They're so many. They've forgotten who they were. *Who were they, Amy?* And she said: Everyone. They're everyone.

Wolgast slept, now, on the first floor of the lodge, in a chair facing the door. They move at night, Carl had told him, in the trees. You get one shot. What were they, these things in the trees? Were they people, as Carter had once been a person? What had they become? And Amy. Amy, who dreamed of voices, whose hair did not grow, who seemed rarely to sleep – for it was true, he'd realized she was only pretending – or to eat; who could read and swim as if she were remembering lives and experiences other than her own: was she part of them, too? The virus was inert, Fortes had

303

said. What if it wasn't? Wouldn't he, Wolgast, be sick? But he wasn't; he felt just as he'd always felt, which was, he realized, simply bewildered, like a man in a dream, lost in a landscape of meaningless signs; the world had some use for him he didn't understand.

Then on a night in March he heard an engine. The snow was heavy and deep. The moon was full. He had fallen asleep in the chair. He realized he'd been hearing, as he'd slept, the sound of an engine coming down the long drive toward the lodge. In his dream – a nightmare – this sound had become the roar of the fires of summer, burning up the mountain toward them; he had been running with Amy through the woods, the smoke and fire all around, and lost her.

A blaze of light in the windows, and footsteps on the porch – heavy, stumbling. Wolgast rose quickly, all his senses instantly alert. The Springfield was in his hand. He racked the slide and released the safety. The door shook with three hard pounds.

'Somebody's outside.' The voice was Amy's. Wolgast turned and saw her standing at the bottom of the stairs.

'Upstairs!' Wolgast spoke to her in a harsh whisper. 'Go, quickly!'

'Is anybody inside there?' A man's voice on the porch. 'I can see the smoke! I'll step away!'

'Amy, upstairs, *now*!'

More pounding on the door. 'For godsakes, somebody, if you can hear me, open the door!'

Amy retreated up the stairs. Wolgast moved to the window and looked out. Not a car or truck but a snowmobile, with containers lashed to its chassis. In the headlights, at the foot of the porch, was a man in a parka and boots. He was positioned in a crouch, his hands on his knees.

Wolgast opened the door. 'Keep back,' he warned. 'Let me see your hands.'

The man lifted his arms weakly. 'I'm not armed,' he said. He was panting, and that was when Wolgast saw the blood, a bright ribbon down the side of his parka. The wound was in his neck.

'I'm sick,' the man said.

Wolgast stepped forward and raised his gun. 'Get out of here!'

The man sank to his knees. 'Jesus,' he moaned. 'Jesus Christ.' Then he tipped his face forward and retched onto the snow.

Wolgast turned to see Amy, standing in the doorway.

'Amy, go inside!'

'That's right honey,' the man said, lifting a bloody hand to give a listless wave. He wiped his mouth with the back of his hand. 'Do what your daddy says.'

'Amy, I said inside, *now*.'

Amy closed the door.

'That's good,' the man said. He was on his knees, facing Wolgast. 'She shouldn't see this. Jesus, I feel like shit.'

'How did you find us?'

The man shook his head and spat onto the snow. 'I didn't come looking for you, if that's what you mean. Six of us were holed up about forty miles west of here. A friend's hunting camp. We'd been there since October, after they took out Seattle.'

'Who's they?' Wolgast asked. 'What happened to Seattle?'

The man shrugged. 'Same thing as everywhere else. Everybody's sick, dying, ripping each other to shreds, the Army shows up, then poof, the place goes up in smoke. Some people say it's the UN or the Russians. It could be the man in the moon, for all I know. We headed south, into the mountains, thought we'd ride out the winter and then try to make it into California. Then those fuckers came. None of us even got a shot off. I hauled ass out of there, but one of them bit me. Bitch just swooped down out of nowhere. I don't know why she didn't kill me like the rest, but they say they do that.' He smiled weakly. 'I guess it was my lucky day.'

'Were you followed?'

'Fuck if I know. I smelled your smoke at least a mile from

here. Don't know how I did that. Like bacon in a pan.' He lifted his face with a look of abject wretchedness. 'For god-sakes, I'm begging you. I'd do it myself if I had a gun.'

It took Wolgast a moment to understand what the man was asking. 'What's your name?' Wolgast asked.

'Bob.' The man licked his lips with a dry, heavy tongue. 'Bob Saunders.'

Wolgast gestured with the Springfield. 'We have to move away from the house.'

They walked into the woods, Wolgast following at five paces. The man's progress was slow in the deep snow. Every few steps he paused to brace himself with his hands on his knees, breathing hard.

'You know what's funny?' he said. 'I used to be an actuarial analyst. Life and casualty. You smoke, you drive without a seat belt, you eat Big Macs for lunch every day, I could tell you when you were going to die pretty much to the month.' He was clutching a tree for balance. 'I guess nobody ever ran the tables on this, did they?'

Wolgast said nothing.

'You're going to do this thing, aren't you?' Bob said. He was looking away, into the trees.

'Yes,' Wolgast said. 'I'm sorry.'

'That's all right. Don't beat yourself up about it.' He breathed heavily, licking his lips. He turned and touched his chest as Carl had done, all those months ago, to show Wolgast where to shoot. 'Right through here, okay? You can shoot me through the head first, if you want, but make sure you put one in here.'

Wolgast could only nod, caught short by the man's frank-ness, his matter-of-fact tone.

'You can tell your daughter I drew on you,' he added. 'She shouldn't know about this. And burn the body when you're done. Gasoline, kerosene, something hot like that.'

They were approaching the bank above the river. In the moonlight, the scene possessed an unearthly stillness, bathed in blue. Wolgast could hear, beneath the snow and ice, the river's quiet gurgle. As good a place as any, Wolgast thought.

'Turn around,' he said. 'Face me.'

But the man, Bob, seemed not to have heard him. He took two more steps forward in the snow and stopped. He had begun, unaccountably, to undress, removing his bloody parka and dropping it into the snow, then unfolding the suspenders of his bibbed snowpants to pull his sweatshirt over his head.

'I said, turn around.'

'You know what sucks?' Bob said. He had removed his thermal undershirt and was kneeling to unlace his boots. 'How old's your daughter? I always wanted to have kids. Why didn't I do that?'

'I don't know, Bob.' Wolgast raised the Springfield. 'Get up and face me, now.'

Bob rose. Something was happening. He was fingering the bloody tear on his neck. Another spasm shook him, but the expression on his face was pleasurable, almost sexual. In the moonlight, his skin seemed almost to glow. He arched his back like a cat, his eyes heavy-lidded with pleasure.

'Whoa, that's good,' Bob said. 'That's really . . . something.'

'I'm sorry,' Wolgast said.

'Hey, wait!' With a start, Bob opened his eyes; he held out his hands. 'Hang on a second here!'

'I'm sorry, Bob,' Wolgast repeated, and then he squeezed the trigger.

The winter ended in rain. For days and days the rain poured down, filling the woods, swelling the river and lake, washing away what remained of the road.

He'd burned the body just as Bob had instructed, dousing it with gasoline and, when the flames died out, soaking the ashes with laundry bleach and burying it all beneath a mound of rocks and earth. The next morning he searched the snowmobile. The containers strapped to the frame turned out to be gas cans, all empty, but in a leather pouch slung from the handlebars he found Bob's wallet. A driver's license with Bob's picture and a Spokane address, the usual credit cards, a few dollars in cash, a library card. There was also a photograph, shot in a studio: Bob in a holiday sweater, posed with a pretty blond woman who was obviously pregnant and two children, a little girl in tights and a green velvet dress and an infant in pajamas. All of them were smiling fiercely, even the baby. On the back of the photograph was written, in a feminine hand, 'Timothy's first Christmas.' Why had Bob said he'd never had children? Had he been forced to watch them die, an experience so painful that his mind had simply erased them from his memory? Wolgast buried the wallet on the hillside, marking the spot with a cross he fashioned from a pair of sticks bound together with twine. It didn't seem like much, but it was all he could think to do.

Wolgast waited for others to come; he assumed Bob was just the first. He left the lodge only to perform the most necessary chores, and only in the daytime; he kept the Springfield with him at all times and left Carl's .38, loaded, in the glove compartment of the Toyota. Every few days he turned the engine over and let it run, to keep the battery charged. Bob had said something about California. Was it still safe there? Was any place safe? He wanted to ask Amy: *Do you hear them coming? Do they know where we are?* He had no map to show her where California was. Instead he took her up to the roof of the lodge one evening, just after sunset. See that ridge? he said, pointing to the south. Follow my hand, Amy. The Cascades. If anything happens to me, he said, follow that ridge. Run and keep on running.

But the months passed, and still they were alone. The rains ended, and Wolgast stepped from the lodge one morning to the taste and smell of sunshine and the feeling that something had changed. Birdsong swelled the trees; he looked toward the lake and saw open water where before had been a solid disk of ice. A sweet green haze dressed the air, and at the base of the lodge, a line of crocuses was pushing from the dirt. The world could be blowing itself apart, yet here was the gift of spring, spring in the mountains. From every direction came the sounds and smells of life. Wolgast didn't even know what month it was. Was it April or May? But he had no calendar, and the battery in his watch, unworn since autumn, had long since died.

That night, sitting in his chair by the door with the Springfield in his hand, he dreamed of Lila. Part of him knew this was a dream about sex, about making love, and yet it did not seem so. Lila was pregnant, and the two of them were playing Monopoly. The dream had no particular setting – the area beyond the place where the two of them sat was veiled in darkness, like the hidden regions of a stage. Wolgast was gripped by the irrational fear that what they were doing would hurt the baby. 'We have to stop,' he told her urgently. 'This is dangerous.' But she seemed not to hear him. He rolled the dice and moved his piece to find he had landed on the square with the image of the policeman blowing his whistle. 'Go to jail, Brad,' Lila said, and laughed. 'Go directly to jail.' Then she stood and began taking off her clothes. 'It's all right,' she said, 'you can kiss me if you want. Bob won't mind.' 'Why won't he mind?' Brad asked. 'Because he's dead,' Lila said. 'We're all dead.'

He awoke with a start, sensing he wasn't alone. He turned in his chair and saw Amy, standing with her back toward him, facing the wide windows that looked toward the lake. In the glow of the woodstove, he watched as she lifted a hand and touched the glass. He rose.

'Amy? What is it?'

He was stepping forward when a blinding light, immense and pure, filled the glass, and in that instant Wolgast's mind seemed to freeze time: like a camera shutter his brain caught and held a picture of Amy, her hands lifting against the light, her mouth open wide to release its cry of terror. A rush of wind shook the cabin, and then, with a concussive thump, the windows burst inward and Wolgast felt himself lifted off the floor and hurled back across the room.

One second later, or five, or ten: time reassembled itself. Wolgast found himself on his hands and knees, pushed against the far wall. Glass was everywhere, a thousand pieces of it on the floor, their edges twinkling like shattered stars in the alien light that bathed the room. Outside, a bulbous glow was swelling the horizon to the west.

'Amy!'

He went to where she lay on the floor.

'Are you burned? Are you cut?'

'I can't see, I can't see!' She was thrashing violently, waving her arms in formless panic before her face. There were pieces of glass glimmering all over her, affixed to the skin of her face and arms. And blood, too, soaking her T-shirt as he leaned over her and tried to calm her.

'Please, Amy, hold still! Let me look to see if you're hurt.'

She relaxed in his arms. Gently he brushed the bits of glass away. There were no cuts anywhere. The blood, he realized, was his own. Where was it coming from? He looked down then to find a long shard, curved like a scimitar, buried in his left leg, halfway between his knee and groin. He pulled; the glass exited cleanly, without pain. Three inches of glass in his leg. Why hadn't he felt it? The adrenaline? But as soon as he thought this, the pain arrived, a late train roaring into the station. Motes of light dappled his vision; a wave of nausea surged through him.

'I can't see, Brad! Where are you!'

'I'm here, I'm here.' His head was afloat in agony. Could you bleed to death from a cut like that? 'Try to open your eyes.'

'I can't! It hurts!'

Flash burns, he thought. Flash burns on the retina, from looking into the heart of the blast. Not Portland or Salem or even Corvallis. The explosion was straight west. A stray nuke, he thought, but whose? And how many more were there? What could it accomplish? The answer, he knew, was nothing; it was just one more violent spasm of the world's excruciating extinguishment. He realized that he'd allowed himself to think, when he'd stepped out into the sun and tasted spring, that the worst was behind them, that they would be all right. How foolish he'd been.

He carried Amy to the kitchen and lit the lamp. The glass in the window over the sink had somehow held. He sat her on a chair, found a dishrag, and quickly tied it around his wounded leg. Amy was crying, pressing her palms to her eyes. The skin of her face and arms, where she'd faced the blast, was a bright pink, already beginning to peel.

'I know it hurts,' he told her, 'but you have to open them for me. I have to see if there's any glass in there.' He had a flashlight on the table, ready to scan her eyes the moment she opened them. An ambush, but what else could he do?

She shook her head, pulling away from him.

'Amy, you have to. I need you to be brave. Please.'

Another minute of struggle, but at last she relented. She let him pull her hands away and opened her eyes, the thinnest crack, before closing them again.

'It's bright!' she cried. 'It hurts!'

He struck a bargain with her: he would count to three; she would open her eyes and keep them open for another count of three.

'One,' he began. 'Two. Three!'

She opened her eyes, every muscle in her face taut with fear. He began to count again, running the flashlight's beam over her face. No glass, no trace of visible injury: her eyes were clear.

'Three!'

She closed her eyes again, shaking and fiercely weeping.

He dressed Amy's skin with burn cream from the first aid kit, wrapped her eyes with a bandage, and carried her upstairs to bed. 'Your eyes are going to be fine,' he assured her, though he didn't know if this was so. 'I think it's just temporary, from looking at the flash.' For a while he sat with her, until her breathing quieted and he knew she was asleep. They should try to get away, he thought, to put some distance between themselves and the blast, but where would

311

they go? First the fires and then the rain, and the road off the mountain had all but washed away. They could try it on foot, but how far could he hope to get, barely able to walk himself, leading a blind girl through the woods? The best he could hope for was that the blast was small, or farther away than he thought it was, or that the wind would push the radiation in the other direction.

In the first aid kit he found a small sewing needle and a ball of black thread. It was just an hour before dawn when he descended the stairs to the kitchen. At the table, by lamplight, he removed the knotted rag and his blood-soaked pants. The cut was deep but remarkably clean, the skin like torn butcher's paper over a blood-red slab of steak. He'd sewed on buttons, once hemmed a pair of his pants. How hard could it be? From the cabinet over the sink he retrieved the bottle of Scotch he'd found at Milton's, all those months ago. He poured himself a glass. He sat and took the Scotch, quickly, tipping his face back to drink without tasting, poured a second, and drank that, too. Then he rose, washed his hands at the kitchen sink, taking his time, and dried them on a rag. He sat once more, wadded the rag, and put it in his mouth; he took the bottle of Scotch in one hand and the threaded needle in the other. He wished he had more light. He drew a long breath and held it. Then he poured Scotch over the cut.

This, it turned out, was the worst part. After that, sewing the wound closed was almost nothing.

He awoke to find he'd slept with his head on the table; the room was ice-cold, and the air held a strange chemical smell, like burning tires. Outside a gray snow was falling. On his bandaged leg, throbbing with pain, Wolgast hobbled from the lodge onto the porch. Not snow, he realized: ashes. He descended the steps. Ashes fell onto his face, into his hair. Strangely, he felt no fear, not for himself or even for Amy. It was a wonder. He tipped his face upward, receiving them. The ashes were full of people, he knew. A raining ash of souls.

*

He could have moved them to the basement, but there seemed no point. The radiation would be everywhere, in the air they breathed, in the food they ate, in the water that ran from the lake to the pump in the kitchen. They kept to the second floor, where at least the boarded-up windows offered some protection. Three days later, the day he removed Amy's bandages – she could see after all, just as he'd promised – Wolgast began to vomit and couldn't stop. He retched long after the only thing left to come up was a thin black mucus, like roofing tar. The leg was infected, or else the radiation had done something to it. Green pus ran from the wound, soaking the bandages. It gave off a foul smell, a smell that was in his mouth too, in his eyes and nose. It seemed to be in every part of him.

'I'll be fine,' he told Amy, who was, after everything that had happened, the same. Her scalded skin had peeled away, exposing, beneath it, a new layer, white as moonlit milk. 'Just a few days off my feet and I'll be right as rain.'

He took to his cot under the eaves in the room next to Amy's. He felt the days passing around him, through him. He was dying, he knew. The fast-dividing cells of his body – the lining of his throat and stomach, his hair, the gums that held his teeth – were being killed off first, because wasn't that what radiation did? And now it had found the core of him, reaching into him like a great, lethal hand, black and bird-boned. He felt himself dissolving, like a pill in water, the process irrevocable. He should have tried to get them off the mountain, but that moment was long past. At the periphery of his consciousness, he was aware of Amy's presence, her movements in the room, her watchful, too-wise eyes upon him. She held cups of water to his broken lips; he did his best to drink, wanting the moisture but wanting, even more, to please her, to offer some assurance that he would become well. But nothing would stay down.

'I'm all right,' she told him, again and again, though perhaps he was dreaming this. Her voice was quiet, close to his ear. She stroked his forehead with a cloth. He felt her soft breath on his face in the darkened room. 'I'm all right.'

She was a child. What would become of her, after he was gone? This girl who barely slept or ate, whose body knew nothing of illness or pain?

No, she wouldn't die. That was the worst of it, the terrible thing they'd done. Time parted around her, like waves around a pier. It moved past her while Amy stayed the same. *And all the days of Noah were nine hundred and fifty years.* However they had done it, Amy would not, could not die.

I'm sorry, he thought. I did my best and it wasn't enough. I was too afraid from the start. If there was a plan, I couldn't see it. Amy, Eva, Lila, Lacey. I was just a man. I'm sorry, I'm sorry, I'm sorry, I'm sorry.

Then one night he awoke and he was alone. He sensed this right away: a feeling in the air around him of departure, of absence and flight. Just lifting the blanket required all the strength he could muster; the feel of its weave in his hand was like sandpaper, like spikes of fire to the touch. He rose to a sitting position, a monumental effort. His body was an immense, dying thing his mind could scarcely contain. And yet it was still his – the same body he'd lived in all the days of his life. How strange it was to die, to feel it leaving him. Yet another part of him had always known. *To die*, his body told him. *To die. That is why we live, to die.*

'Amy,' he said, and heard his voice, the palest croak. A weak and useless sound, without form, speaking a name to no one in a dark room. 'Amy.'

He managed his way down the stairs to the kitchen and lit the lamp. Under its flickering glow, everything appeared just as it had been, though somehow the place seemed changed – the same room where he and Amy had lived together a year, yet someplace completely new. He could not have said what hour it was, what day, what month. Amy was gone.

He stumbled from the lodge, down the porch, into the dark forest. A lidded eye of moon was hanging over the tree line, like a child's toy suspended on a wire, a smiling moon face dangling above a baby's crib. Its light spilled over a landscape of ashes, everything dying, the world's living surface peeled away to reveal the rocky core of all. Like a stage set, Wolgast thought, a stage set for the end of all things, all memories of things. He moved through the broken white dust without direction, calling, calling her name.

He was in the trees now, in the woods, the lodge some nameless distance behind him. He doubted he could find his way back, but this didn't matter. It was over; he was over. Even weeping was beyond his power. In the end, he thought, it came down to choosing a place. If you were lucky, that's what you got to do.

He was above the river, under the moon, among the naked, leafless trees. He sank to his knees and sat with his back against one and closed his weary eyes. Something was moving above him in the branches, but he sensed this only vaguely. A rustling of bodies in the trees. Something someone had told him once, many lifetimes past, about moving in the trees at night. But to recall the meaning of these words required a force of will he no longer possessed; the thought left him, alone.

A new feeling moved through him then, cold and final, like a draft from an open door onto the deepest hour of winter, onto the stilled space between stars. When daybreak found him he would be no more. *Amy*, he thought as the stars began to fall, everywhere and all around; and he tried to fill his mind with just her name, his daughter's name, to help him from his life.

Amy, Amy, Amy.

III

THE
LAST CITY

2 A.V.

Music, when soft voices die,
Vibrates in the memory;
Odors, when sweet violets sicken,
Live within the sense they quicken.

Rose leaves, when the rose is dead,
Are heaped for the beloved's bed;
And so thy thoughts, when thou art gone,
Love itself shall slumber on.

— PERCY BYSSHE SHELLEY,
'Music, When Soft Voices Die'

*************NOTICE OF EVACUATION*************
US Military Forces Command
Eastern Quarantine Zone, Philadelphia, PA

By order of Gen. Travis Cullen, Acting General of
the Army and Supreme Commander of the Eastern
Quarantine Zone, and His Honor George Wilcox,
Mayor of the City of Philadelphia:

All minor children between four (4) and thirteen (13) years
of age and residing in the uninfected areas MARKED IN
GREEN ('Safe Zones') within the City of Philadelphia and
the three counties west of the Delaware River (Montgomery, Delaware, Bucks) are ordered to report to AMTRAK
30th STREET STATION for immediate embarkation.

Each child **MUST** bring:

- A birth certificate, Social Security card, or valid United
  States passport.
- Proof of residency, such as a utility bill in the name of
  parent or legal guardian, or a valid refugee card.
- Current immunization record.
- A responsible adult to assist with evacuation processing.

Each child **MAY** bring:

- ONE container for personal effects, measuring no larger
  than 22" x 14" x 9". DO NOT BRING PERISHABLES. Food
  and water will be provided on the train.
- A bedroll or sleeping bag.

The following items will **NOT** be permitted on the trains
or within the EVACUEE PROCESSING AREA:

- Firearms
- Any knife or penetrating weapon longer than 3 inches
- Pets

- *No parents or guardians will be allowed to enter Amtrak 30th Street Station.*
- *Any person or persons interfering with the evacuation will be SHOT.*
- *Any unauthorized person attempting to board the trains will be SHOT.*

**God Save the People of the United States and the
City of Philadelphia**

EIGHTEEN

From the Journal of Ida Jaxon ('The Book of Auntie')
Presented at the Third Global Conference on the North
 American Quarantine Period
Center for the Study of Human Cultures and Conflicts
University of New South Wales, Indo-Australian Republic
April 16–21, 1003 A.V.

[Excerpt begins.]

*. . . and it was chaos. So many years gone by, but you never forget a
sight like that, the thousands of people, all of them so frightened,
pressing against the fences, the soldiers and dogs trying to keep folks
calm, the shots fired in the air. And me, not more than eight years old,
with my little suitcase, the one my mama had packed for me the night
before, bawling the whole time, because she knew what she was doing,
that she was sending me away forever.*

*The jumps had taken New York, Pittsburgh, DC. Most the whole
country, as far as I recall. I had folks in all those places. There was
lots we didn't know. Such as what happened to Europe or France or
China, though I'd heard my daddy talking to some other men from
our street about how the virus was different there, it just flat-out killed
everyone, so I'm supposing it was possible that Philadelphia was the
last city left with people in it in the whole world at that time. We were
an island. When I asked my mama about the war, she explained that
the jumps were people like you and me, just sick. I'd been sick myself
so it scared me about out my skin when she told me this, I just started
crying my eyes out, thinking I would wake up one day and kill her and
my daddy and my cousins the way the jumps liked to do. She hugged
me hard and told me, no no, Ida, it's different, that's not the same
kind of a thing at all, you hush now and stop your crying, which I did.
But even so for a while it didn't make no sense to me, why there was a
war on and there was soldiers everywhere if folks had just come down
with a sniffle or something in they throat.*

That's what we called them, jumps. Not vampires, though you heard the word said. That's what my cousin Terrence said they were. He showed me in a comic that he had, which was a kind of picture book as I recall, but when I asked my daddy about that and showed him the pictures he told me no, vampires were just something in a made-up story, nice-looking men in suits and capes with good manners, and this here's real, Ida. Ain't no story about it. There's lots of names for them now, of course, flyers and smokes and drinks and virals and such, but we called them jumps on account of that's what they did when they got you. They jumped. My daddy said, no matter what you call them, they are some mean sons of bitches. You stay inside like the Army says, Ida. It shocked me to hear him speaking such, because my daddy was a deacon of the A.M.E., and I'd never heard him talk like that, use words of the kind. Nights was the worst of it, especially that winter. We didn't have the lights like we do now. There weren't much food except what the Army gave us, no heat except what you could find to burn. The sun went down and you could feel it, that fear, snapping down like a lid on everything. We didn't know if that would be the night the jumps got in. My daddy had boarded up the windows of our house and he kept a gun, too, kept it with him all night as he sat at the kitchen table by candlelight, listening to the radio, maybe sipping a bit. He'd been a communication officer in the Navy and knew about such things. One night I came in and found him crying there. Just sitting with his face in his hand and shaking and weeping, the tears all running down his cheeks. Don't know what it was that woke me except maybe the sound of him. He was a strong man, my daddy, and it shamed me to see him in such a state as that. I said Daddy, what is it, why you crying like you are, did something scare you? And he shook his head and said, God don't love us no more, Ida. Maybe it was something we did. But he don't. He's up and flown the coop on us. Then my mama came in and told him to hush up Monroe, you're drunk, and shooed me back to bed. That was my daddy's name, Monroe Jaxon the Third. My mama was Anita. At the time I didn't know it, but I think maybe the night he was crying was when he heard about the train. It could have been something else.

Only the good Lord knows why he spared Philadelphia long as he

did. I barely remember it now, except the feeling of it, time to time.
Little things, like stepping out with my daddy at night to get a water
ice up the corner, and my friends at school, Joseph Pennell
Elementary, and a little girl named Sharise who lived down the corner
from us, the two of us could just keep each other going for hours and
hours. I looked for her on the train but I never did find her.

I remember my address: 2121 West Laveer. There was a college
near there, and stores, and busy streets, and all sorts of people going to
and fro in the day to day. And I remember a time when my daddy took
me downtown, out of our neighborhood, on the bus to see the windows
at Christmastime. I couldn't have been much more than five years old
at the time. The bus carried us past the hospital where my daddy
worked, taking X-rays, which were photographic pictures of people's
bones, he'd had that job since he'd gotten out of the service and met
my mama, and he always said it was the perfect job for a man like
him, how he got to look at the insides of things. He'd wanted to be a
doctor but taking the X-rays was the next best thing. Outside the store
he showed me the windows, all done up fancy for Christmas, with
lights and snow and a tree and moving figures inside them, elves and
reindeer and such. I'd never been happy like that in all my life, just to
see so beautiful a sight, standing in the cold like we were, the two of us
together. We were going to pick up a present for Mama, he told me, his
big hand on my head like he did, a scarf or maybe gloves. The streets
were all full of people, so many people, all different ages and looks to
them. I like to think about it even now, to send my mind back to that
day. No one remembers Christmas anymore, but it was a bit like First
Night is now. I don't recall if we got the scarf and gloves or not.
Probably we did.

That's all gone now, all of it. And stars. Time to time I think that's
what I miss seeing most of all, back in the Time Before. From the
window of my bedroom I could look over the roofs of the buildings and
the houses and see them, these points of light in the sky, hanging there
like God his own self had strung the sky for Christmas. It was my
mama who told me the names for some and how you could watch
them awhile and start to see pictures up there, simple things like
spoons and people and animals. I used to think you could look at the
stars and that was God, right there. Like looking straight into his face.

You needed the dark to see him plain. Maybe he forgot us and maybe he didn't. Maybe it was us who forgot, when we couldn't see the stars no more. And to tell the truth they're the one thing I'd like to see again before I die.

There were other trains, I do believe. We'd heard about trains leaving from all over, that other cities had sent them before the jumps got in. Maybe it was just people talking like they do when they're scared, grasping at any bit of hope that floats on past. I don't know how many made it all the way to where they were going. Some were sent to California, some to places with names I don't just now recall. There was only one we ever heard from, back in the early days. Before the Walkers and the One Law, when radio was still allowed. Someplace in New Mexico, I do believe it was. But something happened to their lights and we didn't hear from them again after that. From what Peter and Theo and the others tell me, I do believe we are the only one left now.

But the train and Philadelphia and what all happened that winter was what I meant to write on. Folks was in the worst way. The Army was everywhere, not just soldiers but tanks and other things of the kind. My daddy said they were there to protect us from the jumps, but to me they were just big men with guns, most of them white, and my daddy had always told me to look on the bright side, Ida, but not to trust the white man – that's how he said it, like they was all one man – though of course that seems funny now, folks all blended together like they are. Probably whoever is reading this doesn't even know what I'm talking about. We knew a fellow from up the way got himself shot, just for trying to catch a dog. I suppose he thought eating a dog was better than nothing. But the Army shot him and strung him up on a light post on Olney Avenue with a sign pinned to his chest that said 'looter.' Don't know what he was trying to loot except maybe a dog that was half starved and going to die anyway.

Then one night we heard the loudest boom and then another and another and planes screaming over our heads, and my daddy told me they'd blown the bridges, and all the next day we saw more planes and smelled fire and smoke, and we knew the jumps was close. Whole parts of the city were on fire. I went to bed and woke up later to the sounds of a set-to. Our place was just four rooms and voices had a way of carrying, you couldn't sneeze in one room without somebody in another saying bless you. I heard my mama crying and crying, and my father saying to her, you can't, we have to, you be strong, Anita, things of the kind, and then the door to my room swung open and I saw my daddy standing there. He was holding a candle and I'd never in my life seen him with such a look upon his face. Like he'd seen a ghost, and the ghost was his own self. He dressed me quick for the cold and said, be good now, Ida, and go say goodbye to your mother, and when I did she held me a long, long time, crying so hard it makes me hurt to think of it, even now, all these years gone by. I saw the little suitcase by the door and said, are we going somewhere, Mama? We leaving? But she didn't answer me, she just went on crying and crying and holding me like she did, until my daddy made her let go. Then we left, my daddy and me. Just the two of us.

It wasn't till we were outside that I realized it was still the middle of the night. It was cold and blowing. Flakes were falling and I thought it was snow but when I licked one off my hand I realized it was ashes. You could smell the smoke and it was stinging my eyes and throat. We had to walk a long way, most of the night. The only things moving on the streets were the Army trucks, some of them with horns on top and voices coming out of them, telling people not to steal, stay calm, about the evacuation. There were some folks about but not many, though we saw more and more the farther we went, until the streets were thick with people, no one saying a word, all walking the same direction as us, carrying they things. I don't think I'd even figured it out in my mind that it was just the Littles who were going.

It was still dark when we got to the station. I've already said a thing or two about that. My father told me we'd got there early so as to avoid the lines, he always hated lines, but it was like half the city had the same idea. We waited a long time, but things were turning ugly, you could feel it. Like a storm was coming, the air whizzing and cracking with it. Folks was too afraid. The fires were going out, the jumps were coming, that's what people were saying. We could hear great booms in the distance, like thunder, and planes flying overhead, fast and low. And each time you saw one your ears would pop and you'd hear a boom a second after, and the ground would shake below your feet. Some folks had Littles with them but not all. My father held *my hand tight. There was an opening in the fence where the soldiers were letting people in and that's what we had to get through. It was so tight with the people pressed together I could hardly take a breath. Some of the soldiers had dogs. Whatever happens, you hold on to me, Ida, my daddy said. Just hold on.*

We got close enough that we could see the train, down below us. We were on a bridge, the rails running under it. I tried to follow its length with my eyes but I couldn't, that's how long it was. It seemed to stretch forever, a hundred cars long. It didn't look like any train I ever saw. The cars didn't have no windows, and long poles stuck out from the sides with nets hanging from them, like the wings of a bird. On the roof there were soldiers with big guns in metal cages, like something you'd put a canary in. At least I supposed they were soldiers, on account of they were wearing shiny silver suits, to protect them from the fires.

I don't remember what happened to my father. Certain things you can't remember because your mind won't take them up once they're done and gone. I remember a woman who had a cat in a box and a soldier saying, lady, what do you think you're doing with that cat, and then something happened quick and believe it or not that soldier shot her, right there. And then there was more shooting, and folks tearing about and pushing and screaming, and my daddy and me got separated in all of it. When I reached for my daddy his hand wasn't there no more. The crowd was moving like a river, dragging me along with it. It was a horrible thing. People was yelling that the train wasn't full but it was leaving anyway. If you can imagine I'd lost my suitcase and that's what I was thinking of, I've lost my suitcase and my daddy's going to be hopping mad at me for that. He was always saying, look after your things, Ida, don't be careless. We work hard to have the things we do, so don't go treating them like nothing. So I had just about figured I was in the worst trouble of my life all on account of the suitcase when something knocked me to the ground and when I got up I saw all the dead folks around me. And one was a boy I thought I knew from school. Vincent Gum, that's what we always called him, Vincent Gum, both names together, and wouldn't you know, that boy was always getting in trouble on account of he liked to chew gum and always had a piece in his mouth at school. But now he had a hole in him right in the center of his chest and he was lying on his back on the ground in a puddle of blood. There was more blood coming out of the hole in his chest in little bubbles, like soap in a bath. I remember thinking, that's Vincent Gum, lying dead right there. A bullet went through his body and killed him. He's never going to move or talk or chew his gum or do nothing at all, and he'll be right there in that spot forever with that forgetful look on his face.

I was still on the bridge over the train, and folks was starting to leap down to it. Everyone was screaming. A lot of the soldiers were shooting at them, like somebody had told them to just shoot anything no matter what it was. I looked over the edge and saw the bodies piled up there like logs on a fire and blood everywhere, so much blood you'd think the world had sprung a leak.

Somebody picked me up then. I thought it was my daddy, he'd come to find me after all, but it wasn't, it was just a man. A big fat white man with a beard. He snatched me up by the waist and ran to the other side of the bridge, where there was a kind of pathway down through some weeds. We were at the top of a wall above the tracks and the man held me by the hands and lowered me down and I thought, he's going to drop me and I'm going to die like Vincent Gum did. I was looking right at that man and I'll never forget his eyes. They were the eyes of a person who knew he was good as dead. When you have that look, you're not young or old, or black or white, or even a man or a woman. You're gone from all those things. He was yelling, somebody take her, somebody take this girl here. And then somebody grabbed my legs from below and lifted me down and the next thing I knew I was on the train and it was moving. And somewhere in there I came to think I'd never be seeing any of them again, not my mama or daddy or anybody I had known in my life to that day.

What I remember after that is more like a feeling than any actual thing. I remember children crying, and being hungry, and the dark and heat and smell of bodies all crammed in. We could hear gunfire outside and feel the heat from the fires passing through the walls of the train like the whole world was aflame. They got to be so hot you couldn't even touch them without burning the skin of your hand. Some of the children weren't no more than four years old, practically babies. We had two Watchers in the car with us, a man and a woman. Folks think the Watchers were Army but they weren't, they were from the FEMA. I remember that because it was written in big yellow letters on the backs of their jackets. My daddy had people down in New Orleans, he'd grown up there before the service, and he always said that FEMA stood for 'Fix Everything My Ass.' I don't remember what became of the woman but that man was First Family, a Chou. He married another Watcher, and after she died, he had two other wives. One of those wives was Mazie Chou, Old Chou's grandmother.

The thing was, the train didn't stop. Not for anything. Time to time we'd hear a great big boom and the car would shake like a leaf in the wind but still we kept right on. One day the woman left the car and went back to help with some of the other children and came back all crying. I heard her tell the man that the other cars behind us were gone. They'd built the train so that if the jumps got into a car, they could leave it behind, and those were the booms we'd heard, one car after another falling away. I didn't want to think about those cars and the children inside them, and to this day I don't. So I'm not going to write anything more about that here.

What you'll want to know about is when we got here, and I do remember something of that, because that was how I found Terrence, my cousin. I didn't know he was on the train with me, he was in one of the other cars. And it was a lucky thing he hadn't been in one of the cars at the back, because by the time we arrived there weren't more than three, and two mostly empty. We were in California, the Watchers told us. California wasn't a state like it used to be, they said, it was a whole different country. Buses would be meeting us to take us up the mountain, someplace safe. The train slowed to a stop and everyone was afraid but excited too, to be getting off the train after all the days and days, and then the door opened and the light was so bright we all had to hold our hands over our faces. Some of the children were crying because they thought it was the jumps, the jumps were coming to get us, and someone else said, don't be stupid, it ain't the jumps, and when I opened my eyes I was relieved to see a soldier standing there. We were someplace in the desert. They took us off and there were lots more soldiers around and a line of buses parked in the sand and helicopters thwocking overhead, stirring up the dust all around and making every kind of a racket. They gave us water to drink, cold water. All my days I've never been so glad just to taste cold water. The light was so bright to my eyes it still hurt me even to look around but that's when I saw Terrence. He was standing there in the dust like the rest of us, holding a suitcase and a dirty pillow. I'd never hugged a boy so hard or long in my life and we were both laughing and crying and saying, look at you. We weren't first cousins but more like second, as I recall. His father was my daddy's nephew, Carleton Jaxon. Carleton was a welder at the shipyard, and Terrence later told me his daddy was one of the men who built the train. A day before the evacuation, Uncle Carleton had taken Terrence to the station and put him in the engine car, closest to Driver, and told him to stay there. You stay put, Terrence. Do what Driver tells you. So that was how Terrence had come to be with me now. He was just three years older than me but it seemed like more at the time, so I said to him, you'll look after me, won't you Terrence? Say you'll do that. And he nodded and said yes he would, and that was just what he did, until the day he died. He was the first Jaxon who was Household and a Jaxon's been Household ever since.

They loaded us onto the buses. Everything felt different to me with Terrence there. He lent me his pillow to use and I fell asleep with my head leaned against him. So I couldn't say how long we were in the buses, though I don't think it was more than a day. Then before I knew it Terrence was saying, wake up, Ida, we're here, wake up now, and right away I could smell how different the air was, where we were. More soldiers took us off, and for the first time I saw the walls, and the lights above us, standing high on their poles – though it was still the daytime so they weren't on. The air was fresh and bright, and so cold all of us were stamping our feet and shivering. There was Army everywhere and FEMA trucks of all sizes full of every kind of thing, food and guns and toilet paper and clothes, and some with animals in them, sheep and goats and horses and chickens in cages, even some dogs. The Watchers put us all in lines like they'd done before and took our names and gave us clean clothes and took us to the Sanctuary. The room they put us in was the one most everyone knows, where all the Littles sleep to this very day. I took a cot next to Terrence and asked him the question that was on my mind, which was, what is this place, Terrence? Your daddy must have told you if he built the train. And

Terrence was very still for a moment and said, this is where we live now. The lights and walls will keep us safe. Safe from the jumps, safe from everything until the war is over. It's like the story of Noah, and this here's the ark. I asked him what ark and what are you talking about and will I ever see my mama and daddy again and he said, I don't know, Ida. But I'll look after you like I said. Sitting on the bed on the other side was a girl no older than me, who was just crying and crying, and Terrence went to her and said, quietly, what's your name, and I'll look after you too if you want, which made her stop. She was a beauty, that one, you could see it plain as day, even as dirty and worn down as all of us were. The sweetest little face and hair so light and wispy it was like a baby's, the way they do. She nodded to what he said and answered, yes, would you please do that, and if it's not much trouble can you look after my brother too. And wouldn't you know that girl, Lucy Fisher, became my very best friend and was the one that Terrence married later on. Her brother was Rex, a little bit of a thing who was just as pretty as Lucy except in the manner of a boy, and I'm guessing you probably know that Fishers and Jaxons been mixed up together one way or the other ever since.

Nobody said it was my job to remember all these things, but it seems to me that without me to put them down, they'd all be gone by now. Not just how we came to be here but that world, the old world of the Time Before. Buying gloves and a scarf at Christmas and walking with my daddy up the block for water ice and sitting in a window on a summer night to watch the stars come on. They're all dead now, of course, the First Ones. Most been dead so long, or else taken up, that no one even remembers their names no more. When I think back on those days it's not sadness I feel. A little sadness, for missing folks, like Terrence, who was taken up at twenty-seven, and Lucy, who died in childbirth not long after, and Mazie Chou, who did live a good while but passed in a manner I don't just now recall. Pendicitis, I think it was, or else the cancer. The hardest to think on are the ones who let it go, the way so many did over the years. The ones who took it into their own hands, from sadness or worry or just not wanting to carry the weight of this life no more. They the ones I dream on. Like they left the world unfinished and don't even know they've gone. But I suppose it's part of being old to feel that way, half in one world and half in the other, all of it mixed together in the mind. No one's left who even knows my name. Folks call me Auntie, on account of I never could have no children of my own, and I guess that suits me fine. Sometimes it's like I've got so many people inside me I'm never alone at all. And when I go, I'll be taking them with me.

The Watchers told us the Army would be coming back, bringing more children and soldiers, but they never did. The buses and trucks pulled away, and as darkness settled down they sealed the gates, and then the lights came on, bright as day, so bright they blotted out the stars. It was a sight to see. Terrence and I had gone outside to look, the two of us shivering in the cold, and I knew then that what he'd said was so. This was where we would live from now on. We were there, together, on First Night, when the lights came on and the stars went out. And in all the years since then, the years and years and years, I never have seen those stars again, not once.

IV

ALL EYES

First Colony
San Jacinto Mountains
California Republic

92 A.V.

O sleep! O gentle sleep!
Nature's soft nurse, how have I frighted thee,
That thou no more wilt weigh my eyelids down
And steep my senses in forgetfulness?

– SHAKESPEARE,
Henry IV, Part II

Slide No. 1: Reconstruction of First Colony Site (33°74' N, 116°71' W)

Presented at the Third Global Conference on the North American Quarantine Period
Center for the Study of Human Cultures and Conflicts
University of New South Wales, Indo-Australian Republic
April 16–21, 1003 A.V.

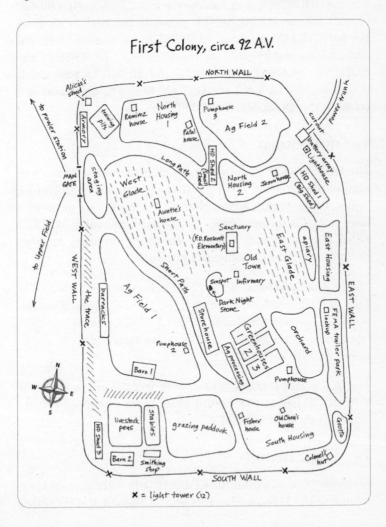

First Colony, circa 92 A.V.

DOCUMENT OF ONE LAW

KNOW ALL COLONISTS BY THESE PRESENT:

We, the HOUSEHOLD, in order to safeguard DOMESTIC ORDER; provide for the EQUAL SHARE; promote the PROTECTION of the SANCTUARY; establish FAIRNESS in all matters of WORK and TRADE; and provide for the COMMON DEFENSE of the COLONY, its MATERIAL ASSETS and all SOULS who dwell within its WALLS, until the DAY OF RETURN, do ordain and establish this DOCUMENT OF ONE LAW.

THE HOUSEHOLD

The HOUSEHOLD shall be composed of the oldest member of each of the surviving FIRST FAMILIES (Patal, Jaxon, Molyneau, Fisher, Chou, Curtis, Boyes, Norris), not to exclude those who have joined a second family by marriage, including WALKER FAMILIES; or, in such cases as the oldest surviving member declines to serve, by another of his surname;

The HOUSEHOLD shall act in consultation with the BOARD OF THE TRADES to oversee all matters of defense, production, illumination, and distribution of EQUAL SHARES, final authority to be retained by the HOUSEHOLD in all matters of dispute and in times of CIVIL EMERGENCY;

The HOUSEHOLD shall elect one of its members to be HEAD OF THE HOUSEHOLD, that person alone to serve without encumbrance of a secondary TRADE.

THE SEVEN TRADES

All duties of work within the COLONY, and without its WALLS, including the POWER STATION and TURBINES and GRAZING

336

FIELDS and PITS, shall be divided into the SEVEN TRADES, to include: the Watch, Heavy Duty, Light and Power, Agriculture, Livestock, Commerce and Manufacturing, and Sanctuary-Infirmary;

Each of the SEVEN TRADES ('Works') shall be self-administering, the HEADS of TRADE to form the BOARD OF TRADES, reporting to the HOUSEHOLD in such manner as the HOUSEHOLD determines and at its sole discretion.

THE WATCH

The WATCH is henceforth known to be one of the SEVEN TRADES, equal to all others, and comprised of no fewer than one FIRST CAPTAIN, three SECOND CAPTAINS, fifteen FULL WATCH, and a number of runners to be determined.

All FIREARMS and PIERCING WEAPONS (longbows, crossbows, blades longer than 10 cm) within the WALLS of the COLONY are to be kept and stored in the ARMORY, under the protection of the WATCH.

THE SANCTUARY

Each child shall remain in the safety of the SANCTUARY ('F. D. Roosevelt Elementary School'), never to leave its walls, until the age of 8 years, to depart its confines on the advent of her 8th birthday, whereupon that child shall select a TRADE, subject to the needs of the COLONY and the approval of the HOUSEHOLD and the BOARD OF TRADES.

That child's EQUAL SHARE shall upon his release from the SANCTUARY revert to the HOUSEHOLD of which he is a part, to be carried with him at the time of his MARRIAGE.

Children in the SANCTUARY are to know nothing of the world in its present form outside the COLONY's walls, including any mention of the VIRALS, the duties of the WATCH, and the event known as the GREAT VIRAL CATACLYSM. Any person found to knowingly provide such information to any MINOR CHILD is subject to the penalty of PUTTING WITHOUT THE WALLS.

RIGHTS OF WALKERS

WALKERS, or souls not of the FIRST FAMILIES, are fully endowed with EQUAL SHARES, not to be deprived of such shares by any person, with the exception of unmarried males who choose to dwell within the BARRACKS under the shares of their TRADES.

LAW OF QUARANTINE

Any soul, whether FIRST FAMILY or WALKER, who comes into direct physical contact with a VIRAL must be quarantined for a period of no fewer than 30 days.

Any soul, whether quarantined or at liberty, who exhibits symptoms of VIRAL INFECTION, including but not limited to SEIZURES, VOMITING, AVERSION TO LIGHT, CHANGES IN EYE COLORATION, BLOOD HUNGER, or SPONTANEOUS DISROBING, may be subject to immediate confinement and/or MERCIFUL EXECUTION by the WATCH.

Any soul who opens the gates, whether wholly or in part, by accident or design, alone or in the company of others, between SECOND EVENING BELL and FIRST MORNING BELL is subject to the penalty of PUTTING WITHOUT THE WALLS.

Any soul who owns, operates, or encourages the operation of a RADIO or other SIGNALING DEVICE is subject to the penalty of PUTTING WITHOUT THE WALLS.

Any soul who commits the crime of murdering another soul, such act to be defined as deliberately causing the physical death

of another without sufficient provocation of infection, is subject
to the penalty of PUTTING WITHOUT THE WALLS.

THUS ENACTED AND RATIFIED IN THE YEAR
OF OUR WAITING,
17 A.V.

Devin Danforth Chou
Federal Emergency Management Agency
Deputy Regional Administrator of the Central Quarantine Zone
HEAD OF HOUSEHOLD

Terrence Jaxon
Lucy Fisher Jaxon
Porter Curtis
Liam Molyneau
Sonia Patal Levine
Christian Boyes
Willa Norris Darrell

FIRST FAMILIES

NINETEEN

On a fading summer evening, late in the last hours of his old
life, Peter Jaxon – son of Demetrius and Prudence Jaxon, First
Family; descendant of Terrence Jaxon, signatory of the One
Law; great-great-nephew of the one known as Auntie, Last of
the First; Peter of Souls, the Man of Days and the One Who
Stood – took his position on the catwalk above Main Gate,
waiting to kill his brother.

He was twenty-one years old, Full Watch, tall though he did not think of himself as tall, with a narrow, high-browed face and strong teeth and skin the color of late honey. He had his mother's eyes, green with flecks of gold; his hair, which was Jaxon hair, coarse and dark, was pulled away from his brow in the style of the Watch, compressed into a tight, nutlike knob at the base of his skull with a single leather loop. A web of shallow creases fanned from the corners of his eyes, squinting into the yellowing light; there was, at the margin of his left temple, a single, hard-won streak of gray. He wore a pair of scavenged gaps, motley-patched at the knees and seat, and, cinched at his slender waist, a jersey of soft wool, beneath which he could feel the day's scrim of dirty perspiration, prickling his skin. He had taken the gaps from the Storehouse three seasons ago, at Share; they had cost him an eighth – he had bargained Walt Fisher down from a quarter, a ridiculous price for a pair of gaps, but that's how Walt did things, the price was never the price – and were too long in the legs by a hand, gathering in bunches at the tops of his feet, shod in sandals of cut canvas and old tire; he always wore sandals in the heat of the year or else went barefoot, reserving his one pair of decent boots for winter. Resting at an angle against the edge of the rampart was his weapon, a crossbow; at his waist, in its sheath of soft leather, a blade.

Peter Jaxon, twenty-one, armed at Full Watch. Standing the Wall as his brother had done, and his father, and his father before him. Standing to serve the Mercy.

It was the sixty-third of summer, the days still long and dry under wide blue skies, the air fresh with the scents of juniper and Jeffrey pine. The sun stood two hands; First Evening Bell had sounded from the Sanctuary, summoning the night shift to the Wall and calling in the herd from Upper Field. The platform on which he stood – one of fifteen distributed along the catwalk that ringed the top of the Wall – was known as Firing Platform One. Usually it was reserved to the First Captain of the Watch, Soo Ramirez, but not tonight;

tonight, as for each of the last six nights, it was Peter's alone. Five meters square, it was edged by an overhanging net of cabled steel. To Peter's left, rising another thirty meters, stood one of the twelve light assemblies, rows of sodium-vapor bulbs in a grid, dim now in the last of day; to his right, suspended over the nets, was the crane with its block and tackle and ropes. This Peter would use to lower himself to the base of the Wall, should his brother return.

Behind him, forming a comforting cloud of noise and smells and activity, lay the Colony itself, its houses and stables and fields and greenhouses and glens. This was the place where Peter had lived his whole life. Even now, facing away to watch the herd come home, he could hold each meter of it in his mind, a mental inventory in three dimensions with complete sensory accompaniment: the Long Path from the gate to Old Town, past the Armory with its music of hammering metal and the shaded recesses of West Glade, where Auntie lived; the fields with their rows of corn and beans, the backs of the workers bent low over the black earth, tilling and hoeing; the broad, semicircular plaza known as the Sunspot, where the trading days and open meetings of the Household were held; the Sanctuary, with its ringing bell-tower and bricked-in windows and coils of concertina wire, barricades that somehow failed to suppress the voices of the Littles playing in the courtyard; the pens and barns and grazing fields and coops, alive with the sound and smell of animals; the three greenhouses, their interiors obscured by a fog of humidity, and, standing adjacent, the vast scavenged bounty of the Storehouse, where Walter Fisher presided over the stalls of clothes and tools and food and fuel; the blocks of houses in various states of repair, from crumbling cabins long abandoned to those that, like Peter's, had been continuously occupied since The Day; the orchard and buzzing apiary and old trailer park, where nobody lived anymore, and, beyond it, past the last houses of the North Quarter and the Big Shed, at the base of the cutout between the north and east walls in a zone of perpetual cooling shade, the battery stack, three

341

gray bulks of humming metal wrapped by wire and pipe, still resting on the sunken wheels of the semi-trailers that had pulled them up the mountain in the Time Before.

The herd had crested the rise; Peter watched from above as they approached, a jostling, bleating mass that flowed like liquid up the hill, followed by the riders, six in all, tall on their mounts. The herd moved as one toward him through the gap in the fireline, their hooves kicking up a cloud of dust. As the riders passed under his post, each gave Peter a tight nod of acknowledgment, as they had for each of the last six evenings.

No words would pass between them. It was bad luck, Peter knew, to speak to someone waiting on the Mercy.

One of the riders broke away: Sara Fisher. Sara was a nurse by trade; Peter's own mother had been the one to train her. But like many people, she had more than one job. And Sara was built to ride – slender but strong, with an alert physical presence in the saddle and a quick, supple style on the reins. She was dressed, as all the riders were, in a loose jersey cinched at the waist, above leggings of patched denim. Her hair, a sun-warmed blond cut short to the shoulders, was tied away, a single loose strand swaying over her eyes, deep-set and dark. A leather bow guard sheathed her left arm from elbow to wrist; the bow itself, a meter long, was slung diagonally across her back like a single jouncing wing. Her horse, a fifteen-year-old gelding known as Dash, was said to prefer her above all others, pinning his ears and flicking his tail at anyone else who attempted to ride him. But not Sara; under Sara's command he moved with a responsive grace, horse and rider seeming to share each other's thoughts, becoming one.

As Peter watched, she cut through the gate again, against the current, back onto open ground. He saw what had drawn her away: a single lamb, a cosset born in spring, had wandered off, diverted by a patch of summer grass just inside the fireline. Setting her horse square to the tiny animal, Sara swung to the ground and in a burst of dexterous motion rolled the lamb onto its back, roping its legs three times around. The last of the herd was passing through the gate now, a roiling wave of horses and sheep and riders heading down the trace that followed the curve of the west wall toward the pens. Sara straightened and lifted her face toward the place where Peter stood on the catwalk; their eyes met quickly across the gap. On any other occasion, he thought, she would have smiled. As Peter looked on, she hoisted the lamb to her chest and draped it across the horse's back, holding it in place with a steadying hand while she swung up into the saddle. A second meeting of the eyes, long enough to hold a sentence: *I hope Theo doesn't come, either.* Then, before Peter could consider this further, Sara flicked her heels and rode briskly through the gate, leaving him alone.

Why did they do it? Peter wondered – as he had wondered through all the nights he'd stood. Why did they come home, the ones who'd been taken up? What force drove the mysterious impulse to return? A last, melancholy memory of the person they'd once been? Did they come home to say goodbye? A viral, it was said, was a being without a soul. When Peter had turned eight and been released from the Sanctuary, it was Teacher, whose job this was, who had explained all of this to him. In its blood was a tiny creature, called a virus, that stole the soul away. The virus entered through a bite, typically to the neck but not always, and once it was inside a person, the soul was gone, leaving the body behind to walk the earth forever; the person they had been was no more. These were the facts of the world, the one truth from which all other truths descended; Peter might just as well have been wondering what made the rain fall; and yet, standing on the catwalk in the sharpening dusk – the seventh and final night of the Mercy, after which his brother would be declared dead, his name etched into the Stone, his belongings carted off to the Storehouse to be patched and repaired and redistributed at Share – he thought it. Why would a viral come home if it had no soul?

The sun stood just one hand above the horizon now, descending quickly into the wavy line where the foothills declined to the valley floor. Even in high summer the days seemed to end this way, in a kind of plunge. Peter cupped his eyes against the glare. Somewhere out there – past the fire-line, with its loose jumble of felled timber, and the grazing grounds of Upper Field and the dump with its pit and piles, and the scrubby woodland hills beyond – lay the ruins of Los Angeles and, farther still, the unimaginable sea. When Peter was a Little and still living in the Sanctuary, he had learned about this, in the library. Although it had been decided, long ago, that most of the books the Builders had left behind were of no value, and potentially confusing to the Littles, who were not to know anything about the virals or what had happened to the world of the Time Before, a few were allowed to remain. Sometimes Teacher would read to them, stories about children and fairies and talking animals who lived in a forest behind the doors of a closet, or else allow them to select a book on their own, to look at the pictures and read as best they could. *The Oceans Around Us*: that had been Peter's favorite, the book he'd always chosen. A faded volume, its pages dank-smelling and cool to the touch, the cracked binding held together by bits of curling yellow tape. On the cover was the name of the author, Ed Time-Life, and inside, page after wondrous page of pictures and photos and maps. One map was called the World, which was everything, and most of the World was water. Peter asked Teacher to help him read the names: Atlantic, Pacific, Indian, Arctic. Hour after hour he sat on his mat in the Big Room, the book cradled in his lap, turning the pages, his eyes locked onto these blue spaces on the maps. The World, he gathered, was round, a great watery ball – a dewdrop hurtling through the sky – and all the water was connected. The rains of spring and snows of winter, the water that poured from the pumps, even the clouds above their heads – that was all part of the oceans, too. Where was the ocean? Peter asked Teacher one day. Could he see it? But Teacher only laughed, as she always did when he asked too many questions, dismissing his concerns with a shake of her head. *Maybe there's an ocean and maybe there isn't. It's only a book, Little Peter. Don't you go worrying about oceans and such.*

But Peter's father had seen the ocean: his father, the great Demetrius Jaxon, Head of the Household, and Peter's uncle Willem, First Captain of the Watch. Together they'd led the Long Rides farther than anyone had ever gone, since before the Day. Eastward, toward the morning sun, and west to the horizon line and farther still, into the empty cities of the Time Before. Always his father returned with stories of the great and terrible sights he'd seen, but none was more wondrous than the ocean, in a place he called the Long Beach. Imagine, Peter's father told the two of them – for Theo was there as well, the two Jaxon brothers sitting at the kitchen table of their small house in the hour of their father's return, raptly listening, drinking his words like water – imagine a place where the ground simply stopped, and beyond that place an endless tumbling blueness, like the sky turned upside down. And sunk down in it, the rusting ribs of great ships, a thousand thousand of them, like a whole drowned city of man's creation, jutting from the ocean's waters as far as the eye could see. Their father was not a man of words; he communicated only with the most sparing phrases and parceled his affections the same way, letting a hand on a shoulder or a well-timed frown or, in moments of approval, a terse nod from the chin do most of his speaking for him. But the stories of the Long Rides brought out the voice in him. Standing on the ocean's edge, his father said, you could feel the bigness of the world itself, how quiet and empty it was, how alone, with no man or woman to look at it or say its name through all the years and years.

Peter was fourteen when his father returned from the sea. Like all the Jaxon males, including his older brother, Theo, Peter had apprenticed to the Watch, hoping someday to join his father and uncle on the Long Rides. But this never happened. The following summer, the scouting party was ambushed in a place his father called Milagro, deep in the eastern deserts. Three souls lost, including Uncle Willem, and there were no more Long Rides after that. People said that it was his father's fault, that he had gone too far, taken too many chances, and for what? None of the other Colonies had been heard from in years; the last, Taos Colony, had fallen almost eighty years ago. Their final transmission, back before the Separation of the Trades and the One Law, when radio was still permitted, said their power plant was failing, the lights were going out. Surely they'd been overrun like all the others. What was Demo Jaxon hoping to accomplish, leaving the safety of the lights for months at a time? What did he hope to find, out there in the dark? There were those who still spoke of the Day of Return, when the Army would come back to find them, but never in all his travels had Demo Jaxon found the Army; the Army was no more. So many men dead now, to learn what they already knew.

And it was true that from the day Peter's father returned from the last Long Ride, there was something different about him. A great weary sadness, as if he'd leapt abruptly forward in age. It was as if a part of him had been left in the desert with Willem, whom Peter knew his father loved most of all, more than Peter or Theo or even their mother. His father stepped down from the Household, passing his seat to Theo; he began to ride alone, leaving with the herds at first light, returning just minutes before Second Evening Bell. He never told anyone where he went, as far as Peter knew. When he asked his mother, all she could say was that his father was in his own time now. When he was ready, he would return to them.

The morning of his father's final ride, Peter – a runner of the Watch by this time – was standing on the catwalk near Main Gate when he saw his father preparing to leave. The lights had just gone down; Morning Bell was about to sound. It had been a quiet night, without sign, and for an hour before dawn, a light snow had fallen. The day broke slowly, gray and cold. As the herd was gathering at the gate, Peter's father appeared on his mount, the great roan mare he always rode, headed down the trace. The horse was called Diamond because of the marking on her brow, an orphaned splash of white beneath the swishing mask of her long forelock; not an especially fast mount, his father always said, but loyal and tireless, and quick when you needed her to be quick. Now, watching his father holding her reins, standing at the rear of the herd while he waited for the gate to open, Peter saw Diamond do a little quickstep, tamping down the snow. Jets of steam puffed from her nostrils, swirling like a wreath of smoke around her long, self-possessing face. His father bent low and stroked the side of her neck; Peter saw his lips moving as he whispered something, some gentle encouragement, into her ear.

When Peter thought of that morning, five years ago, he still wondered if his father had known he was there, observing him from the snow-slickened catwalk. But he had never lifted his eyes to find him, nor had Peter done anything to alert his father to his presence. Watching him as he spoke to Diamond, stroking the side of her neck with his calming hand, Peter had thought of his mother's words, and knew them to be true. His father was in his own time now. Always, in the last moments before Morning Bell, Demo Jaxon would retrieve his compass from his waist pouch and open it once to examine it, then snap it closed as he called his head count to the Watch: 'One out!' he would call, in his deep, barrel-chested voice. 'One back!' the gatekeeper would reply. Always the same ritual, meticulously observed. But not that morning. It was only after the gates had opened and his father had passed, taking Diamond down the power station road, away from the grazing fields, that Peter realized his father had carried no bow, that the sheath at his belt was empty.

That night, Second Bell rang without him. As Peter would soon learn, his father had taken water at the power station midday and was last seen heading out under the turbines, into open desert. It was generally held that a mother could not stand for one of her own children, nor a wife for a husband; though nothing was written, the job of the Mercy had naturally fallen to a chain of fathers and brothers and eldest sons, performing this duty since the Day. So it was that Theo had stood for their father, as Peter now stood for Theo – just as someone, perhaps a son of his own, would stand for Peter should that day come.

Because if the person wasn't dead, if they'd been taken up, they always came home. It might be three days or five or even a week, but never longer than that. Most were Watchers, taken on scavenging parties or trips to the power station, or else riders with the herd or the Heavy Duty crews, who went outside to log or do repairs or drag garbage to the dump. Even in broad daylight, people were killed or taken; you were never really safe as long as the virals had shade to move in. The youngest homecomer that Peter knew of had been the little Boyes girl – Sharon? Shari? – nine years old when she was taken up on Dark Night. The rest of her family had been killed outright, either in the quake itself or the attack that followed; with no one left to stand for her, it had been Peter's uncle Willem, as First Captain, who had done this awful job. Many, like the Boyes girl, were fully taken up by the time they returned; others appeared in the midst of their quickening, sick and shuddering, tearing the clothing from their bodies as they staggered into view. The ones furthest along were the most dangerous; more than one father or son or uncle had been killed in this manner. But generally they offered no resistance. Most just stood there at the gate, blinking into the spotlights, waiting for the shot. Peter supposed that some part of them still remembered being human well enough to want to die.

His father never returned, which meant he was dead, killed by the virals out in the Darklands, at a place called Milagro. Their father had claimed he'd seen a Walker there, a solitary figure darting in the moonlit shadows, just before the virals attacked. But by that time, with the Household and even Old Chou having turned against the Long Rides, and

Peter's father in disgrace, having resigned to pursue his mysterious, solitary expeditions without the Wall – moving in the expanding orbit that even then had seemed to Peter a rehearsal for something final – no one had believed him. A claim as bold as that: surely it was just Demo Jaxon's desire to continue the rides that made him claim something so absurd. The last Walker to come in had been the Colonel, almost thirty years ago, and he was an old man now. With his great white beard and wind-bit face, brown and thickened as tanned hide, he seemed nearly as old as Old Chou, or even Auntie herself, Last of the First. A single Walker, after all these years? Impossible.

Even Peter hadn't known what to believe, until six days ago.

Now, standing on the catwalk in the fading light, Peter found himself wishing his mother were still alive, as he often did, to talk about these things. She'd taken sick just a season after their father's final ride, the onset of her illness so gradual that Peter had at first failed to notice the raspy cough from deep in her chest, how thin she was becoming. As a nurse, she had probably understood only too well what was happening, how the cancer that took so many had made its lethal home inside her, but had chosen to hide this information from Peter and Theo as long as she could. By the end not much was left of her but a shell of flesh on bone, fighting for a single taste of breath. A good death, everyone agreed, to die at home in bed as Prudence Jaxon had. But Peter had been at her side through the final hours and knew how terrible it had been for her, how much she'd suffered. No, there was no such thing as a good death.

The sun was folding into the horizon now, laying the last of its golden road across the valley below. The sky had turned a deep blue-black, drinking up the darkness that was spilling from the east. Peter felt the temperature drop, a quick, decisive notch of cooling; for a moment everything seemed held in a thrumming stillness. The men and women of the night shift were ascending the ladders now – Ian Patal and

Ben Chou and Galen Strauss and Sunny Greenberg and all the rest, fifteen in sum, crosses and longbows slung over their backs – calling out to one another as they thumped and clanged down the catwalks to the firing posts, Alicia barking orders from below, sending the runners scurrying. A small comfort, but real enough, the sound of Alicia's voice; it was she who had stood by Peter through all the nights of waiting, leaving him be but never venturing far, so that he'd know she was there. And should Theo return, it would be Alicia who would ride down the Wall with Peter, to do what needed to be done.

Peter drew in a deep breath of evening air and held it. The stars, he knew, would soon be out. Auntie had spoken often of the stars, as his father had – spread out over the sky like glowing grains of sand, more stars than all the souls who had ever lived, their numbers impossible to count. Whenever his father had spoken of them, telling the stories of the Long Rides and the sights he'd seen, the light of the stars had been in his eyes.

But Peter was not to see the stars tonight. The bell commenced to ring again, two hard peals, and Peter heard Soo Ramirez calling from below: 'Clear the gate! Clear the gate for Second Bell!' A deep, bone-shaking shudder below him as the weights engaged; with a shriek of metal, the doors, twenty meters tall and half a meter thick, began to slide from their walled pockets. As he lifted his cross from the platform, Peter made a silent wish that morning would find it unfired. And then the lights came on.

TWENTY

Log of the Watch
Summer 92

Day 41: No sign.

Day 42: No sign.

Day 43: 23:06: Single viral sighted at 200 m, FP 3. No approach.

Day 44: No sign.

Day 45: 02:00: Pod of 3 at FP 6. One target breaks off and attempts the Wall. Arrows released from FP 5 + 6. Target retreats. No further contact.

Day 46: No sign.

Day 47: 01:15: Runner Kip Darrell reports movement at fireline NW between FP 9 and FP 10, unconfirmed by Watch on station, officially logged as no sign.

Day 48: 21:40: Pod of 3 at FP 1, 200 m. One target makes approach to 100 m but retreats without engagement.

Day 49: No sign.

Day 50: 22:15: Pod of 6 at FP 7. Hunting small game, no approach. 23:05: Pod of 3 at FP 3. 2 males, 1 female. Full engagement, 1 KO. Kill at the nets made by Arlo Wilson, assist to Alicia Donadio, 2nd Capt. Body disposal referred to HD. Note to HD crew to repair split seam toehold at FP 6. Received by Finn Darrell for HD.

During this period: 6 contacts, 1 unconfirmed, 1 KO. No souls killed or taken.

Respectfully submitted to the Household,
S. C. Ramirez, First Captain

To the extent that any singular occurrence may be meaningfully placed within a local framework of events, the disappearance of Theo Jaxon, First Family and Household, a Second Captain of the Watch, could be said to have been set in motion twelve days prior, on the morning of the fifty-first of summer, after a night in which a viral had been killed in the nets by the Watcher Arlo Wilson.

The attack had come in the early evening from the south, near Firing Platform Three. Peter, stationed at his post on the opposite side of the Colony's perimeter, had seen nothing; it wasn't until the early-morning hours, as the resupply detail was assembling at the gate, that he received a full recounting.

The attack was in most ways typical, of the kind that occurred nearly every season, though most often in summer. A pod of three, two males and one large female; it was thought by Soo Ramirez – and others were in agreement – that this was probably the same pod that had been sighted twice over the previous five nights, prowling near the fireline. It often happened this way, in discrete stages, spread over several nights. A group of virals would appear at the edge of the lights, as if scouting the Colony's defenses; this would be followed by a couple of nights of no sign; then they would appear again, closer this time, perhaps one breaking away to draw fire but always retreating; then, on a third night, an attack. The Wall was far too high for even the strongest viral to mount it in a single leap; the only way for them to ascend was along the metal seams between the plates, employing these slender cracks, caused by the inevitable shifting of the plates, as toeholds. The firing platforms, with their overhanging steel nets, were positioned at the tops of these seams. Any viral who made it this far was usually fogged by the lights, sluggish and disoriented; many simply retreated at this point. Those who didn't would find themselves hanging in an inverted position under the nets, giving the Watcher on station ample opportunity to shoot them in the sweet spot with a crossbow or, failing this, to take them on a blade. Only rarely did a viral make it past the net – Peter had seen this occur only once during his five years on the Wall – but when one did, it invariably meant the Watcher was dead. After that, it was simply a question of how weakened the viral was by the lights and how long it took the Watch to bring him down, and how many people died before this happened.

That night, the pod had made a run straight for Platform Six; only one, a female – a detail Peter always found it curious to note, since the differences seemed so slight and served no purpose, as virals did not reproduce, as far as anybody was aware – had made it as far as the net. She was large, a good two meters; most distinctively, she possessed a single shock of white hair on her otherwise bald head. Whether this hair indicated that she had been old when she was taken up, or was a symptom of some biological change that had occurred in the years since then – the virals were thought to be immortal, or something close to it – was impossible to say; but no one Peter knew had ever seen a viral with hair before. Scrambling up the seam, a channel no wider than half a centimeter, she had quickly ascended to the underside of the platform. There she turned, leaping away from the Wall, into space, and grasped the outer edge of the net. All of this had unfolded in at most a couple of seconds. Suspended now, hanging twenty meters above the hardpan, she had rocked her body like a pendulum and, with a quick tucking motion, vaulted out and over the net, landing on her clawed feet on the platform, where Arlo Wilson had shoved his cross against her chest and shot her, point-blank through the sweet spot.

In the lifting morning light, Arlo related these events to Peter and the others with vigorously specific detail. Arlo, like all the Wilson men, liked nothing more than a good story. He was not a Captain, but he seemed like one: a large man with a heavy beard and powerful arms and a genial manner that communicated confident strength. He had a twin brother, Hollis, identical in all respects except that he kept his face clean-shaven; Arlo's wife, Leigh, was a Jaxon, Peter's and Theo's cousin, which made them cousins, too. Sometimes in the evenings, when he wasn't standing the Watch,

Arlo would sit under the lights in the Sunspot and play guitar for everyone, old folk tunes from a book left behind by the Builders, or go to the Sanctuary and play for the children as they readied for bed – funny, made-up songs about a pig named Edna who liked to wallow in the mud and eat clover all day. Now that Arlo had a Little of his own in the Sanctuary – a mewing bundle named Dora – it was generally assumed that he would serve at most a couple more years on the Wall before standing down to work some other, safer job.

That it was Arlo who had gotten credit for the kill was a matter of chance, as he himself was quick to point out. Any one of them could have been stationed at Platform Six; Soo liked to move people around so much you never knew where you might be on a given night. And yet there was more than luck involved, Peter knew, even if Arlo's modesty prevented him from saying so. More than one Watcher had frozen in the moment, and Peter, who had never taken a viral close in like that – all his kills had been dozers, shot in broad daylight – couldn't say for sure that it wouldn't happen to him. So if there was luck involved, it was everyone's good luck that it had been Arlo Wilson who had been there.

Now, in the aftermath of these events, Arlo was among a group who had gathered at the gate, part of the resupply detail that would travel to the power station to swap out the maintenance crews and restock supplies. The standard party of six: a pair of Watchers front and rear and in between, on muleback, two members of the Heavy Duty crew – everyone called them wrenches – whose job was to maintain the wind turbines that powered the lights. A third mule, a jenny, pulled the small cart of supplies, mostly food and water but also tools and skins of grease. The grease was manufactured from a mixture of cornmeal and rendered sheep fat; already a cloud of flies had gathered around the cart, drawn by the smell.

In the last moments before Morning Bell, the two wrenches, Rey Ramirez and Finn Darrell, went over their supplies, while the Watchers waited on their mounts. Theo, the officer in charge, took first position, next to Peter; at the rear were Arlo and Mausami Patal. Mausami was First Family; her father, Sanjay, was Head of the Household. But the previous summer, she had paired with Galen Strauss, making her a Strauss now. Peter still couldn't quite figure that. Galen, of all people: a likable enough guy, but when it came down to it, there was a vagueness about him, as if some essential substance inside him had failed to harden completely. As if Galen Strauss were an approximation of himself. Maybe it was his squinty way of looking at you when you spoke (everyone knew his eyes were bad) or his generally distracted air. But whatever it was, he seemed like the last person Mausami would choose. Though Theo had never said as much, Peter believed that his brother had hoped, someday, to pair with Mausami himself – Theo and Mausami had come up in the Sanctuary together, been released the same year, and apprenticed straight to the Watch – and the news of her marriage to Galen had hit Theo badly. For days after the announcement he'd moped about it, barely uttering a word to anyone. When Peter had finally raised the subject, all Theo would say was that he was fine with it, he guessed he'd waited too long. He wanted Maus to be happy; if Galen was the one to do that, so be it. Theo wasn't one to talk about such things, even with his brother, so Peter had been forced to take him at his word. But even so, Theo hadn't looked at him as he'd spoken.

Which was Theo's way: like their father, he was a man of compact expression who communicated with silence as much as with words. And when, in the days that followed, Peter recalled that morning at the gate, he would find himself wondering if there had been anything different about his brother, any indication that he might have known, as their father had seemed to know, what was about to happen to him – that he was leaving for the last time. But there was nothing; everything about the morning was as usual, a standard resupply detail, Theo sitting atop his mount with his customary impatience, fingering the reins.

Waiting for the bell that would signal their departure, his mount jostling restlessly under him, Peter was letting his mind drift in these thoughts – it was only later that he would come to fully understand their bearing – when he lifted his eyes to see Alicia headed their way on foot from the Armory, moving at a purposeful clip. He expected her to stop in front of Theo's mount – two Captains conferring, perhaps to discuss the night's events and the possibility of mounting a smokehunt, to chase out the rest of the pod – but this was not what happened. Instead she moved straight past Theo to the back of the line.

'Forget it, Maus,' Alicia said sharply. 'You're not going anywhere.'

Mausami looked around – a gesture of puzzlement that Peter perceived at once as false. Everyone said Maus was lucky to have taken her looks from her mother – the same soft, oval face, and rich black hair that, when she undid it, fell to her shoulders in a dark wave. She carried more weight than many women did, but most of it was muscle.

'What are you talking about? How come?'

Alicia, standing below them, rested her hands on her slender hips. Even in the cool dawn light, her hair, which she wore tied back in a long braid, glowed a rich, honeyed red. She was, as always, wearing three blades on her belt. Everybody joked that she hadn't paired yet because she slept with her blades on.

'Because you're pregnant,' Alicia declared, 'that's how come.'

The group was stunned into a momentary silence. Peter couldn't help it; turning in his saddle, he let his eyes fall quickly to Mausami's belly. Well, if she was carrying, she wasn't showing yet, though it was hard to tell under the loose fabric of the jersey. He glanced at Theo, whose eyes betrayed nothing.

'Well, how about that,' Arlo said. His lips curled into a broad grin inside the pocket of his beard. 'I wondered when you two would get around to it.'

A deep crimson had bloomed across Mausami's copper-colored cheeks. 'Who told you?'

'Who do you think?'

Mausami looked away. *'Flyers.* I'm going to kill him, I swear it.'

Theo had shifted on his mount to face Mausami. 'Galen's right, Maus. I can't let you ride.'

'Oh, what does he know? He's been trying to get me off the Wall all year. He can't do this.'

'Galen's not doing it,' Alicia interjected. 'I am. You're off the Watch, Maus. That's it, end of story.'

Behind them, the herd was coming down the trace. In another few moments they'd be subsumed in a noisy chaos of animals. Looking at Mausami, Peter did his best to imagine her as a mother, but couldn't quite. It was customary for women to stand down when the time came; even a lot of the men did when their wives became pregnant. But Mausami was a Watcher, through and through. A better shot than half the men and cool in a crisis, each movement calm and purposeful. Like Diamond, Peter thought. Quick when she needed to be quick.

'You should be happy,' Theo said. 'It's great news.'

A look of utter misery was on her face; Peter saw that her eyes were pooled with tears.

'Come on, Theo. Can you really see me sitting around the Sanctuary, knitting little booties? I think I'll lose my mind.'

Theo reached for her. 'Maus, listen—'

Mausami jerked away. 'Theo, don't.' She averted her face to wipe her eyes with the back of her wrist. 'Okay, everybody. Show's over. Happy, Lish? You've got your wish. I'm going.' And with that, she rode away.

When she was out of earshot, Theo folded his hands on the horn of the saddle and looked down at Alicia, who was wiping a blade on the hem of her jersey.

'You know, you could have waited until we got back.'

Alicia shrugged. 'A Little's a Little, Theo. You know the rules as well as anyone. And, frankly, I'm a little irritated she didn't tell me. It's not like this could stay a secret.' Alicia gave the blade a quick spin around her index finger and pushed it back into its sheath. 'It's for the best. She'll come around.'

Theo frowned. 'You don't know her like I do.'

'I'm not going to argue with you, Theo. I already spoke with Soo. It's done.'

The herd was pressing upon them now. The morning light had warmed to an even glow; in another moment Morning Bell would sound and the gates would open.

'We'll need a fourth,' Theo said.

Alicia's face lit up with a grin. 'Funny you should mention that.'

Alicia Blades. She was the last Donadio, but everyone called her Alicia Blades. Youngest Captain Since The Day.

Alicia had been just a Little when her parents were killed on Dark Night; from that day it was the Colonel who had raised her, taking her under his wing as if she were his own. Their stories were inextricably bound together, for whoever the Colonel was – and there was considerable disagreement on this question – he had made Alicia into the image of himself.

His own history was vague, more myth than fact. It was said he had simply appeared one day out of the blue at Main Gate, carrying an empty rifle and wearing a long necklace of shimmering, sharp objects that turned out to be teeth – viral teeth. If he'd ever had another name, no one knew it; he was simply the Colonel. Some said he was a survivor from the Baja Settlements, others that he had belonged to a group of nomadic viral hunters. If Alicia knew the real story, she'd never told anyone. He never married and he kept his own company, living in the small shack he'd constructed under the east wall of discarded scraps; he declined all invitations to join the Watch, choosing to work in the apiary instead. It was rumored that he had a secret exit that he used to hunt, sneaking out of the Colony just before dawn, to catch the virals as the sun rose. But no one had ever actually seen him do this.

There were others like him, men and women who for one

reason or another never married and kept to themselves, and the Colonel might have slipped into a hermit's anonymity if not for the events of Dark Night. Peter had been just six years old at the time; he couldn't be sure if his memories were real or just stories people had told him, embellished by his imagination over the years. He felt certain that he remembered the quake itself, though. Earthquakes happened all the time, but not like the one that had struck the mountain that night as the children were preparing for bed: a single, massive jolt, followed by a full minute of shaking so violent it seemed the earth would tear itself apart. Peter remembered the feeling of helplessness as he was lifted up, tossed like a leaf in the wind, and then the shouts and screams, Teacher yelling and yelling, and the great rush of noise and the taste of dust in his mouth as the west wall of the Sanctuary collapsed. The quake had hit just after sunset, taking out the power grid; by the time the first virals breached the perimeter, the only thing to do was light the fireline and retreat to what was left of the Sanctuary. Many of those killed had been left trapped in the rubble of their houses to die. By morning, 162 souls had been lost, including nine whole families, as well as half the herd, most of the chickens, and all of the dogs.

Many of those who survived owed their lives to the Colonel. He alone had left the safety of the Sanctuary to search for survivors. Carrying many of the injured on his back, he had brought them to the Storehouse, where he made a final stand, holding off the virals through the night. This group included John and Angel Donadio, Alicia's parents. Of the nearly two dozen people he rescued, they were the only ones to die. The next morning, covered in blood and dust, the Colonel had walked into what remained of the Sanctuary, taken Alicia by the hand, declared simply, 'I will take care of this girl,' and walked back out with Alicia in tow. None of the adults present in the room had been able to summon the energy to object. The night had made an orphan of her, as it had so many others, and the Donadios were Walkers, not First Family; if somebody was willing to see to her care, this seemed like a reasonable bargain. But it was also true, or so people said at the time, that in the little girl's compliance they had felt the workings of fate, of something no less than the settling of a cosmic debt. Alicia was meant, or so it seemed, to be his.

In the Colonel's hut under the Wall and, later, as she grew, in the training pits, he taught her all the things he'd learned out in the Darklands – not just how to fight and kill but how to give it up. Which was what you had to do: when the virals came, the Colonel taught her, you had to say to yourself, I'm already dead. The little girl had learned her lessons well; at the age of eight, she had apprenticed to the Watch, quickly outdistancing everyone in her skills with bow and blade, and by fourteen she was on the catwalk, working as a runner, moving up and down between the firing platforms. Then one night a pod of six virals – they always traveled in multiples of three – came in over the south wall just as Alicia was headed down the catwalk toward them. As a runner, Alicia wasn't supposed to engage – she was supposed to do just that, run, and sound the alarm. Instead she got the first one with a throwing blade, dead on through the sweet spot, drew her cross, and dropped the second one in midair. The third she took with a knife close in, using his weight to shove it under his breastbone as he fell upon her, their faces so close she could taste the breath of night washing over her as he died. The remaining three scattered, back over the Wall and into the dark.

No one had ever taken three like that, single-handedly. Certainly not a fifteen-year-old girl. Alicia stood the Watch from that day forward; by the time she was twenty, the rank of Second Captain was hers. Everyone expected that when Soo Ramirez stepped down, Lish would be the one to take her place as First. And ever since that night, she'd worn three blades at all times.

She told Peter about it late one night under the lights, the two of them standing the Watch. The third viral: that was when it happened, when she'd given it up. Though Alicia was

Peter's commanding officer, they had formed a bond that seemed to make the question of authority moot. So he knew she wasn't telling him to make a point; she was telling him because they were friends. Not the first or second, she explained, but the third. That was when she knew, absolutely knew, that she was dead. And the strange thing was, once she knew this, drawing the second blade was easy. All her fear was gone. Her hand found the knife like it wanted to be there, and as the creature fell upon her, all she'd thought was, *Well, here you go. As long as I'm headed out the door of the world, I might as well take you with me for the trip.* Like it was a fact, like she'd already done it.

The herd had departed by the time Alicia returned on her mount, a small canvas bag and a canteen of water slung from the saddle. Alicia had no proper home to live in; there were lots of vacant houses, but she preferred to bunk in a small metal shed behind the Armory, where she kept a cot and the few things she owned. Peter had never known her to sleep more than a couple of hours at a stretch, and if he ever went in search of her, the Armory was always the last place to look; she was always on the Wall. She was carrying a longbow, lighter than a cross and more comfortable on horseback, but she wore no guard; the bow was just for show. Theo offered to cede first position to her, but Alicia declined, taking Mausami's spot at the rear instead. 'Don't mind me. I'm just out to take the air,' she said, guiding her mount into the slot next to Arlo. 'This is your ride, Theo. No point in confusing the chain of command. Plus, I'd rather ride with the big fellow back here. All the talk keeps me awake.'

Peter heard his brother sigh; he knew Theo found Alicia overbearing at times. *She should worry a little more*, he had said to Peter on more than one occasion, and it was true: her confidence bordered on recklessness. Theo turned in his saddle, looking past Finn and Rey, who had offered only wordless indifference through the entire scene. This was Watcher business, who rode with whom. What did they care?

'That okay by you, Arlo?' Theo asked.

'Sure thing, cuz.'

'You know, Arlo,' Alicia said, her exuberant mood lighting up her voice, 'I always wondered. Is it true that Hollis shaved his beard so Leigh could tell you apart?'

It was commonly known that as young men the two Wilson brothers had swapped girlfriends more than once, allegedly without anyone being the wiser.

Arlo gave a knowing smile. 'You'd have to ask Leigh.'

The time for talk was over; they were running late as it was. Theo gave the order, but as they were approaching the gate, they heard a shout from behind:

'Hold up! Hold at the gate!'

Peter turned to see Michael Fisher jogging toward them. Michael was a First Engineer of Light and Power. Like Alicia, he was young for this job, just eighteen. But all the Fisher men had been engineers, and Michael had been trained by his father straight out of the Sanctuary. No one really understood what the engineers did – Light and Power was by far the most specialized of all the trades – beyond the fact that they kept the lights on, the batteries humming, the current coming up the mountain, a feat that seemed both as remarkable as magic and also completely ordinary. The lights, after all, came on, night after night.

'I'm glad I caught you.' He paused to catch his breath. 'Where's Maus? I thought she was riding with you.'

'Never you mind about it, Circuit,' Alicia called from behind. Her mount, a chestnut-colored mare named Omega, was pawing the dust, eager to ride. 'Theo, can we please just go?'

A flicker of exasperation crossed Michael's face. At such moments, his eyes pinching under his thatch of blond hair, his pale cheeks reddening, he managed to look even younger than he was. He said nothing but instead reached up to pass Theo the object he'd brought with him: a rectangle of green plastic with shining dots of metal decorating its surface.

'Okay,' Theo said, turning it in his hand to examine it, 'I give up. What am I looking at?'

'It's called a motherboard.'

'Hey,' Alicia called, 'watch your language.'

Michael turned toward her. 'You know, it wouldn't kill you to pay a bit more attention to how we keep the lights on.'

Alicia shrugged. Her mutual antagonism with Michael was a matter of record; the two of them squabbled like squirrels. 'You push a button, they come on. What's to understand?'

'Enough, Lish,' Theo said. He tipped his eyes toward Michael. 'Just ignore her. You need one of these things?'

Michael pointed to the board to show him. 'See this here? The little black square? That's the microprocessor. Never mind what it does. Just look for these same numbers if you can, but anything that ends in a nine ought to work. You could probably find the exact same one in almost any desktop computer, but roaches eat the glue, so try to find one that's clean and dry, no droppings. You might try the offices at the south end of the mall.'

Theo examined the board once more before depositing it in his saddlebag. 'Okay. This isn't a scavenging trip, but if we can fit it in, we will. Anything else?'

Michael frowned. 'A nuclear reactor would come in handy. Or about three thousand cubic meters of negatively ionized hydrogen in a proton exchange stack.'

'Oh, for godsakes,' Alicia moaned, 'speak English, Circuit. Nobody knows what the hell you're talking about. Theo, can we just please *ride*?'

Michael shot Alicia one last look of annoyance before returning his eyes to Theo. 'Just the motherboard. Get more than one if you can, and remember what I said about the glue. And Peter?'

Peter's attention had wandered toward the open gate, where the last of the herd was still faintly visible as a cloud of dust in the morning light, flowing up and over the hill toward Upper Field. But it wasn't the herd he'd been thinking of. He'd been thinking of Mausami, the look of panic on her face when his brother had reached out his hand – as if she'd been afraid to let him touch her, that this would be too much to bear.

He shook the image away and returned his gaze to Michael, standing below him.

'My sister asked me to give you a message,' Michael said.

'Sara did?'

'Just, you know,' Michael said, and gave an awkward shrug. 'Be careful.'

The distance to the power station was forty kilometers, nearly a full day's ride. Within an hour of leaving, the group fell silent, even Arlo, lulled by the heat and the prospect of the day ahead. Portions of the roadway down the mountain were washed away, and they had to stop and lead the animals by hand across these sections. The grease had begun to stink, and Peter was glad to be riding up front, out of the plume of its smell. The sun was high and hot, the air breathless, without the slightest breeze. The desert floor shined below them like hammered metal.

At half-day they stopped to rest. The HD crew watered the animals, while the others took positions on a rocky outcrop above the cart, Theo and Peter on one side, Arlo and Alicia on the other, to scan the tree line.

'See there?'

Theo was using the binoculars and pointing toward the shadow of the trees. Peter held a hand over his eyes against the glare.

'I don't see anything.'

'Be patient.'

Then Peter saw it. Two hundred meters distant, a barely detectable movement, no more than a rustling, in the branches of a tall pine, and a gentle shower of needles, floating down. Peter drew in a breath, willing it to be nothing. Then it came again.

'He's hunting, keeping to the shade,' Theo said. 'Squirrel, probably. Not much else around here. He must be one hungry son of a bitch to be out in the day like this.'

Theo whistled a long, windy note through his teeth to signal the others. Alicia turned sharply at the sound; Theo pointed two fingers at his own eyes, then a single outstretched digit toward the tree line. Then he held up his hand, cupping it in the shape of a question mark: *Do you see it?*

Alicia replied with a closed fist. *Yes.*

'Let's go, brother.'

They clambered down the rocks and rendezvoused at the cart, where Rey and Finn were sprawled over the grease bags, chewing on hardtack and passing a plastic jug of water between them.

'We can draw him out with one of the mules,' Alicia said quickly. With a long stick she began to draw in the dirt at their feet. 'Switch out the water for grease, move her down a hundred meters closer to the trees, see if he takes the bait. He probably already smells it. We set up three positions, here, here, and here' – she scratched these in the dirt – 'and catch him in the cross fire. Out in the sun like that he'd be easy.'

Theo frowned. 'This isn't a smokehunt, Lish.'

For the first time Rey and Finn looked up from the cart.

'What the hell,' Rey said, 'are you serious? How many are there?'

'Don't worry, we're moving out.'

'Theo, there's just the one,' Alicia said. 'We can't just leave him there. The herd's only, what, ten clicks?'

'We can and we will. And where there's one, there are others.' Theo arched his eyebrows at Rey and Finn. 'Are we ready to move out?'

'Who cares?' Rey rose quickly from the floor of the cart. 'Flyers, nobody ever tells us anything. Let's get the hell out of here.'

Alicia regarded them another moment, her arms crossed over her chest. Peter wondered how angry she was. But she'd said it herself, at the gate: chain of command.

'Fine, you're the boss, Theo,' she said.

They continued on their way. By the time they reached the foot of the mountain, it was midafternoon. For the last hour they'd descended in full view of the turbine array, hundreds of them spread over the flats of the San Gorgonio Pass, like a forest of man-made trees. On the far side, a second line of mountains shimmered in the haze. A hot, dry wind was blowing, ripping away their words the moment they were uttered, making any conversation impossible. With each meter of their descent the air grew hotter; it felt like they were riding into a smithing furnace. The road ended at the old town of Banning. From there, they'd head inland along the Eastern Road, another ten kilometers to the power station.

'All eyes, everyone,' Theo called over the rush of the wind. He took another moment to scan ahead with the binoculars. 'Let's close it up. Lish on point.'

Peter experienced a quick flash of irritation – he was in second position, the point was his to take – but let the feeling pass without comment; Theo's choice would smooth things over between him and Alicia, and by the time they got to the power station, they'd all be friends again. Theo passed her the binoculars; Alicia heeled her mount and rode briskly ahead an extra fifty meters, her red braid swinging in the sun. Without turning, she held up an open hand, then dropped her palm so that it was parallel to the ground. A thin, birdlike whistle from between her teeth. *Clear. Forward.*

'Let's go,' Theo said.

Peter felt a quickening in his chest as his senses, dulled by the monotony of the long ride down the mountain, revived, bringing him into a heightened awareness of his surroundings, as if he were viewing the scene from several angles at once. They rode forward at an even pace, their bows at the ready. No one spoke except Finn, who had climbed down from the cart and was leading the jenny by hand, murmuring calming words to her. The course they followed was little more than a sand track, rutted from years of use by the carts. Peter felt, like a tingling at his extremities, each bit of sound and movement from the landscape: the soft howl of wind through a broken window; a bit of flapping canvas caught on a tipping utility pole; the creak of a metal sign, its words long since scoured away, tossing to and fro above the fuel pumps of an old garage. They passed a pile of rusted cars, half-buried and twisted in a heap; a block of houses, piled with dunes that reached nearly to their eaves; a cavernous metal shed, bleached and pitted, from which issued the cooing of pigeons and, as they moved downwind, the fetid cloud of their droppings.

'All eyes, everyone,' Theo repeated. 'Let's get through here.'

They moved in silence into the center of town. The buildings here were more substantial, three or four stories, though many had collapsed, carving open spaces between them and filling the street with mounds of undifferentiated debris. Cars and trucks were parked at haphazard angles along the roadway, some with their doors standing open – the moment of their drivers' flight frozen in time – but in others, sealed away beneath the blasting desert sun, were the dried-out corpses known as slims: raggy masses of bones folded over the dashboards or pressed against the windows, their shriveled forms virtually unrecognizable as human beings except for a tuft of stiffened hair still tied with a ribbon, or the glinting metal of a watch on a skinless hand that still, after nearly a hundred years, clutched the steering wheel of a pickup truck sunk to the tops of its wheel wells. All of it unmoving and silent as the grave, all just as it had been since the Time Before.

'Gives me the creeps, cuz,' Arlo murmured. 'I always tell myself not to look, and I always do anyway.'

As they approached the highway overpass, Alicia pulled up sharply. She turned, one hand raised, and rode briskly back to them.

'Three dozers underneath. They're hanging in the rafters on the back side, over the culvert.'

Theo absorbed this news without expression. Unlike the viral they'd seen on the mountain road, there was no question of taking on a whole pod, certainly not this late in the day.

'We'll have to go around. The cart can't make it without a ramp. Lish? Agreed?'

'No argument. We close up and go.'

They turned east, tracing the course of the highway at a distance of a hundred meters. The sun stood four hands; they were cutting it close now. It would be slow going over open ground with the cart. The next entrance ramp was two kilometers away.

'I hate to admit it,' Theo said quietly to Peter, 'but Lish had a point. When we get back, we should put together a hunting party and clear out that pod.'

'If they're still there.'

Theo was frowning pensively. 'Oh, they'll be there. A single smoke bagging squirrels is one thing. This is something else. They know we use this road.'

What the smokes knew and didn't know was always a question. Were they creatures of pure instinct, or were they capable of thought? Could they plan and strategize? And if the latter was true, didn't it follow that they were still, in some sense, people? The people they had been, before they were taken up? A great deal was simply not understood. Why, for instance, some of them would approach the Wall, while others would not; why a handful, such as the one they had seen on the road, would hazard the daylight to hunt; if their attacks, when they came, were simply random occurrences or triggered by something else; the distinctive manner in which they moved, always in groups of three, the actions of their bodies coordinated each to the others, like phrases of a rhyme; even how many there were out there, prowling the dark. It was true that the combination of the lights and walls had kept the Colony secure for most of a hundred years. The Builders seemed to have understood their enemy well, or at least well enough. And yet watching a pod moving at the edge of the lights, appearing out of the night to patrol the perimeter before departing to wherever it was they went, Peter often had the distinct impression of watching a single being, and that this being was alive, soulfully alive, no matter what Teacher said. Death made sense to him, the body joined to the soul in life, ceasing together in death. His mother's final hours had taught him as much. The sounds of her last, ragged breaths, and then the sudden stillness: he knew that the woman she had been was gone. How could a being continue with no soul?

They reached the ramp. To the north, at the base of the foothills, Peter could discern, through a haze of airborne dust, the long, low shape of the Empire Valley Outlet Mall. Peter had been there plenty of times before, on scavenging parties; the place had gotten pretty picked over through the years, but it was so vast you could still find useful stuff. The Gap had been cleared out, and J. Crew too, as had the Williams-Sonoma and the REI and most of the stores on the south end near the atrium, but there was a big Sears with windows that offered some protection and a JC Penney with good exterior access so you could get out fast, both still containing usable things, like shoes and tools and cooking pans. The thought occurred to him that he might go looking for something for Maus, for the baby, and maybe Theo was thinking the same thing. But there was no time for that now.

Standing above the sand at the base of the ramp was a sign, bent with the prevailing winds:

nt   sta e 10 E

P lm   ings 25

In io 55

Alicia rode back to them. 'All clear underneath. We better get a move on.'

The roadway was in passable shape; they were making good time again. A broiling wind was tearing through the pass. Peter's skin and eyes felt scorched, like kindling on the verge of combustion. He realized he hadn't urinated since they'd stopped to water the horses and reminded himself to drink from his canteen. Theo was scanning ahead with the binoculars, one hand loosely holding the reins. They were close enough now that Peter could see the turbines with enough detail to discern which were turning, which not. He tried to count the ones that were but quickly lost track.

The shadow of the mountain had begun to fall over the valley as they moved off the Eastern Road. At last they saw their destination: a concrete bunker, half-submerged in the valley floor, ringed by tall fencing charged with enough current to set anything that touched it aflame, and behind that the power trunk, a great rust-colored tube that ascended the mountain's eastern face, a wall of white rock forming a natural barricade. Theo dismounted and took the leather lanyard that held the key from around his neck. The key opened a metal panel on a post; there were two such panels, one on each side of the fence. Inside was a switch to control the current, another to open the gate. Theo killed the current and stood back while the gate swung open.

'Let's go.'

Adjacent to the station was a small livery, shaded by a metal roof, with troughs for the horses and a pump. They all drank greedily, letting the water stream down their chins and pouring handfuls over their sweat-soaked hair, then left Finn and Rey to see to the animals and went to the hatch. Theo withdrew the key once more. A thunk of metal as the locks freed, and they all stepped inside.

They were met by a blast of cool air and the basal hum of mechanical ventilation. Peter shivered in the sudden chill. A single bulb in a cage provided the only illumination to the flight of metal stairs that took them down below ground level. At the bottom was a second hatch, which stood ajar. Beyond it lay the turbine control room, and, deeper still, a barracks and kitchen and rooms for storage and equipment. At the rear, accessible by a ramp leading to the outside, was the stable where they overnighted the horses and mules.

'Anybody home?' Theo called out. He nudged the door open with his foot. 'Hello!'

No reply.

'Theo—' This was Alicia.

'I know,' Theo said. 'It's weird.'

They stepped cautiously through the hatch. Across the long table in the center of the control room lay an assemblage of guttered beeswax candles and the remains of a hastily departed meal: tins of paste, plates of hardtack, a greasy cast-iron pot that looked like it had contained some kind of meat stew. None of it appeared to have been touched in a day or even longer. Arlo waved his blade over the pot, and a cloud of flies scattered. Despite the whir of the fans the air was close and rank, thick with the smell of men and hot insulation. The only light, a pale yellow glow, came from the meters on the control panel, which monitored the flow of current from the turbines. Above them the station's clock told the hour: 18:45.

'So where the hell are they?' Alicia asked. 'Am I missing something, or is it almost Second Bell?'

They moved through the barracks and storage areas, confirming what they already knew: the station was empty. They climbed the stairs and stepped back into the late-day heat. Rey and Finn were waiting under the shade of the livery's awning.

'Any idea where they might have gone?' Theo asked.

Finn had balled up his shirt to douse it in the trough and was wiping down his chest and armpits. 'One of the tool carts is missing. A jenny, too.' He cocked his head, shifting his eyes to Rey, then back to Theo, as if to say, *Here's a theory.* 'They could still be out on the turbines. Zander likes to play it close sometimes.'

Zander Phillips was the Station Chief. He wasn't much to talk to, or look at, for that matter. All that time out in the sun and wind had dried him like a raisin, and the days of isolation had made him gruff to the point of silence. It was said that nobody had ever heard him say so much as five words in a row.

'How close?'

Finn shrugged again. 'Look, I don't know. Ask him when he gets back.'

371

'Who else is down here?'

'Just Caleb.'

Theo moved out of the shadow of the livery, to face the turbine field. The sun had just begun its dip behind the mountain; soon its shadow would stretch clear across the valley to the foothills on the far side. When that happened, there was no question: they'd have to seal the hatch. Caleb Jones was just a kid, barely fifteen; everyone called him Hightop.

'Well, they've got half a hand,' Theo said finally. Everyone knew this, but still it needed to be said. He looked at each of their party in turn, a quick glance to verify that his meaning was acknowledged. 'Let's get the animals inside.'

They led the animals down the ramp into the stable and sealed the bulkhead for the night. By the time they finished, the sun had dropped behind the mountain. Peter left Arlo and Alicia in the control room and went to join Theo where he was waiting at the gate, scanning the turbine field with his binoculars. Peter felt the first flickering chill of night across his arms, on the sun-baked skin at the back of his neck. His mouth and throat were dry again, tasting of dust and horses.

'How long do we wait?'

Theo didn't answer. The question was rhetorical, just words to fill the silence. Something had happened, or Zander and Caleb would have been back by now. Peter was also thinking of their father, as he believed Theo was as well: Demo Jaxon, gone into the turbine field without a trace, headed out on the Eastern Road. How long had they waited that night to close the hatch on Demo Jaxon?

Peter heard footsteps approaching and turned to find Alicia striding in their direction from the hatch. She took a place beside them, directing her gaze across the darkening field. They stood without speaking for another moment, watching the night march down the valley. As the mountain's shadow touched the foothills on the far side, Alicia drew a blade and wiped it on the hem of her jersey.

'I hate to say it—'

'You don't have to.' Theo turned to face the two of them. 'Okay, we're done here. Let's lock it up.'

The day-to-day. That was the term they used. Thinking neither of a past that was too much a story of loss and death, nor of a future that might never happen. Ninety-four souls under the lights, living in the day-to-day.

Yet it was not always so for Peter. In idle moments, standing the Watch when all was quiet, or lying in his bunk waiting for sleep to come, he would often find himself thinking of his parents. Though there were those in the Colony who still spoke of heaven – a place, beyond physical existence, where the soul went after death – the idea had never made sense to him. The world was the world, a realm of the senses that could be touched and tasted and felt, and it seemed to Peter that the dead, if they went anywhere at all, would pass into the living. Perhaps it was something Teacher had told him; perhaps he had come to the idea on his own. But for as long as he could recall, since he had come out of the Sanctuary and learned the truth of the world, he had believed this to be so. As long as he could hold his parents in his mind, some part of them would go on; and when he himself should die, these memories would pass with him into others still living, so that in this manner, all of them – not just Peter and his parents but everyone who had gone before and those who would come after – would continue.

He could no longer envision his parents' faces. This had been the first thing to go, leaving him in just a matter of days. When he thought of them, it wasn't a question of something seen but something felt – a wash of remembered sensations that flowed through him like water. The milky sound of his mother's voice and the look of her hands, pale and fine-boned but strong too, as she went about her work in the Infirmary, touching here and there, offering what comforts she could; the creak of his father's boots ascending the ladder of the catwalk on a night when Peter was running between the posts, and the way he had passed beside him without speaking, acknowledging Peter only with a hand on his shoulder; the heat and energy of the living room in the days of the Long Rides, when his father and uncle and the other men would gather to plan their routes, and later, the sounds of their voices as they drank shine on the porch well into the night, telling the stories of all they'd seen in the Darklands.

That was what Peter had wanted: to feel himself a part of them. To be one of the men of the Long Rides. And yet he had always known this would never happen. Listening from his bed to the voices on the porch, their rich masculine sound, he knew it about himself. Something was missing. He did not know the name for this thing; he wasn't sure it had a name at all. It was something more than courage, more than giving it up, though these were a part of it. The only word that came to him was *largeness*; that was what the men of the Long Rides possessed. And when the time came for one of the Jaxon boys to join them, Peter knew it would be Theo whom his father would call to the gate. He would be left behind.

His mother had known it about him too. His mother, who had so stoically borne their father's disgrace and then his final ride, everyone knowing but never daring to utter the truth; his mother, who, in the end, even when the cancer had taken everything else from her, had spoken not a single ill word of their father for leaving them. *He's in his own time now.* It was summer, as it was now, the days long and blazing with heat, when she'd taken to her bed. Theo was Full Watch by this time, not yet a Captain though that was soon to follow; the duty of their mother's care had fallen to Peter, who sat with her through the days and nights, helping her eat and dress and even bathe, an awkward intimacy they both endured because it was simply necessary. She might have gone to the Infirmary; that was how things were usually done. But his mother was First Nurse, and if Prudence Jaxon wanted to die at home in her bed, no one was going to tell her otherwise.

Whenever Peter recalled that summer, its long days and

endless nights, it seemed a period of his life from which he had never completely departed. It reminded him of a story Teacher had told them once about a turtle approaching a wall; each time the turtle moved forward, he decreased the distance by half, guaranteeing that he would never reach his destination. That was how it felt to Peter, watching his mother die. For three days she had drifted in and out of a feverish sleep, speaking hardly a word, answering only the simplest questions required for her care. She would take a few sips of water, but that was all. Sandy Chou, the nurse on duty, had been to visit that afternoon, and told Peter to be ready. The room was dim, the light of the spots filtered into dappled shadow by the tree that stood beyond the window. A sheen of sweat gleamed on her pale brow; her hands – the hands that Peter had watched for hours in the Infirmary, going about their careful work – lay motionless at her sides. Since nightfall Peter hadn't set foot from the room, fearing that she would awaken to find herself alone. That she was close to death, within hours, Peter knew; Sandy had made this clear. But it was the stillness of her hands where they rested on the blankets, all their patient labors ended, that told him so.

He wondered: How did you say goodbye? Would it frighten her, to hear him say the word? And what would fill the silence that came after? There had been no chance to do this with his father; in many ways, that had been the worst of it. He had simply slipped away, into oblivion. What would Peter have said to his father if he'd had the chance? A selfish wish, but still he thought it: *Choose me*, Peter would have said. *Not Theo. Me. Before you go, choose me.* The scene was perfectly clear in his mind – as Peter imagined it, the sun was coming up; they were sitting on the porch, just the two of them, his father dressed to ride, holding his compass, flicking the cover open with his thumb and closing it again, as was his habit – and yet the scene did not conclude. Never had he imagined how his father might have answered.

Now here was his mother, dying; if death was a room the

soul entered, she was standing at the threshold; and yet Peter could not find the words to tell her how he felt – that he loved her and would miss her when she was gone. In their family, it had always been true that Peter was hers, as Theo's was their father's. Nothing was ever said about this; it was simply a fact. Peter knew there had been miscarriages, and at least one baby that was born early with something wrong and died within hours. He thought this baby was a girl. It had happened when Peter was just a Little himself, still in the Sanctuary, so he didn't really know. So perhaps that was the missing thing – not something inside him, but inside *her* – and the reason that he had always felt his mother's love so fiercely. He was the one she would keep.

The first soft light of morning was in the windows when he heard her breathing change, catching in her chest like a hiccup. For a terrible instant he believed the moment had come, but then he saw her eyes were open. Mama? he said, taking her hand. Mama, I'm here.

Theo, she said.

Could she see him? Did she know where she was? Mama, he said, it's Peter. Do you want me to get Theo?

She seemed to be looking into some deep place inside herself, infinite and without borders, a place of eternity. *Take care of your brother, Theo*, she said. *He's not strong, like you*. Then she closed her eyes and did not open them again.

He had never told his brother about this. There seemed no point. There were times when he thought, wishfully, that he might have misheard her, or else could attribute these final words to the delirium of illness. But try as he might to construe them otherwise, her words and meaning seemed clear. After everything, the long days and nights he had cared for her, it was Theo she had placed at her bedside in her final hours; Theo to whom she had given the last words of her life.

Nothing more was said of the missing station crew. They fed the animals and then themselves and retired to the barracks, a cramped, foul-smelling room of bunk beds and soiled mattresses stuffed with musty straw. By the time Peter lay down, Finn and Rey were already snoring away. Peter wasn't accustomed to going to bed so early, but he'd been up for twenty-four hours straight and felt himself quickly drifting off.

He awoke disoriented, his mind still swimming in the current of anxious dreams. His internal clock told him it was half-night or later. All the men were still asleep, but Alicia's bunk was empty. He made his way down the dim hall to the control room, where he found her sitting at the long table, turning the pages of a book by the light of the panel. The clock read 02:33.

She lifted her eyes to meet his. 'Don't know how you slept, with all that snoring.'

He took a chair across from her. 'I didn't, not really. What are you reading?'

She closed the book and rubbed her eyes with the tips of her fingers. 'Damned if I know. I found it in the storage room. There's boxes and boxes of them.' She slid it across the table to him. 'Go ahead and look if you want.'

Where the Wild Things Are, the title read. A thin volume, containing mostly pictures. Peter turned the brittle, dusty-smelling pages one by one. A little boy in some kind of animal costume, with ears and a tail, brandishing a fork as he chased a small white dog; the boy's banishment to his room, and the room being enveloped by a forest, magically growing; a moonlit night descending, and a journey across the sea to an island of monsters, unimaginable beings of grasping claws and gnashing teeth and huge yellow eyes. The Wild Things.

'That whole business about the boy looking them in the eyes and telling them to be still,' Alicia said. She yawned into her hand. 'I don't see how that would do any good at all.'

Peter closed the book and put it aside. He had no idea what to make of any of it, but that was the way of most things from the Time Before. How did people live? What did they eat, wear, think? Did they walk in the dark, as if this were nothing? If there were no virals, what made them afraid?

'I think it's all made up.' He shrugged. 'Just a story. I think he's dreaming.'

Alicia lifted her eyebrows, her expression saying, *Who knows? Who can say what the world used to be?*

'I was actually hoping you'd wake up,' she announced then, rising from her chair. She lifted a lantern from the floor. 'I've got something to show you.'

She led him back through the barracks and into one of the storage rooms. The walls were lined with metal shelving, stacked with supplies: greasy tools, coils of wire and solder, plastic jugs of water and alcohol. Alicia placed the lantern on the floor and stepped to one of the shelves and began to move its contents onto the floor.

'Well? Don't just stand there.'

'What are you doing?'

'What does it look like? And keep your voice down – I don't want to wake the others.'

When they'd cleared everything away, Alicia instructed him to stand at one end of the shelf, positioning herself on the opposite side. Peter realized that the back of the shelf was a sheet of plywood, concealing the wall behind it. They pulled the shelf away.

A hatch.

Alicia stepped forward and turned the ring and swung it open. A narrow, tubelike space, with a flight of metal stairs rising in a spiral. Metal crates were stacked against the wall. The stairs vanished in the gloom, some unknowable distance over Peter's head. The air was stale and choked with dust.

'When did you find it?' he asked, amazed.

'Last season. I got bored one night and started poking around. I figure it's some kind of escape route left by the Builders. The stairs go straight to a crawl space on the roof.'

Peter gestured toward the crates with his lantern. 'What's in those?'

'That,' she said, smiling mischievously, 'is the best part.'

Together they dragged one of the crates out onto the floor of the storeroom. A metal locker, a meter long and half as deep, with the words US MARINE CORPS printed on the side. Alicia knelt to undo the hasps and lifted the lid to reveal six sleek black objects, cradled in foam. It took Peter a few seconds to understand what he was seeing.

'Holy shit, Lish.'

She passed him a weapon. A long-bore rifle, cool to the touch and smelling faintly of oil. It was shockingly light in his hands, as if made of some substance that defied gravity. Even in the dim light of the storage room he could detect the lustrous gleam in the finish of the muzzle. The guns he'd seen were all little more than corroded relics, rifles and pistols the Army had left behind; the Watch still kept some in the Armory, but as far as Peter was aware, all the ammunition had been used up years ago. Never in his life had Peter held anything so clean and new, untouched by time.

'How many are there?'

'Twelve boxes, six guns apiece, a little over a thousand rounds. There are six more crates up in the crawl space.'

All his nervousness was gone, replaced by a lusty hunger to use this wonderful new object in his hands, to feel its power. 'Show me how to load it,' he said.

Alicia took the gun from his hands and drew back the bolt and charger. Then she took a magazine of bullets from the box, shoved it into place in front of the trigger guard, pushing forward until it caught, and gave the base two hard taps with her palm.

'Aim it like a cross,' she said, and turned away to demonstrate. 'It's basically the same, only with a lot more kick. Just keep your finger off the trigger unless you mean business. You'll want to, but don't.'

She passed the rifle back to him. A loaded gun! Peter raised it to his shoulder, searching for something in the room that seemed worthy of his aim, and finally selected a coil of copper wire on the far shelf. The urge to fire, to experience the explosive force of its recoil in his arms, was so strong it required an almost physical effort to push the thought away.

'Just remember what I said about the trigger,' Alicia

warned. 'You've got twenty rounds per magazine. Now, load this one so I know you know how.'

He traded the loaded rifle for a new one. Peter did his best to recall the steps: safety, bolt, charger, magazine. When he was done he gave the clip two hard taps, as he had seen Alicia do.

'How's that?'

Alicia was watching him appraisingly, holding her rifle with the stock against her hip. 'Not bad. A little slow. Don't point it down like that, you'll blow your foot off.'

He quickly raised his barrel. 'You know, I'm a little surprised. I thought you didn't believe in these things.'

She shrugged. 'I don't, not really. They're sloppy and they're loud, and they make you too confident by half.' She passed him a second magazine for his waist pouch. 'On the other hand, the smokes believe in them just fine if you do it right.' She tapped a finger against her sternum. 'One shot, through the sweet spot. Closer than three meters you have a little slop, but don't count on it.'

'So you've used these guns before.'

'Did I say that?'

Peter knew better than to press. Six crates of Army rifles. How could Alicia possibly resist?

'So whose guns are they?'

'How should I know? As far as I can tell, they're the property of the United States Marine Corps, just like it says on the box. Quit asking questions and let's go.'

They reentered the hatch and began to climb. He felt the temperature rise with every step of their ascent. Ten meters up they reached a small platform with a ladder. In the ceiling over their heads was another hatch. Alicia rested the lantern on the platform, reached overhead on tiptoes, and began to turn the wheel. They were both sweating hard; the air felt almost too thick to breathe.

'It's stuck.'

He reached up to help her. With a rusty squeal, the mechanism released. Two turns, three; the hatch dropped open on its hinges. Cool night air tumbled through the opening like a current of water, smelling of desert, of dry juniper and mesquite. Above, Peter could see only blackness.

'Me first,' Alicia said. 'I'll call you up.'

He heard her footsteps moving away from the opening. He listened for more but heard nothing. They were up on the roof somewhere, no lights to protect them. He counted to twenty, thirty. Should he follow her?

Then Alicia's face appeared above him, floating over the open hatch. 'Leave the lantern there. It's all clear. Come on.'

He ascended the ladder and found himself in a small crawl space, with pipes and valves and more crates stacked along the walls. He paused, letting his eyes adjust. He was facing an open door. He took a deep breath and stepped forward.

He stepped into the stars.

It hit him in the lungs first, shoving the breath from his chest. A feeling of pure physical panic, as if he'd stepped onto nothing, onto the night sky itself. His knees bent beneath him, his free hand scrabbled at the air, searching for something to hold on to, to give himself a feeling of form and weight, the working dimensions of the world around him. The sky above was a vault of blackness – and everywhere, the stars!

'Peter, breathe,' Alicia said.

She was standing beside him. He realized that her hand was resting on his shoulder. In the dark Alicia's voice seemed to come from very close and far away at once. He did as she said, letting deep gulps of night air fill his chest. Bit by bit his eyes adjusted. Now he could make out the edge of the roof, spilling into nothingness. They were in the southwest corner, he realized, near the exhaust port.

'So what do you think?'

For a long, quiet moment, he let his eyes roam the sky. The longer he looked, the more stars appeared to him, pushing through the blackness. These were the stars his father had spoken of, the stars his father had seen on the Long Rides.

'Does Theo know?'

Alicia laughed. 'Does Theo know what?'

'The hatch. The guns.' Peter shrugged helplessly. 'All of it.'

'I never showed him, if that's what you mean. I'm guessing Zander does, since he knows every inch of this place. But he's never said a word to me about it.'

His eyes searched out her face. She seemed different somehow, in the dark: the same Alicia he had always known, but also someone new. He understood what she had done. She'd saved it for him.

'Thanks.'

'Don't go thinking this means we're friends or anything. If Arlo had woken up first, it'd be him standing here.'

That wasn't true, and he knew it. 'Even so,' he said.

She led him to the edge of the roof. They were facing north, across the valley. Not a breath of wind was blowing. On the far side, the shape of the mountains was etched into the sky as a dark bulk pushed up against a shimmering rim of stars. They took positions, lying side by side with their bellies pressed against the concrete, still warm with the heat of the day.

'Here,' Alicia said, reaching into her pouch. 'You'll want one of these.'

A night scope. She showed him how to fix it to the top of the rifle and adjust the gain. Peter placed his eye to the viewfinder and saw a landscape of shrubs and rocks, all washed in a pale green light, with a pair of hatched crosshairs bisecting his view. At the bottom of the scope he saw a readout: 212 METERS. The numbers rose and fell as he swept the rifle back and forth. Amazing.

'You think they're still alive?'

Alicia took a moment to answer. 'I don't know. Probably not. It can't hurt to wait, though.' She paused again; there wasn't much else to say on the subject. Then: 'You think I was too hard on Maus today?'

The question surprised him. As long as he'd known her, Alicia had never been one to second-guess herself.

'Not the way it worked out. You did the right thing.'

'She's a loss. You can't say she isn't.'

'It doesn't matter. You said it yourself. Maus knows the rules as well as anyone.'

'I'd rather keep her than Galen.' She groaned. 'Flyers. That guy. What the hell could she see in him?'

Peter lifted his face from the scope. The sky was so thick with stars it was as if he could reach out and brush them with his hand. He'd never seen anything so beautiful in his life. It made him think of the oceans, the names in the book like the words of a song – Atlantic, Pacific, Indian, Arctic – and about his father, standing on the edge of the sea. Maybe the stars were what Auntie meant when she spoke of God. The old God, from the Time Before. The God of Heavens who watched the World.

'Do you ever . . .' Alicia began. 'I don't know, think about it?'

Peter shifted to face her. Her eye was still pressed to her scope. 'Think about what?'

Alicia gave a nervous laugh – a sound he'd never heard her make. 'You're going to make me say it? *Pairing*, Peter. Having Littles.'

He had; of course he had. Almost everybody paired by the time they were twenty. But standing the Watch made it hard – up all night, sleeping most of the day or else walking around in a daze of exhaustion. But when Peter faced the question squarely, he knew that wasn't the only reason. Something about the idea simply did not seem possible; it applied to others, but not to him. There had been girls for him, and then a few he would have described as women; each had occupied a few months' time, working him up into such a state that they were, briefly, most of what he thought about. But in the end he had always drifted away or found himself, inexplicably, directing them toward someone he thought of as more suitable.

'Not really, no.'

'What about Sara?'

A feeling of defensiveness rose up inside him. 'What about her?'

'Come on, Peter,' Alicia said, and he heard the exasperation in her voice. 'I know she wants to pair with you. It's no secret. She's First too, it would be a good match. Everyone thinks so.'

'What does that have to do with anything?'

'I'm just saying. It's obvious.'

'Well, it isn't obvious to me.' He paused. They had never spoken like this before. 'Look, I like Sara fine. I'm just not certain I want to pair with her.'

'But you *do* want to? Pair, I mean.'

'Someday. Maybe. Lish, why are you asking this?'

He turned his face toward her again. She was looking through her scope across the valley, slowly sweeping the horizon line with her rifle.

'Lish?'

'Hold on. Something's moving.'

He rolled back into position. 'Where?'

Alicia quickly lifted the barrel of her rifle, pointing. 'Two o'clock.'

He pressed his eye to the scope: a solitary figure, darting from one stand of scrub to another, a hundred meters past the fence line. Human.

'It's Hightop,' Alicia said.

'How do you know?'

'Too small to be Zander. Nobody else out there.'

'He's alone?'

'I can't tell,' Alicia said. 'Wait. No. Ten degrees right.'

Peter looked: a flash of green in the scope, skipping like a stone over the desert floor. Then he saw a second, and a third, two hundred meters and closing. Not closing: circling.

'What are they doing? Why don't they just take him?'

'I don't know.'

Then they heard it.

'Hey!' The voice was Caleb's, high and wild and full of fear.

384

He was up and running toward the fence, waving his arms. 'Open the gate, open the gate!'

'*Flyers.*' Alicia rolled to her feet. 'Come on.'

They raced back to the crawl space; Alicia quickly opened one of the containers stacked by the hatch. She withdrew a pistol of some kind – short, with a fat, snub-nosed barrel. Peter had no time to ask. They ran back to the edge and Alicia pointed it up and over the turbine field and fired.

The flare shot skyward, dragging a hissing tail of light. Peter instinctively knew he shouldn't look but he couldn't stop himself, he looked anyway, his vision instantly seared by the image of the flare's white-hot center. At its apex the flare seemed to stop, suspended in space. Then it exploded, bathing the field in light.

'We've bought him a minute,' Alicia said. 'There's a ladder down the back.'

They slung their weapons over their shoulders; Alicia descended the ladder first, taking it like a pair of poles, her feet not even touching the rungs. As Peter scrambled down, she shot another flare, arcing it over the station toward the field. Then they ran.

Caleb was standing on the far side of the metal gate. The virals had scattered, back into the shadows. 'Please! Let me in!'

'Shit, we don't have a key,' Peter said.

Alicia shouldered her rifle and aimed it at the panel. A burst of fire and noise; a shower of sparks poured forth as the panel shot from its pole.

'Caleb, you'll have to climb over!'

'I'll fry!'

'No you won't, the current's off!' She looked at Peter. 'You think it's off?'

'How should I know?'

Alicia stepped forward and, before Peter could say anything, pressed her palm to the fence. Nothing happened.

'Hurry, Caleb!'

Caleb curled his fingers between the wires and began to

climb. Around them the shadows flattened as the second flare completed its descent. Alicia withdrew a fresh flare from her waist pouch, loaded the pistol, and fired. Up and up it sailed, riding its tail of smoke, and burst above them in a shower of light.

'That's the last,' she said to Peter. 'We've got about ten seconds before they figure out the current's off.' Caleb was straddling the top of the fence now. 'Caleb,' she yelled, 'move your ass!'

He took the last five meters at a drop, rolling as he landed and vaulting to his feet. His cheeks were wet from crying, smeared with dirt and snot; his feet were bare. In another few seconds they'd be in the dark again.

'Are you hurt?' Alicia said. 'Can you run?'

The boy nodded.

They took off toward the station. Peter felt the virals coming before he saw them. He turned in time to see one launching toward them from the top of the fence. A blast of gunfire went off next to his ear: the creature twisted in the air and went down, skidding across the hardpan. He turned to see Alicia, her rifle shouldered, her eyes fixed on the fence. She let off three more shots in quick succession.

'Get him out of here!' she yelled.

He raced with Caleb to the ladder. Behind them, Alicia continued to fire, the sound of her rifle shots reaching him as muffled pops that echoed through the yard. More virals were inside the fence line now. Slinging his rifle, Peter mounted the ladder; when he reached the top, he turned to look. Alicia was backing toward the wall of the station, shooting into the shadows. When her gun went silent she cast it aside and began to climb; Peter shouldered his rifle and aimed in the same general direction and squeezed the trigger. The barrel kicked up, his shots sailing uselessly into the dark. His whole body shook with the feel of it, its wild force.

'Watch what you're doing!' Alicia cried, pressing her body to the ladder below him. 'And for godsakes, aim!'

'I'm trying!' There were three now, coming out of the

shadows toward the ladder's base; Peter took a step to his right, clamping the stock hard against his shoulder. *Aim it like a cross.* He had very little chance of hitting them, but maybe he could scare them off. He squeezed the trigger and they jumped away, rolling across the yard and skittering into the dark. He'd bought a few seconds at most.

'Shut up and climb!' he yelled.

'I will if you stop shooting at me!'

Then she was at the top. He found her hand and pulled hard, vaulting her onto the concrete surface of the roof. Caleb was waving to them from the mouth of the hatch.

'Behind you!'

As Alicia clambered down the hatch, Peter turned; a single viral was standing on the edge of the roof. Peter raised his gun and fired, but too late. The place where the creature had stood was empty.

'Forget the smokes!' Alicia yelled from below. 'Come on!'

He dropped straight through the opening, tumbling into Caleb, who folded under him with a grunt. A sharp pain sliced his ankle as he hit the platform; the rifle clattered away. Alicia stepped over the two of them and reached up to seal the hatch. But something was pressing down on the other side. Alicia's face clenched with exertion; her feet scrabbled at the ladder, fighting for leverage.

'I . . . can't . . . close it!'

Peter and Caleb leapt to their feet and pushed. But the force on the far side was too great. Peter had done something to his ankle when he'd fallen, but the pain was vague now, unimportant. He scanned the platform below for his rifle and found it, lying at the top of the stairs.

'Let go,' he said. 'Drop the hatch. It's the only way.'

'Are you crazy?' But then he saw, in Alicia's eyes, that she understood his intentions. 'Good, do it.' She turned to Caleb, who nodded. 'Ready?'

'One . . . two . . .'

'Three!'

They released the hatch. Peter dropped to the platform,

the pain exploding in his ankle as he made impact; he lunged for the rifle and swung around, thrusting the muzzle upward through the opening. There was no time to aim, but he hoped he wouldn't have to.

He didn't. The end of the barrel went straight into the viral's open mouth. The barrel speared him like an arrow, sliding past the rows of glossy teeth, coming to rest where it pressed against the bony ridge at the top of his throat, and Peter looked him in the eyes and thought, *Be still*, giving the rifle one hard shove to drive it home before he shot Zander Phillips through the brain.

TWENTY-ONE

There was one great difference between the world as it was now and the world of the Time Before, Michael Fisher thought, and it wasn't the virals. The difference was electricity.

The virals were a problem, sure – about forty-two and a half *million* problems, if the old documents in the HD shed behind the Lighthouse were correct. A whole history of the epidemic in its final hours, for Michael the Circuit to read. 'CV1–CV13 National and Regional Summary of Select Surveillance Components,' Centers for Disease Control and Prevention, Atlanta, Georgia; 'Civilian Resettlement Protocols for Urban Centers, Zones 6-1,' Federal Emergency Management Agency, Washington, DC; 'Efficacy of Postexposure Protection Against CV Familial Hemorrhagic Fever in Nonhuman Primates,' United States Army Medical Research Institute for Infectious Diseases, Fort Detrick, Maryland. And so on, in that vein. Some of which he understood, some of which he didn't, but all saying the same basic thing. One person in ten. One person taken up for every nine that died. So, assuming a human population of 500 million at the time of the outbreak – the combined populations of the United States, Canada, and Mexico – and forestalling, for the moment, the question of the rest of the world, about which very little seemed to be known – and even assuming some kind of mortality rate for the virals themselves, say a modest 15 percent – that still left 42.5 million of the bloodthirsty bastards bouncing around between the Panamanian Isthmus and the Bering Frontier, gobbling up everything with hemoglobin in its veins and a heat signature between 36 and 38 degrees, i.e., 99.96 percent of the mammalian kingdom, from voles to grizzly bears.

So, okay. A *problem.*

But just give me enough current, Michael thought, and I can keep the virals out forever.

The Time Before: he sometimes trembled just to think of it, the great buzzing man-made electrical juiciness of it all. The millions of miles of wire, the billions of amps of current. The vast generating plants turning the bottled energy of the planet itself into the eternally affirmative question that was a single amp of current shooting down a line, saying, *Yes? Yes? Yes?*

And the machines. The wondrous, humming, glowing machines. Not just computers and Blu-rays and handhelds – they had dozens of these devices, scavenged over the years from trips down the mountain, socked away in the shed – but simple things, ordinary everyday things, like hair dryers and microwaves and filament lightbulbs. All wired up, plugged in, connected to the grid.

Sometimes it was like the current was still out there, waiting for him. Waiting for Michael Fisher to throw the switch and turn the whole thing – human civilization itself – back on.

He spent too much time alone in the Lighthouse. Fair enough. Just him and Elton, which most of the time was like being alone, in the social sense of things. In the let's-chat-about-the-weather and what's-for-chow sense of things. He didn't say he didn't.

And there was lots of juice still out there, Michael knew. Diesel generators the size of whole towns. Huge LNG plants fat with gas and waiting to go. Acres of solar panels giving their unblinking gaze to the desert sun. Pocket-sized nukes humming away like atomic harmonicas, the heat in the control rods slowly building over decades until someday the whole thing would just go sailing through the floor, exploding in a shower of radioactive steam that somewhere, high above, a long-forgotten satellite, powered by a tiny nuclear cell of its own, would record as the final agonies of a dying brother – before it, too, darkened, soaring headlong to earth in a streak of unacknowledged light.

What a waste. And time was running out.

Rust, corrosion, wind, rain. The nibbling teeth of mice and the acrid droppings of insects and the devouring jaws of years. The war of nature upon machines, of the planet's chaotic forces upon the works of humankind. The energy that men had pulled from the earth was being inexorably pulled back into it, sucked like water down a drain. Before long, if it hadn't happened already, not a single high-tension pole would be left standing on the earth.

Mankind had built a world that would take a hundred years to die. A century for the last lights to go out.

The worst of it was, he'd be there when it happened. The batteries were decaying. Decaying *badly*. He could see it happening before his eyes, on the screen of his old battle-hardened CRT with its thrumming bars of green. The cells had been built to last how long? Thirty years? Fifty? That they could hold any kind of charge after almost a century was a miracle. You could keep the turbines spinning forever in the breeze, but without the batteries to store and regulate the current, one windless night was all it would take.

Fixing the batteries was impossible. The batteries weren't made to be *fixed*. They were made to be *replaced*. You could retrofit all the gaskets you wanted, clear away the corrosion, rewire the controllers till the herd came home. All basically busywork, because the membranes had had it. The membranes were cooked, their polymer pathways hopelessly gummed up with sulfonic acid molecules. That's what the monitor was telling him with that little-bitty hiccup in the day-to-day. Short of the US Army showing up with a brand-new stack fresh from the factory – Hey, sorry, we forgot about you guys! – the lights were going to fail. A year, two at the outside. And when that happened, it would be he, Michael the Circuit, who'd have to stand up and say, *Listen, everybody, I've got some not-great news. Tonight's forecast? Darkness, with widespread screaming. It's been fun keeping the lights on, but I have to die now. Just like all of you.*

The only person he'd told was Theo. Not Gabe Curtis, who was technically head of Light and Power but had mostly checked out when he got sick, leaving Michael and Elton to run the shop; not Sanjay or Old Chou or anyone else; not even Sara, his sister. Why had Michael chosen Theo to tell? They were friends. Theo was Household. Sure, there had always been a touch of the gloom about him – Michael of all people knew this when he saw it – and it was a heavy thing, to tell a man that he and everybody he knew was dead, basically. Maybe Michael was just thinking of the day when he'd have to explain the situation, hoping Theo would break the news instead, or at least back him up somehow. Yet even to Theo, who was better informed than most, the batteries were more like a permanent fixture of nature than something man-made, governed by physical laws. Like the sun and sky and walls, the batteries just *were*. The batteries drank up the juice from the turbines and spit it out into the lights, and if something went wrong, well, Light and Power would fix it. *Right, Michael?* Theo had said. *This problem with the batteries, you can repair it?* Around and around like this for some time, until Michael in complete exasperation had sighed and shaken his head and spelled out the situation in words of exactly one syllable.

Theo, you're not hearing me. You're not hearing what I'm saying. The Lights. Will. Go. Off.

391

They were sitting on the porch of the small, one-story frame house Michael shared with Sara, who was off somewhere for the afternoon, riding herd or taking temperatures in the Infirmary or visiting Uncle Walt to make sure he was actually eating and washing – mooning around restlessly, in other words, the way she always did. It was late afternoon. The house stood at the edge of the short-grass meadow where they turned out the horses to graze, though the dry days of summer had come on early, and the field was the color of bread crust, burned clear through to the dirt in places, forming bare spots that pillowed with dust when you walked across them. Everybody knew the house as the Fisher place.

'Off,' Theo repeated. 'The lights.'

Michael nodded. 'Off.'

'Two years, you say.'

Michael studied Theo's face, watching the information taking hold. 'It could be longer, but I don't think so. It could be less, too.'

'And there's nothing you can do to fix it.'

'No one can.'

Theo exhaled sharply, as if he'd just taken a punch. 'Okay, I get it.' He shook his head. 'Flyers, I get it. Who else have you told?'

'Nobody.' Michael lifted his shoulders in a shrug. 'You're it.'

Theo rose and moved to the edge of the porch. For a moment neither spoke.

'We'll have to move,' Michael said. 'Or else find another power source.'

Theo was looking away, toward the field. 'And just how do you suggest we do that?'

'I don't. I'm just stating it as a fact. When the batteries drop below twenty percent—'

'I know, I know, that's it, no lights,' Theo said. 'You've made that clear.'

'What should we do?'

Theo gave a hopeless laugh. 'How in hell should I know?'

'I mean, should we tell people?' Michael paused, searching his friend's face. 'So they can, you know, prepare themselves.'

Theo thought a moment. Then he shook his head. 'No.'

And that was all. They'd never spoken of it again. When had that been? Over a year ago, about the time Maus and Galen had gotten married – the first wedding in a long, long time. It felt strange, everyone so happy, and Michael knowing what he did. People were surprised that it was Galen up there with Mausami, instead of Theo; only Michael knew the reason, or could guess at it. He'd seen the look in Theo's eyes that afternoon on the porch. Something had gone out of him, and it didn't seem to Michael like the kind of thing a person could get back.

There was nothing to do now but wait. Wait, and listen.

Because that was the thing: the radio was forbidden. The problem, as Michael understood it, had boiled down to too many people. It was the radio that had led the Walkers to the Colony in the early days, nothing the Builders had ever planned on, since the Colony wasn't supposed to last as long as it had. So the decision had been made that right then, in the year 17 – seventy-five years ago – the radio should be destroyed, the antenna taken down from the mountain, its parts chopped up and scattered in the dump.

At the time, it might have made sense. Michael could see how that was possible. The Army knew where to find them, and there was only so much food and fuel to go around, so much room under the lights. But not now. Not with the batteries the way they were, the lights about to fail. Blackness and screaming and dying, et cetera.

It wasn't long after Michael's conversation with Theo, not more than a few days as he recalled, that he had happened upon the old logbook – 'happened' being not quite the correct word, as things turned out. It was the quiet hour, just before dawn. Michael had been sitting at the panel in the Lighthouse like always, minding the monitors and flipping through Teacher's copy of *What to Name the Baby* (that's how desperate he'd become for something new to read; he'd just made it to the I's), when, for some unknown reason, restlessness or boredom or the discomfiting thought that if the winds had blown a little differently his parents might have named him Ichabod (Ichabod the Circuit!), his eyes had drifted upward to the shelf above his CRT, and there it was. A notebook with a thin black spine. Standing there among the usual whatnot, tucked between a spool of solder and a stack of Elton's CDs (*Billie Holiday Sings the Blues*, *Sticky Fingers* by the Rolling Stones, *Superstars #1 Party Dance Hits*, a group called Yo Mama that sounded to Michael like a bunch of people yelling at each other, not that he understood the first thing about music). Michael must have looked right at it a thousand times, and yet he couldn't remember seeing it before; that was curious, the thought that gave him pause. A book, something he hadn't read. (He'd read everything.) He rose and took it from its place on the shelf, and when he cracked the spine the first thing he saw, inscribed in a precise hand, an engineer's hand, was a name he knew: Rex Fisher. Michael's great (great-great?) grandfather. Rex Fisher, First Engineer of Light and Power, First Colony, California Republic. What the hell? How had he missed *this*? He turned the pages, crinkled with moisture and age; it took only a moment for his mind to parse the information, to break it into its components and reassemble it into a coherent whole that told him what this slender, ink-filled volume was. Columns of numbers, with dates written in the old style, followed by the hour and another number Michael understood to be the frequency of transmission, and then, in the spaces to the right, short notations, rarely more than a few words but heavy with suggestion, whole stories folded into them: 'unmanned distress beacon' or 'five survivors' or 'military?' or 'three en route from Prescott, Arizona.' There were other place names, too: Ogden, Utah. Kerrville, Texas. Las Cruces, New Mexico. Ashland, Oregon. Hundreds of such notations, filling page after page, until they simply stopped. The final entry read, simply, 'All transmission ceasing by order of the Household.'

A glow was paling the windows by the time Michael finished. He doused the lantern and rose from his chair as Morning Bell began to peal – three solid rings followed by a pause of identical duration, then three more in case you didn't get the message the first time (it's morning; you're alive) – and crossed the mazelike clutter of the narrow room with its plastic bins of parts and scattered tools and dirty dishes in teetering piles (why Elton couldn't just eat in the barracks Michael had no idea; the man was just flat-out disgusting), stepped to the breaker panel, and powered down the lights. A wave of weary satisfaction washed through him, as it always did at Morning Bell: one more night's work accomplished, all souls safe and sound to face another day. Let's see Alicia and her blades do *that*. (And wasn't it true that when he'd lifted his face to see the log-book, it had been the image of Alicia in his mind that had distracted him? As it sometimes – often – did? And not just Alicia but the specific picture of sunlight flaring her hair as she had stepped from the Armory that very evening, Michael moving down the path toward her, unseen? An image that was, as he considered it again, quite striking? All this despite the fact that Alicia Donadio was, in point of fact, the single most annoying woman on earth, not that there was such a vast field of competitors?) He returned to the panel and moved through the steps, flipping the cells to charge, turning on the fans and opening the vents; the meters, which stood at 28 percent across the board, began to flicker and rise.

He swiveled to look at Elton, who appeared to be dozing in his chair, though it was sometimes hard to tell. Waking and sleeping, Elton's eyes were always the same, two thin strips of yellow jelly, peeking through slitted eyelids of perpetually tearing dampness that never quite managed to close. His pale hands were folded over the curve of his belly, the ear-phones, as always, clamped to the sides of his scaly head, pumping out the music he listened to all night. The Beatles.

Boyz-B-Ware. Art Lundgren and his All-Girl Polka-Party Orchestra (the only one that Michael sort of liked).

'Elton?' No answer. Michael turned his voice up a notch. *'Elton?'*

The old man – Elton was fifty at least – startled to life. 'Flyers, Michael. What time is it?'

'Relax. It's morning. We're down for the night.'

Elton screwed himself up in his chair, setting the hinges creaking, and drew the earphones down into the folds of his neck. 'Then what you wake me up for? I was just getting to the good part.'

Next to the CDs, Elton's nightly forays into imagined sexual adventure constituted his major pastime – dreams of women, conveniently long dead, which he would recount to Michael in excruciating detail, claiming that these were actually memories of things that had happened to him in his younger days. It was all bullshit, Michael figured, since Elton hardly ever set foot outside the Lighthouse, and to look at him now, with his dandruffy head and tangled beard and gray teeth clotted with the remains of a meal he had probably eaten two days ago, Michael didn't see how any of it was even remotely possible.

'Don't you want to hear about it?' The old man gave his eyebrows a suggestive wag. 'It was the hay dream. I know you like that one.'

'Not now, Elton. I . . . found something. A book.'

'You woke me up because you found a book?'

Michael scooted his chair down the length of the panel and placed the log in the old man's lap. Elton ran his fingers over the cover, his sightless eyes turned upward, then drew it to his nose and gave a long sniff.

'Now, I'd say that would be your great-grandfather's logbook. Thing's been floating around here for years.' He passed it back to Michael. 'Can't say I've read it myself. Find anything good in there?'

'Elton, what do you know about this?'

'Couldn't say. Things do have a way of popping up right when you need them, though.'

Which was when Michael realized why he hadn't seen the book before. He hadn't seen it before because it wasn't there.

'You put it on the shelf, didn't you?'

'Now, Michael. Radio's forbidden. You know that.'

'Elton, did you talk to Theo?'

'Theo who?'

Michael felt his irritation mount. Why couldn't the man just answer a question? 'Elton—'

The old man cut him off with a raised hand. 'Okay, don't get your gaps in a twist. No, I didn't talk to Theo. Though I'm guessing you did. I didn't talk to anyone, except for you.' He paused. 'You know, you're more like your old man than you think, Michael. He wasn't a very good liar, either.'

Somehow, Michael wasn't surprised. He slumped down into his chair. Part of him was glad.

'So how bad are they?' Elton asked.

'Not good.' He shrugged; for some reason, he was looking at his hands. 'Number five is the worst, two and three a little better than the others. We've got irregular charge on one and four. Twenty-eight this morning across the board, never over fifty-five by First Bell.'

Elton nodded. 'So, brownouts within the next six months, total failure within thirty. More or less like your father figured.'

'He *knew*?'

'Your old man could read those batteries like a book, Michael. He could see this coming a long time ago.'

So there it was. His father had known, and probably his mother too. A familiar panic rose within him. He didn't want to think about this, he *didn't*.

'Michael?'

He took a deep breath to calm himself. One more secret for him to carry. But he would do what he always did, pushing the information down inside himself as far as it could go.

'So,' said Michael, 'how exactly do you build a radio?'

Radio wasn't the problem, Elton explained; it was the mountain that was the problem.

The original beacon had run off an antenna that stood at the peak of the mountain; an insulated cable, five kilometers long, had run the length of the power trunk to connect it to the transmitter in the Lighthouse. All taken down and destroyed by the One Law. Without the antenna, they were hopelessly blocked to the east, and any signal they might have picked up would be overwhelmed by electromagnetic interference from the battery stack.

That left two choices: go to the Household and ask for permission to run an antenna up the mountain; or say nothing and try to boost the signal somehow.

It was, in the end, no contest. Michael couldn't ask for permission without explaining the reason, which meant telling the Household about the batteries; and to tell them about the batteries was simply out of the question, because then everyone would know, and once that happened, the rest wouldn't matter. It wasn't just the batteries that Michael was in charge of; it was the glue of hope that held the place together. You couldn't just tell people they had no chance. The only thing to do was find somebody still alive out there – find them with a radio, which would mean they had power and therefore light – before he said another word to anyone. And if he found nothing, if the world really was empty, then what would happen would happen anyway; it was better if nobody knew.

He got to work that morning. In the shed, piled among the old CRTs and CPUs and plasmas and bins of cell phones and Blu-rays, was an old stereo receiver – just AM and FM bands, but he could open that up – and an oscilloscope. A copper wire up the chimney served as their antenna; Michael refitted the guts of the receiver into a plain CPU chassis, to camouflage it – the only person who might have noticed an extra CPU sitting on the counter would be Gabe, and from what Sara had told him, the poor guy wasn't ever coming back –

and jacked the receiver into the panel, using the audio port. The battery control system had a simple media program, and with a little work he was able to configure the equalizer to filter out the battery noise. They wouldn't be able to broadcast; he had no transmitter and would have to figure out how to build one from the bottom up. But for the time being, with a little patience, he'd be able to scoop out any decent signal from the west.

They found nothing.

Oh, there was plenty to hear out there. A surprising range of activity, from ULF to microwaves. The odd cell phone tower powered by a working solar panel. Geothermals still pushing juice back into the grid. Even a couple of satellites, still in their orbits, dutifully transmitting their cosmic hellos and probably wondering where everybody on planet Earth had run off to.

A whole hidden world of electronic noise. And nobody, not one single person, home.

Day by day, Elton would sit at the radio, the headphones clamped to his ears, his sightless eyes turned upward in their sockets. Michael would isolate a signal, clear out the noise, and send it to the amplifier, where it would be filtered a second time and pushed through the phones. After a moment of intense concentration, Elton would nod, maybe take a moment to give his crumby beard a thoughtful rub, and then proclaim, in his gentle voice:

'Something faint, irregular. Maybe an old distress beacon.'

Or: 'A ground signal. A mine, maybe.'

Or, with a tight shake of the head: 'Nothing here. Let's move on.'

So they sat through the days and nights, Michael at the CRT, Elton with the earphones clamped to the sides of his head, his mind seemingly adrift in the leftover signals of their all-but-vanished species. Whenever they found one, Michael would record it in the logbook, noting the time and frequency and anything else about it. Then they'd do it all again.

Elton had been born blind, so Michael didn't really feel sorry for him, not on that score. Elton's being blind was just a part of who he was. It was the radiation that had done it; Elton's parents were Walkers, part of the Second Wave to come in, fifty-odd years ago, when the settlements in Baja had been overrun. The survivors had walked straight through the irradiated ruins that had once been San Diego, and by the time the group arrived, twenty-eight souls, those who could still stand were carrying the others. Elton's mother was pregnant, delirious with fever; she delivered just before she died. His father could have been anyone. No one even learned their names.

And for the most part, Elton got along fine. He had a cane he used when he left the Lighthouse, which wasn't all that often, and he seemed content to spend his days at the panel, making use of himself in the only way he knew how. Apart from Michael, he knew more about the batteries than anyone – a miraculous feat, considering the fact that he'd never actually seen them. But according to Elton, this gave him an advantage, because he wasn't fooled by what things merely appeared to be.

'Those batteries are like a woman, Michael,' he liked to say. 'You've got to learn to listen.'

Now, on the evening of the fifty-fourth of summer, First Evening Bell about to sound – four nights since a viral had been killed in the nets by the Watcher Arlo Wilson – Michael called up the battery monitors, a line of bars for each of the six cells: 54 percent on two and three, a whisper under 50 on five and four, a flat 50 on one and six, temperature on all of them in the green, thirty-one degrees. Down the mountain the winds were blowing at a steady thirteen kph with gusts to twenty. He ran through the checklist, charging the capacitors, testing all the relays. What had Alicia said? You push the button, they come on? That's how little people understood.

'You should double-check the second cell,' Elton said from his chair. He was spooning curds of sheep's cheese from a cup into his mouth.

'There's nothing wrong with the second cell.'

'Just do it,' he said. 'Trust me.'

Michael sighed and called the battery monitors back up on the screen. Sure enough: the charge on number two was dropping: 53 percent, 52. The temperature was nudging up as well. He would have asked Elton how he'd known but his answer was always the same – an enigmatic cock of the head, as if to say, *I could hear it, Michael.*

'Open the relay,' Elton advised. 'Do it again and see if it settles down.'

Second Evening Bell was moments away. Well, they could run on the other five cells if they had to, then figure out what the problem was. Michael opened the relay, waited a moment to vent any gas in the line, and closed it again. The meter stayed flat at 55.

'Static is all,' said Elton, as Second Bell began to ring. He gave his spoon a little wave. 'That relay's a bit squirrelly, though. We should swap it out.'

The door of the Lighthouse opened then. Elton lifted his face.

'That you, Sara?'

Michael's sister stepped inside, still dressed to ride and covered in dust. 'Evening, Elton.'

'Now, what's that I smell on you?' He was smiling from ear to ear. 'Mountain lilac?'

She pushed a strand of sweat-dampened hair from behind an ear. 'I smell like sheep, Elton. But thanks.' She directed her words to Michael. 'Are you coming home tonight? I thought I'd cook.'

Michael thought he should probably stay where he was, with one of the cells acting up. Night was also the best time for the radio. But he hadn't eaten all day, and at the thought of warm food, his stomach let loose an empty rumble.

'You mind, Elton?'

The old man shrugged. 'I know where to find you if I need you. You go now if you like.'

'You want me to bring you something?' Sara offered as Michael was rising from his chair. 'We've got plenty.'

But Elton shook his head, as he always did. 'Not tonight, thanks.' He took the earphones from their place on the counter and held them up. 'I've got the whole wide world for company.'

Michael and his sister stepped out into the lights. After so many hours in the dim hut, Michael had to pause on the step and blink the glare away. They moved down the path past the storage sheds, toward the pens; the air was rich with the organic funk of animals. He could hear the bleating of the herd and, as they walked, the nickering of horses from the stables. Continuing onto the narrow path that edged the field, underneath the south wall, Michael could see the runners moving back and forth along the catwalks, their shapes silhouetted against the spots. Michael saw Sara watching also, her eyes distant and preoccupied, shining with reflected light.

'Don't worry,' Michael said. 'He'll be fine.'

His sister didn't respond; he wondered if she'd heard him. They said nothing more until they reached the house. At the kitchen pump, Sara washed up while Michael lit the candles; she stepped out onto the back porch and returned a moment later, swinging a good-sized jackrabbit by the ears.

'Flyers,' Michael said, 'where'd you get him?'

Sara's mood had lifted; her face wore a proud smile. Michael could see the wound where Sara's arrow had skewered the animal through the throat.

'Upper Field, just above the pits. I was riding along and there he was, right out in the open.'

How long had it been since Michael had eaten rabbit? Since anyone had even *seen* a rabbit? Most of the wildlife was long gone, except for the squirrels, which seemed to multiply even faster than the virals could kill them off, and the smaller birds, the sparrows and wrens, which they either didn't want or couldn't catch.

'You want to clean him?' Sara asked.

'I'm not even sure I'd remember how,' Michael confessed.

Sara made a face of exasperation and drew her blade from her belt. 'Fine, make yourself useful and set the fire.'

They made the rabbit into a stew, with carrots and potatoes from the bin in the cellar, and cornmeal to thicken the sauce. Sara claimed to remember their father's recipe, but Michael could tell she was guessing. It didn't matter; soon the savory aroma of cooking meat was bubbling from the kitchen hearth, filling the whole house with a cozy warmth that Michael hadn't felt in a long time. Sara had taken the empty skin out to the yard to scrape it while Michael tended the stove, waiting for her return. He had bowls and spoons set when she stepped back inside, wiping her hands on a rag.

'You know, I know you're not going to listen to me, but you and Elton should be careful.'

Sara knew all about the radio; the way she came in and out of the Lighthouse, it had been impossible to avoid this. But he had kept the rest from her.

'It's just a receiver, Sara. We're not even transmitting.'

'What do you listen to out there, anyway?'

Sitting at the table, he offered a shrug, hoping to kill the conversation as fast as possible. What was there to say? He was looking for the Army. But the Army was dead. Everyone was dead, and the lights were going out.

'Just noise, mostly.'

She was looking at him closely, her hands on her hips as she stood with her back to the sink, waiting him out. When Michael said nothing more, she sighed and shook her head.

'Well, don't get caught,' his sister said.

They ate without speaking at the table in the kitchen. The meat was a little stringy but so delicious Michael could barely stop himself from moaning as he chewed. Usually he didn't go to bed until after dawn, but he could have lain down right there at the table, his head cradled in his folded arms, and fallen instantly asleep. There was something familiar as well – not just familiar but also a little sad – about eating jack stew at the table. Just the two of them.

He lifted his eyes to find Sara's looking back at him.

'I know,' she said. 'I miss them too.'

He wanted to tell her then. About the batteries, and the logbook, and their father, and what he'd known. Just to have one other person carry this knowledge. But this was a selfish wish, Michael knew, nothing he could actually allow himself to do.

Sara pushed back from the table and carried their dishes to the pump. When she was finished washing up, she filled an earthenware pot with the leftover stew and wrapped it with a piece of heavy cloth to keep it warm.

'You taking that to Walt?' Michael asked.

Walter was their father's older brother. As the Storekeeper, he was in charge of Share, a member of the Board of Trade, and Household too – the oldest living Fisher – a three-legged stool of responsibilities that made him one of the most powerful citizens of the Colony, second only to Soo Ramirez and Sanjay Patal. But he was also a widower who lived alone – his wife, Jean, had been killed on Dark Night – and he liked the shine too much and often neglected to eat. When Walt wasn't in the Storehouse, he could usually be found fussing with the still he kept in the shed behind his house, or else passed out somewhere inside.

Sara shook her head. 'I don't think I could face Walt right now. I'm taking it to Elton.'

Michael watched her face. He knew she was thinking of Peter again. 'You should get some rest. I'm sure they're okay.'

'They're late.'

'Just a day. It's routine.'

His sister said nothing. It was terrible, Michael thought, what love could do to a person. He couldn't see the sense in it.

'Look, Lish is riding with them. I'm sure they're safe.'

Sara scowled, looking away. 'It's Lish I'm worried about.'

She headed first to the Sanctuary, as she often did when sleep eluded her. Something about seeing the children, tucked in

404

their beds. She didn't know if it made her feel better or worse. But it made her feel *something*, besides the hollow ache of worry.

She liked to recall her own days there as a Little, when the world seemed like a safe place, even a happy place, and all there was to concern her was when her parents would come to visit, or if Teacher was in a good mood that day or not, and who was friends with whom. For the most part, it hadn't seemed odd that she and her brother lived in the Sanctuary and their parents somewhere else – she'd never known a different existence – and at night when her mother or father or the two of them together came to say good night to her and Michael, she never thought to ask them where they went when the visit was over. *We have to go now*, they'd say, when Teacher announced it was time, and that one word, *go*, became the whole of the situation in Sara's mind, and probably Michael's too: parents came, and stayed for a bit, and then they had to go. Many of her best memories of her parents came from those brief bedtime visits when they would read her and Michael a story or just tuck them into their cots.

And then one night she'd ruined it, quite by accident. *Where do you sleep?* she asked her mother as she was preparing to depart. *If you don't sleep here, with us, where do you go?* And when Sara asked this, something seemed to fall behind her mother's eyes, like a shade being quickly drawn down a window. Oh, her mother said, gathering her expression into a smile that Sara detected as false, I don't sleep, not really. Sleep is something for you, Little Sara, and for your brother, Michael. And the look on her mother's face as she said these words was the first time, Sara now believed, that she'd glimpsed the terrible truth.

It was true, what everyone said: you hated Teacher for telling you. How Sara had loved Teacher, until that day. As much as she loved her own parents, maybe even more. Her eighth birthday: she knew something would happen, something wonderful, that the children who turned eight went someplace special, but nothing more specific than that. The ones who returned – to visit a younger sibling or to have Littles of their own – were older, so much time having passed that they had become different people entirely, and where they'd been and what they'd done was a secret you couldn't know. It was precisely *because* it was a secret that it was so special, this new place that awaited outside the walls of the Sanctuary. Anticipation gathered inside her as her birthday approached. So keen was her excitement that never did it occur to her to wonder what would happen to Michael without her; his own day would come. You were warned by Teacher never to talk about this, but of course the Littles did, when Teacher wasn't around. In the washroom or dining hall or at night in the Big Room, whispers passing up and down the lines of cots, the talk was always of release and who was next in line. What was the world like, outside the Sanctuary? Did people live in castles, like the people in books? What animals would they find, and could they speak? (The caged mice Teacher kept in the classroom were, to a one, discouragingly silent.) What wonderful foods were there to eat, what wonderful toys to play with? Never had Sara been so excited, waiting for this glorious day when she would step into the world.

She awoke on the morning of her birthday feeling as if she were floating on a cloud of happiness. And yet somehow she would have to contain this joy until rest time; only then, when the Littles were asleep, would Teacher take her to the special place. Though no one said as much, all through morning meal and circle time she could tell that everyone was delighted for her, except for Michael, who did nothing to hide his envy, grumpily refusing to speak with her. Well, that was Michael. If he couldn't be happy for her, she wasn't going to let it spoil her special day. It wasn't until after lunch, when Teacher called everyone around to say goodbye, that she began to wonder if maybe he knew something she didn't. What is it, Michael? asked Teacher. Can't you say goodbye to your sister, can't you be happy for her? And

Michael looked at her and said, It's not what you think, Sara, then hugged her quickly and ran from the room before she could say a word.

Well, that was strange, she'd thought at the time, and still did, even now, all these years gone by. How had Michael known? Much later, when the two of them were alone again, she'd remembered this scene and asked him about it. How did you know? But Michael could only shake his head. I just did, he said. Not the details, but the kind of thing it was. The way they spoke to us, Mom and Dad, at night, tucking us in. You could see it in their eyes.

But back then, the afternoon of her release, with Michael darting away and Teacher taking her hand, she hadn't wondered for long. Just chalked it up to Michael being Michael. The final goodbyes, the embraces, the feeling of the moment arriving: Peter was there, and Maus Patal, and Ben Chou and Galen Strauss and Wendy Ramirez and all the rest, touching her, saying her name. Remember us, everyone said. She was holding the bag that contained her things, her clothing and slippers and the little rag doll that she'd had since she was small – you were allowed to take one toy – and Teacher took her by the hand and led her out from the Big Room, into the little courtyard ringed by windows where the children played when the sun was high in the sky, with the swings and the seesaw and the piles of old tires to climb, and through another door into a room she'd never seen before. Like a classroom but empty, the shelves barren, no pictures on the walls.

Teacher sealed the door behind them. A curious and premature pause; Sara had expected more. Where was she going? she asked Teacher. Would it be a long journey? Was someone coming for her? How long was she to wait here, in this room? But Teacher seemed not to hear these questions. She crouched before her, positioning her large, soft face close to Sara's. Little Sara, she asked, what do you suppose is out there, outside this building, beyond these rooms where you live? And what of the men you sometimes see, the ones who come and go at night, watching over you? Teacher was smiling, but there was something different about this smile, thought Sara, something that made her afraid. She didn't want to answer, but Teacher was looking straight at her, her face expectant. Sara thought of her mother's eyes, the night she'd asked her where she slept. A castle? she said, for in her sudden nervousness that was the only thing she could think of. A castle, with a moat? A castle, Teacher said. I see. And what else, Little Sara? The smile was suddenly gone. I don't know, Sara said. Well, Teacher said, and cleared her throat. It's not a castle.

And that was when she told her.

Sara hadn't believed her at first. But not exactly that: she felt as if her mind had split in two, and one half, the half that didn't know, that believed she was still a Little, sitting in circle and playing in the courtyard and waiting for her parents to tuck her in at night, was saying goodbye to the half that somehow always had. Like she was saying goodbye to herself. It made her feel dizzy and sick, and then she started to cry, and Teacher took her by the hand once more and led her down another hallway and out of the Sanctuary, where her parents were waiting for her, to take her home – the home that Sara and Michael lived in still, that she'd never known existed until that very day. *It isn't true*, Sara was saying through her tears, *it isn't true*. And her mother, who was crying too, picked her up and held her close, saying, *I'm sorry, I'm sorry, I'm sorry. It is, it is, it is.*

This was the memory that always replayed in her mind whenever she approached the Sanctuary, which seemed so much smaller to her than it had back then, so much more ordinary. An old brick schoolhouse with the name F. D. Roosevelt Elementary etched in stone over the door. From the path she could see the figure of a single Watcher standing on the top of the front steps: Hollis Wilson.

'Howdy, Sara.'

'Evening, Hollis.'

Hollis was balancing a crossbow on his hip. Sara didn't like them; they had a lot of power but were too slow to reload, and heavy to carry besides. Everyone said how it was just about impossible to tell Hollis apart from his brother until he'd shaved his beard, but Sara didn't see why; even as Littles – the Wilson brothers had come up three years ahead of her – she had always known which was which. It was the little things that told her, details that a person might not notice at first glance, like the fact that Hollis was just a little taller, a little more serious in the eyes. But they were obvious to her.

As she ascended the steps, Hollis tipped his head at the pot she was carrying, his lips turned up in a grin. 'Whatcha bring me?'

'Jack stew. But it's not for you, I'm afraid.'

His face was amazed. 'I'll be damned. Where'd you get him?'

'Upper Field.'

He gave a little whistle, shaking his head. Sara could read the hunger in his face. 'I can't tell you how much I miss jack stew. Can I smell it?'

She drew the cloth aside and opened the lid. Hollis bent to the pot and inhaled deeply through his nose.

'I couldn't maybe talk you into leaving it here with me while you go inside?'

'Forget it, Hollis. I'm taking it to Elton.'

A jaunty shrug; the offer wasn't serious. 'Well, I tried,' said Hollis. 'Okay, let's have your blade.'

She withdrew her knife and passed it to him. Only Watchers were allowed to carry weapons into the Sanctuary, and even they were supposed to keep them out of sight of the children.

'Don't know if you heard,' Hollis said, tucking it into his belt. 'We've got a new resident.'

'I was out with the herd all day. Who is it?'

'Maus Patal. No big shock there, I guess.' Hollis gestured with his cross toward the path. 'Galen just left. I'm surprised you didn't see him.'

She'd been too lost in thought. Gale could have walked

right past her and she wouldn't have noticed. And Maus, pregnant. Why was she surprised?

'Well.' She managed a smile, wondering what she was feeling. Was it envy? 'That's great news.'

'Do me a favor and tell *her* that. You should have heard the two of them arguing. Probably woke up half the Littles.'

'She's not happy about it?'

'It was more Galen, I think. I don't know. You're a girl, Sara. You tell me.'

'Flattery will get you nowhere, Hollis.'

He laughed wryly. She liked Hollis, his easy manner. 'Just passing the time,' he said, and motioned with his head toward the door. 'If Dora's awake, tell her hi from her uncle Hollis.'

'How's Leigh doing? With Arlo gone.'

'Leigh's been down this road. I told her, lots of reasons they might not be back today.'

Inside, Sara left the stew in the empty office and went to the Big Room, where all the Littles slept. At one time it had been the school's gymnasium. Most of the beds were empty; it had been years since the Sanctuary had operated at anything close to capacity. The shades were drawn over the room's tall windows; the only illumination came from narrow slices of light that fell over the sleeping forms of the children. The room smelled like milk, and sweat, and sun-warmed hair: the smell of children, after a day. Sara crept between the rows of cots and cribs. Kat Curtis and Bart Fisher and Abe Phillips, Fanny Chou and her sisters Wanda and Susan, Timothy Molyneau and Beau Greenberg, whom everyone called 'Bowow,' a mangling of his own name that had stuck to him like glue; the three J's, Juliet Strauss and June Levine and Jane Ramirez, Rey's youngest.

Sara came to a crib at the end of the last row: Dora Wilson, Leigh and Arlo's girl. Leigh was sitting in a nursing chair beside her. New mothers were allowed to stay in the Sanctuary up to a year. Leigh was still a little heavy from her pregnancy; in the pale light of the room, her wide face

410

seemed almost transparent, the skin pallid from so many months indoors. In her lap was a fat skein of yarn and a pair of needles. She lifted her eyes from her knitting at Sara's approach.

'Hey,' she said quietly.

Sara acknowledged her with a silent nod and bent over the crib. Dora, wearing only a diaper, was sleeping on her back, her lips parted in a delicate O shape; she was snoring faintly through her nose. The soft, damp wind of her breathing brushed Sara's cheekbones like a kiss. Looking at a sleeping baby, you could almost forget what the world was, she thought.

'Don't worry, you won't wake her.' Leigh yawned into her hand and resumed her knitting. 'That one, she sleeps like the dead.'

Sara decided not to look for Mausami. Whatever was going on between her and Galen, it was none of her business. In a way she felt sorry for Gale. He had always had a thing for Maus – it was like an illness he could never quite shake off – and everyone said that when he'd asked Maus to pair with him, she'd said yes only because Theo had already refused her. That, or he'd never gotten around to asking, and Maus was trying to goad him into action. She'd hardly be the first woman who'd ever made that mistake.

But as she moved down the path, Sara wondered: Why couldn't some things just be easy? Because it was the same with her and Peter. Sara loved him, she always had, even back when they were just Littles in the Sanctuary. There was no explaining it; as long as she could remember, she had felt it, this love, like an invisible golden thread that bound the two of them together. It was more than physical attraction; it was the broken thing inside him she loved most of all, the unreachable place where he kept his sadness. Because that was the thing about Peter Jaxon that nobody knew but her, because she loved him like she did: how terribly sad he was. And not just in the day-to-day, the ordinary sadness

411

everyone carried for the things and people they had lost; his was something more. If she could find this sadness, Sara believed, and take it from him, then he would love her in return.

Which was the reason she had chosen to become a nurse; if she couldn't be Watch – and she absolutely couldn't – the Infirmary, where Prudence Jaxon presided, was the next best place to be. A hundred times she'd almost asked the woman: What can I do? What can I do to make your son love me? But in the end Sara had kept silent. She had gone about the work of learning her trade as best she could and waited for Peter, hoping he would know what she was offering him, simply by being in that room.

Peter had kissed her, once. Or maybe Sara had kissed him. The question of who had kissed whom, exactly, seemed unimportant in the face of the thing itself. They had kissed. It was First Night, late and cold. They'd all been drinking shine, listening to Arlo strum his guitar under the lights, and as the group dispersed in the last hour before dawn, Sara had found herself walking with Peter alone. She was a little light-headed from the shine, but she didn't think she was drunk, and she didn't think that he was, either. A nervous silence fell over them as they moved down the path, not an absence of sound or speech but something palpable and faintly electric, like the spaces between the notes from Arlo's guitar. It was in this bubble of expectancy that they walked together under the lights, not touching but connected nonetheless, and by the time they reached her house, neither one having acknowledged that this was their destination – the silence was a bubble but it was also a river, pulling them along in its current – there seemed no stopping what would happen next. They were against the wall of her house, standing in a wedge of shadow, first his mouth and then the rest of him pressed against her. Not like the kissing games they'd all played in the Sanctuary, or the first clumsy fumblings of puberty – sex was not discouraged, you pretty much got around to anyone you were even vaguely interested in; the unwritten rule was *this and no more*, all of it, in the end, feeling like a kind of rehearsal – but something deeper, full of promise. She felt herself enveloped by a warmth she almost didn't recognize: the warmth of human contact, of truly being with another, no longer alone. She would have given herself to him right then, whatever he wanted.

But then it was over; suddenly he pulled away. 'I'm sorry,' he managed, as if he believed she wished he hadn't done it, though the kiss should have told him that she did, she did; but by then something had shifted in the air, the bubble had popped, and both of them were too embarrassed, too flustered, to say anything else. He left her at her door, and that was the end of it. They hadn't been alone together since that night. They'd barely spoken a word.

Because she knew; she knew it when he kissed her, and then after, and more and more as the days went by. Peter wasn't hers, could never be hers, because there was another. She'd felt it like a ghost between them, in his kiss. It all made sense now, a hopeless kind of sense. While she'd been waiting for him in the Infirmary, showing him what she was, he had been on the Wall with Alicia Donadio the entire time.

Now, on her way to the Lighthouse with the stew, Sara remembered Gabe Curtis and decided to stop at the Infirmary. Poor Gabe – just forty, and already the cancer. There wasn't much anyone could do for him. Sara guessed it had started in the stomach, or else the liver. It didn't really matter. The Infirmary, located across the Sunspot from the Sanctuary, was a small frame structure in the part of the Colony they called Old Town – a block of half a dozen buildings that had once held various stores and shops. The building that served as the Infirmary had once been a grocery store; when the afternoon sun hit the front windows just right, you could still make out the name – Mountaintop Provision Co., Fine Foods and Spirits, Est. 1996 – etched into its frosted glass.

A single lantern lit the outer room, where Sandy Chou – everyone called her Other Sandy, since there had once been two Sandy Chous, the first being Ben Chou's wife, who had died in childbirth – was bent over the nurse's desk, crushing dillonweed seeds with a mortar and pestle. The air was hot and heavy with moisture; behind the desk, a kettle was chuffing out a plume of steam from on top of the stove. Sara put the stew aside and removed the kettle from the heat, placing it on a trivet. Returning to the desk, she tipped her head toward the dillonweed, which Sandy was shaking out into a strainer.

'Is that for Gabe?'

Sandy nodded. Dillonweed was thought to be an analgesic, though they employed it to treat a variety of ailments – head colds, diarrhea, arthritis. Sara couldn't say for a fact that it accomplished anything at all, but Gabe claimed it helped with the pain, and it was the only thing he was keeping down.

'How's he doing?'

Sandy was pouring the water through the strainer into a ceramic mug, the lip chipped and worn. On it were the words NEW DADDY, the letters spelled with the image of safety pins.

'He was asleep a while ago. The jaundice is worse. His boy just left, Mar's in there with him now.'

'I'll bring him the tea.'

Sara took the mug and stepped through the curtain. The ward had six cots in it, but only one was occupied. Mar was sitting in a ladder-backed chair beside the cot on which her husband lay, covered by a blanket. A thin, almost birdlike woman, Mar had shouldered the load of Gabe's care through the months of his illness, a burden plain to see in the crescents of sleeplessness hung beneath her eyes. They had one child, Jacob, sixteen or so, who worked in the dairy with his mother: a large, hulking boy with a face of perpetually vacant sweetness, who could neither read nor write and never would, who was capable of basic tasks as long as someone was there to direct him. A hard, unlucky life, and now this. Past forty, and with Jacob to look after, it was unlikely that Mar would marry again.

As Sara approached, Mar looked up, holding a finger to her lips. Sara nodded and took a chair beside her. Sandy was right: the jaundice was worse. Before he'd gotten sick, Gabe had been a large man – large as his wife was small – with great knotty shoulders and bulky forearms made for work and a prosperously round belly that hung over his belt like a meal sack: a solidly useful man whom Sara had never once seen in the Infirmary until the day he'd come in complaining of back pain and indigestion, apologizing for this fact as if it were a sign of weakness, a failure of character rather than the onset of a serious illness. (When Sara had palped his liver, the tips of her fingers instantly registering the presence that was growing there, she realized he must have been in agony.)

Now, half a year later, the man Gabe Curtis had once been was gone, replaced by a husk that clung to life by will alone. His face, once as full and richly hued as a ripe apple, had withered to a collection of lines and angles, like a hastily drawn sketch. Mar had trimmed his beard and nails; his cracked lips were glazed with glistening ointment from a wide-mouthed pot on the cart beside his bed – a small comfort, small and useless as the tea.

She sat awhile with Mar, the two of them not speaking. It was possible, Sara understood, for life to go on too long, as it was also possible for it to end too soon. Maybe it was his fear of leaving Mar alone that was keeping Gabe alive.

Eventually Sara rose, placing the mug on the cart. 'If he wakes up, see if he'll drink this,' she said.

Tears of exhaustion hung on the corners of Mar's eyes. 'I told him it's all right, he can go.'

It took Sara a moment. 'I'm glad you did,' she said. 'Sometimes that's what a person needs to hear.'

'It's Jacob, you see. He doesn't want to leave Jacob. I told him, We'll be fine. You go now. That's what I told him.'

'I know you will, Mar.' Her words felt small. 'He knows it too.'

'He's so damn stubborn. You hear that, Gabe? Why do you

have to be so goddamn stubborn all the time?' Then she dropped her face to her hands and wept.

Sara waited a respectful time, knowing there was nothing she could do to ease the woman's pain. Grief was a place, Sara understood, where a person went alone. It was like a room without doors, and what happened in that room, all the anger and the pain you felt, was meant to stay there, nobody's business but yours.

'I'm sorry, Sara,' Mar said finally, shaking her head. 'You shouldn't have had to hear that.'

'It's all right. I don't mind.'

'If he wakes up, I'll tell him you were here.' Through her tears, she managed a sad smile. 'I know Gabe always liked you. You were his favorite nurse.'

It was half-night by the time Sara got to the Lighthouse. She quietly opened the door and stepped inside. Elton was alone, fast asleep at the panel, earphones clamped to his head.

He twitched awake as the door closed behind her on its springs. 'Michael?'

'It's Sara.'

He removed the earphones and turned in his chair, sniffing the air. 'What's that I smell?'

'Jack stew. It's probably ice-cold by now, though.'

'Well, I'll be.' He sat up straight in his chair. 'Bring it here.'

She placed it before him. He took a dirty spoon from the counter that faced the panel. 'Light the lamp if you want.'

'I like the dark. If you don't mind.'

'It's all the same to me.'

For a while she watched him eat in the glow of the panel. There was something almost hypnotic about the motions of Elton's hands, guiding the spoon into the pot and then to his waiting mouth with smooth precision, not a single gesture wasted.

'You're watching me,' Elton said.

She felt the heat rising to her cheeks. 'Sorry.'

He polished off the last of the stew and wiped his mouth

on a rag. 'Nothing to be sorry about. You're about the best thing that ever comes in here, as far as I'm concerned. Pretty girl like you, you watch me all you want.'

She laughed – out of embarrassment or disbelief, she didn't know. 'You've never seen me, Elton. How can you possibly know what I look like?'

Elton shrugged, his useless eyes rolling upward behind their drooping lids – as if, in the darkness of his mind, her image was there for him to see. 'Your voice. How you speak to me, how you speak to Michael. How you look after him like you do. Pretty is as pretty does, I always say.'

She heard herself sigh. 'I don't feel like it.'

'Trust old Elton,' he said, and gave a quiet laugh. 'Somebody's going to *love* you.'

There was always something about being around Elton that made her feel better. He was a shameless flirt, for starters, but that wasn't the real reason. He simply seemed happier than anyone she knew. It was true what Michael said about him: his blindness wasn't something missing; it was simply something different.

'I just came back from the Infirmary.'

'Well, there you are,' he said, nodding along. 'Always looking after folks. How's Gabe doing?'

'Not so good. He looks really terrible, Elton. And Mar's taking it hard. I wish there was more I could do for him.'

'Some things you can, and some things you can't. It's Gabe's time now. You've done all you could.'

'It's not enough.'

'It never is.' Elton turned to search the counter with his hands, locating the earphones, which he held out to her. 'Now, since you've brought me a present, I've got one for you. A little something to cheer you up.'

'Elton, I wouldn't have a clue what I was hearing. It's all static to me.'

A cagey smile was on his face. 'Just do like I say. Close your eyes, too.'

The phones were warm against her ears. She sensed Elton

moving his hands over the panel, his fingers gliding here and there. Then she heard it: music. But not like any music she knew. It reached her first as a distant, hollow sound, like a breath of wind, and then, rising behind it, high birdlike notes that seemed to dance inside her head. The sound built and built, seeming to come from all directions, and she knew what she was hearing, that it was a storm. She could picture it in her mind, a great storm of music sweeping down. She had never heard anything so beautiful in her life. When the last notes died away, she pulled the headphones from her ears.

'I don't get it,' she said, astounded. 'This came through the radio?'

Elton chuckled. 'Now, that would be something, wouldn't it?'

He did something to the panel again. A small drawer opened, ejecting a silver disc: a CD. She'd never paid much attention to them; Michael told her they were just noise. She took the disc in her hand, holding it by the edges. Stravinsky, *The Rite of Spring*. The Chicago Symphony Orchestra, Erich Leinsdorf conducting.

'I just thought you should hear what you look like,' said Elton.

TWENTY-TWO

'The thing I don't understand,' Theo was saying, 'is why the three of you aren't dead.'

The group was sitting at the long table in the control room, all except Finn and Rey, who had returned to the barracks to sleep. Peter's daze of adrenaline had worn off, and the pain in his ankle, which did not seem to be broken, had settled to a low throb; someone had chipped a piece of ice off one of the condensers, and Peter was holding this, wrapped in a sodden rag, to the injured joint. The fact that he had just killed Zander Phillips, a man he had known, had yet to produce in him any emotion he could actually name. The information was simply too strange to process. But the station key had still been around Zander's neck, so there could be no doubt who it was. There had been no choice, of course; Zander had been fully turned. Strictly speaking, the viral who had tried to force its way through the hatch hadn't been Zander Phillips anymore. And yet Peter could not suppress the feeling that at the last instant before he'd squeezed the trigger, he'd detected a glimmer of recognition in the viral's eyes – a look, even, of relief.

In the aftermath of the attack, Theo had questioned Caleb carefully. The boy's story didn't quite add up, but it was also clear that he was suffering from exhaustion and exposure. His lips were swollen and cracked, he had a big purple bruise on his forehead, and both of his feet were laced with cuts. The lost shoes seemed to pain him most of all; they were black Nike Push-Offs, he explained, brand-new in their box from the Foot Locker at the mall. They'd come off somehow in his race across the valley, but he'd been so scared he'd barely noticed.

'We'll get you a new pair,' Theo had said. 'Just tell me about Zander.'

Caleb was eating as he spoke, gnawing off bites of hardtack and washing them down with gulps of water. Well, everything had been normal, Caleb explained, until about six days ago, when Zander had begun to act . . . odd. Very odd. Even for Zander, which was saying something. He didn't want to go outside the fence, and he wasn't sleeping at all. All night long he'd be up pacing the control room, muttering to himself. Caleb thought it was just too much time at the station, that when the relief crew showed, Zander would snap out of it.

'So then one day he announces we're going out to the field, and tells me to get the cart packed and ready. I was sitting here eating my lunch, and he just marches in and announces this. He wants to swap out one of the governors in the west section. Okay, I say, but what's the big emergency? Isn't it a little late in the day to be going to the field? He's got this crazy look in his eyes, and he smelled bad. I mean, he *stank*. You feeling okay, I ask him, and he says, Just get your gear, we're going.'

'When was this?'

Caleb swallowed. 'Three days ago.'

Theo leaned forward in his chair. 'You've been outside three *days*?'

Caleb nodded. He'd finished off the last of the hardtack and started on a dish of soybean paste, scooping it out with his fingers. 'So we ride out with the jenny, but here's the thing. We don't go to the west field. We go to the *east* field. Nothing's worked over there for years; they're all dead sticks. And it takes forever to get there, two hours with the cart at least. It's past half-day, we're cutting it close as it is. I'm like, Zander, west is that way, buddy, what the hell are we doing out here? Are you *trying* to get us killed? So we get to the tower he says he wants to fix, and the thing's a rust bucket. Completely backblown. I can see that from the ground. No chance swapping the governor's going to do anything. But that's what he wants to do, so I haul my ass up the ladder and set the winch and start stripping out the old housing, working as fast as I can. I'm thinking, Okay, this doesn't make a lot of sense, as far as I can tell we're risking our necks for nothing, but maybe he knows something I don't. Anyway, that was when I heard the scream.'

'Zander screamed?'

Caleb shook his head. 'The jenny. I'm not kidding, that was exactly what it sounded like. I'd never heard anything like it. When I looked down she's just keeling over, going down like a bag of rocks. It takes me a second to figure what I'm seeing. It's blood. A lot of it.' He wiped his greasy mouth with the back of his hand and pushed the empty dish of paste aside. 'Zander always said this stuff tasted like balls. I was like, When did you eat balls, Zander, like I really want to know? But after three days, it's really not half bad.'

Theo sighed impatiently. 'Caleb, please. The blood—'

He took a long swig of water. 'Right, okay, so. The blood. Zander's kneeling by her and I yell, Zander, what the hell happened? When he gets up I see he's stripped to the waist, he's got a blade in his hand, and there's blood all over him. Somehow I missed the signs. I've got about five seconds before he comes up the ladder for me, too. But he doesn't. He just sits down at the base of the tower, in the shade of one of the struts, where I can't see him. Zander, I yell down, listen to me. You got to fight this thing. I'm all alone up here. I'm thinking that maybe if I can get him to snap out of it long enough, I can make a run for it.'

'I don't get it,' Alicia said. 'When would he have gotten infected?'

'That's the thing,' Caleb went on. 'I couldn't figure that either. I'd been with him just about every minute of the day.'

'What about at night?' Theo offered. 'You said he didn't sleep. Maybe he went outside.'

'I suppose that's possible, but why would he? And plus, he didn't really *look* any different, apart from the blood.'

'What about his eyes?'

'Nothing. No oranging at all, from what I could see. I'm telling you, it was *weird*. So I'm stuck on the tower, Zander's at the bottom, maybe taken up and maybe not, but either way it's going to get dark eventually. Zander, I yell, look, I'm coming down, one way or the other. I'm not armed, all I've got is the wrench, but maybe I can brain him with it and get away. I've also got to get the key from him somehow. I can't see him from the ladder, so when I'm about three meters from the bottom I decide what the hell, I'm just going to jump. I've already tipped my hand, but I figure I'm dead anyway. I drop and come up with the wrench ready to swing. But it's gone. Snatched right out of my hand. Zander's right behind me. That's when he says to me, Go back up.'

'Go back up?' This was Arlo.

Caleb nodded. 'No kidding, that's what he said. And if he was flipping, I still couldn't tell. But he's got the blade in one hand, the wrench in the other, there's blood all over him, and without the key there's no way I'm getting back inside the station. I ask him, What do you mean go back up, and he says, You're safe if you go back up the tower. So that's what I did.' The boy shrugged. 'That's where I was for the last three days, until I saw you on the Eastern Road.'

Peter looked at his brother; Theo's expression indicated he didn't know what to make of Caleb's story either. What had Zander intended? Had he already been taken up or not? It had been many years, and not in living memory, since anyone had directly witnessed the effects of the infection's early stages. But there were plenty of stories, from the early days especially, the time of the Walkers, of bizarre behaviors – not just the blood hunger and spontaneous disrobing that everyone knew to be a sign. Strange utterances, public speechmaking, manic feats of athleticism. One Walker, it was said, had broken into the Storehouse and actually eaten himself to death; another had killed all his children in their beds before setting himself aflame; a third had stripped naked, ascended to the catwalk in full view of the Watch, and recited, at the top of his lungs, both the entire Gettysburg Address – there was a copy of it hanging on the wall in one of the classrooms in the Sanctuary – and twenty-five verses of 'Row, Row, Row Your Boat' before hurling himself over, twenty meters to the hardpan.

'So what about the smokes?' Theo asked.

'Well, that's the funny thing. It was just like Zander said. There weren't any. At least none that came close. I could see them once in a while at night, moving out in the valley. But they pretty much just left me alone. They don't like to hunt in the turbine fields, Zander always thought the movement screwed them up, so maybe that's got something to do with it, I don't know.' The boy paused; Peter could see the weight of his ordeal finally catching up with him. 'Once I got used to it, it was actually kind of peaceful. I didn't see Zander after that. I could hear him, scuffling around at the base of the tower. But he never answered me. By then I figured my best chance was to wait for the relief crew to show up and try to get away.'

'So you saw us.'

'Believe me, I yelled my lungs out, but I guess you were just too far away to hear me. That's when I realized Zander was gone. The jenny, too. The virals must have dragged it off. By then I only had a hand of daylight at the most. But I was out of water, and there was no way anyone was coming to look for me in the east field, so I decided to climb down and make a run for it. I got to within maybe a thousand meters when suddenly the smokes were just *everywhere.* I thought, That's it, I'm meat for sure. I hid under the base of one of the towers and pretty much waited to die. But for some reason, they kept their distance. I couldn't tell you how long I was under there, but when I looked out they were gone, not a smoke in sight. By then I knew the gate was closed, but I guess I just thought I could get inside somehow.'

Arlo turned to Theo. 'It doesn't make sense. Why would they leave him alone like that?'

'Because they were following him,' Alicia cut in. 'We could see them from the roof. Using him as bait maybe, to draw us out? Since when do they do that?'

'They don't.' Something hardened in Theo's expression then; he stiffened in his chair. 'Look, I'm glad Caleb's safe, don't get me wrong. But that was some stupid stunt, both of you. This station goes off-line, the lights go out, that's it for *everybody*. I don't know why I have to explain this, but apparently I do.'

Peter and Alicia were silent; there was nothing to say. It was true. If Peter's rifle had gone just a few centimeters to the left or right, they'd probably all be dead now. It had been a lucky shot and he knew it.

'None of which explains how Zander got infected,' Theo went on. 'Or what he was doing, leaving Caleb on the tower.'

'The hell with that,' Arlo said, and slapped his knees. 'What I really want to know about are those guns. How many are there?'

'Twelve crates under the stairs,' Alicia answered. 'Six more in the crawl space on the roof.'

'Which is exactly where they're going to stay,' Theo said.

Alicia laughed. 'You can't be serious.'

'Oh, yes, I can. Look what almost happened. Can you honestly tell me you would have gone outside there without those guns?'

'Maybe not. But Caleb's alive because of them. And I don't care what you say, I'm glad we went outside. These aren't just *guns*, Theo. They're like brand-new.'

'I know they are,' Theo said. 'I've seen them. I know all about them.'

'You do?'

He nodded. 'Of course I do.'

For a moment no one spoke. Alicia leaned forward over the table. 'So whose guns are they?'

But it was Peter to whom Theo gave his answer. 'Our father's.'

So, in the last hour of the night, Theo told the story. Caleb, unable to keep his eyes open another minute, had gone to the barracks to sleep, and Arlo had broken out the shine, as they sometimes did after a night on the Wall. He poured it into each of their cups, two fingers, and passed it around the table.

There was an old Marine Corps base east of there, Theo explained, about a two-day ride. A place called Twentynine Palms. Most of it was gone, he said, pretty much sanded up. You could hardly tell there was anything there unless you knew where to look. Their father had found the weapons in an underground bunker – all boxed up, tight and dry, and not just rifles. Pistols and mortars. Machine guns and grenades. A whole garage of vehicles, even a couple of tanks. They had no way to move the heavier weapons, and none of the vehicles would run, but their father and Uncle Willem had been moving the rifles back to the station a cartload at a time – three trips total before Willem had been killed.

424

'So why didn't he tell anyone?' Peter asked.

'Well, he did. He told our mother, and a few others. He didn't ride alone, you know. I'm guessing the Colonel knew. Probably Old Chou. Zander had to know, since he was stashing them here.'

'But not Sanjay,' Alicia cut in.

Theo shook his head, frowning. 'Believe me, Sanjay was the last person my father would tell. Don't get me wrong: Sanjay is fine at what he does. But he was always dead set against the rides, especially after Raj was killed.'

'That's right,' Arlo said. 'He was one of the three.'

Theo nodded. 'I think it was always a sore spot with Sanjay, that his brother wanted to ride with our father. I never really understood it, but there was some bad blood between them from way back. After Raj was killed, it only got worse. Sanjay turned the Household against our father, voted him out as Head, put an end to the rides. That was when our father stepped down and began to ride alone.'

Peter held his cup of shine to his nose, felt its acrid fumes burning his nostrils, and put it down on the table. He didn't know what was more discouraging – that his father had kept this secret from him or that Theo had.

'So why hide the guns in the first place?' he asked. 'Why not just bring them up the mountain?'

'And do what with them? Think about it, brother. We all heard you out there. By my count, the two of you shot off thirty-six rounds to kill, what, two virals? Out of how many? Those guns'd last about a season if he just handed them over to the Watch. People would be shooting at their own shadows. Hell, half the time they'd probably be shooting each *other*. I think that's what he was most afraid of.'

'How many are left?' Alicia asked.

'In the bunker? I don't know. I've never seen it.'

'But you know where it is.'

Theo sipped his shine. 'I see where you're going with this, and you can stop right there. Our father, well, he had ideas. Peter, you know this as well as I do. He just couldn't accept the fact that we're all that's left, that there's no one out there. And if he could find others, and if they had guns . . .' His voice trailed away.

Alicia lifted in her chair. 'An army,' she said, her eyes moving over all of them. 'That's it, isn't it? He wanted to make an army. To fight the smokes.'

'Which is pointless,' Theo said, and Peter heard the bitterness in his brother's voice. 'Pointless and crazy. The Army *had* guns, and what happened to them? Did they ever come back for us? With their guns and rockets and helicopters? No, they didn't, and I'll tell you why. Because they're all dead.'

Alicia was undeterred. 'Well, I like it,' she said. 'Hell, I think it's a great idea.'

Theo gave a bitter laugh. 'I knew *you* would.'

'And I don't think we're alone, either,' she pressed. 'There *are* others. Out there, somewhere.'

'Is that right? What makes you so sure?'

Alicia appeared suddenly at a loss. 'Nothing,' she said. 'I just am.'

Theo frowned into his cup, giving the contents a long swirl. 'You can believe anything you want,' he said quietly, 'but that doesn't make it true.'

'Our father believed it,' Peter said.

'Yes, he did, brother. And it got him killed. I know it's not something we talk about, but those are the facts. You stand the Mercy and you figure some things out, believe me. Our father didn't go out there to let it go. Whoever thinks so doesn't understand the first thing about him. He went out there because he just couldn't stand not *knowing*, not for one more minute of his life. It was brave, and it was stupid, and he got his answer.'

'He saw a Walker. At Milagro.'

'Maybe he did. If you ask me, he saw what he wanted to see. And it doesn't matter either way. What difference would one Walker make?'

Peter felt badly shaken by Theo's hopelessness; it seemed not just defeated but disloyal.

'Where there's one, there are others,' Peter said.

'What there are, brother, are smokes. All the guns in the world won't change that.'

For a moment no one spoke. The idea was in the air, unspoken but palpable. How long did they have before the lights went out? Before no one remembered how to fix them?

'I don't believe that,' Arlo said. 'And I can't believe you do either. If that's all there is, what's the point of anything?'

'The point?' Theo peered into his cup again. 'I wish I knew. I suppose the point is just staying alive. Keeping the lights on as long as we can.' He tipped the shine to his lips and drained it in one hard swallow. 'On that note, it'll be daybreak soon, everyone. Let Caleb sleep, but wake the others. We've got bodies to take care of.'

There were four. They found three in the yard and one, Zander, on the roof, lying face-up on the concrete by the hatch, his naked limbs sprawled in a startled-looking X. The bullet from Peter's rifle had blasted through the top of his head, shearing off the crown of his skull, which was hanging kitty-corner by a flap of skin. Already the morning sun had begun to shrivel him; a fine, gray mist was rising from his blackening flesh.

Peter had gotten used to the virals' appearance but still found it unnerving to see one close up. The way the facial features seemed to have been buffed away, smoothed into an almost infantile blandness; the curling expansion of the hands and feet, with their grasping digits and razor-sharp claws; the dense muscularity of the limbs and torso and the long, gimballed neck; the slivered teeth crowding the mouth like spikes of steel. In rubber boots and gloves, wearing a rag around his face, Finn used a long pitchfork to lift the key by its cord and drop it in a metal bucket. They doused the key with alcohol and set it aflame, then left it to dry in the sun; what the flames hadn't killed, the sun's rays would. Then they rolled Zander, his body stiff as wood, onto a plastic tarp, which they folded over him, making a tube. Arlo and Rey hoisted it to the edge of the roof and dropped it to the yard below.

By the time they'd dragged all four past the fence line, the sun was high and hot. Peter, leaning on a length of pipe, watched from the upwind side as Theo poured alcohol over the bodies. He felt useless, but with his ankle the way it was, there wasn't much he could do to help. Alicia was standing watch, holding one of the rifles. Caleb had finally awakened and had come outside to watch with the others. Peter saw that he was wearing a pair of tall leather boots.

'Zander's,' Caleb explained. The boy shrugged, a little guiltily. 'His extra pair. I didn't think he'd mind.'

Theo removed a tin of sulfur matches from his pouch and drew down his mask. In his other hand he held a torch. Huge circles of sweat stained his shirt at the throat and armpits. The shirt was an old one from the Storehouse, the sleeves long gone, the collar frayed to threads; on the breast pocket, embroidered in a curving script, was the name *Armando*.

'Anybody want to say anything?'

Peter thought he should, but couldn't find the words. Seeing the body on the roof had done nothing to change the disquieting feeling that, at the end, Zander had made it easy for him – that Zander had still been Zander. But all of the bodies in the pile had been somebody once. Maybe one of them was Armando.

'Okay, I'll do it,' Theo said, and cleared his throat. 'Zander, you were a good engineer, and a good friend. You never had a bad word for anyone, and we thank you for that. Sleep well.' Then he struck the match, held the flame to the torch until it caught, and touched it to the pile.

The skin went quickly, vaporizing like paper, followed by the rest, the bones caving in on themselves to burst into puffing clouds of ash. It was over in a minute. When the last of the flames had died down, they shoveled the remains into the shallow pit Rey and Finn had dug, pushing a layer of earth on top.

They were tamping down the dirt when Caleb spoke. 'I

just want to say, I think he fought it. He could have killed me out there.'

Theo put his shovel aside. 'Don't take this the wrong way,' he said, 'but what worries me is that he didn't.'

In the days that followed, Peter thought about the events of that night, replaying them in his mind. Not only what had happened on the roof and Caleb's strange story of the tower, but also his brother's bitter tone when they'd spoken of the guns. Because Alicia was right; the guns *meant* something. His whole life Peter had thought of the world of the Time Before as something gone. It was as if a blade had fallen onto time itself, cleaving it into halves, that which came before and that which came after. Between these halves there was no bridge; the war had been lost, the Army was no more, the world beyond the Colony was an open grave of a history no one even remembered. Peter, in fact, had never given much thought to what his father had actually been looking for, out there in the dark. He supposed this was because it had seemed so obvious: people, other survivors. But holding one of his father's rifles – and even now, lying in the barracks while his ankle mended and remembering the feel of it – he sensed something more, how the past and all its powers seemed to have flowed into him. So maybe that was what his father had been doing all along, on the Long Rides. He'd been trying to remember the world.

Surely Theo had known that; that was the largeness inside him, inside all the men of the Long Rides. Peter had made up his mind, long ago, not to hold it against Theo, what his mother had said on the morning she'd died. *Take care of your brother, Theo. He's not strong, like you.* The truth was the truth, and as the years went by, Peter discovered that knowing this about himself was bearable; at times it almost came as a relief. It was a difficult and desperate thing their father had attempted, built on a faith that flew in the face of every fact, and if Theo was to be the Jaxon to shoulder this burden – shoulder it for the two of them – Peter could accept that. But telling Arlo that there was no point, that the only thing left to do was keep the lights on as long as they could – saying this to Arlo, of all people, who had a Little in the Sanctuary – this was not the Theo he knew. Something had changed in his brother. He wondered what it could be.

They stayed at the station five days. Finn and Rey spent the first day restoring power to the fence, then got to work on the west field, regreasing the turbine housings. Arlo, Theo, and Alicia took turns escorting them, in shifts of two, always returning well before sundown to lock the place down tight. With nothing else to occupy his time, Peter resorted to playing solo from a deck with three missing cards and leafing through a box of books in the storage room. A random assemblage of titles: *Charlie and the Chocolate Factory*, *A History of the Ottoman Empire*, *Zane Grey's Riders of the Purple Sage* (Classics of Western Literature). In the back of each book was a cardboard pocket, printed with the words PROPERTY OF RIVERSIDE COUNTY PUBLIC LIBRARY, and tucked inside it a card with a list of dates in faded ink: April 3, 2012; September 7, 2014; December 21, 2016.

'Who got these?' he asked Theo one night, after the group had returned from the field. A pile of books was stacked on the floor by Peter's bunk.

Theo was rinsing his face at the washbasin. He turned, drying his hands on the front of his shirt. 'I think they've been here a long time. I don't know if Zander could read much, so he put them away. Anything good?'

Peter held up the book he had been reading: *Moby-Dick; or, The Whale*.

'To tell you the truth, I'm not even sure this is English,' Peter said. 'It's taken me most of today to get through a page.'

His brother gave a tired-sounding laugh. 'Let's see that ankle.'

Theo sat on the edge of Peter's cot. Gently he took Peter's foot in his hands and rolled it on the joint. The two of them had barely spoken since the night of the attack. None of them had, really.

'Well, it looks better.' Theo rubbed his stubbled chin. His eyes, Peter saw, were hollowed with exhaustion. 'The swelling's down. Think you can ride?'

'I'd crawl if I had to, to get out of here.'

They set out after breakfast the next morning. Arlo had agreed to stay behind with Rey and Finn until the next relief party arrived. Caleb said he wanted to stay too, but Theo convinced him otherwise – with Arlo there, and as long as they stayed inside the fence, a fourth was unnecessary. And Caleb had been through more than enough.

The other question was the guns. Theo wanted to leave them where they were; Alicia argued that it made no sense to leave them all behind. They still didn't know what had happened to Zander or why the smokes hadn't killed Caleb when they'd had the chance. In the end, they reached a compromise. The party would ride back armed but hide their guns outside the Wall for safekeeping. The rest would stay under the stairs.

'I doubt I'll need 'em,' Arlo said, as the group was mounting up. 'Any smokes show up, I can just talk them to death.' Though it was also true that he was wearing a rifle over his shoulder. Alicia had shown him how to load and clean it and let him fire off a few rounds in the yard for practice. 'Holy damn!' he'd yelled in his big voice, and squeezed off another round, knocking the target can clean off its post. 'Is that ever something!' Theo was right, Peter thought; once you had a gun, it was a hard thing to let go of.

'I mean what I say, Arlo,' Theo warned. The horses, after so many days without exercise, were antsy to go, shifting beneath them, tamping down the dust. 'Something's not right. Stay inside the fence. Lock it down each night before you see the first shadow. Agreed?'

'No worries, cuz.' Grinning through his beard, Arlo looked at Finn and Rey, whose faces, Peter thought, did nothing to conceal their feeling of doom. Stuck in the station with Arlo and his stories; probably he'd just break down and sing for them, guitar or no guitar. Hanging from Arlo's neck was the key they'd taken from Zander's body. Theo had the other one.

'Oh, come on, guys,' Arlo called to the wrenches, and clapped his hands. 'Buck up. It'll be like a party.' But as he stepped to Theo's horse, his expression sobered abruptly. 'Put this in your pouch,' Arlo said quietly, slipping him a folded sheet of paper. 'For Leigh and the baby, if anything happens.'

Theo tucked the paper away without looking at it. 'Ten days. Stay inside.'

'Ten days, cuz.'

They rode out into the valley. Without a cart to pull, they cut across the fields toward Banning, bypassing the Eastern Road to shave a few kilometers off the route. No one was talking; they were saving their energies for the long ride ahead.

As they approached the edge of town, Theo drew up.

'I almost forgot.' He reached into his saddlebag and removed the curious object that Michael had given him at the gate, six days ago. 'Anybody remember what this thing is?'

Caleb drew his mount alongside, taking the board from Theo to examine it. 'It's a motherboard. Intel chip, Pion series. See the nine? That's how you can tell.'

'You know about this stuff?'

'Have to.' With a shrug, Caleb handed the board back to Theo. 'The turbine controls use Pions. Ours are hardened military, but basically the same. They're tough as nails and faster than snot. Sixteen gigahertz without overclocking.'

Peter was watching Theo's expression: he had no idea what this meant, either.

'Well, Michael wants one.'

'You should have said something. We have plenty of extras at the station.'

Alicia laughed. 'I have to say, you surprise me, Caleb. You sound like the Circuit. I didn't even know you wrenches could read.'

Caleb twisted in the saddle to face her; but if he was

432

offended, he gave no sign. 'Are you kidding me? What else is there to do down here? Zander was always sneaking off to the library to get more books. There're, like, boxes and boxes of them stacked in the toolshed. And not just technical stuff. Guy would read anything. Said books were more interesting than people.'

For a moment, no one spoke.

'What did I say?' asked Caleb.

The library was located near the Empire Valley Outlet Mall on the north edge of town: a squat, square building surrounded by hardpan tufted with tall weeds. They took shelter behind a filling station and dismounted; Theo retrieved the binoculars from his saddlebag and scanned the building.

'It's pretty sanded up. The windows are still intact above ground level, though. The building looks tight.'

'Can you see inside?' Peter asked.

'The sun's too bright, reflecting off the glass.' He passed the binoculars to Alicia and turned to Hightop. 'You're certain?'

'That Zander came here?' The boy nodded. 'Yes, I'm certain.'

'Did you ever go with him?'

'Are you serious?'

Alicia had clambered up a dumpster to the roof of the filling station to have a better look.

'Anything?'

She drew down the binoculars. 'You're right, the sun's too bright. I don't see how there'd be anything inside, though, with all those windows.'

'That's what Zander always said,' Caleb added.

'I don't get it,' Peter said. 'Why would he come out here alone?'

Alicia dropped down. She dusted off her hands on the front of her jersey and pushed a sweat-dampened strand of hair off her face. 'I think we should check it out. Middle of the day like this, we're not going to have a better chance.'

Theo's face said, *Why am I not surprised?* He turned toward Peter. 'What's your vote?'

'Since when do we vote?'

'Since now. If we do this, everyone has to agree.'

Peter tried to read Theo's expression, to guess what he wanted to do. In the question before him, he felt the weight of challenge. He thought, Why this? Why now?

He nodded his assent.

'Okay, Lish,' Theo said, and reached for his rifle. 'You've got your smokehunt.'

They left Caleb with the horses and approached the building in a loose line. The sand was pushed high against the windows, but the front entrance, at the top of a short flight of stairs, was clear. The door opened easily; they stepped inside. They were in some kind of entryway. Hung on the wall just inside the door was a bulletin board covered with paper signs, faded but still legible. CAR FOR SALE, '14 NISSAN SERATA, LOW MILES. LOSE WEIGHT NOW, ASK ME HOW! BABYSITTER WANTED, AFTERNOONS, SOME EVENINGS, MUST HAVE CAR. CHILDREN'S STORY HOUR, TUESDAYS AND THURSDAYS 10:30–11:30. And, larger than the rest, on a sheet of curling yellow paper:

STAY ALIVE. STAY IN WELL-LIGHTED AREAS.
REPORT ALL SIGNS OF INFECTION.
DO NOT LET STRANGERS INTO YOUR HOME.
ONLY LEAVE SAFE ZONES IF INSTRUCTED BY A
GOVERNMENT OFFICIAL.

They moved inside, into a wide room lit by tall windows that faced the parking lot. The air was sharp and thick with heat.

Sitting at the front desk was a body.

The woman – Peter could tell it was a woman – appeared to have shot herself. The gun, a small revolver, was still clutched in her hand where it had fallen to her lap. The corpse was brown as leather, the woman's desiccated flesh stretched taut over the bones, but the bullet hole in the side of her skull was plainly visible. Her head was tipped to the side, as if she had dropped something and had taken a moment to look.

'I'm glad Arlo isn't here to see that,' Alicia murmured.

They moved in silence into the stacks. Books were strewn everywhere on the floor, so many it was like walking on drifts of snow. They circled back around to the front; Theo gestured with the barrel of his rifle toward the stairs.

'All eyes.'

The stairs opened on a large room flooded with sunlight that poured from the windows. A feeling of spaciousness: the shelves had all been pushed aside to make room for the lines of cots that had taken their place.

Each cot bore a body.

'There must be fifty of them,' Alicia whispered. 'Is it some kind of infirmary?'

Theo moved deeper into the room, sliding between the rows of cots. An odd muskiness clung to the air. Halfway down the column, Theo paused beside one of the cots and reached down to remove a small object. Something floppy, made of disintegrating cloth. He held it up for Peter and Alicia to see. A stuffed doll.

'I don't think that's what this is.'

The images began to resolve in Peter's mind, forming a pattern. The smallness of the bodies. The stuffed animals and toys clutched by tiny hands of leathered bone. As Peter stepped forward, he felt and heard the crunch of plastic. A syringe. There were dozens of them, scattered over the floor.

The meaning hit him like a fist.

'Theo, this is . . . these are . . .' The word stopped in his throat.

His brother was already headed to the stairs. 'Let's get the hell out of here.'

They didn't stop until they were outside. They stood on the front stoop, breathing in great gulps of fresh air. In the distance, Peter could see Caleb standing on the roof of the filling station, still scanning the scene with the binoculars.

'They must have known what was happening,' Alicia said quietly. 'Decided it was better this way.'

Theo slung his rifle and took a long drink of water. His face was ashen; Peter saw that his brother's hands were trembling. 'Goddamn Zander,' Theo said. 'Why the fuck would he come here?'

'There's a second flight of stairs at the back,' Alicia said. 'We should check it.'

Theo spat and shook his head, hard.

'Let it go, Lish,' Peter said.

'What's the point of checking the building if we don't check the whole thing?'

Theo turned sharply. 'I don't want to spend another second in this place.' He was resolved, his words would be final. 'We torch it. No discussion.'

They pulled books from the shelves and fashioned a pile near the front desk. The paper caught swiftly, flames leaping from book to book. They retreated through the door and stood back fifty meters to watch the building burn. Peter took a drink from his canteen, but nothing would wash away the taste in his mouth; the taste of bodies, of death. He knew his eyes had beheld something that would stay with him for all the days of his life. Zander had come here, but not just for books. He'd come to see the children.

And that was when the drifted sand at the base of the building began to move.

Alicia, standing beside him, saw this first.

'Peter . . .'

The sand collapsed; the virals poured forth, clawing from

the sand where it had covered the basement windows. A pod of six, chased into the blazing light of midday by the flames.

They screamed. A great, high-pitched wail that shattered the air with pain and fury.

The library was fully engulfed now. Peter raised his rifle and fumbled for the trigger. His movements felt vague, without focus. Everything about the scene seemed only half real, his mind finding no traction on any of it. More virals were emerging through the heavy black smoke that roiled from the upper windows, the glass exploding in a glittering rain of shards, their flesh blazing, trailing liquid fronds of flame. It seemed that whole stretches of time had passed since he'd lifted his rifle, intending to fire. The first group had taken refuge in a pocket of shade where the library steps rose from the sand, a single huddled mass, their faces pressed to the ground like Littles in a game of hide-and-seek.

'Peter, we can't stay here!'

He shook off his torpor at the sound of Alicia's voice. Beside him, Theo appeared frozen in place, the barrel of his gun pointed uselessly at the ground, his face slack, eyes wide and impassive: *What's the use?*

'Theo, listen to me,' Alicia said, shaking him roughly by the arm; for a moment Peter thought she was actually about to strike him. The virals at the base of the steps had begun to stir. A collective twitch passed through them, like wind rippling the surface of a pool of water. 'We have to go, *right now.*'

Theo shifted his gaze toward Peter. 'Oh, brother,' he said. 'I think we're fucked.'

'Peter,' Alicia pleaded, 'help me.'

They each took him by an arm; by the time they were halfway across the lot, Theo was running on his own. The feeling of unreality was gone now, replaced by one desire only: to get away, to escape. They rounded the corner of the filling station to see Caleb, on his horse, barreling away. They mounted their horses and kicked to a gallop, tearing after him across the hardpan. In their wake, Peter could hear more explosions of glass. Alicia was pointing, yelling over the wind: the mall. That's where Caleb was headed. At full speed they tore up a ridge of crested sand and down into the empty lot in time to see Caleb leaping from his horse by the building's west entrance. He slapped its hindquarters and darted through the opening while his horse raced away.

'Inside!' Alicia yelled. She was in command now; Theo said nothing. 'Go, leave the horses!'

The animals were bait, an offering. There was no chance to say goodbye; they dismounted and dashed inside. The best place, Peter knew, would be the atrium. The glass roof had been torn away, there was sunlight and cover, they could make some kind of defense. Down the darkened hall they ran. The air was heavy and sour, the walls bulging with mold, exposing rusted beams, dangling wires, encrusted pipes. Most of the stores were shuttered but others stood open like amazed faces, their dim interiors clogged with debris. Peter could see Caleb running up ahead, fat beams of golden daylight falling down.

They emerged into the atrium, into sun so bright they blinked against it. The room was like a forest. Nearly every surface was choked with fat green vines; in the center a stand of palms reached toward the open ceiling. More vines dripped from the exposed struts of the ceiling, like coils of living rope. They took cover behind a barricade of overturned tables at the base of the trees. Caleb was nowhere to be seen.

Peter looked at his brother, crouched beside him. 'Are you okay?'

Theo nodded uncertainly. They were all breathing hard. 'I'm sorry. About back there. I just . . .' He shook his head. 'I don't know.' He wiped the sweat from his eyes. 'I'll take the left. Stay with Lish.' He skittered away.

Kneeling beside him, Lish checked the load on her rifle and pulled the bolt. Four hallways met the atrium: the attack, if it came, would come from the west.

'Do you think the sun got them?' Peter asked.

'I don't know, Peter. They seemed pretty mad. Maybe

some but not all.' She wrapped the rifle's sling tightly around her forearm. 'I need you to promise me something,' she said. 'I won't be one of them. If it comes to that, I need you to take care of it.'

'Flyers, Lish. It won't. Don't even say it.'

'I'm saying if it does.' Her voice was firm. 'Don't hesitate.'

There was no more time for words; they heard footsteps racing toward them. Caleb careened into the atrium, clutching an object to his chest. As he dove behind the tables, Peter saw what he was holding. A black shoe box.

'I don't believe it,' Alicia said. 'You went *scavenging*?'

Caleb lifted the lid and tossed it aside. A pair of bright yellow sneakers, still wrapped in paper. He kicked off Zander's boots and shoved his feet into them.

'Shit,' he said, wearing a crestfallen frown, 'they're way too big. They're not even *close*.'

And then the first viral fell, a blur of movement first above and then behind them, dropping through the atrium roof; Peter rolled in time to see Theo being lifted up, tossed toward the ceiling, his rifle dangling where the sling had tangled in his arm, his hands and feet scrabbling at space. A second viral, hanging upside down from one of the ceiling struts, snatched Peter's brother by the ankle as if he weighed nothing at all. Theo's body was fully inverted now; Peter saw the look on his brother's face, an expression of pure astonishment. He'd made no sound at all. His rifle fell away, spinning to the floor below. Then the viral flung Peter's brother through the open roof and he was gone.

Peter scrambled to his feet, his finger finding the trigger. He heard a voice, his voice, calling his brother's name, and the sound of Alicia firing. Three virals were on the ceiling now, launching from strut to strut. Peter detected, at the periphery of his vision, Alicia shoving Caleb up and over the counter of a restaurant on the far side of the atrium. Peter fired at last, fired again. But the virals were too fast; always the spot where he aimed was empty. It seemed to Peter as if they were playing a kind of game, trying to trick them into expending their ammunition. *Since when do they do that?* he thought, and wondered when he'd heard these words before.

As the first one let go, Peter saw, in his mind's eye, the fatal dimension of its arc. Alicia was standing with her back to the counter now. The viral descended straight for her, arms outstretched, legs bent to absorb the impact, a being of teeth and claws and smoothly muscled power. In the instant before it landed, Alicia stepped forward, positioning herself directly under it, holding the rifle away from her body, like a blade.

She fired.

A mist of red, a confusion of bodies tumbling, the rifle clattering away. In the time it took Peter to realize that Alicia was not dead, she was on her feet again. The viral lay where he'd come to rest, the back of his head cratered with blood. She'd shot it through the mouth. Above them, the other two had come to an abrupt halt, stiffening, teeth flashing, their heads swiveling toward Alicia as if pulled by a single string.

'Get out of here!' she called, and vaulted over the counter. 'Just run!'

He did. He ran.

He was deep inside the mall now. There seemed to be no way out. All the exits were barricaded, blocked by mountains of debris: furniture, shopping carts, dumpsters full of trash.

And Theo, his brother, was gone.

His only option was to hide. He tore down a hall of shuttered storefronts, yanking upward at their grates, but none would open; all were locked tight. Through the fog of his panic, a single question emerged: Why wasn't he dead yet? He had fled from the atrium not expecting to make it more than ten steps. A flash of pain and it would all be over. At least a full minute had passed before he'd realized the virals weren't pursuing him.

Because they were busy, he thought. He had to clutch one of the grates just to keep standing. He dug his fingers between the slats and pressed his forehead against the metal, fighting for breath. His friends were dead. That was the only explanation. Theo was dead, Caleb was dead, Alicia was dead. And when the virals were done, when they had drunk their fill, they'd be coming for him.

Hunting him.

He ran. Down one hall and into another, tearing past shuttered storefront after shuttered storefront. He wasn't even bothering with the grates now; his mind was seized with one thought: to get outside, onto open ground. Daylight ahead, and a feeling of openness: he turned a corner and emerged, skidding on the tiles, into a wide, domelike space. A second atrium. The area was clear of debris. Sunshine descended in smoky shafts from a ring of windows, high above.

In the center of the room, standing motionless, was a herd of tiny horses.

They were grouped in a tight circle beneath some kind of freestanding shelter. Peter froze, expecting them to scatter. How had a herd of horses gotten into the mall? He stepped cautiously forward. Now it was obvious: the horses weren't real. A carousel. Peter had seen a picture of one, in a book in the Sanctuary. The base would turn and music would play, and children would ride the horses around and around. He stepped onto the decking; a heavy layer of dust encased them, dulling their features. He squared his shoulders to one of the animals and brushed the grime away, revealing the bright colors beneath, the precisely painted-on details: the lashes of its eyes, the grooves of its teeth, the long slope of its nose and the flaring nostrils.

He felt it then, a sudden awareness at his extremities, like a touch of cold metal. He startled, lifting his face.

Standing before him was a girl.

A Walker.

He couldn't have said how old she was. Thirteen? Sixteen? Her hair was long and dark, and thick with mats; she was wearing a pair of threadbare gaps cut off at the ankles and a T-shirt stiff with dirt, all of it too large on her boyish frame.

Her pants were cinched to her waist with a length of electric cord; on her feet she wore a pair of sandals with plastic daisies poking between the toes.

Before Peter could speak, she raised a finger to her lips: *Don't speak.* She moved briskly toward the center of the platform and turned to wave him on, to tell him to come with her.

He heard them then. A skittering in the hall, the rattle of metal grates on the shuttered storefronts.

The virals were coming. Searching. Hunting.

The girl's eyes were very wide. *Hurry*, her eyes said. She took his hand and pulled him to the center of the platform. There she dropped to her knees and dug at a metal ring in the floor. A trapdoor, flush with the wooden decking. She climbed inside so that only her face was showing.

Quickly, quickly.

Peter followed her down the hole and sealed the trapdoor above him. They were under the carousel now, in some kind of crawl space. Angled blades of light, spangled with dust motes, fell through the slats of the decking over their heads, revealing a dark bulk of machinery and, on the floor beside it, a rumpled bedroll. Plastic bottles of water and tins of food stacked in rows, their paper labels long since worn away. Did she live here?

The decking shuddered. The girl had dropped to her knees. A shadow moved across them. She was showing him what to do.

Lie down. Be still.

He did as she asked. Then she climbed on top of him, onto his back. He could feel the heat of her body, the warmth of her breath on his neck. She was covering his body with her own. The virals were all over the carousel now. He could feel their minds searching, probing, hear the soft clicking in their throats. How long before they discovered the trapdoor?

Don't move. Don't breathe.

He closed his eyes tightly, willing himself into absolute stillness, waiting for the sound of the door being ripped off its hinges. The rifle was on the floor beside him. He might get off a shot or two, but that would be all.

Seconds passed. More shudders above, the sharp, excited breathing of virals with human scent in their nostrils. Tasting the blood in the air. But something was wrong; he sensed their uncertainty. The girl was pressing down upon him. Screening him, protecting him. Silence from above; had the virals gone? A minute moved by, and then another. His sense of expectation shifted from the virals to what the girl would do next. At last she climbed off him. He rose to his knees. Their faces were just inches apart. The soft curve of her cheek was like a child's, but her eyes were not, not at all. He could smell her breath; there was something sweet to it, like honey.

'How did you—'

She shook her head sharply to silence him, pointing to the ceiling, then pressed her fingers to her lips again.

They're gone. But they'll be back.

She rose to her feet and opened the trapdoor. A quick turn of the head to show him her meaning.

Follow me. Do it now.

They emerged onto the decking of the carousel. The room was empty, but he could feel the virals' departed presence, the air swirling in unseen eddies around the places they had stood. Moving quickly, the girl led him to a door across the atrium. It was propped open, held in place with a wedge of concrete. They stepped inside and she let the door close behind them, sealing them inside; he heard the click of a lock.

Blackness.

A new panic gripped him, a feeling of complete disorientation. But then he felt her taking his hand. Her grip was tight, meant to reassure; she pulled him farther in.

I have you. It's all right.

He tried to count his steps, but it was useless. He could feel in her grip that she wanted him to go faster, that his uncertainty was holding them back. He stumbled on something in his path and the rifle fell away, lost in the darkness.

'Wait—'

A *wang* from behind, and the groan of bending metal. The virals had found them. Ahead he detected a glow of daylight; his surroundings began to emerge to his vision. They were in a long, high-ceilinged hallway; slims were shoved against the walls, a chorus of grinning skeletons, their limbs contorted in what seemed to be postures of warning. Another crash from behind; the door was failing, caving in on its hinges. The hallway ended at another door, which stood open. A stairwell. From high above came a glow of yellow daylight, and the sound and smell of pigeons. On the wall was a sign: ROOF ACCESS.

He turned. The girl was still standing in the hallway, just outside the stairwell door. Their eyes met briefly, hauntingly. Before another second passed, the girl stepped forward and, rising on her toes, pressed her closed mouth – a bird pecking water – against his face.

Just that: she kissed him on the cheek.

Peter was too stunned to speak. The girl backed away, into the dark hall. *Go now*, her eyes said.

Then she closed the door.

'Hey!' He heard the click of the lock. He gripped the handle, but it was immovable. He pounded on the sealed metal. 'Hey! Don't leave me!'

But the girl was gone, a departed spirit. He saw the sign again: ROOF ACCESS. That's where she wanted him to go.

He began to climb. The air was roasting, nearly asphyxiating with the gas of pigeon. Long streaks of guano smeared the walls, encrusting the stairs and banister like layers of paint. The birds seemed to take scant notice of him, fluttering here and there as he made his ascent, as if his presence were no more than a curiosity. Three flights, four; he was panting with exertion, the taste in his mouth and nose was excruciating in its foulness, his eyes stung as if splashed by acid.

At last he reached the top. A final door and, on the wall

above it, far out of reach, a tiny window, its edges scalloped by broken glass, yellowed by soot and time.

The door was padlocked.

A dead end. After everything, the girl had led him to a dead end. A furious clang shook the stairwell as the first viral hit the door below him. Birds lifted off and scattered all around him, swirling the air with feathers.

That was when he saw it, so encrusted with guano it had blended invisibly into the wall around it. He used his elbow to smash the glass, then yanked the axe free. A second crash from below. One more push and the virals would be through the door and streaming up the stairs.

Peter lifted the axe over his head and gave it a hard swing, aiming for the padlock. The blade glanced off, but he could tell he'd done some damage. He took a deep breath, calculating the distance, and gave the axe another swing, putting everything he had behind it. A clean hit: the lock split and shattered. He leaned into the door with all his might and with a groan of age and rust it fell open, spilling him into sunlight.

He was on the roof at the north side of the mall, facing the mountains. He hobbled quickly to the edge.

The drop was fifteen meters at least. He'd break his leg or worse.

Lying immobile on the hardpan, waiting for the virals to take him. It wasn't how he wanted things to end. He was bleeding freely from his elbow; a trail of his blood had followed him from the open door. Though he had no memory of pain, he must have cut it when he'd smashed the panel. But a little blood would hardly make a difference now. At least he had the axe.

He was turning to face the door, preparing to swing, when a cry reached him from below.

'Jump!'

Alicia and Caleb, coming around the corner of the building on horseback, riding fast. Alicia was waving to him, her body arched forward from the stirrups. 'Jump!'

He thought of Theo, lifted up. He thought of his father, standing at the edge of the sea, and of the sea and stars. He thought of the girl, covering his body with her own, the warmth and sweetness of her breath on his neck and on his cheek where she had kissed him.

His friends were calling and waving from below, the virals were coming up the stairs, the axe was in his hand.

Not now, he thought, *not yet*, and he closed his eyes and jumped.

TWENTY-THREE

It was summer again and she was alone. Alone with no one but the voices she heard, everywhere and all around.

She remembered people. She remembered the Man. She remembered the other man and his wife and the boy and then the woman. She remembered some more than others. She remembered no one at all. She remembered one day thinking: I am alone. There is no I but I. She lived in the dark. She taught herself to walk in the light, though it was not easy. For a time it pained her, made her sick.

She walked and walked. She followed the mountains. The Man had told her to follow the mountains, to run and keep on running, but then one day the mountains ended; the mountains were no more. She never could find them again, those same ones. Some days she went nowhere at all. Some days were years. She lived here and there, with these and those, with the man and his wife and the boy and then the woman and finally with no one at all. Some of the people were kind to her, before they died. Others were not so. She was different, they said. She was not like them, not of them. She was apart and alone and there were no others like her in all the world. The people sent her away or they did not, but in the end they always died.

She dreamed. She dreamed of voices, and the Man. For some time of months or years she could hear the Man in the howl of the wind and the scrape of the stars if she listened just so, and it gave her a longing in her heart for his care. But over time's passage his voice became all mixed in her mind with the voices of the others, the dreaming ones, both there and not there, as the dark was a thing but not a thing, a presence and an absence joined. The world was a world of dreaming souls who could not die. She thought: there is the ground below my feet, there is the sky over my head, there are the empty buildings and the wind and rain and stars and everywhere the voices, the voices and the question.

Who am I? Who am I? Who am I?

She was not afraid of them, as the Man had been, and the others also, the man and his wife and the boy and then the woman. She had tried to lead the dreaming ones away from the Man and she had, she had done it. They followed her with their question, dragging it like a chain, like the one she'd read about in the story of the ghost, Jacob Marley. For a time she thought they might be ghosts, but they were not so. She had no name for them. She had no name for herself, for the thing she was. One night she awoke and she beheld them all around, their needful eyes, glowing like embers in the dark. She remembered the place because it was a barn and cold and raining out. Their faces crowded around her, their dreaming faces, so sad and lost, like the lonely world she walked in. They needed her to tell them, to answer the question. She could smell their breath on her, the breath of night, and of the question, a current in the blood. *Who am I?* they asked her.

who am I who am I

She ran from that place then. She ran and kept on running.

The seasons changed. They rolled round and round, and round some more. It was cold and then it was not. The nights were long and then they were not. She carried on her back a pack of things she needed, as well as the things she wanted to have because they were a comfort. They helped her to remember, to hold the time of years in her mind, both the good and the bad. Such things as: the story of the ghost, Jacob Marley. The locket of the woman, which she had taken from around her neck after the woman had died in the manner of all people dying, with great commotion. A bone from the field of bones and a stone from the beach where she had seen the ship. From time to time she ate. Some of the things in the cans she found were not good anymore. She would open a can with the tool in her pack and a terrible smell would rise from within it like the insides of the buildings where the dead people lay in rows or not in rows, and she knew she couldn't eat that one but would have to eat another. For a time there was the ocean beside her, huge and gray, and a beach of smooth, wave-rubbed stones, and tall pines stretching their long arms above the surface of the water. At night she watched the stars turning, she watched the moon soaring and dipping over the sea. It was the same moon as over all the world and she was happy in that place for a time. It was in that place she saw the ship. *Hello!* she cried, for she had seen no one in ever and ever, and was joyful at the very sight of it. *Hello, ship! Hello, you big boat, hello!* But the ship said no words back to her. It went away for some time of days, past the edge of the sea, and then returned, moving on the tides of the moon at night. Like a dream of a boat with no one to dream it but her. She followed it over the days and nights to the place of the rocks and the broken bridge the color of blood, where its great bow came to rest, among the others large and small, and by then she knew the ship like its fellows upon the rocks was empty with no people on it; and the sea was black with a foul smell like that which came from the cans that were no good. And she moved on from that place also.

Oh, she could feel them, feel them all. She could stretch out her hands and stroke the darkness and feel them in it, everywhere. Their sorrowful forgetting. Their great and terrible brokenheartedness. Their endless needful questioning. It moved her to a sorrow that was a kind of love. Like the love she'd felt for the Man, who in his care for her had told her to run and keep on running.

The Man. She remembered the fires and the light like an exploding sun in her eyes. She remembered his sadness and the feeling of the Man. But she could not hear him anymore. The Man, she thought, was gone.

There were others she did hear, in the dark. And she knew who these were, too.

I am Babcock.

I am Morrison.

I am Chávez.

I am Baffes-Turrell-Winston-Sosa-Echols-Lambright-Martínez-Reinhardt-Carter.

She thought of them as the Twelve, and the Twelve were everywhere, inside the world and behind the world and threaded into the darkness itself. The Twelve were the blood running below the skin of all things in the world at that time.

All this, through the years and years. She remembered one day, the day of the field of bones, and another, the day of the bird and the not-talking. This was in a place with trees, so tall. There it was, just a small fluttering thing in the air before her face. Her feet were bare on the grass in the sunshine that she had learned to walk in. To and fro it moved on a blur of wings. She looked and looked. It seemed to her as if she had been beholding this small thing for many a day. She thought the word for what it was, but when she tried to say it, she realized she had forgotten how. *Bird.* The word was inside her but there was no door for it to come out of. *Humming . . . bird.* She thought of all the other words she knew and it was just the same. All the words, all locked away inside.

And one night in the moonlight and after much time had passed, she was lonesome and without a friend in the world for company and she thought: *Come here.*

They came. First one and then another and more and more.

Come to me.

They stepped from the shadows. They dropped from the sky above and the high places all around, and soon they were a company without number, as they had been in the barn, only more so. They crowded around her with their dreaming faces. She touched them, caressed them, and did not feel alone. She asked: *Are we the all? For I have seen no one, no man or woman, in all the years and years. Is there no I but I?* But as long as she asked, they had no answer for her, only the question, fierce and burning.

Go now, she thought, and closed her eyes; and when she opened them again she found she was alone.

That was how she learned to do it.

Then, through the seasons of nights and the years of nights, she came upon the place of the buried city, where in the paling light of dusk she saw the men on their horses. Six of them, atop six dark horses of great muscularity. The men had guns, like other men that she recalled, in the time after the man and his wife and the boy and then the woman; and she hid herself away in the shadows, waiting for night to fall. What she would do then she did not know, but then the forgetful ones came to her as they always did in the dark and although she told them not to, they descended upon the men swiftly and with a great commotion and in this fashion the men began to die and then did so, three of their number.

She moved to where the bodies lay, the men and also their horses who were dead with no blood in them as was the case with all things that had died in this manner. Three of the men were nowhere to be found but the soul of one man was still near, watching from some nameless place without the form of solid things as she bent to regard his face and the look written upon it. It was the same look she had seen upon the face of the man and his wife and the boy and then the woman. Fear, and pain, and the letting go. It came to her that the man's name had been Willem. And the ones who had done it to Willem were sorry, so sorry, and she rose and said to them, *It's all right, go now and do not do this again if you can help it*, though she knew that they could not. They could not help it because of the Twelve who filled their minds with their terrible dreams of blood and no answer to the question but this:

I am Babcock.

I am Morrison.

I am Chávez.

I am Baffes-Turrell-Winston-Sosa-Echols-Lambright-Martínez-Reinhardt-Carter.

I am Babcock.

Babcock.

Babcock.

She followed them across the sand, even though the light was a great brightness to her eyes and on some days she could not hide from it. She wrapped herself in a cloth she had found and on her face she had the glasses. The days were long, the sun in its arc cutting a swath in the sky above and plowing the earth below it with the long blade of its light. At night the desert grew still with only the sound of her moving across it and the beating of her heart and the dreaming world around.

Then it was a day when there were mountains once again. She never had found those men on their horses or where they had come from that some of their number should have died in the buried city before her eyes. The floor of the valley between the mountains was dotted with trees that turned with the wind, and that was where she came upon the building with the horses inside; and when she beheld them in their stillness and solitude she thought, Perhaps these are the horses I saw. The horses weren't alive but they seemed so, and the look of them brought a peacefulness to her mind and a feeling of the Man and his cares for her that made her think she should stay in that place, that the time for running was ended. That this was the place where she had come to rest.

But now that time had ended, too. The men had returned at last on their horses and she had saved one of their company; she had covered his body with her own as her instincts had dictated in the moment and she'd told the dreaming ones to *go, go now and do not kill this one*; and for a while these urgings had worked upon them, but the other voice within their minds was strong and the hunger was strong also.

In her space in the dark and dust below the horses she thought of the one she had saved, hoping he was not dead, and listened for the sounds of the men and their horses and guns returning. And after a certain time of days, when she had detected no trace of them, she departed that place as she had departed all the others before it and stepped into the moonlit night of which she was a part, one and indivisible.

—Where are they? she asked the darkness. Where are the men on their horses that I should go to them and find them? For I have been alone through all the years and years, no I but I.

And a new voice came to her from the night sky, saying, *Go into the moonlight, Amy.*

—Where? Where should I go?

Bring them to me. The way will show you the way.

She would. She would do it. For she had been alone too long, no I but I, and she was filled then with a sorrow and a great desire for others of her kind, that she should be alone no longer.

Go into the moonlight and find the men that I should know them as I know you, Amy.

—Amy, she thought. Who is Amy?

And the voice said, *You are.*

V

GIRL FROM
NOWHERE

You who do not remember
Passage from the other world
I tell you I could speak again: whatever
returns from oblivion returns
to find a voice.

— LOUISE GLÜCK,
'The Wild Iris'

TWENTY-FOUR

Log of the Watch
Summer 92

Day 51: No sign.
Day 52: No sign.
Day 53: No sign.
Day 54: No sign.
Day 55: No sign.
Day 56: No sign.
Day 57: Peter Jaxon stationed at FP 1 (M: Theo Jaxon). No
    sign.
Day 58: No sign.
Day 59: No sign.
Day 60: No sign.
During this period: 0 contacts. No souls killed or taken.
    Second Captain vacancy (T. Jaxon, deceased)
    referred to Sanjay Patal.

Respectfully submitted to the Household,
S. C. Ramirez, First Captain

Dawn of the eighth morning: Peter's eyes snapped open at the sound of the herd, coming down the trace.

He remembered thinking, some time after half-night: *Just a few minutes. Just a few minutes off my feet, to gather my strength.* But the moment he'd allowed himself to sit, bracing his back against the rampart, and rested his weary head upon his folded arms, sleep had taken him fast.

'Good, you're up.'

Lish was standing above him. Peter rubbed his eyes and rose, accepting without comment the canteen of water she was handing him. His limbs felt heavy and slow, as if his bones had been replaced by tubes of sloshing liquid. He took a drink of tepid water and cast his gaze over the edge of the rampart. Beyond the fireline, a faint mist was rising slowly from the hills.

'How long was I out?'

She squared her shoulders toward him. 'Forget it. You'd been up seven nights without a break. You had no business being out here as it was. Anybody who says different can take it up with me.'

Morning Bell sounded. Peter and Alicia watched in silence as the gates commenced to retract into their pockets. The herd, restless and ready to move, began to surge through the opening.

'Go home and sleep,' Alicia said, as the logging crews were preparing to leave. 'You can worry about the Stone later.'

'I'm going to wait for him.'

She steadied her eyes on his face. 'Peter. It's been seven nights. Go home.'

They were interrupted by the sound of footsteps ascending the ladder. Hollis Wilson hoisted himself onto the catwalk and looked at the two of them, frowning.

'You standing down, Peter?'

'All yours,' Alicia answered. 'We're done here.'

'I said, I'm staying.'

The day shift was commencing. Two more Watchers clambered up the ladder, Gar Phillips and Vivian Chou. Gar was telling some kind of story, Vivian laughing along, but when they saw the three of them standing there, they abruptly fell silent and moved briskly down the catwalk.

'Listen,' Hollis said, 'if you want to take this post, it's okay with me. But I'm the OD, so I'll have to tell Soo.'

'No, he's not,' Alicia said. 'I mean it, Peter. It's not a request. Hollis won't say it, but I will. Go home.'

The urge to protest rose within him. But as he opened his mouth to speak he was met with a blast of grief that stunned him into surrender. Alicia was right. It was over; Theo was gone. He should have felt relieved, but all he felt was exhausted – a bone weariness that ran so deep he felt as if he'd be dragging it for the rest of his life like a chain. It took nearly all of his strength just to lift his cross from the floor of the rampart.

'I'm sorry about your brother, Peter,' Hollis said. 'I guess I can say that now since it's been seven nights.'

'I appreciate that, Hollis.'

'I guess that makes you Household now, huh?'

Peter had barely considered this. He supposed he was. His cousins, Dana and Leigh, were both older, but Dana had taken a pass when Peter's father had stepped down, and he doubted Leigh would be interested in the job now, with a baby to look after in the Sanctuary.

'I guess it does.'

'Well, um, congratulations?' Hollis gave an awkward shrug. 'Funny to say it, but you know what I mean.'

He'd told no one about the girl, not even Alicia, who might have actually believed him.

The distance from the mall roof to the ground had been less than Peter had thought. He had been unable to detect, as Alicia could from below, how high the sand was piled against the base of the building – a tall, sloping dune that had absorbed the impact of his fall as he tumbled headlong down it. Still clutching the axe, he'd climbed onto Omega's back behind Alicia; it wasn't until they were clear on the other side of Banning, and could reasonably conclude that no pursuit was forthcoming, that he'd thought to wonder how they'd gotten away, and why the horses themselves were not dead.

Alicia and Caleb had fled the atrium through the kitchen of the restaurant. This connected through a series of hallways to a loading dock. The big bay doors were rusted tight, but one was open a crack, letting in a thin beam of sunlight. Using a length of pipe as a wedge, the two of them had managed to force it open wide enough to scramble through.

They rolled out into sunlight to find themselves on the south side of the mall. That was when they spotted two of the horses, obliviously chewing on a stand of tall weeds. Alicia couldn't believe their luck. She and Caleb were making a circuit around the building when she heard the crash of the door and saw Peter on the edge of the roof.

'Why didn't you just go when you found the horses?' Peter asked her.

They had stopped on the power station road to water the animals, not far from the place where they had seen the viral in the trees, six days earlier. They had only what was in their canteens, but after they had each taken some, they poured what was left into their hands and let the horses lick it off. Peter's bleeding elbow was wrapped in a bandage they'd cut from his jersey; the wound wasn't deep but would probably need stitches.

'I don't second-guess these things, Peter.' Alicia's voice was sharp; he wondered if he'd offended her. 'It seemed like the right thing to do, and it was.'

That was when he could have told them about the girl. And yet he'd hesitated, feeling the moment pass away. A young girl alone, and the thing she'd done under the carousel, covering him with her body; the look that passed between them, and the kiss on his cheek, and the suddenly slamming door. Maybe in the heat of the moment he had simply imagined all of it. He told them he'd found a stairwell and let it go at that.

They returned to a great commotion; they were four days overdue, on the verge of being declared lost. At the news of their return, a crowd had assembled at the gate. Leigh actually fainted before anyone could explain that Arlo was not dead, that he had stayed behind at the station. Peter didn't have the heart to go find Mausami in the Sanctuary, to give her the news about Theo. In any case, someone would tell her. Michael was there, and Sara too; it was she who washed and stitched his elbow while he sat on a rock, wincing at the pain and feeling cheated that the trancelike numbness brought on by the loss of his brother did not also apply to having one's skin sewn closed with a needle. She wrapped it in a proper bandage, hugged him quickly, and burst into tears. Then, as darkness fell, the crowd parted, making room for him to pass, and as Second Bell began to ring, Peter ascended the rampart, to stand the Mercy for his brother.

He left Alicia at the bottom of the ladder, promising that he'd go home and sleep. But home was the last place he wanted to go. Only a few of the unmarried men still used the barracks; the place was filthy and reeked as bad as the power station. But that would be where Peter lived from now on. He needed a few things from the house, that was all.

The morning sun was already warm on his shoulders when he arrived at the house, a five-room cabin facing the East Glade. It was the only home that Peter had ever known, since coming out of the Sanctuary; he and Theo had barely done more than sleep there since their mother's death. They certainly hadn't done much to keep the place tidy. It always bothered Peter what a mess it was – dishes piled in the sink, clothing on the floor, every surface tacky with grime – and yet he could never quite bring himself to do anything about this. Their mother had been nothing if not neat, and had kept the house well – the floors washed and rugs beaten, the hearth swept of ashes, the kitchen clear of debris. There were two bedrooms on the first floor, where he and Theo slept, and one, his parents', tucked under the eaves on the second. Peter went to his room and quickly packed a rucksack with a few days' worth of clothing; he'd look over Theo's belongings later, deciding what to keep for himself before carting the rest to the Storehouse, where his brother's clothes and shoes would be sorted and stowed, to await redistribution among the Colony at Share. It was Theo who had seen to this chore after their mother's death, knowing that Peter could not; one winter day, almost a year later, Peter had seen a woman – Gloria Patal – wearing a scarf he recognized. Gloria was in the market stalls, sorting jars of honey. The scarf, with its bit of fringe, was unmistakably his mother's. Peter had been so disturbed he'd darted away, as if from the scene of some misdeed in which he was implicated.

He finished his packing and stepped into the main room of the house, a combined kitchen and living area under exposed beams. The stove hadn't been lit in months; the woodpile out back was probably full of mice by now. Every surface in the room was coated in a sticky skin of dust. Like nobody lived there at all. Well, he thought, I guess they don't.

A last impulse took him upstairs to his parents' bedroom. The drawers of the small dresser were vacant, the sagging mattress stripped of bedding, the shelves in the old wardrobe barren except for a filigree of cobwebs that swayed in the shifting air when he opened the door. The small bedside table where his mother had kept a cup of water and her glasses – the one thing of hers Peter would have liked to keep, but couldn't; a decent pair of glasses was worth a full share – was ringed with ghostly stains. Nobody had opened the windows in months; the atmosphere of the room felt trapped and ill-used, one more item that Peter had dishonored with his neglect. It was true: he felt like he'd failed them, failed them all.

He toted his pack out into the gathering heat of the morning. From all around him came the sounds of activity: the tamp and whinny of the horses in the stables, the ringing music of a hammer from the smithing shop, the calls of the day shift from the Wall, and, as he moved into Old Town, the laughing squeals of the children, playing in the courtyard of the Sanctuary. Morning recess, when for an exhilarating hour Teacher would let them all run wild as mice; Peter recalled a winter day, sunlit and cold, and a game of take-away in which he had, with miraculous effortlessness, seized the stick from the hands of a much older, larger boy – in his memory it was one of the Wilson brothers – and managed to keep it to himself until Teacher, clapping and waving her mittened hands, had summoned them all inside. The sharpness of cold air in his lungs, and the dry, brown look of the world in winter; the steam of his sweat rising on his brow and the pure physical elation as he had dodged and weaved his way through the grasping hands of his attackers. How alive he'd felt. Peter searched his memory for his brother – surely Theo had been among the Littles on that winter morning, part of the galloping pack – but could find no trace of him. The place where his brother should have been was empty.

He came to the training pits then. A trio of wide depressions in the earth, twenty meters long, with high earthen walls to constrain the inevitable stray bolts and arrows, the wildly misthrown blades. At the close end of the middle trench, five new trainees were standing at attention. Three girls and two boys, ranging in ages from nine to thirteen: in their rigid postures and anxious faces, Peter could read the same effortful seriousness he'd felt when he'd come into the pits, an overwhelming desire to prove himself. Theo was ahead of him, three grades; he recalled the morning his brother had been chosen as a runner, the proud smile on his face as he turned and made his way to the Wall for the first time. The glory was reflected, but Peter had felt it, too. Soon he would follow.

The trainer this morning was Peter's cousin Dana, Uncle Willem's girl. She was eight years older than Peter and had stood down to take over the pits after the birth of her first daughter, Ellie. Her youngest, Kat, was still in the Sanctuary, but Ellie had come out a year ago and was one of the trainees in the pit, first grade, tall for her age and slender like her mother, with long black hair plaited in a Watcher braid.

Dana, standing before the group, examined them with a stony expression, as if she were picking a ram for slaughter. All part of the ritual.

'What do we have?' she asked the group.

They answered with one voice. 'One shot!'

'Where do they come from?'

Louder this time: 'They come from above!'

Dana paused, rocking back on her heels, and caught sight of Peter. She sent him a sad smile before facing her charges once again, her face hardening into a scowl. 'Well, that was horrible. You've just earned yourselves three extra laps before chow. Now, I want two lines, bows up.'

'What do you think?'

Sanjay Patal: Peter had been so lost in thought he hadn't heard the man approach. Sanjay was standing beside him, arms folded over his chest, his gaze directed over the pits.

'They'll learn.'

Below them the trainees had begun their morning drills. One of the youngest, the little Darrell boy, misfired, burying his arrow in the fence behind the target with a thunk. The others began to laugh.

'I'm sorry about your brother.' Sanjay turned to face him, drawing Peter's attention back away from the pits. He was a physically slight man, though the impression he gave was one of compactness. He kept his face clean-shaven, his hair, wisped with gray, trimmed tightly to his scalp. Small white teeth and deep-set eyes darkened by a heavy, wool-like brow. 'Theo was a good man. It shouldn't have happened.'

Peter didn't reply. What was there to say?

'I've been thinking about what you told me,' Sanjay continued. 'To be honest, not all of it makes complete sense. This thing with Zander. And what you were doing at the library.'

Peter felt the quick shiver of his lie. They had all agreed to hold to the original story and not tell anyone about the guns, at least for the time being. But this had quickly proved itself a far more complex undertaking than Peter had anticipated. Without the guns, their story was full of holes – what they were doing on the roof of the power station, how they'd rescued Caleb, Zander's death, their presence in the library.

'We told you everything,' Peter said. 'Zander must have gotten bitten somehow. We thought it might have happened at the library, so we went to check it out.'

'But why would Theo take a risk like that? Or was it Alicia's idea?'

'Why would you think that?'

Sanjay paused, clearing his throat. 'I know she is your friend, Peter, and I do not doubt her skills. But she's reckless. Always quick with the hunt.'

'It wasn't her fault. It wasn't anyone's. It was just bad luck. We decided as a group.'

Sanjay paused once more, casting a meditative gaze over the pits. Peter said nothing, hoping his silence would bring about an end to the conversation.

'Still, I find it hard to understand. Out of character for your brother, to take a chance like that. I suppose we'll never know.' Sanjay gave his head a preoccupied shake and turned to face Peter again, his expression softening. 'I'm sorry, I shouldn't be interrogating you like this. I'm sure you're tired. But as long as I have you here, there's something else I need to speak with you about. It concerns the Household. Your brother's spot.'

Just the thought made Peter suddenly weary. But the duty was his to perform. 'Let me know what you want me to do.'

'That is the thing I want to talk to you about, Peter. Your father erred, I believe, in passing his seat to your brother. His seat rightfully belonged to Dana. She was, and is, the oldest Jaxon.'

'But she turned it down.'

'That's true. But confidentially, I will tell you that we have not always been . . . comfortable with the way this came about. Dana was upset. Her father, as you recall, had just been killed. Many of us think she would have been glad to serve if your father hadn't pressured her to stand aside.'

What was Sanjay saying? That the job was Dana's? 'I don't know what you're talking about. Theo never said a word to me about it.'

'Well, I doubt that he would have.' Sanjay let a silent moment pass. 'Your father and I did not always see eye to eye. I'm sure you know this. I opposed the Long Rides from the start. But your father never could quite let go of the idea, even after he'd lost so many men. It was his intention that

463

your brother should revive the rides. That is why he wanted Theo on the Household.'

The trainees had moved out of the pits now, jogging down the path to begin their laps around the perimeter. What was it Theo had said, that night in the control room? That Sanjay was good at what he did? All of which only served to make Peter, at that moment, fiercely protective of a job that minutes ago he would have gladly given away to the first person he saw.

'I don't know, Sanjay.'

'You don't have to know, Peter. The Household has met. We are all in agreement. The seat is rightfully Dana's.'

'And she wants it?'

'When I explained everything to her, yes.' Sanjay put a hand on Peter's shoulder – a gesture meant to be consoling, Peter supposed, though it wasn't, not at all. 'Please don't take it badly. It's not a reflection on you. We were willing to overlook this irregularity because everyone held Theo in such high regard.'

Just like that, Peter thought, the waters had closed over his brother. Theo's shirts were still folded in the drawers, his spare boots sitting under the bed, and it was as if he'd never even existed.

Sanjay lifted his face past the pits. 'Well. Here's Soo.'

Peter turned to see Soo Ramirez striding toward them from the gate; with her was Jimmy Molyneau. A tall, sandy-haired woman in her early forties, Soo had risen to the rank of First Captain after Willem's death – a supremely competent woman with a temper that could flare at a moment's notice, producing outbursts that made even the most hardened Watcher cower in fear.

'Peter, I've been looking for you. Take a few days off the Wall if you want. Let me know when you're going to do the etching; I'd like to say a few words.'

'I was just thinking the same thing,' Sanjay interjected. 'Let us know. And by all means, take a few days. There's no hurry.'

Soo's arrival at precisely this moment was no accident, Peter realized; he was being handled.

'Okay,' Peter managed. 'I guess I will.'

'I really liked your brother,' Jimmy offered then, evidently thinking his presence warranted some comment. 'Karen, too.'

'Thanks. I'm hearing that a lot.'

The remark came off as too bitter; Peter regretted it immediately, seeing the look on Jimmy's hawk-nosed face. Jimmy had been Theo's friend, too – a Second Captain, just as Theo was – and knew what it meant to lose a brother. Connor Molyneau had been killed five years ago on a smoke-hunt to clear out a pod in Upper Field. After Soo, Jimmy was the oldest of the officers, in his midthirties with a wife and two girls; he could have stood down years ago without an ill thought from anyone but had chosen to stay on. Sometimes his wife, Karen, would bring him hot meals on the Wall, a gesture that embarrassed him and earned him no end of jokes from the Watch, even as everyone could tell he liked it.

'Sorry, Jimmy.'

He shrugged. 'Forget it. I've been there, believe me.'

'He's saying it because it's true, Peter. Your brother was someone very important to all of us.' With this final declaration, Sanjay lifted his chin officiously in Soo's direction. 'Captain, if you have a minute?'

Soo nodded, her eyes still fixed on Peter's face. 'I mean it,' she said, and touched him again, gripping his arm just above the elbow. 'Take whatever time you need.'

Peter waited a few minutes to put some distance between himself and the three of them. He felt peculiarly agitated, alert but without focus. What had transpired was only talk, nothing, in the end, that should have surprised him all that much: the expected, awkward condolences he knew so well, and then the news that he wouldn't have to be Household after all – a fact he should have welcomed, wanting nothing whatsoever to do with the daily duties of running things in the first place. And yet Peter had felt a deeper current running under the surface of the conversation. He had the distinct impression of being maneuvered, of everybody knowing something he didn't.

Hoisting his pack over one shoulder – the thing was practically empty, why had he bothered? – he decided not to go to the barracks straight off and instead moved down the path in the opposite direction.

The Dark Night Stone sat at the far end of the plaza: a pear-shaped granite boulder twice the height of a man, grayish white with jewel-like flecks of pink quartzite, in the surface of which were engraved the names of the missing and the dead. This was why he had come. One hundred and sixty-two names: it had taken months to etch them all. Two whole families of Levines and Darrells. The entire Boyes clan, nine all told. A host of Greenbergs and Patals and Chous and Molyneaus and Strausses and Fishers and two Donadios – Lish's parents, John and Angel. The first Jaxons to be named on the stone were Darla and Taylor Jaxon, Peter's grand-parents, who'd died in the rubble of their house under the north wall. It was easy for Peter to think of them as old since they'd been dead for fifteen years, the entirety of their lives consigned to a time before his living memory, a region of existence that Peter simply thought of as 'ago.' But, in fact, Taylor hadn't been much older than forty, and Darla, Taylor's second wife, just thirty-six at the time of the quake.

The Stone had originally been meant for the victims of Dark Night, but since then it had seemed only natural to keep with this custom, to record the dead and lost. Zander's name, Peter saw, had already been inscribed. It did not stand alone: it came below his father and his sister and the woman to whom, Peter recalled, Zander had been married, years ago. It seemed so out of character for Zander to even speak to anyone, let alone be married, that Peter had forgot-ten all about her. The woman, whose name was Janelle, had died in childbirth with their baby, just a few months after Dark Night. The child hadn't been named yet, so there was nothing to write, and his brief stay on earth had gone unrecorded.

'If you want, I can do the engraving for Theo.'

Peter swiveled to find Caleb standing behind him, wearing the bright yellow sneakers. They were far too large on him, giving the impression of something webbed, like the paddled feet of a duck. Looking at them, Peter felt a jab of guilt. Caleb's huge, ridiculous sneakers: they were evidence – the only evidence, really – of the whole misbegotten episode at the mall. But somehow Peter also knew that Theo would have taken one look at Caleb's sneakers and laughed. He would have gotten the joke before Peter had even realized it *was* a joke.

'Did you do Zander's name?'

Caleb shrugged. 'I'm pretty good with the chisel. Nobody else around to take care of it, I guess. He should have tried to make more friends.' The boy paused, glancing past Peter's shoulder. For a second, his eyes seemed to be actually misting over. 'It's a good thing you shot him like you did. Zander really hated the virals. He thought the worst thing in the world would be to be taken up. I'm glad he didn't have to be one of them for long.'

Peter decided it then. He wouldn't write Theo's name in the Stone, and no one else would either. Not until he was sure.

'Where are you bunking these days?' he asked Caleb.

'The barracks. Where else?'

Peter lifted one shoulder to indicate the knapsack. 'Mind if I join you?'

'It's your appetite.'

It was only later, after Peter had unpacked his belongings and lain down at last on the caved-in, too soft mattress that he realized what Caleb's eyes had sought out, past Peter's shoulder, on the Stone. Not Zander's name but above it, a group of three: Richard and Marilyn Jones, and, beneath that, Nancy Jones, Caleb's older sister. His father, a wrench, had been killed in a fall from the lights during the first frantic hours of Dark Night; his mother and sister had died in the Sanctuary, crushed by the collapsing roof. Caleb had been just a few weeks old.

That was when he realized why Alicia had taken him up to the roof of the power station. It had nothing to do with the stars. Caleb Jones was an orphan of Dark Night, as she was. No one to stand for him but her.

She'd taken Peter to the roof to wait for Caleb Jones.

TWENTY-FIVE

Michael Fisher, First Engineer of Light and Power, was sitting in the Lighthouse, listening to a ghost.

That's what Michael was calling it, the ghost signal. Peeking from the haze of noise at the top of the audible spectrum – where nothing, as far as he could tell, should be. A fragment of a fragment, there and not there. The radio operator's manual he'd found in the storage shed listed the frequency as unassigned.

'I could have told you that,' said Elton.

They'd heard it the third day after the supply party's return. Michael still couldn't believe Theo was gone. Alicia had assured him that it wasn't his fault, the motherboard had nothing to do with Theo's death, but still Michael felt responsible, part of a chain of events that had led to the loss of his friend. And the motherboard – the worst part was, Michael had practically forgotten all about it. The day after Theo and the others had departed for the station, Michael had successfully cannibalized an old battery flow control for what he needed. Not a Pion, but enough extra processing power to squeeze out any signal at the top end of the spectrum.

And even if he hadn't, what was one more processor? Nothing for Theo to die for.

But this signal: 1,432 megahertz. Faint as a whisper, but it was *saying* something. It nagged at him, its meaning always seeming to dart away from his vision whenever he looked at it. It was digital, a repeating string, and it came and went mysteriously, or so it had appeared, until he'd realized – okay, Elton had realized – that it was coming every ninety minutes, whereupon it would transmit for exactly 242 seconds, then go silent again.

He should have figured that out on his own. There really was no excuse.

And it was growing stronger. Hour by hour, with each cycle, though more so at night. It was like the damn thing was moving straight up the mountain. He'd stopped looking for anything else; he just sat at the panel and counted off the minutes, waiting for the signal to return.

It wasn't anything natural, not at ninety-minute cycles. It wasn't a satellite. It wasn't anything from the battery stack. It wasn't a lot of things. Michael didn't know what it *was*.

Elton was in a mood, too. The ain't-it-great-to-be-blind Elton that Michael had gotten accustomed to after so many years in the Lighthouse – *that* Elton was nowhere to be found. In his place sat this dandruffy grump who barely uttered hello. He'd clamp the phones to his head, listening to the signal when it came, pursing his lips and shaking his head, maybe say a thing or two about needing more sleep than he was getting. He could barely be bothered to power up the lights at Second Bell; Michael could have let enough gas build up to blast them all to the moon, and he had the feeling that Elton wouldn't have said word one about it.

He could have used a bath too. Hell, they both could.

What was it? Theo's death? Since the supply party's return, an anxious hush had settled over the whole Colony. The thing with Zander made no sense to anyone. Stranding Caleb on the tower like that. Sanjay and the others had tried to keep it quiet, but gossip traveled quickly. People were saying they'd always known there was something a little off about that guy, that all those months down the mountain had done something to his brain. That he hadn't been right since that thing with his wife and the baby who had died.

And then that peculiar business with Sanjay. Michael didn't know what the hell to make of it. Two nights ago he had been sitting at the panel when suddenly the door had swung open and there was Sanjay, standing there with a round-eyed look on his face that seemed to say: *Aha!* That's it, Michael had thought, the earphones still clamped to his head – his crime couldn't have been more obvious – I'm dead meat now. Somehow Sanjay found out about the radio; I'm going to be put out for sure.

But then a funny thing happened. Sanjay didn't say anything. He just stood in the doorway, looking at Michael, and as the silent seconds passed, Michael realized that the expression on the man's face wasn't quite what he'd thought at first glance: not the righteous indignation of crimes uncovered in the night but an almost animal dumbfoundedness, a blank amazement at nothing. Sanjay was wearing bedclothes; his feet were bare. Sanjay didn't know where he was; Sanjay was sleepwalking. Lots of folks did it, there were times when it seemed half the Colony was up and cruising around. It had something to do with the lights, the way it was never quite dark enough to really settle in. Michael had taken a turn or two himself, once awakening to find himself in the kitchen, smearing his own face with honey from a jar. But Sanjay? Sanjay Patal, Head of the Household? He hardly seemed the type.

Michael's mind was working fast. The trick would be to get Sanjay out of the Lighthouse without waking him up. Michael was concocting various strategies for this – he wished he had some honey to offer him – when Sanjay suddenly frowned sharply, cocked his head to the side as if processing some distant sound, and shuffled rigidly past him.

'Sanjay? What are you doing?'

The man had come to a halt before the breaker panel. His right hand, which hung loosely at his side, gave a little twitch.

470

'I don't . . . know.'

'Isn't there,' Michael ventured, 'I don't know, someplace else you have to be?'

Sanjay said nothing. He lifted his hand and held it before his face, turning it slowly back and forth as he gazed at it with the same mute puzzlement, as if he couldn't quite decide whom it belonged to.

'Bab . . . cock?'

More footsteps outside; suddenly Gloria was in the room. She, too, was wearing her bedclothes. Her hair, which she tied up in the daytime, fell halfway down her back. She seemed a little out of breath, having evidently run from their house to follow him. She ignored Michael, who by now felt less alarmed than embarrassed, like an incidental witness to some private marital drama, and marched straight to her husband's side, taking him firmly by the elbow.

'Sanjay, come to bed.'

'This is my hand, isn't it?'

'Yes,' she replied impatiently, 'it's your hand.' Still holding her husband by the elbow, she glanced toward Michael and mouthed the word 'sleepwalking.'

'It's definitely, definitely mine.'

She heaved a sigh. 'Sanjay, come on now. Enough of this.'

A flicker of awareness came into the man's face. He turned to look about the room, his eyes alighting on Michael.

'Michael. Hello.'

The earphones were gone, hidden under the counter. 'Hey, Sanjay.'

'It seems I have . . . taken a walk.'

Michael stifled a laugh; though what, he wondered, had Sanjay been doing at the breaker box?

'Gloria has been good enough to come after me to take me home. So that is where I'm going to go now.'

'Okay.'

'Thank you, Michael. I'm sorry to have disturbed you in your important work.'

'It's no problem.'

471

And with that, Gloria Patal had led her husband from the room, taking him, presumably, back to bed to finish whatever it was he'd started in his restless, dreaming mind.

Now, what to make of that? When Michael had told Elton about it the next morning, all he'd said was, 'I guess it's getting to him like the rest of us.' And when Michael had said, 'What *it*? What do you mean by *it*?' Elton had said nothing at all; he seemed to have no answer.

Brood, brood, brood – Sara was right, he spent far too much time with his head stuck down the hole of worry. The signal was between cycles; he'd have to wait another forty minutes to listen to it again. With nothing else to occupy his mind, he called up the battery monitors on the screen, hoping for good news, not finding it. Bell plus two, a hard wind blowing all day through the pass, and the cells were below 50 percent *already*.

He left Elton in the hut and went to take a walk, to clear his mind. The signal: 1,432 megahertz. It meant something, but what? There was the obvious thing, namely that the numbers were the first four positive integers in a repeating pattern: 1432143214321432 and so on, the 1 closing out the sequence, which reloaded with the 4. Interesting, and probably just a coincidence, but that was the thing about the ghost signal: nothing about it *felt* like a coincidence.

He came to the Sunspot, where often there would be people milling about well into the night. He blinked into the light. A single figure was sitting at the base of the Stone, dark hair tumbling over her folded arms, which rested on top of her knees. Mausami.

Michael cleared his throat to alert her of his approach. But as he neared, she glanced his way with only passing curiosity. Her meaning was clear: she was alone and wanted to stay that way. But Michael had been in the hut for hours – Elton hardly counted – chasing ghosts in the dark, and was more than willing to risk a little rejection for even a few meager crumbs of company.

'Hey.' He was standing above her. 'Would it be okay if I sat?'

She lifted her face then. He saw that her cheeks were streaked with tears.

'Sorry,' Michael said. 'I can go.'

But she shook her head. 'It's all right. Sit if you want.'

Which he did. It was awkward, because the only way to sit properly was to take a place beside her, their shoulders practically touching, his back braced by the Stone as hers was. He was beginning to think this hadn't been such a great idea after all, especially as the silence lengthened. He realized that by staying he had tacitly agreed to ask what was bothering her, even, perhaps, to find the right words to comfort her. He knew that being pregnant could make women act moodily, not that they weren't moody to begin with, their behavior at any given moment as changeable as the four winds. Sara made sense to him most of the time, but that was only because she was his sister and he was used to her.

'I heard the news. I guess, congratulations?'

She wiped her eyes with her fingertips. Her nose was running, but he didn't have a rag to offer her. 'Thanks.'

'Does Galen know you're out here?'

She gave a dismal laugh. 'No, Galen does not.'

Which made him think that what was bothering her wasn't just a mood at all. She had come to visit the Stone because of Theo; her tears were for him.

'I just . . .' But he couldn't find the words. 'I don't know.' He shrugged. 'I'm sorry. We were friends too.'

She did something that surprised him then. Mausami placed her hand on top of his, twining their fingers together where they rested at the top of his knee. 'Thank you, Michael. People don't give you enough credit, I don't think. That was exactly the right thing to say.'

For a while they sat without speaking. Mausami didn't withdraw her hand but left it where it was. It was strange – not until this moment had Michael truly felt Theo's absence. He felt sad, but something else, too. He felt alone. He wanted to say something, to put this feeling into words. But before he could, two more figures appeared at the far end of the plaza. The pair came striding toward them. Galen and, behind him, Sanjay.

'Listen,' Mausami said, 'my advice is, don't let any of Lish's shit get to you. That's just how she does things. She'll come around.'

Lish? Why was she talking about Lish? But there was no time to consider this; Galen and Sanjay were suddenly towering over them. Galen was perspiring and breathing hard, as if he'd been running laps around the walls. As for Sanjay: the befuddled sleepwalker of two nights ago was nowhere to be seen. Standing in his place was a scowling figure of pure paternal self-righteousness.

'What do you think you're doing?' Galen's eyes were pulled into an angry squint, as if trying to bring the image of her into focus. 'You're not supposed to be out of the Sanctuary, Maus. You're *not*.'

'I'm fine, Gale.' She banished him with a wave. 'Go home.'

Sanjay shouldered forward so he was standing above the two of them, an imperious presence, bathed in the lights. His skin seemed to glow with his fatherly disappointment. He glanced down at Michael once, casting his presence aside with a quick clenching of his generous eyebrows – dashing, with this single gesture, any hope Michael might have had for some lighthearted acknowledgment of the other night's events.

'Mausami. I've been patient with you, but that is at its end. I don't understand why you have to be so difficult about this. You know where you're supposed to be.'

'I'm staying right here with Michael. Anybody who thinks different will have to take it up with him.'

Michael felt his stomach drop. 'Listen—'

'You stay out of this, Circuit,' Galen snapped. 'And while we're at it, what do you think you're doing out here with my wife?'

'What am I doing?'

'Yeah. Was this your idea?'

'For godsakes, Galen,' Mausami sighed. 'Do you know how you sound? No, it wasn't Michael's idea.'

Michael became aware that everyone was looking at him now. That he'd come to find himself in the middle of this scene, when all he'd wanted was a little company and fresh air, seemed like the cruelest trick of fate. The expression on Galen's face was pure burning humiliation; Michael considered whether the man was, in fact, capable of doing him real harm. There was something vaguely ineffectual about the way he carried himself, his attention always seeming to lag a step behind the goings-on around him, but Michael wasn't fooled: Galen had a good thirty pounds on him. On top of which, and more to the point, Galen viewed himself at this moment as defending something like his honor. Michael's knowledge of male combat was limited to a few childhood skirmishes in the Sanctuary over not very much, but he had swapped enough punches to know that it helped if your heart was in it. Which Michael's certainly wasn't. If Galen could actually manage to aim a blow, it would all be over fast.

'Listen, Galen,' he began again, 'I was just taking a walk—'

But Mausami didn't let him finish. 'It's all right, Michael. He knows you were.'

She rolled her face to look at him; her eyes were swollen and heavy-lidded from crying. 'We've all got our jobs to do, right?' She took his hand again and squeezed it, as if to seal a bargain between them. 'Mine apparently is to do as I'm told and not be difficult. So for now, that's what I'm going to do.'

Galen reached down to help her to her feet, but Mausami ignored him, rising on her own. Still glowering, Sanjay had stepped back, his hands on his hips.

'I don't see why this has to be so hard, Maus,' Galen said.

But Mausami acted like she hadn't heard him, turning away from the two men to face Michael instead, still seated with his back against the Stone. In the glance that passed

475

between them, Michael could feel the diminishment of her surrender, the shame of marching to her orders.

'Thanks for keeping me company, Michael.' She gave him a sad smile. 'That was nice, what you said.'

Sara, in the Infirmary, was waiting for Gabe Curtis to die.

She had just returned from riding when Mar had appeared at her door. It was happening, Mar said. Gabe was moaning, thrashing, fighting for breath. Sandy didn't know what to do. Could she come? For Gabe?

Sara retrieved her med kit and followed Mar to the Infirmary. As she stepped through the curtain into the ward, the first thing she saw was Jacob, awkwardly leaning over the cot on which his father lay, pressing a cup of tea to his lips. Gabe was choking, coughing up blood. Sara moved quickly to his side and gently took the tea from Jacob's hand; she rolled Gabe onto his side – the poor man weighed almost nothing, just skin and bones – and with her free hand reached to the cart to retrieve a metal basin, which she tucked under his chin. Two more hacking gasps: the blood, Sara saw, was a rich red, and spotted with small black clumps of dead tissue.

Other Sandy stepped from the shadowed recess behind the door. 'I'm sorry, Sara,' she said, her hands fluttering nervously. 'He just started coughing like that and I thought maybe the tea—'

'You let Jacob do this by himself? What's wrong with you?'

'What's the matter with him?' the boy wailed. He was standing by the cot, his face stricken with confused helplessness.

'Your dad is very sick, Jacob,' Sara said. 'No one's mad at you. You did the right thing, helping him.'

Jacob had begun to scratch himself, digging the fingernails of his right hand into the scraped flesh of his forearm.

'I'm going to do my best to take care of him, Jacob. You have my word.'

Gabe was bleeding internally, Sara knew. The tumor had ruptured something. She ran her hand over his belly and felt

476

the warm distension of pooling blood. She reached into her kit for a stethoscope, clamped it to her ears, pulled Gabe's jersey aside, and listened to his lungs. A wet rattle, like water sloshed in a can. He was close, and yet it might take hours. She lifted her eyes to Mar, who nodded. Sara understood what Mar had meant when she'd said that Sara was Gabe's favorite, what she was asking her to do now.

'Sandy, take Jacob outside.'

'What do you want me to do with him?'

Flyers, what was wrong with the woman? 'Anything.' Sara allowed herself a breath, to steady her nerves; it was not a time for anger. 'Jacob, I need you to go with Sandy now. Can you do that for me?'

In his eyes Sara saw no real comprehension – only fear, and a long habit of obedience to the decisions that others made for him. He would go, Sara knew, if he was asked.

A reluctant nod. 'Okay, I guess.'

'Thank you, Jacob.'

Sandy led the boy from the ward; Sara heard the front door opening and closing. Mar, sitting on the opposite side of the cot, was holding her husband's hand.

'Sara, do you . . . have something?'

It was not something that was ever discussed in the open. The herbals were all kept in the basement in the old freezer, stored in jars stacked on metal shelves. Sara excused herself to go downstairs and retrieved the ones she needed – digitalis, or common foxglove, to slow the respiration; the small black seeds of the plant they called angel's trumpet, to stimulate the heart; the bitter brown shaving of hemlock root, to numb the awareness – and set them on the table. She mortared them into a fine brown dust, poured it onto a sheet of paper, and, angling this over a cup, dumped the mixture into it. She put everything away, swept the table clean, and ascended the stairs.

In the outer room, she put water on to boil; the kettle was already warm, and soon the drink was ready. It had a faint greenish cast, like algae, with a bitter, earthen smell. She carried it into the ward.

'I think this will help.'

Mar nodded, taking the cup from Sara. Part of their unfolding understanding was that Sara would only provide the means; she could not do the rest.

Mar gazed into the cup's interior. 'How much?'

'All of it, if you can.'

Sara positioned herself at the head of the bed to lift Gabe's shoulders; Mar held the cup to his mouth, telling her husband to sip. His eyes were still closed; he seemed completely unaware of them. Sara was worried that he wouldn't be able to manage it, that they had waited too long. But then he took a first, tender sip from the cup, then another, pecking at it steadily like a bird drinking from a puddle. When the tea was gone, Sara eased him back down onto the pillow.

'How long?' Mar wasn't looking at her.

'Not long. It's quick.'

'And you'll stay. Until it's over.'

Sara nodded.

'Jacob can never know.' Mar looked at her beseechingly. 'He wouldn't understand.'

'I promise,' said Sara.

And then, just the two of them, they waited.

Peter was dreaming of the girl. They were under the carousel, in that low-ceilinged prison of dust, and the girl was on his back, breathing her honeyed breath onto his neck. *Who are you*, he was thinking, *who are you*, but the words felt trapped in his mouth, bunched inside it like a woolen rag. He was thirsty, so thirsty. He wanted to roll over to see her face but he couldn't move, and it wasn't the girl on him anymore, it was a viral, the teeth were sinking into the flesh of his neck and he was trying to scream for his brother but no sound came and he began to die, one part of him thinking, How strange, I've never died before. So this is what it's like.

He awoke with a start, his heart thumping, the dream

dispersing at once, leaving in its wake a vague but poignant impression of panic, like the echo of a scream. He lay motionless, reassembling his sense of where and when he was. He arched his neck to look out the window over his bunk and saw the lights shining. His mouth was bone dry, his tongue swollen and fibrous-feeling; he'd dreamed of being thirsty because he was. He fumbled for the canteen on the floor beside his cot, lifted the spout to his mouth, and drank.

Caleb was sleeping in the bunk beside him. Peter counted four other men in the room, snoring piles in the shadows. All had come in without his once awakening. How long since he'd slept like that?

Now, lying in the dark, he felt the first stirring of antsiness, a low-grade hum of physical impatience that seemed to have taken up a permanent residence in his chest since his return up the mountain. The obvious course was to report for duty on the catwalk. But Soo had made it clear that she wouldn't have him on the Watch until at least a few days had gone by.

He decided to go see Auntie. He hadn't told her about Theo yet. Probably she knew, but still he wanted her to hear the news from him, even if the information was repeated.

Sometimes it was possible to forget all about her, over in her little house in the glade. *Oh, Auntie*, people would say when her name came up, as if they'd only just remembered her existence. And the truth was, the old woman got on surprisingly well without much help. Peter or Theo would chop wood for her, or do small repairs on her house, and Sara might assist her at the Storehouse. But her needs were few, as she kept a large vegetable and herb patch in the sunlit plot behind her house, which she still managed to tend with virtually no aid from anyone. With the exception of her gardening, which she performed from a seated position on a stool, she spent most of her days inside her house, among her papers and mementos, her mind adrift in the past. She wore three different pairs of eyeglasses on a tangle of lanyards around her neck, alternating between them for whatever task she was attending and, except in winter, went barefoot everywhere she walked. By all accounts, Auntie was close to a hundred. She had married, or so it was said, not once but twice, but because she could never have children of her own, her life span seemed a natural marvel without purpose, like a horse that could count by stamping its hooves. No one could quite figure out how she'd survived Dark Night; her house had weathered the quake with very little damage, and in the morning they had discovered her sitting in her kitchen drinking a cup of her famously awful tea, as if nothing had happened at all. 'Maybe they just don't want my old blood' was all she'd said.

The night had cooled; the windows of Auntie's cottage were glowing faintly as Peter approached. She claimed never to sleep, that day and night were all the same to her, and in fact Peter could not recall a time when he'd failed to find her up and working. He knocked at the door and opened it a crack.

'Auntie? It's Peter.'

From deep within he heard a shuffling of paper and the scrape of a chair on the old wood floor. 'Peter, come in, come in.'

He stepped into the room. The only light came from a lantern in the kitchen, a hammered-on shack attached to the rear of the house. The space was densely cluttered but neat, the arrangement of furniture and other objects – books in towering piles, jars of stones and old coins, various knick-knacks he couldn't even identify – appearing not merely considered but possessing the intrinsic orderliness of having occupied their current position for decades, like trees in a forest. In the doorway to the kitchen, the old woman appeared, waving him in.

'You're just in time. I've made some tea.'

Auntie had always 'just made tea.' She brewed it from a mixture of miscellaneous herbaceous jetsam, some of which she grew and some of which she merely picked along the paths. She had been known, out walking, to make a slow, long bend to the ground to pluck out a nameless weed and pop it straight into her mouth. But drinking Auntie's tea was simply the price one paid for her company.

'Thanks,' Peter said, 'I'd be glad to take some.'

She was fussing with her glasses, picking out the right pair. She found them and slid them onto her weathered, nut-brown face – her head possessed a slightly shrunken appearance, as if the physical reductions of advanced age had moved from the top down – and located him with her eyes, smiling her toothless smile, as if then and only then had she become convinced that he was whom she believed him to be. She was clothed, as always, in a loose, scoop-necked frock of quilted fabrics, bits and pieces harvested from any number of other dresses over the years. What was left of her hair formed a vaporous tangle of white that seemed not so much to grow from her head as float in its vicinity, and her cheeks were sprayed by spots that were neither freckles nor moles but something in between.

'Come into the kitchen with you then.'

He followed her shuffling, barefooted progress down the narrow hallway to the rear of the house. The space was small, crowded by an oak table that left barely enough room to maneuver and oppressive with the heat of the stove and the steam that rose from a battered aluminum teapot resting atop it. Peter felt his pores opening with sweat. While Auntie went about her pouring, Peter raised the sash of the room's lone window, allowing a breeze to trickle in, and took a chair. Auntie carried the pot to the table, where she placed it on an iron trivet; at the sink, she primed the pump and rinsed out a pair of mugs, which she brought to the table also.

'And to what do I owe this come-by, Peter?'

'I'm afraid I have some news. About Theo.'

But the old woman waved this away. 'Oh,' she said, 'I know all about that.'

Auntie sat across from him, straightening her dress on her bony shoulders as she stretched out her legs beneath her, and poured the tea into cups through a strainer. It had a thin, yellow color, like urine, and left behind in the strainer small, disturbingly biological bits of green and brown, like smashed insects.

'How it happen?'

Peter sighed. 'It's a long story.'

'I ain't got nothing but time for stories, Peter. As long as you care to tell them, I got ears to hear by. Go on now, tea's ready. No point letting it get cold.'

Peter took a scalding sip. It tasted vaguely like dirt, leaving behind an aftertaste of such bitterness it didn't even seem like food. He managed a respectful swallow. On the table at his elbow was her book, the one she was always writing in. Her memory book, she called it: a fat, hand-stitched volume wrapped in lambskin, the pages covered with the tiny print she wrote in, using a crow feather and homemade ink. She made her own paper as well, boiling sawdust into pulp and forming sheets on squares of old window screens. Peter knew she was hard at work when he saw pages of this material stiffening on a line behind her house.

'How's the writing going, Auntie?'

'It never ends.' She offered a wrinkled smile. 'So much to put down, and me with nothing but time on my hands. What all that happened. The world from before. The train that brought us here in the fire. Terrence and Mazie and all those ones. All of it, I just write it down as it comes to me. I figure if there weren't no one to do it but one old lady, then that's what they'll get. Someday someone will want to know what happened here, in this place.'

'You think so?'

'Peter, I *know* so.' She sipped, smacking her colorless lips, and frowned at the flavor. 'I reckon that needs more dandelion than I put in it.' She pointed her eyes at Peter again, squinting through her glasses. 'But you didn't ask that, did you? What all do I write in there, wasn't it?'

Her mind was like this: doubling back, forming strange connections, dipping into the past. She spoke often of Terrence, who had ridden with her on the train. Sometimes he seemed to be her brother, sometimes her cousin. There were others. Mazie Chou. A boy named Vincent Gum, a girl named Sharise. Lucy and Rex Fisher. But these wanderings through time could be interrupted, at any moment, by intervals of startling lucidity.

'Have you written about Theo?'

'Theo?'

'My brother.'

Auntie's eyes drifted a moment. 'He told me he was going down to the station. When he coming back?'

So, she didn't know. Or perhaps she had simply forgotten, the news blending in her mind with other such stories.

'I don't think he's coming back,' Peter said. 'That's what I came to tell you. I'm sorry.'

'Oh, don't go being sorry now,' she said. 'The things you don't know would fill a book. That's a joke now, ain't it? A book. Go on now. Drink your tea.'

Peter decided not to press. What good would it do the old woman to hear about one more person dying? He took another sip of the bitter liquid. If anything, it actually tasted worse. He felt a little burble of nausea.

'That the birch bark you feeling. For the digestion.'

'It's good, really.'

'No it ain't. But it does the trick all right. Clean you out like a white tornado.'

Peter remembered his other news then. 'I meant to tell you, Auntie. I saw the stars.'

At this, the old woman brightened. 'Well, there you go.' She quickly touched the back of his hand with the tip of a weathered finger. 'There's something good to talk about. Tell me now, how they look to you?'

His thoughts returned to that moment on the roof, lying on the concrete next to Lish. The stars so thick above their faces it was as if he could brush them with his hand. It seemed like something that had happened years ago, the final minutes of a life he'd left behind.

'It's hard to put into words, Auntie. I never knew.'

'Well, ain't that a thing.' Her eyes, pointed to the wall behind his head, seemed to twinkle, as if with remembered starlight. 'I ain't seen them since I was a girl. Your father used to come in just like you're doing now and tell me all about them. I saw them, Auntie, he'd say, and I'd say to him, How they doing, Demo? How those stars of mine? And the two of us would have a nice visit about them, just like we're doing now.' She sipped her tea and returned her mug to the table. 'Why you looking so surprised?'

'He did?'

A quick frown of correction; but her eyes, still lit with an inner brightness, seemed to be laughing at him. 'Why you think he wouldn't?'

'I don't know,' Peter managed. And it was true: he didn't. But when Peter tried to imagine this scene – his father, the great Demetrius Jaxon, drinking tea with Auntie in her over-heated kitchen, talking about the Long Rides – he somehow couldn't. 'I guess I never realized he told anyone else.'

She gave a little laugh. 'Oh, your father and me, we *talked*. About a lot of things. About the *stars*.'

It was all so confusing. More than confusing: it was as if, in the space of just a few days – since the night the viral had been killed in the nets by Arlo Wilson – some fundamental precept of the world had changed, only nobody had told Peter what this change might be.

'Did he ever tell you . . . about a Walker, Auntie?'

The old woman sucked in her cheeks. 'A Walker, you say? Now, I don't recall anything about that. Theo see a Walker?'

He heard himself sigh. 'Not Theo. My father.'

But she had given up listening; her eyes, pointed at the wall behind him, had gone far away again. 'Now, Terrence, I believe he did tell me something about a Walker. Terrence and Lucy. She always was the littlest thing. It was Terrence who made her stop crying, you know. He always could do that.'

It was hopeless. Once Auntie went off like this, it could be hours, even days, before she came back to the present. He almost envied her, this power.

'Now, what was it you wanted to ask me?'

'That's okay, Auntie. It can keep.'

She lifted her bony shoulders in a shrug. 'You say so.' A silent moment passed. Then: 'Tell me something. You believe in God almighty, Peter?'

The question caught him short. Though she'd spoken of God often, never had she asked him what he believed. And it was true that looking at the stars from the station roof, he'd felt something – a presence behind them, their vast immensity. As if the stars were watching *him*. But the moment, and the feeling it gave him, had slipped away. It would have been nice to believe in something like that, but in the end, he just couldn't.

'Not really,' he admitted, and heard the gloom in his voice. 'I think it's just a word people use.'

'Now, that's a shame. A *shame*. Because the God I know about? He wouldn't give us no chance.' Auntie took a final sip, smacking her lips. 'Now you think on that some and then tell me about Theo and where he gone to.'

The conversation seemed to end there; Peter rose to go. He bent to kiss the top of her head.

'Thanks for the tea, Auntie.'

'Anytime. You come back and tell me your answer when it comes to you. We'll talk about Theo then. Have us a good talk. And Peter?'

He turned in the kitchen doorway.

'Just so you know. She comin'.'

He was taken aback. 'Who's coming, Auntie?'

A teacherly frown. 'You know who, boy. You known it since the day God dreamed you up.'

For a moment Peter said nothing, standing in the door.

'That's all I'm saying now.' The old woman gave a dismissive wave, as if shooing a fly away. 'You go on and come back when you ready.'

'Don't write all night, Auntie,' Peter managed. 'Try to get some sleep.'

A smile creased the old woman's face. 'I got eternity for that.'

He showed himself out, stepping into a breath of cool night air that brushed his face, chilling the sweat that had gathered beneath his jersey in the overheated kitchen. His stomach was still churning under the spell of the tea. He stood a moment, blinking into the lights. It was strange, what Auntie had said. But there was no way she could have known about the girl. The way the old woman's mind worked, stories all piled on top of stories, the past and present all mixed together, she could have meant anyone. She could have been talking about someone who'd died years ago.

Which was just when Peter heard the shouts coming from Main Gate, and all hell began to break loose.

TWENTY-SIX

It had begun with the Colonel. That much everyone was able to ascertain in the first few hours.

No one could recall seeing the Colonel for days, not in the apiary or stables or on the catwalks, where he sometimes went at night. Peter certainly hadn't seen him over the seven nights he'd stood, but he hadn't thought this absence strange; the Colonel came and went according to his own mysterious designs and sometimes didn't show his face for days.

What people did know, and this was reported first by Hollis but confirmed by others, was that the Colonel had appeared on the catwalk shortly after half-night, near Firing Platform Three. It had been a quiet night, without sign; the moon was down, the open ground beyond the walls bathed in the glow of the spots. Only a few people noticed him standing there, and no one thought anything about it. Hey, there's the Colonel, people might have said. Old guy never could quite make himself stand down. Too bad there's nothing doing tonight.

He lingered a few minutes, fingering his necklace of teeth, giving his gaze to the empty field below. Hollis supposed he'd come to speak with Alicia, but he didn't know where she was, and in any event, the Colonel made no move to look for her. He wasn't armed, and he didn't speak with anyone. When Hollis looked again, he was gone. One of the runners, Kip Darrell, claimed later to have seen him descending the ladder and heading down the trace, toward the pens.

The next time anyone saw him, he was running across the field.

'Sign!' one of the runners yelled. 'We have sign!'

Hollis saw it, saw *them*. At the edge of the field, a pod of three, leaping into the light.

The Colonel was running straight toward them.

They fell on him swiftly, swallowing him like a wave, snapping, snarling, while on the catwalk high above a dozen bows released their arcing arrows, though the distance was too great; only the luckiest of shots would have accomplished anything.

They watched the Colonel die.

Then they saw the girl. She was at the edge of the field, a lone figure appearing out of the shadows. At first, Hollis said, they all thought she was another viral, and everyone was completely trigger-happy besides, all of them ready to shoot at anything that moved. As she broke across the field toward Main Gate, under a hail of arrows and bolts, one caught her in the shoulder with a meaty thunk that Hollis actually *heard*, spinning her around like a top. Still she kept on coming.

'I don't know,' Hollis admitted later. 'It might have been me who got her.'

By now Alicia was on the scene, screaming at everyone as she raced down the catwalk, yelling at them to hold fire, it was a person, *a human being goddamnit*, and get the ropes, *get the fucking ropes now!* A moment of confusion: Soo was nowhere to be seen, and the order to go over the Wall could only come from her. All of which apparently gave Alicia no pause whatsoever. Before anyone could say another word she hopped to the top of the rampart, clutching the rope in her hand, and stepped out.

It was, Hollis said, the damnedest thing he'd ever laid eyes on.

She descended in a rush, swinging down the face of the Wall, her feet skimming the surface in an airborne run, the rope buzzing through the block at the top of the Wall while three pairs of hands frantically tried to set the brake before she hit. As the mechanism caught with a scream of bending metal Alicia landed, rolling end over end in the dust, and came up running. The virals were twenty meters away, still huddled over the Colonel's body; at the sound of Alicia's impact, they gave a collective twitch, twisting and snarling, tasting the air.

Fresh blood.

The girl was at the base of the Wall now, a dark shape huddled against it. A glistening hump sat at the center of her back – her knapsack, now pinned to her body by the bolt embedded in her shoulder, all of it slick and shining with the gleaming wetness of her blood. Alicia snatched her like a sack, hurled her over her shoulders, and did her best to run. The rope was useless now, forgotten behind her. Her only chance was the gate.

Everybody froze. Whatever else you did, you didn't open the gate. Not at night. Not for anyone, not even Alicia.

It was at this moment that Peter reached the staging ground, running from Auntie's porch toward the commotion. Caleb came sprinting from the barracks, arriving at Main Gate just ahead of him. Peter didn't know what was taking place on the other side, only that Hollis was yelling from the catwalk.

'It's Lish!'

'What?'

488

'It's Lish!' Hollis cried. 'She's outside!'

Caleb got to the wheelhouse first. It was this fact that would later be used to implicate him, while exonerating Peter of blame for what occurred. By the time Alicia reached the gate, it was open just wide enough for her to scramble through with the girl. If they had been able to close the doors then, probably none of the rest would have happened. But Caleb had released the brake. The weights were dropping, picking up speed as they slipped down the chains; the doors' opening was now ordained by the simple fact of gravity. Peter grabbed hold of the wheel. Behind and above him he heard the shouts, the volley of bolts unleashed from their crosses, the pinging footsteps of Watchers racing down the ladders into the staging ground. More hands appeared, fastening onto the wheel – Ben Chou and Ian Patal and Dale Levine. With excruciating slowness, it began to turn in the opposite direction.

But it was too late. Of the three virals, only one made it through the doors. But that was enough.

He headed straight for the Sanctuary.

Hollis was the first to reach the building, just as the viral vaulted to the roof. It crested the roof's apex like a stone skipping on water and dropped into the interior courtyard. As he tore through the front door, Hollis heard a crash of breaking glass inside.

He reached the Big Room at the same instant Mausami did, the two of them arriving by different hallways onto opposite sides of the room. Mausami was unarmed; Hollis had his cross. An unexpected silence met them. Hollis had braced himself for screams and chaos, the children running everywhere. But nearly all were still in their beds, their eyes wide with terrified incomprehension. A few had managed to scramble under their cots; as Hollis crossed the threshold, he detected a flurry of movement from the nearest row, as one of the three J's, June or Jane or Juliet, rolled off her bed and scurried beneath it. The only light in the room came from the

489

broken window, its shade ripped and hanging kitty-corner, still quivering with movement.

The viral was standing over Dora's crib.

'Hey!' Mausami yelled. She waved her arms above her head. 'Hey, look over here!'

Where was Leigh? Where was Teacher? The viral jerked its face toward the sound of Mausami's voice. It blinked its eyes, tipping its head to the side on its long neck. A wet clicking sound rose from somewhere in the taut curve of its throat.

'Over here!' Hollis yelled, following Mausami's lead and waving to draw the creature's attention. 'Yeah, look this way!'

The viral spun toward him, facing him squarely. Something was glinting at the base of its neck, some kind of jewelry. But there was no time to wonder about this; Hollis had his angle, his opening. Leigh entered the room then. She'd been sleeping in the office and heard nothing. As Leigh broke into a scream, Hollis aimed the crossbow and fired.

A good shot, a clean shot, dead center on the sweet spot: he felt its rightness, its perfection, the instant it leapt from the stock. And in the split second of the arrow's flight, a distance of fewer than five meters, he knew. The glinting key on the lanyard; the look of mournful gratitude in the viral's eyes. The thought came to Hollis fully formed, a single word that arrived on his lips at the same instant that the arrow – the merciful, awful, unrecallable arrow – struck home in the center of the viral's chest.

'Arlo.'

Hollis had just killed his brother.

Sara – though she did not remember this and never would – first learned about the Walker in a dream: a confusing and unpleasant dream in which she was a little girl again. She was making johnnycake. The kitchen where she worked – she was standing on a stool, beating the heavy batter in a wide, wooden bowl – was both the kitchen of the house where she lived and the kitchen in the Sanctuary, and it was snowing: a gentle snow that did not fall from the sky, because there was no sky, but seemed to appear out of the air before her face. Strange, the snow; it almost never snowed and certainly not indoors that Sara could recall, but she had more important things to worry about. It was the day of her release, Teacher would come for her soon, but without the johnnycake, she would have nothing to eat in the outside world; in the outside world, Teacher had explained to her, that was the only thing people ate.

Then there was a man. It was Gabe Curtis. He was sitting at the kitchen table before an empty plate. 'Is it ready?' he asked Sara, and then, turning to the girl sitting next to him, said, 'I always liked johnnycake.' Sara wondered, with vague alarm, who this girl was – she tried to look at her but somehow could not see her; wherever Sara looked for her was always the very spot the girl had just departed – and the fact reached her mind, slowly and then all at once, that she was in a new place now. She was in the room Teacher had brought her to, the place of the telling, and her parents were there, waiting; they were standing at the door. 'Go with them, Sara,' Gabe said. 'It's time for you to go. Run and keep on running.' 'But you're dead,' said Sara, and when she looked at her parents, she saw that where their faces should have been were regions of blankness, as if she were viewing them through a current of water; something was wrong with their necks. There was a pounding sound now, without the room, and the sound of a voice, calling her name. 'You're all dead.'

Then she was awake. She had fallen asleep in a chair by the cold hearth. It was the door that had awakened her; someone was outside, calling her name. Where was Michael? What time was it?

'Sara! Open up!'

Caleb Jones? She opened the door as he was reaching to hit it again, his fist freezing in the air.

'We need a nurse.' The boy was breathing hard. 'Someone's been shot.'

She was instantly awake, reaching for her kit on the table by the door. 'Who?'

'Lish brought her in.'

'Lish? Lish is shot?'

Caleb shook his head, still trying to catch his breath. 'Not her. The girl.'

'What girl?'

His eyes were amazed. 'She's a Walker, Sara.'

By the time they reached the Infirmary the sky beyond the lights had begun to pale. No one was there, which struck her as strange. From what Caleb had told her, she'd expected a crowd. She mounted the steps and rushed into the ward.

Lying on the nearest cot was a girl.

She was lying face-up, the bolt still embedded in her shoulder; a dark shape was pinned beneath her back. Alicia was standing over her, her jersey spattered with blood.

'Sara, do something,' Alicia said.

Sara moved quickly forward and eased her hand behind the girl's neck to check her airway. The girl's eyes were closed. Her breathing was rapid and shallow, her skin cool and clammy to the touch. Sara felt her neck for a pulse; her heart was banging like a bird's.

'She's in shock. Help me roll her over.'

The bolt had entered the girl's left shoulder just below the spoon-shaped curve of her clavicle. Alicia wedged her hands under the girl's shoulders while Caleb took her feet, and together they eased the girl onto her side. Sara retrieved a pair of scissors and sat behind her to cut the blood-soaked knapsack away, then the girl's flimsy T-shirt, snipping it at the neck and tearing the rest of it free, revealing the slender frame of an early adolescent – the small, curving buds of her breasts and her pale skin. The bolt's barbed tip was poking through a star-shaped wound just above the line of her scapula.

'I have to clip this off. I'll need something bigger than these shears.'

Caleb nodded and ran from the room. As he passed

through the curtain, Soo Ramirez rushed in. Her long hair had come undone; her face was streaked with dirt. She stopped abruptly at the foot of the cot.

'I'll be goddamned. She's just a kid.'

'Where the hell is Other Sandy?' Sara demanded.

The woman appeared dazed. 'Where on earth did she come from?'

'Soo, I'm all alone in here. Where's *Sandy*?'

Soo lifted her face, focusing on Sara. 'She's . . . in the Sanctuary, I think.'

Footsteps and voices, a buzz of commotion from without: the outer room was filling with onlookers now.

'Soo, get these people out of here.' Sara lifted her voice to the curtain. 'Everybody, out! I want this building cleared now!'

Soo nodded and darted outside. Sara checked the girl's pulse again. Her skin appeared to have taken on a faintly mottled appearance, like a winter sky on the edge of snow. How old was she? Fourteen? What was a fourteen-year-old girl doing out in the dark?

She turned to Alicia. 'You brought her in?'

Alicia nodded.

'Did she say anything to you? Was she alone?'

'God, Sara.' Her eyes seemed to float. 'I don't know. Yes, I think she was alone.'

'Is that blood yours or hers?'

Alicia dropped her eyes to the front of her jersey, seeming to notice the blood for the first time. 'Hers, I think.'

More commotion from without the room, and Caleb's voice yelling, 'Coming through!' He burst through the curtain, waving a heavy cutter, and thrust it into Sara's hands.

A greasy old thing, but it would do. Sara poured spirits over the blades of the cutter and then her hands, wiping them dry on a rag. With the girl still lying on her side, she used the cutters to clip the arrowhead free, and poured more alcohol over everything. Then she directed Caleb to wash his hands as she had done while she took a skein of wool from the shelf and snipped off a long piece, rolling it into a compress.

'Hightop, when I back the bolt out, I want you to hold this against the entry wound. Don't be gentle, press hard. I'm going to suture the other side, see if I can slow this bleeding.'

He nodded uncertainly. He was in over his head, Sara knew, but the truth was they all were. Whether or not the girl survived the next few hours depended on the extent of the bleeding, how much damage there was inside. They rolled the girl onto her back again. While Caleb and Alicia braced her shoulders, Sara took hold of the bolt and began to pull. Sara could sense, through the bolt's metal shaft, the fibrous gristle of destroyed tissue, the clack of fractured bone. There was no way to be gentle; it was best to do it fast. With a hard tug, the bolt pulled away in a sighing gush of blood.

'Flyers, it's her.'

Sara turned her head to see Peter standing in the doorway. What did he mean, *it's her*? As if he knew her, as if he knew who this girl was? But of course that was impossible.

'Turn her on her side. Peter, help them.'

Sara positioned herself behind the girl, taking up a needle and a spool of thread, and began to stitch the wound. There was blood everywhere now, pooling on the mattress, dripping onto the floor.

'Sara, what should I do?' Caleb's compress was sodden already.

'Just keep pressure on it.' She drew the needle through the girl's skin, pulling a stitch taut. 'I need more light over here, someone!'

Three stitches, four, five, each one pulling the edges of the wound together. But it was no use, she knew. The bolt must have nicked the subclavian artery. That's where all the blood was coming from. The girl would be dead within minutes. Fourteen years old, Sara thought. Where did you come from?

'I think it's stopping,' Caleb said.

Sara was tying off the last stitch. 'That can't be right. Just keep pressure on it.'

'No, really. Look for yourself.'

They rolled the girl onto her back again, and Sara pulled the sodden compress aside. It was true: the bleeding had slowed. The entry wound even looked smaller, pink and puckered at the edges. The girl's face was gently composed, as if she were napping. Sara placed her fingers at the girl's throat; a hard, regular beat met her fingertips. What in the world?

'Peter, hold that lantern over here.'

Peter swung the lantern over the girl's face; Sara gently peeled back the lid of her left eye – a dark, dewy orb, the disklike pupil contracting to reveal the ribbed iris, the color of wet earth. But something was different; something was there.

'Bring it closer.'

As Peter shifted the lantern, blazing the eye with light, she felt it. A sensation like falling, as if the earth had opened under her feet – worse than dying, worse than death. A terrible blackness all around and she was falling, falling forever into it.

'Sara, what's wrong?'

She was on her feet, backing away. Her heart was lurching in her chest, her hands were shaking like leaves in the wind. Everyone was looking at her; she tried to speak but no words came. What had she seen? But it wasn't something she'd seen, it was something she'd *felt*. Sara thought the word: alone. Alone! That's what she was, what they all were. That was what her parents were, their souls falling forever in blackness. They were alone!

She became aware that others were in the ward now. Sanjay and, beside him, Soo Ramirez. Two more Watchers hovered behind them. Everyone was waiting for her to say something; she could feel the heat of all their eyes upon her.

Sanjay stepped forward. 'Will she live?'

She took a breath to calm herself. 'I don't know.' Her voice felt weak in her throat. 'It's a bad wound, Sanjay. She's lost a lot of blood.'

Sanjay regarded the girl a moment. He appeared to be deciding what to think of her, how to account for her impossible presence. Then he turned toward Caleb, who was standing by the cot with the blood-soaked compress in his hands. Something seemed to harden in the air; the men at the door came forward, hands on their blades.

'Come with us, Caleb.'

The two men – Jimmy Molyneau and Ben Chou – grabbed the boy by the arms; he was too surprised to resist.

'Sanjay, what are you doing?' Alicia said. 'Soo, what the hell is this about?'

It was Sanjay who answered. 'Caleb is under arrest.'

'Arrest?' the boy squealed. 'What am I under arrest for?'

'Caleb opened the gate. He knows the law as well as anyone. Jimmy, get him out of here.'

Jimmy and Ben began to pull the struggling boy toward the curtain. 'Lish!' he cried.

She quickly blocked their way, positioning herself in front of the door. 'Soo, tell them,' Alicia said. 'It was me. I was the one who went over. If you want to arrest someone, arrest me.'

Standing beside Sanjay, Soo said nothing.

'Soo?'

But the woman shook her head. 'I can't, Lish.'

'What do you mean you can't?'

'Because it isn't up to her,' Sanjay said. 'Teacher is dead. Caleb is under arrest for murder.'

TWENTY-SEVEN

By midmorning, everyone in the Colony knew the story of the night before, or some version of it. A Walker had appeared outside the walls; Caleb had opened the gate, letting in a viral. The Walker, a young girl, was in the Infirmary,

496

dying, shot by a bolt from a Watcher's cross. The Colonel was dead, an apparent suicide – how he'd gotten over the Wall, no one knew – and Arlo too, killed in the Sanctuary by his brother.

But worst of all was Teacher.

They found her under the window in the Big Room; Hollis's line of sight had been obscured by a line of empty cots. Probably she had heard the viral coming down off the roof and tried to make a stand. A blade was in her hand.

There had been many Teachers, of course. But in a truer sense there had only been one. Each woman who took the job down through the years became that person. The Teacher who had died that night was actually a Darrell – April Darrell. She was the woman Peter remembered laughing at his questions about the ocean, though she had been younger then, not much older than he was now, and pretty in a soft, pale way, like an older sister who was kept indoors by some physical ailment; she was the woman Sara recalled from the morning of her release, leading her with her chain of questions, like a flight of stairs taking her down to a dark basement in which lay the terrible truth, then giving her into her mother's arms, to weep over the world and what it was. It was a hard job, being Teacher, everyone knew that, a thankless job, to live locked away with the Littles with barely any grown-up company except for women who were pregnant or nursing, with nothing on their minds but babies; and it was also true that because Teacher was the one to tell you – tell everyone – she bore the collective resentment of this trauma. Except for First Night, when she might make a brief appearance in the Sunspot, Teacher hardly ever set foot outside the Sanctuary, and when she did, it was as if she moved in an invisible container of betrayal. Peter felt sorry for her, but it was also true that he could barely bring himself to meet her eye.

The Household, which assembled at first light, had declared a state of civil emergency. Runners were dispatched from house to house, passing the word. Until more was known, all activities beyond the Wall would be suspended; the herd would stay inside, as well as any HD crews; the gate would remain closed. Caleb had been remanded to the lockup. For the time being, it was agreed, with so many souls lost, and such fear and confusion having gripped the Colony, no sentence would be passed.

And then there was the question of the girl.

In the early-morning hours, Sanjay had led the members of the Household to the Infirmary to examine her. The wound to her shoulder was obviously serious; she had yet to regain consciousness. There was no sign of viral infection, but it was also the case that her appearance was completely inexplicable. Why had the virals not attacked her? How had she survived, all alone in the dark? Sanjay ordered anyone who had been in contact with her to be stripped and washed, their clothing burned. The girl's backpack and clothing went into the fire as well. The girl had been placed under strict quarantine; no one but Sara would be allowed in the Infirmary until more was known.

The inquest was held in an old classroom in the Sanctuary – the same room, Peter realized, that Teacher had taken him to on the day of his release. An inquest: that was the term Sanjay had used, a word Peter had never heard before. It seemed to Peter that it was a fancy name for looking for someone to blame. Sanjay had instructed the four of them – Peter, Alicia, Hollis, and Soo – not to speak to one another until each had been questioned in turn. They waited outside in the hall, wedged into undersized desks shoved in a line against the wall, with a single Watcher – Sanjay's nephew, Ian – waiting with them. Around them the building was oddly silent; all the Littles had been moved upstairs while the Big Room was washed down. Who knew what they would make of the night's events – what Sandy Chou, who had stepped in for Teacher, would tell them. Probably she would tell them they had simply all dreamed it; with the youngest children, that likely would do the trick. As for the older ones,

Peter had no idea. Maybe they would have to be released early.

Soo had been called first, emerging from the room a short time later and striding down the hall with a harried look. Hollis was then summoned inside. Unfolding his long legs from under the desk, he appeared completely devoid of energy, as if some essential piece of him had been carved away. Ian was holding the door open, eyeing the group with a look of impatient warning. At the threshold Hollis stopped and turned to look at all of them, uttering the first words any of them had spoken in an hour.

'I just want to know it wasn't for nothing.'

They waited. Through the door to the classroom, Peter could hear the murmur of voices. Peter wanted to ask Ian if he knew anything, but the expression on the man's face told him not to try. Ian was Theo's age, part of a group that had come up at around the same time; he and his wife, Hannah, had one young daughter, Kira, in the Sanctuary. So, Peter thought, that explained the look on Ian's face: it was the look of a parent, a father.

Hollis emerged, briefly meeting Peter's eyes and giving him a curt nod before retreating down the hall. Peter began to rise but Ian said, 'Not you, Jaxon. Lish is next.'

Jaxon? Since when did anybody call him Jaxon – especially someone on the Watch? And why did it sound suddenly different to him, coming from Ian's mouth?

'It's all right,' Lish said, and got to her feet wearily. He had never seen her looking so defeated. 'I just want to get this over with.'

Then she was gone, leaving Peter and Ian alone. Ian had awkwardly fixed his gaze on the square of wall above Peter's head.

'It really wasn't her fault, Ian. It wasn't anybody's.'

Ian stiffened but said nothing.

'If you'd been there, you might have done the same thing.'

'Look, save it for Sanjay. I'm not supposed to talk to you.'

By the time Lish appeared, Peter had actually managed to

doze off. She stepped from the room with a wordless look he knew: *I'll find you.*

Peter felt it the moment he stepped into the room. Whatever was going to happen had already been decided. His appearance, whatever he had to say for himself, would make very little difference. Soo had been asked to recuse herself from the proceedings, leaving only five members of the Household in attendance: Sanjay, who was seated at the center of a long table, and, on either side of him, Old Chou, Jimmy Molyneau, Walter Fisher, and Peter's cousin Dana, occupying the Jaxon seat. He noted the odd number; Soo's absence had effectively prevented any kind of deadlock. An empty desk had been positioned to face the table. The tension in the room was palpable; no one was speaking. Only Old Chou seemed willing to meet Peter's eye; everyone else was looking away, even Dana. Slumped in his chair, Walter Fisher seemed hardly to know where he was, or to care. His clothing seemed unusually filthy and rumpled; Peter could actually smell the shine coming off him.

'Have a seat, Peter,' Sanjay said.

'I'd rather stand, if that's all right.'

He felt the small pleasure of defiance, a point being scored. But Sanjay did not react. 'I suppose we should get on with it.' He cleared his throat before continuing. 'Though there is some confusion on this point, the general opinion of the Household, based in large part on what Caleb has told us, is that you were not responsible for opening the gate, that this was his doing entirely. Is this your version?'

'My version?'

'Yes, Peter,' Sanjay said. He sighed with unconcealed impatience. 'Your version of events. What you believe occurred.'

'I don't *believe* anything. What did Hightop tell you?'

Old Chou held up a hand and leaned forward. 'Sanjay, if I may.'

Sanjay frowned but said nothing.

Old Chou leaned forward over the table, a gesture of

command. He had a soft, wrinkled face and damp eyes that gave him an appearance of absolute earnestness. He had been Head of the Household for many years before yielding the position to Theo's father, a history that still gave him considerable authority if he cared to use it. For the most part, he didn't; after his first wife had been killed on Dark Night, he had taken a second, much younger wife, and now passed most of his days in the apiary, among the bees he loved.

'Peter, no one doubts that Caleb thought he was doing the right thing. Intention is not the issue here. Did you open the gate or not?'

'What are you going to do with him?'

'That hasn't been decided. Please answer the question.'

Peter tried to meet Dana's eye but couldn't; she was still looking at the table.

'I would have, if I'd gotten there first.'

Sanjay gave an indignant lift in his chair. 'You see? This is what I'm saying.'

But Old Chou paid this interruption no mind, keeping his eyes locked on Peter's face. 'So am I correct in understanding that your answer is no? You *would* have, but in fact you did not.' He folded his hands on the table. 'Take a moment to think if you need to.'

It seemed to Peter that Old Chou was trying to protect him. But saying what had happened would shift all the blame to Caleb, who had simply done what Peter himself would have, if he'd gotten to the wheelhouse first.

'No one doubts your loyalty to your friends,' Old Chou went on. 'I would expect nothing less from you. But the greater loyalty here must be to the safety of everyone. I'll ask you again. Did you help Caleb in opening the gate? Or did you, in fact, try to close it, once you saw what was happening?'

Peter had the feeling of standing at the edge of a great abyss: whatever he said next would be final. But the truth was all he had.

He shook his head. 'No.'

'No what?'

He took a long breath. 'No, I didn't open the gate.'

Old Chou visibly relaxed. 'Thank you, Peter.' His gaze passed over the group. 'If nobody has anything else—'

'Wait,' Sanjay cut in.

Peter felt the air in the room tighten; even Walter seemed suddenly alert. Here it comes, thought Peter.

'Everyone here knows of your friendship with Alicia,' Sanjay said. 'She is someone who confides in you. Would that be fair to say?'

Peter nodded warily. 'I guess.'

'Has she in any way indicated to you that she knows this girl? Has seen her before, perhaps?'

A knot tightened in his stomach. 'Why would you think that?'

Sanjay glanced at the others before returning his eyes to the front of the room. 'There is a question, you see, of coincidence. You three were the last to return from the power station. And the story you tell, first about Zander and then Theo . . . well, you must admit it's pretty strange.'

The anger Peter had been holding in check gave way. 'You think we *planned* this? I lost my brother down there. We were lucky to get back alive.'

The room had grown very quiet again. Even Dana was looking at Peter with frank suspicion.

'So, for the record,' Sanjay said, 'you are saying you don't know the Walker, you've never seen her before.'

Suddenly it wasn't about Alicia, he realized. The question was about him.

'I have no idea who she is,' he said.

Sanjay held his eyes on Peter's face for what seemed like an unnaturally long moment. Then he nodded.

'Thank you, Peter. We appreciate your candor. You're free to go.'

Just like that it was over. 'That's all?'

Sanjay had already busied himself with the papers before

him. He looked up, frowning, as if surprised to find Peter still in the room. 'Yes. For now.'

'You're not going to . . . do anything to me?'

Sanjay shrugged; his mind had already moved on. 'What do you want us to do?'

Peter felt an unexpected disappointment. Sitting outside with Alicia and Hollis, he'd felt a bond, a shared stake in the outcome. Whatever was going to happen would happen to them all. Now they had been separated.

'If it happened as you say, you're not to blame. The blame is Caleb's. Soo has said, and Jimmy agrees, that the stress of standing for your brother could be considered a factor here. Take a few more days before returning to the catwalk. After that, we'll see.'

'What about the others?'

Sanjay hesitated. 'I suppose there's no reason not to tell you, since everyone will know soon enough. Soo Ramirez has offered her resignation as First Captain, which the Household has, with reluctance, agreed to accept. But she was out of position when the attack occurred and shares some of the blame. Jimmy will serve as new First Captain. As for Hollis, he's off the Wall for the time being. He can return when he's ready.'

'And Lish?'

'Alicia has been ordered to stand down from the Watch. She's been reassigned to Heavy Duty.'

Of everything that had happened, this development was actually the most difficult for him to process. Alicia as a wrench: it was simply beyond Peter's power to imagine such a thing. 'You're joking.'

Sanjay gave a correcting lift of his generous eyebrows. 'No, Peter. I promise you, I am not joking.'

Peter exchanged a quick glance with Dana: *Did you know anything about this?* Her eyes said she did.

'Now, if that's all . . .' Sanjay said.

Peter stepped toward the door. But as he reached the

threshold, a sudden doubt occurred to him. He turned to face the group once more.

'What about the power station?'

Sanjay heaved a weary sigh. 'What about it, Peter?'

'If Arlo's dead, shouldn't we be sending someone down there?'

Peter's first impression, considering the startled looks on everyone's faces, was that he'd somehow implicated himself at the last second. But then he understood: they had failed to consider this.

'You didn't send somebody down there at first light?'

Sanjay swiveled toward Jimmy, who shrugged nervously, evidently caught short. 'It's too late now,' he said quietly. 'They'd never make it before dark. We'll have to wait till tomorrow.'

'Flyers, Jimmy.'

'Look, I just missed it, all right? There was a lot going on. And Finn and Rey could still be all right.'

Sanjay seemed to take a moment just to breathe, composing himself. But Peter could tell he was furious.

'Thank you, Peter. We'll take this under advisement.'

There was nothing more to say; Peter stepped from the room, into the hall. Ian was just where he'd left him, leaning against the wall with his arms folded across his chest.

'I guess you heard about Lish, huh?'

'I heard.'

Ian shrugged; the stiffness had gone out of him. 'Look, I know she's your friend. But you can't say she didn't have it coming. Going over like she did.'

'What about the girl?'

Ian startled, a blaze of anger in his eyes. 'Flyers, what about her? I've got a *kid*, Peter. What do I care about some Walker?'

Peter said nothing. As far as he could see, Ian had every reason to be angry.

'You're right,' he said finally. 'It was stupid.'

But Ian's expression softened then. 'Look,' he said, 'people are just upset is all. I'm sorry I got mad. Nobody thinks it's your fault.'

But it was, Peter thought. It was.

The answer had come to Michael just after dawn: 1,432 megahertz – of *course*.

The bandwidth was officially unassigned, because it really had been assigned – to the military. A short-range digital signal, cycling every ninety minutes, looking for its mainframe.

And all night long, the signal had been growing stronger. It was practically on their doorstep.

The encryption would be the easy part. The trick would be finding the handshake, broadcasting the one reply that would cause the signal's transmitter, wherever and whatever it was, to link up with the mainframe. Once he did this, the rest would be just a question of uploading the data.

So what was the signal looking for? What was the digital answer to the question it was posing, every ninety minutes?

Something Elton had said, just before he'd gone to bed: *Someone's calling us.*

That was when he'd figured it out.

He knew just what he needed. The Lighthouse was full of all kinds of crap, stored in bins on the shelves; there was at least one Army handheld that he knew of. They had some old lithium cells that could still hold a charge – not more than a few minutes' worth, but that was all he'd need. He worked quickly, keeping an eye on the clock, waiting for the next ninety-minute interval to pass so he could grab the signal. Dimly he sensed some kind of commotion going on outside, but who knew what that was. He could jack the handheld into the computer, snatch the signal as it came in, capture its embedded ID, and program the handheld from the panel.

Elton was asleep, snoring on his cratered cot in the back of the Lighthouse. Flyers, if the old man didn't take a bath soon, Michael didn't know what he'd do. The whole place stank like socks.

By the time he was through it was almost half-day. How long had he been working, barely rising from his chair? After that whole thing with Mausami, he'd been too restless to sleep and returned to the hut; that might have been ten hours ago. His ass felt like he'd been sitting that long at least. He really had to pee.

He stepped from the hut, too quickly, unprepared for the blast of daylight that filled his eyes.

'Michael!'

Jacob Curtis, Gabe's boy. Michael saw him jogging up the path with a lumbering gait, waving his arms. Michael took a breath to prepare himself. It was hardly the boy's fault, but talking to Jacob could be a trial. Before Gabe had gotten sick, he would sometimes bring Jacob around the Lighthouse, asking Michael if he could find something for the boy to do to make himself useful. Michael had done his best, but there really wasn't much Jacob could understand. Whole days could be swallowed up by explaining the simplest tasks to him.

He came to a halt before Michael, dropping his hands to his knees and heaving for breath. Despite his size, his movements possessed a childlike disorderliness, the parts never quite seeming in sync. 'Michael,' he gulped, 'Michael—'

'Easy, Jacob. Slow down.'

The boy was flapping a hand before his face, as if to push more oxygen into his lungs. Michael couldn't tell if he was upset or simply excited. 'I want to see . . . Sara,' he gasped.

Michael told him she wasn't there. 'Did you try at the house?'

'She's not there either!' Jacob lifted his face. His eyes were very wide. 'I *saw* her, Michael.'

'I thought you said you couldn't find her.'

'Not *her*. The *other one*. I was sleeping and I saw her!'

Jacob didn't always make perfect sense, but Michael had never seen the boy like this. His face wore a look of complete panic.

'Did something happen to your dad, Jacob? Is he okay?'

A frown creased the boy's damp face. 'Oh. He died.'

'Gabe's *dead*?'

Jacob's tone was disturbingly matter-of-fact; he might have been telling Michael what the weather was. 'He died and he won't wake up anymore.'

'Flyers, Jacob. I'm sorry.'

That was when Michael saw Mar hurrying down the path. He felt a gush of relief.

'Jacob, where have you been?' The woman stopped before them. 'How many times do I have to tell you? You can't run off like that, you *can't*.'

The boy backed away, his long arms flailing. 'I have to find Sara!'

'*Jacob!*'

Her voice seemed to hit him like an arrow: he froze where he stood, though his face was still animated by a strange, unknowable dread. His mouth was open and he was breathing fast. Mar moved toward him cautiously, as if she were approaching some large, unpredictable animal.

'Jacob, look at me.'

'Mama—'

'Hush now. No more talk. Look at me.' She reached up to his face, placing a hand on each of his cheeks, focusing her eyes on his face.

'I saw her, Mama.'

'I know you did. But it was just a dream, Jacob, that's all. Don't you remember? We went back to the house and I put you to bed and you were sleeping.'

'I was?'

'Yes, honey, you were. It was nothing, just a dream.' Jacob was breathing more easily now, his body stilling beneath his mother's touch. 'I want you to go home now and wait for me there. No more looking for Sara. Can you do that for me?'

'But, Mama—'

'No buts, Jacob. Can you do as I ask?'

Reluctantly, Jacob nodded.

'That's my good boy.' Mar stepped back, releasing him. 'Straight home, now.'

The boy looked at Michael once, a quick, furtive glance, and jogged away.

Finally Mar turned to Michael. 'It always works when he gets like this,' she said with a weary shrug. 'It's the only thing that does.'

'I heard about Gabe,' he managed. 'I'm sorry.'

Mar's eyes looked as if she had cried so much there were no tears left in her at all. 'Thank you, Michael. I think Jacob wanted to see Sara because she was there, at the end. She was a good friend. To all of us.' Mar halted a moment, a look of pain skittering across her face. But she shook her head, as if to ward this thought away. 'If you can get her a message, tell her we're all thinking of her. I don't think I had a chance to properly thank her. Will you do that?'

'I'm sure she's around here someplace. Did you check the Infirmary?'

'Of course she's in the Infirmary. That was the first place Jacob went.'

'I don't understand. If Sara's in the Infirmary, why didn't he find her?'

Mar was looking at him strangely. 'Because of the quarantine, of course.'

'Quarantine?'

Mar's face fell. 'Michael, where have you been?'

TWENTY-EIGHT

Alicia didn't find him, after all; it was the other way around. Peter knew just where she'd be.

She was sitting in a wedge of shade outside the Colonel's hut, her back braced against a stack of wood, knees pulled to her chest. At the sound of Peter's approach, she looked up, wiping her eyes with the back of her hand.

'Oh, damn, damn,' she said.

He took a seat beside her on the ground. 'It's okay.'

Alicia sighed bitterly. 'No it isn't. You tell anyone you saw me like this I will *blade* you, Peter.'

They sat in silence for a while. The day was cloudy, cast with a pale and smoky light, carrying with it a strong, acrid odor – the body detail, burning the corpses outside the Wall.

'You know, I always wondered something,' Peter said. 'Why did we call him the Colonel?'

'Because that was his name. He didn't have another one.'

'Why do you think he went out there? He didn't seem like the type. To, you know, let it go like that.'

But Alicia didn't respond. Her relationship with the Colonel was something she rarely spoke of, and never in detail. It was a region of her life, perhaps the one region, that withheld from Peter's view. And yet its presence was something he was always aware of. He did not believe she thought of the Colonel as a father – Peter had never detected any trace of that kind of warmth between them. On those rare occasions when his name arose, or he appeared on the catwalk at night, Peter felt a rigidity come into her, a cold distance. It was nothing overt, and probably he was the only person who would have noticed. But whatever the Colonel had been to her, their bond was a fact; he understood that her tears were for him.

'Can you believe it?' Alicia said miserably. 'They fired me.'

'Sanjay will come around. He's not stupid. It's a mistake – he'll figure it out.'

But Alicia seemed to be barely listening. 'No, Sanjay's right. I never should have gone over the Wall the way I did. I totally lost my head, seeing the girl out there.' She shook her head hopelessly. 'Not that it matters now. You saw that wound.'

The girl, Peter thought. He'd never learned anything about her. Who was she? How had she survived? Were there others like her? How had she gotten away from the virals? But now it looked as if she would die, taking the answers with her.

'You had to try. I think you did the right thing. Caleb, too.'

'You know, Sanjay's actually thinking of putting him out? Putting out Hightop, for godsakes.'

To be put out: it was the worst fate imaginable. 'That can't be right.'

'I'm serious, Peter. I promise you, they're talking about it right now.'

'The others would never stand for it.'

'Since when do they really have a say about anything? You were in that room. People are *scared*. Somebody's got to take the blame for Teacher's death. Caleb's all alone. He's easy.'

Peter drew a breath and held it. 'Look, I know Sanjay. He can be pretty full of himself, but I really don't think he's like that. And everybody likes Caleb.'

'Everybody liked Arlo. Everybody liked your brother. It doesn't mean the story won't end badly.'

'You're beginning to sound like Theo.'

'Maybe so.' She was gazing ahead, squinting into the light. 'All I know is, Caleb saved me last night. Sanjay thinks he's going to put him out, he's going to have to deal with me.'

'Lish.' He paused. 'Be careful. Think about what you're saying.'

'I have thought about it. Nobody's putting him out.'

'You know I'm on your side.'

'You may not want to be.'

Around them, the Colony was eerily quiet, everyone still stunned by the events of the early hours of the morning. Peter wondered if this was the silence that came after something, or before. If it was the silence of blame being tallied. Alicia wasn't wrong; people were frightened.

'About the girl,' Peter said. 'There's something I should have told you.'

* * *

510

The lockup was an old public bathroom in the trailer park on the east side of town. As they made their approach, Peter and Alicia heard a swell of voices on the air. They picked up the pace as they moved through the maze of tipping hulks – most had long since been stripped for parts – and arrived to find a small crowd at the entrance, about a dozen men and women gathered tightly around a single Watcher, Dale Levine.

'What the hell is going on?' Peter whispered.

Alicia's face was grim. 'It's started,' she said. 'That's what.'

Dale was not a small man, but at that moment, he seemed so. Facing the crowd, he looked like a cornered animal. He was a little hard of hearing and had a habit of turning his head slightly to the right in order to point his good ear at whoever was talking to him, giving him a slightly distracted air. But he didn't seem distracted now.

'I'm sorry, Sam,' Dale was saying, 'I don't know anything you don't.'

The person he was addressing was Sam Chou, Old Chou's nephew – a thoroughly unassuming man whom Peter had heard speak only a few times in his life. His wife was Other Sandy; between them they had five children, three in the Sanctuary. As Peter and Alicia moved to the edge of the group, he realized what he was seeing: these were parents. Just like Ian, everyone standing outside the lockup had a child, or more than one. Patrick and Emily Phillips. Hodd and Lisa Greenberg. Grace Molyneau and Belle Ramirez and Hannah Fisher Patal.

'That boy opened the gate.'

'So what do you want me to do about it? Ask your uncle if you want to know more.'

Sam pointed his voice to the high windows of the lockup. 'Do you hear me, Caleb Jones? We all know what you did!'

'Come on, Sam. Leave the poor kid alone.'

Another man moved forward: Milo Darrell. Like his brother, Finn, Milo was a wrench, with a wrench's solid build and taciturn demeanor: tall and slope-shouldered, with a woolly beard and unkempt hair that fell in a tangle to his eyes. Behind him, dwarfed by his height, was his wife, Penny.

'You've got a kid, too, Dale,' Milo said. 'How can you just stand there?'

One of the three J's, Peter realized. Little June Levine. Dale's face, Peter saw, had gone a little white.

'You think I don't know that?' Whatever wedge of authority had separated him from the crowd was dissolving. 'And I'm not just standing here. Let the Household handle this.'

'He should be put out.'

The voice, a woman's, had risen from the center of the crowd. It was Belle Ramirez, Rey's wife. Their little girl was Jane. Peter saw that the woman's hands were trembling; she looked close to tears. Sam moved toward her and put his arm around her shoulder. 'You see, Dale? You see what that boy did?'

Which was the moment Alicia shouldered her way through the crowd. Without looking at Belle, or anyone at all, she stepped up to Dale, who was gazing at the stricken Belle with an expression of utter helplessness.

'Dale, hand me your cross.'

'Lish, I can't do that. Jimmy says so.'

'I don't care. Just give it to me.'

She didn't wait, but snatched it away. Alicia turned to face everyone, holding the cross loosely at her side – a deliberately unthreatening posture, but Alicia was Alicia. Her standing there meant something.

'Everyone, I know you're upset, and if you ask me, you have a right to be. But Caleb Jones is one of us, as much as any of you.'

'That's easy for you to say.' Milo was standing with Sam and Belle now. 'You were the one outside.'

A murmur of agreement flickered through the crowd. Alicia eyed the man coolly, allowing the moment to pass.

'You have a point there, Milo. If not for Hightop, I'd be dead. So if you were maybe thinking about doing something to him, I'd think long and hard.'

'What are you going to do?' Sam sneered. 'Stick us all with that cross?'

'No.' Alicia frowned, not seriously. 'Just you, Sam. I thought I'd take Milo here on the blade.'

A nervous laugh from a few of the men; but it just as quickly died. Milo had taken a step back. Peter, still at the edge of the crowd, realized his hand had dropped to his blade. Everything seemed to depend on what would happen next.

'I think you're bluffing,' Sam said, his eyes held tightly on Alicia's face.

'Is that so? You must not know me very well.'

'The Household will put him out. You wait and see.'

'You could be right. But that's not for either of us to decide. Nothing's happening here except you upsetting a lot of people for no reason. I won't have it.'

The crowd had grown suddenly silent. Peter felt their uncertainty; the momentum had shifted. Except for Sam, and maybe Milo, their anger had no weight. They were simply afraid.

'She's right, Sam,' Milo said. 'Let's get out of here.'

Sam's eyes, burning with righteous anger, were still locked on Alicia's face. The cross had yet to move from Alicia's side, but it didn't have to. Peter, standing behind the two men, still had his hand on his blade. Everyone else had moved away.

'Sam,' Dale said, finding his voice again, '*please*, just go home.'

Milo reached for Sam then, meaning to take him by the elbow. But Sam jerked his arm away. He appeared rattled, as if the touch of Milo's hand had nudged him from a trance.

'All right, all right. I'm coming.'

It wasn't until the two men had disappeared into the maze of trailers that Peter allowed himself to expel the breath of air he realized he'd been holding in his chest. Just a day ago, he never would have imagined that such a thing was possible, that fear could turn these people – people he knew, who did their work and went about their lives and visited their children in the Sanctuary – into an angry mob. And Sam Chou: he'd never seen the man so angry. He'd never seen him angry at all.

'What the hell, Dale?' Alicia said. 'When did this start?'

'About as soon as they moved Caleb over here.' Now that they were alone, the full magnitude of what had occurred, or almost occurred, could be read in Dale's face. He looked like a man who had fallen from a great height only to discover that he was, miraculously, uninjured. 'Flyers, I thought I was going to have to let them in. You should have heard the things they were saying before you got here.'

From inside the lockup came the sound of Caleb's voice. 'Lish? Is that you?'

Alicia pointed her voice to the windows. 'Just hang tight, Hightop!' She fixed her eyes on Dale again. 'Go and get some other Watchers. I don't know what Jimmy was thinking, but you need at least three out here. Peter and I can stand guard till you get back.'

'Lish, you know I can't leave you here. Sanjay will have my ass. You're not even Watch anymore.'

'Maybe not, but Peter is. And since when did you start taking orders from Sanjay?'

'Since this morning.' He gave them a puzzled look. 'Jimmy says so. Sanjay declared a . . . what do you call it? A civil emergency.'

'We know all about that. That doesn't mean Sanjay gives the orders.'

'You better tell Jimmy. He seems to think so. Galen too.'

'Galen? What does Galen have to do with anything?'

'You haven't heard?' Dale scanned their faces quickly. 'I guess you wouldn't have. Galen's Second Captain now.'

'Galen *Strauss*?'

Dale shrugged. 'It doesn't make sense to me, either. Jimmy just called everyone together and told us Galen had your slot, and Ian has Theo's.'

'What about Jimmy's? If he's moved up to First Captain now, who has his slot at second?'

'Ben Chou.'

Ben and Ian: It made sense. Both were in line for second. But Galen?

'Give me the key,' Alicia said. 'Go get two more Watchers. No captains. Find Soo if you can, and tell her what I told you.'

'I don't know who that leaves—'

'I mean it, Dale,' Alicia said. 'Just go.'

They opened the lockup and stepped inside. The room was barren, a featureless concrete box. Old toilet stalls, long since emptied of their fixtures, stood along one wall; facing these was a line of pipes and above it a long mirror, fogged with tiny cracks.

Caleb was sitting on the floor under the windows. They'd left him a jug of water and a bucket, but that was all. Lish balanced her cross against one of the stalls and crouched before him.

'Are they gone?'

Alicia nodded. Peter could see how frightened the boy was. He looked like he'd been crying.

'I'm so screwed, Lish. Sanjay's going to put me out for sure.'

'That's not going to happen. I promise you.'

He wiped his runny nose with the back of a hand. His face and hands were filthy, his nails encrusted with grime. 'What can you do?'

'Let me worry about that.' She drew a blade off her belt. 'You know how to use this?'

'Flyers, Lish. What am I going to do with a blade?'

'Just in case. Do you?'

'I can whittle some. I'm not very good.'

She pressed it into his hand. 'Put it out of sight.'

'Lish,' Peter said quietly, 'you think that's such a good idea?'

'I'm not leaving him unarmed.' She fixed her eyes on

Caleb again. 'You just hold tight and be ready. Anything happens, and you have a chance to get away, don't hesitate. You run like hell for the cutout. There's cover there, I'll find you.'

'Why there?'

They heard voices outside. 'It'll take too long to explain. Are we clear?'

Dale stepped back into the room, a single Watcher trailing behind him, Sunny Greenberg. She was just sixteen, a runner. Not even a season on the Walls.

'Lish, I'm not fooling,' Dale said. 'You have to get out of here.'

'Relax. We're leaving.' But when Alicia rose to her feet and saw Sunny standing in the doorway, she stopped. Her eyes flashed with anger. 'This is the best you could do? A runner?'

'Everybody else is on the Wall.'

Twelve hours ago, Peter realized, Alicia could have gotten anyone she wanted, a full detail. Now she had to beg for scraps.

'What about Soo?' Alicia pressed. 'Did you see her?'

'I don't know where she is. She's probably up there too.' Dale's eyes darted to Peter. 'Will you just get her out of here?'

Sunny, who so far had said nothing, moved farther into the room. 'Dale, what are you doing? I thought you said Jimmy ordered another guard. Why are you taking orders from *her*?'

'Lish was just helping out.'

'Dale, she's not a captain. She's not even *Watch*.' The girl acknowledged Alicia with a quick, faintly embarrassed shrug. 'No offense to you, Lish.'

'None taken.' Alicia gestured toward the cross the girl was holding at her side. 'Tell me something. You any good with that thing?'

A falsely modest shrug. 'Highest scores in my grade.'

'Well, I hope that's true. Because it looks like you just got promoted.' Alicia turned to Caleb again. 'You'll be all right in here?'

The boy nodded.

'Just remember what I told you. I won't be far.'

And with that, Alicia looked at Dale and Sunny one last time, using her eyes to communicate her meaning – *Make no mistake, this is personal* – and led Peter from the lockup.

TWENTY-NINE

Sanjay Patal, Head of the Household, might have said that it had all started years ago. It had started with the dreams.

Not about the girl: he'd never dreamed about her, of that he was certain. Or mostly certain. This Girl from Nowhere – that's what everyone was calling her, even Old Chou; the phrase had, in the space of just a morning, become her name – had arrived in their midst full blown, like an apparition borne from the darkness as a being of flesh and blood. Her sheer impossibility refuted by the fact of her existence. He'd searched his mind but could find her nowhere in it, not in the part he knew as himself, as Sanjay Patal, nor in the other: the secret, dreaming part of him.

For the feeling had lain within him as long as Sanjay could remember. The feeling that was like a whole other person, a separate soul that dwelled within his own. A soul with a name and a voice that sang inside him, *Be my one. I am yours and you are mine and together we are greater than the sum, the sum of our parts.*

Since he was a Little in the Sanctuary, the dream had come to him. A dream of a long-gone world and a voice that sang inside him. It was, in its way, a dream like any other, made of sound and light and sensation. A dream of a fat woman in her kitchen, breathing smoke. The woman shoving food into her wide, wobbling cave of a mouth, talking into her telephone, a curious object with a place to talk into and another to listen. Somehow he knew what this thing was, that it was a telephone, and in this manner Sanjay had come to understand that this wasn't just a dream he was having. It was a vision. A vision of the Time Before. And the voice inside him singing its mysterious name: *I am Babcock.*

I am Babcock. We are Babcock.

Babcock. Babcock. Babcock.

He'd thought of Babcock, back then, as a kind of imaginary friend – no different, really, than a game of pretend, though the game did not end. Babcock was always with him, in the Big Room and the courtyard and taking his meals and climbing into his cot at night. The events of the dream had felt no different to him than the other dreams he had, the usual sorts of things, silly and childish, like taking a bath or playing on the tires or watching a squirrel eating nuts. Sometimes he dreamed those things and sometimes he dreamed about a fat woman in the Time Before, and there was no rhyme or reason to it.

He remembered a day, long ago, sitting in circle in the Big Room when Teacher had said, *Let's talk about what it means to be a friend.* The children had just had lunch; he was full of the warm, sleepy feeling of having eaten a meal. The other Littles were laughing and fooling around though he was not, he wasn't like that, he did as he was told, and then Teacher clapped her hands to silence them and because he was so good, the only one, she turned to him, her kind face wearing the expression of someone about to bestow a present, the wonderful present of her attention, and said, *Tell us, Little Sanjay, who are your friends?*

'Babcock,' he replied.

No thought was involved; the word had simply popped out on its own. At once he realized the scope of his error, saying this secret name. Out in the air it seemed to wither, diminishing with exposure. Teacher was frowning uncertainly; the word meant nothing to her. Babcock? she repeated. Had she heard him correctly? And Sanjay understood that not everyone knew who this was, of course they didn't, why had he thought they did? Babcock was something special and private, all his own, and saying his name the way he had, so thoughtlessly, wishing only to please and be good, was a mistake. More than a mistake: a violation. To say the name was to take its specialness away. *Who is Babcock, Little Sanjay?* In the awful silence that followed – the children had all stopped talking, their attention snapping to this alien word – he heard someone snicker; in his memory it was Demo Jaxon, whom he hated even then – and then another and another, the sounds of their ridicule leaping around the circle of seated children like sparks around a fire. Demo Jaxon: of course it would be him. Sanjay was First Family too, but the way Demo acted, with his smooth, easy smile and effortless way of being liked, it was as if there was a second, rarer category, First of the First, and he, Demo Jaxon, was the only one in it.

But most hurtful of all was Raj. Little Raj, two years Sanjay's junior – who should have respected him, who should have held his tongue – had joined in the laughter too. He was seated on his folded legs to Sanjay's left – if Sanjay was at six o'clock and Demo at high noon, Raj was somewhere in the middle of the morning – and as Sanjay watched in horror, his brother shot Demo a quick inquiring glance, seeking his approval. *You see?* Raj's eyes said. *See how I can make fun of Sanjay, too?* Teacher was clapping her hands again, trying to restore order; Sanjay knew that if he didn't do something fast, he'd never hear the end of it. Their shrill chorus would ring in his ears, at meals and after lights-out and in the courtyard when Teacher had stepped away. *Babcock! Babcock! Babcock!* Like a bathroom word or worse. *Sanjay has a little Babcock!*

He knew what he had to say.

'I'm sorry, Teacher. I meant Demo. Demo is my friend.' He gave his most earnest smile to the little boy across from him, with his cap of dark hair – Jaxon hair – and pearl-like teeth and restless, roving eyes. If Raj could do it, so could he. 'Demo Jaxon is my best friend of all.'

Strange to recall that day now, so many years later. Demo

519

Jaxon gone without a trace, and Willem, and Raj, too; half the children who'd sat in the circle that afternoon were dead or taken up. Dark Night would get the majority; the others would find their own ways to vanish, each in his time. A kind of slow nibbling, of being eaten away; that's what life did, that was how it felt. So many years gone by – the passage of time itself a kind of marvel – and Babcock a part of it all. Like a voice inside him, quietly urging, being a friend to him when others could not, though not always speaking in words. Babcock was a feeling he had about the world. Not since that day in the Sanctuary had he spoken of Babcock again.

And it was true that, over time, the feeling of Babcock, and the dreams, had become something else again. Not the fat woman in the Time Before, though that still happened every now and then. (And come to think of it, what *had* Sanjay been doing in the Lighthouse that strange night? He no longer recalled.) Not the past but the future, and his place, Sanjay's place, within its new unfolding. Something was about to happen, something large. He didn't know quite what. The Colony couldn't last forever, Demo had been right about that, and Joe Fisher too; someday, the lights were going out. They were living on borrowed time. The Army was gone, dead, never to return; a few people still clung to the idea, but not Sanjay Patal. Whatever was coming wasn't the Army.

He knew all about the guns, of course. The guns that weren't a secret, quite. It wasn't Raj who had told him; Sanjay should have expected this, but still it came as a disappointment, to know that Raj had chosen Demo over him. But Raj had told Mimi, who had told Gloria – Raj's chattering gossip of a wife couldn't keep a secret longer than about five seconds; she was a Ramirez, after all – who, one morning over breakfast, in the days right after Demo Jaxon had disappeared, slipping out the gate when no one was looking without so much as a blade in his belt, had let it drop, then

520

flat-out blurted the story, saying, I'm not sure you're supposed to know.

Twelve crates of them, Gloria told him, her voice lowered confidentially, her face radiating the earnestness of an eager pupil. Down at the station, behind a wall that pulled away. Shiny new guns, *Army* guns, from a bunker Demo and Raj and the others had found. Was it important? Gloria wanted to know. Had she done the right thing, telling him? Her anxiety was all pretense; her voice said one thing, but her eyes told him the truth. She knew what the guns meant. Yes, he said, nodding equably. Yes, I think it may be. I think it's best if we keep this to ourselves. Thank you, Gloria, for letting me know.

Sanjay had no illusions that he was the only one. He'd gone straight to Mimi that morning, explaining to her in no uncertain terms that she mustn't tell anyone else. But surely a secret like that would be impossible to keep. Zander had to know; the station was his domain. Probably Old Chou too, since Demo told him everything. Sanjay didn't think Soo knew, or Jimmy, or Dana, Willem's girl. Sanjay had probed around the edges, never detecting a thing. But certainly there were others – Theo Jaxon, for one – and whom had they told? To whom had they, in confidence, as Gloria had that morning at breakfast, whispered, 'I have a secret you should know'? So it wasn't a question of whether the guns would come out, only when, and under what circumstances, and – a lesson he had learned that morning in the Sanctuary – who was friends with whom.

Which was why Sanjay had wanted Mausami off the Watch, away from Theo Jaxon.

Since the day she'd been born, Sanjay had known it about her: she was the reason for everything. True, there had been times, even recently, when Sanjay had found himself wishing for a son, sensing that this would have bestowed a completeness that his life would otherwise lack. But Gloria was simply not able; the usual miscarriages and false alarms, and her bleeding had faded away. Mausami had been born after a pregnancy that itself had seemed like yet one more disaster in the making – Gloria had spotted nearly the entire time – and a torturous, two-day labor that had seemed to Sanjay, forced to listen to her desperate moans from the outer room of the Infirmary, like nothing a person could possibly withstand.

And yet Gloria had prevailed. It was Prudence Jaxon, of all people, who had brought Sanjay's daughter to him where he sat with his head in his hands, his mind wiped clean by the hours of waiting and the terrible sounds from the ward. He had by then given himself over to the idea that the child would die, and Gloria as well, leaving him alone; it was with complete incomprehension that he received the swaddled bundle, believing for a moment that what Prudence had actually handed him was his own dead baby. *It's a girl*, Prudence was saying, *a healthy girl*. And even then it had taken a moment for the idea to sink in, for Sanjay to connect these words with this strange new thing he held in his arms. *You have a daughter, Sanjay.* And when he drew the swaddling aside and saw her face, so startling in its human-ness, her tiny mouth and crown of dark hair and tender, bulging eyes, he knew that what he was feeling, for the first and only time in his life, was love.

And then he'd almost lost her. A bitter irony, for her to take up with Theo Jaxon, the son so like the father; Mausami had done her best to hide it from him, and Gloria too, to protect him from this knowledge. But Sanjay could see what was happening. So it had come to him with a feeling of rescue when, just as he was expecting to hear that she had decided to pair with Theo, Gloria had told him the news. After everything, Galen Strauss! It wasn't that Galen was whom he would have chosen for his daughter – far from it. He would have preferred someone sturdier, like Hollis Wilson or Ben Chou. But Galen wasn't Theo Jaxon, that was the important thing; he wasn't any kind of Jaxon, and it was obvious to everyone that he loved Mausami. If this love had, at its core, a quality of weakness, even of desperation, that was something Sanjay could accept in the bargain.

All of which was on his mind as he stood in the Infirmary at half-day, gazing upon the girl. This Girl from Nowhere. As if all the strands of Sanjay's life, Mausami and Babcock and Gloria and the guns and all the rest, were braided together in her impossible person, the mystery that she was.

She appeared to be sleeping. Or something *like* sleeping. Sanjay had banished Sara to the outer room with Jimmy; Ben and Galen were guarding the door outside. Why he'd done this he couldn't quite say, but something in him wanted to examine the girl alone. The wound was obviously serious; everything Sara had told him led Sanjay to believe the girl would not survive. Yet as she lay before him, her eyes closed and her body still, no trace of struggle or distress in her face or the gentle rise and fall of her breathing, Sanjay could not shake off the impression that she was more resilient than she looked. Stuck by a Watcher's cross: such an injury would have killed a grown man, let alone a girl her age, which was what? Sixteen? Thirteen? Was she younger or older? Sara had done her best to clean the girl off and had gotten her a gown to wear, a cotton shift that opened in the front, the not-quite-sheer fabric dulled to a wintry gray by so many years of washing. It was held on her body only by the right sleeve; the left hung with disturbing emptiness, as if holding an invisible limb. The gown had been left open to expose the thick woolen dressing that encased her chest and one slender shoulder, rising to the base of her pale white neck. Her body wasn't a woman's body, her hips and chest were as compact as a boy's, her legs, where they appeared below the frayed hem of the gown, possessing a coltish sleekness and an adolescent's knobby knees. It was surprising, on knees such as those, not to see a scar or two, the evidence of some small childhood mishap – a fall from a swing, a game of rough-house in the yard.

And her skin, Sanjay thought, looking at her knees, then her arms, and finally her face, his eyes traveling upward to take in the whole of her once more. Not white, not pale;

neither word seemed to capture its quality of muted radiance. As if the lightness of its tone were not an absence of color but something in its own right. A lightness, Sanjay decided; that's what her skin was, a lightness. But, in fact, he could see some color where the sun had touched her, her hands and arms and face, leaving a saddle of faded freckles across her cheeks and nose. It moved him to a feeling of fatherly tenderness, grounded in memory: Mausami, when she was just a girl, had had freckles like those.

The girl's clothing and pack had gone into the fire, but not before the Household, wearing heavy gloves, had examined the meager, blood-soaked contents. Sanjay didn't know what he'd expected, but it wasn't what he'd found. The pack itself was ordinary green canvas, maybe military, but who could say? A few items, they'd all agreed, seemed genuinely useful – a pocketknife, a can opener, a ball of heavy twine – but most seemed arbitrary, their collective significance impossible to know. A rock of surprisingly rounded smoothness; a hunk of sun-bleached bone; a necklace with an empty locket; a book bearing the mysterious title *Charles Dickens' A Christmas Carol Illustrated Edition*. The bolt had passed straight through it, skewering it like a target; the pages were swollen with the girl's blood. Old Chou recalled that Christmas was a kind of gathering in the Time Before, like First Night. But no one really knew.

Which left only the girl herself to tell her story. This Girl from Nowhere, encased in her bubble of silence. The significance of her appearance was obvious: someone out there was still alive. Whoever and wherever these people were, they had cast off one of their own into the wilderness, a defenseless girl, who had somehow made her way here. A fact that, as Sanjay considered it, should have been good news, a cause for outright celebration, and yet in the hours since her arrival had produced nothing more than anxious silence. Not once had he heard anyone say: *We are not alone. That's what this means. The world is not a dead place after all.*

Because of Teacher, he thought. And not just the fact that

Teacher was dead; it was because of what Teacher told you, the day you came out of the Sanctuary. It was common for people, looking back, to laugh this off, telling the story of their release. *I can't believe what a fuss I made!* they'd all say. *You should have seen how I cried!* As if they were speaking not of their childhood selves, innocent creatures to be regarded with compassion and understanding, but of some other being entirely, viewed at a distance and faintly ridiculous. And it was true: once you knew that the world was a place that swarmed with death, the child you'd been no longer seemed like you at all. Seeing the pain in Mausami's face, the day she'd come out, had been one of the worst experiences of Sanjay's life. Some people never managed to get over it – these were the ones who let it go – but most found a way to carry on. You found a way to put hope aside, to bottle it and put it on a shelf somewhere and get on with the duties of your life. As Sanjay himself had done, and Gloria and even Mausami; all of them.

But now there was this girl. Everything about her flew straight into the face of the facts. For a person – a defenseless child – to materialize out of the dark was as fundamentally disturbing as a snowfall in midsummer. Sanjay had seen it in the eyes of the others, Old Chou and Walter Fisher and Soo and Jimmy and all the rest: everyone. It was *wrong*; it made no *sense*. Hope was a thing that gave you pain, and that's what this girl was. A painful sort of hope.

He cleared his throat – how long had he been standing there, looking at her? – and spoke.

'Wake up.'

No response. Yet he believed he detected, behind her eyelids, an involuntary flicker of awareness. He spoke again, louder this time:

'If you can hear me, wake up now.'

His train of thought was broken by movement behind him. Sara entered through the curtain, Jimmy trailing behind.

'Please, Sanjay. Let her rest.'

'This woman is a prisoner, Sara. There are things we need to know.'

'She's not a prisoner, she's a *patient*.'

He regarded the girl again. 'She doesn't look like she's dying.'

'I don't know if she is or not. It's a miracle she's still alive, all the blood she lost. Now will you please go? It's a wonder I can keep this place clean with all of you trooping through here.'

Sanjay could see how worn down Sara was, her hair sweaty and askew, her eyes bleary with exhaustion. It had been a long night for everyone, leading to an even longer day. And yet her face radiated authority; in here she made the rules.

'And you'll let me know if she wakes up?'

'Yes. I told you.'

Sanjay turned to Jimmy where he stood by the curtain. 'All right. Let's go.'

But the man made no response. He was looking at the girl – staring, really.

'Jimmy?'

He broke his gaze away. 'What did you say?'

'I said let's go. Let's let Sara do her work.'

Jimmy shook his head vaguely. 'Sorry. Guess I went away for a second there.'

'You should get some sleep,' Sara said. 'You too, Sanjay.'

They exited onto the porch, where Ben and Galen were standing guard, sweating in the heat. Earlier, there had been a crowd, people eager for some glimpse of the Walker, but Ben and Galen had managed to send them all away. It was past half-day; only a few people were moving about. Across the way, Sanjay saw an HD crew with masks and heavy boots and buckets headed to the Sanctuary, to wash the Big Room down again.

'I don't know what it is,' Jimmy said. 'But something about that girl . . . Did you see her eyes?'

Sanjay startled. 'Her eyes were closed, Jimmy.'

Jimmy was squinting down at the floor of the porch, as if

he'd dropped something and couldn't find it. 'Come to think of it, I guess maybe they *were* closed,' he said. 'So why would I think she was looking at me?'

Sanjay said nothing. The question made no sense. And yet something about Jimmy's words hit a nerve. Watching the girl, he'd had the distinct feeling of being observed.

He looked toward the other two men. 'Do either of you know what he's talking about?'

Ben shrugged. 'Beats me. Maybe she's got a thing for you, Jimmy.'

Jimmy turned sharply. His face, glowing with sweat, was actually panicked. 'Will you be serious? You go in there and see what I mean. It's weird, I'm telling you.'

Ben flicked his eyes quickly to Galen, who offered only a helpless shrug. 'Flyers,' said Ben, 'it was just a joke. What are you getting so riled up for?'

'It wasn't funny, goddamnit. And what are you smirking at, Galen?'

'Me? I didn't say anything.'

Sanjay felt his impatience boiling over. 'The three of you, enough. Jimmy, no one gets in here. Is that understood?'

Jimmy gave a chastened nod. 'Sure. Like you say.'

'I mean it. I don't care who it is.'

Sanjay focused his eyes on Jimmy's face, holding them there an extra moment. The man was no Soo Ramirez, that was obvious; he was no Alicia, either. Sanjay wondered if that was why, in the end, he'd chosen him for the job.

'What do you want us to do about Hightop?' Jimmy asked. 'I mean, we're not really putting him out, are we?'

The boy, Sanjay thought wearily. The last thing he wanted to think about, suddenly, was Caleb Jones. Caleb had given the first hours of the crisis a kind of clarity it demanded; people needed something to focus their anger on. But in the light of day, putting the boy out had begun to seem simply cruel, a pointless gesture that everyone would regret later. And the boy had real courage. When the charges were read, he'd stood before the Household and taken full blame

527

without hesitation. Sometimes you found courage in the strangest places, and Sanjay had seen it in the wrench named Caleb Jones.

'Just keep a guard on him.'

'What about Sam Chou?'

'What about him?'

Jimmy hesitated. 'There's talk, Sanjay. Sam and Milo and some others. About putting him out.'

'Where did you hear this?'

'I didn't. Galen did.'

'That's what I *heard*,' Galen volunteered. 'It was actually Kip who told me. He was at his folks' place and heard a bunch of them talking.'

Kip was a runner, Milo's oldest boy. 'Well? What did he say?'

Galen shrugged uncertainly, as if to distance himself from his own story. 'That Sam says if we don't put him out, he will.'

He should have seen this coming, Sanjay thought. It was the last thing he needed, people taking the situation into their own hands. But Sam Chou – it seemed completely out of character for the man, as mild a fellow as Sanjay had ever known, to go off half-cocked like that. Sam ran the greenhouses, a Chou always had; it was said that he fussed over the banks of peas and carrots and lettuce like pets. He supposed all those Littles had something to do with it. Every time Sanjay turned around, it seemed, Sam was passing out the celebratory shine and Other Sandy was pregnant again.

'Ben, he's your cousin. You hear anything about this?'

'When would I? I've been here all morning.'

Sanjay told them to double the guard at the lockup and stepped down onto the path. It really was awfully damn quiet, he thought. Not even the birds were singing. It made him think again of looking at the girl, the feeling he'd had of being seen. As if, behind her sweetly sleeping face – and there was something *sweet* about it, he thought, a babyish kind of sweetness; it reminded him of Mausami when she was just a

Little, climbing into her cot in the Big Room and waiting for Sanjay to bend toward her to kiss her good night – as if her mind, the girl's mind, behind her eyelids, that veil of soft flesh, was seeking his out in the room. Jimmy wasn't wrong; there was something about her. Something about her eyes.

'Sanjay?'

He realized his thoughts were drifting, carrying him away on a current. He swiveled to find Jimmy standing on the top step, his eyes pulled into a squint and his body leaning forward expectantly, the words of some unspoken declaration stalled on his lips.

'Well?' Sanjay's mouth was suddenly dry. 'What is it?'

The man opened his mouth to speak, but no words came; the effort seemed lost.

'It's nothing,' Jimmy said finally, looking away. 'Sara's right. I really could use some sleep.'

THIRTY

There would come a time, many years later, when Peter would recall the events surrounding the girl's arrival as a series of dancelike movements: bodies converging and separating, flung for brief periods into wider orbits, only to be drawn back again under the influence of some unknown power, a force as calm and inevitable as gravity.

When he'd come into the Infirmary the night before and seen the girl – so much blood, blood everywhere, Sara frantically trying to seal off the wound and Caleb with the soaked compress in his hands – he'd felt not horror or surprise but a blast of pure recognition. Here was the girl of the carousel; here was the girl of the hallway and the mad dash in darkness; here was the girl of the kiss and the closing door.

The kiss. In the long hours on the catwalk, standing the Mercy for Theo, Peter's mind had returned to it, again and again, to the puzzle of its meaning, the kind of kiss it was. Not a kiss like Sara's, that night under the lights; not the kiss of a friend or even, strictly speaking, the chaste kiss of a child, though there had been something childlike about it: its furtive haste and embarrassed quickness, ending almost before it had begun, and the girl's abrupt reversal, stepping back into the hallway before he could say a word and sealing the door in his face. It was all of these and none, and it wasn't until he'd come into the Infirmary and seen her lying there that he understood what it was: a promise. A promise as clear as words from a girl who hadn't any. A kiss that said: *I'll find you.*

Now, hidden behind a stand of junipers at the base of the Sanctuary wall, Alicia and Peter watched Sanjay depart. Jimmy left a moment later – there was something odd about his movements, Peter thought, a directionless lassitude, as if he didn't quite know where to go or what to do with himself – leaving Ben and Galen standing guard in the shade of the porch.

Alicia shook her head. 'I don't think we're going to be able to talk our way past them.'

'Come on,' he said.

He led her around to the rear of the building, a protected alleyway running between the Infirmary and the greenhouses. The back door of the building and its windows were all bricked in, but behind a pile of empty crates was a metal bulkhead. Inside was an old delivery chute, leading to the basement; sometimes at night, when his mother had been working alone and he was still young enough to take enjoyment from such a thing, she'd let him come over and ride the chute.

He swung the metal door open. 'In you go.'

He heard her body banging off the sides of the tube, then her voice from below: 'Okay.' Gripping the edges of the door, he eased himself inside, drawing the bulkhead down over his head – a sudden, enveloping blackness; it had been part of the thrill, he recalled, to ride the chute in darkness – and let go.

A quick, rattling plunge; he landed on his feet. The room was as he recalled, full of crates and other supplies and to his right the old walk-in freezer with its wall of jars, and at the center the wide table, with its scale and tools and guttered candles. Alicia was standing at the base of the stairs that led to the Infirmary's front room, angling her head upward into the shaft of light that fell from above. The steps emerged, at the top, in full view of the porch. Getting past the windows would be the tricky part.

Peter ascended first. Near the top he peeked out, lifting his eyes over the final step. The angle was wrong, he was too low, but he could hear the muffled sound of the two men's voices; they were facing away. He turned back to Alicia, signaling his intentions, then quickly rose and moved furtively across the room and down the hall to the ward.

The girl was awake and sitting up. That was the first thing he saw. Her bloody clothing was gone, replaced by a thin gown that revealed the white swath of her dressing. Sara, positioned on the edge of the narrow cot, was facing away; the girl's wrist was in her hand.

The girl's eyes flicked up then, meeting his own. A burst of panicked movement: she yanked her hand away and scrambled to the head of the cot, as Sara, sensing his presence behind her, vaulted to her feet and spun to face him.

'Flyers, Peter.' Her whole body seemed clenched; she spoke in a hoarse whisper. 'How the hell did you get in here?'

'Through the basement.' The voice came from behind him: Alicia. The girl had pulled herself into a ball, her knees defensively compressed to her chest to form a barricade, the loose fabric of her gown drawn down over her legs, which she was gripping with her hands.

'What happened?' Alicia said. 'That shoulder was torn to shreds a few hours ago.'

Only then did Sara's posture relax. She huffed a weary sigh and dropped onto one of the adjacent cots.

'I might as well tell you. As far as I can see, she's perfectly okay. The wound is practically healed.'

'How can that be?'

Sara shook her head. 'I can't explain it. I don't think she wants anyone to know, though. Sanjay was just in here with Jimmy. Anybody comes in here, she pretends to be asleep.' She shrugged. 'Maybe she'll talk to you. I can't get a word out of her.'

Peter heard this exchange only distantly; it seemed to be occurring in another room of the building. He had moved forward, toward the cot. The girl was peering at him warily over the tops of her knees, her eyes hooded by a tangle of her hair; he had the sense of moving into the presence of a skittish animal. He sat on the edge of the bed, facing her.

'Peter.' This was Sara. 'What are you . . . doing?'

'You followed me. Didn't you?'

A tiny nod, almost imperceptible. *Yes. I followed you.*

He lifted his face. Sara was standing at the foot of the bed, staring at him.

'She saved me,' Peter explained. 'At the mall, when the virals attacked. She protected me.' He gave his eyes to the girl again. 'That's right, isn't it? You protected me. You sent them away.'

Yes. I sent them away.

'You *know* her?' Sara said.

He hesitated, struggling to assemble the story in his mind. 'We were under a carousel. Theo was already gone. The smokes were coming, I thought it was all over. Then she . . . climbed on top of me.'

'She climbed on top of you.'

He nodded. 'Yes, on my back. Like she was shielding me. I know I'm not telling it right, but that's how it happened. Next thing I knew, the smokes were gone. She led me to a hallway and showed me the stairs that led to the roof. That's how I got out.'

For a moment Sara said nothing.

'I know it sounds strange.'

'Peter, why didn't you tell anyone?'

He shrugged, at a loss. He had no defense, at least not a good one. 'I should have. I wasn't even sure the whole thing had actually happened. And once I didn't say anything, it became harder and harder to actually do it.'

'What if Sanjay finds out?'

The girl had inched her face above the barricade of her knees; she appeared to be studying him, probing his face with a dark and knowing look. The feeling of wildness was still there, an animal jitteriness in the way she moved and held herself. But in the few minutes since they had entered the ward, a shift had occurred, a perceptible lessening of fear.

'He's not going to,' Peter said.

'Oh my God,' a voice behind them said. 'It's true.'

They all turned to see Michael standing at the curtain.

'Circuit, how did you get in here?' Alicia hissed. 'And keep your voice down.'

'Same as you. I saw the two of you going down the alley.' Michael moved cautiously toward the cot, his eyes locked on the girl. He was clutching something in his hand. 'Seriously, who *is* that?'

'We don't know,' Sara said. 'She's a Walker.'

For a moment Michael fell silent, his expression unreadable. Yet Peter could detect the workings of his mind, the swift calculations. He seemed, all of a sudden, to take notice of the object he was carrying.

'Holy shit. Holy *shit*. It's just like Elton said.'

'What are you talking about?'

'The signal. The ghost signal.' He shushed them with a hand. 'No, wait . . . hang on. I can't *believe* this. Everybody ready?' His face lit up with a triumphant smile. 'Here it comes.'

And just like that, the device began to buzz.

'Circuit,' said Alicia, 'what the hell is that?'

He held it up to show them. A handheld.

'That's what I came to tell you,' Michael said. 'That girl? The Walker? She's *calling* us.'

The transmitter had to be somewhere on her person, Michael explained. He couldn't say exactly what it would look like. Large enough to have a power source, but beyond that he couldn't say.

Her knapsack and its contents had gone into the fire. This left something on the girl herself as the source of the signal. Sara sat beside her on the cot and explained what she wanted to do, asking the girl to hold still. Moving from her feet, Sara ran her hands up the girl's body, gently touching every surface, examining her legs and arms and hands and neck; when this was done she rose and moved behind her, positioning herself at the head of the cot, and pulled her fingers slowly through the matted nest of her hair. Through all of it the girl held herself with a motionless compliance, lifting her arms and legs when Sara asked, her eyes floating about the room with a neutral inquisitiveness, as if she was not quite sure what to make of it all.

'If it's here, it's well hidden.' Sara paused to push a strand of hair from her face. 'Michael, are you sure?'

'Yes, I'm sure. It has to be inside her then.'

'Inside her *body*?'

'It should be near the surface. Probably just under the skin. Look for a scar.'

Sara considered this. 'Well, I'm not doing it in front of a crowd. Peter and Michael, both of you turn around. Lish, get over here. I might need you.'

Peter used this moment to step to the curtain and peek through. Ben and Galen were still outside, blurred figures facing away on the far side of the windows. He wondered how much longer they had. Surely someone else would come, Sanjay or Old Chou or Jimmy.

'Okay, you can look now.'

The girl was sitting on the edge of the bed, her head bent forward at the neck. 'Michael was right; I didn't have to look very long.' Sara lifted the tangle of the girl's hair to show them: a distinct white line at the base of her neck, no more than a couple of centimeters long. Above it was the telltale bulge of some foreign object.

'You can feel the edges.' Sara pressed her fingers against it to demonstrate. 'Unless there's more to it, I think it should come out clean.'

Peter asked, 'Will it hurt?'

Sara nodded. 'It'll be quick, though. After last night it should feel like nothing. Like removing a big splinter.'

Peter sat on the cot and spoke to the girl. 'Sara needs to remove something from under your skin. A kind of radio. Is that okay?'

He saw a flicker of apprehension in her face. Then she nodded.

'Just be careful,' said Peter.

Sara went to the storage cabinet and returned with a basin, a scalpel, and a bottle of spirits. She wet a cloth and cleaned the area. Then, positioned behind the girl once more, holding her hair away, she took the scalpel from the basin.

'This will sting.'

With a stroke of the scalpel's blade she traced the line of the scar. If the girl felt any pain, she made no indication. A single bead of blood appeared at the wound, running down the long line of the girl's neck to disappear into her gown. Sara dabbed the wound with the cloth and angled her head toward the basin.

'Somebody hand me those tweezers. Don't touch the tines.'

Alicia was the one to do this. Sara eased the ends of the tweezers through the jacketlike opening in the girl's skin, holding the blood-tinged cloth below it. So intense was Peter's focus that he could feel – actually feel in the tips of his fingers – the moment when the ends of the tweezers caught hold of the object. With a slow pulling motion, Sara drew it free, a dark shadow emerging, and placed it on the cloth. She held it up for Michael to see.

'Is this what you're looking for?'

Resting on the bed of cloth was a small, oblong-shaped disk, made of some shiny metal. A fringe of tiny wires, like hairs, beaded at the tips, encircled its edges. Altogether it looked to Peter like some kind of flattened spider.

'That's a radio?' Alicia said.

Michael was frowning, his brow furrowed. 'I'm not sure,' he confessed.

'You're not sure? How is it you could make the phone ring but you don't know what this is?'

Michael rubbed the object with a clean rag and held it to the light. 'Well, it's some kind of transmitter. That's what these wires are probably for.'

'So what's it doing inside her?' Alicia asked. 'Who could have done something like that?'

'Maybe we should ask *her* what it is,' Michael said.

But when he held the object out to show her, lying on its bed of bloodstained cloth, the girl responded with a look of puzzlement. Its very existence in her neck seemed as mysterious to her as it was to them.

'You think the Army put it in there?' Peter asked.

'It could be,' Michael said. 'It was broadcasting on a military frequency.'

'But you can't tell by looking at it.'

'Peter, I don't even know what it's transmitting. It could be reciting the alphabet for all I know.'

Alicia frowned. 'Why would it be reciting the alphabet?'

Michael let this pass without comment. He looked at Peter again. 'That's all I can tell you. If you want to know more, I'll have to open it.'

'Then open it,' said Peter.

THIRTY-ONE

Sanjay Patal had left the Infirmary intending to find Old Chou. There were things that needed to be decided, things to be discussed. Sam and Milo, for starters – that was a wrinkle Sanjay hadn't planned on – and what to do about Caleb, and the girl.

The girl. Something about her eyes.

But as he moved away from the Infirmary, into the afternoon, an unexpected heaviness came over him. He supposed it was only natural – up half the night and then a morning like the one he'd had, so much to do and say and worry over, so many things to consider. People often joked about the Household, that it wasn't a real job, one of the trades, Watch or HD or Ag – it had been Theo Jaxon who had dubbed it 'the plumbing committee,' a joke that had cruelly stuck – but that was because they didn't know the half of it, the responsibility. It weighed on a person; it was a load you carried and never quite put down. Sanjay was forty-five years old, which wasn't young, but as he moved down the gravel path, he felt much older.

At this time of day, Old Chou would be in the apiary – never mind that the gates were closed; the bees would care nothing about that. But the thought of the long walk over there, under the high, hot sun of midday, and whom Sanjay might encounter along the way and be forced to talk to, filled him with a sudden weariness like a gray mist in his brain. He decided it then: he had to get off his feet. Old Chou would keep. And almost before he knew it, Sanjay found himself moving at a slow trudge through the shadowed glade in the direction of his house, then stepping through the door (he listened for the sounds of Gloria elsewhere in the house, detecting nothing), climbing the creaking stairs under the eaves with their cobwebby corners, and lying down in bed. He was tired, so tired. Who knew how long it had been since he had let himself take a nap in the middle of the day.

He was asleep almost before he'd finished asking himself this question.

He awoke sometime later with a savagely sour taste in his mouth and a rush of blood in his ears. He felt not so much awake as ejected bodily from sleep; his mind felt beaten clean. Flyers, how he'd slept. He lay motionless, savoring the feeling, floating in it. He realized he'd heard voices down-stairs, Gloria's and someone else's, deeper, a man's; he thought it might be Jimmy or Ian or maybe Galen, but as he lay and listened he realized more time had passed, and the voices had gone away. How nice it was, simply to lie there. Nice and a little strange, because in fact it seemed to him that he should have gotten up some time ago; night was falling, he could see this through the window, the whiteness of the summer sky pinkening with dusk, and there were things to do. Jimmy would want to know about the power station, and who should ride down in the morning (though Sanjay couldn't, at that moment, recall precisely why this had to be decided), and there was still the question of the boy, Caleb, whom everyone called Hightop for some reason, it had some-thing to do with his shoes. So many things like this. And yet the longer he lay there, the more these concerns seemed distant and indistinct, as if they applied to someone else.

'Sanjay?'

Gloria was standing in the doorway. Her presence touched him less as a person than as a voice: a disembodied voice, calling his name in the dark.

'Why are you in bed?'

He thought: I don't know. How strange I don't know why I'm lying in this bed.

'It's late, Sanjay. People are looking for you.'

'I was . . . napping.'

'Napping?'

'Yes, Gloria. Napping. Taking a nap.'

His wife appeared above him, the image of her smooth round face floating bodiless in the gray sea of his vision. 'Why are you holding the blanket like that?'

'Like what? How am I holding it?'

'I don't know. Look for yourself.'

The effort, imagined in advance, seemed huge, nothing he wished to attempt. And yet somehow he managed it, tipping his head forward from the sweat-moistened pillow to troll the length of his body. It appeared that in his sleep he had pulled the blanket from their bed and twisted it into the form of rope, which he was now holding across his waist, clutching it tightly with his hands.

'Sanjay, what's the matter with you? Why are you talking like that?'

Her face was still above him and yet he could not seem to focus on it, to bring it fully into view. 'I'm fine. I was just tired.'

'But you're not tired anymore.'

'No. I don't think so. But perhaps I will sleep some more.'

'Jimmy was here. He wants to know what to do about the station.'

The station. What about the station?

'What should I tell him if he comes back?'

He remembered then. Somebody had to go down to the station to secure it, from whatever it was that might be happening there.

'Galen,' he said.

'Galen? What about him?'

But her question touched him only vaguely. His eyes had closed again, the image of Gloria's face shifting before him, resolving, replaced by another: the face of a girl, so small. Her eyes. Something about her eyes.

'What about Galen, Sanjay?'

'It would be good for him, don't you think?' he heard a voice saying, for one part of him was still there in the room while the other part, the dreaming part, was not. 'Tell him to send Galen.'

THIRTY-TWO

The hours passed and night came on.

They'd heard no word yet from Michael. After the three of them had slipped out the back of the Infirmary, the group

539

had separated: Michael to the Lighthouse, Alicia and Peter to the trailer park, to watch over Caleb from one of the empty hulks, in case Sam and Milo returned. Sara was still inside with the girl. For the time being, the only thing to do was wait.

The trailer where they hid was two rows away from the lockup, far enough that they could go undetected but still with a view of the door. It was said the trailers had been left by the Builders, who had used them to house the workers who had built the walls and lights; as far as Peter knew, no one else had ever lived there. Most of the paneling had been stripped away to get at the pipes and wires, and all the fixtures and appliances had been taken out, chopped up and dispersed. There was a space in the back where a mattress had sat on a platform, separated by a flexible, sliding door on a track, and a couple of sleeping cubbies tucked into the walls; a tiny table was situated at the other end with a pair of benches facing each other. These were covered in cracked vinyl, the gaps in the fabric disgorging a brittle foam that crumbled to dust when you touched it.

Alicia had brought a deck of cards to pass the time. Between hands of go-to, she would shift restlessly on the bench, glancing out the window toward the lockup. Dale and Sunny were gone, replaced by Gar Phillips and Hollis Wilson, who evidently had decided not to stand down after all. Sometime in the late afternoon, Kip Darrell had appeared, bearing a tray of food. Otherwise they'd seen no one.

Peter dealt a fresh hand. Alicia turned away from the window, took her cards from off the table, and looked at them quickly, frowning.

'Flyers. Why'd you give me such junk?'

She sorted her cards while Peter did the same, and led with a red jack. Peter matched the suit and countered with the eight of spades.

'Go to.'

He had no more spades; he drew from the deck. Alicia was gazing out the window again.

'Stop it, will you?' he said. 'You're making me nervous.'

Alicia said nothing. It took Peter four draws to match the suit; his hands were now hopelessly full of cards. He played a deuce and watched while Alicia played out the two of hearts, rolling the suit, and ran with four cards in a row, flipping on a queen to bring him back to spades.

He drew again. She was long in spades, he could feel it, but there was nothing he could do. She had him completely boxed. He played a six and watched while she dealt out a sequence of cards, flipping to diamonds on a nine, and emptied the rest of her hand.

'You always do that, you know,' she said, as she was scooping up the cards. 'Play out your weakest suit first.'

Peter was still looking at his hand, as if there was something left to play. 'I didn't know that.'

'Always.'

First Bell was moments away. How strange it would be, Peter thought, not to spend this night on the catwalk.

'What will you do if Sam comes back?' Peter asked.

'I really don't know. Try to talk him out of it, I guess.'

'And what if you can't?'

She tipped a shoulder, frowning. 'Then I'll deal with it.'

They heard First Bell.

'You don't have to do this, you know,' Alicia said.

He wanted to say: Neither do you. But he knew this wasn't so.

'Trust me,' Alicia said, 'nothing's going to happen after Second Bell. After last night, everybody's probably hiding in their houses. You should go look in on Sara. The Circuit, too. See if he's found anything.'

'What do you think she is?'

Alicia shrugged. 'As far as I can see, she's just a frightened kid. That doesn't explain that thing in her neck, or how she survived out there. Maybe we'll never figure it out. Let's see what Michael comes up with.'

'But you believe me? About what she did at the mall.'

'Of course I believe you, Peter.' Alicia was frowning at him. 'Why wouldn't I believe you?'

'It's a pretty crazy story.'

'If you say that's what happened, then that's what happened. I've never doubted you before, and I'm not going to start now.' She examined him closely for a moment. 'But that's not what you were asking about, is it?'

He let a silence pass. Then: 'When you look at her, what do you see?'

'I don't know, Peter. What should I see?'

Second Bell began to ring. Alicia was still studying him, waiting for his reply. But he had no words for what he felt, at least none that he trusted.

A blaze from outside: the lights were on. Peter unfolded his legs from under the table and rose to his feet.

'Would you really have stuck Sam with that cross today?' he asked her.

Alicia was below him now, illuminated from behind, her face sunk in shadow. 'Honestly? I don't really know. I might have. I'm sure I'd be sorry if I had.'

He waited, saying nothing. Resting on the floor was Alicia's pack – food and water and a bedroll, her cross beside it.

'Go on,' she urged, tipping her head toward the door. 'Get out of here.'

'You're sure you'll be okay?'

'Peter,' she said with a laugh, 'when wasn't I?'

In the Lighthouse, Michael Fisher was having more than his share of problems. But worst of all was the smell.

It had gotten bad, really bad. A sour, armpitty reek of unwashed body and old socks. A moldy-cheese-and-onions sort of smell. The air was so rank that Michael could barely concentrate.

'Flyers, Elton, just get out of here, will you? You're stinking the whole place up.'

The old man was sitting in his usual spot at the panel to

Michael's right, his hands lying heavily on the arms of his old wheeled chair, face turned slightly to the side, away. After they'd powered up for the night – levels all green as far as that went; the station, whatever might have happened down there, was still sending current up the mountain – Michael had resumed work on the transmitter, which now lay in pieces on the counter, their images bulging through the articulated magnifying glass he'd carried out from the shed. He'd been nervously anticipating a visit from Sanjay, to ask him about the batteries; he was ready at a moment's notice to scoop the whole thing into a drawer. But the only official visit had come from Jimmy, late in the afternoon. Jimmy didn't look so hot, sort of flushed and out of it, like maybe he was coming down with something, and he'd asked about the batteries sheepishly, as if he'd forgotten all about them and was almost too embarrassed to bring it up now. He hadn't gotten farther than a meter from the door, though the smell would keep anyone away, a barricade of human stink, and had appeared to take no notice of the magnifier, sitting out there for anyone with half a brain to see, nor the open slot on the panel with its colored cables and exposed circuitry and the soldering iron resting beside it on the counter.

'I mean it, Elton. If you're going to sleep, go do it in back.'

The old man twitched to life, fingers tightening on the arms of his chair. He turned his blind, rigid face to Michael.

'Right. Sorry.' He rubbed a hand over his face. 'Did you solder it?'

'I'm going to. Seriously, Elton. You're not *alone* in here. When was the last time you took a bath?'

The old man said nothing. Come to think of it, he didn't look so great himself, not that the standards where Elton was concerned were all that high to begin with. Sweaty and washed out and somehow not *there*. While Michael watched, Elton drifted a slow hand toward the surface of the counter, his fingers tapping lightly in a searching way until they alighted on the headphones, though he didn't pick them up.

'Are you feeling all right?'

'Hmmm?'

'I'm just saying you don't look so great is all.'

'Are we lights up?'

'That was an hour ago. How asleep were you?'

Elton licked his lips with a heavy tongue. Flyers, what was it? Something in his teeth?

'Maybe you're right. Maybe I will go lie down.'

The old man lumbered to his feet and shuffled down the narrow hallway that connected the work area with the back of the hut. Michael heard the creak of springs as his big body hit the cot.

Well, at least he wasn't in the room.

Michael turned his attention back to the work that lay before him. He'd been right about the thing in the girl's neck. The transmitter was connected to a memory chip, but not any kind he'd ever seen, much smaller and without any obvious ports except for a pair of tiny gold brads. One was linked to the transmitter, the other to the filigree of beaded wires. So either the wires were an antenna array and the transmitter ran off the chip, which didn't seem likely, or the wires themselves were sensors of some kind, the source of the data the chip was recording.

The only way to find out for sure was to read the data on the chip. And the only way to do that was to solder it hard to the mainframe's memory board.

It was a risk. Michael was hard-soldering a piece of unknown circuitry to the control panel itself. Maybe the system wouldn't see it. Maybe the system would crash and the lights would all go out. Probably the wisest course would be to wait until morning. But by this point he was moving forward on sheer momentum, his mind clamped onto the problem like a squirrel with a nut in his teeth; he couldn't have waited if he'd wanted to.

He'd have to take the mainframe off-line first. This meant shutting down the controllers to run straight off the batteries. You could do this for a while but not for long; without the system to monitor the current, any fluctuation could flip a breaker. So once the mainframe was off-line, he'd have to work fast.

He took a deep breath and called up the system menu.

Shut down?

He clicked on: **Y**

The hard drive began to spin down. Michael darted from his chair and shot across the room to the breaker box.

None of the breakers moved.

He got quickly to work, pulling the motherboard free, placing it on the counter under the magnifier, taking up the hot iron in one hand and the strip of solder in the other. He touched it to the tip of the iron – a waft of smoke curling in the air above it – and watched as a single drop descended toward the open channel on the motherboard.

Bull's-eye.

He tweezered the chip; he had one shot to get this right. Gripping his right wrist to keep it steady, he gently lowered the chip's exposed contacts into the solder, freezing it in place for a count of ten while the bead of liquid solder cooled and stiffened around it.

Only then did he let himself breathe. He slid the board back into the panel, locked it in place, and booted the mainframe back up.

In the long minute that followed as the system came back online, the hard drive clicking and whirring, Michael Fisher closed his eyes and thought: *Please.*

And there it was. When he opened his eyes he saw it, sitting in the system directory. UNKNOWN DRIVE. He selected the image and watched as the window sprang open. Two partitions, A and B. The first was tiny, just a few kilobytes. But not B.

B was huge.

It contained two files, identical in size; one was probably a backup of the other. Two identical files of such immensity it simply boggled the mind. This chip: it was like the whole world was written inside it. Whoever had made this thing and put it inside the girl, that person was not like anyone he knew; they did not seem to be from a world he was part of. He wondered if he should maybe get Elton, ask him what he thought. But the snores coming from the back of the hut told him this would be a waste of his energy.

When Michael opened the file, as he did in due course, he did it almost furtively, one hand raised before his eyes, which were peeking through his fingers.

THIRTY-THREE

A lucky stroke: approaching the Infirmary, Peter saw a single Watcher standing guard. He marched straight up the steps.

'Evening, Dale.'

Dale's cross hung loosely at his side. He sighed with exasperation, cocking his head a little, giving Peter his good ear. 'You know I can't let you in.'

Peter craned his neck to look past Dale through the front windows. A lantern was glowing on the desk.

'Sara inside?'

'She left a little while ago. Said she was getting something to eat.'

Peter held his ground, saying nothing more. It was a waiting game, he knew. He could see the indecision moving through Dale's face. At last he huffed in surrender and stood aside.

'Flyers. Just be quick about it.'

Peter stepped through the door and moved back into the ward. The girl was curled on the cot, her knees tucked against her chest, facing away. At the sound of his entry, she made no movement; Peter guessed she was asleep.

He positioned a chair by the cot and sat with his chin in his hands. Under the tousle of her hair, he could see the mark on her neck where Sara had cut away the transmitter – a barely detectable line, almost completely healed.

She roused then, as if to meet his thoughts, and shifted on the cot to face him. The whites of her eyes were moist and full, shining in the lamplight that leaked through the curtain.

'Hey,' he said. His voice felt thick in his throat. 'How are you feeling?'

Her hands were pressed together, buried to her slender wrists in the crevice between her knees. Everything about the way she held her body seemed conceived to make her appear smaller than she was.

'I came to thank you, for saving me.'

A quick tightening of her shoulders under the gown. *You're welcome.*

How strange it was, speaking this way – strange because it *wasn't* so strange. He had never heard the sound of the girl's voice, and yet he did not feel this as a lack. There was something calming about it, as if she had put aside the noise of words.

'I don't suppose you feel like talking,' Peter ventured. 'Like maybe telling me your name? We could start with that, if you want.'

The girl said nothing, indicated nothing. *Why would I tell you my name?*

'Well, that's okay,' Peter said. 'I don't mind. We can just sit here.'

Which was what he did; he sat with her, in the dark. After a time, a slackness came into the girl's face. More minutes passed, and without any further acknowledgment of his presence, she closed her eyes again.

As Peter waited in the quiet, a sudden weariness came over him, and with it a memory: of a night, long ago, when he had come into the Infirmary and seen his mother watching over one of her patients – just as he was doing now. He couldn't remember who this person was or if, in fact, the memory was several memories, folded over one another. It could have been one night or many. But on the night he recalled, he had stepped through the curtain and found his mother sitting in a chair by one of the cots, her head tipped to the side, and knew she was asleep. The person on the cot was a child, a small form hidden in darkness; the only light came from a candle on a tray by the bed. He moved forward, not speaking; no one else was in the room. His mother stirred, tilting her face toward him. She was young, and healthy, and he was glad, so glad, to see her again.

Take care of your brother, Theo.

—Mama, he said. I'm Peter.

He's not strong, like you.

He was jarred by voices outside and the clatter of the opening door. Sara strode into the ward, the lantern swinging from her hand.

'Peter? Is everything okay?'

He blinked into the sudden blaze. It took him a moment to reassemble his sense of where he was. He had slept only a minute, and yet it felt like longer. Already the memory, and the dream it had produced, were gone.

'I was just . . . I don't know.' Why was he apologizing? 'I think I must have dozed off.'

Sara was busying herself with the lantern, moving a wheeled tray to the side of the cot, where the girl was sitting up, an alert and watchful expression on her face.

'How'd you talk Dale into letting you in?'

'Oh, Dale's all right.'

Sara sat on the girl's cot and opened her kit to reveal what she'd brought: flatbread, an apple, a wedge of cheese.

'Hungry?'

The girl ate quickly, polishing off her meal with darting bites: first the bread and then the cheese, which she sniffed suspiciously before tasting, and finally the apple, right down to the core. When it was gone she wiped her face with the back of her hand, smearing juice over her cheeks.

'Well, I guess that settles it,' Sara declared. 'Not the best table manners I've ever seen, but your appetite is normal enough. I'm going to check your dressing, okay?'

Sara untied the gown, drawing it aside to expose the girl's

bandaged shoulder while leaving the rest covered. With a pair of shears, she snipped the cloth away. Where the bolt had entered, tearing skin and muscle and bone, all that remained was a small pink depression. It reminded Peter of a baby's flesh, that soft freshness of new skin.

'All my patients should heal so fast. No point in leaving those stitches in, I guess. Turn around so I can do the back.'

The girl complied, swiveling on the cot; Sara took up a pair of tweezers and began pulling the sutures from the exit wound, dropping them one by one into a metal basin.

'Does anybody else know about this?' Peter asked.

'About the way she heals? I don't think so.'

'So nobody else has been in to see her since this afternoon.'

She clipped off the final stitch. 'Just Jimmy.' She pulled the girl's gown back over her shoulder. 'There you go, all set.'

'Jimmy? What did he want?'

'I don't know, I assume Sanjay sent him.' Sara shifted on the cot to look at Peter. 'It was kind of strange, actually. I never heard him come in, I just looked up and there he was, standing in the doorway with this . . . look on his face.'

'A look?'

'I don't know how else to describe it. I told him she hadn't said anything, and then he left. But that was hours ago.'

Peter felt suddenly rattled. What did she mean by a look? What had Jimmy seen?

Sara took up her tweezers again. 'Okay, your turn.'

Peter was about to say, My turn for what? But then he remembered: his elbow. The bandage had long since worn down to a filthy rag. He guessed the cut was healed by now; he hadn't looked at it for days.

He sat on one of the empty cots. Sara took a place beside him and unwrapped the bandage, releasing a sour odor of stale skin.

'Did you bother keeping this thing clean at all?'

'I guess I forgot.'

She took hold of the arm, bending closely with the

549

tweezers. Peter was aware of the girl's eyes, intently watching them.

'Any news from Michael?' He felt a jab of pain as she tugged the first suture. 'Ow, be careful.'

'It would help if you held still.' Sara repositioned his arm, not looking at him, and resumed her work. 'I stopped by the Lighthouse on the way back from the house. He's still working. Elton's helping him.'

'Elton? Is that so smart?'

'Don't worry, we can trust him.' Her eyes flicked upward with a troubled glance. 'Funny how we're all talking like that, all of a sudden. Who can trust who.' She gave his arm a pat. 'There, move it around a little.'

Balling his hand into a fist, he pumped his arm back and forth. 'Good as new.'

Sara had stepped to the pump to clean her tools. She turned and faced him, drying her hands on a rag.

'Honestly, Peter. Sometimes I worry about you.'

He realized that he was still holding his arm away from his body. He awkwardly dropped it to his side. 'I'm fine.'

She raised her eyebrows doubtfully but said nothing. That one night after the music, Arlo and his guitar and everybody drinking shine; something had come over him, a sudden, almost physical loneliness, but then, the moment he kissed her, a puncturing jab of guilt. It wasn't that he didn't like her, nor that she had failed to make her interest less than plain. Alicia was right, what she'd said on the roof of the power station. Sara was the obvious choice for him. But he couldn't will himself to feel something he didn't. There was a part of him that simply didn't feel alive enough to deserve her, to offer in kind what she was offering him.

'As long as you're here,' Sara said, 'I'm going to go look in on Hightop. Make sure somebody remembered to feed him.'

'What do you hear?'

'I've been inside all day. You probably know more than I do.' When Peter said nothing, Sara shrugged. 'I expect people are divided. There's going to be a lot of anger about last night. The best thing would be for a little time to pass.'

'Sanjay better think twice about doing anything with him. Lish will never stand for it.'

Sara seemed to stiffen. She drew her kit from the floor and hung it on her shoulder again, not looking at him.

'What did I say?'

But she shook her head. 'Forget it, Peter. Lish is not my problem.'

Then she was gone, the curtain shifting with her departure. Well, Peter thought, what to make of that? It was true that Alicia and Sara couldn't have been two more different women, and nothing said they had to get along. Maybe it was simply the case that Sara blamed Alicia for Teacher's death, which would hit Sara harder than most. It was sort of obvious, now that Peter considered it. He didn't know why he hadn't thought of it before.

The girl was looking at him again. She gave a quizzical lift of her eyebrows: *What's wrong?*

'She's just upset is all,' he said. 'Worried.'

He thought it again: How strange it all was. It was as if he could hear her words in his head. Anybody who saw him talking like this would think he'd lost his mind.

Then the girl did something he hadn't expected at all. Aroused by some unknown purpose, she rose from her cot and moved to the sink. She primed the pump, three hard pushes, and filled a basin with water. This she carried back to the cot where Peter sat. She placed it on the dusty floor at his feet and took a cloth from the cart and sat beside him, bending at the waist to dip the rag in the water. Then she took his arm in her hand and began to dab the place where the sutures had been with the moistened cloth.

He could feel her breath on him, breezing over his damp flesh. She had unfolded the cloth against her open hand to increase the surface area. Her gesture was more thorough now, not a cautious dabbing but a smooth, even stroking motion, rubbing the dirt and desiccated skin away. An ordinary kindness, to wash his skin, and yet completely surprising: it was full of sensation, of memory. His senses seemed to have gathered around it, the feel of the washcloth on his arm, her breath on his skin, like moths around a flame. As if he were a boy again, a boy who had fallen and scraped his elbow and run inside, and she was washing him clean.

She misses you.

Every nerve in his body seemed to jump. The girl was holding his arm in a firm grip, immovable. Not words, not spoken words. The words were in his mind. She was gripping his arm; their faces were inches apart.

'What did you—?'

She misses you she misses you she misses you.

He was on his feet, lurching away. His heart was pounding in his chest like a great caged animal. He had backed with his full weight into some kind of glass cabinet, sending the contents spilling off the shelves behind him. Someone had stepped through the curtain, a figure at the periphery of his vision. For a moment his mind came mercifully into a wider focus. Dale Levine.

'What the hell is going on in here?'

Peter swallowed, trying to answer. Dale was standing at the curtain, wearing a look of confusion, his emotions unable to coalesce around any single point in the unfolding scene. He shifted his face toward the girl, who was still seated on the cot with the basin at her feet, then looked at Peter again.

'She's awake? I thought she was *dying*.'

Peter found his voice at last. 'You can't . . . tell anyone.'

'Flyers, Peter. Does Jimmy know about this?'

'I mean it.' He knew suddenly that if he didn't leave the room at once he would dissolve. 'You can't.'

Then he turned, brushing past Dale, practically knocking him over; he was through the curtain and out the door and stumbling down the steps into the spotlit yard, his mind still caught in the flow of words in his head – *she misses you she misses you* – his vision wavering through the tears that were rising to his eyes.

THIRTY-FOUR

For Mausami Patal, the night began in the Sanctuary.

She was sitting alone in the Big Room, trying to teach herself to knit. All the cots and cribs had been taken out; the children had bedded down upstairs. The broken window was boarded up, the glass swept away, the room and all its surfaces washed down with spirits. The smell would linger for days.

It wasn't anyplace she should have been. The aroma of alcohol was so strong it was making her eyes tear up. Poor Arlo, Maus thought. And Hollis, having to kill his brother like that, though it was lucky that he had. She didn't want to think about what would have happened if he'd missed. And of course Arlo wasn't really Arlo anymore, just as Theo, if he was still alive out there, wasn't Theo. The virus took the soul, the person you loved, away.

The chair where she sat was an old nursing rocker she'd found in the storage closet. She'd positioned a small table beside it; resting on this was a lantern, giving her enough light to work by. Leigh had instructed her in the basic stitches, which had seemed easy enough when she'd started, but somewhere along the way she had taken a wrong turn. The stitches weren't coming out even, not at all, and her left thumb, when she tried to draw the yarn around the needle, as Leigh had demonstrated, kept getting in the way. Here she was, a woman who could bolt-load a crossbow in under a second, put half a dozen long arrows in the air in fewer than five, blade a target dead through the sweet spot at six meters, on the run, on an off day; and yet knitting a pair of baby booties seemed completely beyond her power. She'd gotten so distracted that twice the ball of yarn in her lap had dropped to the floor to roll across the room, and by the time she'd gotten it rolled back up, she'd forgotten where she was and had to start over.

Part of her simply couldn't absorb the notion that Theo was gone. She had planned to tell him about the baby on the ride, their first night at the station. With its warren of rooms and heavy walls and doors that sealed, it was easy to find an occasion to be alone there. A fact that, as long as she was being honest with herself, was the reason the whole situation existed in the first place.

Pairing with Galen: why had she done it? Cruel in a way, because he wasn't a bad person; it was hardly his fault that she didn't love him, or even much like him, not anymore. A bluff. That's what it had been. To jar Theo out of his gloom. And when she'd said to him that night on the Wall, *Maybe I just will marry Galen Strauss*, and Theo had said, *All right, if that's what you want, I only want you to be happy*, the bluff had hardened into something else, something she *had* to do, to prove that he was wrong. Wrong about her, wrong about himself, wrong about everything. You had to *try*. You had to *act*. You had to get on with things and make do. A feat of stubbornness, that's what it was, marrying Galen Strauss, and all for Theo Jaxon.

For a time, most of that summer and into the fall, she had tried to make the marriage work. She had hoped she could will the right emotions into being, and for a while she had almost done it, simply because the sheer fact of her existence seemed to make Galen so happy. They were both Watch, so it wasn't like they saw each other all that much or kept any kind of regular hours; it proved, in fact, pretty easy to avoid him, because he was on the day shift most of the time, a subtle but unmistakable comment on the fact that he had come up last in his grade, and with his eyes the way they were, no good in the dark. Sometimes when he looked at her, squinting like he did, she wondered if in fact she was the girl he really loved at all. Maybe it was some other woman he saw, one he had made up in his mind.

She'd found a way to almost never let him near her.

Almost: because you couldn't not lie with your husband. *Is he tender with you?* her mother had asked her. *Is he kind? Does*

he care about what's happening to you? That's all I want to know.
But Galen was too happy to be tender. *I can't believe it!* his
face and body said. *I can't believe you're mine!* Which she
wasn't; while Galen huffed and puffed above her in the dark,
Mausami was miles away. The harder he tried to be a husband, the less she felt like a wife to him, until – and this was
the bad part, the part that didn't seem fair of her – she'd
found herself actually disliking him. By the first snowfall
she'd caught herself imagining she could close her eyes and
simply wish him off the face of the earth. Which only made
Galen try harder, and left her disliking him even more.

How could he not know the baby wasn't his? Could the
man not do basic math?

True, she'd fudged the numbers. The morning he'd caught
her throwing up her breakfast into the compost pile, she'd
told him three periods, when it was really two. Three and it
was Galen's baby; two and it was not. Galen had come to her
only one time the month she'd gotten pregnant; she had
refused him on some pretense, she couldn't even remember
what. No, it was all perfectly clear to Mausami, the when and
who. She had been down at the station when it happened;
Theo was there, and Alicia, and Dale Levine. The four of
them had stayed up late playing hands of go-to in the control
room, and then Alicia and Dale had gone to bed, and the
next thing she knew, she and Theo were sitting alone together, the first time since her wedding. She began to cry,
surprised at how much she wanted to and by the sheer
volume of her tears, and Theo had taken her in his arms to
comfort her, which was what she wanted too, both of them
saying how sorry they were, and after that it had taken all of
about thirty seconds. They never stood a chance.

She'd barely seen him after that. They'd ridden back the
next morning, and life returned to normal – though it wasn't
normal, not at all. She was a person with a secret. It lay like a
warm stone inside her, a private glowing happiness. Even
Galen seemed to detect the change, remarking something
along the lines of Well, I'm glad to see your mood has picked

up. It's nice to see you smiling. (Her response, wholly absurd and nothing that could be acted upon, was a friendly desire to tell him, so he could share in her good news.) She didn't know what would happen; she didn't think about it at all. When she missed her period, she gave it scarcely any thought. It wasn't like she was anything close to regular; she'd always been that way, it came and went as it pleased. All she could think about was the next trip down to the station, when she could make love to Theo Jaxon again. She saw him on the catwalk, of course, and at evening assembly, but that wasn't the same, it wasn't the time and place to touch or even talk. She would have to wait. But even this, the waiting, the torturous crawl of days – the date of their next departure for the station was plainly listed on the duty roster, where anyone could see it – was part of her happiness, the blur of love.

Then she missed another period, and Galen caught her throwing up into the compost pile.

Of course she was pregnant. Why hadn't she anticipated this? How had this eventuality escaped her attentions? Because the one thing Theo Jaxon wouldn't want was a baby. Maybe under the right circumstances she could have won him over to the idea. But not like this.

Then another thought had come to her, dawning with a simple clarity: a baby. She was going to have a baby. Her baby, Theo's baby, their baby together. A baby wasn't an idea, as love was an idea. A baby was a fact. It was a being with a mind and a nature, and you could feel about it any way you liked, but a baby wouldn't care. Just by existing, it demanded that you believe in a future: the future it would crawl in, walk in, live in. A baby was a piece of time; it was a promise you made that the world made back to you. A baby was the oldest deal there was, to go on living.

Maybe the thing Theo Jaxon needed most of all was a baby.

That's what Mausami would have told him down at the station, in the little room of shelves that was now theirs. She had imagined the scene unfolding a number of ways, some good and some not so good, the worst of all being the one in which she lost her nerve and said nothing. (The second worst: Theo guessed, her courage failed her anyway, and she told him it was Galen's.) What she hoped was that she'd see a light in his eyes come on. The light that had gone out, long ago. A baby, he would say. Our baby. What should we do? What people always do, she would have told him, and that was when he would take her in his arms again, and in this zone of sheltering safety she would know that everything would be all right, and together they would ride back to face Galen – to face everyone – together.

But now this would never happen. The story she had told herself was just that, a story.

She heard footsteps coming down the hall behind her. A heavy, loose-limbed tread she knew. What did she have to do to get a moment's peace? But it wasn't his fault, she reminded herself again; nothing was Galen's *fault*.

'What are you doing down here, Maus? I've been all over.'

He was standing above her. She shrugged, still giving her eyes to her horrible knitting.

'You shouldn't be in here.'

'It's washed down, Galen.'

'I mean you shouldn't be here alone.'

Mausami said nothing. What *was* she doing here? Just a day ago, she'd felt so suffocated by the place that she thought she'd lose her mind. What made her think she could ever learn to knit?

'It's fine, Gale. I'm perfectly fine where I am.'

She wondered if it was guilt that made her torment him so. But she didn't think it was. It felt more like anger – anger at his weakness, anger that he loved her like he did when she'd clearly done nothing to deserve it, anger that she would have to be the one to look him in the eye after the baby was born – a baby that would, as long as life was being so ironic, look just like Theo Jaxon – and explain the truth to him.

'Well.' He paused, clearing his throat. 'I'm leaving in the morning. I just came to tell you.'

She put her needles down to look at him. He was squinting at her in the dim light, giving his face a scrunched, boyish appearance. 'What do you mean, "leaving"?'

'Jimmy wants me to secure the station. With Arlo gone, we don't know what's going on down there.'

'Flyers, Galen. Why is he sending you?'

'You think I can't handle it?'

'I didn't say that, Gale.' She heard herself sigh. 'I'm just wondering why you, is all. You've never been down there before.'

'Someone has to go. Maybe he thinks I'm the best man for the job.'

She did her best to look agreeable. 'Be careful, okay? All eyes.'

'You say that like you actually mean it.'

Mausami didn't know how to answer that. She felt suddenly tired.

'Of course I mean it, Gale.'

'Because if you don't, you should probably just say so.'

Tell him, she thought. Why didn't she just tell him?

'Go on, it's all right.' She took up her knitting again. 'I'll be here when you get back. Go to the station.'

'You really think I'm so stupid?'

Galen was standing with his hands at his sides, glaring at her. One hand, his right, closest to his blade, gave a small, involuntary-seeming twitch.

'I didn't . . . say that.'

'Well, I'm not.'

A silent moment passed. His hand had moved to his belt, perched beside the handle of his knife.

'Galen?' she asked gently. 'What are you doing?'

The question appeared to jar him. 'What makes you say that?'

'The way you're staring at me. What you're doing with your hand.'

He dropped his gaze to look. A little *hmm* sound rose in the back of his throat. 'I don't know,' he said, frowning. 'I guess you've got me there.'

'Won't they be looking for you on the catwalk? Aren't you supposed to be there?'

There was, she thought, something strangely inward about his expression, as if he wasn't quite seeing her. 'I guess I better go,' he said.

But still he made no effort to leave, nor to move his hand away.

'So I'll see you in a few days,' Mausami said.

'What do you mean?'

'Because you're going to the station, Galen. Isn't that what you said?'

A glimmer of recognition came into his face. 'Yeah, I'm going down there tomorrow.'

'So take care of yourself, okay? I mean it. All eyes.'

'Right. All eyes.'

She listened to his footsteps receding down the hall, the sound abruptly muffled as the door to the Big Room sealed in his wake. Only then did Mausami realize that she had slid one of her knitting needles free and was clutching it in her fist. She looked around the room, which suddenly seemed too large, a place abandoned, empty of its cribs and cots. All the Littles gone.

The feeling touched her then, a cold shiver from within: something was about to happen.

VI

THE NIGHT
OF BLADES
AND STARS

Swift as a shadow, short as any dream,
Brief as the lightning in the collied night,
That, in a spleen, unfolds both heaven and earth,
And ere a man hath power to say, 'Behold!'
The jaws of darkness do devour it up:
So quick bright things come to confusion.

– SHAKESPEARE,
A Midsummer Night's Dream

THIRTY-FIVE

For ninety-two years, eight months, and twenty-six days, since the last bus had driven up the mountain, the souls of First Colony had lived in this manner:

Under the lights.

Under the One Law.

According to custom.

According to instinct.

In the day-to-day.

With only themselves, and those they had made, for company.

Under the protection of the Watch.

Under the authority of the Household.

Without the Army.

Without memory.

Without the world.

Without the stars.

For Auntie, alone in her house in the glade, the night – the Night of Blades and Stars – commenced like so many nights before it: she was sitting at the table in her steam-fogged kitchen, writing in her book. That afternoon she had taken a batch of pages off the line, stiff with the sun – they always felt to her like squares of captured sunlight – and had passed the remainder of the daylight hours preparing them: trimming the edge on her cutting board, opening the binding and its covers of stretched lambskin, carefully undoing the stitching that held the pages in place, taking up her needle and thread to sew the new ones in. It was slow work, satisfying in the way of all things that required time and concentration, and by the time she was finished, the lights were coming on.

Funny how everyone thought she had just the one book.

The volume she was writing in, by her closest recollection, was the twenty-seventh of its kind. It seemed she was always opening a drawer or stacking cups in a cabinet or sweeping under the bed and coming across another one. She supposed that was the reason she put them away like she did, here and there, not in a neat line on some shelf to look at. Whenever she found one, it felt like bumping into an old friend.

Most told the same stories. Stories she remembered of the world and how it was. Time to time a bit of something would sail out of the blue, a memory she'd forgotten she had, like television, and the silly things she used to watch (its flickering blue-green glow and her daddy's voice: *Ida, turn that damn thing off, don't you know it rots your brain?*); or something would set her off, the way a ray of sunshine drizzled over a leaf or a breeze with a certain smell in its currents, and the feelings would start to move through her, ghosts of the past. A day in a park in autumn and a fountain billowing water and the way the afternoon light seemed to catch in its spray, like a huge sparkling flower; her friend Sharise, the girl from down the corner, sitting beside her on a step to show her a tooth she'd lost, holding it with its bloody stump in her palm for Auntie to see. (*Ain't no such thing as the tooth fairy, I know it, but she always brings me a dollar.*) Her mama folding laundry in the kitchen, wearing her favorite summer dress of pale green, and the puff of scent from the towel she was snapping and folding against her chest. When this happened, Auntie knew it would be a good night of writing, memories opening into other memories, like a hall of doors her mind could walk down, keeping her busy till the morning sun was rising in the windows.

But not tonight, thought Auntie, dipping the nib of her pen into the cup of ink and smoothing the page flat beneath her hand. Tonight was not a night for these old things. It was Peter she meant to write on. She expected he'd be along directly, this boy with the stars inside him.

Things came to her in their way. She supposed it was because she'd lived so long, like she was a book herself and the book was made of years. She remembered the night Prudence Jaxon had appeared at her door. The woman was sick with the cancer, well on her way, much before her time. Standing there in Auntie's door with the box pressed to her chest, so brittle and thin it was like she could blow away in the wind. Auntie had seen it so many times in her life, this bad thing in the bones, and there was never any right thing to do except to listen and do like the person asked, and that was what Auntie did for Prudence Jaxon that night. She took the box and kept it safe, and it wasn't but a month before Prudence Jaxon was dead.

He has to come to it on his own. Those were the words Prudence had said to Auntie, true words; for it was the way of all things. The things of your life arrived in their own time, like a train you had to catch. Sometimes this was easy, all you had to do was step onto it, the train was plush and comfortable and full of people smiling at you in a hush, and a conductor who punched your ticket and tousled your head with his big hand, saying, *Ain't you pretty, ain't you the prettiest girl now, lucky lady taking a big train trip with your daddy*, while you sank into the dreamy softness of your seat and sipped ginger ale from a can and watched the world float in magical silence past your window, the tall buildings of the city in the crisp autumn light and then the backs of the houses with laundry flapping and a crossing with gates where a boy was waving from his bicycle, and then the woods and fields and a single cow eating grass.

But Peter, she thought; it wasn't the train but Peter she had meant to write on. (Only where had they been going? Auntie wondered. Where had they taken a train to that one time, the two of them together, she and her daddy, Monroe Jaxon? They had been going to visit her gramma and cousins, Auntie remembered, in a place he called *Downsouth*.) Peter, and the train. Because sometimes it was one way, easy, and sometimes it was the other, not easy; the things of your life roared down to you and it was all you could do to grab hold and hang on. Your old life ended and the train took you away to another, and the next thing you knew you were standing in the dust with helicopters and soldiers all around, and all you had to remember folks by was the picture you found in the pocket of your coat, the one your mama, who you would never see again in all the days of your life, had slipped in there when she'd hugged you at the door.

By the time Auntie heard the knock, the screen opening and slapping as the person who'd come calling let themselves in, she'd almost stopped her stupid old crying. She'd sworn to herself she wouldn't do it anymore. Ida, she'd said to herself, no more crying over things you can't do nothing about. But here she was, all these years gone by, and still she could work herself into such a state whenever she thought about her mama, tucking that picture in her pocket, knowing that by the time Ida found it, the two of them would be dead.

'Auntie?'

She'd expected it would be Peter, come with his questions about the girl, but it wasn't. She didn't recognize the face, floating in the fog of her vision. A squished-up narrow man's face, like he'd gotten it jammed in a door.

'It's Jimmy, Auntie. Jimmy Molyneau.'

Jimmy Molyneau? That didn't seem right. Wasn't Jimmy Molyneau dead?

'Auntie, you're crying.'

'Course I'm crying. Got something in my eye is all.'

He slid into the chair across from her. Now that she had found the right pair of glasses from the lanyards around her neck, she saw that he was, as he claimed, a Molyneau. That nose: it was a Molyneau nose.

'What you want then? You come about the Walker?'

'You know about her, Auntie?'

'Runner came by this morning. Said they found a girl.'

She couldn't say for sure what all he wanted. There was something sad about him, defeated seeming. Usually Auntie would have welcomed a bit of company, but as the silence continued, this strange, sullen man she only vaguely recalled sitting across from her with a hangdog look on his face, she began to feel impatient. Folks shouldn't just come barging into a place with nothing on their minds.

'I don't really know why I came by. There was something I think I was supposed to tell you.' He sighed heavily, rubbing a hand over his face. 'I really should be on the Wall, you know.'

'You say so.'

'Yeah, well. That's where the First Captain should be, right? On the Wall?' He wasn't looking at her; he was looking at his hands. He shook his head in a way that seemed like maybe the Wall was the last place on earth he wanted to be. 'It's something, huh? Me, First Captain.'

Auntie had nothing to say to that. Whatever was on this man's mind, it had nothing to do with her. There were times when you couldn't fix what was broken with words, and this looked like one of those times.

'You think I could have a cup of tea, Auntie?'

'You want, I make you one.'

'If it's no trouble.'

It was, but there seemed no escaping it. She rose and put the kettle on to boil. All the while the man, Jimmy Molyneau, sat silently at the table, looking at his hands. When the water began to thrum in its kettle she poured it through the strainer into a pair of cups and carried it back.

'Careful. It hot now.'

He took a cautious sip. He seemed to have lost all interest in talking. Which was fine by her, all things considered. Folks came in time to time to talk about a problem, private things, probably thinking since she lived alone like she did and saw almost no one that she'd have nobody to tell. Usually it was women, come to talk about their husbands, but not always. Maybe this Jimmy Molyneau had a problem with his wife.

'You know what people say about your tea, Auntie?' He was frowning into his cup, like the answer he was looking for might be floating in there.

'What's that now?'

'That it's the reason you've lived so long.'

More minutes passed, a weighty silence pressing down. At last he took a final sip of tea, grimacing at the taste, and returned it to the table.

'Thanks, Auntie.' He climbed wearily to his feet. 'I guess I better be going. It's been nice talking to you.'

'Ain't no bother.'

He paused at the door, one hand poised on the frame. 'It's Jimmy,' he said. 'Jimmy Molyneau.'

'I know who you are.'

'Just in case,' he said. 'In case anybody asks.'

The events that began with Jimmy's visit to Auntie's house were destined to be misremembered, beginning with the name. The Night of Blades and Stars was, in fact, three separate nights, with a pair of days between. But as with all such occurrences – those destined to be recounted not only in the immediate aftermath but for many years to come – time seemed compressed; it is a common error of memory to impose upon such events the coherence of a concentrated narrative, beginning with the assignment of a specific interval of time. That season. That year. The Night of Blades and Stars.

The error was compounded by the fact that the events of the night of the sixty-fifth of summer, from which the rest descended, unfolded in a series of discrete compartments with overlapping chronologies, no single piece being wholly aware of the others. Things were happening everywhere. For instance: while Old Chou was rising from the bed he shared with his young wife, Constance, propelled by a mysterious urge to go to the Storehouse, across the Colony, Walter Fisher was thinking the same thing. But the fact that he was too drunk to get out of bed and lace his boots would delay his visit to the Storehouse, and his discovery of what lay there, by twenty-four hours. What these two men had in common was that they had both seen the girl, the Girl from Nowhere, when the Household had visited the Infirmary at first light; but it was also true that not everyone who had encountered her firsthand experienced this reaction. Dana Curtis, for instance, was wholly unaffected, as was Michael Fisher. The girl herself was not a source but a conduit, a way for a certain feeling – a feeling of lost souls – to enter the minds of the most susceptible parties, and there were some, like Alicia, who would never be affected at all. This was not true of Sara Fisher and Peter Jaxon, who had experienced their own versions of the girl's power. But in each case, their encounters had taken a more benign, if still troubling form: a moment of communion with their beloved dead.

First Captain Jimmy Molyneau, lurking in the shadows outside his house at the edge of the glade – he had yet to appear on the catwalk, a cause of considerable confusion for the Watch, leading to the hasty deputizing of Sanjay's nephew Ian as First Captain *pro tem* – was trying to decide whether or not to go to the Lighthouse, kill whomever he found there, and turn the lights off. Though the impulse to perform such a grave and final act had been building in him all day, it was not until he had gazed into his teacup in Auntie's steam-fogged kitchen that the idea had crystallized into a specific shape in his mind, and if anyone had happened upon him standing there and asked what he was doing, he wouldn't have known what to say. He could not have explained this desire, which seemed both to originate from some deep place within him and yet not be entirely his own. Sleeping inside the house were his daughters, Alice and Avery, and his wife, Karen. There were times in the course of his marriage, whole years, when Jimmy had not loved Karen as he should have (he was secretly in love with Soo Ramirez), but he had never doubted her love for him, which seemed boundless and unwavering, finding its physical expression in their two girls, who looked exactly like her. Alice was eleven, Avery nine. In the presence of their gentle eyes and tender, heart-shaped faces and sweetly melancholy dispositions – they were both known to burst into tears at the slightest provocation – Jimmy had always felt a reassuring force of historical continuum and, when the black feelings came, as they sometimes did, a tide of darkness that felt like drowning from within, it was always the thought of his daughters that would lift him from his gloom.

And yet the longer he stood there, skulking in the shadows, the more his impulse to douse the lights seemed wholly unrelated to, and hence beyond the reach of, the idea of his sleeping family. He felt strange within himself, very strange, as if his vision were collapsing. He stepped away from his house and by the time he reached the base of the Wall, he knew what he had to do. He felt an overwhelming relief, soothing as a bath of water, as he ascended the ladder, which connected with Firing Platform Nine. Firing Platform Nine was known as the odd-man post; because of its location above the cutout, an irregularity in the shape of the Wall to accommodate the power trunk, it was not visible from either of the adjacent platforms. It was the worst duty, the loneliest duty, and this was where Jimmy knew Soo Ramirez would be tonight.

Though her emotions had yet to consolidate into anything more specific than a nameless dread, Soo as well had been feeling troubled all night. But these feelings, of something vaguely not right, were diffused by other, more personal recriminations: the array of disappointments brought about by being asked to step down as First Captain. As Soo had discovered in the hours since the inquest, this was not an entirely unwelcome development – the responsibilities had begun to take their toll – and she would've had to step down eventually. But getting herself fired was hardly the way she wanted to do it. She'd gone straight home and sat in her kitchen and cried for a good two hours. Forty-three years old, nothing ahead of her but nights on the catwalk and the odd dutiful meal with Cort, who meant well enough but who'd run out of things to say to her about a thousand years ago; the Watch was all she had. Cort was in the stables like always, and for a minute or two she wished he was at home, though it was just as well he wasn't, since he probably would have just stood there with that helpless look on his face, not moving to comfort her, such gestures being completely beyond his powers of expression. (Three dead babies inside her – three! – and he'd never known what to say even then. But that was years ago.)

She had no one to blame but herself. That was the worst part about it. Those stupid books! Soo had come across them at Share, idly sifting through the bins where Walter kept the stuff nobody wanted. It was all because of those stupid books! Because once she'd cracked the binding on the first one – she'd actually sat down on the floor to read, folding her legs under her like a Little in circle – she'd felt herself being sucked down into it, like water down a drain. (*'Why, if it isn't Mr Talbot Carver,' exclaimed Charlene DeFleur, descending the stairs in her long rustling ball gown, her eyes wide in an expression of frank alarm at the sight of the tall, broad-shouldered man standing in the hallway in his dusty riding breeches, the fabric smoothly taut against his virile form. 'What ever could you intend, coming here while my father is away?' Belle of the Ball* by Jordana Mixon; The Passionate Press, Irvington, New York, 2014.) There was a picture of the author inside the back cover: a smiling woman with flowing handfuls of dark hair, reclining on a bed of lacy pillows. Her arms and throat were bare; atop her head was perched a peculiar, disklike hat – a hat not large enough even to keep the rain off.

By the time Walter Fisher had appeared by the bin, Soo had read to chapter three; the sound of his voice was so intrusive, so alien to her experience of the words on the pages, that she actually jumped. Anything good? Walter asked, his eyebrows lifting inquisitively. You seem pretty interested. Seeing as it's you, Walter went on, I can let you have the whole box for an eighth. Soo should have bargained, that's what you did with Walter Fisher, the price was never the price; but in her heart she'd already bought them. Okay, she said, and hoisted the box off the floor. You've got yourself a deal.

The Lieutenant's Lover, Daughter of the South, The Hostage

Bride, A Lady at Last: never in all her life had Soo read anything like these books. Whenever Soo imagined the Time Before, the thought was synonymous with machines – cars and engines and televisions and kitchen stoves and other things of metal and wire she had seen in Banning but did not know the purpose of. She supposed it had also been a world of people, too, all kinds of people, going about their business in the day-to-day. But because these people were gone, leaving behind only the ruined machines they had made, the machines were what she thought of. And yet the world she found between the covers of these books did not appear so very different from her own. The people rode horses and heated their homes with wood and lit their rooms with candlelight, and this material sameness had surprised her, while also opening her mind to the stories, which were happy stories of love. There was sex, too, lots of sex, and it wasn't at all like the sex she knew with Cort. It was fiery and passionate, and sometimes she found herself wanting to hurry through the pages to get to one of these scenes, though she didn't; she wanted to make it last.

She never should have brought one to the Wall that night, the night the girl had appeared. That was her big mistake. Soo hadn't meant to, not really; she'd been carrying the book around in her pouch all day, hoping for a free minute, and had forgotten it was there. Well, maybe not forgotten, not exactly; but certainly it hadn't been Soo's intention, as things had occurred, that she should decide to make a quick visit to the Armory – where, alone in the quiet with no one to see her, she had pulled it out and started to read. The book she'd brought was *Belle of the Ball* (she'd read them all and started over), and encountering its opening passages for the second time – the impetuous Charlene descending the stairs to find the arrogant and mutton-whiskered Talbot Carver, her father's rival, whom she loved but also hated – Soo found herself instantly reliving the pleasures of her first discovery, a feeling magnified by the knowledge that Charlene and Talbot, after much hemming and hawing, would find each other in the end. That was the best thing about the stories in the books: they always ended well.

These were Soo's thoughts when, twenty-four hours later, busted from First Captain, *Belle of the Ball* still stashed in her pouch (why couldn't she just leave the damn thing at home?), she heard footsteps ascending behind her and turned to see Jimmy Molyneau climbing off the ladder onto Firing Platform Nine. Of course it would be Jimmy. Probably he had come to gloat, or apologize, or some awkward combination of the two. Though he was hardly one to talk, Soo thought bitterly, not showing up at First Bell.

Jimmy? she said. Where the hell have you been?

The night was inhabited by dreams. In the houses and barracks, in the Sanctuary and Infirmary, dreams moved through the dozing souls of First Colony, alighting here and there, like wafting spirits.

Some, like Sanjay Patal, had a secret dream, one they'd been having all their lives. Sometimes they were aware of this dream and sometimes they were not; the dream was like an underground river, constantly flowing, that might from time to time rise to the surface, briefly washing their daylight hours with its presence, as if they were walking in two worlds at the same time. Some dreamed of a woman in her kitchen, breathing smoke. Others, like the Colonel, dreamed of a girl, alone in the dark. Some of these dreams became nightmares – what Sanjay did not remember, had never remembered, was the part of the dream that involved the knife – and sometimes the dream wasn't like a dream at all; it was more real than reality itself, it sent the dreamer stumbling helplessly into the night.

Where did they come from? What were they made of? Were they dreams or were they something more – intimations of a hidden reality, an invisible plane of existence that revealed itself only at night? Why did they feel like memories, and not just memories – someone *else's* memories? And why, on this night, did the entire population of First Colony seem to lapse into this dreamer's world?

In the Sanctuary, one of the three J's, Little Jane Ramirez, daughter of Belle and Rey Ramirez – the same Rey Ramirez who, having found himself suddenly and terrifyingly alone at the power station, and troubled by dark urges he could neither contain nor express, was, at that moment, cooking himself to a crisp on the electrified fence – was dreaming of a bear. Jane had just turned four years old. The bears she knew were the ones in books and in stories Teacher told – large, mild creatures of the forest whose hairy bulk and gentle faces were the seat of a benign animal wisdom – and that was true of the bear in her dream, at least at the beginning. Jane had never seen an actual bear, but she had seen a viral. She was among the Littles of the Sanctuary who had actually beheld the viral Arlo Wilson with her own eyes. She had been rising from her cot, which was positioned in the last row, farthest from the door – she was thirsty and had meant to ask Teacher for a cup of water – when he had burst through the window in a great shattering of glass and metal and wood, landing practically on top of her. She had thought at first it was a man, because it seemed like a man, with a man's displacement and presence. But he wasn't wearing any clothes, and there was something different about him, especially his eyes and mouth, and the way he seemed to glow. He was looking at her in a sad way – his sadness seemed suggestively bearlike – and Jane was about to ask him what was wrong and why he glowed like that when she heard a cry behind her and turned to see Teacher racing toward them. She passed over Jane like a cloud, the blade she kept hidden in a sheath beneath her billowing skirt clutched in her outstretched hand, one arm raised over her head to bring it down upon him like a hammer. The next part Jane did not see – she had dropped to the floor and begun to scramble away – but she heard a soft cry and a ripping sound and the thud of something falling. This was followed by more yelling – 'Over here!' someone was saying, 'look over here!' – and then more screams and shouts and a general commotion of grown-ups, of mothers and fathers coming in and out, and the next thing Jane knew she was being pulled from under her cot and whisked with all the other Littles up the stairs by a woman who was crying. (Only later did she realize that this woman was her mother.)

Nobody had explained these confusing events, nor had Jane told anyone what she'd seen. Teacher was nowhere around; some of the Littles – Fanny Chou and Bowow Greenberg and Bart Fisher – were whispering that she was dead. But Jane didn't think she was. To be dead was to lie down and sleep forever, and the woman whose airborne leap she had witnessed did not seem even slightly tired. Just the opposite: at that moment, Teacher had seemed wondrously, powerfully alive, animated by a grace and strength that Jane had never experienced – that even now, a whole night later, excited and embarrassed her. Hers was a compact existence of compact movements, a place of order and safety and quiet routine. There were the usual squabbles and hurt feelings, and days when Teacher seemed cross from beginning to end, but in general the world Jane knew was bathed in an essential mildness. Teacher was the source of this feeling; it radiated from her person in a blush of maternal warmth, as the rays of the sun heated the air and earth; but now, in the perplexing aftermath of the night's events, Jane sensed she had glimpsed something secret about this woman who had so selflessly cared for all of them.

That was when it had occurred to Jane that the thing she'd seen was love. It could be nothing less than the force of love that had lifted Teacher into the air, into the waiting arms of the glowing bear-man, whose light was the radiance of royalty. He was a bear-prince who had come to take her away to his castle in the forest. So perhaps that was where Teacher had gone off to now, and why all the Littles had been moved upstairs: to wait for her. When she returned to them, her rightful identity as a queen of the forest revealed, they would

575

be brought back downstairs to the Big Room, to welcome and celebrate her with a grand party.

These were the stories Jane was telling herself as she fell asleep in a room with fifteen other sleeping Littles, all dreaming their various dreams. In Jane's dream, which commenced as a rewriting of the prior night's events, she was jumping up and down on her bed in the Big Room when she saw the bear come in. He did not enter through the window this time but through the door, which seemed small and far away, and he was different than he'd been the night before, fat and woolly like the bears in books, lumbering his wise and friendly way toward her on all fours. When he reached the foot of Jane's bed he sat on his haunches and gradually drew himself upright, revealing the downy carpet of his great smooth tummy, his immense bear head and damp bear eyes and huge, paddled hands. It was a wonderful thing to see, strange and yet expected, like a present Jane had always believed would arrive, and her four-year-old's heart was moved to a rush of admiration for this great noble being. He stood in this manner a moment, taking her in with a thoughtful expression, then said to Jane, who had continued her happy bouncing, addressing her in the rich, masculine tone of his woodland home, Hello, Little Jane. I'm Mister Bear. I have come to eat you up.

This came out as funny – Jane felt a tickling in her stomach that was the beginning of a laugh – but the bear did not react, and as the moment elongated, she noticed there were other aspects to his person, disturbing aspects: his claws, which emerged in white curves from his mittlike paws; his wide and powerful jaws; his eyes, which did not seem friendly or wise anymore but dark with unknowable intention. Where were the other Littles? Why was Jane alone in the Big Room? But she wasn't alone; Teacher was in the dream now also, standing beside the bed. She looked as she always looked, though there was something vague about the features of her face, as if she were wearing a mask of gauzy fabric. Come on now, Jane, urged Teacher. He's already eaten all the other Littles.

Be good and stop that jumping so Mister Bear can eat you up. *I – don't – want – to*, Jane replied, still bouncing, for she did not want to be eaten – a request that seemed more silly than frightening, but even so. *I – don't – want – to*. I mean it, warned Teacher, her voice rising. I am asking you nicely, Little Jane. I am going to count to three. *I – don't – want – to*, Jane repeated, applying the greatest possible vigor to her defiant bouncing. *I – don't – want – to*. Do you see? said Teacher, turning to the bear, who had continued his upright vigil at the foot of the cot. She raised her pale arms in exasperation. Do you see now? This is what I have to put up with, all day long. It's enough to make a person lose her mind. Okay, Jane, she said, if that's how you're going to be. Don't say I didn't warn you.

Which was when the dream took its last, sinister turn into the realm of nightmare. Teacher had seized Jane by the wrists, forcing her down onto the bed. Up close, Jane saw that a piece of Teacher's neck was missing, like a bite snatched from an apple, and there were thready things hanging there, a collection of dangling strips and tubes, wet and glistening and gross. Only then did Jane understand that all the other Littles had indeed been eaten, just as Teacher had said; they'd all been eaten by Mister Bear, bite by bite by bite, though he wasn't Mister Bear anymore, he was the glowing man. *I don't want this*, Jane was screaming, *I don't want this!* But she had no strength to resist, and she watched in helpless terror as first her foot and then her ankle and then the whole of her leg were swallowed into the dark cave of his mouth.

The dreams bespoke a range of concerns, influences, tastes. There were as many dreams as there were dreamers. Gloria Patal dreamed of a massive swarm of bees, covering her body. Part of her understood these bees to be symbolic; each bee that crawled upon her flesh was a worry she had carried in her life. Small worries, like whether or not it would rain on a day when she had planned to work outside, or whether or not Mimi, Raj's widow, her only real friend, was angry with her on a day when she had failed to visit; but larger worries, too. Worries about Sanjay, and about Mausami. The worry that the pain in her lower back and the cough that sometimes woke her at night were harbingers of something worse. Included in this catalog of apprehensions were the worried love she had felt for each of the babies she had failed to carry to term, and the knot of dread that tightened inside her each night at Evening Bell, and the more generalized worry that she – that all of them – might just as well be dead already, for all the chance they had. Because you couldn't not think about it; you did your best to carry on (that's what Gloria had told her daughter when she'd announced her intentions to marry Galen, crying all the while over Theo Jaxon; you had to carry on), but the facts were the facts: someday those lights were going out. So perhaps the greatest worry of all was that one day you would realize that all the worries of your life amounted to one thing: the desire to just stop worrying.

That's what the bees were, they were worries large and small, and in the dream they were moving all over her, her arms and legs and face and eyes, even inside her ears. The setting of the dream was contiguous with Gloria's last moment of consciousness; having tried without success to rouse her husband, and having fended off the inquiries of Jimmy and Ian and Ben and the others who had come to seek his counsel – the matter of the boy Caleb had yet to be determined – Gloria had, against her better instincts, dozed off at the table of her kitchen, her head rocked back, her mouth hanging open, soft snores issuing from deep within her sinuses. This was all true in the dream – the sound of her snoring was the sound of the bees – with the singular addition of the swarm, which had, for reasons that were not entirely clear, entered the kitchen to settle in a single mass upon her, like a great quivering blanket. It seemed obvious now that this was the sort of thing bees did; why had she failed to protect herself against this eventuality? Gloria could feel the prickling scrape of their tiny feet on her skin, the buzzing flutter of their wings. To move, she knew, even to breathe, would arouse them into a lethal fury of simultaneous stinging. In this condition of excruciating stasis she remained – it was a dream of not moving – and when she heard the sound of Sanjay's footsteps descending the stairs, and felt his presence in the room, followed by his wordless departure and the slap of the screen door as he stepped from the house, Gloria's mind lit up with a silent scream that launched her into consciousness while also erasing any memory of what had happened: she awakened having forgotten not only about the bees, but about Sanjay.

On the other side of the Colony, lying on his cot in a cloud of his own smell, the man known as Elton, a lifelong fantasist of splendidly ornate and erotic flights, was having a good dream. This dream – the hay dream – was Elton's favorite, because it was true, taken from life. Though Michael did not believe him – and, really, Elton had to admit, why would he? – there had been a time, many years ago, when Elton, a man of twenty, had enjoyed the favors of an unknown woman who had chosen him, or so it appeared, because his blindness guaranteed his silence. If he didn't know who this woman was – and she never spoke to him – he couldn't say anything, which implied that she was married. Perhaps she wanted a child with a man who wasn't able, or had simply wished for something else in her life. (In self-pitying moments, Elton wondered if she'd done it on a dare.) It didn't really matter; he welcomed these visits, which always came at night. Sometimes he would simply awaken into the experience, its distinctive sensations, as if the reality had been called forth out of a dream, to which it would then return, fueling the empty nights to come; on other occasions the woman would come to him, take him silently by the hand, and lead him elsewhere. This was the circumstance of the hay dream, which unfolded in the barn, surrounded by the whinnying of horses and the sweet dry smell of grass, lately cut from the field. The woman did not speak; the only sounds she made were the sounds of love; and it ended much too quickly, with a final shuddering exhalation and a mound of hair brushing over his cheeks as the woman released herself, rising word-lessly away. He always dreamed these events just as they'd occurred, in all their tactile contours, up to the moment when, lying alone on the floor of the barn, wishing only to have seen the woman, or even just to have heard her speak his name, he tasted salt on his lips and knew that he was crying.

But not tonight. Tonight, just as it was ending, she bent to his face and whispered into his ear:

'Somebody's in the Lighthouse, Elton.'

In the Infirmary, Sara Fisher was not dreaming, but the girl appeared to be. Sitting on one of the empty cots, feeling brightly, almost painfully awake, Sara watched the girl's eyes flickering behind her lids, as if darting over an unseen land-scape. Sara had pretty much convinced Dale to keep his mouth shut, promising that she would tell the Household in the morning; for now the girl needed sleep. As if to support this claim, that was precisely what the girl had done, curling on the cot in that self-protective way she had, while Sara watched her, wondering what the thing in her neck had been, what Michael would find, and why, looking at the girl, Sara believed she was dreaming about snow.

There were others, quite a few, who were not sleeping either. The night was alive with wakeful souls. Galen Strauss, for one: standing at his post on the north wall – Firing Plat-form Ten – squinting into the pooling glow of the lights, Galen was telling himself, for the hundredth time that day, that he wasn't a complete fool. The need to say this – he had actually caught himself muttering the words under his breath – meant of course he was. Even he knew that. He was a fool. He was a fool because he'd believed he could make Mausami love him, as he loved her; he was a fool because he'd married her when everyone knew she was in love with Theo Jaxon; he was a fool because when she'd told him about the baby, spouting her stupid lie about how many months it was, he'd swallowed his pride and plastered an idiotic smile on his face, saying only: A baby. Wow. How about that.

He'd known damn well whose baby it was. One of the wrenches, Finn Darrell, had told Galen about that night down at the station. Finn had gotten up to take a leak and, hearing a noise from one of the storage rooms, had gone to check it out. The door was closed, Finn explained, but you didn't have to open it to know what was happening on the other side. Finn was the kind of guy who took a little too much pleasure from giving you news he thought you needed to hear; from the way he told the story, Galen guessed he'd stood outside the door a lot longer than he needed to. Jeez, Finn said, she always make noises like that?

Fucking Finn Darrell. Fucking Theo Jaxon.

And yet, for a hopeful moment, Galen had entertained the notion that maybe a baby would make things better between them. A dumb idea, but still he'd thought it. But of course the baby only made them fight more. If Theo had returned from that ride down the mountain, probably they would have told him right then; Galen could pretty much imagine the scene. We're sorry, Galen. We should have told you. It just kind of . . . happened. Humiliating, but at least it would have been over by now. The way things stood, he and Maus would have to live with this lie between them forever. Probably they'd end up despising each other, if they didn't despise each other already.

He was thinking these things while also dreading the morning to come, when he was supposed to ride down to the station. The order had come from Ian, though Galen had the feeling it wasn't his idea, that it came from somewhere else – Jimmy, probably, or maybe Sanjay. He could take a runner with him, but that was all; they couldn't spare the hands. Box it up and wait for the next relief crew, Ian had said, three days tops. Okay, Galen? You can handle this? And of course he'd said he could, no problem. He'd even felt a little flattered. But as the hours passed, he'd found himself regretting his quick compliance. He'd been off the mountain only a few times before, and it was awful – all those empty buildings and slims cooking in their cars – but that wasn't the worst of it, not really. The problem was that Galen was afraid. He was afraid all the time now, more and more as the days went by and the world around him continued its slow, hazy dissolving. People didn't really know how bad his eyesight was, not even Maus. They knew, but they didn't really *know*, not the full extent, and every day it seemed to be getting worse. As things stood, his field of vision had shrunk to less than two meters; everything beyond that quickly faded into a gassy blankness, all lurching shapes and formless colors and halos of light. He'd tried a variety of eyeglasses from the Storehouse, but nothing seemed to help; all he'd gotten for his troubles were headaches that felt like someone sticking a blade into his temple, so he had long since stopped trying. He was pretty good with voices and could generally aim his face in the right direction, but he missed a lot of things, and he knew this made him seem slow and stupid, which he wasn't. He was just going blind.

Now here he was, a Second Captain of the Watch, riding down the mountain in the morning to secure the station. A trip that, considering what had happened to Zander and Arlo, pretty much felt like suicide to Galen Strauss. He was hoping he'd have a chance to talk to Jimmy about it, maybe make him see some sense, but so far, the guy had not shown up.

And, come to think of it, where *was* Jimmy? Soo was out there someplace, and Dana Curtis; with Arlo and Theo gone, and Alicia off the Watch for good, Dana had come out of the pits to guard the Wall like everybody else. Galen got along with Dana, and the fact that she was Household now, he reasoned, might give her some sway with Jimmy. Maybe the two of them should talk about this whole go-down-to-the-station thing. Soo was on Nine, Dana on Eight. If he was quick about it, Galen could be back to his post in a matter of just a few minutes. And in point of fact, wasn't that sound he was hearing – a sound of voices nearby, though noises traveled well at night – wasn't that Soo Ramirez? And wasn't the other voice Jimmy's? If Galen could round up Dana too, might it be just a matter of a few right words to get Jimmy to see a little sense? Maybe get Soo or Dana to say, Well, sure, I can go down to the station, I don't see why Galen should be the one?

Just a couple of minutes, Galen thought and, taking up his cross, he began to make his way down the catwalk.

At the same time, hidden away in the old FEMA trailer, Peter and Alicia were playing hands of go-to. With just the light of the spots to see by, the game had an unfocused quality, but both had long since stopped caring who won, if they'd ever cared in the first place. Peter was trying to decide what he should tell Alicia about what had happened in the Infirmary, the voice he'd heard in his mind, but with each passing minute it became more difficult to imagine actually doing this, how he might explain himself. He'd heard *words* in his *head*. His mother *missed him*. I must be dreaming, he told himself, and when Alicia broke his train of thought with an impatient lift of her cards, he only shook his head. It's nothing, he told her. Play your hand.

Also awake at that hour, half-plus-one on the log of the Watch, was Sam Chou. Sam longed for nothing so much as the comfort of his bed and his wife's affectionate arms around him. But with Sandy bedding down in the Sanctuary – she had volunteered to take over for April until someone else could be found – he had suffered a disruption to these customary rhythms, leaving him staring at the ceiling. He was also troubled by a feeling that, as the day had moved into night, he had recognized as embarrassment. That funny business at the lockup: he couldn't quite explain it. In the heat of the moment, he'd honestly believed that something had to be done. But in the intervening hours, and after a trip to the Sanctuary to visit with his children – who seemed none the worse for wear – Sam had discovered that his feelings about the whole Caleb situation had moderated substantially.

Caleb was, after all, just a kid, and Sam could now see how putting the boy out would solve very little. He felt a little guilty about manipulating Belle the way he had – with Rey down at the station, the woman was probably out of her mind with worry – and though there was certainly no love lost between him and Alicia, who was too full of herself by half, Sam had to admit that under the circumstances, with that fool Milo egging him on, it was a good thing she'd been there. Who knows what might have happened if she hadn't. When Sam had spoken to Milo later, following up on the day's conversations, most of which had presupposed that if the Household didn't do anything they would take it upon themselves to put the poor kid out, and suggested that maybe they should rethink the situation, see how things looked tomorrow after a good night's rest, Milo had responded with a look of unconcealed relief. Okay, sure, said Milo Darrell. Maybe you're right. Let's see how we feel in the morning.

So Sam was feeling a little bad now about the whole thing, bad and a little confounded, because it wasn't like him to get so angry. It wasn't like him at all. For a second there, outside the lockup, he really had believed it: somebody had to pay. It didn't seem to matter that it was just a defenseless kid who probably thought someone on the catwalk had told him to open the gate. And the most extraordinary thing, really, was that in all that time, Sam hadn't given much or even any thought to the girl, the Walker, who was the reason the whole thing had happened in the first place. Watching the lights of the spots playing on the eaves above his face, Sam wondered why this should be. My God, he thought, after all these years, a Walker. And not just a Walker – a young girl. Sam wasn't one of those people who believed the Army was still coming – you'd have to be pretty stupid to think so after all these years – but a girl like that, it meant something. It meant somebody was still alive out there. Maybe a whole *lot* of somebodies. And when Sam considered this, he found himself strangely . . . uncomfortable with the idea. He couldn't say quite why that was, except that the notion of this girl, this Girl from Nowhere, felt like a piece that didn't fit. And what if all these somebodies just showed up out of the blue? What if she was the beginning of a whole new wave of Walkers, seeking safety under the lights? There was only so much food and fuel to go around. Sure, back in the early days it had probably seemed too cruel to turn the Walkers away. But wasn't the situation a little different now? So many years gone by? Things having achieved a kind of balance? Because the fact was, Sam Chou liked his life. He wasn't one of the worriers, the fretters, the keepers of bad thoughts. He knew people like that – Milo, for one – and he didn't see the sense in it. Awful things could happen, sure, but that was always true, and in the meantime, he had his bed and his house and his wife and his children, they had food to eat and clothes to wear and the lights to keep them safe, and wasn't that enough? The more Sam thought about it, the more it seemed that it wasn't Caleb that something needed to be done about. It was the girl. So maybe in the morning, that's what he'd say to Milo. Something needs to be done about this Girl from Nowhere.

Also awake was Michael Fisher. In the main, Michael viewed sleep as a waste of time. It was just another case of the body's unreasonable demands upon the mind, and his dreams, when he cared to remember them, all seemed to be lightly retooled versions of his waking state – full of circuits and breakers and relays, a thousand problems to be solved, and he would awaken feeling less restored than rudely shot forward in time, with no discernible accomplishments to show for these lost hours.

But that was not the case tonight. Tonight, Michael Fisher was as awake as he'd ever been in his life. The contents of the chip, having disgorged itself into the mainframe – a veritable flood of data – was nothing less than a rewriting of the world. It was this new understanding that had inspired the risk Michael was now taking, running an antenna up to the top of the Wall. He'd started on the roof of the Lighthouse, connecting a twenty-meter spool of eight-gauge uninsulated copper wire to the antenna they'd stuffed up the chimney, months ago. Two more spools had gotten him to the base of the Wall. That was it for the copper he could spare. For the remainder he had decided to use an insulated high-voltage cable he would have to strip by hand. The trick now would be getting it up to the top of the Wall without being seen by the Watch. Having retrieved two more spools from the shed, he stood in the pocket of shadow underneath one of the supporting struts, weighing his options. The closest ladder, twenty meters to his left, led straight up to Platform Nine; there was no way he could climb this unnoticed. There was a second ladder situated midway between Platforms Eight and Seven, which would be ideal – except for the runners, who sometimes used it as a shortcut between Seven and Ten, it had very little traffic – but he didn't have enough cable to reach that far.

That left only one option. Take a spool up the far ladder, move down the catwalk until he was suspended over the cutout, anchor the end of the wire, drop it to the ground below, and descend once more to connect the second wire to the first. All without anyone seeing him.

Michael knelt in the dirt, removed his wire cutters from the old canvas rucksack he used as a toolbag, and set to work, pulling the cable from its spool and stripping the plastic conduit away. At the same time he was listening for the clanging footsteps above his head that would signify a runner going through. By the time the wire was stripped and spooled back up, he'd heard the runners move through twice; he was reasonably certain he'd have a few minutes before the next one came. Depositing everything into the rucksack, he hurried to the ladder, took a deep breath, and began to ascend.

Heights had always been a problem for Michael – he didn't like so much as standing on a chair – a fact that, in his determined state, he had failed to figure in his calculations, and by the time he reached the top of the ladder, an ascent of twenty meters that felt like ten times that many, he was beginning to doubt the wisdom of the entire enterprise. His heart was galloping with panic; his limbs had turned to gelatin. Getting down the catwalk, an open grate suspended above a maw of space, would mandate every ounce of will he possessed. His eyes had begun to sting with sweat as he pulled himself up from the final rung, sliding belly-first onto the grate. Under the glare of the lights, and without the customary reference points of ground and sky to orient him, everything seemed larger and closer, possessing a bulging vividness. But at least no one had noticed him. He cautiously lifted his face: a hundred meters to his left, Platform Eight appeared to be empty, no Watcher on station. Why that should be, Michael didn't know, but he took it as an encouraging sign. If he acted quickly, he could be back in the Lighthouse before anyone was the wiser.

He began to move down the catwalk, and by the time he was in position, he had begun to feel better – a lot better. His fear had receded, replaced by an invigorated sense of possibility. This was going to work. Platform Eight was still empty; whoever was supposed to be there would probably catch hell, but its vacancy gave Michael the opening he needed. He knelt on the catwalk and pulled the coil of wire from his rucksack. Constructed of a titanium alloy, the catwalk would make a serviceable conductor in its own right, adding its attractive electromagnetic properties to the wire's; in essence, Michael was turning the whole perimeter into a giant antenna. He used a wrench to loosen one of the bolts that attached the catwalk's decking to its frame, curled the stripped wire into the gap, and tightened down the bolt. Then he dropped the spool to the ground below, listening for the soft thud of its impact.

Amy, he thought. Who would have thought the Girl from Nowhere would have a name like Amy?

What Michael didn't know was that Firing Platform Eight was empty because the Watcher on station, Dana Curtis, First

Family and Household, was already lying dead at the base of the Wall. Jimmy had killed her right after he'd killed Soo Ramirez. Whom he honestly hadn't meant to kill; he'd only wanted to tell her something. Goodbye? I'm sorry? I always loved you? But one thing had led to another in the strangely inevitable manner of that night, the Night of Blades and Stars, and now all three of them were gone.

Galen Strauss, approaching from the opposite direction, witnessed these events as if through the fat end of a telescope: a distant splash of color and movement, far beyond the range of his vision. If it had been anybody else on Platform Ten that night, someone whose eyesight was more robust, who was not going blind from acute glaucoma as Galen Strauss was, a clearer picture of events might have emerged. As it was, what occurred on Firing Platform Nine would never be known by anyone except those directly involved; and even they did not understand it.

What happened was this:

The Watcher Soo Ramirez, her thoughts still bobbing in the currents of *Belle of the Ball* and, in particular, a scene set in a moving coach during a thunderstorm so vividly rendered that she could practically recall it word for word (*As the heavens opened, Talbot seized Charlene in his powerful arms, his mouth falling on hers with a searing force, his fingers finding the silken curve of her breast, waves of ardor roiling through her . . .*), turned to see Jimmy hoisting himself onto the platform; and her first impression, punching through her feelings of conflicted irritation (she resented the interruption; he was late) was that something wasn't right. *He doesn't look like himself,* she thought. *This isn't the Jimmy I know.* He stood a moment, his body oddly slack, his eyes squinting with perplexity into the lights; he looked like a man who had come to make an announcement, only to have forgotten his lines. Soo thought maybe she knew what this unspoken declaration was – she'd had a feeling for some time that Jimmy considered the two of them as more than friends – and under different circumstances, she might have been glad to hear this from him. But not now. Not tonight, on Firing Platform Nine.

'It's her eyes,' he said faintly; he seemed to be speaking to himself. 'At least I thought it was her eyes.'

Soo stepped toward him. His face was turned away, as if he couldn't bring himself to look at her. 'Jimmy? Whose eyes?'

But he didn't answer her. One hand reached down to the hem of his jersey and proceeded to tug at it, like a nervous boy fumbling with his clothes. 'Can't you feel it, Soo?'

'Jimmy, what are you talking about?'

He had begun to blink. Fat, jeweled tears were spilling down his cheeks. 'They're all so fucking sad.'

Something was happening to him, Soo knew, something bad. In a burst of motion he yanked his jersey over his head and flung it over the edge of the platform. His chest was glazed with sweat that shone in the lights.

'It's these clothes,' he growled. 'I can't *stand* these clothes.'

She'd left her cross resting against the rampart. She turned to reach for it but she'd waited too long, Jimmy had her from behind, his hands were sliding under her arms, wrapping the back of her neck, and with a sudden twisting motion something snapped at the base of her throat; and just like that her body was gone, her body had drifted away, her body was no more. She tried to cry out but no sound came; flecks of light were drifting in her vision, like shards of silver. (*Oh Talbot, Charlene moaned as he moved against her, his manhood a sweet invasion she could no longer deny, oh Talbot yes, let us end this absurd game . . .*) She was aware that someone else was coming toward her; she heard a sound of footsteps on the catwalk where she now lay helpless; and then the shot of a cross and muffled, breathy cry. She was in the air now, Jimmy was lifting her up; he was going to throw her over the Wall. She wished she'd lived a different life, but this was the one she had, she didn't want to leave it yet, and then she was falling, down and down and down.

She was still alive when she hit the ground. Time had slowed, reversed, started again. The spots were shining in her eyes; in her mouth, a taste of blood. Above her she saw Jimmy standing at the edge of the nets, naked and gleaming, and then he, too, was gone.

And in the last instant before all thought left her, she heard the voice of the runner Kip Darrell crying from the rampart high above: 'Sign, we have sign! Holy shit, they're everywhere!'

But he spoke these words into the darkness. The lights had all gone out.

THIRTY-SIX

The meeting was called for half-day, under a sky bulging with rain that would not fall. All souls had gathered at the Sunspot, where the long table had been carried out from the Sanctuary. Seated before the assembly were just two men: Walter Fisher and Ian Patal. Walter looked his usual, disheveled self, a wreckage of greasy hair and rheumy eyes and stained clothing he had probably worn for a season; that he was now serving as acting Head of the Household, or what remained of it, was, Peter thought, one of the day's more unpromising facts.

Ian looked far better off, but even he, after the night's events, seemed halting and uncertain, at pains even to bring the meeting to order. It was unclear to Peter what, precisely, his role was – was he sitting as a Patal or as First Captain? – but this seemed a small concern, far too technical to worry about. For now, Ian was in charge.

Standing at the edge beside Alicia, Peter scanned the crowd. Auntie was nowhere to be seen, but that did not surprise him. It had been many years since she'd attended an open meeting of the Household. Also among the missing faces he sought were Michael, who had returned to the Lighthouse, and Sara, still in the Infirmary; he saw Gloria, standing close to the front, but not Sanjay, whose where-abouts, along with Old Chou's, were the source of much of the talk around him, a hum of worry from people who simply had no idea what was happening to them. And it was worry that he heard, at least so far. Outright panic had yet to set in, but Peter saw this as only a matter of time; night would come again.

The other faces he saw, wishing he hadn't, belonged to those who had lost someone, a spouse or child or parent, in the attack. Among this group were Cort Ramirez and Russell Curtis, Dana's husband, who was standing with his daughters, Ellie and Kat, all of them looking benumbed; Karen Molyneau with her two girls, Alice and Avery, their faces washed by grief; Milo and Penny Darrell, whose son Kip, a runner, had been just fifteen years old, the youngest killed; Hodd and Lisa Greenberg, Sunny's parents; Addy Phillips and Tracey Strauss, who looked like she had aged ten years over-night, all vitality drained from her; Constance Chou, Old Chou's young wife, who was fiercely clutching their daughter, Darla, to her side – as if she, too, might slip away from her. It was this grieving body of survivors – for they stood as one, the scope of their loss both forming a cohesive bond among them while also separating them from the others, like a magnetic force that both attracted and repelled – to whom Ian seemed to aim his words when the crowd fell quiet long enough to bring the meeting to order.

Ian began with a recitation of the facts, which Peter already knew, or mostly. Shortly after half-night, for reasons unexplained, the lights had failed. This had apparently been caused by a power surge, which had flipped the main breaker. The only person in the Lighthouse at the time of the incident had been Elton, sleeping in the back; the engineer on duty, Michael Fisher, had briefly stepped out to manually reset one of the vents on the battery stack, leaving the panel unmanned. In this, Ian assured the crowd, Michael was not to blame; leaving the Lighthouse to vent the stack was entirely proper and there was no way Michael could have foreseen the surge that would cause the breaker to flip. All told, the lights had been out for less than three minutes – the time it had taken for Michael to race back to the Lighthouse and reset the system – but in that brief interval, the Wall had been breached. The last report was of a large pod massing at the fireline. By the time power was restored, three souls had been taken: Jimmy Molyneau, Soo Ramirez, and Dana Jaxon. All had been sighted at the base of the Wall, their bodies being dragged away.

That was the first wave of the attack. Ian was clearly at pains to maintain his composure as he related what had next occurred. Though the first, large pod had dispersed, a second, smaller pod of three had approached from the south, mounting an assault on the Wall near Platform Six – the same platform where, sixteen days before, the large female with the distinctive shock of hair had been killed by Arlo Wilson. The split seam that had allowed her ascent had since been repaired, so the three had found no purchase; but that, apparently, was not their intention. By now the Watch was in disarray, all hands moving toward Platform Six; under a storm of arrows and cross bolts, the three virals had tried, again and again, to ascend; while meanwhile, at the unmanned Platform Nine, a third pod – perhaps a part of the second, which had split in two; perhaps a wholly different pod in its own right – had managed to make its way over the Wall.

They'd come straight down the catwalk.

It was a melee. There was no other word. Three more Watchers had been killed before the pod had been repelled: Gar Phillips and Aidan Strauss and Kip Darrell, the runner who had first reported the massing pod at the fireline. A fourth, Sunny Greenberg, who had left her post at the lockup to join the fight, was unaccounted for and presumed lost. Also among the missing – and here Ian paused with a deeply troubled look – was Old Chou. Constance had awakened in the early-morning hours to find him gone; nobody had seen him since. So it seemed likely, though there was no

592

direct evidence of this, that he had left his house in the dead of night to go to the Wall, where among the others he'd been taken. No virals had been killed at all.

That's all, Ian said. That's what we know.

Something was happening, Peter thought; the crowd could feel it too. Never had anybody witnessed an attack like this, its tactical quality. The closest analogue was Dark Night itself, but even then, the virals had given no evidence of presenting an organized assault. When the lights had gone out, Peter had run with Alicia from the trailer park to the Wall to fight with everyone else, but Ian had ordered them both to the Sanctuary, which in the confusion had been left undefended. So what they'd seen and heard had been both softened by distance and made worse because of it. He should have been there, he knew. He should have been on the Wall.

A voice cut through the murmuring of the crowd: 'What about the power station?'

The speaker was Milo Darrell. He was holding his wife, Penny, to his side.

'As far as we know, it's still secure, Milo,' Ian said. 'Michael says there's current still flowing.'

'But you said there was a power surge! Somebody should be going down there to check it out. And where the hell is Sanjay?'

Ian hesitated. 'I was coming to that, Milo. Sanjay has taken sick. For now, Walter here is serving as Head.'

'Walter? You can't be serious.'

Walter seemed to regain focus, stiffening in his seat to lift his bleary face toward the assembly. 'Wait just a damn minute—'

But Milo cut back in. 'Walter's a drunk,' he said, his voice rising, becoming bolder. 'A drunk and a cheat. Everybody knows it. Who's really in charge here, Ian? Is it you? Because as far as I can tell, nobody is. I say open the Armory, let everybody stand the Wall who wants to. And let's get somebody down to the station right now.'

A buzz of acknowledgment shivered the crowd. What was

Milo trying to do? Peter thought. Start a riot? He glanced at Alicia; she was staring intently at Milo, her body in a posture of alert, arms held from her sides. All eyes.

'I'm sorry about your boy,' Ian said, 'but this isn't the time to go off half-cocked. Let the Watch handle this.'

But Milo paid him no attention. He swept his gaze over the assembly. 'You heard him. Ian said they were organized. Well, maybe we need to be organized, too. If the Watch won't do anything, I say we should.'

'Flyers, Milo. Calm down. People are scared, you're not helping.'

It was Sam Chou, stepping forward, who spoke next: 'They should be scared. Caleb let that girl in here, and now, what, eleven people are dead? She's the reason they're here!'

'We don't know that, Sam.'

'*I* know it. And so does everybody else. Caleb and that girl, that's where this all started. I say let it end with them, too.'

Peter heard it then, voices rising here and there: *the girl, the girl*, people were saying. *He's right. It was the girl.*

'Just what do you want us to do about it?'

'What do I want you to *do*?' Sam said. 'What you should have done already. They should be put out.' He swiveled to face the crowd. 'Everyone, listen to me! The Watch won't say it, but I will. Crosses can't protect us, not against this. I say we put them out now!'

And with that, the first echoing voice rose from the crowd, then another and another, gathering into a chorus:

Put them out! Put them out! Put them out!

It was, Peter thought, as if a lifetime of worry had come suddenly undammed. Up front, Ian was waving his arms, bellowing for silence. The scene seemed poised on the verge of violence, some terrible act. There was nothing to stop it; the pretense of order had been stripped away.

He knew it then: he had to get the girl out of here. Caleb too, whose fate was now bound up with hers. But where could they go? What place would be safe?

He turned to Alicia, but she was gone.

594

Then Peter saw her. She had barged her way through the roiling mass of people. With an agile hop she mounted the table and spun to face the assembly.

'Everybody!' she cried. 'Listen to me!'

Peter felt the crowd tense around him. A fresh dread bored through his veins. Lish, he thought, what are you doing?

'She's not the reason they're here,' Alicia said. 'I am.'

Sam hurled his voice toward her: 'Get down, Lish! This isn't up to you!'

'All of you. This is my fault. It's not the girl they want, it's me. *I* was the one who torched the library. That's what started this. It was a nest, and I led them all right back here. If you're going to put anybody out, I should be the one. I'm the reason those people are dead.'

It was Milo Darrell who made the first move, lunging toward the table. Whether or not he was trying to get to Alicia, or Ian, or even Walter was unclear; but with this provocation a force of violence was suddenly unleashed in a wave of pushing and shoving, the crowd surging forward, a vaguely coordinated mass propelled only by itself. The table was overrun; Peter saw Alicia tumbling backward, enveloped by the mob. People were screaming, shouting. Those with children seemed to be trying to move away, while others wanted only to get to the front. The only thought in Peter's mind was to reach Alicia. But as he labored to move forward, he, too, was caught in the crush of bodies. He felt his feet snarling up below him – he sensed that he was stepping on someone – and as he tumbled forward he saw who this person was: Jacob Curtis. The boy had dropped to his knees and was holding his hands protectively over his head against the rain of trampling feet. They impacted with a mutual grunt, Peter somersaulting over the boy's broad back; he scrabbled to his knees and launched forward again, rising through a mass of arms and legs, propelling himself like a swimmer through a sea of people, flinging bodies aside. Something struck him then – a blow to the back of the head that felt like a punch – and as his vision flared he turned, swinging, his fist connecting solidly with a bearded, heavy-browed face that only later did he realize belonged to Hodd Greenberg, Sunny's father. He had by this moment neared the front of the crowd; Alicia was on the ground, fleetingly visible through the throng that surrounded her. Like Jacob, she had drawn her hands up over her head, curling her body into a ball as a pummeling storm of hands and feet fell down upon her.

It wasn't even a question. Peter drew his blade.

What might have happened next, Peter never learned. From the direction of the gate came a second rush of figures: the Watch. Ben and Galen, holding crosses. Dale Levine and Vivian Chou and Hollis Wilson and the others. Weapons drawn, they quickly formed a battle line between the table and the crowd, their presence immediately sending everyone scurrying back.

'Go to your homes!' Ian shouted. Blood was soaking his hair, running down the side of his face into the neck of his jersey. His cheeks were crimson with anger; spit was soaring in bright specks from his lips. He swept his cross across the crowd, as if unable to decide whom to fire on first. 'The Household is suspended! I am declaring a state of martial law! An immediate curfew is in effect!'

Everything seemed held in a brittle silence. The mob had separated around Alicia, leaving her exposed. As Peter dropped to his knees beside her, she pivoted her dirt-streaked face toward him, the whites of her eyes enormous in their urgency.

She mouthed a single word: 'Go.'

He rose and backed away, melting into the throng – some standing, some on the ground, a few who had fallen being lifted to their feet. Everybody was covered in dust; Peter realized his mouth was choked with it. Walter Fisher was sitting by the overturned table, clutching the side of his head. Sam and Milo were nowhere visible; like Peter, they had faded away.

A pair of Watchers, Galen and Hollis, came forward and

pulled Alicia upright; she offered no resistance as Ian stripped her of her blades. Peter could tell she was injured but did not know how; her body seemed both limp and rigid at the same time, as if she were holding the pain in check. A smear of blood was on her cheek, another on her elbow. Her braid had come undone; her jersey was torn at the sleeve, hanging by threads. Ian and Galen were holding her now, each on a side, like a prisoner. It was then that Peter understood: by drawing the fury of the crowd down upon herself, she had deflected it away from the girl and bought them some time. If only to keep control of the crowd, Ian would have to put her in the lockup now. *Be ready*, her eyes had told him.

'Alicia Donadio,' Ian said, loudly enough for all to hear, 'you are under arrest. The charge is treason.'

'Put the bitch out now!' someone yelled.

'Quiet!' But Ian's voice was thin, trembling. 'I mean what I say. Go to your homes *now*. The gates will stay closed until further notice. Anyone seen out and about will be subject to arrest by the Watch. Anyone carrying a weapon will be fired on. Don't think I won't do it.'

And while Peter looked on helplessly, in a world that had become completely strange to him, among people he felt he no longer knew, the Watch led Alicia away.

THIRTY-SEVEN

In the Sanctuary, Mausami Patal, having passed a restless night and an even more restless morning in the second-floor classroom among the Littles – the story of the night's terrible events having reached her via Other Sandy, whose husband, Sam, had come in at first light – had made a decision.

The idea had come upon her with quiet suddenness; she hadn't even known she was thinking it. But she had awakened with the distinct impression that something had changed inside her. The decision had made itself known simply, almost arithmetically. She was going to have a baby. The baby was Theo Jaxon's. Because this baby was Theo Jaxon's, Theo could not be dead.

Mausami was going to find him, and tell him about their baby.

The moment to make her exit would be just before Morning Bell, at the changing of the shift. That would afford both the cover she needed and a full day's light to make it on foot down the mountain; from there she could figure out where to go. The best place to exit would be over the cutout, with its limited angles of sight. Once Sandy and the others had gone to sleep, she would slip away to the Storehouse and equip herself for the journey: a strong rope to ride down the Wall, food and water, a cross and blade, a pair of good sturdy boots and a change of clothes and a pack to carry everything in.

With the curfew, no one would be about. She would make her way to the cutout, keeping to the shadows, and wait for dawn to come.

As the plan blossomed in her mind, assuming shape and detail, Mausami came to see what she was doing: that she was staging her own death. She'd actually been doing it for days. Since the resupply party had returned, she had given every indication of a mind in distress: breaking curfew, moping like a crazy person, making everyone scramble around, worried for her safety. She couldn't have built a more convincing case if she'd tried. Even that tearful scene at Main Gate, when Lish had made her stand down, would play its part in the backtracking narrative people would assemble to explain her fate. How did we fail to see this coming? they would all say, mournfully shaking their heads. She gave us all the signs. Because in the morning, when Other Sandy awoke to discover that Mausami's cot was empty, perhaps waiting a few hours before noting the oddness of this fact but eventually reporting it, and others in due course went to search for her, the rope over the cutout would be discovered. A rope with only one possible meaning: a rope to nowhere and nothing.

There would be no other conclusion people could draw. She, the Watcher Mausami Patal Strauss, wife of Galen Strauss, daughter of Sanjay and Gloria Patal, First Family, pregnant and afraid, had chosen to let it go.

Yet here was the day. Here she was, knitting her booties in the Sanctuary – she'd made almost no progress – listening to Other Sandy chattering away, keeping the Littles occupied with games and stories and songs, the news of Mausami's death like a fact delayed – like an arrow that, once launched from its bow, had merely to sink itself into its target to reveal the meaning of its aim. She felt like a ghost. She felt like she was gone already. She thought about visiting her parents one last time, but what was there to say? How could she say goodbye without saying it? There was Galen to consider, but after last night she didn't want to see him ever again in her life. He hadn't gone down to the station after all, Other Sandy had told her, thinking this would be good news to her. Galen was among the Watchers who had arrested Alicia. Mausami wondered if Galen would be the first person they told, or the second, or the third. Would he be sad? Would he cry? Would he imagine her sliding down the Wall and feel relieved?

Her hands had paused over her knitting. She wondered if she really might be crazy. Probably she was. You'd have to be crazy, to think that Theo wasn't dead. But she didn't care.

She excused herself to Other Sandy, who waved her distractedly away – she had cleared a space for the Littles to sit in circle and was trying to quiet them, to begin their lesson for the day – and stepped into the hall, sealing the door and the voices of the children behind her. A blast of quiet that felt like noise; she stood a moment in the hushed corridor. At such a moment, it was almost possible to imagine that the world was not the world. That there was some *other* world in which the virals did not exist, as they did not exist for the Littles, who lived in a dream of the past. Which was probably the reason the Sanctuary had been built in the first place: so there was still a place like that. She moved down the hall, her sandals slapping the cracked linoleum, past the doors of the empty classrooms, and descended the stairs. The odor of spirits was still strong in the Big Room, enough to bring tears to her eyes, and yet as Mausami settled down with her knitting, she knew that she would remain there the rest of the day. She would sit in the quiet and finish knitting the baby booties, so that she could take them with her.

THIRTY-EIGHT

If asked to name the worst moment of his life, Michael Fisher wouldn't have hesitated to give his answer: it was when the lights went out.

Michael had just rolled the spool off the catwalk when it happened: a plunge into blackness so total, so consuming in its three-dimensional nothingness, that for a heart-seizing instant he wondered if he had rolled off after the spool and simply failed to notice – that this was the darkness of death. But then he heard Kip Darrell's voice – 'Sign, we have sign! Holy shit, they're everywhere!' – and the information shot into his brain that not only was he still alive but the lights, in fact, were out.

The lights were out!

That he had managed to make his way back down the catwalk and descend the ladder at something close to a dead run, in utter darkness, was a feat that, in hindsight, seemed completely incredible. He had taken the last few meters at a drop, tool bag swinging, knees bent to absorb the impact, and sprinted toward the Lighthouse. 'Elton!' he was shouting as he skidded around the corner and mounted the porch and blasted through the door. 'Elton, wake up!' He expected to find the system crashed, but when he reached the panel, Elton lumbering into the room from the other side like a big blind horse, and he saw the glow of the CRTs, all meters in the green, he froze.

Why the hell were the lights off?

He lurched across the room to the box, and there he saw the problem. The main breaker was open. All he had to do was close it, and the lights came on again.

Michael made his report to Ian at first light. The story of the power surge was the best he could come up with, to get Ian out of the Lighthouse. And he supposed a surge could do it, although this would have been logged by the system, and there was nothing in the file. The problem could have been a short somewhere, but if that were true, the breaker wouldn't have held; the circuit would have failed again the moment he flipped the switch. He'd spent the morning checking every connection, venting and reventing the ports, charging the capacitors. There was simply nothing wrong.

Was anyone in here? he asked Elton. Did you hear anything? But Elton only shook his head. I was sleeping, Michael. I was sound asleep in the back. I didn't hear a thing until you came in yelling.

It was past half-day before Michael was able to reassemble the frame of mind to return to work on the radio. In all the excitement, he'd almost forgotten about it, but as he exited the Lighthouse in search of the spool he had dropped the night before, then found it lying undisturbed in the dust, the long wire arcing up to the top of the Wall, he was convinced anew of its importance. He spliced the wire to the copper filaments he'd left in place, returned to the Lighthouse, pulled the logbook down off the shelf to check the frequency, and clamped the headphones to his ears.

Two hours later, lit with adrenaline, his hair and jersey drenched with sweat, he found Peter in the barracks. Peter was sitting on a bunk, spinning a blade around his index finger. No one else was in the room; at the sound of Michael's entry, Peter glanced up with only passing interest. He looked like something awful had happened, Michael thought. Like he wanted to use that blade on someone but couldn't decide

601

just who. And come to think of it, Michael wondered, where was everybody? Wasn't it awful damn quiet around here? Nobody ever told him anything.

'What is it?' Peter said, and resumed his melancholy spinning. 'Because whatever it is, I hope it's good news.'

'Oh my God,' said Michael. He was struggling to get the words out. 'You have to hear this.'

'Michael, do you have any idea what's going on around this place? What do I have to hear?'

'Amy,' he said. 'You have to hear Amy.'

THIRTY-NINE

In the Lighthouse, Michael took a seat at his terminal. The device they'd removed from the girl's neck now lay in pieces on a leather mat beside Michael's CRT.

'The power source,' Michael was saying, 'now, that's interesting. *Very* interesting.' With a pair of tweezers, he lifted a tiny metal capsule from inside the transmitter. 'A battery, but not like anything I've seen. Given how long it's been running, my guess is nuclear.'

Peter startled. 'Isn't that dangerous?'

'It wasn't to her, apparently. And it's been inside her a long time.'

'What's long?' Peter looked at his friend, whose face glowed with excitement. So far he'd provided only the vaguest answers to Peter's questions. 'You mean like a year?'

Michael grinned mysteriously. 'You don't know the half of it. Just hang on a minute.' He directed Peter's attention again to the object on the counter, using his tweezers to identify the parts. 'So you've got a transmitter, a battery, and then – the rest. My first guess was a memory chip, but it was way too small to fit into any of the ports on the mainframe, so I had to solder it hard.'

602

With a couple of quick strokes on his keyboard, Michael called up a page of information on the screen.

'The information on the chip is divided into two partitions, one much smaller than the other. What you're looking at is the first partition.'

Peter saw a single line of text, letters and numbers all run together. 'I can't really read it,' he confessed.

'That's because the spaces have been removed. For some reason, some of it's transposed, too. I think it's just a bad sector on the chip. Maybe something happened when I soldered it to the board. Either way, it looks like a lot of it is gone. But what's here tells us a lot.'

Michael called up a second screen. The same figures, Peter saw, but the numbers and letters had reorganized themselves.

AMY NLN
SUB 13
ASSTO NOAH USAMRIID SWD
G:F W:22.72K

'Amy NLN.' Peter lifted his eyes from the screen. 'Amy?'

Michael nodded. 'That's our girl. I don't know for sure what NLN stands for, but I'm thinking "no last name." I'll get to the stuff in the middle in a second, but the bottom line is pretty clear. Gender, female. Weight, 22.72 kilos. That's about the size of a five- or six-year-old kid. So I'm figuring she was about that age when the transmitter was put in.'

None of it was clear to Peter, and yet Michael spoke with such confidence he could only take his friend's word for it. 'So it's been in there, what, ten years?'

'Well,' Michael said, still grinning, 'not exactly. And don't jump ahead, I've got a lot to show you. It's better if you just let me walk you through it. Now, that's all I can get from the first partition, and it isn't much, but it's not nearly the most interesting stuff by a long shot. The second partition is the real storehouse. Close to sixteen terabytes. That's sixteen *trillion* bytes of data.'

He pressed another key. Dense columns of numbers began to fly up the screen.

'It's something, isn't it? I thought at first it was some kind of encryption, but it actually isn't. Everything's right here, it's just all run together like the first partition.' Michael did something to freeze the rush of columns and tapped a finger against the glass. 'The key was this number here, first in the sequence, repeated down the column.'

Peter squinted at the screen. 'Nine hundred eighty-six?'

'Close. Ninety-eight *point* six. Ring any bells?'

Peter could only shake his head. 'Not really, no.'

'Ninety-eight point six is a normal human body temperature, using the old Fahrenheit scale. Now look at the rest of the line. The seventy-two is probably heart rate. You've got respiration and blood pressure. I'm guessing the rest has to do with brain activity, kidney function, that sort of thing. Sara would probably understand it better than I do. But the most important thing is that they come in discrete groups. It's pretty obvious if you look for the first number and see where the sequence remounts. I'm thinking this thing is a kind of body monitor, designed to transmit data to a mainframe. My guess is she was a patient of some kind.'

'A patient? Like in an infirmary?' Peter frowned. 'No one could do this.'

'No one could *now*. And here's where it gets more interesting. All told, there are five hundred forty-five thousand four hundred and six groups on the chip. The transmitter was set to cycle every ninety minutes. The rest was just arithmetic. Sixteen cycles a day times three hundred sixty-five days in a year.'

Peter felt like he was trying to take a sip of water from a blasting hose. 'I'm sorry, Michael. You've lost me.'

Michael turned to face him. 'I'm telling you that this thing in her neck has been taking her temperature every hour-and-a-half for a little more than ninety-three years. Ninety-three years, four months, and twenty-one days, to be exact. Amy NLN is a hundred years old.'

By the time his mind was able to bring Michael's face back into focus, Peter realized he had collapsed into a chair.

'That's impossible.'

Michael shrugged. 'Okay, it's impossible. But there's no other way I can figure it. And remember the first partition? That word, USAMRIID? I recognized it right away. It stands for United States Army Medical Research Institute for Infectious Diseases. There's tons of stuff with USAMRIID all over it in the shed. Documents about the epidemic, lots of technical material.' He turned in his chair and directed Peter's attention to the top of the screen. 'See this here? This long string of numbers in the first line? That's the mainframe's digital signature.'

'The what?'

'Think of it as an address, the name of the system this little transmitter is looking for. You might think it was just gibberish, but if you look closely the numbers actually tell you more. This thing had to have some kind of onboard locator system, probably linked to a satellite. Old military stuff. So what you're seeing are actually coordinates on a grid, and not anything fancy. It's just longitude and latitude. Thirty-seven degrees, fifty-six minutes north by one hundred seven degrees, forty-nine minutes west. So, we go to the map—'

Michael cleared the screen again, tapping briskly at the keys. A new image sprang into view. It took Peter a moment to understand what he was seeing, that it was a map of the North American continent.

'We type in the coordinates, like so . . .'

A grid of black lines appeared over the map, breaking it into squares. With a flourish, Michael lifted his fingers from the keyboard and slapped Enter. A bright yellow dot appeared.

'. . . and there we have it. Southwestern Colorado. A town called Telluride.'

The name meant nothing to Peter. 'So?'

'*Colorado*, Peter. The heart of the CQZ.'

'What's the CQZ?'

Michael sighed impatiently. 'You really need to brush up on your history. The Central Quarantine Zone. It's where the epidemic *began*. The first virals all came out of Colorado.'

Peter felt like he was being dragged from a runaway horse. 'Please, just slow down. Are you telling me she comes from there?'

Michael nodded. 'Basically, yeah. The transmitter was short-range, so she had to be within a few clicks when they put it in. The real question is why. '

'Flyers. You're asking like I know?'

His friend paused, searching Peter's face for a long moment. 'Let me ask you something. Have you ever really thought about what the virals are? Not just what they *do*, Peter. What they *are*.'

'A being without a soul?'

Michael nodded. 'Right, that's what everybody says. But what if there's more to it? This girl, Amy, she's not a viral. We'd all be dead if she were. But you've seen the way she heals, and she survived out there. You said it yourself, she protected you. And how do you explain the fact that she's almost a hundred years old but doesn't look a day over, what, fourteen? The Army did something to her. I don't know how they did it, but they did. This transmitter was broadcasting on a military frequency. Maybe she was infected and they did something to her that made her normal again.' He paused once more, his eyes fixed on Peter's face. 'Maybe she's the cure.'

'That's . . . a big leap.'

'I'm not so sure.' Michael lifted in his chair to remove a book from the shelf above his terminal. 'So I went back through the old logbook to see if we had ever picked up a signal from those coordinates. Just a hunch. And sure enough, we did. Eighty years ago, we picked up a beacon broadcasting these same coordinates. Military distress frequency, old-style Morse. But then there's this notation.'

Michael opened the log to the page he'd marked. He

placed the book in Peter's lap, pointing at the words written there.

If you found her, bring her here.

'And here's the clincher,' Michael went on. 'It's still transmitting. That's what took me so long. I had to run a cable up the Wall to get a decent signal.'

Peter lifted his eyes from the page. Michael was still looking at him with the same intense gaze.

'It's what?'

'*Transmitting.* Those same words. "If you found her, bring her here."'

Peter felt a kind of dizziness, gathering at the fringes of his brain. 'How could it be transmitting?'

'Because somebody's *there*, Peter. Don't you get it?' He smiled victoriously. 'Ninety-three years. That's year zero, the start of the outbreak. That's what I'm telling you. Ninety-three years ago, in the spring of the year zero, in Telluride, Colorado, somebody put a nuclear-powered transmitter inside a six-year-old-girl's neck. Who's still alive and sitting in quarantine, like she walked straight out of the Time Before. And for ninety-three years, whoever did this has been asking for her back.'

FORTY

It was nearly half-night, no one about, everyone but the Watch inside because of the curfew. All seemed quiet on the Wall. During the intervening hours, Peter had done all he could to get a handle on the situation. He hadn't reported for duty, and nobody had come looking for him, though probably they wouldn't have thought to look in the Lighthouse or in the FEMA trailer, from which he had scouted the lockup. With the coming of night, and the Watch so depleted, Ian had posted only a single guard there, Galen Strauss. But Peter doubted Sam and the others would try anything before first light. By then he planned to be gone.

The Infirmary was under heavier guard – a pair of Watchers, one in the front and one in the rear. Dale had been moved up to the Wall, so there was no way Peter could get inside, but Sara was still free to come and go. He had hidden in the shrubbery at the base of the courtyard wall and waited for her to appear. A long time passed before the door opened and she stepped onto the porch. She spoke briefly to the Watcher on duty, Ben Chou, before descending the stairs and making her way down the path, evidently headed to her house to get something to eat. Peter followed her at a discreet distance until he was sure they were out of sight and made his quick approach.

'Come with me now,' he said.

He led her to the Lighthouse, where Michael and Elton were waiting. Moving through the same explanation he had given Peter, Michael told his sister what he knew. When he came to the part about the signal and showed her the words in the logbook, Sara took it from his hands and examined it.

'Okay.'

Michael frowned. 'What do you mean "okay"?'

'Michael, it's not that I doubt you. I've known you too long. But what are we supposed to do with this information? Colorado is, what, a thousand kilometers from here?'

'About sixteen hundred,' Michael said. 'Give or take.'

'So how are we supposed to get there?'

Michael paused. He glanced past his sister to Elton, who nodded.

'The real problem is what happens if we don't.'

And that was when Michael told them about the batteries.

Peter absorbed this news with a strange detachment, a feeling of inevitability. Of course the batteries were failing; the batteries had been failing all along. He could feel it in everything that had happened; he felt it in the core of him, as if he'd always known. Like the girl. This girl, Amy, the Girl from Nowhere. That she had arrived in their midst when the batteries were failing was more than coincidence. All that remained was for him to act upon this knowledge.

He became aware that no one had spoken for a while. 'Who else knows about this?' he asked Michael.

'Just us.' He hesitated. 'And your brother.'

'You told Theo?'

Michael nodded. 'I always wished I hadn't. He was the one who told me not to tell anyone. Which I didn't, until now.'

Of course, Peter was thinking. Of course Theo had known.

'I think he didn't want people to be afraid,' Michael explained. 'As long as there wasn't anything we could do.'

'But you think there is.'

Michael paused to rub his eyes with the tips of his fingers. Peter could see the long hours catching up with him. None of them had slept at all.

'You know what I'd do, Peter. The signal's probably automated. But if the Army's still out there, I don't see how we can just do nothing. If she did what you said at the mall, maybe she could protect us.'

Peter turned his face toward Sara. After what Michael had just told them, he was surprised to find her so composed, her face revealing no emotion. But she was a nurse; Peter knew that toughness.

'Sara? You haven't said anything.'

'What do you want me to say?'

'You've been with her all this time. What do you think she is?'

Sara released a weary sigh. 'All I know is what she isn't. She's not a viral, that's obvious. But she's not an ordinary human being, either. Not the way she heals.'

'Is there any reason she can't speak?'

'Nothing I can find. If she's as old as Michael says, maybe she's forgotten how.'

'And no one else has been in to see her.'

'Not since yesterday.' She hesitated. 'I get the feeling everyone's sort of . . . afraid of her.'

609

'Are you?'

Sara frowned. 'Why would I be afraid of her, Peter?'

But he didn't know. The question had felt strange to him even as he'd asked it.

Sara rose to her feet. 'Well, I'm going to have to get back. Ben will start to wonder.' She placed a hand on Michael's shoulder. 'Try to get some rest. You too, Elton. The two of you, you look like hell.'

She had nearly reached the door when she turned, focusing her attention on Peter again.

'You're not really serious about this, are you? Going to Colorado.'

The question seemed too simple. And yet everything they'd been saying pointed to this conclusion. Peter felt much as he had outside the library, Theo asking him, What's your vote?

'Because if you were,' Sara said, 'with the way things are going, I wouldn't wait much longer to get her out of here.' And then she slipped from the Lighthouse.

In Sara's absence, a deeper silence settled over the room. Peter knew she was right. And yet his mind still could not grasp the totality of what they were contemplating, to bring it into focus. The girl, Amy, and the voice in his head, telling him his mother missed him; the failing batteries, which Theo had known about; the message on Michael's radio, like a transmission that had crossed not just a width of space but time itself, speaking to them out of the past. It was all of a piece, and yet its shape remained elusive, as if some crucial bit of information was still absent from its design.

Peter found himself looking at Elton. The old man hadn't spoken a word; Peter thought he might have fallen asleep.

'Elton?'

'Hmm?'

'You're pretty quiet.'

'Nothing to say,' he replied, his blank eyes roaming upward. 'You know who you need to talk to. You Jaxon boys, it's always the same. I don't have to tell you.'

Peter rose to his feet.

'Where are you going?' Michael asked.

'To get the answer,' he said.

Sanjay Patal couldn't sleep. Lying in his bed, he couldn't even close his eyes.

It was the girl. This Girl from Nowhere. She'd gotten into him somehow, into his mind. The girl was there with Babcock and the Many – what Many? he wondered; why was he thinking about the Many? – and it was as if he was somebody else now, somebody new and strange to himself. He'd wanted . . . what? A little peace. A little order. To stop the feeling that everything wasn't what it seemed to be, that the world was not the world. What had Jimmy said about the girl's eyes? But her eyes were closed, he'd seen that plainly; her eyes were closed and never opened. They were inside him, those eyes, as if he were viewing everything from two angles at once, within and without, Sanjay and not Sanjay, and what he saw was a rope.

Why was he thinking about a rope?

He'd meant to find Old Chou. That was why he'd left the house last night, leaving Gloria asleep in the kitchen. The need to find Old Chou was the force that had called him from bed, down the stairs and out the door. The lights, Sanjay remembered. As soon as he'd stepped into the yard they had filled his eyes like a bomb, the brightness exploding on his retinas, searing his mind with a pain that wasn't real pain, exactly, it was like a memory of pain, washing away any thoughts of Old Chou or the Storehouse or what he'd intended there. What he had next done seemed to have unfolded in a state without volition. The images in his memory lacked any coherence, like a pack of cards spilled on the floor. It was Gloria who had found him afterward, huddled in the bushes at the base of their house, whimpering like a child. Sanjay, she was saying, what did you do? What did you do, what did you do? He could not answer her – at that point, he honestly had no idea – but he could tell from her face and voice that it was awful, unthinkable, as if he might have killed someone, and he let her lead him back inside and up to bed. It wasn't until the sun was rising that he remembered what he'd done.

He was going mad.

So the day had passed. It was only by remaining awake – not merely awake but lying absolutely still, bringing all the force of his will to bear – that he believed he might restore some coherence to his troubled mind and avoid a repetition of the previous night's events. This was his new vigil. For a time, shortly after dawn and then later, as darkness was coming on, there had been a commotion of voices downstairs (Ian's and Ben's and Gloria's; he wondered what had happened to Jimmy). But this had ended too. He felt himself to be in a kind of bubble, everything unfolding at a distance, beyond his reach. At intervals he became aware of Gloria's presence in the room, her worried face hovering above him, asking questions he could not bring himself to answer. *Should I tell them about the guns, Sanjay? Should I? I don't know what to do, I don't know what to do. Why won't you speak to me, Sanjay?* But still he could say nothing. Even to speak would break the spell.

Now she was gone. Gloria was gone, Mausami was gone, everyone was gone. His Mausami. It was her image he was holding in his mind now – not the grown woman she had become but the tiny baby she'd been, this bundle of warm new life that Prudence Jaxon had placed into his arms – and as this image faded away, and Sanjay closed his eyes at last, he heard the voice, the voice of Babcock, coming out of the darkness.

Sanjay. Be my one.

He was in the kitchen now. The kitchen of the Time Before. Part of him was saying: You have closed your eyes, Sanjay. Whatever you do, you must not close your eyes. But it was too late, he was in the dream again, the dream of the woman and the telephone and her laughing voice of smoke and then the knife; the knife was in his hand. A great, heavy-handled knife that he would use to cut the words, the laughing words, from her throat. And the voice rose to him out of the darkness.

Bring them to me, Sanjay. Bring me one and then another. Bring them to me that you should live in this way and no other.

She was sitting at the table looking at him with her great padded face, smoke puffing from her lips in tiny clouds of gray. Watchoo doing with that knife? Huh? Is that supposed to scare me?

Do it. Kill her. Kill her and be free.

He lunged toward her and brought the knife down hard, all his force behind it.

But something was wrong. The knife had stopped, its gleaming brilliance frozen mid-plunge. Some force had come into the dream and stayed his hand; he felt its grip upon him. The woman was laughing. He was tugging and pulling, straining to bring the knife down, but it was no use. The smoke was pouring from her mouth and she was laughing at him, laughing laughing laughing . . .

He jerked awake. His heart was lurching in his chest. Every nerve in his body seemed to be firing at once. His heart! His heart!

'Sanjay?' Gloria had come into the room, carrying a lantern. 'Sanjay, what is it?'

'Get Jimmy!'

Her face, disturbingly close to his own, was distorted with fear. 'He's dead, Sanjay. Don't you remember? Jimmy's dead!'

He hurled the covers aside, was standing, now, in the middle of the bedroom, a wild force galloping through him. This world, with its little things. This bed, this dresser, this woman named Gloria, his wife. What was he doing? Where had he meant to go? Why had he been calling for Jimmy? But Jimmy was dead. Jimmy was dead, Old Chou was dead, Walter Fisher and Soo Ramirez and the Colonel and Theo Jaxon and Gloria and Mausami and even he himself – all of them were dead! Because the world was not the world, that was the thing, that was the terrible truth he had discovered.

It was a dream world, a veil of light and sound and matter that the real world hid behind. Walkers in a dream of death, that's what they were, and the dreamer was the girl, this Girl from Nowhere. The world was a dream and she was dreaming them!

'Gloria,' he croaked. 'Help me.'

A lantern was still on in Auntie's kitchen, spilling mullioned rectangles of yellow light onto the ground. Peter knocked on the door first, then quietly let himself in.

Peter found the old woman sitting at her kitchen table. She was neither writing nor drinking her tea, and as he entered she lifted her face toward him, simultaneously reaching into the tangle of eyeglasses around her neck. The right pair found her face.

'Peter. Been thinking I'd see you.'

He took a chair across from her. 'How did you know about her, Auntie?'

'Who that now?'

'You know who, Auntie. Please.'

She gave a little wave. 'The Walker, you mean? Oh someone must have come by and told me. That Molyneau man, I think it was.'

'I meant two nights ago. You said something. Told me she was coming. That I knew who she was.'

'I said that?'

'Yes, Auntie. You did.'

The old woman frowned. 'Can't imagine what was on my mind. Two night ago, you say?'

He heard himself sigh. 'Auntie—'

She held up a hand to quiet him. 'Okay, don't work yourself up into a condition. I was just having a bit of fun. Haven't done that in so long I couldn't resist it. You looking like you do.' She met his eye with an unblinking gaze. 'So tell me. Before I go offering my own opinion. What you think she is? This girl?'

'Amy.'

'Don't know what she's called. You want to call her Amy, go right on with it.'

'I don't know, Auntie.'

Her eyes grew suddenly wide. 'Of course you don't!' She chuckled to herself, then broke into a spasm of coughing. Peter rose to help her, but she waved him back down. 'Go on, sit,' she croaked. 'My voice just gets rusty is all it is.' She took a moment to settle herself, clearing her throat with a wet harrumph. 'That's what you have to find out. Everybody got something to find out in they lives, and this is your one thing.'

'Michael says she's a hundred years old.'

The old woman nodded. 'Best look out then. A *older* woman. Careful this Amy don't boss you around too much.'

He was getting nowhere. Talking to Auntie was always a challenge, but he'd never seen her quite like this, so weirdly cheerful. She hadn't even offered him tea.

'Auntie, you said something else the other night,' he pressed. 'Something about chance. *A* chance.'

'Reckon I might have. Sounds like something I'd say.'

'Is she?'

Her pale lips curled into a frown. 'I'd say that depends.'

'On what?'

'On you.'

Before Peter could speak, the woman continued: 'Oh, don't be looking like that, all woebegone like you are. Feeling lost is just a part of it.' She pushed away from the table and rose stiffly to her feet. 'Come on with you then. Got something to show you. Might help you make up your mind.'

He followed her down the hall to her bedroom. Like the rest of the house, the space was cluttered but clean, everything in its place. Pushed against the wall was an old four-poster bed, the mattress sagging in a manner that told him the ticking was just loose straw; beside it was a wooden chair bearing a lantern. He saw that the top of the dresser, the room's only other piece of furniture, was decorated with a collection of apparently random objects: an old glass bottle with the words *Coca-Cola* written in faded lettering of elaborate script; a metal tin that, when he picked it up, made a sound suggesting pins; the jawbone of some small animal; a pyramidal pile of flat, smooth stones.

'Those my worry things,' said Auntie.

Now that they were standing together in the cramped room, Peter felt her smallness; the crown of her white head reached barely to his shoulder.

'That's what my mama called them. Keep your worry things nearby, she always said.' She gestured with a crooked finger toward the bureau. 'Don't remember where most of it comes from, excepting the picture, of course. Brought that with me on the train.'

The picture was positioned in the center of the bureau top. Peter lifted it from its place and tipped it toward the window to catch the light of the spots. The photo was too small for the frame, which was tarnished and pitted; Peter supposed the frame had come later. Two figures were standing on a flight of stairs that ascended to the door of a brick house, the man behind and above the woman, his arms wrapping her waist as she leaned her weight against him. They were dressed for the cold, in bunchy coats; Peter could see a dusting of snow on the pavement in the foreground. The tones had been bleached by the years so that everything was a muted tan color, but he could tell that they were both dark-skinned, like Auntie, with Jaxon hair; the woman's was cut nearly as short as the man's. She wore a long scarf around her neck and was smiling straight into the camera; the man was looking away with an expression that seemed to Peter like three-quarters of a laugh – a laugh the camera had stopped. It was a haunting image, full of hope and promise, and Peter sensed, in the man's misdirected attention and the woman's smile and the way his arms enfolded her, pulling her into his body, the presence of a secret the two of them shared; and then, as more of its details came into focus – the way the woman's body curved and the thickness of her, beneath her coat – he realized what this secret was. It was a picture not of two people but three; the woman was pregnant.

'Monroe and Anita,' said Auntie. 'Those were their names. That there's our house, 2121 West Laveer.'

Peter touched the glass over the woman's belly. 'That's you, isn't it?'

'Course it's me. Who you think it was?'

Peter returned the picture to its place on her dresser. He wished he had something like that, to remember his parents by. With Theo it was different; he could still see his brother's face and hear his voice, and when he thought of Theo now, the image that came to his mind was from their time together at the power station, the day before they'd left. Theo's tired, troubled eyes as he sat on Peter's cot to examine his ankle and then, as he lifted his gaze, an expectant smile of challenge. *The swelling's down. Think you can ride?* But Peter knew that over time, even just a few months' worth, this memory would fade, like all the others – like the colors of Auntie's photograph. First the sound of Theo's voice would be lost, and then the picture itself, the details dissolving into visual static until all that remained was an empty space where his brother had been.

'Now, I know it's under here someplace,' Auntie was saying.

She had lowered herself to her knees, pulling the skirt of the bed aside to look beneath it. With a grunt she reached under the bed and withdrew a box, sliding it across the floor. 'Help me up, Peter.'

He took her by an elbow and eased her to her feet, then lifted the box from the floor. An ordinary cardboard shoe box, with a hinged lid and a flap that sealed it tight.

'Go on now.' Auntie was sitting on the edge of the bed, her naked feet dangling like a Little's, skimming the floor. 'Open it.'

He did as she'd said. The box was full of folded paper – he had already figured that out. But not just paper, he saw. Maps.

The box was full of maps.

Carefully he lifted the first one free of the box. Its surface was worn smooth, so brittle at its creases he worried that it might dissolve in his hands. At the top were the words AUTOMOBILE CLUB OF AMERICA, LOS ANGELES BASIN AND SOUTHERN CALIFORNIA.

'These were my father's. The ones he used on the Long Rides.'

He gently withdrew the others, placing each on top of the bureau. SAN BERNARDINO NATIONAL FOREST. LAS VEGAS STREET ATLAS. SOUTHERN NEVADA AND ENVIRONS. LONG BEACH, SAN PEDRO AND THE PORT OF LOS ANGELES. CALIFORNIA DESERT REGION, MOJAVE NATIONAL RESERVE. And, at the bottom, its folded edges squeezed against the sides of the box: FEDERAL EMERGENCY MANAGEMENT AGENCY, MAP OF THE CENTRAL QUARANTINE ZONE.

'I don't understand,' he said. 'Where did you get them?'

'Your mother brought them to me. Before she died.' Auntie was still watching him from the bed, her hands resting in her lap. 'That woman knew you better than you know yourself. Give them to him when he's ready, she said.'

A familiar sadness washed over him. 'I'm sorry, Auntie,' he said after a moment. 'You've made a mistake. She must have meant Theo.'

But she shook her head. 'No, Peter.' She smiled a toothless smile; her vaporous cloud of hair, backlit by the spots pouring down outside the windows, seemed to glow around her face – a halo of hair and light. 'It was you. She told me to give them to you.'

Later Peter would think: how strange it was. How, standing in the quiet of Auntie's room, among her things of the past, he had felt time opening before him, like the pages of a book. He thought of his mother's final hours – of her hands, and the close heat of the bedroom where Peter had cared for her; of her sudden struggle for breath, and the last imploring words she'd spoken. *Take care of your brother, Theo. He's not strong, like you.* Her intentions had seemed so clear. And yet as

Peter searched this moment, the memory began to shift, his mother's words forming a new shape and emphasis and, with that, a different meaning entirely.

Take care of your brother Theo.

His thoughts were broken by a burst of knocking from the porch.

'Auntie, are you expecting anyone?'

The old woman frowned. 'At this hour?'

Peter quickly returned the maps to the box and slid them beneath the bed. It wasn't until he reached the front door and saw Michael standing behind the screen that he wondered why he'd done this. Michael eased himself into the room, darting a glance past Peter to the old woman, who was standing behind him, her arms folded disapprovingly over her chest.

'Hey, Auntie,' he said breathlessly.

'Hey yourself, rude boy. You come knocking at my door in the middle of the night, I expect a how-do-you-do.'

'Sorry.' His cheeks reddened with embarrassment. 'How are you this evening, Auntie?'

She nodded. 'I'm expecting I'm all right.'

Michael directed his attention to Peter again, lowering his voice confidentially. 'Could I speak to you? Outside?'

Peter stepped onto the porch behind Michael, in time to see Dale Levine appearing out of the shadows.

'Tell him what you told me,' said Michael.

'Dale? What is it?'

'Look,' the man said, glancing around nervously, 'I probably shouldn't be saying this, and I have to get back to the Wall. But if you're planning on getting Alicia and Caleb out of here, I'd do it at first light. I can help you at the gate.'

'Why? What's happened?'

It was Michael who answered. 'The guns, Peter. They're going to get the guns.'

FORTY-ONE

In the Infirmary, Sara Fisher, First Nurse, was waiting with the girl.

Amy, Sara thought. Her name was Amy. This impossible girl, this one-hundred-year-old girl, was named Amy. Is that you? she'd asked her. Is that your name? Are you Amy?

Yes, her eyes said. She might have actually smiled. How long since she had heard the sound of her name? *That's me. I'm Amy.*

Sara wished she had some clothing for the girl, instead of the gown. It didn't seem right for a girl who had a name not to have clothing to wear, and a pair of shoes. Sara should have thought of that before returning to the Infirmary. The girl was shorter than she was, lighter-boned and slimmer-hipped, but Sara had a pair of gaps she liked to ride in, snug at the waist and seat, that would fit the girl well enough if she cinched them tight. She needed a bath, too, and a haircut.

Sara didn't question anything Michael had told her. Michael was Michael, that's what everyone said, meaning he was too smart by half – too smart for his own good. But the one thing he wasn't, not ever, was wrong. There would come a time, Sara supposed, when this would happen – a person couldn't be right all the time – and she wondered what would become of her brother on that day. The ceaseless effort he applied to being right, to fixing every problem, would suddenly collapse inside him. It made Sara think of a game they had played as Littles, building towers of blocks and then pulling them away from the lower tiers, one by one, daring the whole thing to fall; and when it fell, it happened swiftly, all at once. She wondered if that's what would happen to Michael, if there would be any part left standing. He would need her then, as he had needed her that morning in the shed when they'd found their parents – the day when Sara had failed him.

Sara had meant it, when she'd told Peter she wasn't afraid of the girl. She had been, at first. But as the hours and then days had moved by, the two of them locked away, she'd begun to feel something new. In the girl's watchful and mysterious presence – silent and unmoving, and yet not – she'd begun to feel a quality of reassurance, even of hope. A feeling that she was not alone, but even more: that the world was not alone. As if they were all waking from a long night of terrible dreams to step back into life.

Dawn would soon come. The attack of the night before had evidently not repeated; Sara would have heard the shouts. It was as if the night were holding the last of its breath, waiting for what would come next. Because what Sara hadn't told Peter, or anyone at all, was what had occurred in the Infirmary in the moments just before the lights had gone out. The girl had suddenly sat bolt upright on her cot. Sara, exhausted, had just lain down to sleep; she was roused by a sound she realized was coming from the girl. A low moaning, a single continuous note, rising at the back of her throat. What is it? Sara said, rising quickly to go to her. What's wrong? Are you hurt, has something hurt you? But the girl gave no reply. Her eyes were very wide, and yet she seemed not to see Sara at all. Sara had sensed that something was happening outside – the room was strangely dark, there were shouts coming from the Wall, the sounds of a commotion, voices calling and feet racing past – but while this seemed important, a fact worthy of her attention, Sara could not look away; whatever was going on outside was being waged here also, in this room, in the vacancy of the girl's eyes and the tautness of her face and throat and in the mournful melody that she was playing from somewhere deep within her. Things continued this way for some unknown numbers of minutes – two minutes and fifty-six seconds, according to Michael, though it felt like an eternity – and then, as quickly and alarmingly as it had begun, it was over; the girl fell silent. She lay back down on the cot, pulling her knees to her chest, and that had been the end of it.

Sara, sitting at the desk in the outer room, was remembering this, wondering if she should have told Peter about it, when her attention was taken by a sound of voices on the porch. She lifted her face toward the window. Ben was still sitting at the rail, facing away – Sara had carried out a chair for him – the end of his cross visible where it protruded from his lap; whomever he was speaking to was standing below him, Sara's view obscured by the angle. *What are you doing there?* she heard Ben say, his voice gathering into a tone of warning. *Don't you know there's a curfew?*

And as Sara rose to her feet, to see whom Ben was speaking to, she saw Ben rising also, sweeping his cross before him.

Peter and Michael, moving through the trailer park, darting from shadow to shadow: they made their final approach to the lockup in the cover of the trees.

No guard.

Peter gently pushed open the door, which stood ajar. As he stepped inside, he saw a body pushed against the far wall, its arms and legs bound, just as Alicia, moving from his left, dropped the cross she was pointing at his back.

'Where the hell have you been?' she said.

Caleb was standing behind her, holding the blade.

'A long story. I'll tell you on the way.' He gestured toward the body on the floor, which he now recognized as Galen Strauss. 'I see you decided to get started without me. What did you do to him?'

'Nothing he'll remember when he wakes up.'

'Ian knows about the guns,' said Michael.

Alicia nodded. 'So I figured.'

Peter explained the plan. First to the Infirmary to get Sara and the girl, then to the stables, for mounts. Just before First Bell, Dale, on the Wall, would call sign. In all the confusion, they should be able to slip out the gate, just as the sun was rising, and make their way down to the power station. From there they could figure out what to do.

'You know, I think I misjudged Dale,' Alicia said. 'He's got more stones than I thought.' She looked at Michael. 'You too, Circuit. I wouldn't have figured you as someone ready to storm the lockup.'

The four of them stepped out. Dawn was fast approaching; Peter didn't think they had more than a few minutes. They moved in quick silence toward the Infirmary and circled around to the west wall of the Sanctuary, giving them cover and a clear view of the building.

The porch was empty; the door stood open. Through the front windows came a flicker of lamplight. Then they heard a scream.

Sara.

Peter got there first. The outer room was empty. Nothing was disturbed except the chair at the front desk, which was lying on its side. From the ward Peter heard a groan. As the others entered behind him, he raced down the hallway and tore through the curtain.

Amy was huddled at the base of the far wall, her arms folded over her head as if to ward off a blow. Sara was on her knees, her face covered in blood.

The room was full of bodies.

The others had burst in behind him. Michael rushed to his sister's side.

'Sara!'

She tried to speak, opening her bloodied lips, but no sound came. Peter dropped to his knees beside Amy. She appeared uninjured, but at his touch she flinched, pulling farther away, waving her arms protectively.

'It's okay,' he was saying, 'it's okay,' but it wasn't okay. What had happened here? Who had killed these men? Had they slaughtered one another?

'It's Ben Chou,' Alicia said. She was kneeling by one of the bodies. 'Those two are Milo and Sam. The other one is Jacob Curtis.'

Ben had been taken on a blade. Milo, face-down in a spreading puddle of blood, had been killed by a blow to the head; Sam appeared to have gone down the same way, his skull caved in from the side.

Jacob was lying at the foot of Amy's cot, the bolt from Ben's cross jutting from his throat. A bit of blood was still bubbling from his lips; his eyes were open, wearing a look of surprise. In his outstretched hand he was clutching a length of iron pipe, smeared with blood and brain, white flecks among the red, clinging to its surface.

'Holy shit!' Caleb said. 'Holy shit, they're all dead!'

Everything about the scene had taken on a horrifying vividness. The bodies on the floor, the pooling blood. Jacob with the pipe in his hand. Michael was helping Sara to her feet. Amy was still cowering against the wall.

'It was Sam and Milo,' Sara croaked. Michael had helped his sister onto one of the cots. She spoke haltingly, through cracked and swollen lips, her teeth lined in crimson. 'Ben and I tried to stop them. It was all . . . I don't know. Sam was hitting me. Then someone else came in.'

'Was it Jacob?' Peter said. 'He's lying dead here, Sara.'

'I don't know, I don't know!'

Alicia took Peter by the elbow. 'It doesn't matter what happened,' she said urgently. 'No one will ever believe us. We have to go *now*.'

They couldn't risk the gate; Alicia explained what she wanted everyone to do. The important thing was to keep out of sight of the Wall. Peter and Caleb would go to the Storehouse, for ropes and packs and shoes for Amy; Alicia would lead the others to the rendezvous.

They crept from the Infirmary and fanned out. The main door to the Storehouse stood ajar, the lock hanging on its hasp – an odd detail, but nothing they had time to worry about now. Caleb and Peter moved into the dim interior with its long rows of bins. That was where they found Old Chou and, beside him, Walter Fisher. They were hanging side by side from the rafters, the ropes tight around their necks, their bare feet suspended above a bin of crated books. Their skin had taken on a grayish cast; both men's tongues were hanging from their mouths. They had evidently used the crates as a kind of stepladder, assembling them into a pile and then, once the ropes were in place, kicking them away. For a moment Peter and Caleb just stood there, looking at the two men, the improbable image they made.

'Fuck . . . me,' said Caleb.

Alicia was right, Peter knew. They had to go now. Whatever was happening was vast and terrible, a force to sweep over them all.

They assembled their supplies and stepped outside. Then Peter remembered the maps.

'Go ahead,' he told Caleb. 'I'll catch up.'

'They'll already be there.'

'Just go. I'll find you.'

The boy darted away. At Auntie's house, Peter didn't bother to knock; he stepped inside and moved straight to the bedroom. Auntie was asleep. He paused for a moment in the doorway, watching her breathe. The maps were where he'd left them, under the bed. He bent to retrieve them and slid the box into his pack.

'Peter?'

He froze. Auntie's eyes were still closed. Her hands lay still at her sides.

'I was just lying here to rest some.'

'Auntie—'

'No time for goodbyes,' the old woman intoned. 'You go on now, Peter. You're in your own time now.'

By the time he reached the cutout, filaments of pink were rising from the east. Everyone was there. Alicia was climbing from under the trunk line, dusting herself off.

'Everybody ready?'

Footsteps behind them: Peter wheeled around, drawing his blade. But then he saw, stepping from the undergrowth, the figure of Mausami Patal. A cross was slung from one shoulder; she was wearing a pack.

'I tracked you from the Storehouse. We better hurry.'

'Maus—' Alicia began.

'Save your breath, Lish. I'm going.' Mausami focused her eyes on Peter. 'Just tell me one thing,' she said. 'Do you believe your brother's dead?'

He felt as if he had been waiting for someone to ask him this very question. 'No.'

'Neither do I.'

Her hand moved toward her belly, an unconscious gesture. Its meaning came upon him with such completeness it felt less like something discovered than remembered, as if he'd known all along.

'I never got the chance to tell him,' Mausami said. 'I still want to.'

Peter turned to Alicia, who was studying the two of them with a look of exasperation.

'She comes.'

'Peter, this is not a good idea. Think about where we're going.'

'Mausami's blood now. It's not a discussion.'

For a moment Alicia said nothing; she appeared to be at a loss for words.

'The hell with it,' she said finally. 'We don't have time to argue.'

Alicia went first, showing them the way. Sara followed, then Michael, then Caleb and Mausami, dropping into the tunnel one by one, leaving Peter to guard the rear.

Amy was the last. They'd found a jersey and a pair of gaps for her, and a pair of sandals. As she lowered herself through the hatch, her eyes found Peter's with a sudden, beseeching force. *Where are we going?*

Colorado, he thought. The CQZ. They were just names on a map, bits of colored light on the screen of Michael's CRT. The reality behind them, the hidden world of which they were a part, was nothing Peter could imagine. When they'd spoken of such a journey earlier that night – had it really been that same night, the four of them crowded into the Lighthouse? – Peter had envisioned a proper expedition:

a large armed detail, carts of supplies, at least one scouting party, a meticulously plotted route. His father would spend whole seasons planning the Long Rides. Now here they were, fugitives on foot, scurrying away with little more than a pile of old maps and the blades on their belts. How could they possibly hope to get to such a place?

'I don't really know,' he told her. 'But if we don't leave now, I think we'll all die here.'

She ducked into the tunnel and was gone. Peter tightened the straps of his pack and scrambled in behind her, pulling the hatch closed over his head, sealing himself in darkness. The walls were cool and smelled of earth. The tunnel had been dug long ago, perhaps by the Builders themselves, to make it easier to service the trunk line; except for the Colonel, no one had used it for years. It was his secret route, Alicia had explained, the one he used to hunt. So at least one mystery was solved.

Twenty-five meters later, Peter emerged into a copse of mesquite. Everyone was waiting. The lights were down, revealing a gray dawn sky. Above them, the face of the mountain rose like a single slab of stone, a silent witness to all that had occurred. Peter heard the calls of the Watch from the top of the Wall, sounding off their posts for Morning Bell and the changing of the shift. Dale would be wondering what had happened to them, if he didn't know already. Surely it wouldn't be long before the bodies were found.

Alicia closed the hatch behind him and turned the wheel, then knelt to cover it with underbrush.

'They'll come after us,' Peter said quietly, crouched beside her. 'They'll have horses. We can't outrun them.'

'I know.' Her face was set. 'It's a question of who gets to the guns first.'

And with that Alicia rose, turned on her heels, and began to lead them down the mountain.

VII

THE
DARKLANDS

I saw eternity the other night
Like a great ring of pure and endless light,
All calm as it was bright,
And round beneath it time in hours, days, years,
Driven by the spheres,
Like a vast shadow moved in which the world
And all her train were hurled.

– HENRY VAUGHAN,
'The World'

FORTY-TWO

They reached the foot of the mountain before half-day. The pathway, a switchback zigzagging down the eastern face of the mountain, was too steep for horses; in places it wasn't a path at all. A hundred meters above the station a portion of the mountain seemed to have been carved away; a pile of rubble lay below. They were above a narrow box canyon, the station obscured to the north by a wall of rock. A hot, dry wind was blowing. They climbed back up, searching for another route as the minutes ticked away. At last they found a way down – they had drifted off the path – and made their final, creeping descent.

They approached the station from the rear. Inside its fenced compound they detected no sign of movement. 'You hear that?' Alicia said.

Peter stopped to listen. 'I don't hear anything.'

'That's because the fence is off.'

The gate stood open. That was when they saw a dark hump on the ground, beneath the awning of the livery. As they moved closer the hump seemed to atomize, breaking apart into a swirling cloud.

A jenny. The cloud of flies scattered as they approached. The ground around her was darkened with a stain of blood.

Sara knelt beside the body. The jenny was lying on her side, exposing the swollen curve of her belly, bloated with putrefying gas. A long gash, alive with squirming maggots, followed the line of her throat.

'She's been dead a couple of days, I'd say.' Sara's bruised face was wrinkled against the smell. Her lower lip was split; her teeth were outlined with crusted blood. One eye, her left, was swollen with a huge, purple shiner. 'It looks like someone used a blade.'

Peter turned to Caleb. His eyes were open very wide, locked on the animal's neck. He'd pulled the neck of his jersey over the lower half of his face, a makeshift mask against the stench.

'Like Zander's jenny? The one in the field?'

Caleb nodded.

'Peter—' Alicia was gesturing toward the fence. A second dark shape on the ground.

'Another jenny?'

'I don't think so.'

It was Rey Ramirez. There wasn't much left, just bones and charred flesh, which still exuded a faint smell of grilled meat. He was kneeling against the fence, his stiffened fingers locked in the open spaces between the wires. The exposed bones of his face made him appear to be smiling.

'That explains the fence,' Michael said after a moment. He looked like he might be ill. 'He must have shorted it out, holding on like that.'

The hatch was open: they descended into the station, moving through its darkened spaces, room by room. Nothing seemed disturbed. The panel still glowed with current, flowing up the mountain. Finn was nowhere to be seen. Alicia led them to the back; the shelf that hid the escape hatch was still in place. It was only when she opened the door and he saw the guns, still in their boxes, that Peter realized he'd feared they'd be gone. Alicia pulled a crate free and opened it.

Michael gave an admiring whistle. 'You weren't kidding. They're like brand-new.'

'There's more where this came from.' Alicia glanced up at Peter. 'Think you can find the bunker on those maps?'

They were interrupted by footsteps banging down the stairs: Caleb.

'Someone's coming.'

'How many?'

'Looks like just one.'

Alicia quickly doled out weapons; they ascended into the

yard. Peter could see a single rider in the distance, pulling a boiling plume of dust. Caleb passed the binoculars to Alicia.

'I'll be damned,' she said.

Moments later, Hollis Wilson rode through the gate and dismounted. His arms and face were caked with dust. 'We better hurry.' He paused to take a long drink from his canteen. 'There's a party of at least six behind me. If we want to make it to the bunker, we should leave right now.'

'How do you know where we're going?' Peter asked.

Hollis wiped his mouth with the back of his wrist. 'You forget. I rode with your father, Peter.'

The group had gathered in the control room; they were loading gear as fast as they could, whatever they hoped to carry. Food, water, weapons. Peter had spread the maps over the central table for Hollis to examine. He found the one he wanted: *Los Angeles Basin and Southern California.*

'According to Theo, the bunker was a two-day ride,' Peter said.

Hollis frowned, his brow furrowed as he studied the map. Peter noticed for the first time that he'd begun to let his beard come in. For a second, it felt to him as if it were Arlo standing there.

'I remember it as more like three, but we were pulling the carts. On foot, I'd say we could do it in two.' He bent over the map, pointing. 'We're here, at the San Gorgonio Pass. The time I rode with your father, we followed this road, Route 62, north from the Eastern Road, Interstate 10. It's quaked out in spots but on foot that should be no problem. We overnighted here' – again he pointed – 'in the town of Joshua Valley. About twenty kilometers, but it could be as much as twenty-five. Demo fortified an old fire station and laid in supplies there. It's tight, and there's a working pump, so we can take water if we need it, which we will. From Joshua it's another thirty clicks east on the Twentynine Palms Highway, another ten due north across open country to the bunker. A hell of a walk, but you could do it in another day.'

'If the bunker's underground, how do we find it?'

'I can find it, all right. And believe me, you've got to see this place. Your old man called it the war chest. There's vehicles, too, and fuel. We never could figure out how to get one running, but maybe Caleb and the Circuit can.'

'What about the smokes?'

'We never saw much of any through this stretch. Doesn't mean they aren't there. But it's high desert, which they don't like. Too hot, not enough cover, no real game that we ever saw. Demo called it the golden zone.'

'And farther east?'

Hollis shrugged. 'Your guess is as good as mine. The bunker's as far as I ever went. If you're serious about Colorado, I'd say our best bet is to stay off I-40 and work our way north to Interstate 15. There's a second supply cache in Kelso, an old railroad depot. It's rough terrain through there, but I know your old man got at least that far.'

Alicia would ride point; the rest of the group would follow on foot. Caleb was still signaling the all clear from the roof of the station as they loaded up their gear in the shade of the livery. The jenny was gone; Hollis and Michael had dragged it to the fence.

'They should be in sight by now,' Hollis said. 'I didn't think they were more than a few clicks behind me.'

Peter turned his eyes to Alicia. Should they go look? But she shook her head.

'It doesn't matter,' she said, with an air of finality. 'They're on their own now. Same as us.'

Caleb descended the ladder at the rear of the station and joined them in the shade. They were a group of eight now. Peter was suddenly aware how depleted they all were. None of them had slept at all. Amy was standing close to Sara, wearing a pack like the others. She was squinting with a kind of fierce bravery in the sunlight, beneath an old visored cap somebody had found in the supply room. Whatever else was true about her, she wasn't used to the brightness. But there wasn't anything he could do about that now.

Peter stepped away from the awning. He counted out the hands; seven hours until darkness fell. Seven hours to cover twenty-five kilometers, on foot, across the open valley. Once they started, there would be no turning back. Alicia, her rifle slung from her shoulder, swung up onto Hollis's horse, a huge, sandy-colored mare built like a house. Caleb passed her the binoculars.

'Everybody ready?'

'You know,' Michael said, 'technically, it's not too late to surrender.' He was standing next to his sister, awkwardly holding a rifle across his chest. He looked at their silent faces. 'Hey, it was just a joke.'

'Actually, I think Circuit has a point,' Alicia declared from atop her mount. 'There's no shame in staying. Anybody who wants to should speak up now.'

No one did.

'All right then,' Alicia said. 'All eyes.'

He wasn't cut out for this, Galen decided. He just wasn't. The whole thing had been a huge mistake from the beginning.

The heat was killing him, the sun like a white explosion in his eyes. His ass was so sore from riding he wouldn't walk for a week. He had a screaming headache, too, where Alicia had clobbered him with the cross. And nobody in the party was listening to him. Nobody was doing a goddamn thing he said. *Hey, guys, maybe we should close it up a little. We might want to slow down. What's the goddamn hurry?*

'Kill them,' Gloria Patal had said. This little mouse of a woman, scared of her own shadow as far as Galen could tell; but from the looks of things, there were whole sides of Gloria Patal that he had never seen before. Standing at the gate, the woman was seething with rage. 'Bring my daughter back here, but kill the rest of them. I want them *dead*.'

The girl had done it, that's what everyone was saying, the girl and Alicia and Caleb and Peter and Michael and . . . Jacob Curtis. Jacob Curtis! How could that half-wit Jacob Curtis be responsible for anything? It made no sense to

Galen, but nothing about the situation did; sense was no longer the point as far as he could tell. Not at the gate where everyone had gathered, all of them shouting and waving their arms; it was as if half the Colony wanted to kill someone, anyone, that morning. If Sanjay had been there, he might have been able to talk a little sense into people, get them to calm down and think. But he wasn't. He was in the Infirmary, Ian said, babbling and weeping like a baby.

That was about the time that the crowd had gone to get Mar Curtis and dragged her to the gate. She wasn't the person they really wanted, but there was nothing to be done about it. The crowd was going wild. A pitiful scene, the poor woman who'd never had a bit of luck in her life, who didn't have an ounce of strength to resist, hustled up the ladder by a hundred hands and thrown over the Wall as everyone broke into cheers. It might have ended there, but the crowd was just getting started, Galen could feel it, the first one had simply given them a taste for more, and Hodd Greenberg was yelling, 'Elton! Elton was with them in the Lighthouse!' And the next thing Galen or any of them knew, the crowd was rushing to the Lighthouse and under a storm of cheers they hustled the old guy, the blind old guy, to the Wall. And they threw him over, too.

Galen, for his part, was keeping his mouth *shut*. How long before somebody said, Hey, Galen, where's your wife? What about Mausami? Was she part of this too? Let's throw Galen over next!

Finally Ian had given the order. Galen didn't see the sense in going after them, but he was the only Second Captain now, since all the other Seconds were dead, and he could tell Ian wanted to maintain at least the illusion that the Watch was still in charge. Something had to be done or the crowd would be throwing everyone over the Wall. This was when Ian had taken him aside and told him about the guns. Twelve crates of them, behind a wall in the storage room. Personally, I don't care one way or the other about the Walker, Ian said. Your wife is up to you. Just bring me those fucking guns.

They were a party of five: Galen in command, Emily Darrell and Dale Levine in the second slot, with Hodd Greenberg and Cort Ramirez bringing up the rear. His first command outside the Wall, and what did he have? That idiot Dale and a sixteen-year-old runner and two men who weren't even Watch.

A fool's errand, that's what this was. He released a heavy sigh – loud enough for the runner Emily Darrell, riding beside him, to ask him what was wrong. She had been the first to volunteer for the ride, the only one from the Watch besides Dale. A girl with something to prove. He told her, Nothing, and let it go at that.

They were almost through Banning now. He was glad he couldn't make out much in the way of detail, but the glimpses he got as they rode through town – you couldn't not look – creeped him to the bone. A bunch of caved-in buildings and dried-out slims roasting in their cars like strips of mutton, never mind the smokes, who were probably skulking around somewhere. *One shot. They come from above.* The Watch drilled those words into your head from the time you were eight years old, never once letting you in on the big secret, what nonsense it all was. If a smoke dropped down on Galen Strauss, he wouldn't stand a chance. He wondered how much it would hurt. Probably a lot.

The truth was, the way things were, the whole Mausami thing finally felt over. He wondered why he hadn't seen that before. Well, maybe he had and just hadn't been able to bring himself to accept it. He didn't even feel angry. Sure, he had loved her. Probably he still did. There would always be a place in his mind where Mausami was, and the baby, too. The baby wasn't his, but still he found himself wishing it were. A baby could make you feel better about just about anything, even going blind. He wondered if Maus and the baby were okay. If he found them, he hoped that he'd be man enough to say that. I hope that you're okay.

They approached the ramp to the Eastern Road, riding in two lines. Flyers, his fucking head was pounding. Maybe it was just the knock Alicia had given him, but he didn't think so. His whole vision seemed to be collapsing. Funny motes of light had begun to dance in his eyes. He felt a little sick.

He was so wrapped up in his thoughts he didn't realize where he was, that he'd reached the top of the ramp. He paused to take a drink. The turbines were out there, somewhere, spinning in the wind that was pushing into his face. All he wanted was to get to the station and lie down in the dark and close his eyes. The dancing specks were worse now, descending through his narrowed field of sight like a glowing snowfall. Something was really wrong. He didn't see how he would be able to continue; someone else would have to take the point. He turned to Dale, who had moved up behind him, saying, 'Listen, do you think—'

The space beside him was empty.

He swiveled in his saddle. No one was behind him. Not one rider. Like a giant hand had plucked them, mounts and all, right off the face of the earth.

A wave of bile rose in his throat. 'Guys?'

That was when he heard the sound, coming from beneath the overpass. A soft, wet ripping, like sheets of damp paper being torn in half, or the skin being pried off an orange fat with juice.

FORTY-THREE

They made Joshua Valley with just minutes to spare; by the time they reached the fire station, the light was nearly gone. The station was located on the western edge of town, a squat, square structure with a concrete roof and a pair of arched doors facing the street, sealed with cement blocks. Hollis led them to the rear, where the water tank sat in a thicket of tall weeds. The water that poured from the pump was warm and tasted of rust and earth. They all drank greedily, dumping great cascades over their heads. Never had water tasted so good, Peter thought.

They gathered in the shade of the building while Hollis and Caleb pried loose the boards that covered the back entrance of the station. With a shove the door spilled open on its rusted hinges, exhaling a wash of trapped air as dense and warm as human breath. Hollis took up his rifle again.

'Wait here.'

Peter listened to Hollis's echoing footsteps moving through the dark space within. He was strangely unconcerned; they had come this far, it seemed impossible that the fire station would refuse them shelter for the night. Then Hollis returned.

'All clear,' he said. 'It's hot, but it'll do.'

They followed him into a large, high-ceilinged room. The windows were sealed by more concrete blocks, with narrow slits at the top for ventilation, through which issued a yellow-tinted glow of fading daylight. The air smelled of dust and animals. A miscellaneous assemblage of tools and building supplies was pushed against the walls: sacks of concrete, plastic troughs and hoes encrusted with cement, a wheelbarrow, coils of rope and chain. The bays where the engines had once been were empty. Now the area served as a make-shift stable, with half a dozen stalls and tack hung on the boards. Along the far wall, a flight of wooden stairs ascended into nothing – the second floor was gone.

'Cots in the back,' Hollis explained. He had knelt to fill a lantern from a plastic jug. Peter saw the liquid's pale golden color and recognized the smell. Not alcohol: petroleum. 'All the comforts of home. There's a kitchen and bath, too, though there's no running water and the chimney's sealed.'

Alicia was leading the horse inside. 'What about this door?' she asked.

Hollis lit the lantern with a match, paused to adjust the wick, and passed it to Mausami, who was standing beside him. 'Hightop, give me a hand.'

Hollis retrieved a pair of wrenches and passed one to

Caleb. Hanging from the joists over the front entrance, suspended by a pair of blocked chains, was a barricade of thick metal plates, framed by heavy timbers. They lowered it into position and bolted it to receivers set in the jamb, sealing themselves inside.

'Now what?' Peter asked.

The big man shrugged. 'Now we wait till morning. I'll take first watch. You and the others should sleep.'

In the back room were the cots Hollis had spoken of, a dozen mattresses on sagging springs. A second door led to the kitchen and bathroom, with a row of rust-stained sinks below a cracked mirror and four toilet stalls. All of the windows were sealed. One of the toilets had been pulled out and now sat, its bowl tipped forward like the face of a drunken man, in the far corner of the room. In its place was a plastic bucket and, on the floor beside it, a pile of old magazines. Peter picked up the top one: *Newsweek*. On the cover was a blurry photo of a viral. There was something oddly flattened about the image, as if it had been taken from a great distance and very close at the same time. The creature was standing in some sort of alcove, in front of a device with the letters ATM written at the top. Peter didn't know what this was, though he'd seen one like it in the mall. On the ground behind the viral lay a single, empty shoe. The two-word caption said, BELIEVE IT.

He returned with Alicia to the garage. 'Where are the rest of the supplies?' he asked Hollis.

Hollis showed him where the floorboards lifted up, revealing a recess about a meter deep, its contents covered by a heavy plastic tarp. Peter dropped down and pulled the tarp free. More jugs of fuel and water and, packed tightly together, rows of crates like the ones they'd found under the stairs at the power station.

'These ten here are more rifles,' Hollis said, pointing. 'Pistols over there. We only moved the smaller weapons, and no explosives. Demo didn't know if maybe they'd just blow up on their own and wreck the place, so we left them in the bunker.'

Alicia had opened one of the crates, removing a black pistol. She pulled the slide, sighted down the barrel, and squeezed the trigger; they heard the sharp click of the hammer falling on an empty chamber. 'What kind of explosives?'

'Grenades, mostly.' Hollis tapped one of the crates with the toe of his boot. 'But the real surprise is this one here. Give me a hand.'

The others had gathered around the hole. Hollis and Alicia stood on either side of the locker and hoisted it to the floor of the garage. Hollis knelt and opened it. Peter had expected more weaponry, so he was surprised to see a collection of small gray pouches. Hollis handed one to Peter. It weighed barely a kilo; on one side was a white label, covered with tiny black writing. At the top were the letters MRE.

'It stands for Meal, Ready to Eat,' Hollis explained. 'Army food. There are thousands of them in the bunker. You've got . . . let's see,' he said, and took the pouch Peter was holding, squinting at the tiny print. ' "Soyloaf with gravy." I've never had that one.'

Alicia was holding one of the pouches, frowning at it skeptically. 'Hollis, these things have been "ready" for about ninety years. They *can't* still be good.'

The big man shrugged and began passing the pouches around. 'A lot aren't. But if it's still airtight, you can eat it. Believe me, you'll know when you pull the tab. Most are pretty good, but look out for the beef Stroganoff. Demo called it "Meal Refusing to Exit." '

They were reluctant but, in the end, too hungry to refuse. Peter had two: the soyloaf and a sweet, gluey pudding called 'mango cobbler.' Amy sat on the edge of one of the cots to nibble suspiciously on a handful of yellow crackers and a wedge of what appeared to be cheese. From time to time she lifted her eyes warily; then she returned to her furtive eating. The mango cobbler was so sugary it made Peter's head buzz, but when he lay down he felt his fatigue uncoiling in his chest and knew that sleep would grab him fast. His last thought was of Amy, nibbling on the crackers, her eyes darting over the room. As if she were waiting for something to happen. But this idea was like a rope in his hands he could not hold, and soon his hands were empty; the thought was gone.

Then Hollis's face was floating above him in the dark. He blinked the fog of his disorientation away. The room was stifling; his shirt and hair were soaked with sweat. Before Peter could speak, Hollis silenced him with a finger held to his lips.

'Get your rifle and come on.'

Hollis, carrying the lantern, led him to the garage. Sara was standing against the wall of concrete blocks where the bay doors had once been. A small observation port had been built into one of the doors – a metal plate that pulled aside in a track, bolted into the concrete.

Sara stepped away. 'Take a look,' she whispered.

Peter pressed his eyes to the opening. He could smell the wind in his nostrils, the cooling desert night. The window faced the town's main street, Route 62. Across from the fire station stood a block of buildings, ruined hulks, and behind them a softly undulating line of hills, all of it bathed in a bluish moonlight.

Crouched in the roadway was a single viral.

Peter had never seen one so motionless, at least not at night. It was facing the building, resting on its chiseled haunches, gazing at the building. While Peter watched, two more appeared out of the darkness, moving along the road and stopping to take up the same, vigilant posture, facing the firehouse. A pod of three.

'What're they doing?' Peter whispered.

'Just standing there,' Hollis said. 'They move around a bit but never come any closer.'

Peter pulled his face from the window.

'You think they know we're in here?'

'It's tight but not that tight. They can smell the horse for sure.'

'Sara, go wake up Alicia,' Peter said. 'Keep quiet – it's best if everyone else stays asleep.'

Peter returned his face to the window. After a moment he asked, 'How many did you say there were?'

'Three,' Hollis answered

'Well, there's six now.'

Peter stood aside for Hollis to look.

'This is . . . bad,' Hollis said.

'What are the weak spots?' Alicia was beside them now. She freed the safety on her rifle and, making an effort to keep quiet, pulled the bolt. Then they heard it: a thump from above.

'They're on the roof.'

Michael stumbled from the back room. He looked them over, frowning, his eyes blurry with sleep. 'What's going on?' he said, too loudly. Alicia touched a finger to her lips, then pointed urgently to the ceiling.

More sounds of impact came from overhead. In his gut Peter felt it, a soft bomb exploding. The virals were searching for a way in.

Something was scratching at the door.

A thump of flesh on metal, of bone on steel. It was as if the virals were testing it, Peter thought. Gauging its strength before they made a final push. He tightened the stock against his shoulder, ready to fire, just as Amy stepped into his line of vision. Later he would wonder if she'd been in the room all along, hiding in a corner, silently observing. She stepped to the barricade.

'Amy, get back—'

She knelt before the door, placing her palms against it. Her head was bowed, her brow touching the metal. Another thump from the far side, though softer this time, searching. Amy's shoulders were trembling.

'What's she doing?'

It was Sara who answered. 'I think she's . . . crying.'

No one moved. There were no more sounds coming from the far side of the door now. Finally Amy shifted off her knees and stood, facing them all. Her eyes were distant, unfocused; she seemed not to be seeing any of them.

Peter held up a hand. 'Don't wake her.'

While they watched in silence, Amy turned and walked, with the same otherworldly air, to the door to the bedroom, just as Mausami, the last sleeper, emerged. Amy pushed past her without appearing to notice her. The next thing they heard was the squeak of rusted springs as she lay down on her cot.

'What's going on?' Mausami said. 'Why is everybody looking at me like that?'

Peter went to check the window. He pressed his face against the slot. It was as he expected. Nothing was moving outside; the moonlit field was empty.

'I think they're gone.'

Alicia frowned. 'Why would they just leave like that?'

He felt strangely calm; the crisis, he knew, had passed. 'Look for yourself.'

Alicia slung her rifle and pressed her eyes to the window, her neck straining as she tried to widen her field of vision through the opening.

'He's right,' she reported. 'There's nothing out there.' She drew her face away and turned toward Peter, her eyes narrowed. 'Like . . . pets?'

He shook his head, searching for the right word. 'Like friends, I think.'

'Will somebody *please* tell me what's going on?' Mausami said.

'I wish I knew,' said Peter.

They raised the barricade just after daybreak. All around they saw the creatures' tracks in the dust. None of them had slept much, but even so, Peter felt a new energy coursing through him. He wondered what this was, and then he knew. They had survived their first night out in the Darklands.

The map spread out on a boulder, Hollis went over their route.

'After Twentynine Palms, it's open desert through here, no real roads. The trick to finding the bunker is this range of mountains to the east. There are two distinct peaks at the south end, and a third behind them. When the third stands right in the middle of the two, turn due east, and you're going the right way.'

'What if we don't make it before dark?' he asked.

'We could hole up in Twentynine if we had to. There are a few structures still standing. But as I remember it they're just hulks, nothing like the fire station.'

Peter glanced toward Amy, who was standing with the others. She was still wearing the brimmed cap from the supply room; Sara had also given her a man's long-sleeved shirt to wear, frayed at the sleeves and collar, and a pair of desert glasses they'd found in the firehouse. Her black hair was pushed away from her face, a nimbus of dark tangles flapping under the brim of the cap.

'Do you really think she did it?' Hollis said. 'Sent them away.'

Peter turned back toward his friend. He thought of the magazine in the bathroom, the two stark words on its cover.

'Truthfully, Hollis? I don't know.'

'Well, we better hope she did. After Kelso, it's open country clear to the Nevada line.' He drew his blade and wiped it on the hem of his jersey. When he resumed speaking his voice was quiet, confidential. 'Before I left, you know, I heard people talking, saying things about her. The Girl from Nowhere, the last Walker. People were saying she was a sign.'

'Of what?'

Hollis frowned. 'The end, Peter. The end of the Colony, the end of the war. The human race, or what's left of it. I'm not saying they were right. It was probably just more of Sam and Milo's bullshit.'

Sara stepped toward them. The swelling on her face had

eased overnight; the worst of the bruising had faded to a greenish purple.

'We should let Maus ride,' she said.

'Is she okay?' Peter asked.

'A little dehydrated. In her condition, she has to keep her fluids up. I don't think she should be walking in the heat. I'm worried about Amy, too.'

'What's wrong with her?'

She shrugged. 'The sun. I don't think she's used to it. She's got a bad burn already. The glasses and shirt will help, but she can stay covered only so long in this heat.' She cocked her head and looked at Hollis. 'So what's this Michael tells me about a vehicle?'

They marched.

The mountains fell away behind them; by half-day, they were deep in open desert. The roadway was little more than suggestion, but they could still follow its course, tracing the bulge it made in the hardpan, through a landscape of scattered boulders and strange, stunted trees, beneath a boiling sun and a limitless sky bleached of all color. The breeze hadn't so much died as collapsed; the air was so motionless it seemed to hum, the heat vibrating around them like an insect's wings. Everything in the landscape looked both close and far away, the sense of perspective distorted by the immeasurable horizon. How easy it would be, Peter thought, to get turned around in such a place, to wander aimlessly until darkness fell. Past the town of Mojave Junction – no town at all, just a few empty foundations and a name on the map – they crested a small rise to discover a long line of abandoned vehicles, two abreast, facing the direction they had come. Most were passenger cars but there were some trucks as well, their rusted, sand-scoured chassis sunk in the drifting sand. It felt as if they'd stumbled on an open grave, a grave of machines. Many of the roofs had been peeled away, the doors torn off their hinges. The interiors looked melted; if there had once been bodies inside, they were long gone, scattered to the desert winds. Here and there in the undifferentiated debris, Peter detected a recognizable item of human scale: a pair of eyeglasses, an open suitcase, a child's plastic doll. They passed in silence, not daring to speak. Peter counted over a thousand vehicles before they ended in a final plume of wreckage, the indifferent desert sands resuming.

It was midafternoon when Hollis announced that it was time to leave the road and turn north. Peter had begun to doubt that they would ever make it to the bunker. The heat was simply overwhelming. A blazing wind was blowing from the east, pushing dust into their faces and eyes. Since the line of cars, no one had said much of anything. Michael seemed the worst off; he'd begun, discernibly, to limp. When Peter questioned him, Michael removed his boot without comment to show him a fat, blood-filled blister on his heel.

They paused to rest in the sparse shadow of a yucca grove. 'How much farther?' Michael asked. He'd taken off his boot for Sara to attend to his blister; he winced as she pierced it with a small scalpel from the med kit she had found at the station. From the incision came forth a single bead of blood.

'From here, about fifteen kilometers,' Hollis said. He was standing away from them, at the edge of the shade. 'See that line of mountains? That's what we're looking for.'

Caleb and Mausami had fallen asleep, their heads propped on their packs. Sara wrapped Michael's foot in a bandage; he wedged it back into his boot, grimacing with pain. Only Amy seemed little worse for the wear. She was sitting apart from the others, her skinny legs folded under her, watching them warily from behind her dark glasses.

Peter went to where Hollis was standing. 'Will we make it?' he asked quietly.

'It'll be close.'

'Let's give everyone half a hand.'

'I wouldn't go longer.'

Peter's first canteen was empty. He allowed himself a sip from his second, vowing to hold the rest in reserve. He lay down with the others in the shade. It was as if he'd only just closed his eyes when he heard his name and opened them again to find Alicia standing over him.

'You said half a hand.'

He rose on his elbows. 'Right. Time to go.'

Another hand had passed before they saw the sign, rising out of the wavering heat. First a long line of fencing, tall chain-link with coils of barbed wire at the top, and then, a hundred meters inside the open gate, the small sentry house and the sign standing beside it.

**YOU ARE ENTERING THE TWENTYNINE PALMS
MARINE CORPS AIR GROUND COMBAT CENTER.
DANGER. UNEXPLODED ORDNANCE.
DO NOT LEAVE THE ROAD.**

'Unexploded ordnance.' Michael's face was compacted in a fierce squint. 'What does that mean?'

'It means watch your step, Circuit.' Alicia directed her voice to everyone. 'It could be bombs, or maybe mines. Single file, try to step in the footprints of the person in front of you.'

'What's that?' Mausami was pointing with one hand, the other held over her brow against the glare. 'Are they buildings?'

They were buses: thirty-two of them parked in two closely spaced lines, their yellow paint almost entirely rubbed away. Peter stepped toward the closest bus, at the rear of the line. The breeze had died; the only sound came from their footsteps on the hardpan. Below windows covered in heavy-gauge wire were the words DESERT CENTER UNIFIED SCHOOL DISTRICT. He clambered up the dune of sand that was pushed against it and peered inside. More sand had blown through, subsuming the benches in wavelike drifts. Birds had roosted in the ceiling, staining the walls with the white paint of their droppings.

'Hey! Look at this!' Caleb called.

They followed his voice around to the far side. Tipped onto its side was the shell of some kind of small aircraft.

'It's a helicopter,' said Michael.

Caleb was standing on top of the fuselage. Before Peter could speak, Caleb had pulled the door open, like a hatch, and dropped down inside it.

'Hightop,' Alicia called, 'be careful!'

'It's okay! It's empty!' They heard him rummaging around the interior; a moment later, his head popped through the hatch. 'Nothing here, just a couple of slims.' He chinned himself up. He slid down the fuselage and showed them what he'd found. 'They were wearing these.'

A pair of necklaces, tarnished from exposure. To each was attached a silver disk. Peter used some of his water to rinse the tags clean.

Sullivan, Joseph D. O+ 098879254 USMC Rom. Cath.
Gomez, Manuel R. AB– 859720152 USMC No pref.

'USMC – that's Marine Corps,' Hollis said. 'You should put these back where you found them, Caleb.'

Caleb snatched the necklaces from Peter's hand, clutching them protectively against his chest. 'No way. I'm keeping these. I found them, fair and square.'

'Hightop, they were soldiers.'

Caleb's voice was suddenly shrill. 'So what? They never came back, did they? The soldiers were supposed to come back for us, and they never did.'

For a moment, no one spoke. 'That's what this place is, isn't it?' Sara said. 'Auntie used to tell stories about it. How the First Ones came from the cities, to ride the buses up the mountain.'

Peter had heard these stories, too. He'd always thought of them as just that, stories. But Sara was right; that's what this place was. More than the buses themselves, or the fallen helicopter with its dead soldiers inside, the stillness told him so. It was more than the simple absence of sound; it was the silence of something stopped.

A feeling jarred him then, a prickling alertness. Something was wrong.

'Where's Amy?'

They fanned out through the lines of buses, calling her name. By the time Michael found her, Peter was completely frantic. He had never considered that she might wander off like this.

Michael was standing beside one of the sunken buses, peering through an open window.

'What's she doing?' Sara said.

'I think she's just sitting there,' said Michael.

Peter clambered up and pulled himself inside. The wind had pushed the sand to the rear of the vehicle; the first few lines of benches were exposed. Amy was sitting on the bench directly behind the driver's seat, holding her pack on her lap. She had removed her glasses and hat.

'Amy, it'll be dark soon. We have to go.'

But the girl made no move to leave. She appeared to be waiting for something. She glanced around, her eyes pulled into a squint, as if noticing for the first time that the bus was empty, a ruin. Then she rose, drawing her pack onto her shoulders, and climbed out through the window.

The bunker was just where Hollis had promised.

He led them to a spot where the third mountain stood between the other two, turned east again, and in half a click he stopped. 'This is it,' he announced.

They were facing a wall of rock. Behind them, the setting sun cut a final sliver of light across the horizon.

'I don't see anything,' Alicia said.

'You're not supposed to.'

Hollis slung his rifle and began to scramble up the wall. Peter watched him with a hand over his eyes against the reflected glare. Ten meters up he disappeared.

'Where did he go?' Michael said.

The face of the mountain began to move. A pair of doors, Peter realized, made to blend with the surface as camouflage: they backed into the face of the hillside, revealing a dark cavern and the figure of Hollis standing before them.

It took Peter a moment to absorb the full dimensions of what he was seeing: a vast vault, carved from the mountain itself. Rows of shelving extended into its dark recesses, stacked with pallets of crates that reached high above their heads. A forklift was parked near the entrance, where Hollis had opened a metal panel in the wall. As the group moved inside, he flipped a switch and the room suddenly thrummed with light, issuing from a network of glowing ropes on the walls and ceiling. Peter heard the airy hum of mechanical ventilation coming on.

'Hollis, these are fiber optics,' Michael said, his voice lit with amazement. 'What's the power source?'

Hollis flipped a second switch. A yellow warning beacon sprang to life, swiveling with a mad urgency over the doors. With a clunk of gears engaging, the doors began to slide from their pockets, dragging blades of shadow across the floor.

'You can't see them the way we came,' Hollis explained, lifting his voice over the racket, 'but there's a solar array on the south face of the mountain. That's how Demo found the place.'

A hard bang as the doors closed, the echo ricocheting deep within. They were sealed away now, in safety.

'The stack won't hold much of a charge anymore, but you can run straight off the panels for a few hours. There are some portable generators too. There's a fuel depot just a short walk north of here. Gas, diesel, kerosene. If you bleed it off right it's still usable. There's more than we could ever use.'

Peter advanced into the room. Whoever had constructed this place, he thought, they had built it to last. The room reminded him of the library, only the books were crates, and the crates contained not words but weapons. The leftovers of the last, lost war, boxed and stored for the war to come.

He moved to the nearest shelf, where Alicia was standing

with Amy. Since the incident at the buses, the girl had stayed close, never venturing more than a few meters away. Alicia had pulled the base of her sleeve over her wrist to wipe away a layer of dust from the side of one of the crates.

'What's an RPG?' Peter asked.

'I have no idea,' Alicia said. She turned, smiling, to look at him. 'But I think I want one.'

FORTY-FOUR

From the Journal of Sara Fisher ('The Book of Sara')
Presented at the Third Global Conference on the North
    American Quarantine Period
Center for the Study of Human Cultures and Conflicts
University of New South Wales, Indo-Australian Republic
April 16–21, 1003 A.V.

[*Excerpt begins.*]

Day 4
So I guess I'll just begin. Hello. My name is Sara Fisher, First Family. I am writing to you from an army bunker somewhere north of the town of Twentynine Palms, California. I am one of eight souls traveling from the San Jacinto Mountains to the town of Telluride, Colorado. It's strange to say these things to a person I don't even know, who may not even be alive when I'm writing this. But Peter says someone should keep a record of what happens to us. Maybe someday, he said, someone will want to know.

We have been at the bunker two days. All things considered it's pretty comfortable, with electricity and plumbing and even a shower that works if you don't mind cold water (I don't). Not counting the barracks, the bunker has three main chambers: one that seems to contain mostly weapons ('the storeroom'), another with vehicles ('the garage'), and a third, smaller room with food and clothing and medical supplies (we don't have a name for it yet, we just call it the third room). This was where I found the notebooks and the pencils. Hollis says there's enough stuff here to outfit a small army, and I don't doubt it.

Michael and Caleb are going to try to fix one of the Humvees, which is a kind of car. Peter thinks two of them should be able to carry the eight of us with supplies and enough extra fuel, though Michael says he doesn't know if he can salvage more than one from the parts we have. Alicia is helping them, though from the looks of it she doesn't do much more than hand them the tools they ask for. It's nice to see her not bossing everyone around for a change.

All of this belonged to the Army, who are all dead now. I think I should say that. Also that the reason we are here is the girl, named Amy, who is a hundred years old, according to Michael. Though if you met her you might not know this. You'd think she was just a girl. There was something in her neck, a kind of radio, which told us she comes from Colorado, in a place called the CQZ. This is a long story, and I'm not quite sure how to tell it. She can't talk, but we think there may be more people out there like her, because Michael heard them on the radio. And that is why we are going to Colorado.

Everybody here has a job to do, and mine is to help Hollis and Peter figure out what's in the crates on the shelves. Peter says that as long as we're waiting on the Humvee we might as well make use of the time, in case we need to come back here someday. Plus, we might find things we can use now, such as the walkie-talkies. Michael thinks he can make a couple of them work if there are any batteries that will still take a charge. Off the storeroom there's a kind of alcove we call the office, full of desks and computers that don't work anymore and shelves stacked with binders and manuals, and that was where we found the inventory lists, pages and pages of them, with everything from rifles and mortars to pairs of pants and bars of soap. (I hope we find the soap soon.) Each item is followed by a bunch of numbers and letters, which match the numbers and letters on the shelves, though not always. Sometimes you open a crate and think it will be blankets or batteries and what you've got is shovels or more guns. Amy is helping us, and though she still hasn't said anything, today I realized

she could read the lists as well as anyone. I don't know why this
surprised me, but it did.

Day 6
Michael and Caleb are still working on the Humvees. Michael says
there's two he can probably fix, but he's still not sure. He says the
problem is anything rubber – a lot of it is cracked and falling apart.
But I have never seen Michael so happy, and everyone thinks he will
figure it out.

Yesterday I took inventory of the medical supplies. A lot of it is no
good, but there are some things I think I can use, real bandages and
splints and even a blood pressure cuff. I took Maus's pressure and it
was 120/80 and I told her to remind me to take it every day and be
sure to drink a lot of water. She said she would, but it makes her have
to pee about every five minutes.

This morning Hollis took all of us out to the desert to show us how
to shoot and throw a grenade. There's so much ammo he said it was
okay to use and everyone ought to know. So for a while we all shot off
rifles at piles of rocks and threw grenades into the sand, and now my
ears are ringing with the sound of it. Hollis thinks the area south of us
is full of mines and says no one should go there. I think he was
speaking mostly to Alicia because she's been taking the horse to hunt
in the early mornings before it gets too hot, though so far she hasn't
got anything except a couple of jacks, which we cooked last night.
Peter found a deck of cards in the barracks and after dinner we all
played go-to, even Amy, who won more hands than anyone, even
though no one explained the rules to her. I guess she figured out just by
watching.

Real leather boots! We're all wearing them now except for Caleb,
who still has his sneakers. They're way too big but he says he doesn't
mind, he likes the way they look, and he thinks they're lucky, since he
hasn't died since he put them on. Maybe we'll find a crate of lucky
sneakers?

Day 7
Still no progress on the Humvees. Everyone is beginning to worry we'll
have to walk out of here.

Apart from the boots, the best thing we've found so far are the light sticks. These are plastic tubes you snap over your knee and give them a hard shake and light comes out, a pale glowing green. Last night Caleb broke one open and put the glowing stuff all over his face and said, 'Look at me, I'm a smoke now!' Peter said that wasn't funny but I thought it was, and most of us laughed anyway. I'm glad Caleb is here.

Tomorrow I'm going to boil water and take a real bath, and give Amy a haircut while I'm at it, at least do something about those tangles. Maybe I can get her to take a bath, too.

Day 9

Michael said today they were going to try to start one of the Humvees so we all gathered around while they hooked it up to one of the generators, but when they tried to turn the engine over there was a loud bang and smoke and Michael said they'll have to start from scratch. It was probably bad gas, he says, but I could tell he didn't really know. To make matters worse, the toilets backed up in the barracks and Hollis said, How is it the United States Army can make food that lasts a hundred years but they can't make a decent toilet?

Hollis asked me to give him a haircut too and I have to say, with a little cleaning up he doesn't look half bad. Maybe I can get him to shave off the beard, but I think it means too much to him, with Arlo gone. Poor Arlo. Poor Hollis.

Day 11

The horse was killed today. It was completely my fault. During the day we've been keeping her staked outside in the shade where there's some brush and weeds to graze on. I decided to walk her a bit but then something spooked her and she got away. Hollis and I ran after her but of course we couldn't catch her and then we saw her out in the field where the mines were and before I could say anything there was a terrible boom, and when the dust cleared she was lying on the ground. I was going to go after her but Hollis stopped me, and I said, We can't leave her like that, and he said, No we can't, and he went back to the barracks to get his rifle and that was what he did. Both of us were crying and after I asked him if he'd had a name for her and he said yes, her name was Sweetheart.

We've been here just nine days but it feels like much longer and I have begun to wonder if we are ever leaving this place.

Day 12
The horse's body was taken away in the night. So now we know there are smokes around. Peter has decided to close the doors an hour before sunset just to be safe. I'm a little worried about Mausami. In just the last few days she's started to show. Probably no one else would notice, but I can tell. What everybody knows but isn't saying is that Theo is probably dead. She's tough but I'm sure this is all very hard for her as the days drag by. I wouldn't want to have a baby out here.

Day 13
Good news – Michael says he may try to start one of the Humvees tomorrow. We all have our fingers crossed. Everyone is anxious to get going.

I came across a crate in the third room marked Human Remains Pouch and when I opened it and saw what was there I realized they were bags the Army used to put dead soldiers in. I repacked the crate and hope no one asks me about it.

Day 16
I haven't written for a couple of days because I've been learning to drive.

Two days ago Michael and Caleb finally got the first of the Humvees running, tires and all. Everyone was shouting and laughing, we were all so happy. Michael said he wanted to go first and with just a few scrapes he managed to back it out of the bunker. We all took turns at the wheel with Michael telling us what to do, but none of us is very good.

The second Humvee rolled out this morning. Caleb says that's it, that's what we're going to get, but we don't really need more than two anyway. If one breaks down we can use the other as a backup. Michael thinks we can carry enough diesel to get to Las Vegas, maybe farther, before we have to find more.

We're off in the morning to the fuel depot.

Day 17

Gassed and ready to go. We spent the morning shuttling back and forth to the depot, filling the Humvees and the extra cans.

Everyone is exhausted but excited, too. It's like the trip has finally, truly begun. We're riding as two groups of four. Peter is going to drive one Humvee, and I'm going to drive the other, with Hollis and Alicia riding up top to man the guns, fifty-caliber machine guns, which we mounted this afternoon. Michael found some batteries to hold a charge so we can talk to each other with the walkie-talkies, at least until the batteries run out. Peter thinks we should try to go around Las Vegas, stay to the backcountry, but Hollis says it's the quickest way if we want to get to Colorado, and the interstates are best, because they follow the easiest terrain. Alicia sided with Hollis, and Peter finally agreed, so Las Vegas it will be, I guess. Everyone is wondering what we will find there.

I feel like we're a proper expedition now. We threw away our old clothing and everyone is wearing Army clothes, even Caleb, though they're much too big on him. (Maus is hemming a pair of pants for him.) After dinner Peter gathered everyone around and showed us our route on the map, and then he said, I think we should celebrate, Hollis, don't you, and Hollis nodded and said, I think that's right, and held up a bottle of whiskey he'd found in one of the desks in the office. It tasted a little like shine and felt the same, and before long everyone was laughing and singing, which felt wonderful but was a little sad too, because we were all remembering Arlo and his guitar. Even Amy drank some, and Hollis said, Maybe it will put her in the mood to say something, and at that she smiled, the first time I think I've ever seen her do this. It really feels like she's one of us now.

It's late now, and I have to go to bed. We're setting out at first light. I can't wait to leave, but I think I will miss this place, too. None of us knows what we'll find or if we'll ever see home again. I think without our realizing it, we've become a family here. So, to whoever is reading this, that's really all I have to say.

Day 18

We made it to Kelso in plenty of time. The landscape we're in seems totally dead – the only living creatures seem to be lizards, which are everywhere, and spiders, huge hairy ones the size of your hand. No other buildings besides the depot. After the bunker, it feels like we're out in the open, totally exposed, even though the windows and doors are all boarded up. There's a pump but no water, so we are running on what we brought. If it stays this hot we better find more soon. I can tell no one's going to sleep much. I hope Amy can keep them away, like Peter says.

Day 19
They came last night, a pod of three. They entered through the roof, tearing the wood apart like paper. When it was over, two of them were dead and the third had scattered. But Hollis had been shot. Alicia says she thinks she did it, but Hollis said he actually shot himself, trying to load one of the pistols. Probably he was just saying that to make her feel better. The bullet passed through his upper arm, just a nick really, but any wound is serious, especially out here. Hollis is too tough to show it, but I can tell he's in a lot of pain.

I'm writing this in the early-morning hours, just before dawn. Nobody's going back to sleep. We're all just waiting for sunrise so we can get out of here. Our best chance is to make it to Las Vegas with enough time to find shelter for the night. What everybody's thinking, but not saying, is that there's no real safety from here on out.

The funny thing is, I don't mind so much, not really. I hope we don't all die out here, of course. But I think I'd rather be here than anywhere else, with these people. It's different being afraid when there's the hope that it will amount to something. I don't know what we'll find in Colorado, if we ever get there. I'm not even sure it matters. All those years, waiting for the Army, and it turns out the Army is us.

FORTY-FIVE

They drove in from the south, into the fading day, into a vision of towering ruins.

Peter was at the wheel of the first Humvee, Alicia up top,

scanning the terrain with the binoculars; Caleb sat beside him in the passenger seat with the map over his lap. The highway had all but disappeared, its course vanished under waves of cracked, pale earth.

'Caleb, where the hell are we?'

Caleb was twisting the map this way and that. He arched his neck and shouted up to Alicia, 'Do you see the 215?'

'What's the 215?'

'Another highway, like this one! We should be crossing it!'

'I didn't know we were even *on* a highway!'

Peter brought the vehicle to a halt and picked up the radio from the floor. 'Sara, what's your fuel gauge say?'

A crackle of static, and then Sara's voice came through: 'A quarter tank. Maybe a little more.'

'Let me talk to Hollis.'

He watched in the rearview as Hollis, his injured arm wrapped in a sling, scrambled down from the gun post and took the radio from Sara. 'I think we may have lost the road,' Peter told him. 'We both need fuel, too.'

'Is there an airport anywhere?'

Peter took the map from Caleb to examine it. 'Yes. If we're still following Highway 15, it should be ahead of us, to the east.' He shouted up to Alicia: 'Do you see anything that looks like an airport?'

'How the hell should I know what an airport looks like?'

Through the radio, Hollis said, 'Tell her to look for fuel tanks. Big ones.'

'Lish! Do you see any fuel tanks?'

Alicia dropped down into the cabin. Her face was coated with dust. She rinsed out her mouth from her canteen and spat out the window. 'Dead ahead, about five clicks.'

'You're sure?'

She nodded. 'There's a bridge up ahead. I'm thinking that could be the overpass at Highway 215. If I'm right, the airport is just on the other side.'

Peter picked up the radio again. 'Lish says she thinks she sees it. We're going ahead.'

'All eyes, cuz.'

Peter put the vehicle in gear and drew forward. They were on the city's southern outskirts, an open plain tufted with weeds. To the west, purpling mountains lifted against the desert sky like the backs of great animals rising from the earth. Peter watched as the cluster of buildings at the heart of the city began to take shape beyond his windshield, resolving into a pattern of discrete structures, bathed in a golden light. It was impossible to tell how big they were or how far away. In the backseat, Amy had removed her glasses and was squinting at the landscape outside her window. Sara had done a thorough job of cutting the mats away; what remained of her hair, that wild tangle, was a trim, dark helmet, tracing the lines of her cheeks.

They came to the overpass; the bridge was gone, collapsed in sheets of broken concrete. The highway below was a choked gulley of cars and debris, completely impassable. There was nothing to do but try to go around. Peter guided the Humvee east, tracing the highway below them. A few minutes later they came to a second bridge, which appeared intact. A gamble, but they were running out of time.

He radioed Sara. 'I'm going to try to get across. Wait until we're over.'

Their luck held; they traversed it without incident. Pausing on the far side for Sara to cross, Peter took the map from Caleb once again. If he was correct, they were on Las Vegas Boulevard South; the airport, with its fuel tanks, would be due east.

They pressed on. The landscape began to change, thickening with structures and abandoned vehicles. Most were pointed south, away from the city.

'Those are Army trucks,' said Caleb.

A minute later they saw the first battle tank. It was resting upside down in the center of the road, like a huge capsized turtle; both of its tracks had been blown off its wheels.

Alicia crouched to peek her head back into the cabin. 'Pull forward,' she said. 'Slowly.'

He turned the wheel to navigate around the overturned tank. By now it was obvious what lay ahead: the city's defensive perimeter. They were moving through a vast debris field of tanks and other vehicles. Peter saw, beyond it, a line of sandbags backed against a concrete barrier, topped with coils of wire.

'What do you want to do now?' Sara asked over the radio.

'We'll have to go around somehow.' He released the Talk button and lifted his voice to Alicia, who was scanning with the binoculars. 'Lish! East or west?'

She ducked down again. 'West. I think there's a break in the wall.'

It was getting late; the attack the night before had left them all shaken. The last hands of daylight were like a funnel, drawing them down toward night. With each passing minute, the decisions they made became more irrevocable.

'Alicia says west,' Peter radioed.

'That'll take us away from the airport.'

'I know. Put Hollis on again.' He waited for Hollis's acknowledgment, then continued: 'I think we have to use the gas we've got to find shelter for the night. All those buildings up ahead, there has to be something we can use. We can backtrack to the airport in the morning.'

Hollis's voice was calm, but Peter could detect the underlying note of worry. 'It's your call.'

He glanced through the rearview at Alicia, who nodded.

'We're going around,' Peter said.

The break in the perimeter was a ragged gap twenty meters across. The remains of a burned-out tanker truck lay on its side near the opening. Probably, Peter thought, the driver had tried to run the blockade.

They continued on. The landscape was changing again, thickening with structures as they moved into the city. No one was talking; the only sounds were the low rumble of the engine and the scrape of weeds on the underside of the Humvee's carriage. They had somehow gotten on Las Vegas

Boulevard again; a creaking sign, still held aloft on its wires above the street, jostled in the wind. The buildings were larger now, monumental in scope, towering above the roadway with their great ruined faces. Some were burned, empty cages of steel girders, others half-collapsed, their facades fallen away to reveal the honeycombed compartments within, dressed with dripping gardens of wire and cable. They passed beneath signs bearing mysterious names: Mandalay Bay. The Luxor. New York New York. Rubble of all kinds littered the spaces between the buildings, forcing Peter to move at a creep. More Humvees and tanks and sandbagged positions; there had been a battle here. Twice he had to stop completely and search for an alternate route around some obstacle.

'This is too dense,' Peter said finally. 'We'll never make it through. Caleb, find me a way out of here.'

Caleb directed him west, onto Tropicana. But a hundred meters later the road disappeared, subsumed once again under a mountain of rubble. Peter reversed direction, returned to the intersection, and fought his way north again. They were stopped this time by a second perimeter of concrete barricades.

'It's like a maze in here.'

He tried one more route, heading farther east. This, too, was impassable. The shadows were lengthening; they had maybe half a hand of good light left. It had been a mistake, he knew, to head through the heart of the city. Now they were trapped.

He took the radio from the dashboard. 'Any ideas, Sara?'

'We can go back the way we came.'

'It'll be dark by the time we get out of here. We don't want to be caught out in the open, not with all these high points.'

Alicia dropped down from the roof. 'There's one building that looks tight,' she said quickly. 'Back down this road about a hundred meters. We passed it coming in.'

Peter relayed this information to the second Humvee. 'I don't see that we have a lot of options.'

It was Hollis who answered. 'Let's do it.'

They reversed course. Angling his eyes upward through the windshield, Peter identified the structure Alicia had indicated: a white tower, fantastically tall, rising from the lengthening shadows into sunlight. It appeared solid, though of course he couldn't see the other side; the rear of the building might be completely peeled away, for all they knew. The structure was separated from the roadway by a masonry wall and a broad, bowl-like depression, with pipes extruding from the drifts of sand and debris that littered the bottom. Peter was worried they would have to traverse this somehow, or else leave the Humvees on the street, but then they came to a break in the wall just as Alicia called down, 'Turn here.'

He was able to pull the Humvee right up to the base of the tower, parking beneath a kind of portico, wreathed with skeletal vines. Sara pulled in behind him. The front of the building was boarded up, the entrance barricaded by sandbags. Exiting the vehicle, Peter felt a sudden chill; the temperature was dropping.

Alicia had opened the rear compartment and was hurriedly passing out packs and rifles. 'Just take what we'll need for tonight,' she ordered. 'Whatever we can carry. Bring as much water as you can.'

'What about the Humvees?' Sara asked.

'They're not going anywhere on their own.' Alicia, after drawing a belt of grenades over her head, checked the load on her rifle. 'Hightop, do you have a way in yet? We're losing the light here.'

Caleb and Michael were furiously working to pry loose the covering from one of the windows. With a crack of splitting plywood it yanked loose from the frame, revealing the glass behind it, caked with grime. A single stroke from Caleb's pry bar and the glass shattered.

'Flyers,' he exclaimed, wrinkling his nose, 'what's that *stink*?'

'I guess we'll find out,' Alicia said. 'Okay, everybody, let's move.'

Peter and Alicia climbed through the window first. Hollis would bring up the rear with Amy and the others in between. Dropping inside, Peter found himself in a dark hallway, running parallel with the front of the building. To his right stood a pair of metal doors, chained shut through the handles. He stepped back to the open window.

'Caleb, pass me a hammer. The pry bar, too.'

He used the sharp end of the pry bar to shatter the chain. The door swung free, revealing a wide, open space, more region than room, remarkably undisturbed. Apart from the smell – a tart chemical scent, vaguely biological – and a heavy layer of dust that coated every surface, the impression it gave was less of ruin than abandonment, as if its inhabitants had departed days ago, not decades. At the center of the space stood a large stone structure, evidently some kind of fountain, and on a raised platform in the corner, a piano, tented with cobwebs. A long counter was positioned to the left.

Peter tilted his gaze upward to the ceiling, which was bisected by elaborately carved molding into discrete, convex panels. Each was ornately painted: winged figures with sad, dewy eyes and plump-cheeked faces, set against a sky of billowing clouds.

Caleb whispered, 'Is it . . . some kind of church?'

Peter didn't answer; he didn't know. Something about the winged figures on the ceiling was disquieting, even a little ominous. He turned to see Amy standing by the cobwebbed piano, gazing upward like the rest of them.

Then Hollis was beside him. 'We better get to higher ground.' He felt it, too, Peter could tell, this ghostlike presence hovering over them. 'Let's try to find the stairs.'

They advanced into the building's interior down a second, wider hallway, lined with stores – Prada, Tutto, La Scarpa, Tesorini – the names meaningless but strangely musical. There was more damage here, windows shattered, shards of glinting glass scattered over the stone floor and crunching under the soles of their boots. Many of the stores appeared to have been ransacked – counters smashed, everything overturned – while others seemed untouched, their peculiar, useless wares – shoes no one could actually walk in, bags that were too small to carry anything – still displayed in the windows. They passed signs that said SPA LEVEL and POOL PROMENADE, with arrows pointing down other, adjacent hallways, and banks of elevators, their gleaming doors sealed, but nothing that said STAIRS.

The hallway ended in a second open area, as large as the first, receding into darkness. There was something subterranean about it, as if they had stumbled upon the entrance to an immense cave. The smell was stronger here. They broke their light sticks and moved forward, sweeping the area with their rifles. The room appeared to be filled with long banks of machines, like nothing Peter had ever seen before, with video screens and various buttons and levers and switches. Before each was a stool, presumably where the machines' operators had sat, performing their unknown function.

Then they saw the slims.

First one and then another and then more and more, their frozen figures resolving out of the gloom. Most were seated around a series of tall tables, their postures grimly comical, as if they'd been overcome in the midst of some desperate, private act.

'What the hell is this place?'

Peter approached the nearest table. Three seated figures occupied it; a fourth lay on the floor beside his overturned stool. Holding up his light stick, Peter bent to the closest body, a woman. She had toppled facefirst; her head was turned to the side, her cheekbone resting on the table's surface. Her hair, bleached of all color, formed a snarl of parched fibers around the knob of her skull. Where her teeth should have been were a pair of dentures, their plastic gums still retaining an incongruously lifelike pinkness. Ropes of golden metal wreathed her neck; the bones of her fingers, where they rested on the tabletop – she seemed to have reached out to stop her fall – were bedecked with rings, fat shining stones of every color. On the table before her was a pair of playing cards, face-up. A six and a jack. It was the same with the others, he saw: each player had two cards showing. There were more cards strewn over the table. Some kind of game, like go-to. In the center lay a heaping mound of more jewelry, rings and watches and bracelets, as well as a pistol and a handful of shells.

'We better keep moving,' Alicia said, coming up beside him.

Something was here, he thought, something he was meant to find.

'It'll be dark soon, Peter. We have to find those stairs.'

He pulled his gaze away, nodding.

They emerged into an atrium, domed in glass. The sky above was cooling, night falling. Escalators led down to another dark recess; to the right they saw a bank of elevators, and yet another hallway, and more shops.

'Are we going in circles?' This was Michael. 'I swear we came right though here.'

Alicia's face was grave. 'Peter—'

'I know, I know.' The moment of decision was upon them: keep looking for the stairs or seek shelter on the ground floor. He turned to face the group, which seemed, suddenly, too small.

'Damnit, not *now*.'

Mausami pointed toward the windows of the closest shop. 'There she is.'

DESERT GIFT EMPORIUM, the sign read. Peter opened the door and moved inside. Amy was facing a wall of shelves by the counter, bearing a display of spherical glass objects. Amy had taken one in her hand. She gave it a hard shake, filling its interior with a flurry of movement.

'Amy, what is that?'

The girl turned, her face bright – *I have found something*, her eyes seemed to say, *something wonderful* – and held it out for him to take. An unexpected weight filled his hand:

the sphere was full of liquid. Suspended in this fluid, bits of glittering white matter, like flakes of snow, were settling down upon a landscape of tiny buildings. Rising at the center of this miniaturized city was a white tower – the same tower, Peter realized, in which they now stood.

The others had crowded around. 'What is it?' Michael asked.

Peter passed it to Sara, who showed it to the others.

'Some kind of model, I think.' Amy's face was still wearing a look of glowing happiness. 'Why did you want us to see this?'

But it was Alicia who provided the answer.

'Peter,' she said, 'I think you better look at this.'

She had turned the globe upside down, revealing the words that were printed on its base.

Milagro Hotel and Casino
Las Vegas

The smell had nothing to do with the slims, Michael explained. It was sewer gas. Mostly methane, which was why the place smelled like an outhouse. Somewhere beneath the hotel was a sea of one-hundred-year-old effluent, the pooled waste of an entire city, trapped like a giant fermentation tank.

'We don't want to be here when that lets go,' he warned. 'It'll be the biggest fart in history. The place will go up like a torch.'

They were on the fifteenth floor of the hotel, watching the night come on. For a few, panicked minutes it had begun to look as if they'd have to take refuge on the hotel's lower levels. The only stairwell they'd found, on the far side of the casino, was clogged with debris – chairs, tables, mattresses, suitcases, all of it bent and smashed, as if hurled from a great height. It was Hollis who had suggested jimmying open one of the elevators. Assuming the cable was intact, he explained, they could climb a couple of floors, enough to get around the barricade, and take the stairs the rest of the way.

It worked. Then, at the sixteenth floor, they encountered a second barricade. The floor of the stairwell was littered with shell casings. They exited to find themselves in a darkened hallway. Alicia cracked another light stick. The hall was lined with doors; a sign on the wall said AMBASSADOR SUITE LEVEL.

Peter gestured with his rifle to the first door. 'Caleb, do your thing.'

The room had two bodies in it, a man and a woman, lying on the bed. They were both wearing bathrobes and slippers; on the table by the bed was an open whiskey bottle, its contents long evaporated to a brown stain, and a plastic syringe. Caleb, voicing the words everyone was thinking, said he wasn't going to spend the night with a couple of slims, especially slims that had killed themselves. It wasn't until they had tried five doors that they found one without bodies behind it. Three rooms, two with a pair of beds in each and a third, larger room facing a wall of windows that gazed over the city. Peter stepped to the glass. The last daylight was going, bathing the scene in an orange glow. He wished they were higher, even on the roof, but this would have to do.

'What's that down there?' Mausami asked. She was pointing across the street, where a massive structure of ribbed steel, four legs that tapered to a narrow tip, rose between the buildings.

'I think it's the Eiffel Tower,' said Caleb. 'I saw a picture of it in a book once.'

Mausami frowned. 'Isn't that in Europe?'

'It's in Paris.' Michael was kneeling on the floor, unpacking their gear. 'Paris, France.'

'So what's it doing here?'

'How should I know?' Michael shrugged. 'Maybe they moved it.'

They watched together as night fell – first the street, then the buildings, then the mountains beyond, all sinking into darkness as if into the waters of a filling tub. The stars were coming out. No one was in the mood to talk; the precariousness of their situation was obvious. Sitting on the sofa, Sara rebandaged Hollis's wounded arm. Peter could discern, not from anything she said but from what she didn't, going about her work with tight-lipped efficiency, that she was worried about him.

They divvied up the MREs and lay down to rest. Alicia and Sara volunteered to take first watch. Peter was too exhausted to object. Wake me up when you're ready, he said. Probably I won't even sleep.

He didn't. In the bedroom he lay on the floor, his head propped on his pack, staring at the ceiling. Milagro, he thought. This was Milagro. Amy was sitting in a corner with her back to the wall, holding the glass globe. Every few minutes she would lift it from her lap and give it a shake, holding it close to her face as she watched the snow whirl and settle inside it. At such moments, Peter wondered what he was to her, what all of them were. He had explained to her where they were going and why. But if she knew what was in Colorado, and who had sent the signal, she had made no indication.

At last he gave up trying to sleep and returned to the main room. A wedge of moon had risen over the buildings. Alicia was standing at the window, scanning the street below; Sara was sitting at the small table, playing a hand of solo, her rifle resting across her lap.

'Any sign out there?'

Sara frowned. 'Would I be playing cards?'

He took a chair. For a while he said nothing, watching her play.

'Where'd you get the cards?' On the backs was that name, Milagro.

'Lish found them in a drawer.'

'You should rest, Sara,' Peter offered. 'I can take over.'

'I'm fine.' Frowning again, she swept the cards into a pile and redealt. 'Go back to bed.'

Peter said nothing more. He had the feeling he'd done something wrong, but he didn't know what.

Alicia turned from the window. 'You know, if you don't mind, I think I'll take you up on your offer. Put my head down for a few minutes. If it's okay with you, Sara.'

She shrugged. 'Suit yourself.'

Alicia left them alone. Peter rose and stepped to the window, using the nightscope on his rifle to scan the street: abandoned cars, heaps of rubble and trash, the empty buildings. A world frozen in time, caught at the moment of its abandonment in the last, violent hours of the Time Before.

'You don't have to pretend, you know.'

He turned. Sara was looking at him coolly, her face bathed in moonlight. 'Pretend what?'

'Peter, please. Not now.' Peter could feel her resolve; she had decided something. 'You did your best. I know that.' She gave a quiet laugh, looking away. 'I'd say I was grateful but I'd sound like an idiot, so I won't. If we're all going to die out here, I just wanted you to know it's all right.'

'No one's going to die.' It was all he could think to say.

'Well. I hope that's true.' She paused. 'Still, that one night—'

'Look, I'm sorry, Sara.' He took a deep breath. 'I should have told you that before. It was my fault.'

'You don't have to apologize, Peter. Like I said, you tried. It was a good try, too. But the two of you are meant for each other. I think I've always known that. It was stupid of me not to accept it.'

He was completely confounded. 'Sara, who are you talking about?'

Sara didn't answer. Her eyes grew suddenly wide. She was looking past him, out the window.

He turned sharply. Sara rose and came to stand beside him.

'What did you see?'

She pointed. 'Across the street, up on the tower.'

He pressed the nightscope to his eye. 'I don't see anything.'

'It was there, I know it.'

Then Amy was in the room. She was clutching the globe to her chest. With her other hand she gripped Peter by the arm and began to pull him away from the window.

'Amy, what's wrong?'

The glass behind them didn't so much shatter as explode, detonating in a hail of glinting shards. The air blew from his body as he was knocked across the room. It was only later that Peter would realize that the viral had come in right on top of them. He heard Sara scream – not even words, just a cry of terror. He hit the floor, rolling, his limbs tangled with Amy's, in time to see the creature vaulting back out the window.

Sara was gone.

Alicia and Hollis were in the room now, everyone was there, Hollis was ripping off the sling and taking up his rifle, he was standing at the window, aiming below, sweeping the scene with his barrel. But no shots came.

'Fuck!'

Alicia pulled Peter to his feet. 'Are you cut? Did it scratch you?'

His insides were still churning. He shook his head: no.

'What happened?' Michael cried. 'Where's my sister!'

Peter found his voice. 'It took her.'

Michael had grabbed Amy roughly by the arms. She was still clutching the globe, which had somehow remained unbroken. 'Where is she? Where is she?'

'Stop it, Michael!' Peter yelled. 'You're frightening her!'

The globe fell to the floor with a crash as Alicia yanked Michael away, sending him spilling onto the sofa. Amy stumbled backward, her eyes wide with fear.

'Circuit,' Alicia said, 'you have to calm down!'

His eyes were brimming with furious tears. 'Don't fucking call me that!'

A booming voice: 'Everyone shut the hell up!'

They turned to where Hollis stood by the open window, his rifle at his hip.

'Just. Shut. Up.' He looked them all over. 'I'll get your sister, Michael.'

Hollis dropped to one knee and began rifling through his pack for extra clips, filling the pockets of his vest. 'I saw which way they took her. Three of them.'

'Hollis—' Peter began.

'I'm not asking.' He met Peter's eyes. 'You of all people know I have to go.'

Michael stepped forward. 'I'm coming with you.'

'I'm going too,' said Caleb. He raised his eyes to the group, his face suddenly uncertain. 'I mean, because we're all going. Right?'

Peter looked at Amy. She was sitting on the sofa, her knees pressed protectively to her chest. He asked Alicia for her pistol.

'What for?'

'If we're going out there, Amy needs a weapon.'

She drew it from her waistband. Peter released the clip to check the load, then pushed the clip back into the handle and cocked the slide to put a round in the chamber. He turned it around in his hand and held it out to Amy.

'One shot,' he said. He tapped his breastbone. 'That's all you get. Through here. You know how to do this?'

Amy lifted her eyes from the gun in her hand, nodding.

They were gathering their gear when Alicia pulled Peter aside. 'Not that I'm objecting,' she said quietly, 'but it could be a trap.'

'I know it's a trap.' Peter took up his rifle and pack. 'I think I've known it since we got to this place. All those blocked streets, they led us right here. But Hollis is right. I never should have left Theo behind, and I'm not leaving Sara.'

They cracked their light sticks and stepped into the hall. At the top of the stairwell, Alicia moved to the rail and looked down, sweeping the area with the barrel of her rifle. She gave them the all clear, waving them forward.

They descended in this manner, flight by flight, Alicia and Peter trading the point, Mausami and Hollis guarding the rear. When they reached the third floor they exited the stairwell and moved down the hall, toward the elevators.

The middle elevator stood open, as they'd left it. Peering over the edge, Peter could see the car with its roof hatch standing open below. He swung out onto the cable, his rifle slung across his back, and shimmied to the roof of the car, then dropped inside. The elevator opened on another lobby, two stories tall, with a glass ceiling. The wall facing the open door was mirrored, giving him an angled view of the space beyond. He inched the barrel of his rifle out, holding his breath. But the moonlit space was empty. He whistled up through the hatch to the others.

The rest of the group followed, passing their rifles through the hatch and dropping down. The last was Mausami. She was wearing two packs, Peter saw, one slung from each shoulder.

'Sara's,' she explained. 'I thought she'd want it.'

The casino was to their left, to their right the darkened hall of empty stores. Beyond that lay the main entrance and the Humvees. Hollis had seen the pod taking Sara across the street, to the tower. The plan was to get across the open ground in front of the hotel using the vehicles, with their heavy guns, for cover. Beyond that, Peter didn't know.

They reached the lobby, with its silent piano. All was quiet, unchanged. In the glow of their light sticks, the painted figures on the ceiling seemed to float freely, suspended over their heads without attachment to any physical plane. When Peter had seen them the first time, they had seemed somehow menacing, but as he looked at them now, this feeling was gone. Those dewy eyes and soft, round faces – Peter realized they were Littles.

They reached the entrance and crouched by the open window. 'I'll go first,' Alicia said. She took a drink from her canteen. 'If it's clear, we get in and go. I don't want to hang around the base of the building more than about two seconds. Michael, you take Sara's place at the wheel of the second Humvee; Hollis and Mausami, I want you up on those fifties. Caleb, just run like hell and get inside and make sure Amy's with you. I'll cover you while everybody gets aboard.'

'What about you?' Peter asked.

'Don't worry, I'm not letting you leave without me.'

Then she was up and out the window, dashing for the nearest vehicle. Peter scrambled into position. The darkness beyond was total, the moon obscured by the roof of the portico. He heard a soft impact as Alicia took cover at the base of one of the Humvees. He pressed the stock of his weapon tight against his shoulder, willing Alicia to whistle the all clear.

Beside him, Hollis whispered, 'What the hell's keeping her?'

The lack of light was so complete it felt like a living thing, not an absence but a presence, pulsing all around him. An anxious sweat prickled his hair. He drew a breath and tightened his finger on the trigger of his rifle, ready to fire.

A figure raced toward them out of the darkness.

'Run!'

As Alicia dove headfirst through the window, Peter realized what he was seeing: a roiling mass of pale green light, like a cresting wave, hurtling toward the building.

Virals. The street was full of virals.

Hollis had begun to fire. Peter shouldered his weapon and managed to let off a pair of shots before Alicia seized him by the sleeve and yanked him away from the window.

'There's too many! Get out of here!'

They had made it less than halfway across the lobby when there came a thundering crash and the sound of splintering wood. The front door was failing; the virals would be streaming in at any second. Up ahead, Caleb and Mausami were sprinting down the hall toward the casino. Alicia was firing in quick bursts behind them, covering their retreat, her spent shell casings pinging across the tiled floor. In the flashing light of her muzzle Peter saw Amy on all fours by the piano, probing the ground as if she'd lost something. Her gun. But there was no point in looking for it now. He grabbed her by the arm and pulled her down the hall, chasing the others. His mind was saying: We're dead. We're all dead.

Another crash of breaking glass from deep inside the building. They were being flanked. Soon they'd be surrounded, lost in the dark. Like the mall, only worse, because there was no daylight to run to. Hollis was beside him now. Ahead he saw the glow of a light stick and the figure of Michael ducking through the shattered window of a restaurant. As he reached it he saw that Caleb and Mausami were already inside. He yelled to Alicia, 'This way! Hurry!' and shoved Amy through, in time to see Michael disappearing through a second door at the rear.

'Just follow them,' he cried. 'Go!'

Then Alicia was upon him, yanking him through the window. Without a pause she reached into her pouch and withdrew another light stick and cracked it over her knee. They raced across the room to the rear door, which was still swinging with the force of Michael's exit.

Another hallway, narrow and low-ceilinged, like a tunnel. Peter saw Hollis and the others up ahead, waving to them, shouting their names. The smell of sewer gas was suddenly stronger, almost dizzying. Peter and Alicia swiveled as the first viral burst through the door behind them. The hallway flashed with the light of their muzzles. Peter was firing blind, aiming at the door. The first one fell and then another and another. And still they kept on coming.

He realized he'd been squeezing the trigger but nothing was happening. His gun was empty; he had fired off his last round. Alicia was pulling him down the hall again. A flight of stairs, leading down to another hall. He bumped against the wall and almost fell but somehow kept going.

The hall ended at a pair of swinging doors that opened on a kitchen. The stairs had taken them below ground level, into the deep inner workings of the hotel. Banks of copper pots hung from the ceiling above a wide steel table that shone with the reflected glow of Alicia's light stick. His breath felt tight in his chest; the air was dense with fumes. He dropped his empty rifle and seized one of the pots from the ceiling. A wide copper fry pan, heavy in his hands.

Something had followed them through the door.

He turned, swinging the pan as he lurched backward against the stove – a gesture that would have seemed comical if it weren't so desperate – sheltering Alicia with his body as the viral bounded to the top of the steel table, dropping into a crouch. A female: her fingers were covered in rings like the ones he'd seen on the slims at the card table. She was holding her hands away from her body, the long fingers flexing, shoulders swaying in a liquid motion from side to side. Peter clutched the pan like a shield, Alicia pressed behind him.

Alicia: 'She sees herself!'

What was the viral waiting for? Why hadn't she attacked?

'Her reflection!' Alicia hissed. 'She sees her reflection in the pan!'

Peter became aware of a new sound, coming from the viral – a mournful nasal moaning, like the whine of a dog. As if the image of her face, reflected in the pan's copper bottom, were the source of some deep and melancholy recognition. Peter cautiously moved the pan back and forth, the viral's eyes following, entranced. How long could he hold her like this, before more virals came through the door? His hands were slick with sweat, the air was so dense with fumes he could scarcely breathe.

This place will go up like a torch.

'Lish, do you see a way out of here?'

Alicia swiveled her head quickly. 'A door to your right, five meters.'

'Is it locked?'

'How should I know?'

He spoke through clenched teeth, doing everything he

could to hold his body still, to keep the viral's eyes focused on the pan. 'Does it have a lock you can see, damnit?'

The creature startled, a muscular tautness rippling through her. Her jaw fell open, lips withdrawing to reveal the rows of gleaming teeth. She had given up her moaning; she had begun to click.

'No, I don't see one.'

'Pull a grenade.'

'There's not enough space in here!'

'Do it. The room is full of gas. Toss it behind her and run like hell for the door.'

Alicia slipped a hand between their bodies to her waist, freeing a grenade from her belt. He felt her pull the pin.

'Here you go,' she said.

A clean arc, up and over the viral's head. It was as Peter had hoped; the viral's eyes broke away, her head twisting to follow the airborne parabola of the grenade as it lobbed across the room, clattering on the table behind her before rolling to the floor. Peter and Alicia turned and dashed for the door. Alicia got there first, slamming into the metal bar. Fresh air and a feeling of space – they were on some kind of loading dock. Peter was counting in his head. *One second, two seconds, three seconds . . .*

He heard the first report, the concussive spray of the grenade's detonation, and then a second, deeper boom as the gas in the room ignited. They rolled over the edge of the dock as first the door shot above their heads and then the shock wave, a prow of fire. Peter felt the air being stripped from his lungs. He pressed his face into the earth, his hands held over his head. More explosions as pockets of gas went off, the fire traveling upward through the structure. Debris began to pour down over them, glass falling everywhere, exploding on the pavement in a rain of glinting shards. He breathed in a mouthful of smoke and dust.

'We have to move!' Alicia cried, pulling at him. 'The whole thing is going up!'

His hands and face felt wet, but who knew what that was.

They were somewhere on the south side of the building. They tore across the street under the light of the burning hotel and took cover behind the rusted hulk of an overturned car.

They were breathing hard, coughing out smoke. Their faces were coated with soot. He looked at Lish and saw a long glistening stain on her upper thigh, soaking the fabric of her pants.

'You're bleeding.'

She pointed at his head. 'So are you.'

Above them, a second series of explosions shook the air. A huge fireball ascended upward through the hotel, bathing the scene in a furious orange light, sending more flaming debris cascading to the street.

'You think the others got out?' he asked.

'I don't know.' Alicia coughed again, then took a mouthful of water from her canteen and spat onto the ground. 'Stay put.'

She scooted around the base of the car, returning a moment later. 'I count twelve smokes from here.' She made a vague gesture up and away. 'More on the tower on the far side of the street. The fires pushed them back, but that won't last.'

So there it was. Out in the dark, their rifles gone, trapped between a burning building and the virals. They were resting with their shoulders touching, their backs braced against the car.

Alicia rolled her head to look at him. 'That was a good idea. Using the pan. How'd you know it'd work?'

'I didn't.'

She shook her head. 'It was still some cool trick, anyway.' She paused, a look of pain skittering across her face. She closed her eyes and breathed, then: 'Ready?'

'The Humvees?'

'It's our best shot, I think. Stay close to the fires, use them for cover.'

Fires or no, they probably wouldn't make it ten meters once the virals saw them. From the look of Alicia's leg, he doubted she'd be able to walk at all. All they had were their blades and the five grenades on Alicia's belt. But Amy and the others were still out here, maybe; they had to at least try.

She clipped off two grenades and placed them in his hands. 'Remember our deal,' she said.

She meant would he kill her, if it came to that. The answer came so easily it surprised him. 'Me too. I won't be one of them.'

Alicia nodded. She had removed a grenade and pulled the pin, ready to throw. 'I just want to say, before we do this, I'm glad it's you.'

'Same here.'

She wiped her eyes with her wrist. 'Oh fuck, Peter, now you've seen me cry twice. You can't tell anyone, you can't.'

'I won't, I promise.'

A blaze of light filled his eyes. For an instant he actually believed something had happened and she'd accidentally released the grenade – that death was, in the end, an affair of light and silence. But then he heard the roar of the engine and knew that it was a vehicle, coming toward them.

'Get in!' a voice boomed. 'Get in the truck!'

They froze.

Alicia's eyes widened at the unpinned grenade in her hand. 'Flyers, what do I do with this?'

'Just throw it!'

She tossed it over the top of the car; Peter yanked her to the ground as the grenade went off with a bang. The lights were closing in. They took off at a hobbling run, Peter's arm wrapped around Alicia's waist. Lumbering out of the darkness was a boxy vehicle with a huge plow jutting from the front like a demented smile, the windshield wrapped in a cage of wire; some kind of gun was mounted to the roof, a figure positioned behind it. As Peter watched, the gun sprang to life, shooting a plume of liquid fire over their heads.

They hit the dirt. Peter felt stinging heat on the back of his neck.

'Keep down!' the voice boomed again, and only then did

Peter realize the sound was amplified, coming from a horn on the roof of the truck's cabin. 'Move your asses!'

'Well, which is it?' Alicia yelled, her body pressed to the ground. 'You can't have both!'

The truck ground to a halt just a few meters from their heads. Peter pulled Alicia to her feet as the figure on the roof slid down a ladder. A heavy wire mask obscured his face; his body was covered in thick pads. A short-barreled shotgun clung to his leg in a leather holster. Written on the side of the truck were the words NEVADA DEPARTMENT OF CORRECTIONS.

'In the back! Move it!'

The voice was a woman's.

'There are eight of us!' Peter cried. 'Our friends are still out here!'

But the woman seemed not to hear him or, if she did, to care. She hustled them to the rear of the truck, her movements surprisingly nimble despite her heavy armor. She turned a handle and flung the door wide.

'Lish! Get in!'

The voice was Caleb's. Everybody was there, splayed out on the floor of the dark compartment. Peter and Alicia clambered inside; the door clanged shut behind them, sealing them in darkness.

With a lurch, the truck began to move.

FORTY-SIX

That awful woman. That awful fat woman in the kitchen, her loose round form spilling over her chair like something melted. The tight, close heat of the room and the taste of her smoke in his nose and mouth and the smell of the woman's body, the sweat and crumb-filled creases in the rolls of billowing flesh. The smoke curling around her, puffing from her lips as she spoke, as if her words were taking solid form in the air, and his mind telling him, Wake up. You are asleep and dreaming. Wake up, Theo. But the pull of the dream was too strong; the more he struggled, the deeper he was drawn down into it. Like his mind was a well and he was falling, falling into the darkness of his own mind.

Watchoo looking at? Huh? You worthless little shit. The woman watching him and laughing. *The boy isn't just dumb. I tell you, he's been* struck *dumb.*

He awoke with a jolt, spilling from his dream into the cold reality of his cell. His skin was glazed with rank-smelling sweat. The sweat of his nightmare, which he could no longer recall; all that remained was the feeling of it, like a dark stain spattered over his consciousness.

He rose from his cot and shuffled to the hole. He did his best to aim, listening for the splash of his urine below. He'd begun to look forward to that sound, anticipating it the way he might have waited for a visit from a friend. He'd been waiting for the next thing to happen. He'd been waiting for someone to say something, to tell him why he was here and what they wanted. To tell him why he wasn't dead. He had come to realize, through the empty days, that he was waiting for pain. The door would open, and men would enter, and then the pain would begin. But the boots came and went – he could make out their scuffed toes through the slot at the bottom of the door – delivering his meals and taking away the empty bowls and saying nothing. He pounded on the door, a slab of cold metal, again and again. *What do you want from me, what do you want?* But his pleas met only silence.

He didn't know how many days he'd been here. High out of reach, a dirty window gave a view of nothing. A patch of white sky and at night, the stars. The last thing he remembered was the virals dropping from the roof, and everything turned upside down. He remembered Peter's face receding, the sound of his name being called, and the whip and snap of his neck as he'd been tossed upward, toward the roof. A last taste of the wind and sun on his face and the gun dropping away. Its slow, pinwheeling passage to the floor below.

And then nothing. The rest was a black space in his memory, like the cratered edges of a missing tooth.

He was sitting on the edge of the bed when he heard footsteps approaching. The slot in the door opened and a bowl slid through, across the floor. The same watery soup he'd eaten meal after meal. Sometimes there was a little joint of meat in it, sometimes just a marrowed bone for him to suck. At the beginning he had decided not to eat, to see what they, whoever they were, would do. But this had lasted only a day before his hunger had gotten the better of him.

'How you feeling?'

Theo's tongue was thick in his mouth. 'Fuck off.'

A dry chuckle. The boots shifting and scraping. The voice was young or old, he couldn't tell.

'That's the spirit, Theo.'

At the sound of his name, a chill snaked his spine. Theo said nothing.

'You comfortable in there?'

'How do you know who I am?'

'Don't you remember?' A pause. 'I guess you don't. You *told* me. When you first got here. Oh, we had ourselves a nice talk.'

He willed his mind to remember, but it was all blackness. He wondered if the voice was really there at all. This voice that seemed to know him. Maybe he was just imagining it. It would happen sooner or later, in a place like this. The mind did what it wished.

'Don't feel like talking now, do you? That's all right.'

'Whatever you're going to do, just do it.'

'Oh, we've done it already. We're doing it right now. Look around you, Theo. What do you see?'

He couldn't help it: he looked at his cell. The cot, the hole, the dirty window. There were bits of writing on the walls, etchings in the stone he'd puzzled over for days. Most were senseless figures, neither words nor any kind of image he recognized. But one, situated at eye level above the hole, was clear: RUBEN WAS HERE.

'Who's Ruben?'

'Ruben? Now, I don't believe I know any Ruben.'

'Don't play games.'

'Oh, you mean Ru-*ben*.' Another quiet laugh. Theo would have given his life to reach through the wall and smash the speaker's face. 'Forget Ru-*ben*, Theo. Things did not work out so nicely for Ru-*ben*. Ru-*ben*, you might say, is ancient history.' A pause. 'So tell me. How you sleeping?'

'What?'

'You heard me. You like that fat lady?'

His breath caught in his chest. 'What did you say?'

'The fucking fat lady, Theo. Come on. Work with me here. We've all been there. The fat lady inside your head.'

The memory burst inside his brain like a piece of rotten fruit. The dreams. The fat lady in her kitchen. A voice was outside the door and it knew what his dreams were.

'I have to say, I never did like her very much myself,' the voice was saying. 'Yakkity yakkity yakkity, all day long. And that stink. What the hell is that?'

Theo swallowed, trying to still his mind. The walls around him seemed closer somehow, squeezing him in. He put his head in his hands.

'I don't know any fat lady,' Theo managed.

'Oh, sure you don't. We've all been through it. It's not like you're the only one. Let me ask you something else.' The voice dropped to a whisper. 'You carve her up yet, Theo? With the knife? You get to that part yet?'

A swirl of nausea. His breath caught in his chest. The knife, the knife.

'So you haven't then. Well, you will. All in time. Trust me, when you get to that part, you're gonna feel a *lot* better. That's kind of a turning point, you could say.'

Theo lifted his face. The slot at the bottom of the door was still open, showing the tip of a single boot, leather so scuffed it looked white.

'Theo, you listening to me in there?'

His eyes fixed on the boot with the force of an idea taking

hold. Gingerly he rose from the bed and moved toward the door, stepping around the bowl of soup. He sank into a crouch.

'Are you hearing my words? Because I am talking about some serious *re*-lief.'

Theo lunged. Too late: his hand grabbed empty air. A bright explosion of pain: something came down hard, hard, on his wrist. A boot heel. It smashed the bones flat, compressing his hand into the floor. Grinding and twisting. His face was shoved against the cold steel of the door.

'Fuck!'

'It hurts, don't it?'

Spangled motes were dancing in his eyes. He tried to pull his hand away, but the force holding him in place was too strong. He was pinned now, one hand stuck through the slot. But the pain meant something. It meant the voice was real.

'You . . . go . . . to . . . hell.'

The heel twisted again; Theo yelped in agony.

'That's a good one, Theo. Where did you *think* you were? Hell is your new address, my friend.'

'I'm not . . . your friend,' he gasped.

'Oh, maybe not. Maybe not just at the moment. But you will be. Sooner or later, you will be.'

Then, just like that, the pressure on Theo's hand released – an absence of torment so abrupt it was like pleasure. Theo yanked his arm through the slot and slumped against the wall, breathing hard, cradling his wrist on his lap.

'Because, believe it or not, there are things even worse than me,' the voice said. 'Sleep well, Theo.' And then the slot slammed closed.

VIII
THE HAVEN

The isle is full of noises,
Sounds and sweet airs, that give delight and hurt not.
Sometimes a thousand twangling instruments
Will hum about mine ears; and sometimes voices,
That, if I then had wak'd after long sleep,
Will make me sleep again.

– Shakespeare,
The Tempest

FORTY-SEVEN

They had been on the road for hours. With nothing to lie on but the hard metal floor, sleep was all but impossible. It seemed that every time Michael closed his eyes, the truck would hit a bump or swerve one way or the other, sending some part of his body slamming down.

He lifted his head to see a glow of daylight gathering beyond the compartment's only window, a small porthole of reinforced glass set in the door. His mouth was bone dry; every part of him felt bruised, as if someone had been hitting him with a hammer all night long. He rose to a sitting position, pushing his back against the jostling wall of the compartment, and rubbed the gunk from his eyes. The rest of the group were propped on their packs in various postures of discomfort. Though they were all banged up to some degree, Alicia seemed the worst off. She was facing him, her back resting against the wall of the compartment; her face was pale and damp, her eyes open but drained of energy. Mausami had done her best to clean and bandage Alicia's injured leg the night before, but Michael could tell the wound was serious. Only Amy seemed to be actually sleeping. She was curled on the floor beside him, her knees pulled to her chest. A fan of dark hair lay over her cheek, pushed to and fro by the bouncing of the truck.

The memory hit him like a slap.

Sara, his sister, was gone.

He remembered running as fast as he could, through the kitchen and out onto the loading dock and into the street with the others, only to end up surrounded – smokes *everywhere*, the street was like a goddamn smoke party – and then the truck with its immense plow driving toward them, spewing its jet of flame. *Get in, get in*, the woman on top was yelling at him. And a good thing she had, because Michael had found himself, at just that moment, paralyzed with fear. Nailed to the ground with it. Hollis and the rest of them were yelling, *Come on, come on*, but Michael couldn't move a muscle. Like he'd forgotten *how*. The truck was no more than ten meters away but it could have been a thousand. He turned and as he turned one of the virals locked eyes with him, cocking its head in that funny way they did, and everything seemed to slow down in a way that wasn't good. *Oh boy*, a voice in Michael's head was saying, *oh boy oh boy oh boy oh boy*, and that was when the woman hit the viral with the flamethrower, coating it with a jet of liquid fire. It crisped up like a ball of fat. Michael actually heard the pop. Then someone was pulling him by the hand – Amy of all people, whose strength was surprising, more than he would have guessed from the little thing she was – and she shoved him into the truck.

Now it was morning. Michael felt himself pushed forward as the vehicle decelerated. Beside him, Amy's eyes shot open; she rolled into a sitting position and drew her knees to her chest once more, her gaze fixed on the door.

The truck drew to a halt. Caleb scrambled to the window and peered outside.

'What do you see?' Peter had risen to a crouch; his hair was matted with dried blood.

'There's some kind of structure, but it's too far away.'

Footsteps on the roof, the sound of the driver's door, opening and closing again.

Hollis was reaching for his rifle.

Peter put a hand out to stop him. 'Wait.'

Caleb: 'Here they come—'

The door swung open, blazing their eyes with daylight. Two backlit figures stood before them, clutching shotguns. The woman was young, with dark hair shorn close to her scalp; the man, much older, had a soft, wide face and a nose that looked punched and a few days' growth of beard. Both were still encased in their bulky body armor, making their heads seem strangely undersized.

'Hand over your weapons.'

'Who the hell are you people?' Peter demanded.

The woman cocked her shotgun. 'Everything. Knives, too.'

They disarmed, sliding their guns and blades along the floor in the direction of the door. Michael didn't have much more than a screwdriver left – he'd lost his rifle in the dash from the hotel, never having fired the damn thing once – but he handed it over anyway. He certainly didn't want to get shot over a screwdriver. While the woman collected their weapons, the second figure, who had yet to utter a word, kept his gun trained on all of them. In the distance, Michael could make out the shape of a long, low building set against a bulge of barren hills.

'Where are you taking us?' Peter asked.

The woman lifted a metal pail from the ground and placed it on the floor of the truck. 'If you have to piss, use this.' Then she slammed the door.

Peter slapped the wall of the truck. '*Fuck.*'

They drove on. The temperature was rising steadily. The truck decelerated again, turning west. For a long time the vehicle bounced violently; then they began to climb. By now the air in the cabin had become intolerably hot. They drank the last of their water; no one had used the pail.

Peter pounded on the wall that separated them from the truck's cab. 'Hey, we're roasting back here!'

Time passed, and passed some more. No one spoke; just breathing was an effort. It seemed that some terrible joke had been played on them. They had been rescued from the virals only to be cooked to death in the back of a truck. Michael had begun to drift in and out of a state that felt like sleep but not exactly. He was hot, so hot. At some point he realized they were descending, though this detail seemed trivial, as if it pertained to some other person.

Gradually the fact seeped into Michael's awareness that the vehicle had stopped. He had been lost in a vision of water, cool water. It was pouring over and through him, and his sister was there, and Elton too, smiling that off-kilter smile of his. Everyone was there, Peter and Mausami and Alicia and even his parents, they all were swimming in it together, its healing blueness, and for a moment Michael willed his mind to return to it, this beautiful dream of water.

'My God,' a voice said.

Michael opened his eyes to a harsh white light and the smell, unmistakable, of animal dung. He rolled his face toward the door and saw a pair of figures – he knew he had seen them before but could not say when – and standing between them, brilliantly backlit so that he seemed almost to hover, a tall man with steel-gray hair, wearing what appeared to be an orange jumpsuit. 'My God, my God,' the man was saying. 'Seven of them. It's beyond belief.' He turned to the others. 'Don't just stand there. We need stretchers. *Hurry*.'

The pair jogged away. The thought reached Michael's brain that something was very wrong. Everything seemed to be happening at the far end of a tunnel. He could not have said where he was or why, although he also sensed that this knowledge had abandoned him only recently, a feeling like déjà vu in reverse. It was a kind of joke but the joke wasn't funny, not at all. Some large, dry object was in his mouth, fat as a fist, and he realized this was his own tongue, choking him. He heard Peter's voice, a labored croak: 'Who . . . are . . . you?'

'My name is Olson. Olson Hand.' A smile lit up his wind-chapped face, only it wasn't the silver-haired man anymore, it was Theo – it was Theo's face at the far end of the tunnel – and that was the last thing Michael saw before the tunnel collapsed and all thought left him.

He did not come to so much as slowly surface, ascending through layers of darkness over a period of time that felt both short and long, an hour turned into a day, a day turned into a year. Darkness yielding to a widening whiteness above him, and the gradual reassembly of consciousness, distinct from his surroundings. His eyes were open, blinking. No other part of him seemed capable of movement, just his eyes, the damp plink of his lids. He heard the sound of voices, moving over him like the songs of distant birds, calling to one another across a vast expanse of sky. He thought: Cold. He was cold. Wonderfully, amazingly cold.

He slept, and when he opened his eyes again, some unknown interval of time having passed, he knew that he was in a bed, that the bed was in a room, and that he wasn't alone. Lifting his head was out of the question; his bones felt as heavy as iron. He was in some kind of infirmary, white walls and white ceiling, angled beams of white light falling upon the white sheet that covered his body and beneath which, it seemed, he was naked. The air was cool and moist. From a place somewhere above and behind came the rhythmic throb of machinery and the drip of water falling into a metal pan.

'Michael? Michael, can you hear me?'

Seated next to his cot was a woman – he thought it was a woman – with dark hair short as a man's, and a smooth brow and cheeks and a small, thin-lipped mouth. She was gazing at him with what appeared to be intense concern. Michael felt as if he'd seen her before, but his sense of recognition stopped there. Her slender form was draped in a loose-fitting orange costume that seemed, like everything else about her, vaguely familiar. Behind her was some kind of screen, obscuring his view.

'How do you feel?'

He tried to speak but the words seemed to die in his throat. The woman lifted a plastic cup from the table by his bed and held the straw to his lips: water, crisp and cold, distinctly metallic in taste.

'That's it. Sip slowly.'

He drank and drank. How amazing, the taste of water. When he had finished, she returned the cup to the table.

'Your temperature's down. I'm sure you'll want to see your friends.'

691

His tongue felt slow and heavy in his mouth. 'Where am I?'

She smiled. 'Why don't I let them explain that to you?'

The woman disappeared behind the screen, leaving him alone. Who was she? What was this place? He felt as if he'd been asleep for days, his mind adrift on a current of disturbing dreams. He tried to remember. Some fat woman. A fat woman breathing smoke.

His thoughts were broken by voices and the sound of footsteps. Peter appeared at the foot of his bed. His face glowed with a grin.

'Look who's awake! How are you feeling?'

'What . . . happened?' Michael croaked.

Peter took a seat by Michael's bed. He filled the cup again and held the straw to Michael's lips. 'I guess you don't remember. You had heatstroke. You passed out in the truck.' He angled his head toward the woman, who was standing to one side, silently observing. 'You've already met Billie, I guess. I'm sorry I wasn't here when you woke up. We've all been taking shifts.' He leaned in closer. 'Michael, you've got to see this place. It's fantastic.'

This place, Michael thought. Where was he? He pointed his eyes toward the woman, her serenely smiling face. All at once the memory coalesced in his mind. The woman from the truck.

He flinched, knocking the cup from Peter's hand, sending water splashing all over him.

'Flyers, Michael. What's the matter?'

'She tried to kill us!'

'That's a bit of an exaggeration, don't you think?' He glanced at the woman and gave a little laugh, as if the two of them were in on some private joke. 'Michael, Billie *saved* us. Don't you remember?'

There was something troubling about Peter's good cheer, Michael thought; it seemed completely out of step with the facts. Obviously he was very ill; he might well have died.

'What about Lish's leg? Is she all right?'

Peter waved this concern away. 'Oh, she's fine, everybody's fine. Just waiting for you to get better.' Peter leaned toward him again. 'They call it the Haven, Michael. It's actually an old prison. That's where you are now, in the infirmary.'

'A prison. Like a lockup?'

'Sort of. They really don't use the prison itself much anymore. You should see the size of their operation. Almost three hundred Walkers. Though I guess you could say we're the Walkers now. And here's the best thing, Michael. Are you ready? No smokes.'

His words made no sense. 'Peter, what are you talking about?'

Peter gave a puzzled shrug, as if the question wasn't interesting enough to warrant any real thought. 'I don't know. There just aren't. Listen,' he continued, 'when you're up on your feet, you can look for yourself. You should see the size of the herd. Actual beef cattle.' He was grinning at Michael vacantly. 'So what do you say? Think you can sit up?'

He didn't, but something about Peter's tone made him feel that he should at least try. Michael eased himself up on his elbows. The room began to tip; his brain sloshed painfully inside his skull. He fell back down again.

'Whoa. That hurt.'

'That's okay, that's okay. Just take it easy. Billie says a headache's perfectly normal after a seizure like that. You'll be back on your feet in no time.'

'I had a seizure?'

'You really don't remember much, do you?'

'I guess I don't.' Michael breathed steadily, trying to calm himself. 'How long was I out?'

'Counting today? Three days.' Peter glanced at the woman. 'No, make that four.'

'Four *days*?'

Peter shrugged. 'I'm sorry you missed the party. But the good news is that you're feeling better. Let's focus on that.'

Michael felt his frustration boiling over. 'What *party*? Peter, what's wrong with you? We're stranded in the middle of no place. We've lost all our gear. This woman tried to kill us. You're talking like everything's fine.'

They were interrupted by the sound of the door opening and a burst of cheerful laughter. Alicia, on crutches, swung around the screen. Trailing her was a man that Michael didn't recognize – fierce blue eyes, a chin that looked like it had been chiseled from stone. Was Michael hallucinating or were the two of them playing some sort of chase game, like Littles?

She stopped abruptly at the foot of his bed. 'Circuit, you're up!'

'Well, look at that,' the blue-eyed man declared. 'Lazarus, back from the dead. How you doing, pardner?'

Michael was too startled to respond. Who was Lazarus?

Alicia turned to Peter. 'Did you tell him?'

'I was just getting to that,' Peter said.

'*Tell me what?*'

'It's your sister, Michael.' Peter smiled into his face. 'She's here.'

Tears sprang to Michael's eyes. 'That's not funny.'

'I'm not joking, Michael. Sara's here. And she's perfectly all right.'

'I just don't remember.'

Six of them were gathered around Michael's bed: Sara, Peter, Hollis, Alicia, the woman they called Billie, and the man with the blue eyes, who had introduced himself to Michael as Jude Cripp. After Peter had told Michael the news, Alicia had left to retrieve his sister; moments later she had burst into the room and flung herself upon him, weeping and laughing. It was all so completely inexplicable that Michael hadn't known where to begin, what questions to ask. But Sara was alive. For the moment, that was all that mattered.

Hollis explained how they had found her. The day after

694

their arrival, he and Billie had driven back to Las Vegas, to look for the Humvees. They'd reached the hotel to find a scene of total destruction, a smoking mound of rubble and twisted girders. The whole east side of the building had collapsed, filling the street with a mountain of debris. Somewhere beneath this lay the Humvees, smashed to pieces. The air was thick with soot and dust; a rain of ashes coated every surface. The fires had leapt to an adjacent hotel, which was still smoldering. But the building to the east, where Hollis had seen the viral taking Sara, was intact. This, as it turned out, was something called the Eiffel Tower Restaurant. A long flight of stairs led to the structure at the top, a large round room encircled by windows, many broken or missing, that looked out on the demolished hotel.

Sara was curled under one of the tables, unconscious. At Hollis's touch she seemed to rouse, but her eyes were glazed, unfocused; she appeared to have no notion where she was or what had happened to her. There were scratches on her face and arms; one of her wrists seemed broken from the way she held it, cradling it in her lap. He lifted her into his arms and climbed down the eleven flights of darkened stairs and into the smoke. It wasn't until they were halfway back to the Haven that she had started to come around.

'Is that really how it happened?' Michael asked her.

'If he says so. Honestly, Michael, all I remember is playing solo. The next thing I knew I was in the truck with Hollis. The rest is a big blank.'

'And you're really okay?'

Sara shrugged. It was true: apart from the scratches and the wrist that was not broken after all but merely sprained, wrapped with a splinted bandage, she had no visible injuries at all. 'I *feel* fine. I just can't explain it.'

Jude twisted in his chair toward Alicia. 'I've got to say, Lish, you sure know how to throw a party. I'd have liked to see the looks on their faces when you tossed that grenade.'

'Michael should get some of the credit. He was the one

who told us about the gas. And Peter was the one who used the pan.'

'I still don't completely understand that part,' said Billie, frowning. 'You say it saw its own reflection?'

Peter shrugged. 'All I know is, it worked.'

'Maybe the virals just don't like your cooking,' Hollis suggested.

Everybody laughed.

It was all so strange, Michael thought. Not just the story itself but the way everyone was acting, as if they had no worries in the world.

'What I don't get is what you guys were doing there in the first place,' he ventured. 'I'm glad you were, but it seems like quite a coincidence.'

It was Jude who answered. 'We still send regular patrols down to the city to scavenge up supplies. When the hotel went up, we were just three blocks away. We've got a fortified shelter in the basement of one of the old casinos. We heard the explosion and headed straight for it.' He gave a closed-mouth grin. 'Just dumb luck we saw you when we did.'

Michael paused to consider this. 'No, that can't be right,' he said after a moment. 'I remember it distinctly. The hotel blew up *after* we got out. You were already there.'

Jude shook his head doubtfully. 'I don't think so.'

'No, ask her. She saw the whole thing.' Michael turned his head to look at Billie; she was observing him coolly, that same look of neutral concern on her face. 'I remember it distinctly. You used the gun on one of them, and Amy pulled me into the truck. Then we heard the explosion.'

But before Billie could respond, Hollis broke in: 'I think you've got it a little mixed up, Michael. I was the one who pulled you into the truck. The hotel was already burning. That's probably what you're thinking of.'

'I could have sworn . . .' Michael fixed his eyes on Jude again, his chiseled face. 'And you were in a shelter, you say?'

'That's pretty much it.'

'Three blocks away.'

'About that.' An indulgent smile. 'Like I said, I wouldn't second-guess a stroke of luck like that, my friend.'

Michael felt the nervous heat of everyone's attention. Jude's story didn't add up; that was obvious. Who would leave the safety of a fortified shelter at night and drive *toward* a burning building? And why was everyone going along with it? The streets on three sides of the hotel were all blocked by rubble. That meant Jude and Billie could only have come from the east. He tried to recall which side of the building they'd exited from. The south, he thought.

'Oh hell, I don't know,' he said finally. 'Maybe I'm not remembering it right. To tell you the truth, the whole thing is pretty mixed up in my mind.'

Billie nodded. 'That's to be expected after a long period of unconsciousness. I'm sure in a few days things will start to come back to you.'

'Billie's right,' said Peter. 'Let's let the patient get some rest.' He directed his voice to Hollis. 'Olson said he'd take us out to the fields to look around. See how they do things.'

'Who's Olson?' Michael asked.

'Olson Hand. He's in charge around here. I'm sure you'll meet him soon. So, how about it, Hollis?'

The big man offered a close-lipped smile. 'Sounds great.'

With that, everyone rose to leave. Michael had resigned himself to lying in solitude, puzzling over these strange new circumstances, when at the last instant Sara darted back to his bedside. Jude was observing her from the edge of the screen. Taking hold of Michael's hand, she kissed him quickly on the forehead – the first time in years she had done this.

'I'm glad you're okay,' she said. 'Just focus on getting your strength back, okay? That's what we're all waiting for.'

Michael listened closely for their departure. Footsteps, then the sound of a heavy door, opening and closing again. He waited another minute, to be certain he was alone. Then he opened his hand to examine the folded slip of paper Sara had secreted there.

Tell them nothing.

697

FORTY-EIGHT

The party Peter had spoken of had been held the previous evening, the third night after their arrival. This had been their one chance to see everyone, the whole of the Haven, in one place. And what they saw did not ring true.

Nothing did, beginning with Olson's claim that there were no virals. Just two hundred kilometers to the south, Las Vegas was crawling; they had traveled at least that far from the Joshua Valley to Kelso, through similar terrain, and the virals had followed them the whole way. The stink of that herd, Alicia pointed out, would travel far downwind as well. And yet the only perimeter appeared to be a metal fence, far too insubstantial to protect against an attack. Except for the flamethrowers on the vans, Olson had confessed, they had no useful weapons at all. The shotguns were just for show, all their ammunition having been used up decades ago.

'So you see,' he had told them, 'our existence here is an entirely peaceful one.'

Olson Hand: Peter had never met anybody like him, so apparently at ease with his own authority. Apart from Billie and the man known as Jude, who seemed to function as his aides, and the driver of the truck that had brought them from Las Vegas – Gus appeared to be a kind of engineer, in charge of what they termed 'the physical plant' – Peter could detect no other structures of command. Olson had no title; he was simply in charge. And yet he wore this mantle easily, communicating his intentions with a gentle, even apologetic manner. Tall and silver-haired – like most of the men, Olson wore his hair in a long ponytail, while the women and children were all closely shorn – with a stooped frame that seemed to barely fill his orange jumpsuit and a habit of placing the tips of his fingers together when he spoke, he seemed more like a benevolent father figure than someone responsible for the lives of three hundred souls.

It was Olson who had told them the history of the Haven. This had transpired within the first hours of their arrival. They were in the infirmary, where Michael was being attended by Olson's daughter, Mira – an ethereal, slender-limbed adolescent with close-cropped hair so pale and fine it was almost transparent, who seemed to regard them with a nervous awe. After they had been carried from the van, the seven of them had been stripped and washed, their belongings confiscated; all would be returned, Olson had assured them, except for their weapons. If they chose to move on – and here Olson had paused to note, with his customary mildness, that he hoped they would elect to stay – their weapons would be returned to them. But for now their guns and blades would remain locked away.

As for the Haven: a lot was simply not known, Olson explained, the stories having evolved and changed over time until it was no longer clear what the truth really was. But a few points were generally agreed on. The first settlers had been a group of refugees from Las Vegas who had come there in the last days of the war. Whether they had come by design, hoping that the prison, with its bars and walls and fences, might offer some safety, or had simply stopped here on the way to someplace else, no one could know. But once they realized there were no virals, the surrounding wilderness being too inhospitable – forming, in fact, a kind of natural barrier – they had chosen to remain and eke out an existence from the desert landscape. The prison complex was in fact made up of two separate facilities: Desert Wells State Penitentiary, where the first settlers had housed themselves, and the adjacent Conservation Camp, a low-security agricultural work camp for juvenile offenders. That was where all the inhabitants now lived. The spring from which the prison took its name provided water for irrigation, as well as a steady stream of water to cool some of the buildings, including the infirmary. The prison had provided much of what they needed, right down to the orange jumpsuits nearly everyone still wore; the rest they scavenged from the towns to the south. It was not an easy existence, and there were many things they lacked, but here at least they were free to live their lives without the threat of the virals. For many years they had sent out search parties to hunt for more survivors, hoping to lead them to safety. They had found some, quite a few in fact, but not for many years, and had long since given up hope of ever finding any more.

'Which is why,' Olson had said, smiling benignly, 'your being here is nothing less than a miracle.' His eyes actually misted over. 'All of you. A miracle.'

They had spent that first night in the infirmary with Michael and were moved the next day to a pair of adjacent cinder-block huts on the outskirts of the work camp, facing a dusty plaza with a pile of tires in the center, the edges lined by fire barrels. This was where they would spend the next three days in isolation, a mandatory quarantine. On the far side were more huts, which appeared to be unoccupied. Their quarters were spartan, each of the two huts with just a table and chairs and a room in the back with cots; the air was hot and dense, and the floor crunched underfoot with grit.

Hollis had left with Billie in the morning, to look for the Humvees; working vehicles were in short supply, Olson had said, and if they had survived the explosion, they would be worth the hazards of such a trip. Whether Olson intended to keep them for his own use or return them, Peter did not know. This fact was left ambiguous, and Peter had elected not to press. After their experience in the van, the seven of them nearly cooked to death in the heat, and with Michael still unconscious, the wisest course seemed to be to say as little as they could. Olson had questioned them about the Colony and the purpose of their journey, and there was no avoiding offering some explanation. But Peter had volunteered only that they had come from a settlement in California and had gone looking for survivors. He told Olson nothing about the bunker, his silence suggesting that the place they came from was well armed. There would come a time, Peter thought, when he would probably have to tell Olson the truth, or at least more of it. But that time had not arrived yet, and Olson had appeared to accept the caginess of his explanation.

For the next two days they received only fleeting glimpses of the other inhabitants. Behind the huts stood the growing fields, with long irrigation pipes radiating from a central pumphouse, and beyond that the herd, several hundred head kept in large, shaded pens. From time to time they could see the boiling dust of a vehicle moving against the distant fence line. But apart from this, and a few figures in the fields, they detected virtually no one. Where were the other people? The doors to their huts were not locked, but always across the empty plaza were two men, wearing the orange jumpsuits. It was these men who brought them their meals, usually in the company of Billie or Olson, who reported on Michael's condition. Michael appeared to have lapsed into a deep sleep – not a coma necessarily, Olson assured them, but something like one. They had seen it before, they said, the effects of the heat. But his fever was down, a good sign.

Then, the morning of the third day, Sara was returned to them.

She possessed no memory of what had happened to her. This part of the story that they related to Michael, when he awakened the following day, was not a lie, nor was Hollis's tale of how he had found her. They were very happy and very relieved – Sara seemed fine, if a little slow to come around to the news of their new circumstances – but it was also true that both her capture and her return were deeply puzzling. Like the absence of lights and walls, it simply made no sense.

By this time, whatever happiness they felt at the thought of finding another human settlement had been replaced by a deep unease. Still they had seen almost no one, apart from Olson and Billie and Jude, and the two orange-suited men who watched them, whose names were Hap and Leon. The only other sign of life was a group of four Littles in raggy clothing who appeared each evening to play on the tires in the square, though, strangely, no adults ever appeared to claim them; they simply drifted away when the game was over. If they weren't prisoners, why were they guarded? If they were, why all the pretense? Where was everyone? What was wrong with Michael, why was he still unconscious? Their packs, as Olson had promised, had been returned to them; the contents had obviously been examined, and a number of items, such as the scalpel in Sara's med kit, had been taken. But the maps, which Caleb had tucked into an inner compartment, had apparently been overlooked. The prison itself was not on the Nevada map, but they found the town of Desert Wells, north of Las Vegas on Highway 95. It was bordered to the east by a vast gray region, no roads or town in it at all, marked with the words NELLIS AIR FORCE TEST RANGE COMPLEX. Situated at the western edge of this region, just a few kilometers from the town of Desert Wells, was a small red square and the name YUCCA MOUNTAIN NATIONAL REPOSITORY. If Peter was correct about where they were, they could see this structure plainly, a humped ridge forming a barricade to the north. Hollis's drive south with Billie and Gus had given him the chance to scout out more of the landscape. The fence line, Hollis reported, was more robust than it appeared – twin barricades of heavy-gauge steel, roughly ten meters apart, topped with concertina wire. Hollis had seen only two exits. One stood to the south, at the far edge of the fields – this seemed to connect to a roadway that encircled the compound – and the main gate, which connected the compound with the highway. This was flanked by a pair of concrete towers with observation posts – manned or not, they didn't know, but one of the orange-suited men was stationed in the small guardhouse at ground level; it was he who had opened the gate for Hollis and Billie to pass.

The Haven itself was situated just a few kilometers off the highway that had carried them north. The original prison, a forbidding bulk of gray stone, stood at the eastern edge of the compound, surrounded by a few smaller buildings and Quonset huts. Between the perimeter and the highway, Hollis said, they had crossed railroad tracks, running in a

702

north-south direction. These appeared to head straight toward the ridge of mountains toward the north – odd, Hollis noted, because who would run a pair of tracks straight into a mountain? In their first meeting, Olson had mentioned a railroad depot, in response to Peter's question about where they got fuel for their vehicles. But on the drive south, Hollis said, they hadn't stopped, so he couldn't say if there was a fuel depot or not. Presumably they got fuel somewhere. It was only in the course of this conversation that Peter realized that the idea of leaving was already taking shape in his mind, and that this would require stealing a vehicle and finding fuel to run it on.

The heat was intense; the days of isolation had begun to take their toll. Everyone was antsy and worried about Michael. In their stifling huts, none of them was sleeping. Amy was the most wakeful of them all; Peter didn't think he'd seen the girl close her eyes. All night she sat on her cot, the features of her face gathered in what appeared to be intense concentration. It was as if, thought Peter, she was trying to work out some problem in her mind.

On the third night, Olson came for them. Accompanying him were Billie and Jude. Over the preceding days, Peter had come to suspect that Jude was more than he had first appeared to be. He couldn't say why this was, exactly. But there was something disconcerting about the man. His teeth were white and straight, impossible not to look at, like his eyes, which radiated a piercing blue intensity. They gave his face an ageless quality, as if he had slowed time, and whenever Peter looked at the man, the impression he received was of someone who was looking straight into a gale of wind. Peter had become aware that he had yet to hear Olson give the man a direct order – Olson addressed himself entirely to Billie and Gus and the various orange-suited men who came and went from the hut – and in the back of Peter's mind the idea had begun to form that Jude held some measure of authority, independent of Olson. Several times he had observed Jude speaking to the men who were guarding them.

In the falling dusk, the three appeared across the square, striding toward the hut. With the day's passing heat, the Littles had appeared on the tires; as the three passed by, they abruptly scattered, like a flock of startled birds.

'It is time to see where you are,' Olson said when he reached the door. He was smiling munificently – a smile that had begun to seem false. It seemed like a smile with nothing behind it. Standing next to Olson, Jude was showing his line of perfect teeth, his blue eyes darting past Peter into the dim hut. Only Billie seemed immune to the mood; her stoic face betrayed nothing.

'Please come, all of you,' Olson urged. 'The wait is over. Everyone is very excited to meet you.'

They led the seven of them across the empty plaza. Alicia, swinging on her crutches, kept Amy close to her side. In watchful silence, they moved into a maze of huts. These appeared to be arranged in a kind of grid, with alleyways between the lines of buildings, and were obviously inhabited: the windows were lighted with oil lanterns; in the spaces between the buildings were lines of laundry, stiffening in the desert air. Beyond, the bulk of the old prison loomed like a cutout shape against the sky. Out in the dark, no lights to protect them, not even a blade on his belt; Peter had never felt so odd. From somewhere up ahead came a smell of smoke and cooking food and a buzz of voices, growing as they approached.

They turned the corner then to see a large crowd, gathered beneath a wide roof that was open on the sides and held aloft by thick steel girders. The space was lit by smoky flames from the open barrels that encircled the area. Pushed to the side were long tables and chairs; jumpsuited figures were moving pots of food from an adjacent structure.

Everyone froze.

Then, from the sea of faces gazing at them, first one voice and then another rose in a buzz of excitement. *There they are! The travelers! The ones from away!*

As the crowd enfolded them, Peter had a sense of being

softly swallowed. And for a brief time, subsumed in a wave of humanity, he forgot all about his worries. Here were people, hundreds of people, men and women and children all so apparently joyous at their presence he almost felt like the miracle Olson had said they were. Men were clapping him on the shoulder, shaking his hand. Some of the women pressed babies to him, displaying them as if they were gifts; others merely touched him quickly and darted away – embarrassed or frightened or merely overcome by emotion, Peter couldn't tell. Somewhere at the periphery of his awareness Olson was instructing people to stay calm, not to rush, but these warnings seemed unnecessary. *We're so happy to see you*, everyone was saying. *We're so glad that you have come.*

This went on for some minutes, enough time for Peter to begin to feel exhausted by it all, the smiling and touching, the repeated words of greeting. The idea of meeting new people, let alone a crowd of hundreds, was so new and strange to him that his mind could scarcely capture it. There was something childlike about them, he came to think, these men and women in their threadbare orange jumpsuits, their faces careworn and yet possessing a look of wide-eyed innocence, almost of obedience. The crowd's warmth was undeniable, and yet the whole thing felt staged, not a spontaneous reaction but one designed to elicit the very response it had produced in Peter: a feeling of complete disarmament.

All of these calculations were moving through his mind while part of him was also struggling to keep track of the others, which proved difficult. The effect of the crowd's advance had been to separate them, and he could detect only quick glimpses of the others: Sara's blond hair peeking above the head of a woman with a baby over her shoulder; Caleb's laughter, coming from somewhere out of range. To his right, a nugget of women had encircled Mausami, cooing with approval. Peter saw one dart out her hand to touch Mausami's stomach.

Then Olson was at his side. With him was his daughter, Mira.

'The one girl, Amy,' Olson said, and it was the only time Peter had ever seen the man frown. 'She can't speak?'

Amy was standing close to Alicia, ringed by a group of little girls who were pointing at Amy and pressing their hands to their mouths in laughter. While Peter watched, Alicia lifted one of her crutches to shoo them away, a gesture half playful and half serious, sending them scattering. Her eyes briefly met Peter's. *Help*, she seemed to say. But even she was smiling.

He turned to Olson again. 'No.'

'How strange. I've never heard of that.' He glanced at his daughter before returning his attention to Peter, looking concerned. 'But she's otherwise . . . all right?'

'All right?'

He paused. 'You'll have to forgive my directness. But a woman who can bear a child is a great prize. Nothing is more important, with so few of us left. And I see that one of your females is pregnant. People will want to know.'

Your females, Peter thought. A strange choice of words. He looked toward Mausami, who was still surrounded by the women. He realized that many of them were pregnant, too.

'I suppose.'

'And the others? Sara and the redhead. Lish.'

The line of questioning was so odd, so out of the blue, that Peter hesitated, unsure of what to say or not say. But Olson was looking at him intently now, requiring at least some kind of response.

'I guess.'

The answer seemed to satisfy him. Olson concluded with a brisk nod, the smile returning to his lips. 'Good.'

Females, Peter thought again. As if Olson were speaking of livestock. He had the disquieting sense of having told too much, of having been maneuvered into surrendering some crucial bit of information. Mira, standing beside her father, was facing the crowd, which was moving away; Peter realized she hadn't said a word.

Everyone had begun to gather around the tables. The

706

volume of conversation settled to a murmur as food was passed out – bowls of stew ladled from giant vats, platters of bread, pots of butter and pitchers of milk. As Peter scanned the scene, everyone talking and helping themselves, some assisting with children, women with babies bouncing on their laps or suckling at an exposed breast, he realized that what he was seeing was more than a group of survivors; it was a family. For the first time since they had left the Colony, he felt a pang of longing for home, and wondered if he had been wrong to be so suspicious. Perhaps they really were safe here.

And yet something wasn't right; he felt that, too. The crowd was incomplete; something was missing. He couldn't say what this missing thing was, only that its absence, nibbling at the edge of his consciousness, seemed more profound the longer he looked. Alicia and Amy, he saw, were with Jude now, who was showing them where to sit. Standing tall in his leather boots – nearly everyone else was barefoot – the man seemed to tower over them. While Peter watched, Jude leaned close to Alicia, touching her on the arm, and spoke quickly into her ear; she responded with a laugh.

These thoughts were interrupted when Olson rested his hand on Peter's shoulder. 'I do hope you choose to remain with us,' he said. 'We all do. There's strength in numbers.'

'We'll have to talk about it,' Peter managed.

'Of course,' said Olson, leaving his hand where it was. 'There's no hurry. Take all the time you need.'

FORTY-NINE

It was simple. There were no boys.

Or almost no boys. Alicia and Hollis claimed they'd seen a couple. But when Peter questioned them more closely, they were both forced to confess that they couldn't say for sure if they'd seen any or not. With those short haircuts all the Littles wore, it was difficult to tell, and they'd seen no older children at all.

It was the afternoon of the fourth day, and Michael was finally awake. The five of them had gathered in the larger of the two huts; Mausami and Amy were next door. Peter and Hollis had just returned from their trip out to the fields with Olson. The real purpose of this trip had been to get a second look at the perimeter, because they had decided to leave as soon as Michael was able. There was no question of taking this up with Olson; though Peter had to admit he liked the man and could find no outward reason to distrust him, too much about the Haven simply failed to add up, and the events of the night before had left Peter more uncertain than ever of Olson's intentions. Olson had given a short speech welcoming them all, but as the night had worn on, Peter had begun to find the crowd's empty warmth oppressive, even disturbing. There was a fundamental sameness to everyone, and in the morning, Peter found he couldn't recall anyone in particular; all the faces and voices seemed to blur together in his mind. Not one person, he realized, had asked a single question about the Colony or how they'd come to be there – a fact that, the longer he considered it, made no sense at all. Wouldn't it be the most natural thing, to wonder about another settlement? To question them about their journey and what they had seen? But Peter and the others might just as well have materialized out of thin air. No one, he realized, had so much as told him their name.

They would have to steal a vehicle; on this point, everyone was agreed. Fuel was the next question. They could follow the train tracks south, looking for the fuel depot, or if they had enough, drive south to Las Vegas to the airport before heading north again on Highway 15. Probably they'd be followed; Peter doubted Olson would let go of one of the vans without a fight. To avoid this, they could head straight east instead, across the test range, but with no roads or towns, Peter doubted they could make it, and if the terrain was anything like it was around the Haven, it didn't look like the kind of place where they wanted to get stranded.

This left the matter of weapons. Alicia believed there had to be an armory somewhere – from the beginning she'd maintained that the guns they'd seen were loaded, no matter what Olson said – and she'd done her best to feel out Jude on this question the night before. Jude had stayed close to her all evening – just as Olson had stayed close to Peter – and in the morning he had taken her out in a pickup to show her the rest of the compound. Peter didn't like it, but any chance to glean more information, and to do so in a way that would go undetected, was one they had to take.

But if there was an armory, Jude had given no hint where it might be. Perhaps Olson was telling the truth, but it wasn't anything they could risk. And even if he was, the weapons they had brought with them had to be somewhere – by Peter's count, three rifles, nine blades, at least six magazines of ammunition, and the last of the grenades.

'What about the prison?' Caleb suggested.

Peter had already thought of this. With its fortresslike walls, it seemed the natural place to lock something away. But so far, none of them had been close enough to see how they might get inside. For all intents and purposes, the place seemed abandoned, just as Olson had said.

'I think we should wait till dark and scout it out,' Hollis said. 'We can't know for sure what we're up against if we don't.'

Peter turned to Sara. 'How long do you think until Michael can travel?'

She frowned doubtfully. 'I don't even know what's wrong with him. Maybe it really was heatstroke, but I don't think so.'

She had expressed these misgivings before. Heatstroke serious enough to make him seize, Sara had said, would almost certainly have killed him, because it would have meant the brain had swollen. His protracted state of unconsciousness might follow from that, but now that he was awake, she detected no sign of brain injury at all. His speech and motor coordination were fine; his pupils were normal and reactive. It was as if he had fallen into a profound but otherwise ordinary sleep from which he had simply awakened.

'He's still pretty weak,' Sara went on. 'Some of that is just dehydration. But it could be a couple of days before we can move him, maybe more.'

Alicia sank back on her cot with a groan. 'I don't think I can keep this up that long.'

'What's the problem?' Peter asked.

'Jude is the problem. I know we're supposed to play along here, but I'm wondering how far I'm going to have to take this.'

Her meaning was plain. 'Do you think you can . . . I don't know, hold him off?'

'Don't worry about me. I can take care of myself. But he's not going to like it.' She paused, suddenly uncertain. 'There's something else, nothing to do with Jude. I'm not sure I should even bring this up. Does anybody remember Liza Chou?'

Peter did, at least by name. Liza was Old Chou's niece. She and her family, a brother and her parents, had all been lost on Dark Night – killed or taken up, he couldn't recall. Peter remembered Liza vaguely, from their days together in the Sanctuary. She was one of the older children, practically an adult in his eyes.

'What about her?' Hollis asked.

Alicia hesitated. 'I think I saw her today.'

'That's impossible,' Sara scoffed.

'I *know* it's impossible. Everything *about* this place is impossible. But Liza had a scar on her cheek, I do remember that. Some kind of accident, I forget what it was. And there it was, the same scar.'

Peter leaned forward. Something about this new bit of information seemed important, part of an emerging pattern his mind couldn't quite discern. 'Where was this?'

'In the dairy barns. I'm pretty certain she saw me, too. Jude was with me, so I couldn't really break away. When I looked again she was gone.'

It was conceivable, Peter supposed, that she had escaped, and somehow ended up here. But how would a young girl, as Liza was at the time, travel such a distance?

'I don't know, Lish. Are you sure?'

'No, I'm not sure. I didn't have the chance to be sure. I'm just saying she looked a lot like Liza Chou.'

'Was she pregnant?' Sara asked.

Alicia thought for a moment. 'Come to think of it, she was.'

'A lot of the women are pregnant,' Hollis offered. 'It makes sense, doesn't it? A Little's a Little.'

'But why no boys?' Sara went on. 'And if so many of the women are pregnant, wouldn't there be more children?'

'Aren't there?' asked Alicia.

'Well, I thought so too. But I didn't count more than a couple dozen last night. And the children I see all seem to be the same ones.'

Peter said, 'Hollis, you said there were some kids outside.'

The big man nodded. 'They're playing on that pile of tires.'

'Hightop, check it out.'

Caleb rose from his bunk and moved to the door, opening it a crack.

'Let me guess,' Sara said. 'The one with the crooked teeth and her friend, the little blond girl.'

Caleb turned from the door. 'She's right. That's who's out there.'

'That's what I mean,' Sara insisted. 'It's always the same ones. It's like they're always out there so we *think* there's more than there are.'

'What are we saying here?' This was Alicia. 'Okay, I agree it's strange about the boys. But this . . . I don't know, Sara.'

Sara turned to face Alicia, squaring her shoulders combatively. 'You're the one who thinks she saw a girl who died fifteen years ago. She'd be, what, in her midtwenties now? How would you know it was Liza Chou?'

'I told you. The scar. And I think I know a Chou when I see one.'

'And that means we're supposed to take your word for it?'

Sara's sharp tone seemed to bristle through Alicia. 'I don't care if you do or not. I saw what I saw.'

Peter had heard all he wanted to. 'Both of you, enough.' The two women were glowering at each other. 'This isn't going to solve anything. What's the matter with you?'

Neither woman answered; the tension in the room was palpable. Then Alicia sighed and flopped back on the cot again.

'Forget it. I'm just tired of waiting. I can't sleep at all in this place. It's so goddamn hot, I have nightmares all night long.'

For a moment no one spoke.

'The fat woman?' Hollis said.

Alicia sat up quickly. 'What did you say?'

'In the kitchen.' His voice was grave. 'From the Time Before.'

Caleb stepped toward them from the door. '*I tell you, the boy isn't just dumb . . .*'

Sara finished for him: '*. . . he's been struck dumb.*' Her face was astonished. 'I'm dreaming about her, too.'

Everyone was looking at Peter now. What were his friends talking about? What fat lady?

He shook his head. 'Sorry.'

'But the rest of us are having the same dream,' said Sara.

Hollis rubbed his beard, nodding. 'It would appear so.'

Michael had been drifting in and out of a formless sleep when he heard the door opening. A girl stepped around the screen. Younger than Billie, but with the same funny orange costume and severe haircut. She was holding a tray before her.

'I thought you might be hungry.'

As she advanced into the room, the smell of warm food hit

712

Michael's senses like an electric current. He was suddenly ravenous. The girl placed the tray on his lap: some kind of meat in a brown gravy, boiled greens, and, most wondrous of all, a fat slice of buttered bread. Metal utensils lay beside it, wrapped in a rough cloth.

'I'm Michael,' he offered.

The girl nodded faintly, smiling. Why was everybody always smiling?

'I'm Mira.' She was blushing, he saw. What little hair she possessed was so fair it was practically white, like a Little's. 'I was the one who took care of you.'

Michael wondered what this meant exactly. In the hours since he'd awakened, bits of memory had come floating back to him. The sound of voices, shapes and bodies moving around him, water on his body and moistening his mouth.

'I guess I should say thank you.'

'Oh, I was glad to do it.' She studied him for a moment. 'You're really from away, aren't you?'

'Away?'

She gave a delicate shrug. 'There's here and there's away.' She lifted her nose toward the tray. 'Aren't you going to eat?'

He started with the bread, soft and wonderful in his mouth, then moved on to the meat and finally the greens, stringy and bitter but still satisfying. While he ate, the girl, who had taken a chair beside his bed, kept her eyes on him, her face rapt, as if each bite he took brought her pleasure as well. What strange people these were.

'Thanks,' he said, when all that remained was a smear of grease on his plate. How old was she, anyway? Sixteen? 'That was fantastic.'

'I can get you more. Whatever you want.'

'Really, I couldn't eat another bite.'

She took the tray from his lap and put it aside. He thought she was preparing to leave but instead she moved toward him again, standing close to the cot, which was positioned high off the floor.

'I like . . . watching you, Michael.'

He felt his face grow warm. 'Mira? It's Mira, right?'

Nodding, she took his hand from where it lay on the sheet and wrapped it in her own. 'I like how you say my name.'

'Yes, well, um—'

But he couldn't continue; she was suddenly kissing him. A wave of sweet softness filled his mouth; he felt his senses collapsing. Kissing him! Of all things, she was kissing him! And he was kissing her!

'Poppa says I can have a baby,' she was saying, her breath warm on his face. 'If I have a baby, I won't have to go to the ring. Poppa says I can have anyone I want. Can I have you, Michael? Can I have you?'

He was trying to think, to process what she was saying and what was happening, the taste of her, and also the fact that she had now, it seemed, climbed on top of him, straddling him near the waist, her face still pushed into his own – a collision of impulses and sensations that rendered him into a state of mute compliance. A baby? She wanted to have a baby? If she had a baby she didn't have to wear a ring?

'Mira!'

A moment of complete disorientation; the girl was gone, vaulted away. The room was suddenly full of men, large men in orange jumpsuits, crowding the space with their bulk. One of them caught Mira by the arm. Not a man: Billie.

'I'll pretend,' she said to the girl, 'that I didn't see this.'

'Listen,' Michael said, finding his voice, 'it was my fault, whatever you think you saw—'

Billie nailed him with a cold glare. Behind her, one of the men snickered.

'Don't even pretend this was your idea.' Billie pointed her eyes at Mira again. 'Go home,' she commanded. 'Go home now.'

'He's mine! He's for me!'

'Mira, enough. I want you to go straight home and wait there. Don't talk to anyone. Do I make myself understood?'

'He's not for the ring!' Mira cried. 'Poppa said!'

That word again, Michael thought. The ring. What was the ring?

'He will be unless you get out of here. Now go.'

These last words appeared to work; Mira fell silent and, without looking at Michael again, darted behind the screen. The feelings of the last few minutes – desire, confusion, embarrassment – were still whirling inside him while another part of him was also thinking: just my luck. Now she'll never come back.

'Danny, go bring the truck around back. Tip, you stay with me.'

'What are you going to do with me?'

Billie had withdrawn a small metal tin from somewhere on her person. With thumb and forefinger she pinched a bit of dust from the tin and sprinkled it into a cup of water. She held it out to him.

'Bottoms up.'

'I'm not drinking that.'

She sighed impatiently. 'Tip, a little help here?'

The man stepped forward, towering over Michael's bed.

'Trust me,' Billie said. 'You won't like the taste, but you'll feel better fast. And no more fat lady.'

The fat lady, thought Michael. The fat lady in the kitchen in the Time Before.

'How did you—?'

'Just drink. We'll explain on the way.'

There seemed no way to avoid it. Michael tipped the cup to his lips and poured it down. Flyers, it was awful.

'What the hell is that?'

'You don't want to know.' Billie took the cup from him. 'Feeling anything yet?'

He was. It was as if someone had plucked a long, tight string inside him. Waves of bright energy seemed to radiate from his very core. He'd opened his mouth to declare this discovery when a strong spasm shook him, a gigantic, whole-body hiccup.

'That happens the first time or two,' said Billie. 'Just breathe.'

Michael hiccuped again. The colors in the room seemed unusually vivid, as if all the surfaces around him were part of this new nexus of energy.

'He better shut up,' warned Tip.

'It's fantastic,' Michael managed to say. He swallowed hard, pushing the urge to hiccup down inside him.

The second man had returned from the hallway. 'We're losing the light,' he said briskly. 'We better get a move on.'

'Get him his clothes.' Billie steadied her gaze on Michael again. 'Peter says you're an engineer. That you can fix anything. Is that true?'

He thought of the words on the paper Sara had slipped him. *Tell them nothing.*

'Well?'

'I guess.'

'I don't want you to guess, Michael. It's important. You can or you can't.'

He glanced toward the two men, who were looking at him expectantly, as if everything depended on his answer.

'Okay, yes.'

Billie nodded. 'Then put your clothes on and do everything we tell you.'

FIFTY

Mausami in darkness, dreaming of birds. She awoke to a quick bright fluttering beneath her heart, like a pair of wings beating inside her.

The baby, she thought. This baby is moving.

The feeling came again – a distinct aquatic pressure, rhythmic, like rings widening on the surface of a pool. As if someone were tapping at a pane of glass inside her. *Hello? Hello out there!*

She let her hands trace the curve of her belly under her shirt, damp with sweat. A warm contentment flooded her. Hello, she thought. Hello back, you.

The baby was a boy. She'd thought it was a boy since the start, since the first morning at the compost pile when she'd lost her breakfast. She didn't want to name him yet. It would be harder to lose a baby with a name, that's what everyone always said; but that wasn't the real reason, because the baby would be born. The idea was more than hope, more than belief. Mausami knew it for a fact. And when the baby was born, when he'd made his loud and painful entry into the world, Theo would be there, and they would name their son together.

This place. The Haven. It made her so tired. All she could do was sleep. And eat. It was the baby, of course; it was the baby that made her think about eating all the time. After all the hardtack and bean paste, and that awful strange food they'd found in the bunker – hundred-year-old goop vacuumed in plastic; it was a miracle they hadn't all poisoned themselves – how amazing to have real food. Beef and milk. Bread and cheese. Actual butter so creamy it made the top of her throat tickle. She shoveled it in, then licked her fingers clean. She could have stayed in this place forever, just for the food.

They'd all felt it right away: something wasn't right. Last night, all those women crowding around her, holding babies or pregnant themselves – some actually both – their faces beaming with a sisterly glow at the discovery that she was pregnant too. A baby! How wonderful! When was she due? Was it her first? Were any of the other women in their group also with child? It hadn't occurred to her at the time to wonder how they'd known – she was barely showing, after all – nor why none had asked who the father was or mentioned the fathers of their own children.

The sun was down. The last thing Mausami remembered

717

was lying down for a nap. Peter and the others were probably in the other hut, deciding what to do. The baby was moving again, flipping around inside her. She lay with her eyes closed and let the sensation fill her. Standing the Watch: it seemed like years ago. A different life. That was what happened, she knew, when a person had a baby. This strange new being grew inside you and by the time it was all over, you were someone different, too.

Suddenly she realized: she wasn't alone.

Amy was sitting on the bunk next to hers. Spooky, the way she could make herself invisible like that. Mausami rolled to face her, tucking her knees to her chest as the baby went *thump-thump* inside her.

'Hey,' Maus said, and yawned. 'I guess I took a little nap there.'

Everybody was always talking that way around Amy, stating the obvious, filling the silence of the girl's half of the conversation. It was a little unnerving, the way she looked at you with that intense gaze, as if she were reading your thoughts. Which was when Mausami realized what the girl was really looking at.

'Oh. I get it,' she said. 'You want to feel it?'

Amy cocked her head, uncertain.

'You can if you want. Come on, I'll show you.'

Amy rose, taking a place on the edge of Mausami's cot. Mausami held her hand and guided it to the curve of her belly. The girl's hand was warm and a little damp; the tips of her fingers were surprisingly soft, not like Mausami's, which were callused from years of the bow.

'Just wait a minute. He was flipping around in there a second ago.'

A bright flicker of movement. Amy drew her hand away quickly, startled.

'You feel that?' Amy's eyes were wide with pleasant shock. 'It's okay, that's what they do. Here—' She took Amy's hand and pressed it to her belly once more. At once the baby flipped and kicked. 'Whoa, that was a strong one.'

718

Amy was smiling too now. How strange and wonderful, Mausami thought, in the midst of everything, all that had happened, to feel a baby moving inside her. A new life, a new person, coming into the world.

Mausami heard it then. Two words.

He's here.

She yanked her hand away, scurrying up the cot so she was sitting with her back pushed to the wall. The girl was looking at her with a penetrating stare, her eyes filling Maus's vision like two shining beams.

'How did you do that?' She was shaking; she thought she might be ill.

He's in the dream. With Babcock. With the Many.

'Who's here, Amy?'

Theo. Theo is here.

FIFTY-ONE

He was Babcock and he was forever. He was one of Twelve and also the Other, the one above and behind, the Zero. He was the night of nights and he had been Babcock before he became what he was. Before the great hunger that was like time itself inside him, a current in the blood, endless and needful, infinite and without border, a dark wing spreading over the world.

He was made of Many. A thousand-thousand-thousand scattered over the night sky, like the stars. He was one of Twelve and also the Other, the Zero, but his children were within him also, the ones that carried the seed of his blood, one seed of Twelve; they moved as he moved, they thought as he thought, in their minds was an empty space of forgetting in which he lay, each to a one, saying, *You will not die. You are a part of me, as I am a part of you. You will drink the blood of the world and fill me up.*

719

They were his to command. When they ate, he ate. When they slept, he slept. They were the We, the Babcock, and they were forever as he was forever, all part of the Twelve and the Other, the Zero. They dreamed his dark dream with him.

He remembered a time, before he Became. The time of the little house, in the place called Desert Wells. The time of pain and silence and the woman, his mother, the mother of Babcock. He remembered small things – textures, sensations, visions. A box of golden sunlight falling on a square of carpet. A worn place on the stoop that fit his sneakered foot just so, and the ridges of rust on the rail that cut the skin of his fingers. He remembered his fingers. He remembered the smell of his mother's cigarettes in the kitchen where she talked and watched her stories, and the people on the television, their faces huge and close, their eyes wide and wet, the women with their lips painted and shimmering, like glossy pieces of fruit. And her voice, always her voice:

Be quiet now, goddamnit. Cain't you see I'm trying to watch this? You make such a goddamn racket, it's a wonder I don't lose my goddamn mind.

He remembered being quiet, so quiet.

He remembered her hands, Babcock's mother's hands, and the starry bursts of pain when she struck him, struck him again. He remembered flying, his body lifted on a cloud of pain, and the hitting and the slapping and the burning. Always the burning. *Don't you cry now. You be a man. You cry and I'll give you something to cry about, so much the worse for you, Giles Babcock.* Her smoky breath, close to his face. The look of the red-hot tip of her cigarette where she rolled it against the skin of his hand, and the crisp wet sound of its burning, like cereal when he poured milk into it, the same crackle and pop. The smell of it mingling with the jets of smoke that puffed from her nostrils. And the way the words all stopped up inside him, so that the pain could end – so he could be a man, as she said.

It was her voice he remembered most of all. Babcock's mother's voice. His love for her was like a room without doors, filled with the scraping sound of her words, her talk-talk-talk. Taunting him, tearing into him, like the knife he took from the drawer that day as she sat at the table in the kitchen of the little house in the place called Desert Wells, talking and laughing and laughing and talking and eating her mouthfuls of smoke.

I tell you, the boy isn't just dumb. He's been struck *dumb.*

He was happy, so happy, he'd never felt such happiness in his life as the knife passed into her, the white skin of her throat, the smooth outer layer and the hard gristle below. And as he dug and pushed with his blade, the love he felt for her lifted from his mind so that he could see what she was at last – that she was a being of flesh and blood and bone. All her words and talk-talk-talk moving inside him, filling him up to bursting. They tasted like blood in his mouth, sweet living things.

They sent him away. He wasn't a boy after all, he was a man; he was a man with a mind and a knife, and they told him to die – die, Babcock, for what you have done. He didn't want to die, not then, not ever. And after – after the man, Wolgast, had come to where he was, like a thing foretold; and after the doctors and the sickness and the Becoming, that he should be one of Twelve, the Babcock-Morrison-Chávez-Baffes-Turrell-Winston-Sosa-Echols-Lambright-Martínez-Reinhardt-Carter – one of Twelve and also the Other, the Zero – he had taken the rest the same way, drinking their words from them, their dying cries like soft morsels in his mouth. And the ones he did not kill but merely sipped, the one of ten, as the tide of his own blood dictated, became his own, joining to him in mind. His children. His great and fearful company. The Many. The We of Babcock.

And This Place. He had come to it with a feeling of return, of a thing restored. He had drunk his fill of the world and here he rested, dreaming his dreams in the dark, until he awoke and he was hungry again and he heard the Zero, who was called Fanning, saying: *Brothers, we're dying.* Dying! For there was hardly anyone left in the world, no people and no animals even. And Babcock knew that the time had come to bring those that remained to him, that they should know him, know Babcock and the Zero also, assume their place within him. He had stretched out his mind and said to the Many, his children, *Carry the last of humankind to me; do not kill them; bring them and their words that they should dream the dream and become one of us, the We, the Babcock.* And first one had come and then another and more and more and they dreamed the dream with him and he told them, when the dreaming was done, Now you are mine also, like the Many. You are mine in This Place and when I am hungry you will feed me, feed my restless soul with your blood. You will bring others to me from beyond This Place that they should do the same, and I will let you live in this way and no other. And those that did not bend their wills to his, that did not take up the knife when the time had come in the dark place of dreaming where Babcock's mind met theirs, they were made to die so the others could see and know and refuse no longer.

And so the city was built. The City of Babcock, first in all the world.

But now there was Another. Not the Zero or the Twelve but Another. The same and not the same. A shadow behind a shadow, pecking at him like a bird that darted from sight whenever he tried to fix the gaze of his mind upon her. And the Many, his children, his great and fearful company, heard her also; he sensed her pull upon them. A force of great power, drawing them away. Like the helpless love he had felt so long ago, when he was just a boy, watching the red-hot tip rolling, rolling and burning against his flesh.

Who am I? they asked her. *Who am I?*

She made them want to remember. She made them want to die.

She was close now, very close. Babcock could feel it. She was a ripple in the mind of the Many, a tear in the fabric of night. He knew that through her, all that they had done could be undone, all that they had made could be unmade.

Brothers, brothers. She is coming. Brothers, she is already here.

FIFTY-TWO

'I'm sorry, Peter,' said Olson Hand, 'I can't keep track of all your friends.'

Peter had learned that Michael was missing just before sunset. Sara had gone over to the infirmary to check on him and found that his bed was empty. The whole *building* was empty.

They had fanned out in two groups: Sara, Hollis, and Caleb to search the grounds, Alicia and Peter to look for Olson. His house, which Olson had explained had once been used as the warden's residence, was a small, two-story structure situated on a patch of parched ground between the work camp and the old prison. They had arrived to find him stepping from the door.

'I'll speak with Billie,' Olson continued. 'Maybe she knows where he went.' He seemed harried, as if their visit had caught him in the midst of some important duty. Even so, he took the trouble to offer one of his reassuring smiles. 'I'm sure he's fine. Mira saw him in the infirmary just a few hours ago. He said he was feeling better and wanted to have a look around. I thought he was probably with you.'

'He could barely walk,' Peter said. 'I'm not sure he could walk at all.'

'In that case, he can't have gone far, now could he?'

'Sara said the infirmary was empty. Don't you usually have people there?'

'Not as a general matter. If Michael chose to leave, they'd have no reason to remain.' Something dark came into his face; he leveled his eyes at Peter. 'I'm sure he'll turn up. My best advice would be to return to your quarters and wait for his return.'

'I don't see—'

Olson cut him off with a raised hand. 'As I said, that's my best advice. I suggest you take it. And try not to lose any more of your friends.'

Alicia had been silent until now. Suspended on her crutches, she bumped Peter with her shoulder. 'Come on.'

'But—'

'It's fine,' she said. Then, to Olson: 'I'm sure he's okay. If you need us, you know where to find us.'

They retreated through the maze of huts. Everything was strangely quiet, no one about. They passed the shed where the party had been held, finding it deserted. All the buildings were dark. Peter felt a prickling on his skin as the cooling desert night descended, but he knew this sensation was caused by more than just a change in temperature. He could feel the eyes of people watching them from the windows.

'Don't look,' Alicia said. 'I feel it too. Just walk.'

They arrived at their quarters as Hollis and the others were returning. Sara was frantic with worry. Peter related their conversation with Olson.

'They've taken him somewhere, haven't they?' Lish said.

It seemed so. But where, and for what purpose? Olson was lying, that was obvious. Even more strange was the fact that Olson seemed to have wanted them to *know* he was lying.

'Who's out there now, Hightop?'

Caleb had taken his position by the door. 'The usual two. They're hanging out across the square, pretending they're not watching us.'

'Anyone else?'

'No. It's dead quiet out there. No Littles, either.'

'Go wake up Maus,' Peter said. 'Don't tell her anything. Just bring her and Amy over here. Their packs, too.'

'Are we leaving?' Caleb's eyes shifted to Sara, then back again. 'What about the Circuit?'

724

'We're not going anywhere without him. Just go.'

Caleb darted out the door. Peter and Alicia exchanged a look: something was happening. They would have to move quickly.

A moment later Caleb returned. 'They're gone.'

'What do you mean *gone*?'

The boy's face was gray as ash. 'I mean the hut's empty. There's no one there, Peter.'

It was all his fault. In their haste to find Michael, he'd left the two women alone. He'd left *Amy* alone. How could he have been so stupid?

Alicia had put her crutches aside and was unrolling the bandage from her leg. Inside, secreted there on the night of their arrival, was a blade. The crutch was a ruse: the wound was nearly healed. She rose to her feet.

'Time to find those guns,' she said.

Whatever Billie had put in his drink, the effects hadn't worn off yet.

Michael was lying in the back of a pickup, covered with a plastic tarp. The bed of the truck was full of rattling pipes. Billie had told him to lie still, not to make a sound, but the jumpy feeling inside him was almost more than he could bear. What was she doing, giving him a concoction like that and expecting him to lie perfectly still? The effect was like shine in reverse, as if every cell in his body were singing a single note. Like his mind had passed through some kind of filter, giving each thought a bright, humming clarity.

No more dreams, she'd said. No more fat lady with her smoke and smell and awful, scratchy voice. How did Billie know about his dreams?

They'd stopped once, just a few moments after they'd left the infirmary, which they'd exited through the rear. Some kind of checkpoint. Michael heard a voice he didn't recognize, asking Billie where she was going. From under the tarp Michael had listened anxiously to their exchange.

'There's a broken line out in the eastern field,' she

explained. 'Olson asked me to move these pipes around for the crew tomorrow.'

'It's new moon. You shouldn't be out here.'

New moon, Michael thought. What was so important about the new moon?

'Look, that's what he said. Take it up with him if you want.'

'I don't see how you're going to make it back in time.'

'Let me worry about that. Are you going to let me through or not?'

A tense silence. Then: 'Just be back by dark.'

Now, sometime later, Michael felt the truck slowing once again. He drew the tarp aside. A purpling evening sky and behind them, in the truck's wake, a boiling cloud of dust. The mountains were a distant bulge against the horizon.

'You can come out now.'

Billie was standing at the tailgate. Michael climbed from the truck bed, grateful to move at last. They had parked outside a massive metal shed, at least two hundred meters long, with a bulging convex roof. He saw the rusted shape of fuel tanks behind it. The land was lined with railroad tracks, heading off in all directions.

A small door opened in the side of the building; a man emerged and walked toward them. His skin was covered in grease and oil, so much that his face was practically black with it; he was holding something in his hands, working at it with a filthy rag. He stopped where they were standing and looked Michael up and down. A short-barreled shotgun was holstered to his leg. Michael remembered him as the driver of the van that had brought them from Las Vegas.

'This him?'

Billie nodded.

The man moved forward so their faces were just inches apart and peered into Michael's eyes. First one eye, then the other, shifting his head back and forth. His breath was sour, like spoiled milk. His teeth were lined in black. Michael had to force himself not to pull away.

726

'How much did you give him?'

'Enough,' Billie said.

The man gave him one more skeptical look, then stepped back and shot a jet of brown spit onto the hardpan. 'I'm Gus.'

'Michael.'

'I know who you are.' He held up the object for Michael to see. 'You know what this is?'

Michael took it in his hand. 'It's a solenoid, twenty-four volts. I'd say it comes off a fuel pump, a big one.'

'Yeah? What's wrong with it?'

Michael passed it back, shrugging. 'Nothing I can see.'

Gus looked at Billie, frowning. 'He's right.'

'I told you.'

'She says you know about electrical systems. Wiring harnesses, generators, controller units.'

Michael shrugged again. He was still reluctant to say too much, but something, some instinct, was telling him he could trust these two. They hadn't brought him all this way for nothing.

'Let me see what you've got.'

They crossed the railyard to the shed. Michael could hear, from inside, the roar of portable generators, the clang of tools. They entered through the same door the man had emerged from. The interior of the shed was vast, the space illuminated by spotlights on tall poles. More men in greasy jumpsuits were moving about.

What Michael saw stopped him where he stood.

It was a train. A diesel locomotive. And not some rusted derelict, either. The damn thing looked like it could actually run. It was covered in protective metal plating, three-quarter-inch steel at least. A huge plow jutted from the front of the engine; more steel plates were riveted over the windshield, leaving only a thin slit of exposed glass for the driver to see by. Three boxy compartments sat behind it.

'The mechanicals and pneumatics are all up and running,' Gus said. 'We charged the eight-volts using the portables. It's the electrical harness that's the problem. We can't pull a current from the batteries to the pump.'

The blood was racing through Michael's veins. He took a breath to calm himself. 'Do you have schematics?'

Gus led him to a makeshift desk where he'd laid out the drawings, broad sheets of brittle paper covered in blue ink. Michael looked them over.

'This is a rat's nest,' he said after a moment. 'It could take me weeks to find the problem.'

'We don't have weeks,' Billie said.

Michael lifted his face to look at them. 'How long have you been working on this thing?'

'Four years,' Gus said. 'Give or take.'

'So how much time do I have?'

Billie and Gus exchanged a worried glance.

'About three hours,' said Billie.

FIFTY-THREE

'Theo.'

He was in the kitchen again. The drawer was open; the knife lay gleaming there. Tucked in the drawer like a baby in its crib.

'Theo, come on now. I'm telling you, all you got to do is pick it up and do her. You do her and this will all be over.'

The voice. The voice that knew his name, that seemed to crawl around inside his head, waking and sleeping. Part of his mind was in the kitchen, while another part was in the cell, the cell where he had been for days and days, fighting sleep, fighting the dream.

'Is that so fucking hard? Am I not being absolutely clear here?'

He opened his eyes; the kitchen vanished. He was sitting on the edge of the cot. The cell with its door and its stinking hole that ate his piss and shit. Who knew what time it was, what day, what month, what year. He had been in this place forever.

'Theo? Are you listening to me?'

He licked his lips, tasting blood. Had he bitten his tongue? 'What do you want?'

A sigh from the far side of the door. 'I gotta say, Theo. You do impress me. Nobody holds out like this. I think you've got some kind of record going.'

Theo said nothing. What was the point? The voice never answered his questions. If there even was a voice. Sometimes he thought it was just something in his head.

'I mean some, sure,' the voice went on. 'In some cases you could say it goes against the grain, carving the old bitch up.' A dark chuckle, like something from the bottom of a pit. 'Believe me, I've seen people do the damnedest shit.'

It was terrible, Theo thought, what staying awake could do to a person's mind. You went without sleep long enough, you made your brain stand up and walk around day after day after day no matter how tired you felt – you did push-ups and sit-ups on the cold stone floor until your muscles burned, you scratched and slapped yourself and dug at your own flesh with your bloodied nails to keep awake – and before long you didn't know which was which, if you were awake or asleep. Everything got blended together. A sensation like pain – only worse, because it wasn't a pain in your body; the pain was your mind and your mind was you. You were pain itself.

'You mark my words, Theo. You do not want to go there. That was not a story with a happy ending.'

He felt his awareness folding again, taking him down into sleep. He dug his nails hard into his palm. *Stay. Awake. Theo.* Because there was something worse than staying awake, he knew.

'Sooner or later everybody comes around, is what I'm saying, Theo.'

'Why do you keep using my name?'

'I'm sorry? Theo, did you ask me something?'

He swallowed, tasting blood again, the foulness of his own mouth. His head was in his hands. 'My name. You're always saying it.'

'Just trying to get your attention. You haven't been yourself much these last few days, if you'll pardon my saying so.'

Theo said nothing.

'So okay,' the voice went on. 'You don't want me to use your name. Don't see why not, but I can live with that. Let's change the subject. What are your thoughts on Alicia? Because I do believe that girl is something special.'

Alicia? The voice was talking about Alicia? It simply wasn't possible. But nothing was, that was the thing. The voice was always saying things that were impossible.

'Now, I thought it would be Mausami, the way you described her,' the voice went merrily on. 'Back when we had our little talk. I was pretty sure my tastes would run in her direction. But there's something about a redhead that just gets my blood boiling.'

'I don't know who you're talking about. I told you. I don't know anyone by those names.'

'You *dog*, Theo. Are you trying to tell me you put the wood to Alicia, too? And Mausami in the condition she is?'

The room seemed to tip. 'What did you say?'

'Oh, I'm sorry. You didn't hear? Now, I'm surprised she didn't tell you. Your Mausami, Theo.' The voice lifted to a kind of singsong. 'Got a little *bunski* in the *ovenski*.'

He was trying to focus. To hold the words he was hearing in place so he could grasp their meaning. But his brain was heavy, so heavy, like a huge, slippery stone the words kept sliding off.

'I know, I know,' the voice went on. 'It came as a shock to me, too. But back to Lish. If you don't mind my asking, how does she like it? I'm thinking she's an on-all-fours-howl-at-the-moon kind of girl. How about it, Theo? Set me straight here if I'm wrong.'

'I don't . . . know. Stop using my name.'

A pause. 'All right. If that's how you want it. Let's try a new name, shall we? How about: Babcock.'

His mind clenched. He thought he might be sick. He would have been, if there had been anything in his stomach to come up.

'Now we're getting somewhere. You know about Babcock, don't you, Theo?'

That was what was on the other side, the other side of the dream. One of Twelve. Babcock.

'What . . . is he?'

'Come on, you're a smart fellow. You really don't know?' An expectant pause. 'Babcock is . . . you.'

I am Theo Jaxon, he thought, saying the words in his mind like a prayer. *I am Theo Jaxon, I am Theo Jaxon. Son of Demetrius and Prudence Jaxon. First Family. I am Theo Jaxon.*

'He's you. He's me. He's everyone, at least in these parts. I like to think he's kind of like our local god. Not like the old gods. A new god. A dream of god we all dream together. Say it with me, Theo. *I. Am. Babcock.*'

I am Theo Jaxon. I am Theo Jaxon. I am not in the kitchen. I am not in the kitchen with the knife.

'Shut up, shut up,' he begged. 'You're not making any sense.'

'There you go again, trying to make *sense* of things. You gotta let *go*, Theo. This old world of ours hasn't made sense in a hundred goddamn years. Babcock isn't about making *sense*. Babcock just *is*. Like the We. Like the Many.'

The words found Theo's lips. 'The Many.'

The voice was softer now. It floated toward him from behind the door on waves of softness, calling him to sleep. To just let go and sleep.

'That's right, Theo. The Many. The We. The We of Babcock. You gotta do it, Theo. You've got to be a good boy and close your eyes and carve that old bitch up.'

He was tired, so tired. It was like he was melting from the outside in, his body liquefying around him, around the single overwhelming need to close his eyes and sleep. He wanted to cry but he had no tears to shed. He wanted to beg but he didn't know what for. He tried to think of Mausami's face, but his eyes had closed again; he had let his lids fall shut, and he was falling, falling into the dream.

'It's not as bad as you think. A bit of a tussle at the start. The old gal's got some fight in her, I'll give her that. But in the end, you'll see.'

The voice was somewhere above him, floating down through the warm yellow light of the kitchen. The drawer, the knife. The heat and smell and the tightness in his chest, the silence plugging his throat, and the soft place on her neck where her voice was bobbing in its rolls of flesh. *I tell you, the boy isn't just dumb. He's been* struck *dumb.* Theo was reaching for the knife, the knife was in his hand.

But a new person was in the dream now. A little girl. She was seated at the table, holding a small, soft-looking object in her lap: a stuffed animal.

—This is Peter, she stated in her little girl's voice, not looking at him. He's my rabbit.

—That's not Peter. I know Peter.

But she wasn't a little girl, she was a beautiful woman, tall and lovely, with tresses of black hair that curved liked cupped hands around her face, and Theo wasn't in the kitchen anymore. He was in the library, in that terrible room with its stench of death and the rows of cots under the windows and on each cot the body of a child, and the virals were coming; they were coming up the stairs.

—Don't do it, said the girl, who was a woman now. The kitchen table at which she sat had somehow traveled to the library, and Theo saw that she wasn't beautiful at all; in her place sat an old woman, wizened and toothless, her hair gone ghostly white.

—Don't kill her, Theo.

No.

He jerked awake, the dream popping like a bubble. 'I won't . . . do it.'

The voice broke into a roar. 'Goddamnit, you think this is a *game*? You think you get to choose how this is going to go?'

Theo said nothing. Why wouldn't they just kill him?

'Well, okay then, pardner. Have it your way.' The voice released a great, final sigh of disappointment. 'I got news for you. You're not the only guest in this hotel. You won't like this next part very much, I don't expect.' Theo heard the boots scraping on the floor, turning to go. 'I had higher hopes for you. But I guess it's all the same. Because we're going to have them, Theo. Maus and Alicia and the rest. One way or the other, we're going to have them all.'

FIFTY-FOUR

It was the new moon, Peter realized, as they made their way through the darkness. New moon, and not one soul about.

Getting past the guards had been the easy part. It was Sara who had come up with a plan. *Let's see Lish do this*, she had said, and marched straight out the door across the square to where the two men, Hap and Leon, were standing by a fire barrel, watching her approach. She stepped up to them, positioning herself between them and the door of the hut. A brief negotiation ensued; one of the men, Hap, the smaller of the two, turned and walked away. Sara ran one hand through her hair, the signal. Hollis slipped outside, ducking into the shadow of the building, then Peter. They circled around to the north side of the square and took positions in the alley-way. A moment later, Sara appeared, leading the remaining guard, whose quick step told them what she'd promised. As she walked past them, Hollis rose from his hiding place behind an empty barrel, wielding the leg of a chair.

'Hey,' said Hollis, and hit the one named Leon so hard he simply melted.

They dragged his limp body deeper into the alley.

Hollis patted him down; strapped to the man's leg in a leather sheath, hidden under the jumpsuit, was a short-barreled revolver. Caleb appeared with a length of laundry line; they bound the man's hands and feet and stuffed a wadded rag into his mouth.

'Is it loaded?' Peter asked.

Hollis had opened the cylinder. 'Three rounds.' He snapped it closed with a flick of his wrist and passed the weapon to Alicia.

'Peter, I think these buildings are empty,' she said.

It was true; there were no lights anywhere.

'We better hurry.'

They approached the prison from the south, across an empty field. Hollis believed the entrance to the building was located on the far side, facing the main gate to the compound. There was, he said, a kind of tunnel there, the entrance arched in stone and set into the wall. They would attempt this if they had to, but it stood in full view of the observation towers; the plan was to look for a less risky way in. The vans and pickups were kept in a garage on the south side of the building. It would make sense for Olson and his men to keep their hard assets together, and, in any event, they had to look somewhere first.

The garage was sealed, the doors drawn down and secured with a heavy padlock. Peter looked through a window but could see nothing. Behind the garage was a long concrete ramp leading to a platform with an overhang and a pair of bay doors set in the prison wall. A dark stain ran up the middle of the ramp. Peter knelt and touched it; his fingers came away wet. He brought his fingers to his nose. Engine oil.

The doors had no handles, no obvious mechanism by which they could be opened. The five of them formed a line and pressed their hands against the smooth surface, attempting to draw it upward. They felt no sharp resistance, only the weight of the doors themselves, too heavy to lift without something to grip. Caleb scampered back down the ramp to the garage; a crash of glass and he returned a moment later, holding a tire iron.

They formed a line again, managing to lift the door far enough for Caleb to wedge the iron under it. A blade of light had appeared on the concrete. They drew the door upward and ducked through one by one and let it fall closed behind them.

They found themselves in some kind of loading area. There were coils of chain on the floor, old engine parts. Somewhere nearby water was dripping; the air smelled like oil and stone. The source of the light lay up ahead, a flickering glow. As they moved forward, a familiar shape emerged from the gloom.

A Humvee.

Caleb opened the tailgate. 'Everything's gone, except for the fifty-cal. There are three boxes of rounds for that.'

'So where are the rest of the guns?' Alicia said. 'And who moved this in here?'

'We did.'

They swiveled to see a single figure step from the shadows: Olson Hand. More figures began to emerge, surrounding them. Six of the orange-suited men, all of them armed with rifles.

Alicia had drawn the revolver from her belt and was pointing it at Olson. 'Tell them to back off.'

'Do as she says,' Olson said, holding up a hand. 'I mean it. Guns down, *now*.'

One by one the men dropped the barrels of their weapons. Alicia was the last – though Peter noted that she didn't return the gun to her belt, but kept it at her side.

'Where are they?' Peter asked Olson. 'Do you have them?'

'I thought Michael was the only one.'

'Amy and Mausami are missing.'

He hesitated, appearing perplexed. 'I'm sorry. This isn't what I intended. I don't know where they are. But your friend Michael is with us.'

'Who's "us"?' Alicia demanded. 'What's going on, god-damnit? Why are we all having the same dream?'

Olson nodded. 'The fat woman.'

'You son of a bitch, what did you do with Michael?'

With that, she raised the gun again, using two hands to steady the barrel, which she aimed at Olson's head. Around them, six rifles responded in kind. Peter felt his stomach clench.

'It's all right,' Olson said quietly, his eyes fixed on the barrel of the gun.

'Tell him, Peter,' Alicia said. 'Tell him I will put a bullet in him right here unless he starts talking.'

Olson was gently waving his hands at his sides. 'Everyone, stay calm. They don't *know*. They don't *understand*.'

Alicia drew her thumb down on the hammer of the revolver to cock it. '*What don't we know?*'

In the thin lamplight, Olson appeared diminished, Peter thought. He seemed hardly the same person at all. It was as if a mask had fallen away and Peter was seeing the real Olson for the first time: a tired old man, beset by doubt and worry.

'Babcock,' he said. 'You don't know about Babcock.'

Michael was on his back, his head buried beneath the control panel. A mass of wiring and plastic connectors hung above his face.

'Try it now.'

Gus closed the knife switch that connected the panel to the batteries. From beneath them came the whir of the main generator spinning up.

'Anything?'

'Hang on,' Gus said. Then: 'No. The starter breaker popped again.'

There had to be a short in the control harness somewhere. Maybe it was the stuff in the drink Billie had given him or all that time he'd spent around Elton, but it was as if Michael could actually *smell* it – a faint aerial discharge of hot metal and molten plastic, somewhere in the tangle of wires above his face. With one hand he moved the circuit tester up and down the board; with the other he gave a gentle tug at each connection. Everything was tight.

He shimmied his way out and drew up to a seated position. The sweat was pouring down. Billie, standing above him, eyed him anxiously.

'Michael—'

'I know, I know.'

He took a long swig from a canteen and wiped his face on his sleeve, giving himself a moment to think. Hours of testing circuits, tugging wires, backtracking each connection to the panel. And still he'd found nothing.

He wondered: What would Elton do?

The answer was obvious. Crazy, perhaps, but still obvious. And in any event, he'd already tried everything else he could think of. Michael climbed to his feet and moved down the narrow walkway connecting the cab with the engine compartment. Gus was standing by the starter control unit, a penlight tucked in his mouth.

'Reset the relay,' he instructed.

Gus spat the flashlight into his hand. 'We've already tried that. We're draining the batteries. We do this too many times, we'll have to recharge them with the portables. Six hours at least.'

'Just do it.'

Gus shrugged and reached around the unit, into its nest of pipes, feeling his way blind.

'Okay, for what it's worth, it's reset.'

Michael stepped back to the breaker panel. 'I want everybody to be very, very quiet.'

If Elton could do it, so could he. He took a deep breath and slowly released it as he closed his eyes, trying to empty his mind.

Then he flipped the breaker.

In the instant that followed – a splinter of a second – he heard the spin of the batteries and the rush of current moving through the panel, the sound in his ears like water

737

moving through a tube. But something was wrong; the tube was too small. The water pushed against the sides and then the current began to flow in the wrong direction, a violent turbulence, half going one way and half the other, canceling each other out, and just like that everything stopped; the circuit was broken.

He opened his eyes to find Gus staring at him, mouth open, showing his blackened teeth.

'It's the breaker,' Michael said.

He drew a screwdriver from his tool belt and popped the breaker from the panel. 'This is fifteen amps,' he said. 'This thing wouldn't power a hot plate. Why the hell would it be fifteen amps?' He gazed up at the box, its hundreds of circuits. 'What's this one, in the next slot? Number twenty-six.'

Gus examined the schematic that was spread out on the tiny table in the engine's cab. He glanced at the panel, then back to the drawing. 'Interior lights.'

'Flyers, you don't need thirty amps for that.' Michael jimmied the second breaker free and swapped it for the first one. He closed the knife switch again, waiting for the breaker to pop. When it didn't, he said, 'That's it.'

Gus was frowning doubtfully. 'That's it?'

'They must have gotten switched. It's got nothing to do with the head-end unit. Reset the relay and I'll show you.'

Michael moved forward to the cab, where Billie was waiting in one of the two swiveling chairs at the windshield. Everyone else was gone; the rest of the crew had left just after dark in Billie's pickup, headed for the rendezvous.

Michael took the other chair. He turned the key set in the panel beside the throttle; from below they heard the batteries spinning up. The dials on the panel began to glow, a cool blue. Through the narrow slit between the protective plates, Michael could see a curtain of stars beyond the open doors of the shed. Well, he thought, it's now or never. Either there was current to the starter or there wasn't. He'd found one problem but who knew how many others there might be. It had taken him twelve days to fix one Humvee. Everything he'd done here, he'd done in a little under three hours.

Michael lifted his voice to the rear of the car, where Gus was priming the fuel system, clearing any air from the line: 'Go ahead!'

Gus fired the starter. A great roar rose from below, carrying the satisfying smell of combusting diesel. The engine gave a shuddering lurch as the wheels engaged and began to push against their brakes.

'So,' Michael said, turning to Billie, 'how do you drive this thing?'

FIFTY-FIVE

In the end, they could only take Olson at his word. They simply had no choice.

They divvied up the weapons and split into two groups. Olson and his men would storm the room from ground level while Peter and the others entered from above. The space they called the ring had once been the prison's central courtyard, covered by a domed roof. Part of the roof had fallen away, leaving the space open to the outside, but the original structural girders were intact. Suspended from these girders, fifteen meters above the ring, was a series of catwalks, once used by the guards to monitor the floor below. These were arranged like the spokes of a wheel with ducts running above them, wide enough for a person to crawl through.

Once they had secured the catwalk, Peter and the others would descend by flights of stairs at the north and south ends of the room. These led to three tiers of caged balconies encircling the yard. This would be where most of the crowd would be, Olson explained, with perhaps a dozen stationed on the floor to operate the fireline.

The viral, Babcock, would enter through the opening in

the roof, on the east side of the room. The cattle, four head, would be driven in from the opposite end, through a gap in the fireline, followed by the two people slated for the sacrifice.

Four and two, Olson said, *for each new moon. As long as we give him the four and two, he keeps the Many away.*

The Many: that was what Olson called the other virals. The ones of Babcock, he explained. The ones of his blood. He controls them? Peter asked, not really believing any of it yet; it was all too fantastic – though even as he formed the question, he felt his skepticism giving way. If Olson was telling the truth, a great deal suddenly made sense. The Haven itself, its impossible existence; the strange behavior of the residents, like people carrying a terrible secret; even the virals themselves and the feeling Peter had harbored his whole life that they were more than the sum of their parts. *He doesn't just control them*, Olson answered. As he spoke, a heaviness seemed to come over him; it was as if he'd waited years to tell the story. *He is them, Peter.*

'I'm sorry I lied to you before, but it couldn't be helped. The first settlers who came here weren't refugees. They were children. The train brought them here, from where exactly we don't know. They were going to hide in Yucca Mountain, in the tunnels inside it. But Babcock was already here. That was when the dream began. Some say it's a memory from a time before he became a viral, when he was still a man. But once you've killed the woman in the dream, you belong to him. You belong to the ring.'

'The hotel, with the blocked streets,' Hollis ventured. 'It's a trap, isn't it?'

Olson nodded. 'For many years we sent out patrols, to bring in as many more as we could. A few just wandered through. Others were left there by the virals for us to find. Like you, Sara.'

Sara shook her head. 'I still don't remember what happened.'

'No one ever does. The trauma is simply too great.' Olson

looked imploringly at Peter again. 'You must understand. We've lived this way always. It was our only way to survive. For most, the ring seems a small price to pay.'

'Well, it's a lousy deal, if you ask me,' Alicia cut in. Her face was hardened with anger. 'I've heard enough. These people are *collaborators*. They're like *pets*.'

Something darkened in Olson's expression – though his tone, when he continued, was still almost eerily calm. 'Call us what you like. You can't say anything I haven't said to myself a thousand times. Mira was not my only child. I had a son, too. He would be about your age if he had lived. When he was chosen, his mother objected. In the end, Jude sent her into the ring with him.'

His own son, Peter thought. Olson had sent his own son to die.

'Why Jude?'

Olson shrugged. 'It's who he is. There has always been Jude.' He shook his head again. 'I would explain it better if I could. But none of that matters now. What's past is past, or so I tell myself. There's a group of us who've been preparing for this day for years. To get away, to live our lives as people. But unless we kill Babcock, he'll call the Many. With these weapons we have a chance.'

'So who's in the ring?'

'We don't know. Jude wouldn't say.'

'What about Maus and Amy?'

'I told you, we don't know where they are.'

Peter turned to Alicia. 'It's them.'

'We don't know that,' Olson objected. 'And Mausami is pregnant. Jude wouldn't choose her.'

Peter was unconvinced. Even more: everything Olson had said made him believe that Maus and Amy were the ones in the ring.

'Is there another way inside?'

That was when Olson explained the layout, the ducts above the catwalks, kneeling on the floor of the garage to draw in the dust. 'It will be pitch-black for the first part,' he warned, as his men were passing out rifles and pistols from the cache taken from the Humvee. 'Just follow the sound of the crowd.'

'How many more men do you have inside?' Hollis asked. He was filling his pockets with magazines. Kneeling by an open crate, Caleb and Sara were both loading rifles.

'The seven of us, plus another four in the balconies.'

'That's all?' Peter said. The odds, not good to begin with, were suddenly much worse than he'd thought. 'How many does Jude have?'

Olson frowned. 'I thought you understood. He has all of them.'

When Peter said nothing, Olson continued: 'Babcock is stronger than any viral you've ever seen, and the crowd won't be on our side. Killing him won't be easy.'

'Has anyone ever tried?'

'Once.' He hesitated. 'A small group, like us. It was many years ago.'

Peter was about to ask what had happened. But he heard, in Olson's silence, the answer to this question.

'You should have told us.'

A look of abject resignation came into Olson's face. Peter realized that what he was seeing there was a burden far heavier than sorrow or grief. It was guilt.

'Peter. What would you have said?'

He didn't answer; he didn't know. Probably he wouldn't have believed him. He wasn't sure what he believed now. But Amy was inside the ring, of that he was certain; he felt it in his bones. He popped the clip from his pistol to blow it clean, then reinserted it into the handle and pulled the slide. He looked toward Alicia, who nodded. Everyone was ready.

'We're here to get our friends,' he said to Olson. 'The rest is up to you.'

But Olson shook his head. 'Make no mistake. Once you're in the ring, our fights are the same. Babcock has to die. Unless we kill him, he'll call the Many. The train will make no difference.'

New moon: Babcock felt the hunger uncoiling inside him. And he stretched out his mind from This Place, the Place of Return, saying:

It is time.

It is time, Jude.

Babcock was up. Babcock was flying. Soaring over the desert floor in leaps and bounds, the great joyful hunger coursing through him.

Bring them to me. Bring me one and then another. Bring them that you should live in this way and no other.

There was blood in the air. He could smell it, taste it, feel its essence coursing through him. First would come the blood of the beasts, a living sweetness. And then his Best and Special, his Jude, who dreamed the dream better than all the others since the Time of Becoming, whose mind lived with him in the dream like a brother, would bring the ones of blood that Babcock would drink and be filled by it.

He mounted the wall in a single jump.

I am here.

I am Babcock.

We are Babcock.

He descended. He heard the gasps of the crowd. Around him, the fires blazed up. Behind the flames were the men, come to watch and know. And through the gap he saw the beasts approaching, driven on the whip, their eyes fearless and unknowing, and the hunger lifted him up in a wave and he was sailing down upon them, tearing and ripping, first one and then the other, each in its turn, a glorious fulfillment.

We are Babcock.

He could hear the voices now. The chant of the crowds in their cages, behind the ring of flames; and the voice of his One, his Jude, standing on the catwalk above, leading them, as if in song.

'Bring them to me! Bring me one and then another! Bring them that we should live . . .'

A wall of sound, ascending in fierce unison: '. . . in this way and no other!'

A pair of figures appeared in the gap. They stumbled forward, pushed by men who quickly stepped away. The flames rose again behind them, a door of fire, sealing them inside for the taking.

The crowd roared.

'Ring! Ring! Ring!'

A stampede of feet. The air shuddering, hammering.

'Ring! Ring! Ring!'

And that was when he felt her. In a bright and terrible burst, Babcock felt her. The shadow behind the shadow, the tear in the fabric of night. The one who carried the seed of forever but was not of his blood, was not of the Twelve or the Zero.

The one called Amy.

Peter heard it all from the ventilation shaft. The chanting, the panicked cries of the cattle, and then the silence – of bated breath, of some terrible spectacle about to unfold – and then the explosion of cheers. Heat was rising in waves to his belly and, with it, the choking fumes of diesel smoke. The shaft was just wide enough for a single person crawling on his elbows. Somewhere below him, gathering in the tunnel that connected the ring to the prison's main entrance, were Olson's men. There was no way to coordinate their arrivals, nor to communicate with the others stationed in the crowd. They would simply have to guess.

Peter saw an opening ahead: a metal grate in the floor of the duct. He pressed his face against it, gazing downward. Below the grate he could see the slats of the catwalk and farther still, another twenty meters, the floor of the ring, wrapped by a trench of burning fuel.

The floor was covered in blood.

On the balconies, the crowd had taken up its chanting again. *Ring! Ring! Ring! Ring!* Peter guessed he and the others were positioned over the east end of the room now. They would have to cross the catwalk in full view of the crowd to reach the stairs to the floor below. He glanced back to Hollis, who nodded, and lifted the grate free, pushing it to the side. Then he freed the safety on his pistol and crawled forward so that his feet straddled the vent.

Amy, Peter thought, *it's nothing good, what's down there. Do what you do or we're all dead.*

He pushed himself off, dropping feet first through the opening.

He fell and fell, long enough to wonder: Why am I always falling? The distance to the catwalk was more than he'd expected – not two meters but four or even five – and he hit the metal with a bone-rattling bang. He rolled. The pistol was gone, squirted from his grasp. And it was as he rolled that he glimpsed, from the corner of his eye, a figure below: wrists bound, body slack with submission, wearing a sleeveless shirt that Peter recognized. His mind grabbed hold of this image, which was also a memory – of the smell of pyre smoke on the day they'd burned the body of Zander Phillips, standing in the sunshine outside the power station, and the name stitched over the pocket. *Armando*.

Theo.

The man in the ring was Theo.

His brother wasn't alone. There was someone else beside him, a man on his knees. He was stripped to the waist, slumped forward on the ground so that his face was obscured. And as Peter's vision widened he realized that what he was seeing on the floor of the ring was the cattle, or what had once been the cattle – they were strewn in pieces everywhere, as if they had been situated at the heart of an explosion – and crouched at the center of this heaping mass of blood and flesh and bone, its face bent to bury itself in the remains, its body twitching with a darting motion as it drank, was a viral – but not like any viral Peter knew. It was the largest he had ever seen, that anyone had ever seen, its curled bulk so immense that it was like some new being entirely.

745

'Peter! You're in time to watch the show!'

He had come to rest on his back, useless as a turtle. Jude, standing above him, wearing a look that Peter had no name for, a dark pleasure beyond words, was aiming a shotgun at his head. Peter felt the shudder of footsteps coming toward them – more orange-suited men racing down the catwalks from every direction.

Jude was standing directly below the vent.

'Go ahead,' Peter said.

Jude smiled. 'How noble.'

'Not you,' Peter said, and flicked his eyes upward. 'Hollis.'

Jude lifted his face in time for the bullet from Hollis's rifle to strike him just above the right ear. A misty bloom of pink: Peter felt the air dampen with it. For a moment, nothing happened. Then the shotgun released from Jude's hands, clattering to the catwalk. A large-butted pistol was tucked at his waist; Peter saw Jude's hand grope for it, blindly searching. Then something released inside him, blood began to pour from his eyes, a pitiful weeping of blood, and he dropped to his knees, flopping forward, his face frozen in an expression of eternal wonderment, as if to say: *I can't believe I'm dead.*

It was Mausami who killed the operator manning the fuel pump.

She and Amy had entered from the main tunnel just before the crowd arrived and had hidden under the stairs that connected the floor of the courtyard to the balconies. For many minutes they had waited, huddled together, emerging only when they heard the sound of the cattle being driven in, the wild cheers exploding above. The air was broiling, choked with smoke and fumes.

There was something terrible behind the flames.

As the viral tore into the cattle, the crowd seemed to detonate, everyone pumping their fists, chanting and stomping their feet, like a single being caught in some great and terrible ecstasy. Some were holding children on their shoulders so they could see. The cattle were screaming now, bucking and tearing around the ring, racing toward the flames and backing away in confusion, a mad dance between two poles of death. While Mausami watched, the viral sprang forward and snatched one by its hind legs, lifting upward with a deep cracking sound, twisting until the legs came free, then flinging them through the air to slap against the cages in a spray of blood. The creature left that one where it was – its front legs twitching at the dirt, struggling to pull its ruined body forward – and seized another by the horns, applying the same twisting motion to break its neck, then shoved its face into the stilled flesh at the base of the animal's throat, the viral's whole torso seeming to inflate as it drank, the steer's body contracting with each of the viral's muscular inhalations, shriveling before Mausami's eyes as the blood was pulled from its body.

She did not see the rest; she'd turned her face away.

'Bring them to me!' a voice was calling. 'Bring me one and then another! Bring them that we should live . . .'

'. . . in this way and no other!'

That was when she saw Theo.

In that instant, Mausami experienced a collision of joy and terror so violent it was as if she were stepping from her own body. Her breath seized up inside her; she felt dizzy and sick. Two men in jumpsuits were pushing Theo forward, driving him through a gap in the flames. His eyes had an empty, almost bovine look; he seemed to have no idea what was happening around him. He lifted his face to the crowd, blinking vacantly.

She tried to call out to him, but her voice was drowned in the foam of voices. She looked for Amy, hoping the girl would know what to do, but couldn't see her anywhere. Above and around her the voices were chanting again:

'Ring! Ring! Ring!'

And then the second man was brought in, held at the elbows by two guards. His head was bowed, his feet seemed barely to touch the floor as the men, supporting his weight, dragged him forward and pitched him onto the ground and darted away. The cheers of the crowd were deafening now, a wash of sound. Theo staggered onward, scanning the crowd, as if someone there might be bringing help. The second man had brought himself upright on his knees.

The second man was Finn Darrell.

Suddenly a woman was standing before her: a familiar face, with a long pink scar stitched to the cheekbone like a seam. Her jumpsuit bulged with the belly of her pregnancy.

'I know you,' the woman said.

Mausami backed away, but the woman gripped her by the arm, her eyes locking on Mausami's face with a fierce intensity. 'I know you, I know you!'

'Let me go!'

She pulled away. Behind her, the woman was frantically pointing, shouting, 'I know her, I know her!'

Mausami ran. All thoughts had left her but one: she had to get to Theo. But there was no way past the flames. The viral was almost done with the cattle; the last lay twitching under its jaws. In another few seconds it would rise and see the two men – see Theo – and that would be the end.

Then Mausami saw the pump. A huge greasy bulk, connected by long trailing hoses to a pair of bulging fuel tanks, weeping with rust. The operator was cradling a shotgun across his chest; a blade hung on his belt in a leather sheath. He was facing away, his eyes, like everyone's, trained on the spectacle unfolding beyond the fluttering wall of flame.

She felt a flicker of doubt – she'd never killed a man before – but it was not enough to stop her; in a single motion she stepped behind the guard and drew the blade and shoved it with all her strength into his lower back. She felt a stiffening, the muscles of his frame drawing tight, like a bow; from deep inside his throat came an exhalation of surprise.

She felt him die.

Punching through the din, a voice from high above: Peter's? 'Theo, run!'

The pump was a throbbing confusion of levers and knobs. Where were Michael and Caleb when you needed them?

Mausami picked the largest one – a wild guess, a lever as long as her forearm – and wrapped it in her fist and pulled.

'Stop her!' someone yelled. 'Stop that woman!'

As Mausami felt the shot entering her upper thigh – a strangely trivial pain, like the sting of a bee – she realized she'd done it. The flames were dying, guttering around the ring. The crowd was suddenly backing away from the wires, everyone yelling, chaos erupting. The viral had broken away from the last of the cattle, drawing itself erect – all throbbing light and eyes and claws and teeth, its smooth face and long neck and massive chest bibbed in blood. Its body looked swollen, like a tick's. It stood at least three meters, maybe more. With a flick of its head it found Finn with its eyes, head cocking to the side, body tensing as it took aim, preparing to spring, and then it did; it seemed to cross the air between them at the speed of thought, invisible as a bullet was invisible, arriving all at once where Finn lay helpless. What happened next Mausami did not see clearly and was glad that she did not, it was so fast and terrible, like the cattle but vastly worse, because it was a man. A splash of blood like something bursting, and part of Finn went one way, and part of him another.

Theo, she thought, as the pain in her leg abruptly deepened – a wave of heat and light that bent her double. The leg folded beneath her, sending her pitching forward. *Theo, I'm here. I've come to save you. We have a baby, Theo. Our baby is a boy.*

As she fell she saw a figure sprinting across the ring. It was Amy. Her hair was pulling a trail of smoke; darting tongues of fire were licking at her clothing. The viral had shifted his attention toward Theo now. Amy charged between them, protecting Theo like a shield. Faced with the creature's immense, bloated form, she seemed tiny, like a child.

And in that instant, which felt suspended – the whole world brought to a halt while the viral regarded the small figure before him – Mausami thought: that girl wants to say something. That girl is going to open her mouth and speak.

*

Twenty meters overhead, Hollis had dropped through the vent with his rifle, followed by Alicia, holding the RPG. She swung it toward the floor, pointing its barrel at the place where Amy and Babcock stood.

'I don't have a shot!'

Caleb and Sara dropped through behind them. Peter snatched Jude's shotgun from the floor of the catwalk and fired in the direction of the two men racing down the catwalk toward them. One man uttered a strangled cry and fell away, tumbling headfirst to the floor below.

'Shoot the viral!' he called to Alicia.

Hollis fired and the second man dropped, face-down, onto the catwalk.

'She's too close!' Alicia said.

'Amy,' Peter yelled, 'get out of there!'

The girl stood her ground. How long could she hold him that way? And where was Olson? The last of the fires had gone out; people were streaming down the stairs, an avalanche of orange jumpsuits. Theo, on his hands and knees, was backing away from the viral, but his heart was nowhere in this; he had accepted his fate, he had no strength to resist. Caleb and Sara had made it across the catwalk to the stairs now, descending into the melee on the balconies. Peter heard women screaming, children crying, a voice that sounded like Olson's, rising over the din: 'The tunnel! Everyone run to the tunnel!'

Mausami lurched into the ring.

'Over here!' She stumbled, catching herself with her hands as she fell to the floor. Her pants were soaked in blood. On all fours, she tried to rise. She was waving, screaming: 'Look over here!'

Maus, Peter thought, *keep back*.

Too late. The spell was broken.

The viral rocked its face toward the ceiling and drew down into a crouch, its body gathering energy like a coiled spring, and then it was flying, lofting through the air. It rose toward them with a pitiless inevitability, arcing over their heads and seizing one of the ceiling struts, body rotating like a child swinging on a tree limb – an oddly exhilarating, even joyful image – and landed on the catwalk with a shuddering clang.

I am Babcock.

We are Babcock.

'Lish—'

Peter felt the RPG sailing past his face, the scald of hot gas on his cheek; he knew what was going to happen before it did.

The grenade exploded. A punch of noise and heat and Peter was shoved backward into Alicia, the two of them tumbling onto the catwalk, but the catwalk wasn't there. The catwalk was falling. Something caught and held and they banged down hard, and for a hopeful moment everything stopped. But then the structure lurched again, and with a pop of rivets and a groan of bending metal the end of the catwalk broke away from the ceiling, tilting toward the floor like the head of a hammer, falling.

Leon in the alley, face-down in the dirt. Goddamn, he thought. Where did that girl go?

Some kind of gag was in his mouth; his wrists were bound behind him. He tried to wriggle his feet, but they were tied, too. It was the big one, Hollis; Leon remembered now. Hollis had risen out of the shadows, swinging something, and the next thing Leon knew he was all alone in the dark and couldn't move.

His nose was thick with snot and blood. Probably the son of a bitch had broken it. That was all he needed, a broken nose. He thought he'd cracked a couple of teeth, too, but with the gag in his mouth, his tongue stuffed behind it, he had no way to check.

It was so goddamn dark out here he couldn't see two feet in front of his face. The reek of garbage was coming from somewhere. People were always putting it in the alleys instead of taking it to the dump. How many times had he heard Jude tell people, *Take your fucking garbage to the* dump. What are we, pigs? A joke, sort of, since they weren't pigs but what was the difference, really? Jude was always making jokes like that, to watch people squirm. For a while they'd kept pigs – Babcock liked pork almost as much as he liked the cattle – but some kind of sickness had wiped them out one winter. Or maybe they'd just seen what was coming and decided, What the hell, I'd rather just lie down and die in the mud.

No one would be coming to look for Leon, that was for sure; the problem of standing up was his to solve on his own. He could sort of see a way to do it, by drawing his knees to his chest. It made his shoulders hurt something terrible, twisted back like they were, and pushed his face, with its broken nose and teeth, into the dirt; he gave a yelp of pain through the gag, and by the time he was done with it, he was woozy and breathing hard, the sweat popping out all over. He lifted his face – more pain in his shoulders, what the fuck had that guy done, tying his hands so tight – and raised his upper body until he was sitting up, his knees folded under him, and that was when he realized his mistake. He had no way to stand. He'd sort of thought he could push off with his toes, jumping his way into a standing position. But this would just send him pitching forward onto his face again. He should have scooched over to the wall first, used it to shimmy his way up. But now he was stuck, his legs jammed up under him, frozen in place like a big dumbshit.

He tried to cry for help, nothing fancy, just the word 'Hey,' but it came out as a strangled *Aaaaa* sound and made him want to cough. Already he could feel the circulation going out of his legs, a prickly numbness crawling up from his toes, like ants.

Something was moving out there.

He was facing the mouth of the alley. Beyond it lay the square, a zone of blackness since the fire barrel had gone out. He peered into the dark. Maybe it was Hap, come to look for him. Well, whoever it was, he couldn't see a goddamn thing.

Probably his mind was playing tricks on him. Alone outside on new moon, anybody could get a little jumpy.

No: something *was* moving. Leon felt it again. The feeling was coming from the ground, through his knees.

A shadow streaked above him. He lifted his head quickly, finding only stars, set in a liquidy blackness. The feeling through his knees was stronger now, a rhythmic shuddering, like the flapping of a thousand wings. What the goddamn—?

A figure darted into the alley. Hap.

Aaaaaaaaa, he said through the gag. *Aaaaaaaaa*. But Hap seemed not to notice him. He paused at the edge of the alley, panting for breath, and raced away.

Then he saw what Hap was running from.

Leon's bladder released, and then his bowels. But his mind was unable to register these facts as all thought was obliterated by an immense and weightless terror.

The end of the catwalk impacted the floor with a massive jolt. Peter, clutching one of the guardrails, barely managed to hold on. An object tumbled past him, clattering end over end before bounding into space: the empty RPG, spiraling a meteoric wick of smoke from its tube. Then something heavy struck him from above, ripping his hand away – Hollis and Alicia, tangled together – and that was that: the three of them were falling free, sliding down the angled catwalk to the floor below.

They hit the ground in a confusion of arms and legs and bodies and equipment, scattering across the floor like balls tossed from a hand. Peter came to rest on his back, blinking at the distant ceiling, his mind and body roaring with adrenaline.

Where was Babcock?

'Come on!' Alicia had grabbed him by the shirt and was pulling him to his feet. Sara and Caleb were beside her; Hollis was hobbling toward them, somehow still carrying his rifle. 'We have to get out of here!'

'Where did it go?'

'I don't know! It jumped away!'

The remains of the cattle were strewn everywhere. The air stank of blood, of meat. Amy was helping Maus to her feet. The girl's clothes were still smoking, though she seemed not to notice. A patch of her hair had been scorched away, revealing a raw pinkness of scalp.

'Help Theo,' Mausami said, as Peter crouched before her.

'Maus, you're shot.'

Her teeth were clenched with pain. She shoved him away. *'Help him.'*

Peter went to where his brother was kneeling in the dirt. He seemed dazed, his expression disordered. His feet were bare, his clothing was in tatters, his arms were covered with scabs. What had they done to him?

'Theo, look at me,' Peter commanded, gripping him by the shoulders. 'Are you hurt? Do you think you can walk?'

A small light seemed to go on in his brother's eyes. Not the whole Theo, but at least a glimmer.

'Oh my God,' said Caleb, 'that's *Finn.*'

The boy was pointing toward a bloody shape on the floor a few meters away. Peter thought at first it was a piece of the cattle, but then the details came into focus and he understood that this lump of meat and bone was half a person, a torso and head and a single arm, which lay twisted at an odd angle over the dead man's forehead. Below the waist there was nothing. The face, just as Caleb had said, was Finn Darrell's.

He tightened his grip on Theo's shoulders. Sara and Alicia were lifting Mausami to her feet. 'Theo, I need you to try to walk.'

Theo blinked and licked his lips. 'Is it really you, brother?'

Peter nodded.

'You . . . came for me.'

'Caleb,' Peter said, 'help me.'

Peter pulled Theo upright and wrapped an arm around his waist, Caleb taking him from the other side.

Together, they ran.

They exited into the dark tunnel, into the fleeing crowds. People were tearing toward the exit, pushing and shoving. Up ahead, Olson was waving people through the opening, screaming at the top of his voice: 'Run to the train!'

They burst from the tunnel into the yard. Everyone was making for the gate, which stood open. In the darkness and confusion a bottleneck had formed, too many people trying to shove their way through the narrow opening at once. Some were attempting to scale the fence, hurling themselves against the wires and clawing their way up. As Peter watched, a man at the top fell backward, screaming, one leg tangled in the barbs.

'Caleb!' Alicia cried. 'Take Maus!'

The crowd was surging around them. Peter saw Alicia's head bobbing above the fray, a flash of blond hair he knew to be Sara's. The two of them were moving in the wrong direction, fighting the current of the crowd.

'Lish! Where are you going?' But his voice was overpowered by a blast of sound, a single sustained note that split the air, seeming to come not from one direction but from everywhere at once.

Michael, he thought. Michael was coming.

They were suddenly propelled forward, the energy of the panicked throng lifting them like a wave. Somehow Peter managed to keep hold of his brother. They passed through the gate and into another mob of people compressed into the gap between the two fence lines. Someone banged into him from behind and he heard the man grunt and stumble and fall beneath the feet of the crowd. Peter fought his way through, pushing, shoving, using his body like a battering ram, until, at last, they burst free of the second gate.

The tracks were dead ahead. Theo seemed to be rousing, doing more to carry his own weight as they fought their way forward. In the chaos and darkness Peter couldn't see any of the others. He called their names but heard no answer over the yelling of the figures tearing past him. The road ascended a sandy rise and as they neared the top he saw a glow of light coming from the south. Another blast of the horn and then he saw it.

A huge silver bulk churning toward them, parting the night like a blade. A single beam of light shot from its bow, shining over the masses of figures crowding around the tracks. He saw Caleb and Mausami up ahead, racing toward the front of the train. Still holding Theo, Peter stumbled down the embankment; he heard a squeal of brakes. People were racing alongside the train, trying to grab hold. As the engine drew closer, a hatch opened in the front cab and Michael leaned out.

'We can't stop!'

'What?'

Michael cupped his mouth. 'We have to keep moving!'

The train had slowed to a crawl. Peter saw Caleb and Hollis lifting a woman into one of the three open boxcars trailing the engine; Michael was helping to pull Mausami up the ladder into the cab, Amy pushing from behind. Peter began to run with his brother, trying to match their speed with the ladder; as Amy ducked into the hatch, Theo grabbed hold and began to ascend. When he reached the top, Peter dove for the ladder and pulled himself up, his feet swinging free. Behind him he heard a sound of gunfire, shots pinging off the sides of the cars.

He slammed the door closed behind him to find himself in a cramped compartment, glowing with a hundred tiny lights. Michael was sitting at the control panel, Billie beside him. Amy had withdrawn to the floor behind Michael's chair, her eyes wide, her knees protectively pulled to her chest. To Peter's left, a narrow hallway led aft.

'Flyers, Peter,' Michael said, swiveling in his chair. 'Where the hell did Theo come from?'

Peter's brother was slumped on the floor of the hallway; Mausami was holding his head against her chest, her bloody leg folded under her.

Peter directed his voice to the front of the cab. 'Is there a med kit in this thing?'

Billie passed him a metal box. Peter popped it open and withdrew a cloth bandage, rolling it into a compress. He tore the fabric of Mausami's pant leg away to reveal the wound, a crater of torn skin and bloody flesh, and placed the bandage against it and told her to hold it there.

Theo lifted his face, his eyes flickering. 'Am I dreaming you?'

Peter shook his head.

'Who is she? The girl. I thought . . .' His voice trailed away.

For the first time it struck him: he had done it. *Take care of your brother.*

'There'll be time later, okay?'

Theo managed a weak smile. 'Whatever you say.'

Peter moved to the front of the cab, between the two seats. Through the slit of windshield between the plates he could see a view of desert in the beam of the headlamp and the tracks rolling under them.

'Is Babcock dead?' Billie asked.

He shook his head.

'You didn't kill him?'

The sight of the woman filled him with a sudden anger. 'Where the hell was Olson?'

Before she could answer, Michael broke in. 'Wait, where are the others? Where's *Sara*?'

The last Peter had seen her, she was with Alicia at the gate. 'I think she must be in one of the other cars.'

Billie had opened the cabin door again, leaning out; she ducked her head back inside. 'I hope everybody's on board,' she said, 'because here they come. Hit the gas, Michael.'

'My sister could still be out there!' Michael shouted. 'You said no one gets left!'

Billie didn't wait. She reached across Michael, knocking him back into his chair, and gripped a lever on the panel, pushing it forward. Peter felt the train accelerate. A digital readout on the panel sprang to life, the number swiftly rising: 30, 35, 40. Then she shoved her way past Peter into the hallway, where a ladder in the wall led to a second hatch in the ceiling. She briskly ascended, turning the wheel, directing her voice to the rear of the train. 'Gus! Up top, let's go!'

Gus jogged forward, dragging a canvas duffel bag, which he unzipped to reveal a pile of short-barreled shotguns. He passed one to Billie and took one for himself, then lifted his grease-stained face to Peter, handing him a weapon.

'If you're coming,' he said gruffly, 'you might want to remember to keep your head down.'

They ascended the ladder, Billie first, then Gus. As Peter lifted his head through the hatch, a blast of wind smacked him in the face, making him duck. He swallowed, pushing his fear down inside himself, and made a second attempt, easing through the opening with his face turned toward the front of the train, sliding onto the roof on his belly. Michael passed him the shotgun from below. He eased into a crouch, trying to find his footing while simultaneously cradling the shotgun. The wind was slapping him, a continuous pressure threatening to push him over. The roof of the engine was arched, with a flat strip down the middle. He was facing the rear of the train now, giving his weight to the wind; Billie and Gus were already well ahead of him. As Peter watched, they leapt the gap between the first and second boxcars, making their way aft, into the roaring dark.

He first saw the virals as a region of pulsing green light from the rear. Above the din of the engine and the squeal of the wheels on the rails he heard Billie yelling something, but her words were yanked away. He drew a breath and held it and leapt the gap to the first boxcar. Part of him was wondering, *What am I doing here, what am I doing on the roof of a moving train*, while another part accepted this fact, strange as it seemed, as an inevitable consequence of the night's events. The green glow was closer now, breaking apart as it widened into a wedge-shaped mass of bounding points, and Peter understood what he was seeing – that it was not just ten or twenty virals but an army of hundreds.

The Many.

The Many of Babcock.

As the first one took shape, vaulting through the air toward the rear of the train, Billie and Gus fired. Peter was halfway down the first boxcar now. The train shuddered and he felt his feet begin to slide, and just like that the shotgun was gone, falling away. He heard a scream and when he looked up there was no one – the place where Billie and Gus had stood was empty.

He had barely found his footing again when a huge crash from the front of the train pitched him forward. The horizon collapsed; the sky was gone. He was sliding on his belly down the sloping roof of the car. Just when it seemed he would sail into space, his hands found a narrow lip of metal at the top of one of the armored plates. There was no time even to be afraid. In the whirling darkness he sensed the presence of a wall shooting past him. They were in some kind of tunnel, boring through the mountain. He held on fast, feet swinging, scrabbling at the side of the train, and then he felt the air opening beneath him as the door of the boxcar flew open, and hands grabbing him, pulling him down and in.

The hands belonged to Caleb and Hollis. In a heap of arms and legs they spilled onto the floor of the boxcar. The interior was lit by a single lantern, swaying from a hook. The car was nearly empty – just a few dark figures huddled against the walls, apparently immobilized by fear. Beyond the open door the walls of a tunnel were flying past, filling the space with sound and wind. As Peter climbed to his feet, a familiar figure emerged from the shadows: Olson Hand.

A furious anger broke inside him. Peter seized the man by the scruff of his jumpsuit, shoving him against the wall of the boxcar and pushing his forearm up against his throat.

'Where the hell were you? You left us there!'

All color was drained from Olson's face. 'I'm sorry. It was the only way.'

All at once he understood. Olson had sent them into the ring as bait.

'You knew who it was, didn't you? You knew it was my brother all along.'

Olson swallowed, the point of his Adam's apple bobbing against Peter's forearm. 'Yes. Jude believed others would come. That's why we were waiting for you in Las Vegas.'

Another crash detonated from the front of the train; everyone went spilling forward. Olson was ripped from Peter's grasp. They were out of the tunnel again, back on open ground. Peter heard gunfire from outside and looked to see the Humvee racing past, Sara in the driver's seat, her knuckles clenched to the wheel, Alicia up top on the big gun, firing in concentrated bursts toward the rear of the train.

'Get out!' Alicia was waving frantically toward the last boxcar. 'They're right behind you!'

Suddenly all the people in the car were yelling, shoving, trying to scramble away from the open door. Olson gripped one of the figures by the arm and pushed her forward. Mira.

'Take her!' he yelled. 'Get her to the engine. Even if the cars are overrun, it's safe there.'

Sara had drawn alongside, matching her speed to the train's, trying to narrow the space.

Alicia was waving to them: 'Jump!'

Peter leaned out the door. 'Bring it closer!'

Sara drew in. The racing vehicles were less than two meters apart now, the Humvee positioned below them on the angled rail bed.

'Reach out!' Alicia called to Mira. 'I'll catch you!'

The girl, standing at the edge of the doorway, was rigid with fear. 'I can't!' she wailed.

Another splintering crash; Peter realized the train was barreling through debris on the tracks. The Humvee swayed away as something large and metal went whirling through the space between the vehicles, just as one of the huddled figures leapt to his feet and made a dash for the door. Before

Peter could speak, the man had hurled himself into the widening breach, a desperate plunge. His body slammed into the side of the Humvee, his outstretched hands clawing at the roof; for a moment it seemed possible that he would manage to hold on. But then one of his feet touched the ground, dragging in the dust, and with a wordless cry he was whisked away.

'Hold it steady!' Peter yelled.

Twice more the Humvee approached. Each time, Mira refused to go.

'This won't work,' Peter said. 'We'll have to go over the roof.' He turned to Hollis. 'You go first. Olson and I can push you up.'

'I'm too heavy. Hightop should go, then you. I'll lift Mira up.'

Hollis dropped to a crouch; Caleb climbed aboard his shoulders. The Humvee had swayed away again, Alicia firing in short bursts at the rear of the train. With Hightop on his shoulders, Hollis positioned himself at the edge of the door.

'Okay! Let go!'

Hollis ducked away, keeping one hand gripped on Caleb's foot; Peter grabbed the other. Together they pushed the boy upward, propelling Caleb over the lip of the door.

Peter ascended the same way. From the roof of the car he could see that the mass of virals, having passed through the tunnel, had broken apart into three groups – one directly behind them, two following on either side. They were racing in a kind of gallop, using both their hands and their feet to propel themselves forward in long leaps. Alicia was shooting at the head of the central group, which had closed to within ten meters. Some went down, dead or injured or merely stunned he couldn't tell; the pod closed over them and kept coming. Behind them the other two groups began to merge, passing through one another like currents of water, separating once again to re-form their original shapes.

He lay on his belly beside Caleb and reached down as

761

Hollis lifted Mira up; they found the frightened girl's hands and pulled, drawing her onto the roof.

Alicia, below them: 'Get down!'

Three virals were on the roof of the last boxcar now. A blast of fire erupted from the Humvee and they jumped away. Caleb was already vaulting across the gap to the engine. Peter reached for Mira but the girl was frozen in place, her body pressed to the roof of the car, her arms hugging it as if it were the one thing that might save her.

'Mira,' Peter said, trying to pull her free, 'please.'

Still she held on. 'I can't, I can't, I can't.'

From below, a clawed hand reached up, wrapping around her ankle.

'Poppa!'

Then she was gone.

There was nothing else he could do. Peter dashed toward the gap, took it at a leap, and dropped through the hatch behind Caleb. He told Michael to hold the train steady and swung open the door to the cabin and looked aft.

The virals were all over the third boxcar now, clinging to the sides like a swarm of insects. So intense was their frenzy that they appeared to be fighting with one another, snapping and snarling for the right to be the first ones inside. Even over the wind, Peter could hear the screams of the terrified souls inside.

Where was the Humvee?

Then he saw it, racing toward them at an angle, bouncing wildly over the hardpan. Hollis and Olson were clinging to the vehicle's roof. The big gun was depleted, all its ammo spent. The virals would be all over them any second.

Peter leaned out the door. 'Bring it closer!'

Sara gunned the engine, drawing alongside. Hollis was the first to grab the ladder, then Olson. Peter pulled them through into the cab and called down, 'Alicia, you go!'

'What about Sara?'

The Humvee was drifting away again, Sara fighting to keep them close without colliding. Peter heard a crash as the door of the last boxcar was ripped away, tumbling end over end into the receding darkness.

'I'll get her! Just grab the ladder!'

Alicia jumped from the roof of the Humvee, hurling her body across the gap. But the distance was suddenly too great; in his mind Peter saw her falling, her hands grabbing at nothing, her body tumbling into the crushing rush of space between the vehicles. But then she had done it; her hands had found the ladder, Alicia was climbing hand over hand up the train. When her feet reached the bottom rung, she turned, stretching her body into the gap.

Sara was gripping the wheel with one hand; with the other she was frantically trying to wedge a rifle into place to brace the gas pedal.

'It won't stay!'

'Forget it, I'll grab you!' Alicia called. 'Just open the door and take my hand!'

'It won't work!'

Suddenly Sara gunned the motor. The Humvee shot forward, pulling ahead of the train. Sara was on the edge of the tracks now. The driver's door swung open. Then she hit the brakes.

The edge of the train's plow caught the door and sheared it off like a blade, sending it whirling away. For a breathtaking instant the Humvee rocked onto its two right wheels, skidding down the embankment, but then the left side of the vehicle banged down. Sara was moving away now, rocketing across the hardpan at a forty-five-degree angle to the train; Peter saw a skid in the dust and then she was pulling alongside again. Alicia stretched a hand out into the gap.

Peter: 'Lish, whatever you're going to do, do it now!'

How Alicia managed it, Peter would never fully comprehend. When he asked her about it later, Alicia only shrugged. It wasn't anything she'd thought about, she told him; she had simply followed her instincts. In fact, there would come a time, not much later, when Peter would learn to expect such things from her – extraordinary things, unbelievable things. But that night, in the howling space between the Humvee and the train, what Alicia did seemed simply miraculous, beyond knowing. Nor could any of them have known what Amy, in the engine's aft compartment, was about to do, or what lay between the engine and the first boxcar. Not even Michael knew about that. Perhaps Olson did; perhaps that was why he'd told Peter to take his daughter to the engine, that she'd be safe there. Or so Peter reasoned in the aftermath. But Olson never said anything about this, and under the circumstances, in the brief time they had left with him, none of them would have the heart to ask.

As the first viral launched itself toward the Humvee, Alicia reached out, snatching Sara's wrist off the steering wheel, and pulled. Sara swung out on Alicia's arm in a wide arc, separating from the vehicle as it swerved away. For a horrible instant her eyes met Peter's as her feet skimmed the ground – the eyes of a woman who was going to die and knew it. But then Alicia pulled again, hard, drawing her upward, Sara's free hand found the ladder, and the two of them were climbing; Sara and Alicia were up and rolling into the cab.

Which was when it happened. An earsplitting boom, like thunder: the engine lurched violently forward, free of its weight; everything in the cab was suddenly airborne. Peter, standing by the open hatch, was slapped off his feet and hurled backward, his body slamming into the bulkhead. He thought: *Amy.* Where was Amy? And as he tumbled to the floor he heard a new sound, louder than the first, and he knew what this sound was: a deafening roar and a screech of metal, as the cars behind them jumped the rails, jackknifing into the air and careering like an avalanche of iron across the desert floor, everyone inside them dead, dead, dead.

They came to a stop at half-day. The end of the line, Michael said, powering down. The maps Billie had shown them indicated that the rails petered out at the town of Caliente. They were lucky the train had taken them this far. How far? Peter asked. Four hundred kilometers, give or take, said Michael. See that mountain ridge? He was pointing through the slitted windshield. That's Utah.

They disembarked. They were in some kind of railyard, with tracks all around, littered with abandoned cars – engines, tankers, flatbeds. The land here was less dry; there was tall grass growing, and cottonwoods, and a gentle breeze was blowing, cooling the air. Water was running nearby; they could hear the sound of birds.

'I just don't get it,' Alicia said, breaking the stillness. 'Where did they hope to get to?'

Peter had slept in the train, once it was clear no virals were pursuing them, and awakened at dawn to find himself curled on the floor beside Theo and Maus. Michael had stayed up through the night, but the ordeal of the last few days had eventually caught up with everyone. As for Olson: perhaps he'd slept, though Peter doubted it. The man had spoken to no one and was now sitting on the ground outside the engine, staring into space. When Peter had told him about Mira, he hadn't asked for any details, just nodded and said, 'Thank you for letting me know.'

'Anywhere,' Peter answered after a moment. He wasn't sure what he was feeling. The events of the night before – the whole four days at the Haven – felt like a feverish dream. 'I think they just wanted to get . . . anywhere.'

Amy had stepped away from the group, into the field. For a moment they watched her, moving through the windblown grass.

'Do you think she understands what she did?' Alicia asked.

It was Amy who had blown the coupler. The switch was located in the rear of the engine compartment by the head-end unit. Probably it had been connected to a drum of diesel fuel or kerosene, Michael surmised, with some kind of igniter. That would have been enough to do it. A fail-safe, in case the cars were overrun. It made sense, Michael said, when you thought about it.

Peter supposed it did. But none of them could explain how Amy had known what to do, nor what had led her to actually throw the switch. Her actions seemed, like everything else about her, beyond ordinary understanding. And yet it was because of her, once again, that they were all alive.

Peter watched her for a long moment. In the waist-high grass she appeared almost to float, her hands held out from her sides, grazing the feathered tips. Many days had passed since he'd thought of what had happened in the Infirmary; but watching her now as she moved through the grass, he was washed by the memory of that strange night. He wondered what she had told Babcock when she had stood before him. It was as if she were part of two worlds, one that he could see and one that he could not; and it was within this other, hidden world that the meaning of their voyage lay.

'A lot of people died last night,' Alicia said.

Peter drew a breath. Despite the sun, he felt suddenly cold. He was still watching Amy, but in his mind he saw Mira – the girl's body pressed to the roof of the train, the viral's hand reaching for her, pulling her away. The empty space where she had been and the sound of her screams as she fell.

'I think they'd been dead a long time,' he said. 'One thing's for sure, we can't stay here. Let's see what we've got.'

They inventoried their supplies, spreading them out on the ground by the engine. It didn't amount to much: half a dozen shotguns, a couple of pistols with a few rounds each, one automatic rifle, two spare clips for the rifle plus twenty-five shells for the shotguns, six blades, eight gallons of water in jugs plus more in the train's holding tank, a few hundred gallons of diesel fuel but no vehicle to put it in, a couple of plastic tarps, three tins of sulfur matches, the med kit, a kerosene lantern, Sara's journal – she had removed it from her pack when they'd left the hut and stashed it inside her jersey – and no food at all. Hollis said there was probably game out there; they shouldn't waste their ammo, but they could set some snares. Maybe they'd find something edible in Caliente.

Theo was sleeping on the floor of the engine compartment. He'd managed to give them a rough accounting of events as best he could recall them – his fragmented memory of the attack at the mall, then his time in the cell and the dream of the woman in her kitchen and his struggle to stay awake, and the taunting visits of the man whom Peter believed was almost certainly Jude – but the effort of talking was clearly difficult for him, and he'd eventually fallen into a sleep so profound that Sara had to reassure Peter that his brother was still breathing. The wound to Mausami's leg was worse than she'd claimed but less than life-threatening. The shot had blasted through her outer thigh, cutting a grisly-looking bloody trench but exiting cleanly. The night before, Sara had used a needle and thread from the med kit to sew the wound closed and had cleaned it with spirits from a bottle they'd found under the sink in the engine's tiny lavatory. It must have hurt like hell, but Maus had borne all of it with a stoic silence, gritting her teeth as she clutched Theo's hand. As long as she kept it clean, Sara said, she'd be fine. With luck she'd even be able to walk in a day or two.

The question arose about where to go. It was Hollis who raised it, and Peter found himself taken aback; the thought had never occurred to him that they would fail to press on. Whatever lay ahead of them in Colorado, he felt more strongly than ever that they had to find out what it was, and it seemed far too late to turn back now. But Hollis, he was forced to concede, had a point. Theo, and Finn, and the woman whom first Alicia and now Mausami claimed was Liza Chou – all had come from the Colony. Whatever was happening with the virals – and obviously something *was* happening – it appeared that they wanted people alive. Should they go back and warn the others? And Mausami – even if her leg was all right, could she really continue on foot? They had no vehicles and very little in the way of ammunition for the weapons they possessed; they could probably find food on the way, but this would slow them down, and soon they would be entering the mountains, where the terrain would be more difficult. Could they expect a pregnant woman to walk all the way to Colorado? He was only posing these questions, Hollis said, because someone had to; he wasn't sure what he thought. On the other hand, they had come a long way. Babcock, whatever he was, was still out there, as were the Many. Turning around brought risks of its own.

Sitting on the ground outside the engine, the seven of them – Theo was still sleeping in the train – discussed their options. For the first time since they'd left, Peter sensed uncertainty among the group. The bunker and its bounty of supplies had given them a sense of security – a false one, maybe, but adequate to propel them forward. Now, stripped of their weapons and vehicles, with no food but what they could find, and having been cast four hundred kilometers into an unknown wilderness, the idea of Colorado had become much more tenuous. The events at the Haven had left them all shaken; never had it occurred to them that they would have to count among their obstacles the other human survivors they might encounter, or that a being like Babcock – a viral but also something far more, possessing a power to control the others – could exist.

Alicia, unsurprisingly, said she wanted to press on, as did Mausami – if only, Peter thought, to prove that Alicia was no tougher than she was. Caleb said he would do whatever the group wanted to do, but as he voiced these words his eyes were fixed on Alicia; if it came to a vote, Caleb would side with her. Michael also spoke for continuing, reminding everyone of the Colony's failing batteries. That's what this all comes down to, he said. As far as he was concerned, the message from Colorado was the only real hope they had – especially now, after what they'd seen at the Haven.

This left Hollis and Sara. Hollis plainly believed they should turn back. That he had come short of actually saying so, however, suggested that he believed, as Peter did, that the decision had to be unanimous. Sitting beside him in the shade of the train, her legs folded under her, Sara appeared more uncertain. She was squinting across the field, where Amy was continuing her solitary vigil in the grass. Peter realized it had been many hours since he'd heard her voice.

'I remember some of it now,' Sara said after a moment. 'When the viral took me. Bits and pieces, anyway.' She lifted her shoulders in a gesture that was half shrug, half shudder, and Peter knew she would say no more about this. 'Hollis isn't wrong. And I don't care what you say, Maus, you're in no shape to be out here. But I agree with Michael. If you're asking for my vote, Peter, that's it.'

'So we keep going.'

She shifted her eyes toward Hollis, who nodded. 'Yes. We keep going.'

The other question was Olson. Peter's distrust of the man had not abated, and though no one had said as much, he obviously represented a risk – for suicide, if nothing else. Since the train had stopped, he had barely moved from his place on the ground outside the engine, staring vacantly in the direction they'd come. From time to time he would run his fingers through the loose dirt, scooping up a handful and letting it fall through his fingers. He seemed like a man who was weighing his options, none of them very good, and Peter suspected where his thoughts lay.

Hollis pulled Peter aside as they were packing up the supplies. All the shotguns and the rifle now lay on one of the tarps, beside the piles of ammo. They had elected to spend the night in the train – it was as safe a place as any – and set out, on foot, in the morning.

'What should we do about him?' Hollis asked quietly, tipping his head toward Olson. Hollis was holding one of the pistols; Peter had the other. 'We can't just leave him here.'

'I guess he comes.'

'He may not want to.'

Peter considered this for a moment. 'Leave him be,' he said finally. 'There's nothing we can do.'

It was late afternoon. Caleb and Michael had gone around

to the rear of the engine, to siphon off water from the tanks with a hose they'd found in a closet in the engine's aft compartment. Peter turned to see Caleb examining a hinged panel, about a meter square, hanging off the underside of the train.

'What's this?' he asked Michael.

'It's an access panel. It connects to a crawl space that runs underneath the floor.'

'Anything in there we can use?'

Michael shrugged, busying himself with the hose. 'I don't know. Have a look.'

Caleb knelt and turned the handle. 'It's stuck.'

Peter, watching from five meters away, felt a prickling sensation along his skin. Something clenched inside him. All eyes. 'Hightop—'

The panel flew open, sending Caleb tumbling backward. A figure unfolded from inside the tube.

Jude.

Everyone reached for a weapon. Jude stumbled toward them, lifting a pistol. Half his face had been blasted away, revealing a broad smear of exposed meat and glistening bone; one of his eyes was gone, a dark hole. He seemed, in that elongated moment, a being of pure impossibility, half dead and half alive.

'You fucking people!' Jude snarled.

He fired just as Caleb, reaching for the pistol, stepped in front of him. The bullet caught the boy in the chest, spinning him around. In the same instant, Peter and Hollis found the triggers of their weapons, lighting up Jude's body in a crazy dance.

They emptied both their guns before he toppled.

Caleb was lying face-up on the dirt, one hand clutched at the place where the bullet had entered. His chest rose and fell in shallow jerks. Alicia threw herself onto the ground beside him.

'Caleb!'

Blood was running through the boy's fingers. His eyes,

pointed at the empty sky, were very moist. 'Oh shit,' he said, blinking.

'Sara, do something!'

Death had begun to ease across the boy's face. 'Oh,' he said. 'Oh.' Then something seemed to catch in his chest and he was still.

Sara was crying, everyone was crying. She got on the ground beside Alicia and touched her elbow. 'He's dead, Lish.'

Alicia shrugged her violently away. 'Don't say that!' She pulled the boy's limp form to her chest. 'Caleb, you listen to me! You open your eyes! You open your eyes right now!'

Peter crouched beside her.

'I promised him,' Alicia pleaded, hugging Caleb close. 'I promised him.'

'I know you did.' It was all he could think to say. 'We all know it. It's all right. Let go now.'

Peter gently freed the body from her arms. Caleb's eyes were closed, his body motionless where it lay in the dust. He was still wearing the yellow sneakers – one of the laces had come untied – but the boy he was, was nowhere. Caleb was gone. For a long moment, nobody said anything. The only sounds were the birds and the wind in the tips of the grass and Alicia's damp, half-choked breathing.

Then, in a sudden burst, Alicia shot to her feet, snatched Jude's pistol from the ground, and strode to where Olson was sitting on the dirt. A furious look was in her eyes. The gun was huge, a long-barreled revolver. As Olson looked up, squinting at the dark form looming over him, she reared back and struck him across the face with the butt of the gun, knocking him flat to the ground, cocked the hammer with her thumb, and aimed the barrel at his head.

'Goddamn you!'

'Lish—' Peter stepped toward her, his hands raised. 'He didn't kill Caleb. Put the gun down.'

'We saw Jude die! We all saw it!'

A trickle of blood was running from Olson's nose. He made

771

no motion to defend himself or move away. 'He was familiar.'

'Familiar? What does that mean? I'm sick of your double-talk. Speak English, goddamnit!'

Olson swallowed, licking the blood from his lips. 'It means . . . you can be one of them without being one of them.'

Alicia's knuckles were white where she clutched the butt of the revolver. Peter knew she was going to fire. There seemed no stopping this; it was simply what was going to happen.

'Go ahead and shoot if you want.' Olson's face was impassive; his life meant nothing to him. 'It doesn't matter. Babcock will come. You'll see.'

The barrel had begun to waver, driven by the current of Alicia's rage. 'Caleb mattered! He was worth more than your whole fucking Haven! He never had anyone! I stood for him! I stood for him!'

Alicia howled, a deep animal sound of pain, and then she pulled the trigger – but no shot came. The hammer fell on an empty chamber. 'Fuck!' She squeezed again and again; the gun was empty. *'Fuck! Fuck! Fuck!'* Then she turned to Peter, the useless pistol dropping from her hand, leaned into his chest, and sobbed.

In the morning, Olson was gone. Tracks led away into the culvert; Peter didn't have to look to know which way he was headed.

'Should we go look for him?' Sara asked.

They were standing by the empty train, assembling the last of their gear.

Peter shook his head. 'I don't think there's any point.'

They gathered around the place where they had buried Caleb, in the shade of a cottonwood. They'd marked the spot with a scrap of metal Michael had popped from the hull and etched with the tip of a screwdriver, then affixed to the trunk of the tree with sheet-metal screws.

Everyone was there except Amy, who was standing apart, in the tall grass. Beside Peter were Maus and Theo. Mausami was leaning on a crutch Michael had fashioned from a length of pipe; Sara had examined her wound and said she could travel, as long as they didn't push it. Theo had slept straight through the night, awakening at dawn, and now seemed if not better, then at least on the mend. Yet, standing beside him, Peter could feel something missing in his brother; something had changed, or broken, or been taken away. Something had been stolen from him, in that cell. In the dream. With Babcock.

But it was Alicia who worried him most of all. She was standing at the foot of the grave with Michael, a shotgun cradled across her chest, her face still swollen from crying. For a long time, the rest of the day and all that night, she had said almost nothing. Anyone else might have supposed she was simply grieving for Caleb, but Peter knew differently. She had loved the boy, and that was a part of it. They all had, and Caleb's absence felt not just strange but wrong, as if a piece of them had been cut away. But what Peter saw now, as he looked into Alicia's eyes, was a deeper kind of pain. It was not her fault that Caleb was dead, and Peter had told her so. Still, she believed she had failed him. Killing Olson would not have solved anything, though Peter couldn't help but think it might have helped. Perhaps that was why he hadn't tried harder – tried at all, really – to take Jude's gun away from her.

Peter realized he was waiting out of habit for his brother to speak, to issue the command that would set the day in motion. When he didn't, Peter hitched up his pack and spoke.

'Well,' he said, his throat thick, 'we should probably get going. Use the daylight.'

'Forty million smokes out there,' Michael said glumly. 'What chance do we have on foot?'

Amy stepped into the circle then.

'He's wrong,' she said.

For a moment no one spoke. None of them seemed to know where to look – at Amy, at one another – a flurry of startled and amazed glances passing around the circle.

'She can *talk*?' Alicia said.

Peter stepped gingerly toward her. Amy's face seemed different to him, now that he had heard her voice. It was as if she were suddenly present, fully among them.

'What did you say?'

'Michael is wrong,' the girl stated. Her voice was neither a woman's nor a child's but something in between. She spoke flatly, without intonation, as if she were reading the words from a book. 'There aren't forty million.'

Peter wanted to laugh or cry, he didn't know which. After everything, for her to speak now!

'Amy, why didn't you say anything before?'

'I am sorry. I think I had forgotten how.' She was frowning inwardly, as if puzzling over this thought. 'But now I have remembered.'

Everyone fell silent again, gaping at her in astonishment.

'So, if there aren't forty million,' Michael ventured, 'how many are there?'

She lifted her eyes to them all.

'Twelve,' said Amy.

IX
THE LAST EXPEDITIONARY

I am all the daughters of my father's house,
And all the brothers too.

– SHAKESPEARE,
Twelfth Night

FIFTY-SIX

From the Journal of Sara Fisher ('The Book of Sara')
Presented at the Third Global Conference on the North
   American Quarantine Period
Center for the Study of Human Cultures and Conflicts
University of New South Wales, Indo-Australian Republic
April 16–21, 1003 A.V.

[*Excerpt begins.*]

. . . *and that was when we found the orchard – a welcome sight,
since none of us has had anything like enough to eat since three days
ago, when Hollis shot the deer. Now we are loaded up with apples.
They're small and wormy and if you eat too many of them all at once
you get cramps, but it's good to have a full belly again. We're
bedding down tonight in a rusted metal shed that's full of old cars
and stinks like pigeons. It seems we've lost the road for good now, but
Peter says that if we continue walking straight east, we should hit
Highway 15 in a day or so. The map we found at the gas station in
Caliente is all we have to go by.*

   *Amy is talking a little bit more every day. It all still seems new to
her, just to have someone to talk to, and sometimes she seems to
struggle for the words, like she's reading a book in her mind and
looking for the right ones. But I can tell that talking makes her
happy. She likes to use our names a lot, even when it's clear who
she's speaking to, which sounds funny but by now we are all used to
it and even doing it ourselves. (Yesterday she saw me stepping
behind a bush and asked me what I was doing, and when I said, I
have to pee, she beamed like I'd just given her the best news in the
world and said, too loudly, I have to pee also, Sara. Michael burst
out laughing, but Amy didn't seem to mind, and when we were done
with our business she said, very politely – she is always polite – I'd*

forgotten that was what it's called. Thank you for peeing with me, Sara.)

Which isn't to say that we always understand her, because half the time we don't. Michael says it reminds him of talking to Auntie only worse, because with Auntie you always knew she was fooling with you. Amy doesn't appear to remember anything about where she comes from, except that it was a place with mountains and that it snowed there, which could be Colorado, though we don't really know. She doesn't seem afraid of the virals at all, not even the ones, like Babcock, who she calls the Twelve. When Peter asked her what she did in the ring to make him not kill Theo, Amy shrugged and said, as if this were nothing, I asked him to please not do it. I didn't like that one, she said. He's full of bad dreams. I thought it would be better to use my please and thank you.

A viral, and she actually said please!

But the thing that sticks in my mind most of all is what happened when Michael asked her how she'd known to blow the coupler. A man named Gus told me, Amy said. I never even knew that Gus was on the train, but Peter explained what had happened to Gus and Billie, that they'd been killed by the virals, and Amy said, nodding, That was when. Peter got very quiet for a moment, staring at her. What do you mean that was when? he said, and Amy answered, That was when he told me, after he'd fallen off the train. The virals didn't kill him, I think he broke his neck. But he was around for a little bit after. He was the one who put the bomb between the cars. He saw what was going to happen to the train and thought someone should know.

Michael says there has to be some other explanation, that Gus must have said something to her earlier. But I can tell Peter believes her, and I know I do, too. Peter is more convinced than ever that the signal from Colorado is the key to all of this, and I agree. After what we saw in the Haven, I am beginning to think that Amy is the only hope we have – that any of us has.

Day 31

A real town, the first since Caliente. We are spending the night in some kind of school, like the Sanctuary, with the same little desks in rows in all the rooms. I was worried that it would have more slims

778

in it, but we haven't found any. We've been taking the watch in shifts of two. I'm on second shift with Hollis, which I thought would be hard, sleeping a few hours and then waking up again, then trying to sleep a couple more before dawn. But Hollis makes the time pass easily. For a while we talked of home, and Hollis asked me what I missed the most, and the first thing that came to mind was soap, which made Hollis laugh. I said, What's so funny and he said, I thought you were going to say the lights. Because I sure as hell miss those lights, Sara. And I said, What do you miss and he was quiet for a moment, and I thought he was going to say Arlo, but he didn't. He said, The Littles. Dora and the others. The sounds of their voices in the courtyard, and the smell in the Big Room at night. Maybe it's this place, that it kind of reminds me of them. But that's what I'm missing tonight, the Littles.

Still no virals. Everybody's wondering how long our luck will hold out.

Day 32
It looks like we're going to spend an extra night here – everybody needs to rest.

The big news is the store we found, Outdoor World, full of all kinds of supplies we can use, including bows. (The gun case was empty.) We got knives and a hand axe and canteens and packs with frames and a pair of binoculars and a camp stove and fuel that we can use to boil water. Also maps and a compass and sleeping sacks and warm jackets. Now we all have new gaps to wear, and warm socks for our boots, and thermal underwear, which we don't really need yet but probably will soon. There was one slim in the store, we didn't see him until we were almost done, lying under the counter with the binoculars. It made us all feel a little bad that we'd been pulling stuff off the shelves and not even noticing he was there. I know Caleb would have made a joke about it to cheer everyone up. I can't believe he's gone.

Alicia and Hollis went hunting and came back with another deer, a yearling. I wish we could stay long enough to cure the meat but Hollis thinks there'll be more where we're going. What he didn't say because he didn't need to was that if there's game there's probably smokes, too.

It's cold tonight. I think it must be fall.

Day 33

Walking again. We're on Highway 15 now, headed north. The highway is quaked out but at least we know we're going the right way. Lots of abandoned vehicles. They seem to come in clusters, you see a bunch of them together and then nothing for a while and then you hit a line of twenty or even more. We've stopped to rest by a river. Hoping to make Parowan by late afternoon.

Day 35

Still walking. Peter thinks we are covering about 25 kilometers a day. Exhausted. I am worried about Maus. How can she keep this up? She's clearly showing now. Theo never leaves her side.

It's suddenly hot again, scorching. At night there's lightning to the east, where the mountains are, but never any rain. Hollis got a jack on the bow so that's what we're eating, roast jack split eight ways, plus a few leftover apples. Tomorrow we're going to try to look for a grocery and see if there are any cans there that are still okay to eat. Amy says that you can eat plenty of what's there if you have to. More 100-year-old food.

Why no virals?

Day 36

We smelled the fires last night and by morning we knew the forest was burning over the ridgeline to the east. We debated if we should turn around or wait or try to go around somehow, but that would mean leaving the highway, which no one wants to do. We've decided to press on and if the air gets worse we'll have to make a decision.

Day 36 (again)

A mistake. The fires are close now, no way to outrun them. We have taken shelter in a garage off the highway. Peter isn't sure what town this is, or if there even is a town. We used the tarps and some nails and a hammer we found to cover the broken windows in the front and now all we can do is wait and hope the wind shifts. The air is so thick I can barely see what I'm writing.

[Pages missing.]

Day 38

We're past Richfield now, on Highway 70. In places it's washed away but Hollis was right about the major roads, how they follow the passes. The fire came straight through here. There are dead animals everywhere, and the air smells like charred meat. Everyone thinks the sound we heard that night was the screams of virals, caught in the fire.

Day 39

The first dead virals. They were beneath a bridge, three of them huddled together. Peter thinks we haven't seen any before because they'd driven all the game up into the higher elevations. When the wind changed, they got trapped by the fire.

Maybe it was just the way they looked, all burned up and their faces pressed to the ground, but I found myself feeling sorry for them. If I didn't know they were virals I would have sworn they were human, and I know it could just as easily have been us lying dead there. I asked Amy do you think they were afraid and she said yes, she thought that they had been.

We're going to stay an extra day in the next town we come to, to rest and scavenge supplies. (Amy was right about the cans. As long as the seams are tight and it feels heavy in your hand, they're OK.)

[Pages missing.]

Day 48

Moving east again, the mountains behind us. Hollis thinks we've seen the last game for a while. We are crossing a dry, open tableland, stitched by deep gullies. There are bones everywhere you look – not just small game but deer and antelope and sheep, and something that resembles a cow only larger, with a huge knobby skull (Michael says they're buffalo). At half-day we stopped to rest by an outcrop of boulders and saw, scraped into the rocks, 'Darren loves Lexie 4Ever' and 'Green River SHS '16, PIRATES KICK ASS!!!' The first part everybody understood but nobody knew what to make of the rest. It made me feel a little sad, I can't quite say why, maybe it was just that

781

the words had been there so long with no one to read them. I wonder if Lexie loved Darren back?

We got off the highway and are sheltering near the town of Emery. Nothing really left here, just foundations and a few sheds with rusted farm equipment, full of mice. There's no pump we can find, but Peter says there's a river near here and tomorrow we'll go look for it.

Stars everywhere. A beautiful night.

Day 49
I have decided to marry Hollis Wilson.

Day 52
Going south now from Crescent Junction, on Highway 191. At least we think it's 191. We actually walked straight past the turnoff at least five clicks and had to double back. There's not much of a road to follow, which was why we missed it in the first place. I asked Peter why we had to get off the 70 and he said we're too far north for where we're going. Sooner or later we'll have to head south, so it might as well be now.

Hollis and I have decided not to tell anyone about what's happened. It's funny how when I made up my mind about him I realized I had been thinking it for a long time without knowing it. I wish all the time I could kiss him again but everyone's around or else we're on watch. I still feel kind of guilty about the other night. Also, he really needs a bath. (So do I.)

No towns at all. Peter doesn't think we'll hit one till Moab. We are spending the night in a shallow cave, really just a recess with an overhang, though it's better than nothing. The rocks here are all a kind of orange-pink color, very lovely and strange.

Day 53
Today was the day we found the farmstead.

At first we thought it was just a ruin, like all the others we've seen. But as we got closer, we saw it was in much better shape – a cluster of wood-frame houses, with barns and outbuildings and paddocks for animals. Two of the houses are empty, but one of them, the largest, looks like someone was actually living here not so long ago. The table in the kitchen was actually set with places and cups; there are curtains in the windows, clothing folded in the drawers. Furniture and pots and pans and books on the shelves. In the barn we found an old car, covered in dust, the shelves lined with jugs of lantern fuel, empty jars for canning, tools. There's what looks like a graveyard, too, four plots marked with circles of stones. Michael said we should dig one up to see who's down there. But nobody took this suggestion seriously.

We found the wellhead but the pump was rusted tight; it took three of us to free it, but once we did the water that came out was cold and clear, the best we've had in a long while. There's a pump in the kitchen that Hollis is still trying to free up and a woodstove for cooking. In the basement we found more shelves stacked with cans of beans and squash and corn, the seals still good. We still have the tins we scavenged in Green River, plus some of the smoked venison and a bit of lard we saved. Our first real meal in weeks. Peter says there's a river not far and tomorrow we're going to go look for it. We're all bedding down in the biggest house, using mattresses we dragged from upstairs and set around the fireplace.

Peter believes the place has been abandoned at least ten years, but probably not more than twenty. Who lived here? How did they survive? The place has a haunted feeling to it, more than any of the towns we've seen. It's as if whoever lived here went out one day, expecting to be back for supper, and simply never returned.

Day 54
We are staying an extra day. Theo is insistent, says Maus can't keep up this kind of pace, but Peter says we have to leave soon if we want to make it to Colorado before the snow. Snow. I hadn't thought about that.

Day 56
Still at the farmstead. We decided to stay a few more days, though Peter is antsy and wants to get moving. He and Theo actually argued about this. I think [indecipherable]

[Pages missing.]

Day 59

We are leaving in the morning, but Theo and Maus are staying behind. I think everyone knew this was coming. They made the announcement right after supper. Peter objected, but in the end there was nothing he could say to change Theo's mind. They have shelter, there's plenty of small game around plus the cans in the basement, they can ride out the winter here and have the baby. We'll see you in the spring, brother, Theo said. Just don't forget to stop in on your way back from whatever it is you find.

I'm supposed to be on watch in a few hours, and I really should be sleeping. I think Maus and Theo are doing the right thing, even Peter has to know it. But it's sad to be leaving them behind. I think it's making us all think about Caleb, Alicia especially, who clammed up completely after Maus and Theo gave their news and has yet to say a word to anyone. I think everyone's remembering those graves in the yard, wondering if we'll ever see Maus and Theo again.

I wish Hollis were awake. I told myself I wouldn't cry. Oh damn, damn.

Day 60

Traveling again. Theo was right about one thing – without Maus, we are making better time. The six of us got to Moab well before dusk. There's nothing here; the river has washed everything away. A huge wall of debris is blocking the way, trees and houses and cars and old tires and every kind of thing, filling the narrow canyon where the town once was. We've sheltered for the night in one of the few remaining structures, up in the hills. A complete derelict, just the framing and a patchy roof over our heads. We might just as well be out in the open, and I doubt anyone's going to get much sleep tonight. Tomorrow we're going to walk up the ridge, try to find a way through to the other side.

[Pages missing.]

Day 64

We found another animal carcass today, some kind of large cat. It was hanging in the limbs of a tree, like the others. The body was too rotted to tell, but everyone is thinking it was a viral that killed it.

Day 65

Still in the La Sal Mountains, heading east. The sky has turned from white to blue, the color of autumn. There's a damp, delicious smell to everything. The leaves are coming down, and there's frost at night, and in the morning, a heavy, silver mist hugs the hills. I don't think I've ever seen anything so lovely.

Day 66

Last night Amy had another nightmare. We were sleeping out in the open again, under the tarps. I had just come off watch with Hollis and was prying my boots off when I heard her mumbling in her sleep. I was thinking maybe I should wake her up when suddenly she sat bolt upright. She was all wrapped up in her bag, only her face showing. She looked at me for a long moment, her eyes unfocused, like she didn't know who I was. He's dying, she said. He keeps on dying and can't stop. Who's dying, I said, Amy, who? The man, she said. The man is dying. What man? I asked her. But then she lay back down and was fast asleep again.

Sometimes I wonder if we are heading toward something terrible, more terrible than any of us can imagine.

Day 67

Today we came to a rusted sign by the road that said, 'Paradox pop. 2387.' I think we're here, Peter said, and showed us all on the map.

We are in Colorado.

FIFTY-SEVEN

The mountains declined at last to a broad valley, wide in the autumn sunlight, beneath an azure dome of sky. The grass was tall and parched, the limbs of the trees barren or else dotted with a few remaining leaves, the stragglers, bleached to the color of bone. They lifted in the breeze like waving hands, rustling like old paper. The ground was dry, but in the culverts water ran freely. They filled their canteens with it, cold as ice against their teeth. Winter was in the air.

They were six now. They moved across the empty land like visitors to a forgotten world, a world without memory, stilled in time. Here and there the shell of a farmhouse, the skull-like grille of a rusted truck; no sound but the wind and the creak of the crickets, flicking through the grass as they walked. The terrain was easy, but this wouldn't last. A distant white shape, painted across a far horizon, told a story of mountains to come.

They rested for the night in a barn by a river. Old tack hung on the walls, buckets for milking, lengths of chains. An old tractor sat on flattened tires. The house was gone, collapsed into its foundation, its walls improbably folded one on top of another like the flaps of a box, not so much destroyed as packed away. They divvied the cans they'd found and sat on the floor to eat the contents cold. Through the ragged tears in the roof they could see stars, and then, as the night drew down, the moon, ringed by scudding clouds. Peter took first watch with Michael; by the time Hollis and Sara relieved them, the stars were gone, the moon no more than a region of paleness in the cloud-thickened sky. He slept, dreaming of nothing, and when he awoke in the morning, he saw that it had snowed in the night.

By midmorning the air had warmed again; the snow had melted away. On the map, the next town was named Placerville. Eight days had passed since they'd seen the body of the cat in the trees. The feeling that something was following them had dissipated over the long days of walking, the silent, star-strewn nights. The farmstead was a distant memory; the Haven, and all that had occurred there, seemed like years ago.

They were tracing a river now. Peter thought it was the Dolores, or the San Miguel. The road was long gone, absorbed by the grass, the wash of earth and time. They marched in silence, two rows of three. What were they looking for, what would they find? The journey had acquired a meaning of its own, intrinsic: to move, to keep moving. The thought of stopping, of reaching the end, seemed beyond Peter's power to imagine. Amy was walking beside him, her back sloped forward against the heft of her pack, her sleeping sack and winter jacket lashed to the bottom of the frame. She was dressed, like all of them, in clothing scavenged at Outdoor World: a pair of gaps cinched to her hips and, on her upper body, a loose-fitting blouse of red and white checks, the sleeves unsnapped and flapping around her wrists. On her feet, a pair of leather sneakers; her head was bare. She had given up the glasses long ago. She kept her eyes forward, squinting against the brightness. In the days since they'd left the farmstead, a shift had occurred, subtle but unmistakable. Like the river, she was leading them now; their job was simply to follow. With each passing day, the feeling grew stronger. Peter thought, as he often did, of the message Michael had shown him, that long-ago night in the Lighthouse. Its words formed a backbeat to the rhythm of his walking, each footfall carrying him forward, into a world he didn't know, into the hidden heart of the past, to the place where Amy came from.

If you found her, bring her here. If you found her, bring her here.

He had discovered, in the days since they'd left the farmstead, that he did not miss Theo as he'd thought he would. As with the Haven and all that had happened before it – even the Colony itself – thoughts of his brother seemed to have fallen away, subsumed like the grassy road by the project of simply moving forward. At first, that night when Theo and Maus had called them all together and announced their decision, Peter had been angry. He had not shown this, or hoped he hadn't. Even in the midst of it, he knew this anger was irrational; it was obvious that Maus could not continue. Part of him simply didn't want his brother to leave him again so soon. But Theo had the facts on his side, and in the end, Peter could only agree.

But he had also come to see, over the days, a deeper truth behind his brother's decision. His path and Theo's had been destined to diverge again, because their cause was not the same. Theo did not seem to doubt their story of Amy, or at least he had said nothing to make Peter think so. He had absorbed Peter's explanation, fantastic as it was, with no more or less skepticism than it deserved. Yet Peter could detect in his brother's compliance a feeling of detachment; Amy meant nothing to him, or meant very little. If anything, he seemed a little afraid of her. It was clear that he had come as far as he had only because that's where the group was headed; at the first opportunity, and under the circumstances of Mausami's pregnancy, he had quickly given this up. Selfishly, Peter would have wished for more, if only for Theo to have expressed some regret, however small, at their separation. But he hadn't done this. The morning of their departure, as the six of them had walked away from the farmhouse, Peter had turned to see his brother and Mausami watching them. A small thing, but it had seemed important to Peter that Theo remain where he was, standing on the porch, until the six of them were out of sight. But when Peter looked again, his brother was gone; only Mausami was there.

When the sun was high they stopped to rest. They could see the line of mountains plainly now, a rugged bulk against the eastern skyline, the peaks dolloped in white. The day had grown warm again, enough to make them sweat; but up high, where they were going, winter had already arrived.

'More snow up there,' Hollis said.

He was sitting beside Peter on a fallen log, its rotted bark blackened with dampness. No one had spoken a word in at least an hour. The others were scattered around, all except Alicia, who had gone ahead to scout the terrain. Hollis knifed open a can and began to spoon the contents to his mouth, some kind of shredded meat. A bit got caught in the coarse tangle of his beard; he wiped it away, washed the last of his meal down with a long, throat-pumping drink of water, and passed the can to Peter.

Peter took the can and ate. Sara, sitting across from him with her back against a tree, was writing in her book. She paused, her eyes focused intently on what she'd written; her pencil was just a nub, almost too short to hold. While Peter watched, she drew her blade from her belt, scraped it across the tip, and then resumed her patient scribbling.

'What are you writing about?'

Sara shrugged, hooking a stray strand of hair behind her ear. 'The snow. What we ate, where we slept.' She lifted her face to the trees, squinting into the sunlight descending through the sodden branches. 'How beautiful it is here.'

He felt himself smile. How long had it been since he'd smiled?

'I guess it is, isn't it?'

A new feeling seemed to have come over Sara since they'd left the farmstead, Peter thought, an unhurried calm. It was as if she had decided something and, in so doing, had moved more deeply into herself, into a state beyond worry or fear. He felt a flicker of regret; watching her now, he realized how foolish he'd been. Her hair was long and matted, her face and bare arms streaked with grime. Her nails were blackened with crescents of dirt. And yet she'd never looked more radiant. As if all that she had seen had become a part of her, infusing her with a glowing stillness. It wasn't a small thing, to love a person. That was the gift she had offered him, had always offered him. And yet he had refused it.

Sara met his eyes then. She cocked her head in puzzlement. 'What?'

He shook his head, embarrassed. 'Nothing.'

'You were staring.'

Sara shifted her gaze to Hollis; the corners of her mouth lifted in a quick flash of a smile. Just a moment, but Peter felt it keenly, the invisible line of connection between the two of them. Of course. How could he have been so blind?

'It wasn't anything,' he managed. 'Just . . . you looked happy, sitting there. It surprised me is all.'

Alicia emerged from the brush. Balancing her rifle against a tree, she retrieved a can from the pile of packs and bladed it open, frowning at the contents.

'Peaches,' she groaned. 'Why do I always get peaches?' She took a place on the log and began to spear the soft yellow fruit from the can, straight into her mouth.

'What's down there?' Peter asked.

Juice was dripping down her chin. She gestured with her blade in the direction she had come. 'About half a click east, the river narrows and turns south. There's hills on either side, heavy cover, lots of high points.' The peaches gone, she drained the can into her mouth and cast it aside, wiping her hands on her gaps. 'The middle of the day like this, we're probably okay. But we shouldn't hang around too long.'

Michael was sitting a few meters away on the damp ground, his back braced against a log. The days of walking had made him leaner, harder; his chin now sported a wisp of pale beard. A shotgun was resting across his lap, his finger close to the trigger.

'No sign in what, seven days?' He spoke with his eyes closed, his face tipped toward the sun. He was wearing only a T-shirt; his jacket was tied around his waist.

'Eight,' Alicia corrected. 'That doesn't mean we should let our guard down.'

'I'm just saying.' He opened his eyes and turned toward Alicia, shrugging. 'A lot of things could have killed that cat. Maybe it died of old age.'

Alicia gave a laugh. 'Sounds good to me,' she said.

Amy was standing by herself at the edge of the glade. She was always drifting off like this. For a while this habit had made Peter worry, but she never went very far, and by now they were all accustomed to it.

He rose and went to her. 'Amy, you should eat something. We're moving on soon.'

For a moment the girl said nothing. Her eyes were directed toward the mountains, rising in the sunlight beyond the river and the grassy fields beyond.

'I remember the snow,' she said. 'Lying down in it. How cold it was.' She looked at him, squinting. 'We're close, aren't we?'

Peter nodded. 'A few days, I think.'

'Tell-uride,' Amy said.

'Yes, Telluride.'

She turned away again. Peter saw her shiver, though the sun was warm.

'Will it snow again?' she asked.

'Hollis thinks so.'

Amy nodded, satisfied. Her face had filled with a warm light; the memory was a happy one. 'I would like to lie down in it again, to make snow angels.'

She often spoke like this, in vague riddles. Yet something felt different this time. It was as if the past were rising up before her eyes, stepping into view like a deer from the brush. Even to move would scare it away.

'What are snow angels?'

'You move your arms and legs, in the snow,' she explained. 'Like the ones in heaven. Like the ghost Jacob Marley.'

Peter was aware that the others were listening now. A single strand of black hair pushed over her eyes in the wind. Watching her, he felt himself transported back through the months to that night in the Infirmary when Amy had washed his wound. He wanted to ask her: How did you know, Amy? How did you know my mother misses me, and how much I miss her? Because I never told her, Amy. She was dying, and I never told her how much I would miss her when she was gone.

'Who's Jacob Marley?' he asked.

Her brow furrowed with a sudden grief. 'He wore the chains he forged in life,' she said, and shook her head. 'It was such a sad story.'

They followed the river, into the afternoon. They were in the foothills now, leaving the plateau behind. The land began to rise and thicken with trees – naked, twiglike aspens and huge, ancient pines, their trunks wide as houses, towering over their heads. Beneath their vast canopies, the ground was open and shaded, pillowed with needles. The air was cold

791

with the dampness of the river. They moved, as always, without speaking, scanning the trees. All eyes.

There was no Placerville; it was easy to see what had occurred. The narrow valley, the river carving through it. In spring, when the snowpack melted, it would be a raging torrent. Like Moab, the town had washed away.

They sheltered that night at the river's edge, stretching the tarp between a pair of trees to fashion a roof and laying their sleeping bags in the soft dirt. Peter was on the third shift, with Michael. They took their positions. The night was still and cold, filled with the sound of the river. Standing at his post, trying to keep motionless despite the chill, Peter thought of Sara, and the feeling he had detected between her and Hollis in that private gaze, and realized he was honestly happy for the two of them. He'd had his chance, after all, and Hollis obviously loved her, as she deserved to be loved. Hollis had told him as much, he realized, that night at Milagro, when Sara was taken: *Peter, you of all people should know I have to go.* Not just the words themselves but the look in his eyes – an absolute fearlessness. He'd given it up, right then; he'd given it up for Sara.

The sky was just paling when Alicia stepped from the shelter and walked toward him.

'So,' she said, and gave a loose-jawed yawn. 'Still here.'

He nodded. 'Still here.'

Each night without sign made him wonder how much longer their luck could hold. But he never thought about this for long; it seemed dangerous, like daring fate, to question their good fortune.

Alicia said, 'Turn around, I have to go.'

Facing away, he heard Alicia unbuckle her trousers and lower herself to a squat. Ten meters upstream, Michael was resting on the ground with his back against a boulder. Peter realized he was fast asleep.

'So what do you make of this business?' Alicia asked. 'Ghosts and angels and all that.'

'Your guess is as good as mine.'

'Peter,' she scolded, 'I don't believe that for a second.' A moment passed, then: 'Okay, you can turn around now.'

He faced her again. Alicia was cinching her belt. 'You're the reason we're here, after all,' she said.

'I thought Amy was.'

Alicia turned her eyes away, toward the trees on the far side of river. She let a silent moment pass. 'We've been friends as long as I can remember. Nothing can change that. So what I'm going to tell you is between us. Understood?'

Peter nodded.

'The night before we left, the two of us were in the trailer outside the lockup. You asked me what I saw when I looked at Amy. I don't think I ever answered, and probably I didn't know at the time. But I'll tell you my answer now. What I see is you.'

She was regarding him closely, wearing an expression that was almost pained. Peter fumbled for a response. 'I don't . . . understand.'

'Yes, you do. You may not know it, but you do. You never talk about your father, or the Long Rides. I've never pressed. But that doesn't mean I didn't know what they meant to you. You've been waiting for something like Amy to come along your whole life. You can call it destiny if you want, or fate. Auntie would probably call it the hand of God. Believe me, I've heard those speeches too. I don't think it matters what name you give it. It is what it is. So you ask me why we're here, and I'll say, sure, we're here because of Amy. But she's only half the reason. The funny thing is, everybody knows it but you.'

Peter didn't know what to say. Ever since Amy had come into his life, he had felt himself caught in a strong current, and that this current was pulling him toward something, something he had to find. Every step along the way had told him so. But it was also true that each of them had played a part, and a great deal had simply come down to luck.

'I don't know, Lish. It could have been anyone that day at the mall. It could have been you. Or Theo.'

She dismissed this with a wave. 'You give your brother too much credit, but you always did. And where is he now? Don't get me wrong, I think he did the right thing. Maus was in no shape to travel, and I said so from the start. But that's not the only reason he stayed behind.' She shrugged. 'I'm only saying this because you might need to hear it. This is your Long Ride, Peter. Whatever's up that mountain, it's yours to find. Whatever else happens, I hope you get that chance.'

Another silence fell. Something about the way she was speaking disturbed him. It was as if these words were final ones. As if she were saying goodbye.

'You think they're all right?' he asked. 'Theo and Maus.'

'I couldn't say. I hope so.'

'You know,' he said, and cleared his throat, 'I think Hollis and Sara—'

'Are together?' She gave a quiet laugh. 'And here I was, thinking you hadn't noticed. You should tell them you know. Personally, it will be a load off everyone's mind.'

He was completely astounded. 'Everyone knows?'

'Peter.' She met his eye with a correcting frown. 'This is exactly what I'm talking about. It's all well and good to save the human race. You could say I'm in favor. But you might want to pay a little more attention to what's right in front of you.'

'I thought I was.'

'That's what you *thought*. We're just people. I don't know what's up that mountain, but I do know that much. We live, we die. Somewhere along the way, if we're lucky, we may find someone to help lighten the load. You should tell them it's okay. They're waiting to hear from you.'

It still confounded him, how slow he'd been to detect what was happening with Sara and Hollis. Perhaps, he thought, it was something he hadn't *wanted* to see. Looking at Alicia now, her hair shining in the morning light, he found himself recalling their night together on the roof of the power station, the two of them talking about pairing, having Littles; that strange and amazing night, when Alicia had given him the gift of stars. At the time, just the idea of it, of living a normal life, or what passed for one, had seemed as distant and impossible as the stars themselves. Now here they were, more than a thousand kilometers from home – a home they would probably never see again – the same people they had always been, but also *not* the same, because something had happened; love was among them.

That's what Alicia was telling him now; that's what she had been trying to tell him that night on the roof of the power station, in that last easy hour before everything had happened. That what they did, they did for love. Not just Sara and Hollis; all of them.

'Lish—' he began.

But she shook her head, cutting him off. Her face was suddenly flustered. Behind her, Sara and Hollis were emerging from the shelter, into the morning.

'Like I said, we're all here because of you,' Alicia said. 'Me more than anyone. Now, are you going to wake up the Circuit or am I?'

They broke camp; by the time they were moving downriver, the sun had lifted over the crest of the valley, filling the branches of the trees with a vaporous light.

It was almost half-day when Alicia, at the head of the line, abruptly halted. She raised a hand to silence everyone.

'Lish,' Michael called from the rear, 'why are we stopping?'

'*Quiet.*'

She was sniffing the air. Peter smelled it too: a strange and powerful odor, stinging his nostrils.

Behind him, Sara whispered, 'What *is* that?'

Hollis pointed with his rifle over their heads. 'Look—'

Suspended from the limbs above their heads were dozens of long strands of small, white objects, bunched like fruit.

'What the hell *is* that?'

But Alicia was looking at the ground now, anxiously scanning the carpeted earth beneath their feet. She dropped to a knee and brushed the heavy covering of dead leaves aside.

'Oh, shit.'

Peter heard the groan of the dropping weight. Before he could speak the net had swallowed them; they were rising, lifting through the air, all of them yelling and tumbling, their bodies caught in its weave. It reached the apex of its ascent, everything cradled in suspension for one weightless instant, and then they descended, a hard drop, their bodies jamming together as the ropes compressed them into a single, twisting, captive mass.

Peter was upside down. Somebody, Hollis, was on top of him. Hollis and also Sara and a sneaker, close to his face, which he recognized as Amy's. It was impossible to tell where one body ended and the next began. They were spinning like a top. His chest was compressed so tightly he could barely breathe. The skin of his cheek was pressed against the ropes, which were made of some heavy, fibrous twine. The ground was twirling under him, a rush of undifferentiated color.

'Lish!'

'I can't move!'

'Can anyone?'

Michael: 'I think I'm going to be sick!'

Sara, her voice shrill with panic: 'Michael, don't you dare!'

There was no way Peter could reach his blade; even if he could have, severing the ropes would have sent them all plunging headlong to the ground. The spinning motion slowed, then stopped, then started again, its velocity increasing as they were flung in the opposite direction. Somewhere above him in the jumble of bodies he heard Michael retch.

They spun and spun and spun some more. It was on the sixth rotation that Peter detected, from the corner of his rolling eye, a tremulous motion in the brush. Like the woods were moving, coming to life. But by then he was too disoriented to speak. Part of him felt fear, but the rest of him could not seem to find this part.

'Holy goddamn,' a voice below them said, 'they're *strags*.'

And then Peter saw: they were soldiers.

FIFTY-EIGHT

In the first days, Mausami slept – sixteen, eighteen, twenty hours at a stretch. Theo had chased the mice away from the upstairs bedroom, whisking them down the stairs and out the door with a broom and a great deal of yelling. In a closet they had found, folded with an eerie care, smelling of time and dust, a pile of sheets and blankets, even a couple of pillows, one for her head and a second to fold between her knees to straighten her back. Random electric currents, exquisitely painful, had begun to shoot down one of her legs – the baby, compressing her spine. She took it as a sign that the baby was doing what it was supposed to do, making space for himself in the densely packed room of her body. Theo came and went, fussing over her like a nurse, bringing her meals and water. He slept during the afternoons on the old saggy sofa downstairs, and when evening fell he dragged a chair out to the porch, where he sat through the night, a shotgun on his lap, staring into the dark.

Then one morning she awoke to a fresh, new vigor coursing through her. The drought of energy was over; the days of rest had done their work. She drew up to a sitting position and saw that the sun was shining in the window. The air was cool and dry, pushing a gentle breeze that shifted in the curtains. She did not remember opening the window but perhaps Theo had done this, sometime in the night.

The baby was sitting on her bladder. Theo had left a pail for her, but she didn't want to use this, now that she no longer needed to. She would make the long march to the privy, to show Theo that she was finally awake.

Even now, she could detect his movements somewhere in the house below. She rose, pulled a sweater over her long-tailed shirt – she was suddenly much too big for the only pair of gaps she had – and descended the stairs. Her center of gravity seemed to have shifted overnight; the frank bulge of her stomach made her feel top-heavy and clumsy. She supposed this was just something to get used to. Not even six months, and here she was, huge already.

She stepped into a room she barely remembered; it took her a moment to absorb the fact that a great deal had changed. The sofa and chairs, which before had been pushed against the walls, now stood in the middle of the room at right angles to the fireplace, facing one another. Between them rested a small wooden table atop a threadbare woolen rug. The floor under her bare feet was free of dirt, swept clean. Theo had laid more blankets over the sofa, tucking the edges in, to cover the places where it was worn through and stained.

But what drew her attention were the pictures propped on the mantel. A series of yellowed photographs – the same people, at different ages and in different configurations, all posed before the very house in which she now stood. A man and his wife and three children, a boy and two girls. The photos seemed to have been taken at intervals of a year; in each, the children had grown. The youngest, a baby in the first photograph, held in his mother's arms – a tired-looking woman wearing a pair of dark glasses perched above her forehead – was, by the final image, a boy of five or six. He was standing in front of his older sisters, grinning greedily for the camera, showing the gap in his smile where he had lost a tooth. His T-shirt read, incomprehensibly, UTAH JAZZ.

'They're something, aren't they?'

Mausami turned to discover Theo observing her from the kitchen door.

'Where did you find them?'

He approached the mantel and took the last photograph, with the smiling boy, in his hands. 'They were in a crawl space, under the stairs. See this here?' He tapped the glass to show her: in the background, at the edge of the photo, an automobile, packed to the tops of its windows, with more belongings lashed to the roof. 'It's the same car we found in the barn.'

Mausami regarded the photos another moment. How happy they all looked. Not just the smiling boy but his parents and sisters, as well – all of them.

'You think they lived here?'

Theo nodded, returning the picture to its place on the mantel with the others. 'My guess is, they came here before the outbreak and got stranded. Or else they just decided to stay on. And don't forget the four graves out back.'

Mausami was about to point out that there were four graves, not five. But then she realized her error. The fourth grave would have been dug by the last survivor, who couldn't bury himself.

'Hungry?' Theo asked her.

She ran a hand through her dirty hair. 'What I'd really like is a bath.'

'As it happens, I thought you might.' He was wearing a sly smile. 'Come on.'

He led her out to the yard. A large cast-iron pot now hung from a length of chain over a pile of glowing embers; beside it was a metal trough, long and deep enough for a person to sit in. He used a plastic bucket to fill the trough with water from the pump, then, gripping the handle with a heavy cloth, lifted the metal pot and poured the steaming contents into the trough as well.

'Go on, get in,' Theo said.

She felt suddenly embarrassed.

'It's okay,' he said, laughing gently, 'I won't watch.'

It seemed foolish, after everything, to be shy about her body. And yet she was. With Theo's eyes averted, she removed her clothing quickly, standing naked for a moment in the autumn sunshine. The air was cold against her tightening skin, the taut, round shape of her belly. She eased herself into the water, which rose to cover her stomach, her swollen breasts, laced with a nimbus of blue veins.

'Okay if I turn around?'

'I feel so huge, Theo. I can't believe you want to see me like this.'

'You'll get bigger before you get smaller. Might as well get used to it.'

What was she afraid of? They could have a baby together, but she wouldn't let him see her naked? They hadn't so much as touched in days; she realized she had been waiting for him to do this, to cross the barrier that separated them, now that they were alone.

'It's okay, you can turn around.'

For a moment his eyebrows raised at the sight of her. But just a moment. She saw that he was holding a blackened fry pan, full of some hard, glistening substance. He placed it on the ground by the trough and knelt to carve a wedge-shaped piece with his blade.

'My God, Theo. You made soap?'

'I used to make it with my mother sometimes. I don't know if I used enough ash, though. The fat comes from a pronghorn I shot yesterday morning. They're lean sons of bitches, but I got enough to render one batch.'

'You shot a pronghorn?'

He nodded. 'It was hell dragging him back here, too,' he said. 'At least five clicks. And there's lots of fish in the river. I'm figuring we can put up enough stores to make it through the winter easy.' He rose, dusting his hands on his trouser legs. 'Go ahead and finish and I'll make breakfast.'

By the time she was done, the water was opaque with dirt and filmed with grease from the soap. She rose to her feet and used the rest of the heated water to rinse herself off, standing naked in the yard to let the sun dry her, feeling the moisture wicking off her skin in the arid air. She couldn't remember when she'd felt so clean.

She dressed – her clothing felt filthy against her skin; she'd have to see about doing the laundry – and reentered the house. More surprises from the basement: Theo had set the table – actual china, laid out with utensils and drinking cups, the glass murky with age. He was cooking some kind of steak in a fry pan, with translucent slivers of onion. The room was roaring with heat from the stove, fueled by logs taken from a pile he'd stacked at the door.

'The last of the antelope,' he explained. 'The rest is up for smoking.' He flipped the steaks and turned toward her, drying his hands on a rag. 'It's a little stringy but not bad. There's wild onions down by the river, and bushes I think may be blackberries, though we'll have to wait till spring.'

'Flyers, Theo, what else?' The question wasn't serious; she was amazed at all he'd done.

'Potatoes.'

'Potatoes?'

'They're mostly gone to seed now, but we can still use some. I've moved a bunch down to the bins in the cellar.' With a long fork he speared the steaks onto their plates. 'We won't starve. There's lots, once you look.'

After breakfast, he washed the dishes in the sink while she watched. She wanted to help, but he insisted that she do nothing.

'Feel up to a walk?' he asked.

He disappeared into the barn and returned with a bucket and a pair of fishing poles, still strung with plastic monofilament. He gave her a small spade and the shotgun to carry, and a handful of shells. By the time they reached the river, the sun was high in the sky. They were at a spot where the river slowed and widened into a broad, shallow bend; the banks were dense with vegetation, tall weeds golden with autumnal color. Theo had no hooks but had found, tucked in a kitchen drawer, a small sewing kit, containing a tin of safety pins. While Maus dug in the dirt for worms, Theo tied these to the ends of their lines.

'So, how do you fish, exactly?' Maus said. Her hands were full of wriggling dirt; everywhere she looked, the ground was teeming with life.

'I think you just put them in the water and see what happens.'

They did. But after a while, this seemed silly. Their hooks were sitting in the shallows where they could see them.

'Stand back,' Theo said. 'I'm going to try to get mine farther out.'

He drew back the latch on his reel, lifted the rod over his shoulder, and threw the line forward. It shot out in a long arc over the water, disappearing into the current with a plunk. Almost at once, the tip of the rod bent sharply.

'Shit!' His eyes went wide with panic. 'What do I do?'

'Don't let him get away!'

The fish broke the surface with a shimmering splash. Theo began to reel him in.

'He feels huge!'

As Theo pulled the fish toward shore, Maus stumbled into the shallows – the water was astonishingly cold, filling her boots – and bent to grab him. He darted away, and in another moment her ankles were all wrapped up in the fishing line.

'Theo, help!'

They were both laughing. Theo snatched the fish and rolled him onto his back, which seemed to have the desired effect; the fish gave up his struggles. Maus managed to un-tangle herself and retrieved the bucket from shore while Theo pulled the fish from the river – a long, glimmering thing, like a single slab of muscle flecked with brilliant color, as if hundreds of tiny gems were set into its flesh. The pin was hooked through its lower lip, the worm still on it.

'What part do you eat?' Maus asked.

'I guess that depends on how hungry we get.'

He kissed her then; she felt a flood of happiness. He was still Theo, her Theo. She could feel it in his kiss. Whatever had happened in that cell hadn't taken this away from her.

'My turn,' she said, pushing him away, and took up her rod to cast as he had done.

They filled the bucket with wriggling fish; the abundance of the river seemed almost too much, like an overly extrava-gant present. The wide blue sky and the sun-dappled river and the forgotten countryside and the two of them together, in it: it all seemed, somehow, miraculous. Walking back to the house, Maus found her mind returning to the family in the pictures. The mother and the father and the two girls and the boy with his victorious, gap-toothed smile. They had lived here, died here. But most of all, she felt certain, they had lived.

They cleaned the fish and set the tender meat on racks in the smokehouse; tomorrow they would take them out to dry in the sun. One they saved for dinner, and cooked it in the pan with a bit of onion and one of the seedy potatoes.

As the sun was setting, Theo took up the shotgun from its place in the corner of the kitchen. Maus was putting the last of the dishes away in the cabinets. She turned to see him ejecting the shells, three of them, into his palm, blowing on each to clean the cap of dust, then sliding them back into the magazine. Next he removed his blade and cleaned this also, wiping it on his pants.

'Well.' He cleared his throat. 'I guess it's time.'

'No, Theo.'

She put down the plate she was holding and stepped toward him, taking the gun from his hands and placing it on the kitchen table.

'We're safe here, I know it.' Even as she said the words, she felt their veracity. They were safe because she believed they were safe. 'Don't go.'

He shook his head. 'I don't think that's such a good idea, Maus.'

She leaned her face into his and kissed him again, long and slow, so he would know this about her, about both of them. They were safe. Inside her, the baby had begun to hiccup.

'Come to bed, Theo,' said Mausami. 'Please. I want you to come to bed with me, now.'

It was sleep he feared. He told her that night, as they lay curled together. He couldn't *not* sleep; he knew that. Not sleeping was like not eating, he explained, or not breathing; it was like holding your breath in your chest as long as you could, until motes of light were dancing before your eyes and every part of you was saying one word: *breathe*. That's what it had been like in the cell, for days and days and days.

And now: the dream was gone, but not the feeling of it. The fear that he would close his eyes and find himself in the dream again. Because, at the end, if not for the girl, he would have done it. She'd come into the dream and stayed his hand, but by then it was too late. He would have killed the woman, killed anyone. He would have done whatever they wanted. And once you knew that about yourself, he said, you could never *unknow* it. Whoever you thought you were, you were somebody else entirely.

She held him as he spoke, his voice drifting in the darkness, and then for a long time both of them were silent.

Maus? Are you awake?

I'm right here. Though this wasn't so: she had, in fact, dozed off.

He shifted against her, pulling her arm over his chest like a blanket to keep him warm. Stay awake for me, he said. Can you do that? Until I'm asleep.

Yes, she said. Yes, I can do that.

He was quiet for a while. In the marginless space between their bodies, the baby flipped and kicked.

We're safe here, Theo, she said. As long as we're together, we'll be safe.

I hope that's true, he said.

I know it's true, Mausami said. But even as she felt his breathing slow against her, sleep taking him at last, she kept her eyes open, staring into the dark. It's true, she thought, because it has to be.

FIFTY-NINE

By the time they reached the garrison, it was midafternoon. Their packs had been returned but not their weapons; they were not prisoners, but neither were they free to go as they wished. The term the major had used was 'under protection.'

From the river they had marched straight north over the ridge. At the base of a second valley they'd come to a muddy trace, rutted with hoofprints and tire tracks. It was sheer chance that they had missed it on their own. Heavy clouds had moved in from the west; the air looked and felt like rain. As the first spits commenced to fall, Peter tasted woodsmoke in the wind.

Major Greer came up beside him. He was a tall, well-built man with a brow so furrowed it looked plowed. He might have been forty years old. He was dressed in loose-fitting camouflage spattered in a pattern of green and brown, drawn tight at the waist by a wide belt, pockets fat with gear. His head, covered by a woolen cap, was shaved clean. Like all his men, a squad of fifteen, he'd painted his face with streaks of mud and charcoal, giving the whites of his eyes a startling vividness. They looked like wolves, like creatures of the forest; they looked like the forest itself. A long-range patrol unit; they had been in the woods for weeks.

Greer paused on the path and shouldered his rifle. A black pistol was holstered at his waist. He took a long drink from his canteen and waved it toward the hillside. They were close now; Peter could feel it in the quickening step of Greer's men. A hot meal, a cot to sleep on, a roof over their heads.

'Just over the next ridge,' Greer said.

In the intervening hours they had formed something that felt, to Peter, like the beginnings of a friendship. After the initial confusion of their capture, a situation compounded by the fact that neither group would agree to say who they were until the other blinked first, it was Michael who had broken the stalemate, lifting his vomit-smeared face from the dirt where the net had disgorged them to proclaim, 'Oh, fuck. I surrender. We're from California, all right? Somebody, please just shoot me so the ground will stop spinning.'

As Greer capped his canteen, Alicia caught up to them on the path. From the start she had been unusually silent. She'd voiced no objection to Greer's order that they travel unarmed, a fact that now struck Peter as completely out of character. But probably she was just in shock, as they all were. For the duration of the march to camp she had kept protectively to Amy's side. Perhaps, Peter thought, she was simply embarrassed that she'd led them straight into the soldiers' trap. As for Amy, the girl seemed to have absorbed this new turn of events as she absorbed everything, with a neutral, watchful countenance.

'What's it like?' he asked Greer.

The major shrugged. 'Just like you'd think. It's like a big latrine. It beats being out in the rain, though.'

As they crested the hill, nestled in a bowl-like valley below them, the garrison leapt into view: a cluster of canvas tents and vehicles ringed by a fence of timbers, fifteen meters tall at least and each honed at the top to a sharp point. Among the vehicles Peter saw at least half a dozen Humvees, two large tankers, and a number of smaller trucks, pickups and five-tons with heavy, mud-choked tires. At the perimeter, a dozen large floodlights stood on tall poles; at the far end of the compound horses were grazing in a paddock. More soldiers were moving among the buildings, and along a cat-walk at the top of the wall. At the center of the compound, standing over all, a large flag flapped in the wind, blocks of red, white, and blue with a single white star. The whole thing couldn't have been more than half a square kilometer, and yet, standing on the ridge, Peter felt as if he were gazing into an entire city, the heart of a world he'd always believed in but never actually imagined.

'They've got *lights*,' said Michael. More men from Greer's unit moved past them, headed down the hill.

'Hell, son,' said the one named Muncey – a corporal, bald as the rest of them, with a wide, snaggle-toothed smile. Most of Greer's men bore themselves with a soldierly silence, speaking only when spoken to, but not Muncey, who chat-tered like a bird. His job, fittingly, was to operate the radio, which he carried on his back, a mechanism with a generator run by a hand crank, which stuck from the bottom like a tail.

'Inside that fence?' Muncey said with a grin. 'That dirt is *Texas*. If we ain't got it, you don't need it.'

They weren't regular army, Greer had explained. At least not the US Army. There was no US Army anymore. Then whose army are you? Peter had asked.

That was when Greer had told them about Texas.

By the time they reached the base of the hill, a crowd of men had gathered. Despite the cold, and now the rain, a pattering drizzle, some were bare-chested, exposing their narrow waists, the densely ribboned muscles of their shoulders and chests. All were smooth-shaven, their heads, too. Everyone was armed; rifles and pistols, even a few crossbows.

'Folks'll stare,' Greer said quietly. 'You better get used to it.'

'How many . . . *strags* do you usually bring in?' Peter asked. The term, Greer had explained, was short for *stragglers*.

Greer frowned. They were moving toward the gate. 'None. Farther east you still get some. Up in Oklahoma, Third Battalion once found a whole goddamn *town*. But way out here? We're not even looking.'

'Then what was the net for?'

'Sorry,' Greer said, 'I thought you understood. That's for the dracs. What you all call smokes.' He twirled a finger in the air. 'That twisting motion messes with their heads. They're like ducks in a barrel in that thing.'

Peter recalled something Caleb had told him, about why the virals stayed out of the turbine field. *Zander always said the movement screwed them up.* He related this to Greer.

'Makes sense,' the major agreed. 'They don't like spinning. I haven't heard that about turbines, though.'

Michael was walking beside them. 'So what were those things? Hanging in the trees, with the bad smell.'

'Garlic.' Greer gave a little laugh. 'Oldest trick in the book. The fucking dracs love it.'

The conversation was cut short as they stepped through the gate, into a tunnel of waiting men. Greer's squad had dispersed among the crowd. No one was talking. As Peter passed, he saw their eyes darting quickly over him. That was when he realized what the soldiers were all looking at: they were looking at the women.

'Ten-*shun.*'

Everyone snapped to. Peter saw a figure stepping briskly toward them from one of the tents. At first glance, he was not what Peter would have expected of a high-ranking military officer: an almost barrel-shaped man, a full head shorter than Greer, with a waddling, round-heeled gait. Under the dome of his shorn head, the features of his face seemed scrunched, as if they had been placed too close together. But as he approached, Peter felt the force of his authority, a mysterious energy, like a zone of static electricity that hovered in the air around him. His eyes, small and dark, possessed a frank, piercing intensity, even if, as it appeared, they had been incongruously set in the wrong face.

He regarded Peter a long moment, his hands on his hips, then looked past him toward the others, holding each briefly with the same evaluating gaze.

'I'll be goddamned.'

His voice was surprisingly deep. He spoke with the same loose-jawed accent as Greer and his men.

'At ease, all of you.'

Everyone relaxed. Peter didn't know what to say; best, he thought, to wait to hear from this man first.

'Men of the Second,' he declared, lifting his voice to the gathered men, 'it has come to my attention that some of these strags are women. You are not to look at these women. You are not to speak to them, or come near them, or approach them, or in any way think you have anything to do with them, or they with you. They are not your girlfriends or your wives. They are not your mothers or your sisters. They are nothing, they do not exist, they are not here. Am I clear?'

'Sir yes sir!'

Peter glanced at Alicia, where she was standing with Amy, but couldn't meet her eye. Hollis shot him a skeptical frown: clearly he had no idea what to make of this, either.

808

'You six, drop your packs and come with me. Major, you too.'

They followed him into the tent, a single room with an earthen floor beneath a sagging canvas ceiling. The only furnishings were a potbellied stove, a pair of plywood trestle tables covered with papers, and, along the far wall, a smaller table with a radio manned by a soldier with earphones clamped to the sides of his head. On the wall above him was a large, multicolored map, marked with dozens of beaded pins forming an irregular V. As Peter moved closer, he saw that the base of the V was in central Texas, with one arm reaching north across Oklahoma and into southern Kansas, the other veering west, into New Mexico, before it, too, turned north, ending just across the Colorado border – the place where he now stood. At the top of the map, written in yellow on a dark stripe, were the words UNITED STATES INTER-MEDIATE POLITICAL, and, beneath that, *Fox and Sons Classroom Maps, Cincinnati, Ohio.*

Greer came up beside him. 'Welcome to the war,' he murmured.

The commander, who had entered behind them, directed his voice to the radio operator, who, as the men outside had, was staring frankly at the women. He seemed to have chosen Sara, but then his eyes moved to Alicia, then Amy, in a series of nervous jerks.

'Corporal, excuse us, please.'

With obvious effort, he broke his gaze away, pulling the earphones from his head. His face bloomed with embarrassment. 'Sir. Sorry, sir.'

'Now, son.'

The corporal got to his feet and scampered away.

'So.' The commander's eyes settled on Greer. 'Major. Is there something you neglected to tell me?'

'Three of the strags are women, sir.'

'Yes. Yes, they are. Thank you for letting me know.'

'Sorry, General.' He seemed to wince. 'We should have called that in.'

'Yes, you should have. Since you found them, I'm putting you in charge. Think you can handle that?'

'Of course, sir. No problem.'

'Put together a detail, get them billeted. They'll need their own latrine, too.'

'Yes, General.'

'Go.'

Greer nodded, glancing quickly toward Peter – *Good luck*, his eyes seemed to say – and exited the tent. The general, whose name, Peter realized, he had yet to learn, took another moment to look them over. Now that they were alone, his bearing had relaxed.

'You're Jaxon?'

Peter nodded.

'I'm Brigadier General Curtis Vorhees. Second Expeditionary Forces, Army of the Republic of Texas.' A hint of a smile. 'I'm the big dog around here, in case that was something else Major Greer neglected to mention.'

'He didn't, sir. I mean, he did. Mention it.'

'Good.' Vorhees nodded, regarding them all another moment. 'So, am I to understand – and forgive me if I seem incredulous on this point – that the six of you walked all the way from California?'

Actually, Peter thought, *we drove some of the way. For some of it, we took a train*. But instead he simply answered, 'Yes, sir.'

'And why, may I ask, would anyone attempt such a thing?'

Peter opened his mouth to reply; but once again the answer, the true one, seemed too large. Outside, the rain had begun to fall in earnest, drumming on the tent's canvas roof.

'It's a long story,' he managed.

'Well, I'm sure it is, Mr Jaxon. And I'd be very interested to hear it. For now, we need to concern ourselves with a few preliminaries. You are civilian guests of the Second Expeditionary. For the duration of your stay, you're under my authority. Think you can live with that?'

Peter nodded.

'In another six days, this unit will be moving south to rendezvous with Third Battalion at the town of Roswell, New Mexico. From there, we can send you back to Kerrville with a supply convoy. I suggest you take this offer, but this is entirely your choice. No doubt it is something you will wish to discuss among yourselves.'

Peter broke his gaze away to look at the others, whose faces seemed to mirror his own surprise. He hadn't considered the possibility that their journey might be over.

'Now, as for the other matter,' Vorhees went on, 'which you heard me speak of with the major. I will need you to instruct the women in your party that they are not to have any contact with my men, beyond what is absolutely necessary. They are to remain in their tent, except to go to the latrine. Any needs they have are to go through you or Major Greer. Is this clear?'

Peter had no reason to refuse, other than the fact that the offer struck him as plainly ridiculous. 'I'm not sure I can tell them that, sir.'

'You can't?'

'No sir.' He shrugged. There were no other words for it. 'We're all together. That's just how it is.'

The general sighed. 'Perhaps you misunderstood me. I am asking only as a courtesy. The mission of the Second Expeditionary is such that it would be completely improper, even dangerous, for them to move freely among the unit.'

'Why would they be in danger?'

He frowned. 'They wouldn't. It's not the women I'm thinking of.' Vorhees took a patient breath and began again. 'I will explain this as simply as I know how. We are a volunteer force. To join the Expeditionary is to do so for life, by blood oath, and each of these men is sworn to die. He's cut all ties to the world but this unit and the men within it. Each time a man leaves this compound, he wholly believes he'll never come back. He accepts this. More than that, he embraces it. A man will happily die for his friends, but a woman – a woman makes him want to live. Once that happens, I promise you, he'll walk through that gate and never come back.'

Vorhees was talking, Peter understood, about giving it up. But after all they had been through, it was simply impossible to imagine telling any of them, Alicia especially, that they would have to hide in their tent.

'I'm sure all of these women are fine fighters,' Vorhees continued. 'You couldn't have made it this far if they weren't. But our code is very strict, and I need you to respect it. If you can't, I will return your weapons and send you on your way.'

'Fine,' he said, 'we'll go.'

'Wait, Peter.'

It was Alicia who had spoken. Peter turned to face her.

'Lish, it's all right. I'm with you on this. He says we go, we'll go.'

But Alicia didn't acknowledge him. Her eyes were pointed at the general. Peter realized she was standing at attention, her arms held rigidly at her sides.

'General Vorhees. Colonel Niles Coffee of the First Expeditionary sends his regards.'

'Niles Coffee?' A light seemed to come on in his face. '*The* Niles Coffee?'

'Lish,' Peter said, her meaning dawning upon him, 'do you mean . . . the Colonel?'

But Alicia said nothing. She didn't even look at him. Her expression was set in a way that Peter had never seen before.

'Young lady. Colonel Coffee was lost with all his men thirty years ago.'

'Not true, sir,' Alicia said. 'He survived.'

'Coffee's *alive*?'

'KIA, sir. Three months ago.'

Vorhees glanced around the room before finding Alicia with his eyes again. 'And who, may I ask, are you?'

She gave a crisp nod from her chin. 'His adopted daughter, sir. Private Alicia Donadio, First Expeditionary. Baptized and sworn.'

No one spoke. Something final was occurring, Peter knew.

Something irrevocable. He felt a wave of disorienting panic rising inside him, as if some basic fact of his life, fundamental as gravity, had been suddenly, and without warning, stripped away.

'Lish, what are you saying?'

At last she turned her face to look at him; her eyes were pooled with trembling tears.

'Oh, Peter,' she said, as the first one broke away to descend her dirt-stained cheek, 'I'm sorry. I really should have told you.'

'You can't have her!'

'I'm sorry, Jaxon,' the general said. 'This isn't your decision to make. It's no one's decision.' He stepped briskly to the door of the tent. 'Greer! Somebody get Major Greer to my tent, *now*.'

'What's going on?' Michael demanded. 'Peter, what is she talking about?'

Suddenly everybody was speaking at once. Peter gripped Alicia by the arms, making her look at him. 'Lish, what are you doing? Think about what you're doing.'

'It's already done.' Through her tears, her face seemed to glow with relief, as if a burden long carried had finally been put to rest. 'It was done before I knew you. Long before. The day the Colonel came into the Sanctuary to claim me. He made me promise not to tell.'

He understood, then, what she'd been trying to say to him that morning. 'You were *tracking* them.'

She nodded. 'Yes, for the last two days. When I was scouting downstream I found one of their camps. The ashes of their fire were still warm. Way out here, I didn't think it could be anybody else.' She shook her head faintly. 'Honestly, Peter, I didn't know if I even wanted to find them. Part of me always thought they were just an old man's stories. You have to believe that.'

Greer appeared at the door of the tent, dripping with rain.

'Major Greer,' the general said, 'this woman is First Expeditionary.'

Greer's jaw fell open. 'She's what?'

'Niles Coffee's daughter.'

Greer stared at Alicia, his eyes wide with shock, as if he were looking at some strange animal. 'Holy goddamn. Coffee had a daughter?'

'She says she's sworn.'

Greer scratched his bare head in puzzlement. 'Christ. She's a *woman*. What do you want to do?'

'There's nothing to do. Sworn is sworn. The men will have to learn to live with it. Take her to the barber, get her assigned.'

It was all happening too fast. Peter felt as if something huge were breaking open inside him. 'Lish, tell them you're lying!'

'I'm sorry. This is how it has to be. Major?'

Greer nodded, his face grave, and stepped to her side.

'You can't leave me,' Peter heard himself say, though the voice that spoke these words did not seem to be his own.

'I have to, Peter. It's who I am.'

He had, without realizing it, stepped into her arms. He felt the tears in his throat. 'I can't . . . do this without you.'

'Yes, you can. I know you can.'

It was no use. Alicia was leaving him; he felt her slipping away. 'I can't, I can't.'

'It's all right,' she said, her voice close to his ear. 'Hush now.'

She held him that way a long moment, the two of them wrapped in a bubble of silence, as if they were alone. Then Alicia took his face in her hands and bent him toward her; she kissed him, once and quickly, on the forehead. A kiss that both sought forgiveness and bestowed it: a kiss of goodbye. The air parted between them. She had released him, stepping away.

'Thank you, General,' she said. 'Major Greer, I'm ready now.'

814

SIXTY

The days of rain: Peter told them everything.

For five full days the rain poured down. He sat for hours at the long table in Vorhees's tent, sometimes just the two of them, but usually with Greer as well. He told them about Amy, and the Colony, and the signal they had come to find; he told them about Theo and Mausami, and the Haven, and all that had happened there. He told them that sixteen hundred kilometers away, on a mountaintop in California, ninety souls were waiting for the lights to go out.

'I won't lie to you,' Vorhees said, when Peter asked them if they could send the soldiers there. It was late afternoon. Alicia had left in the morning, on patrol. Just like that, she had been subsumed into the life of Vorhees's men.

'It's not that I don't believe you,' Vorhees explained. 'And this bunker of yours alone sounds like it would be worth the trip. But I'll have to take this up the line, and that means Division. It would be next spring at the earliest before we could think about making such a trip. That's all uncharted ground.'

'I'm not sure they can wait that long.'

'Well, they'll have to. My biggest worry is getting out of this valley before the snow hits. This rain doesn't let up, we could get stuck here. There's only enough fuel to keep our lights going another thirty days.'

'What I want to know more about is this place, the Haven,' Greer cut in. Outside the walls of the tent and in the presence of any of the men, Greer's and Vorhees's relationship was rigidly formal; but inside, as they were now, they visibly relaxed into friendship. Greer looked at the general, his eyes darkening thoughtfully. 'Sounds a little like those folks in Oklahoma.'

'What folks?' Peter asked.

'Place called Homer,' Vorhees replied, picking up the

thread. 'Third Battalion came across them about ten years ago, way the hell and gone out in the panhandle. A whole town of survivors, over eleven hundred men, women, and children. I wasn't there, but I heard the stories. It was like stepping back a hundred years; they didn't even seem to know what the dracs *were*. Just going about their business, nice as you please, no lights or fencing, happy to see you but don't slam the door on your way out. The CO offered them transport but they said no thanks, and in any case, the Third wasn't really equipped to move that many bodies south to Kerrville. It was the damnedest thing. Survivors, and they didn't want to be rescued. Third Battalion left a squad behind and moved on north, up to Wichita, where they got their happy asses handed to them. Lost half their men; the rest hightailed it back. When they got there, the place was empty.'

'What do you mean "empty"?' Peter asked.

Vorhees's eyebrows lifted sharply. 'I mean *empty*. Not a soul, and no bodies. Everything neat as a pin, dinner dishes sitting on the table. No sign of the squad they'd left, either.'

Peter had to admit it was puzzling, but he didn't see what this had to do with the Haven. 'Maybe they decided to go somewhere safer,' Peter offered.

'Maybe. Maybe the dracs just took them so fast they didn't have time to wash the dishes. You're asking something I don't know the answer to. But I will tell you this. Thirty years ago, when Kerrville sent out the First Expeditionary, you couldn't walk a hundred meters without tripping over a drac. The First lost half a dozen men on a good day, and when Coffee's unit disappeared, people pretty much thought it was over. I mean, the guy was a legend. The Expeditionary more or less disbanded right then. But now here you are, having traveled all the way from California. Back in the day, you wouldn't have made it twenty steps to the latrine.'

Peter glanced at Greer, who acknowledged this truth with a nod, then looked back at Vorhees. 'Are you saying they're dying off?'

'Oh, there's plenty, believe me. You just got to know where to look. What I'm saying is something's different. Something's changed. In the last sixty months, we've run two supply lines from Kerrville, one up as far as Hutchinson, Kansas, another through New Mexico into Colorado. What we've seen is that you tend to find them in clusters now. They're burrowing deeper, too, using mines, caves, places like that mountain you found. They're sometimes packed in there so tightly you'd need a crowbar to pry them apart. The cities are still crawling, with all the empty buildings, but there's plenty of open countryside where you could go for days without seeing one.'

'What about Kerrville? Why is that safe?'

The general frowned. 'Well, it isn't. Not a hundred per-cent. Most of Texas is pretty bad, actually. Laredo is no place you'd ever want to go, or Dallas. Houston, what's left of it, is like a goddamn bloodsucker swamp. The place is so polluted with petrochemicals I don't know how they survive there, but they do. San Antonio and Austin were both pretty much leveled in the first war, El Paso, too. Fucking federal govern-ment, trying to burn the dracs out. That's what led to the Declaration, along about the same time California split off.'

'Split off?' Peter asked.

Vorhees nodded. 'From the Union. Declared its independ-ence. The California thing was a real bloodbath, pretty much open warfare for a while, like there wasn't anything else to worry about. But Texas got lost in the shuffle. Maybe the federals just didn't want to fight on two fronts. The governor seized all military assets, which wasn't hard, since the Army by then was in total free fall, everything coming apart. They moved the capital to Kerrville and dug in. Walled it off, like your Colony, but the difference is, we had oil, and lots of it. Down near Freeport, there's about five hundred million barrels sitting in underground salt domes, the old Strategic Petroleum Reserve. You got oil, you got power. You got power, you got lights. We've got over thirty thousand souls inside the walls, plus another fifty thousand acres under

817

irrigation and a fortified supply line running to a working refinery on the coast.'

'The coast,' Peter repeated. The word felt heavy in his mouth. 'You mean the *ocean*?'

'The Gulf of Mexico, anyway.' Vorhees shrugged. 'Calling it the ocean would be polite. It's pretty much a chemical slick. All those offshore platforms still pumping the crap out, plus the discharge from New Orleans. Ocean currents pushed a lot of debris in through there, too. Tankers, cargo ships, you name it. In places you can practically walk across it without getting your feet wet.'

'But you could still leave from there,' Peter tendered. 'If you had a boat.'

'In theory. But I wouldn't recommend it. The problem is getting past the barrier.'

'Mines,' Greer explained.

Vorhees nodded. 'And lots of them. In the last days of the war, the NATO alliance, our so-called friends, banded together and made one last effort to contain the infection. Heavy bombing along the coasts, and not just conventional explosives. They blasted just about anything in the water. You can still see the wreckage down in Corpus. Then they laid mines, just to slam the door.'

Peter remembered the stories his father had told him. The stories of the ocean, and the Long Beach. The rusting ribs of the great ships, stretching as far as the eye could see. Never had he thought to wonder how this had come about. He had lived in a world without history, without cause, a world where things just were what they were. Talking to Vorhees and Greer was like looking at lines on a page and suddenly seeing words written there.

'What about farther east?' he asked. 'Have you ever sent anybody there?'

Vorhees shook his head. 'Not for years. The First Expeditionary sent two battalions that way, one north into Louisiana through Shreveport, another across Missouri toward

St Louis. They never came back.' He shrugged. 'Maybe some-day. For now, Texas is what we've got.'

'I'd like to see it,' Peter said after a moment. 'The city. Kerrville.'

'And you will, Peter.' Vorhees allowed himself a rare smile. 'If you take that convoy.'

They had yet to give Vorhees an answer, and Peter felt torn. They had safety, they had lights, they had found the Army after all. It might not be until spring, but Peter felt confident that Vorhees would send an expedition to the Colony and bring the others in. They had found what they had come for, in other words – more than found it. To ask his friends to continue seemed like an unnecessary risk. And without Alicia, part of him wanted to say yes, to just let the whole thing be over.

But whenever he thought this, his next thought would be of Amy. Alicia had been right: to come so close and turn away felt like something he would regret, probably for the rest of his life. Michael had tried to pick up the signal from the radio in the general's tent, but their radio equipment was all short range, worthless in the mountains. In the end, Vorhees said he had no reason to doubt their story, but who knew what the signal meant?

'The military left all kinds of crap behind. Civilians, too. Believe me, we've seen it before. You can't go chasing every squeak.' He spoke with the weariness of a man who had seen a lot, more than enough. 'This girl of yours, Amy. Maybe she's a hundred years old, like you say, and maybe she isn't. I have no reason to disbelieve you, except for the fact that she looks about fifteen and scared shitless. You can't always explain these things. My guess is she's just some poor traumatized soul who survived somehow and by a stroke of luck just wandered into your camp.'

'What about the transmitter in her neck?'

'Well, what about it?' Vorhees's tone wasn't mocking, merely factual. 'Hell, maybe she's Russian or Chinese. We've

819

been waiting for those people to show up, assuming there's even anyone left alive out there.'

'Is there?'

Vorhees paused; he and Greer exchanged a look of caution.

'The truth is, we don't know. Some people say the quarantine worked, that the rest of the world is just humming right along out there without us. This raises the question as to why we wouldn't hear anything over the wireless, but I suppose it's possible they set up some kind of electronic barricade in addition to the mines. Others believe – and I think the major and I share this opinion – that everybody's dead. This is all conjecture, mind you, but the story goes that the quarantine wasn't quite as tight as people thought. Five years after the outbreak, the continental United States was pretty much depopulated, ripe for the picking. The gold depository at Fort Knox. The vault at the Federal Reserve in New York. Every museum and jewelry shop and bank, right down to the corner savings and loan, all just sitting there, nobody minding the store. But the real prize was all that American military ordnance just lying around, including upwards of ten thousand nuclear weapons, any one of which could shift the balance of power in a world without the United States to babysit it. Frankly, I don't think it's a question of if anyone came ashore, but how many and who. Chances are, they took the virus back with them.'

Peter gave himself a moment to absorb all this. Vorhees was telling him the world was empty, an empty place.

'I don't think Amy's here to steal anything,' he said finally.

'If it's any help, I don't think so either. She's just a kid, Peter. How she survived out there is anybody's guess. Maybe she'll find a way to tell you.'

'I think she already has.'

'That's what you believe. And I won't disagree with you. But I'll tell you something else. I knew a woman growing up, crazy old lady lived in a shack behind our housing section, an old falling-down dump of a place. Wrinkled as a raisin, kept about a hundred cats, place absolutely reeked of cat piss. This woman claimed she could hear what the dracs were *thinking*. We kids would tease the hell out of her, though of course we couldn't get enough of her, either. The kind of thing you feel bad about later, but not at the time. She was what you all call a Walker, just appeared at the gates one day.' Vorhees concluded with a shrug: 'Time to time you hear stories like this. Old people mostly, half-crazy mystics, never a young one like this girl. But it's not a new story.'

Greer leaned forward. He seemed suddenly interested. 'What happened to her?'

'The woman?' The general rubbed his chin as he searched his memory. 'As I recall, she took the trip. Hanged herself in her cat-piss-smelling house.' When neither Peter nor Greer said anything, the general went on: 'You can't overthink these things. Or at least we can't. I'm sure the major will agree with me. We're here to clear out as many dracs as we can, lay in supplies, find the hot spots and burn them out. Maybe someday it'll all add up to something. I'm sure it's nothing I'll live to see.'

The general pushed back from the table, and Greer as well; the time for talk was over, at least for the day. 'In the meantime, think about my offer, Jaxon. A ride home. You've earned it.'

By the time Peter had stepped to the door, Greer and Vorhees were already leaning over the table, where a large map had been unrolled. Vorhees raised his face, frowning.

'Was there something else?'

'It's just . . .' What did he want to say? 'I was wondering about Alicia. How she's doing.'

'She's fine, Peter. However Coffee did it, he taught her well. You probably wouldn't even recognize her.'

He felt stung. 'I'd like to see her.'

'I know you would. But it's just not a good idea right now.' When Peter didn't move from the door, Vorhees said, with barely concealed impatience, 'Is that all?'

Peter shook his head. 'Just tell her I asked for her.'

'I'll do that, son.'

821

Peter stepped through the flap, into the darkening afternoon. The rain had let up, but the air felt completely saturated, heavy with bone-chilling dampness. Beyond the walls of the garrison, a dense fogbank was drifting over the ridge. Everything was spattered with mud. He hugged his jacket around himself as he crossed the open ground between Vorhees's tent and the mess hall, where he caught sight of Hollis, sitting alone at one of the long tables, spooning beans into his mouth from a battered plastic tray. More soldiers were scattered around the room, quietly talking. Peter fetched a tray and filled it from the pot and went to where Hollis was sitting.

'This seat taken?'

'They're all taken,' Hollis said glumly. 'They're just letting me borrow this one.'

Peter took a place on the bench. He knew what Hollis meant; they were like extra limbs here, something vestigial, with nothing to do, no role to play. Sara and Amy had been relegated to their tent, but for all his relative freedom, Peter felt just as trapped. And none of the soldiers would have anything to do with them. The unstated assumption was that they had nothing worth saying and would be leaving soon anyway.

He updated Hollis on all he had learned, then asked the question that was really on his mind: 'Any sign of her?'

'I saw them leaving this morning, with Raimey's squad.'

Raimey's unit, one of six, was doing short recon patrols to the southeast. When Peter had asked Vorhees how long they'd be gone, he had answered, enigmatically, 'However long it takes.'

'How'd she look?'

'Like one of them.' Hollis paused. 'I waved to her, but I don't think she saw me. Know what they're calling her?'

Peter shook his head.

'The Last Expeditionary.' Hollis frowned at this. 'Kind of a mouthful, if you ask me.'

They fell silent; there was nothing more to say. If they

822

were extra limbs, Alicia felt to Peter like a missing one. He kept looking for her in his mind, turning his thoughts to the place where Alicia should be. It wasn't the kind of thing he thought he could ever really get used to.

'I don't think they really believe us about Amy,' Peter said. 'Would you?'

Peter shook his head, conceding the point. 'I guess not.'

Another silence descended.

'So what do you think?' Hollis said. 'About the evac.'

With all the rain, the battalion's departure had been delayed another week. 'Vorhees keeps urging us to go. He may be right.'

'But you don't think so.' When Peter hesitated, Hollis put down his fork and looked him in the eye. 'You know me, Peter. I'll do whatever you want to do.'

'Why am I in charge? I don't want to decide for everyone.'

'I didn't say you were. I think it's just a case of what *is*, Peter. If you don't know yet, you don't know. It'll keep until the rain lets up.'

Peter felt a twinge of guilt. Since they'd arrived at the garrison, he had somehow never quite found the moment to tell Hollis that he knew about him and Sara. With Alicia gone, part of him didn't want to face the fact that the force that held them all together was dissolving. The three men had been billeted in a tent adjacent to the one where Sara and Amy now bided their time, playing hands of go-to and waiting for the rain to stop; for two nights running, Peter had awakened to find that Hollis's bunk was empty. But always he was there in the morning, snoring away. Peter wondered if Hollis and Sara were staging this for his benefit or for Michael's, who was, after all, her brother. As for Amy: after a period of time, a day or so, in which she had seemed nervous, even a little afraid of the soldiers who brought them their meals and escorted them to the latrine, she appeared to have moved into a state of hopeful, even cheerful waiting, content to bide her time but wholly expecting to press forward. *Will we be leaving soon?* she had asked Peter, her voice gently urging. *Because I would like to see the snow.* To which Peter had only said, I don't know, Amy. We'll see, after the rain stops. The truth, yet even as he'd spoken, the words had the hollow taste of a lie.

Hollis tipped his head toward Peter's plate. 'You should eat.'

He pushed the tray aside. 'I'm not hungry.'

They were joined by Michael, who swept down to the table in a rain-beaded poncho, carrying a tray piled high with food. Of all of them, he alone had found some use for his time: Vorhees had assigned him to the motor pool, helping to ready the vehicles for the trip south. He placed the tray on the table, sat before it, and dug in greedily, using a piece of corn bread to shovel beans into his mouth with his oil-stained hands.

'What's the matter?' he said, looking up. He swallowed a mouthful of bread and beans. 'The two of you look like somebody died.'

One of the soldiers moved past their table with his tray. A jug-eared private, his bald head shimmering with a downy fuzz.

'Hey, Lugnut,' he said to Michael.

Michael brightened. 'Sancho. What's the ups?'

'*De nada.* Listen. A bunch of us were talking, thought maybe you'd like to join us later.'

Michael smiled around a mouthful of beans. 'Sure thing.'

'Nineteen hundred in the mess.' The soldier looked at Peter and Hollis as if noticing them for the first time. 'You strags can come too, if you want.'

Peter had never quite gotten used to this term. There was always a note of derision in it.

'Come where?'

'Thanks, Sancho,' Michael said. 'I'll run it by them.'

When the soldier had moved on, Peter narrowed his eyes at Michael. 'Lugnut?'

Michael had resumed eating. 'They're big on names like

824

that. I kind of like it better than Circuit.' He mopped the last of the beans from his plate. 'They're not bad guys, Peter.'

'I didn't say they were.'

'What's tonight?' Hollis asked after a moment.

'Oh, that.' Michael shrugged dismissively, his face reddening. 'I'm surprised no one told you. It's movie night.'

By 18:30, all the tables had been pulled from the mess hall, the benches assembled in rows. With nightfall had come a distinct cooling and drying of the air; the rain had blown through. All the soldiers had gathered outside, noisily talking among themselves in a way that Peter had not seen before, laughing and joking and passing flasks of shine. He took a bench with Hollis at the back of the hall, facing the screen, a sheet of plywood covered in whitewash. Michael was somewhere up forward, among his new friends from the motor pool.

Michael had done his best to explain how the movie would work, but still Peter did not quite know what to expect, and he found the idea vaguely troubling, not rooted in any physical logic he understood. The projector, which rested on a high table behind them, would beam a current of moving images onto the screen – but if that was true, where did these images come from? If they were reflections, what did they reflect? A long electric cable had been run from the projector, out the door of the mess to one of the generators; Peter could not help but think how wasteful it was to use precious fuel for the simple purpose of entertainment. But as Major Greer stepped forward, to the excited hoots of sixty men, Peter felt it too: a pure anticipation, an almost childlike thrill.

Greer held up a hand to quiet the men, which only made them hoot louder.

'Shut up, you bloodbags!'

'Bring on the Count!' someone yelled.

More hooting and shouting. Standing in front of the screen, Greer wore a thinly concealed smile; for the moment, the hard carapace of military discipline had been allowed to crack. Peter had spent enough time in Greer's company to know this was no accident.

Greer allowed the excitement to die down on its own, then cleared his throat and spoke: 'All right, everyone, that'll do. First, an announcement. I know you all have enjoyed your stay out here in the north woods—'

'Fucking A right!'

Greer shot a frown in the direction of the man who'd spoken. 'Interrupt me again, Muncey, and you'll be sucking latrines for a month.'

'Just saying how happy I am to be here poking dracs, sir!'

More laughter. Greer let it go.

'As I was saying, with the break in the weather, we have some news. General?'

Vorhees stepped forward from where he'd been waiting, off to the side. 'Thank you, Major. Good evening, Second Battalion.'

A shouted chorus: 'Good evening, sir!'

'It looks like we've got ourselves a bit of a window here with the weather, so I'm calling it. Oh-five-hundred, report to your squad leaders after morning chow for your sections. We need this place racked and packed by lights tomorrow. When Blue Squad gets back, we're moving south. Any questions?'

A soldier raised his hand. Peter recognized him as the one who had spoken to Michael in the mess hall. Sancho.

'What about the heavy mechs, sir? They won't make it in the mud.'

'The decision's been made to leave them in place. We'll be traveling L and Q. Your squad leaders will go over this with you. Anyone else?'

Silence from the crowd.

'All right then. Enjoy the show.'

The lanterns were doused; at the back of the room, the wheels of the projector began to turn. So there it was, Peter thought; the moment to decide was upon them. A week had suddenly become no time at all. Peter felt someone slip onto the bench next to him: Sara. Beside her was Amy, wearing a dark woolen blanket over her shoulders, against the cold.

'You shouldn't be here,' Peter whispered.

'The hell with that,' Sara said quietly. 'You think I'd miss this?'

The screen blazed with light. Encircled numbers, descending in sequence: 5, 4, 3, 2, 1. Then:

CARL LAEMMLE

PRESENTS

"DRACULA"

by BRAM STOKER

FROM THE PLAY ADAPTED BY
HAMILTON DEANE & JOHN L. BALDERSTON

A TOD BROWNING PRODUCTION

A chorus of cheers rose up from the benches as, incredibly, the screen was filled with the moving image of a horse-drawn carriage, racing along a mountain road. The picture was bleached of all color, composed entirely of tones of gray – the palette of a half-remembered dream.

'Dracs,' said Hollis. He turned to Peter, frowning. 'Dracula?'

'Sound!' one of the soldiers bellowed, followed by others. 'Sound! Sound!'

The soldier operating the projector was frantically checking connections, twisting knobs. He jogged briskly forward and knelt by a box positioned under the screen.

'Wait, there, I think that's it—'

A crackling boom of static: Peter, entranced by the moving image on the screen – the carriage was entering a village now, people running to meet it – reflexively bolted in his chair. But then he realized what had occurred, what the box under the screen was. The clop of horses, the creak of the carriage on its springs and the voices of the villagers, speaking to one another in a strange language he had never heard before: the images were more than pictures, more than light. They were alive and breathing with sound.

On the screen, a man in a white hat waved a walking stick at the carriage man. As he opened his mouth to speak, all the soldiers chimed in as one:

'*Don't take my luggage down, I'm going on to Borgo Pass tonight!*'

An explosion of general hilarity. Peter tore his gaze away to glance at Hollis. But his friend's eyes, glowing with reflected light, were raptly focused on the moving images before them. He turned to Sara and Amy; they were the same.

On the screen, a heavyset man was speaking to the driver of the carriage, a burble of meaningless sounds. He returned to the first fellow, in the hat, his words amplified by the shouted recitation of the men:

'The driii-ver. He eez . . . afraid. Good fellow he eez. He wants me to ask if you can wait, and go on after sunrise.'

The first man waved his cane arrogantly, having none of it. 'Well, I'm sorry, but there's a carriage meeting me at Borgo Pass at midnight.'

'Borgo Pass? Whose carriage?'

'Why, Count Dracula's.'

The mustached man's eyes widened with terror. 'Count . . . *Dracula's*?'

'Don't do it, Renfield!' one of the soldiers yelled, and everybody laughed.

It was a story, Peter realized. A story, like the old books in the Sanctuary, the ones Teacher read to them in circle, all those years ago. The people on the screen looked like they were pretending because they were; their exaggerated motions and expressions called to mind the way Teacher would act out the voices of the characters in the books she read. The heavy man with the mustache knew something that the man in the hat did not; there was danger ahead.

Despite this warning, the traveler resumed his journey, to more mocking shouts from the soldiers. In darkness, the carriage ascended a mountain road, approaching a massive structure of turrets and walls, drenched in a forbidding moonlight. What lay ahead was obvious: the mustached man had more or less explained it. Vampires. An old word, but one Peter knew. He waited for the virals to appear, falling on the carriage and tearing the traveler to shreds, but this didn't happen. The carriage pulled through the gate; the man, Renfield, stepped out to find that he was alone; the driver was gone. A creaking door, opening of its own accord, beckoned him inside, where he found himself in a great ruined cave of a room. Renfield, unaware, his innocence almost laughable, backed toward a massive flight of stairs, where a figure in a dark cloak, holding a single candle, was descending. As the cloaked figure reached the bottom, Renfield turned, the whites of his eyes expanding with such horror it was as if he'd stumbled on a whole pod of smokes, not a single man in a cape.

'I am . . . *Drrrrrac-ulaaah.*'

Another tent-shaking detonation of whoops, whistles, cheers. One of the soldiers in the front row shot to his feet.

'Hey, Count, eat this!'

A flash of spinning steel through the stream of light from the projector: the tip of the blade met the wood of the screen with a meaty thunk, burying itself squarely in the chest of the caped man, who seemed, surprisingly, to take no notice of this.

'Muncey, what the fuck!' the projector operator yelled.

'Get your blade,' someone else shouted, 'it's in the way!'

But the voices weren't angry; everybody thought it was hilarious. Under a storm of catcalls, Muncey bounded to the screen, the images washing over him, to yank his blade free of the wood. He turned, grinning, and gave a little bow.

Despite it all – the chaotic interruptions, the laughter and mocking recitations of the soldiers, who anticipated every line – Peter soon found himself sliding into the story.

He sensed that some pieces of the film were missing; the narrative leapt ahead in confusing jerks, leaving the castle behind for a ship at sea, then for a place called London. A city, he realized. A city from the Time Before. The Count – some kind of viral, though he didn't look like one – was killing women. First a girl handing out flowers in the street, then a young woman asleep in her bed, with great sleepy curls of hair and a face so composed she looked like a doll. The Count's movements were comically slow, as were his victim's; everyone in the movie seemed trapped in a dream in which they couldn't make themselves move fast enough, or even at all. Dracula himself possessed a pale, almost womanly face, his lips painted to look bowed, like the wings of a bat; whenever he was about to bite someone, the screen would hold for a long, lingering moment on his eyes, which were lit from below to glow like twin candle flames.

Part of Peter knew it was all fake, nothing to take seriously, and yet as the story continued, he found himself worried for the girl, Mina, the daughter of the doctor – Dr Seward, owner of the sanatorium, whatever that was – and whose husband, the ineffectual Harker, seemed to have no idea how to help her, always standing around with his hands in his pockets, looking helpless and lost. None of them knew what to do, except for Van Helsing, the vampire hunter. He wasn't like any hunter Peter had ever seen – an old man with thick, distorting eyeglasses, given to vast, windy pronouncements that were the object of the soldiers' most outspoken mockery. 'Gentlemen, we are dealing with the unthinkable!' and 'The superstitions of tomorrow can become the scientific reality of today!' The catcalls flew each time, and yet a great deal of what Van Helsing said seemed true to Peter, especially the part about a vampire being 'a creature whose life has been unnaturally prolonged.' If that didn't describe a smoke, he didn't know what did. He found himself wondering if Van Helsing's trick with the jewelry-box mirror wasn't some version of what had happened with the pans in Las Vegas, and if, as Van Helsing claimed, a vampire 'must sleep each night in his native soil.' Was that why they always came home, the ones who'd been taken up? At times the movie seemed almost to be a kind of instruction manual. Peter wondered if it wasn't a made-up tale at all but an account of something that had actually happened.

The girl, Mina, was taken up; Harker and Van Helsing pursued the vampire to his lair, a dank basement. Peter realized where the story was headed: they were going to perform the Mercy. They were going to hunt down Mina and kill her, and it was Harker, Mina's husband, who would have to perform this terrible duty. Peter braced himself. The soldiers had finally grown quiet, their antics put aside as they were caught up, despite themselves, in the story's final, grim unfolding.

He never got to see the end. A single soldier dashed into the tent.

'Lights up! Extraction at the gate!'

The movie was instantly forgotten; all the soldiers bolted from their chairs. Weapons were coming out, pistols, rifles, blades. In the rush to get to the door, someone tripped over the projector's power cable, sinking the room into darkness. Everyone was pushing, shouting, calling out orders; Peter heard the pop of rifle fire from outside. As he followed the crowd from the tent, he saw a pair of flares rocketing over the walls toward the muddy field beyond the gate. Michael was running past him with Sancho; Peter seized him by the arm.

'What is it? What's happening?'

Michael barely broke his stride. 'It's Blue Squad!' he said. 'Come on!'

From the chaos of the mess hall had emerged a sudden orderliness; everyone knew what to do. The soldiers had broken into distinct groups, some quickly ascending the ladders to the catwalk at the tops of the pickets, others taking positions behind a barricade of sandbags just inside the gate. More men were swiveling the spotlights to aim them across the muddy field beyond the opening.

'Here they come!'

'Open it now!' Greer shouted from the base of the wall. 'Open the goddamn gate!'

A deafening barrage of cover fire from the catwalk as half a dozen soldiers leapt into the space over the yard, holding the ropes that connected through a system of pulleys and blocks to the gate's hinges. Peter was momentarily arrested by the coordinated grace of it all, the practiced beauty of their synchronized movements. As the soldiers descended, the gates began to part, revealing the light-bathed ground beyond the walls and a group of figures racing toward them. Alicia was leading the way. They hit the gate at a dead sprint, six of them, dropping and rolling in the dust as the men behind the sandbags opened fire, releasing a stream of rounds over their heads. If there were virals back there, Peter didn't see any. It was all too fast, too loud, and then, just like that, it was over: the gates were sealed behind them.

Peter ran to where Alicia lay with the others. She was on all fours in the dirt, breathing hard; the paint was dripping down her face, her bald head shining like polished metal under the harsh glare of the spotlights.

As she rocked back onto her knees, their eyes met quickly. 'Peter, get the hell out of here.'

From above, a few last halfhearted shots. The virals had scattered, retreating from the lights.

'I mean it,' she said fiercely. Every part of her seemed clenched. 'Go.'

Others were crowding around. 'Where's Raimey?' Vorhees bellowed, moving through the men. 'Where the hell's Raimey?'

'He's dead, sir.'

Vorhees turned to where Alicia was kneeling in the mud. When he saw Peter, his eyes flashed with anger. 'Jaxon, you don't belong here.'

'We found it, sir,' Alicia said. 'Stumbled right into it. A regular hornets' nest. There must be hundreds of them.'

Vorhees waved to Hollis and the others. 'All of you, back

832

to your quarters, *now*.' Without waiting for an answer, he turned back to Alicia. 'Private Donadio, report.'

'The mine, General,' she said. 'We found the mine.'

All that summer Vorhees's men had been looking for it: the entrance shaft to an old copper mine, hidden somewhere in the hills. It was thought that this was one of the hot spots Vorhees had spoken of, a nest where the virals slept. Using old geological survey maps and tracking the creatures' movements with the nets, they had narrowed their search to the southeast quadrant, an area of roughly twenty square kilometers above the river. Blue Squad's mission had been one last attempt to locate it before the evac. It was sheer chance that they had; as Peter heard the story from Michael, Blue Squad had simply wandered into it, just before sundown – a soft depression in the earth, into which the point man had vanished with a scream. The first viral who emerged took two more men before anyone could get off a shot. The rest of the squad was able to form some kind of firing line, but more virals swarmed out, braving the last of daylight in their blood fury; once the sun went down, the unit would be quickly overwhelmed, the location of the mine shaft lost with them. The flares they carried would buy them a few minutes, but that was all. They broke into two groups; the first would make a run for it while the second, led by Lieutenant Raimey, would cover their escape, holding the creatures off as long as they could, until the sun went down and all the flares were gone, and that would be the end of it.

All night long, the camp buzzed with activity. Peter could feel the change: the days of waiting, of hunt-and-peck missions in the forest, were over; Vorhees's men were preparing themselves for battle. Michael was gone, helping to ready the vehicles that would carry the explosives, drums of diesel fuel and ammonium nitrate with a grenade-cluster igniter, known as a 'flusher.' These would be lowered by winch straight into the exposed shaft. The explosion would no doubt kill many of the virals inside; the question was, where would the survivors emerge? In a hundred years the topography might have changed, and for all Vorhees and the others knew, a landslide or earthquake had opened an entirely new access point. While one squad put the explosives in place, the rest of the men would do their best to sniff out any other openings. With luck, everyone would be in position when the bomb went off.

The lights came down to a gray dawn. The temperature had dropped in the night, and all the puddles in the yard were encrusted with ice. The vehicles were being loaded; Vorhees's soldiers were assembled at the gate, all but a single squad, which would stay behind to man the garrison. Alicia had spent many of the intervening hours in Vorhees's tent. It was she who had led the survivors back to the garrison, using the route they had first traveled along the river. Now Peter saw her up front with the general, the two of them with a map spread over the hood of one of the Humvees. Greer, on horseback, was supervising the final loading of supplies. Watching from the sidelines, Peter felt a growing unease, but something else, too – a strong attractive force, instinctual as breathing. For days he had drifted between the poles of his uncertainty, knowing he should press on but unable to leave Alicia behind. Now, as he watched the soldiers completing their preparations at the gate, Alicia among them, a single desire pushed itself forward. Vorhees's men were going to war; he wanted to be part of it.

As Greer moved down the line, Peter stepped forward. 'Major, I'd like to speak with you.'

Greer's face and voice were distracted, hasty. He looked over Peter's head as he spoke: 'What is it, Jaxon?'

'I'd like to go, sir.'

Greer regarded him a moment. 'We can't take civilians.'

'Just put me at the rear. There must be something I can do. I can, I don't know, be a runner or something.'

Greer's focus shifted to the back of one of the trucks, where a group of four men, including Michael, were winching the drums of fuel into place over the tailgate.

'Sergeant,' Greer barked to the squad sergeant, a man named Withers, 'can you take over for me here? And Sancho, watch that chain – it's all wrapped up.'

'Yes, sir. Sorry, sir.'

'These are *bombs*, son. For Christsakes, be careful.' Then, to Peter: 'Come with me.'

The major dismounted and took Peter aside, out of earshot. 'I know you're worried about her,' he said. 'Okay? I get it. If it were up to me, I'd probably let you come.'

'Maybe if we talked to the general—'

'That's not going to happen. I'm sorry.' A curious expression came into Greer's face, a flickering indecision. 'Look. What you told me about the girl, Amy. You should know something.' He shook his head, glancing away. 'I can't believe I'm about to tell you this. Maybe I really have been out in these woods too long. What's that thing called? When you think something's happened before, like you dreamed it. There's a name for it.'

'Sir?'

Greer still wasn't looking at him. 'Déjà vu. That's it. I've been feeling that way since I first found you guys. A big bad case of déjà vu. I know it doesn't look like it now, but when I was a kid, I was a scrawny little thing, sick all the time. My parents died when I was small, I never even really met them, so probably it was just the orphanage where I was raised, fifty kids all crammed together, all that snot and dirty hands. You name it, I caught it. About a dozen times the sisters were ready to write me off. Fever dreams like you wouldn't believe, too. Nothing I could really describe, or even remember. Just the feeling of it, like being lost in the dark for a thousand years. But the thing was, I wasn't alone. That was part of the dream, too. I hadn't thought about it for a long time, not until you all showed up. That girl. Those eyes of hers. You think I didn't notice that? Jesus, it's like I'm right back there, six years old and sweating my brains out with fever. I'm telling you, she was the one. I know it sounds crazy. She was in the dream with me.'

An expectant silence hung around his final words. Peter felt a shiver of recognition.

'Did you tell Vorhees this?'

'Are you kidding? What would I say? Hell, son, I'm not even telling *you*.'

To show Peter that the conversation was over, Greer took his mount by the reins and swung back up into the saddle. 'That's all. But you ask me why you can't go, there's my answer. We don't come back, Red Squad has orders to evacuate you down to Roswell. That's *official*. Unofficially, I will tell you they won't stop you if you decide to press on.'

He heeled his mount to take his place at the head of the line. A roar of engines; the gates swung open. Peter watched as the men, five squads plus the horses and vehicles, moved slowly through. Alicia was somewhere in there, Peter thought, probably up front with Vorhees. But he couldn't find her anywhere.

The line had long since passed when Michael came up beside him.

'He didn't let you go, huh?'

Peter could only shake his head.

'Me neither,' said Michael.

SIXTY-ONE

They waited, through that day and into the next. With just a single squad remaining to man the walls, the camp felt strange, empty and alone. Amy and Sara were now free to move through the garrison as they wished, but there was nowhere to go, nothing to do but wait. Amy had lapsed into a silence so profound that Peter had begun to wonder if he had dreamed her voice in the first place; all day long she sat on her bunk in her tent, her eyes drawn into an intense look of concentration. When Peter could stand it no longer, he asked her if she knew what was happening out there.

Her voice when she answered was vague; she seemed to be looking at him and also not. 'They're lost. Lost in the woods.'

'Who is, Amy? Who's lost?'

She seemed to discover him only then, to enter into the present moment and its circumstances. 'Will we be leaving soon, Peter?' she asked again. 'Because I would like to leave soon.' An airy smile. 'To make the snow angels.'

It was more than puzzling; it was maddening. For the first time, Peter actually felt anger at her. Never had he felt so helpless, pinned in place by his own hesitancy and the delay it had created. They should have departed days ago; now they were trapped. To leave without knowing if Alicia was safe was simply impossible for him. He stormed from the women's tent and resumed his haunted walks around the compound, filling the useless hours. He made no effort even to speak with the others, keeping his distance. The sky was clear, but to the east, the peaks of the mountains glinted with ice. It had begun to seem possible they would never leave the garrison at all.

Then, on the morning of the third day, they heard it: the sound of engines. Peter raced to the ladder and ascended to the catwalk, where the squad commander, whose name was Eustace, was looking south through a pair of binoculars. Eustace alone had deigned to talk to any of them, though he kept such exchanges brief and to the point.

'It's them,' Eustace said. 'Some of them, anyway.'

'How many?' Peter asked.

'Looks like two squads.'

The men who moved through the gate were filthy, exhausted; everything about them spoke of defeat. Alicia was nowhere among them. At the rear of the line, still on horseback, was Major Greer. Hollis and Michael had come running from their tent. Greer dismounted, looking dazed, and took a long drink of water before speaking.

'Are we the first?' he asked Peter. He seemed to not quite know where he was.

'Where's Alicia?' Peter demanded.

'Christ, what a mess. The whole fucking hillside caved in. They came at us from everywhere. We were totally flanked.'

Peter could contain himself no longer. He grabbed Greer roughly by the shoulders, forcing the major to look him in the eye. 'Goddamnit, tell me where she is!'

Greer made no resistance. 'I don't know, Peter. I'm sorry. Everybody got split up in the dark. She was with Vorhees. We waited a day at the fallback point, but they never showed.'

More waiting; it was unbearable, infuriating. Peter had never felt so powerless. A short time later, a cry went up from the wall.

'Two more squads!'

Peter was sitting in the mess hall in a haze of worry. He dashed outside, arriving at the gate as the first truck pulled into the compound. It was the one that had carried the explosives; the winch was still attached to the bed, the empty hook swinging. Twenty-four men, three squads reconstituted as two. Peter searched for Alicia among their benumbed faces.

'Private Donadio! Does anyone know what happened to Private Donadio!'

No one did. Everyone told the same story: the bomb exploding, the ground tearing open beneath them, the virals pouring forth, everyone scattering, lost in the dark.

Someone claimed they'd seen Vorhees die, others that he was with Blue Squad. But no one had seen Alicia.

The day dragged on. Peter paced the parade ground, talking to no one. As senior officer, Greer was now in charge. He spoke briefly to Peter, telling him not to abandon hope. The general knew what he was doing; if anyone could bring his unit back alive, it was Curtis Vorhees. But Peter could see in Greer's face that he, too, had begun to believe that no one else was coming back.

His hopes ended with the fall of darkness. He returned to

the tent, where Hollis and Michael were playing hands of go-to. Both glanced up as he entered.

'Just keeping busy,' Hollis said.

'I didn't say anything.'

Peter lay down on his bunk and drew a blanket over himself, not even bothering to remove his muddy boots. He was filthy, wrung out with fatigue; the last, unreal hours seemed to have transpired in a kind of trance. He had barely eaten for days, but the thought of food was impossible. A cold wind – a winter wind – was shaking the walls of the tent. His last thoughts before he slept were of Alicia's final words to him: *Get the hell out of here.*

He was awakened by a distant cry that sent him lurching upright. Hollis's face ducked through the flap of the tent.

'Someone's at the gate.'

He threw the blanket aside and tore outside, into the glare of the spotlights. His doubts turned to certainty, and by the time he was halfway across the parade ground he knew what was waiting for him.

Alicia. Alicia had come back.

She was standing at the gate. His first impression, as he moved toward her, was that she was alone. But as he pushed his way through the gathering men, he saw a second soldier, kneeling on the dirt. It was Muncey. His wrists were bound before him. Under the blaze of the spotlights, Peter could see that his face was glazed with sweat. He was shivering, but not from the cold; one of his hands was wrapped in a rag sodden with blood.

The two were surrounded by soldiers now, everyone keeping their distance. A reverential hush had descended. Greer stepped forward to Alicia.

'The general?'

She shook her head: no.

The private was holding his bloody hand away from his body, breathing rapidly. Greer crouched before him. 'Corporal Muncey.' His voice was quiet, soothing.

'Yes, sir.' Muncey licked his lips with a slow tongue. 'Sorry, sir.'

'It's all right, son. You've done well.'

'Don't know how I missed the one that did it. Chewed me like a dog before Donadio got him.' He raised his head toward Alicia. 'You wouldn't know she was a girl from the way she fights. Hope you don't mind I asked her to truss me up and bring me home.'

'That's your perfect right, Muncey. That's your right as a soldier of the Expeditionary.'

Muncey's body shook then, a series of three hard spasms. His lips curled away, showing the gaps in his teeth. Peter felt the soldiers tense; all around him, hands dropped to their blades, a quick, unconscious movement. But Greer, crouched before the ailing soldier, didn't flinch.

'Well, I guess that's it now,' Muncey said when the spasms had passed. Peter could find no fear anywhere in the soldier's eyes, only a calm acceptance. All the color had seeped from his face, like water down a drain. He lifted his bound hands to wipe the sweat from his brow with the bloody rag. 'It's like they say, the way it comes on. If it's no trouble, I'd like it on the blade, Major. I want to feel it coming out of me.'

Greer nodded his approval. 'Good man, Muncey.'

'Donadio should be the one to do it, if that's all right. My mama always said you should dance with the one who brung you, and she was kind enough to bring me back. She didn't have to do that.' His eyes were blinking now, the sweat was pouring down. 'I just wanted to say it's been an honor, sir. The general, too. I wanted to come home to say that. But I think you better step to it, Major.'

Greer rose to his feet and backed away. Everyone snapped to attention. He raised his voice to all of them:

'This man is a soldier of the Expeditionary! It is time for him to take the trip! All hail, Corporal Muncey. Hip hip . . .'

'Hooray!'

'Hip hip—'

'Hooray!'

'Hip hip—'

'Hooray!'

Greer drew his blade and passed it to Alicia. Her face was composed, lacking all emotion: a soldier's face, a face of duty. She gripped the blade in her fist and knelt before Muncey, who had bowed his head now, waiting, his bound hands slack in his lap. Alicia bent her head toward Muncey's until their foreheads were touching. Peter saw that her lips were moving, murmuring quiet words to him. He felt no horror, only a sense of astonishment. The moment seemed frozen, not part of a flow of events but something fixed and singular – a line that, once crossed, could never be uncrossed. That Muncey would die was only a part of its meaning.

The knife did its work almost before Peter realized what had happened; when Alicia dropped her hand, it was buried to the hilt in Muncey's chest. His eyes were open, wide and damp, his lips parted. Alicia was holding his face now, tenderly, like a mother with her child. 'Go easy now, Muncey,' she said. 'Go easy.' A bit of blood had risen to his lips. He breathed once more, holding the air in his chest, as if it were not air but something far more – a sweet taste of freedom, of all cares lifted, everything over and done. Then his life left him and he slumped forward, Alicia receiving him in her arms to ease his body's passage to the muddy ground of the garrison.

Peter did not see her all through the next day and then the day after. He thought of sending her a message through Greer, but he didn't know what to say. In his heart he knew the truth: Alicia was gone. She had slipped into a life he had no part of.

They'd lost a total of forty-six men, including General Vorhees. It stood to reason that some were not dead but had been taken up; the talk among the men was of sending out search parties. But Greer said no. The window for their departure was closing, if they were going to make their rendezvous with Third Battalion. Seventy-two hours, he announced, and that would be the end of it.

By the end of the second day, the camp was nearly buttoned up. Food, weapons, gear, most of the larger tents except the mess – all were packed and ready to go. The lights would remain, as would the large fuel tankers, now mostly empty, and a single Humvee. The battalion would be traveling south in two groups: a small scouting party on horseback, led by Alicia, with the rest following in the trucks and on foot. Alicia was now an officer; with so many men lost, including all but two squad leaders, the ranks had thinned, and Greer had given her a battlefield commission. She was now Lieutenant Donadio.

Greer had lifted the order to keep Sara and Amy segregated; a body was a body, he said, no reason at this point to split hairs. A lot of men had been injured in the raid; mostly small things, cuts and scratches and sprains, but one soldier had a broken collarbone, and two more, Sancho and Withers, had been badly burned in the detonation. The battalion's two medical corpsmen had been killed, so with Amy helping her, Sara had taken over caring for the wounded, preparing them as best she could for the trip south. Peter and Hollis had been assigned to the packing crews, whose job was to sort through the contents of two large supply tents, culling what would travel with them and moving the rest to storage in a series of dugouts spread through the compound. Michael had more or less disappeared into the motor pool; he slept in the barracks, took his meals elbow to elbow with the other oilers. Even his name was gone, replaced by Lugnut.

Over everything, the question of the evacuation hung like a blade. Peter had yet to give Greer his answer, because the truth was, he didn't know. The others – Sara and Hollis and Michael and even Amy, in her quiet, inward way – were all waiting, giving him the space to decide. That they said nothing on the subject made this fact all the more obvious. Or maybe they were simply avoiding him, for all he knew. Either way, leaving the safety of the garrison now seemed more perilous than ever. Greer had cautioned him that with the mine disturbed, the woods would be crawling; perhaps, he suggested, it would be best to wait until they returned next summer. He'd talk to Division, persuade them to mount a proper expedition. Whatever's up that mountain, Greer said, it's been there a long time. Surely it can wait another year.

The evening of the second day after Alicia's return, Peter came into his tent to find Hollis alone, sitting on his cot. A winter parka was draped over his shoulders; he was holding a guitar in his lap.

'Where'd you find that?'

Hollis was idly plucking notes, his face drawn in concentration. He looked up and gave a smile through his heavy beard, which by now climbed halfway up his cheeks. 'One of the oilers had it. Friend of Michael's.' He blew on his hands and plucked a few more notes, nibbling around the edges of a melody that Peter couldn't quite discern. 'It's been so long I thought I'd forgotten how to play.'

'I didn't know you could.'

'I can't, not really. Arlo was always the one.'

Peter sat on the bunk across from him. 'Go on. Play something.'

'I don't remember much. Just a song or two.'

'Then play that. Play anything.'

Hollis shrugged; but Peter could tell he was happy to be asked. 'Don't say I didn't warn you.'

Hollis did something with the strings, tightening and testing, then began. It took Peter a moment to realize what he was hearing: one of Arlo's funny, made-up songs, the ones he used to play for the Littles in the Sanctuary, yet different somehow. The same but not the same. Under Hollis's fingers, it was deeper and richer, full of an aching sadness. Peter lay back on his cot and let the notes wash over him. Even when the song had ended, he could still feel it inside him, like an echo of longing in his chest.

'It's all right,' he said. He took a deep breath, fixing his eyes on the tent's sagging ceiling. 'You and Sara should take

that convoy. Michael, too. I doubt she'll go without him.'
When Hollis said nothing, Peter rose on his elbows and faced
his friend. 'It's okay, Hollis. I mean it. That's what I want you
to do.'

'It's what Vorhees said, when we first got here. About his
men, the oath they take. He was right. I'm no good for this
anymore, if I ever was. I really love her, Peter.'

'You don't have to explain. I'm glad for you both. I'm glad
you have this chance.'

'What will you do?' Hollis asked.

The answer was obvious. Still, it needed to be said. 'What
we came to do.'

It was strange. Peter felt sad, but something else as well. He
felt at peace. The decision was behind him now; he was free
of it. He wondered if this was how his father had felt the
night before his final ride. Watching the ceiling of the tent
shaking in the wintry wind, Peter recalled Theo's words that
night in the power station, all of them sitting around the
table in the control room, drinking shine. *Our father didn't go
out there to let it go. Whoever thinks so doesn't understand the
first thing about him. He went out there because he just couldn't
stand not knowing, not for one more minute of his life.* It was the
peace of truth that Peter felt, and he was glad for it, down to
his bones.

Beyond the walls of the tent, Peter could hear the roar of
the generators, the calls of Greer's men on the pickets, standing the watch. One more night and all would be silent.

'There's not any way I can talk you out of this, is there?'
Hollis asked.

Peter shook his head. 'Just do me a favor.'

'Whatever you want.'

'Don't follow me.'

He found the major in the tent that once had been Vorhees's.
Peter and Greer had barely spoken since Alicia's return; a
heaviness seemed to have come over the major since the
abortive raid, and Peter had kept his distance. It was more

than the burden of command that was weighing on him, Peter knew. In those long hours he had spent with the two men, Peter had seen the depth of their bond. It was grief Greer was feeling now, grief for his lost friend.

A lamp was glowing in the tent.

'Major Greer?'

'Enter.'

Peter stepped through the flap. The room was blazing with warmth from the woodstove; the major, wearing his camo pants and an olive-drab T-shirt, was sitting at Vorhees's desk, sorting through papers by lantern light. An open locker, half full of various belongings, rested on the floor at his feet.

'Jaxon. I was wondering when I'd hear from you.' Greer leaned back in his chair and rubbed his eyes wearily. 'Come here and look at this.'

A pile of loose papers lay on the desk. On the top was a sheet bearing the image of three figures, a woman and two young girls. The image was so precisely rendered that Peter thought at first he was looking at a photograph, something from the Time Before. But then he realized that it was a drawing, rendered in charcoal. A portrait, done from the waist up; the bottom seemed to fade away, into nothing. The woman was holding the smaller girl, who couldn't have been older than three, with a soft, baby-cheeked face, in her lap; the other, just a couple of years older than her sister, stood behind the two of them, over the woman's left shoulder. Greer pulled more pages from the pile: the same three figures, in an identical pose.

'Vorhees did these?'

Greer nodded. 'Curt wasn't a lifer, like most of us. He had a whole life before the Expeditionary, a wife, two little girls. He was a farmer, if you can believe that.'

'What happened to them?'

Greer answered with a shrug. 'What always happens, when it happens.'

Peter bent to examine the drawings again. He could feel the painstaking care of their creation, the force of concentration that lay behind each detail. The woman's wry smile; the younger girl's eyes, wide and refractive like her mother's; the lift of the older one's hair, caught on a sudden breeze. A bit of gray dust still floated on the surface of the paper, like ashes, pushed on this remembered wind.

'I guess he drew all these so he wouldn't forget them,' Greer said.

Peter felt suddenly self-conscious – whatever these images had meant to the general, Peter knew they were private. 'If you don't mind my asking, Major, why are you showing these to me?'

Greer gathered them carefully together in a cardboard folder and placed them in the trunk at his feet. 'Someone once told me that part of you lives on so long as somebody remembers you. Now you remember them, too.' He sealed the locker with a key he took from around his neck and leaned back in his chair. 'But that's not why you came to see me, is it? You've made your decision.'

'Yes, sir. I'll be leaving in the morning.'

'Well.' A thoughtful nod, of something expected. 'All five, or just you?'

'Hollis and Sara are going with the evac. Michael, too, though he may not know that yet.'

'So, the two of you, then. You and the mystery girl.'

'Amy.'

Greer nodded again. 'Amy.' Peter waited for Greer to try to talk him out of it, but instead he said, 'Take my mount. He's a good horse, he won't let you down. I'll leave word at the gate to let you pass. You need weapons?'

'Whatever you can spare.'

'I'll leave that too, then.'

'I appreciate that, sir. Thank you for everything.'

'Seems the least I can do.' Greer regarded his hands where they were folded in his lap. 'You know it's probably suicide, don't you? Going up that mountain alone like that. I have to say it.'

'Maybe so. But it's the best idea I've got.'

A moment of silent acknowledgment passed between them. Peter thought how he would miss Greer, his calm, steadfast presence.

'Well, this is goodbye then.' Greer rose and offered his hand to shake. 'Look me up if you're ever in Kerrville. I want to know how it ends.'

'How what ends?'

The major smiled, his big hand still wrapped around Peter's. 'The dream, Peter.'

A light was burning inside the barracks; Peter could hear murmuring behind the canvas walls. There was no proper door, no way to knock. But as he approached, a soldier appeared through the flap, drawing his parka around him. The one they called Wilco; he was one of the oilers.

'Jaxon.' He gave a startled look. 'If you're looking for Lugnut, he's with some of the other guys, moving the last of the fuel off the tanker. I was just going over there.'

'I'm looking for Lish.' When Wilco met this request with an empty stare, Peter clarified. 'Lieutenant Donadio.'

'I'm not sure—'

'Just tell her I'm here.'

Wilco shrugged and ducked back through the flap. Peter strained his ears to hear what, if anything, was being said inside. But all the voices had gone suddenly silent. He waited, long enough to wonder if Alicia would simply fail to appear. But then the flap drew aside and she stepped through.

It would not have been quite true, Peter thought, to say that she looked changed; she simply *was* changed. The woman who stood before him was both the same Alicia he had always known and someone entirely new. Her arms were crossed over her chest; on her upper body she was wearing nothing more than a T-shirt, despite the cold. A bit of her hair had grown back over the days, a ghostly scrim that clung to her scalp like a glowing cap under the lights. But it wasn't any of these things that made the moment strange. It was the way she stood, holding herself apart from him.

'I heard about your promotion,' he said. 'Congratulations.'

Alicia said nothing.

'Lish—'

'You shouldn't be here, Peter. I shouldn't be talking to you.'

'I just came to tell you that I understand. For a while I didn't. But I do now.'

'Well.' She paused, hugging herself in the cold. 'What changed your mind?'

He didn't know quite what to say. Everything he'd meant to tell her seemed to have abruptly fled from his mind. Muncey's death had something to do with it, and his father, and Amy. But the real reason wasn't anything he possessed the words for.

He said the only thing he could think of. 'Hollis's guitar, actually.'

Alicia gave him a blank look. 'Hollis has a guitar?'

'One of the soldiers gave it to him.' Peter stopped; there was no way to explain. 'I'm sorry. I'm not making much sense.'

A space seemed to have opened in Peter's chest, and he realized what it was; it was the pain of missing someone he had not yet left.

'Well, thank you for telling me. But I really have to get back inside.'

'Lish, wait.'

She turned to face him again, her eyebrows raised.

'Why didn't you ever tell me? About the Colonel.'

'Is that why you came here? To ask me about the Colonel?' She sighed, looking away; it wasn't anything she wanted to discuss. 'Because he didn't want anyone to know. About who he was.'

'But why wouldn't he?'

'What would he have said, Peter? He was all alone. He'd lost all his men. As far as he was concerned, he should have died with them.' She paused to breathe. 'As for the rest, I think he raised me the only way he knew how. For a long time, I thought it was fun, to tell you the truth. Stories about brave men crossing the Darklands to fight and die. Taking the oath, a bunch of mumbo jumbo that meant nothing to me, just words. Then I was angry. I was eight, Peter. Eight years old, and he took me outside the walls, underneath the power trunk, and left me there. At night, with nothing, not even a blade. You haven't heard about that part.'

'Flyers, Lish. What happened?'

'Nothing. I'd be dead if it had. I just sat under a tree and cried all night. To this day I don't know if he was testing my courage or my luck.'

Part of the story seemed missing. 'He must have been out there with you. Watching you.'

'Maybe.' She angled her face to the wintry sky. 'Sometimes I think he was, sometimes I don't. You didn't know him like I did. I hated him after that, for the longest time. Really and truly hated him. But you can only hate somebody for so long.' She breathed again – deeply, resignedly. 'I hope that's true for you, Peter. That someday you can find it in your heart to forgive me.' She sniffed and wiped her eyes. 'That's all. I've said too much as it is. I'm just glad I had you as long as I did.'

He looked at her, her stricken face, and he knew.

The Colonel wasn't the real secret. He was. He was the secret she had kept. That they had kept from each other, even from themselves.

He reached for her. 'Alicia, listen—'

'Don't do this. Don't.' And yet she did not back away.

'Those three days, when I thought you'd die and I wouldn't be there.' A fist-sized lump had formed in his throat. 'I always thought I'd be there.'

'Peter, goddamnit.' She was trembling; he felt the weight of her struggle. 'You can't do this now. It's too late, Peter. It's too late.'

'I know.'

'Don't say it. Please. You said you understood.'

He did; he understood. All that they were to each other seemed cradled within this simple fact. He felt no surprise or even regret but, rather, a deep and sudden gratitude and, with it, a force of clarity, filling him like a breath of winter air. He wondered what this feeling was and then he knew. He was giving her up.

She let him put his arms around her then, pulling her into the open flaps of his jacket. He held her, as she had held him, all those days ago in Vorhees's tent. The same goodbye reversed. He felt her stiffen and then relax against him, becoming smaller in his embrace.

'You're leaving,' she said.

'I need you to promise me something. Keep the others safe. Get them to Roswell.'

A faint but discernible nod against his chest. 'What about you?'

How he loved her. And yet the words themselves could never be spoken. Holding her in his arms, he closed his eyes and tried to inscribe the feeling of her into his mind, into memory, so that he could take this with him.

'I think you've looked after me long enough, don't you?' He pulled away to see her face a final time. 'That's all,' he said. 'I just wanted to thank you.'

And then he turned and walked away, leaving her standing alone in the icy wind outside the silent barracks.

He did his best to sleep, turning restlessly through the night, and in the last hour before dawn, when he could wait no more, rose and quickly packed his gear. It was the cold he was thinking of; they would need blankets, extra socks, anything that could keep them warm and dry. Sleeping sacks and ponchos and a tarp with a good sturdy rope. The night before, on his way back from the barracks, he had ducked into the supply tent and pilfered an entrenching tool and a hand axe, and a pair of heavy parkas. Hollis was softly snoring on his cot, a bearded face buried in blankets, oblivious. When he awoke, Peter would be gone.

He hoisted the pack to his shoulder and stepped outside, into a cold so sharp it stunned him, sucking the air from his lungs. The garrison was quiet, just a few men moving about; the smells of wood smoke and warm food reached him from the mess, making his stomach rumble. But there was no time for that. In the women's tent he found Amy sitting on her bunk, her small pack resting on her lap. He'd told her nothing. She was alone; Sara was still with Sancho and the others, in the infirmary.

'Is it time?' she asked him. Her eyes were very bright.

'Yes, it's time.'

They crossed together to the paddock. Greer's horse, a large black gelding, his coat heavy for winter, was grazing with the others, noses angled to the wind. Peter retrieved a bridle from the shed and led him to the fence. He wished he could use a saddle, but it wouldn't work with two. He lashed their packs together, draping them over the animal's withers. His fingers were already stiff with the cold. He lifted Amy up, then used the fence to climb aboard. They rode around the edge of the paddock to the shadows under the pickets, headed for the gate. Dawn was just breaking, a gray softening, as if the darkness were not lifting but dissolving; a pale, almost invisible snow had begun to fall, flakes that seemed to materialize in the air before their faces.

They were met at the gate by a single sentry: Eustace, the lieutenant who had first alerted Peter to the raiding party's return.

'Major says to let you pass. He also asked me to give you this.' Eustace dragged a duffel bag from the sentry hut and lay it on the ground before the horse. 'Says to take whatever you need.'

Peter swung down and knelt to open it. Rifles, magazines, a couple of pistols, a belt of grenades. Peter looked through all of it, thinking about what to do.

'Thanks anyway,' he said, drawing upright. He drew his

blade from his belt and held it out for Eustace to take. 'Here. A present for the major.'

Eustace frowned. 'I don't get it. You want to give me your blade?'

Peter pushed it toward him. 'Take it,' he said.

Reluctantly, Eustace accepted the blade. For a moment he just looked at it, as if it were some strange artifact he'd found in the forest.

'Give it to Major Greer,' Peter said. 'I think he'll understand.'

He turned to address Amy, sitting high above him. She had tipped her chin upward to the falling snow.

'Ready?'

The girl nodded. A faint smile shone on her face; flakes had caught on her lashes, in her hair, like jeweled dust. Eustace gave Peter a leg up; he swung onto the horse's back, taking the reins in his hand. The gate drew open before them. He allowed himself one last look toward the barracks, but all was quiet, unchanged. Goodbye, he thought, goodbye. Then he heeled his mount and they rode out, into the breaking day.

X

THE ANGEL
OF THE
MOUNTAIN

Like to a Hermite poore in place obscure,
I meane to spend my daies of endles doubt,
To waile such woes as time cannot recure,
Where none but Loue shall euer finde me out.

– SIR WALTER RALEIGH,
from *The Phoenix Nest*

SIXTY-TWO

By half-day they had found the river again. They rode in silence under the snow, which was falling steadily now, filling the woods with a muffling light. The river had begun to freeze at its edges, dark water flowing freely in its narrowed channel, oblivious. Amy, leaning against Peter's back, her pale wrists slack in his lap, had fallen asleep. He felt the warmth of her body, the slow rise and fall of her chest against him. Plumes of warm vapor flowed back from the horse's nostrils, smelling of grass and earth. There were birds in the trees, black birds; they called to one another from the branches, their voices dimmed by the smothering snow.

As he rode, memories came to him, a disordered assemblage of images that drifted across his consciousness like smoke: his mother, on a day not long before the end, as he stood in the door to her room to watch her sleep, and saw her glasses sitting on the table, and knew that she would die; Theo at the station, when he'd sat on the cot to take Peter's foot in his hand, and again, standing on the porch of the farmstead, Mausami at his side, watching them leave; Auntie in her overheated kitchen, and the taste of her terrible tea; the last night at the bunker, everyone drinking whiskey and laughing at something funny Caleb had done or said, the great unknown unfolding before them; Sara on the morning after the first snowfall, sitting against the log, her book in her lap, her face bathed in sunlight and her voice saying, 'How beautiful it is here'; Alicia.

Alicia.

They turned east. They were in a new place now, the landscape rising ruggedly around them, wrapping them in the forested embrace of the mountains, mantled in white. The snow eased, then stopped, then started up once more.

They had begun to climb. Peter's attention had narrowed to the smallest things. The slow, rhythmic progress of the horse, the feel of worn leather in his fist where he held the animal's reins, the gentle brush of Amy's hair on his neck. All somehow inevitable, like details from a dream he'd had once, years ago.

When darkness came on, Peter used the shovel to clear a spot and pitched their tarp at the edge of the river. Most of the wood on the ground was too wet to burn, but beneath the heavy canopy of trees they found enough dry kindling to get a fire going. Peter had no blade, but in his pack was a small pocketknife that he could use to open the cans. They ate their dinner and slept, huddled together for warmth.

They awoke to bone-numbing cold. The storm had passed, leaving, in its wake, a sky of fierce cold blueness. While Amy built a fire, Peter went to look for the horse, which had broken loose and wandered away in the night – a situation that under different circumstances would have brought him to outright panic and yet somehow, on this morning, did not alarm him. He tracked the animal a hundred meters downstream, where he found him nibbling on some grassy shoots at the river's edge, his great black muzzle bearded with snow. It did not seem like the kind of thing Peter ought to disturb, so he stood awhile, watching the horse eat its breakfast, before leading him back to camp, where Amy's efforts had produced a small, smoky fire of damp needles and crackling twigs. They ate from more cans and drank cold water from the river, then warmed themselves together by the fire, taking their time. It would be their last morning, he knew. To the west, behind them, the garrison would be empty and silent now, all the soldiers moving south.

'I think this is it,' he told Amy as he was tying the bags onto the horse. 'I don't think we have more than ten kilometers to go.'

The girl said nothing, merely nodded. Peter led the horse to a fallen log, a great sodden thing at least a meter high, and used this to step up. He got himself situated, pulling the packs tight against him, and reached out to pull her aboard.

'Do you miss them?' Amy asked. 'Your friends.'

He lifted his face toward the snowy trees. The morning air was calm and sunlit.

'Yes. But it's all right.'

They came, sometime later, to a fork. For a period of some hours they had been following a road, or what had once been a road. Beneath the snow, the ground was firm and even, the route marked here and there by a rusted sign or a weather-beaten guardrail. They were moving deeper into a narrowing valley, walled cliffs rising on either side, showing their rocky faces. That was when they came to the place where the road split in two directions: straight, along the river, or across it on a bridge, an arched span of exposed girders, covered with snow. On the opposite side, the roadway rose again and angled into the trees, away.

'Which direction?' he asked her.

A silent moment passed. 'Across,' she said.

They dismounted. The snow was deep, a loose powder that rose nearly to the tops of Peter's boots. As they approached the riverbank, Peter saw that the connecting roadway was gone; the bridge's decking, which had probably once been wood, was all rotted away. Fifty meters: they could probably manage it, balancing on the exposed beams, but the horse would never make it.

'You're sure?' She was standing beside him, squinting intently in the light. Her hands, like his own, were drawn up protectively into the sleeves of her coat.

She nodded.

He returned to the horse to unhitch their packs. There was no question of leaving Greer's horse tied up to wait for them. It had brought them this far; Peter couldn't leave it defenseless. He finished unloading their gear, unhitched the bridle, and stepped to the animal's hindquarters. 'Ha!' he yelled, giving the animal a firm slap on its haunches. Nothing. He tried again, louder this time. '*Ha!*' He slapped and yelled and waved his arms. '*Go on! Git!*' Still the animal refused to budge, gazing at them impassively with his huge, gleaming eyes.

'He's a stubborn son of a bitch. I guess he doesn't want to leave.'

'Just tell him what you want him to do.'

'He's a horse, Amy.'

And yet what happened next, strange as it was, did not feel wholly unexpected. Amy took the animal's face in her hands, placing her palms against the side of his long head. The horse, which had begun to fidget, quieted under her touch; his wide nostrils flared with a heavy sigh. For a long, hushed moment, girl and horse stood there, locked in some deep and mutual regard. Then the animal broke away, turned in a wide circle, and began to walk in the direction they had come. His pace quickened to a trot as he vanished in the trees.

Amy lifted her pack off the snow and hoisted it to her shoulders. 'We can go now.'

Peter didn't know what to say; there was no reason to say anything.

They clambered down the embankment to the river's edge. The reflected sunlight dancing on the surface of the water was almost explosively brilliant, as if, on the edge of freezing solid, its reflective powers had been magnified. Peter sent Amy up first, giving her a knee to send her through a hatchlike opening in the exposed beams. Once she was situated he passed her the packs, then chinned himself up.

The safest route would be along the edge of the bridge, where they could hold onto the guardrail as they stepped from beam to beam. The feel of the cold metal on his hands was like fire, an exquisite sharpness. They couldn't get this done fast enough. Amy went first, skipping with confident grace over the gaps. As he made to follow her, it became instantly clear that the problem wasn't the beams themselves, which seemed solid, but what encased them, under the snow: a hidden skin of ice. Twice Peter felt himself losing traction, his feet slipping out from under him, his hand biting into the frigid rail, barely holding on. But to come this far, only to drown in an icy river – he couldn't imagine it. Slowly, beam by beam, he made his way across. By the time he reached the far side, Peter's hands felt utterly numb; he had begun to shiver. He wished they could stop to build a fire, but there was no delaying their progress now. Already the shadows had begun to lengthen; the brief winter day would soon be over.

They ascended the bank of the river and began to climb. Wherever they were going, he hoped there would be shelter. He didn't see how they would last the night without it. Never mind the virals; cold like this could kill them just as easily. The important thing was to keep moving. Amy had taken the lead, her strides carrying her up the mountain. It was all Peter could do to keep up. The air felt thin in his lungs; around him the trees were moaning in the wind. After a period of time had passed he looked back and beheld the valley far below them, the river curling through it. They were in shadow now, a zone of twilight, but on the far side of the valley, the faces of the mountains, receding to the north and east, thrummed with golden light. The top of the world, Peter thought, that's where Amy is taking me. The very top of the world.

The day drained away. In the descending gloom, the landscape appeared as a confusing jumble; what Peter had thought would be the apex of their climb revealed itself to be a crest in a series of ascents, each more exposed and windblasted than the last. To the west the mountain fell away sharply, an almost sheer drop. The cold seemed to have reached some deeper place inside him, dulling his senses. It had been a mistake, he realized, to send the horse away. If push came to shove, they could at least have hiked back down and used his body for warmth and shelter. It was a grave thing, to kill such an animal, nothing he could have imagined doing before; but now, as darkness was falling on the mountain, he knew he could have done it.

He realized Amy had come to a stop. He struggled forward

and halted at her side, breathing great gulps of air. The snow was thinner here, pushed away by the wind. She was scanning the sky, her eyes narrowed, as if she were listening to some distant sound. Beads of ice clung to her pack, her hair.

'What is it?'

Her gaze settled on the line of trees to their left, away from the open valley.

'There,' she said.

But there was nothing, only the wall of trees. The trees and the snow and the indifferent wind.

Then he saw it: a gap in the undergrowth. Amy was already moving toward it. As they neared, he realized what he was seeing: the gate of a half-fallen fence. It ran the length of the woods on either side of them, entwined with a dense mass of camouflaging vines, now denuded of leaves and covered in snow, making the fence all but invisible, a part of the landscape. Who knew how long they had been walking along it without his noticing. Beyond the opening stood a small hut, more suggestion than actual structure. The building, not more than five meters square, seemed tipped, one part of its foundation having collapsed beneath it; the door stood half open, angled on its hinges. He peered inside. Nothing, only snow and leaves, rivers of rot running down the walls.

He turned. 'Amy, where—'

He saw her darting through the trees, away, and lumbered after her. Amy was moving more quickly now, practically running. Through the fog of his exhaustion and the trudge of his frozen feet, Peter had become aware that they had reached the end of their journey, or nearly. Something was leaving him; his strength, stripped away by the cold, was leaving him at last.

'Amy,' he called. 'Stop.'

She seemed not to hear him.

'Amy, please.'

She turned to face him.

'What's here?' he pleaded. 'There's nothing here.'

'There is, Peter.' Her face was lit with joy. 'There is.'

'Then where is it?' he said, and heard the anger in his voice. His hands were on his knees; he was panting for breath. 'Tell me where it is.'

She lifted her face to the darkening sky, letting her eyes fall shut. 'It's . . . everywhere,' she said. 'Listen.'

He did his best; with every ounce of his remaining strength he sent his mind outward. But all he heard was the wind.

'There's nothing,' he said again, and felt his hopes collapsing. 'Amy, there's nothing here.'

But then he heard it.

A voice. A human voice.

Somebody, somewhere, was singing.

They saw the beacon first, rising in the trees.

They had come into a clearing, the forest parting. All around them Peter could discern evidence of human habitation, the suggestive shapes of ruined buildings and abandoned vehicles under the snow. The antenna stood at the edge of a wide depression in the earth, full of debris – a foundation of some kind, for a building long since gone. The antenna was positioned to the side of it, a four-legged metal tower rising high above them, anchored in place by steel cables sunk in concrete. Affixed to its apex was a gray orb studded with spikes. Beneath the orb, encircling the tower and jutting from the sides like the petals of a flower, was a series of paddle-like objects. Perhaps these were solar panels; Peter didn't know. He placed a hand on the cold metal. Something appeared to be written on one of the struts. He brushed the snow aside, revealing the words UNITED STATES ARMY CORPS OF ENGINEERS.

'Amy—'

But the place beside him was empty. He detected movement at the edge of the clearing and quickly followed her, into the underbrush. The sound of singing was stronger now. Not words but a wash of notes in phrased patterns, rising and falling. It seemed to be drifting toward them from all directions on the wind. They were close now, very close. He sensed the presence of something up ahead, an openness. The trees separating, the sky exposed. He reached the place where Amy stood, and then stopped.

It was a woman. She was facing away, standing in the dooryard of a small log house. The windows of the house were lighted, and curls of smoke coiled from the chimney. She was shaking out a blanket; more blankets sagged on a line that stretched between a pair of trees. The incredible thought reached him that this woman, whoever she was, was taking in her laundry. Taking in her laundry and singing. The woman was wearing a heavy woolen cloak; her hair, dense and dark with streaks of snowy white, flowed over her shoulders in a cloudlike mass. The lines of her bare legs descended from the edge of the cloak to her feet, on which she appeared to be wearing nothing more than a pair of rope sandals, her toes in the snow.

Peter and Amy moved toward her, the words of her song resolving as they approached. Her voice had a rich, full-throated sound to it, full of a mysterious contentment. She sang and went about her work, placing the blankets in a basket at her feet, apparently oblivious to their presence. The two of them were standing just a few meters behind her now. *Sleep, my child, and peace attend thee*, the woman sang,

> *All through the night.*
> *Guardian angels God will send thee,*
> *All through the night.*
> *Soft the drowsy hours are creeping,*
> *Hill and dale in slumber sleeping,*
> *I my loved ones' watch am keeping,*
> *All through the night.*

She halted, her hands poised over the line.

'Amy.'

The woman turned. She had a broad, handsome face and

dark skin, like Auntie's. But it was not an old woman he saw. Her skin was firm, her eyes clear and bright. Her face bloomed with a radiant smile.

'Oh, it is good to see you.' Her voice was like music, as if she were singing the words. She advanced toward them on her sandaled feet and took Amy by the hands, holding them with a maternal tenderness. 'My little Amy, all grown up.' She let her eyes drift past Amy toward Peter, appearing to notice him for the first time. 'And here he is, your Peter.' She gave her head a little shake of wonder. 'Just as I knew he would be. Do you remember, Amy, when I said to you, Who is Peter? It was when I first met you. You were very small.'

Tears had begun to fall from Amy's eyes. 'I left him.'

'Hush now. It is as it had to be.'

'He told me to run!' she cried out. 'I left him! I left him!'

The woman jostled Amy's hands. 'And you will find him again, Amy. That's what you have come to find out, isn't it? I was not the only one to watch over you, through all the years and years. That sadness you feel is not your own. It's his sadness you feel in your heart, Amy, for missing you.'

The sun was down. Cold darkness crowded around them, standing in the snow outside the woman's house. And yet Peter could make himself neither move nor speak. That he was a part of what had just unfolded he did not doubt, and yet he did not know what part.

He found his voice at last. 'Tell me,' he said. 'Please. Tell me who you are.'

The woman's eyes sparkled with sudden mischief. 'Shall we tell him, Amy? Shall we tell your Peter who I am?'

Amy nodded; the woman raised her face, wearing a shining smile.

'I am the one who's been waiting for you,' she said. 'My name is Sister Lacey Antoinette Kudoto.'

SIXTY-THREE

Private Sancho was dying.

Sara was riding at the back of the convoy, in one of the big trucks. Bunks had been slung from the sides of the rear compartment to carry the injured men. The space was crowded with crates of supplies; it was all Sara could do to wedge herself between them, to offer what comfort she could.

The other one, Withers, wasn't as bad off; most of the burns were on his arms and hands. Probably he would survive, if sepsis didn't set in. But not Sancho.

Something had happened when they'd winched down the bomb. A cable had jammed. The fuse wouldn't light. Something. The story had come to Sara in bits and pieces from a dozen different sources, all with a slightly different version of events. It was Sancho who had entered the mine shaft, shimmying down the cable on a harness, to fix whatever had gone wrong; he had either still been down the hole or was just emerging, Withers running toward him, reaching for him, pulling him free, when the drums of fuel exploded.

The flames had engulfed him utterly. She could see the path the fire had taken, moving up his body, fusing his uniform to his flesh. That he had survived was a miracle, though not, Sara thought, a happy one; she could still hear the screams that had torn from his lips as, with the help of two soldiers, she had peeled the blackened remains of his uniform from his body, taking most of the skin of his legs and chest with it, and again, as she had done her best to scrub away the debris, revealing a raw, red flesh beneath it. Already the burns on his legs and feet had begun to suppurate, mixing the sick-sweet odor of charred skin with the stink of infection. His chest and arms and hands and shoulders: the fire had consumed them all. His face was a smooth pink nub, like the eraser on a pencil. After she'd finished the abrasion – a horrible ordeal – he'd made scarcely any sound at all, lapsing into a fitful sleep from which he awoke only to beg for water. She was surprised when, in the morning, he was still alive, and then the next day also. The night before their departure, she had offered, in a moment of bravery that surprised her, to stay behind with him. But Greer would have none of it. We've left enough men in these woods, he said. Do your best to make him comfortable.

For a while the convoy had traveled east, but now they were moving south again, on what felt to Sara like a road; the worst of the bouncing, the lurching from side to side and the sound of spinning mud and snow, spattering against the wheel wells beneath her, had stopped. She felt nauseated and cold, chilled to the core, her limbs achy from the hours of banging in the back of the truck. The convoy of vehicles and horses and men proceeded in fits and starts, as Alicia's scouting party gave the all clear. The goal for their first day of travel was Durango, where a fortified shelter in an old grain elevator, one of nine such refuges along the supply road to Roswell, offered safety for the night.

She had decided she wasn't angry that Peter had left without telling her. She had been at first, when Hollis came to the mess to give her the news; but with Sancho and Withers to take care of, she hadn't dwelt on these feelings for long. And the truth was, she'd sensed it coming – if not Peter's and Amy's departure exactly, then something like it. Something final. When she and Hollis had discussed leaving with the convoy, always in the background, unstated, was the feeling that Peter and Amy wouldn't be going with them.

But Michael had been angry. More than angry – furious. Hollis had practically had to restrain him from heading off after the two of them, into the snow. Strange how Michael had become so brave, almost recklessly so, over the months. She had always felt herself to be a kind of stand-in parent, responsible for him in some deep, incontrovertible way. Somewhere along the way, she had let these feelings go. So maybe it wasn't Michael who had changed; perhaps it was she herself.

She wanted to see Kerrville. The name hung in her mind with a shimmering weightlessness. To think: thirty thousand souls. It gave her a hope she hadn't felt since the day Teacher had taken her out the door of the Sanctuary, into the broken world. Because it wasn't broken, after all; the little girl Sara had been, the one who slept in the Big Room and played with her friends and felt the sun on her face as she swung on the tire in the courtyard, believing the world to be a fine place that she could be a part of – that little girl had been right all along. Such a simple thing to want. To be a person; to live a human life. That was what she would have in Kerrville, with Hollis. Hollis, who loved her, and told her so, again and again. It was as if he'd opened something up inside her, something long clenched; for the feeling had filled her at once, that first night on watch, somewhere in Utah, when he'd put his rifle down and kissed her; and again each time he said the words in his quiet, almost embarrassed way, their faces so close she could feel the tangles of his beard on her cheeks, as if he were confessing the deepest truth of himself. He told her he loved her and she loved him in return, at once and infinitely. She did not believe in fate; the world seemed far chancier than that, a series of mishaps and narrow escapes you somehow managed to survive until, one day, you didn't. Yet that's what loving Hollis felt like: like fate. As if the words were already written down someplace, and all she had to do was live out the story. She wondered if her parents had felt that way about each other. Though she did not like to think about them and avoided this whenever she could, she found herself, riding in the back of the cold truck, wishing they were still alive, so she could ask this question.

It wasn't fair, what they had done. It was Michael, poor Michael, who had found the two of them in the shed that terrible morning. He was eleven; Sara had just turned fifteen. Part of her believed that their parents waited until she was old enough to look after her brother, that her age was part of the rationale for what they'd done. By the time Michael's yells had pulled her out of bed and down the stairs and across the yard to the shed behind their house, he had flung his arms around their legs, trying to hold them up; she'd stood in the door, speechless and immobile, Michael crying and begging her to help him, and known that they were dead. What she had felt at that moment was not horror or grief but something like wonder – a mute amazement at the factually declarative nature of the scene, its merciless mechanics. They had used ropes and a pair of wooden stools. They had tied the ropes around their necks, slipping the knots tight, and kicked the stools aside, employing the weight of their bodies to strangle themselves. She wondered: Did they do it together? Had they counted to three? Did first one go and then the other? Michael was pleading, *Please Sara, help me, help me save them,* and yet that was all she saw. The night before, her mother had made johnnycake; the pan was still sitting on the kitchen table. Sara had searched her mind for some evidence that her mother had gone about this task in any way that seemed different, knowing, as she must have, that she was preparing a breakfast she would not eat, for children she would never see again. And yet Sara could remember nothing.

As if obeying some final, tacit command, she and Michael had eaten it all, every bite. And by the time they were done, Sara knew, as Michael surely did as well, that she would take care of her brother from that day forward, and that part of this care was the unspoken agreement that they would never speak of their parents again.

The convoy had slowed. Sara heard a shout from up ahead, calling them to halt, and then the sound of a single horse, galloping past them through the snow. She climbed to her feet and saw that Withers's eyes were open and looking about. His bandaged arms lay over his chest, on top of the blankets. His face was flushed, damp with sweat.

'Are we there?'

Sara felt his forehead with the base of her wrist. He didn't seem to have a fever; if anything, his skin was too cold. She retrieved a canteen from the floor and dribbled a bit into his waiting mouth. No fever, and yet he looked much worse; he couldn't seem to lift his head at all.

'I don't think so.'

'This itching is driving me crazy. Like my arms are crawling with ants.'

Sara capped the canteen and put it aside. Fever or no fever, his color had her worried.

'That's a good sign. It means you're healing under there.'

'It doesn't feel like it.' Withers took a long breath and let the air out slowly. 'Fuck.'

Sancho was in the berth beneath him, swaddled in bandages; only the small pink circle of his face was showing. Sara knelt and took a stethoscope from her med kit to listen to his chest. She heard a wet rattle, like water sloshing in a can. It was dehydration, as much as anything, that was killing him; and yet he was drowning in his own lungs. His cheeks were blazing to the touch; the air around him was sharp with the smell of infection. She tucked the blanket around him and moistened a rag and held it to his lips.

'How's he doing?' Withers asked from above.

Sara rose.

'He's close, isn't he? I can see it in your face.'

She nodded. 'I don't think it will be long now.'

Withers closed his eyes once more.

She pulled on her parka and climbed from the back of the truck, into the snow and sunlight. The orderly lines of soldiers had dissolved into clusters of three or four men, standing around with scowls of bored impatience on their faces, hoods drawn up over their heads, their noses runny from the cold. Up ahead, she saw where the problem lay. One of the trucks sat with its hood open, exhaling a plume of steam into the air. It was ringed by a group of soldiers, who were looking at it with bewilderment, as if it were a giant carcass they'd happened upon in the road.

Michael was standing on the bumper, his arms buried to the elbows in the engine. Greer, from atop his horse, said, 'Can you fix it?'

Michael's head emerged from under the hood. 'I think it's just a hose. I can replace it if the housing isn't cracked. We'll need more coolant, too.'

'How long?'

'Not more than half a hand.'

Greer lifted his head and shouted to the men, 'Let's tighten that perimeter! Blue up front, and mind that line of trees! Donadio! Where the hell's Donadio?'

Alicia came riding from the front, her rifle slung, wreaths of steam swirling around her face. Despite the cold she had shucked her parka and was wearing only a compartmented vest over her jersey.

Greer said, 'Looks like we're stuck here for a while. Might as well have a look at what's down the road. We're going to have to make up some time.'

Alicia heeled her horse and galloped away, riding without a glance past Hollis, who was advancing toward them from the front of the line. Greer had assigned him to one of the supply trucks, handing out food and water to the men.

'What's going on?' he asked Sara.

'Hang on a minute. Major Greer,' she called.

Greer was already moving down the line. He turned his horse to face her.

'It's Sancho, sir. I think he's dying.'

Greer nodded. 'I see. Thank you for telling me.'

'You're his CO, sir. I thought he might appreciate a visit from you.'

His face showed no emotion. 'Nurse Fisher. We've got four hours of light to cover six hours of open ground. That's what I'm thinking about right now. Just do the best you can. Is that all?'

'Did he have anyone he was close to? Somebody who could be with him?'

'I'm sorry, I can't spare the men right now. I'm sure he'd understand. Now, if you'll excuse me.' He rode away.

Standing in the snow, Sara realized she was suddenly fighting back tears.

'Come on,' Hollis said, and took her by the arm. 'I'll help you.'

They made their way back to the truck. Withers had fallen asleep again. They pulled a couple of crates beside Sancho's berth. His breathing had gotten more ragged; a bit of foam had collected on his lips, which were blue with hypoxia. Sara didn't need to check his pulse to know his heart was racing, running out the clock.

'What can we do for him?' asked Hollis.

'Just be with him, I guess.' Sancho was going to die, she'd known that since the start, but now that it was actually happening, all her efforts seemed too meager. 'I don't think it will be long now.'

It wasn't. While they watched, his breathing began to slow. His eyelids fluttered. Sara had heard it said that, in the last moments, a person's life would pass before his eyes. If that was true, what was Sancho seeing? What would she be seeing, if she were the one lying there? Sara took his bandaged hand and tried to think of what to say, what words of kindness she could offer. But nothing came to her. She didn't know anything about him, only his name.

When it was over, Hollis drew the blanket over the dead soldier's face. Above them they heard Withers rousing. Sara stood to find his eyes open and blinking, his gray face shining with sweat.

'Did he—?'

Sara nodded. 'I'm sorry. I know he was your friend.'

But he did nothing to acknowledge her; his mind was somewhere else.

'Goddamn,' he groaned. 'What a fucking dream. Like I was really there.'

Hollis was standing beside Sara now. 'What did he say?'

'Sergeant,' Sara pressed, 'what dream?'

He shuddered, as if trying to loosen its hold from his memory. 'Just horrible. Her voice. And that stink.'

'Whose voice, Sergeant?'

'Some fat woman,' Withers answered. 'Some big ugly fat woman, breathing smoke.'

At the head of the line, lifting his head from the engine of the disabled five-ton, Michael saw Alicia – racing down the ridge, galloping through the snow. She tore past him toward the back of the line, calling for Greer.

What the hell?

Wilco was standing beside Michael, mouth open, eyes following the path of Alicia's horse. The rest of Alicia's squad was coming down the ridge now, riding toward them.

'Finish this,' Michael said, and when Wilco said nothing, he pressed the wrench into his hand. 'Just do it and be quick. I think we're moving out.'

Michael took off after her, following the tracks she had made in the snow. With every step the feeling grew: Alicia had seen something, something bad, over the ridge. Hollis and Sara climbed from the back of the truck, all of them converging on Greer and Alicia, who had both dismounted; Alicia was pointing over the ridge, her arm swinging in a broad swath, then kneeling, drawing frantically in the snow. As Michael came upon them, he heard Greer saying, 'How many?'

'They must have moved through last night. The tracks are still fresh.'

'Major Greer—' This was Sara.

Greer held up a hand, cutting her off. 'How many, goddamnit?'

Alicia rose. 'Not many,' she said. '*The* Many. And they're headed straight for that mountain.'

SIXTY-FOUR

Theo awoke not with a start but with a feeling of tumbling; he was rolling and falling, into the living world. His eyes were open. They had been open, he realized, for some time. The baby, he thought. He reached for Mausami and found her beside him. She shifted under his touch, drawing her knees upward. That's what it was. He'd been dreaming of the baby.

He was chilled to the bone, and yet his skin was slick with sweat. He wondered if he had a fever. You had to sweat to break a fever; that's what Teacher had always said, and his mother, too, her fingers stroking his face as he lay in bed, burning up. But that was long ago, a memory of a memory. He hadn't had a fever in so many years he'd forgotten what it felt like.

He pushed the blankets aside and rose to his feet, shivering in the cold, the moisture on his body sucking the last heat from him; he was wearing the same thin shirt he'd worn all day, stacking wood in the yard. They were ready at last for winter, everything battened down and put up and locked away. He drew off his sweat-soaked shirt and took another from the bureau. In one of the outbuildings he had found lockers full of clothes, some still in their packaging from the store: shirts and pants and socks and thermal underwear and sweaters made of a material that felt like cotton but wasn't. The mice and moths had gotten into some of it but not all. Whoever had stocked this place had stocked it for the long haul.

He retrieved his boots and the shotgun from their place by the door and descended the stairs. The fire in the living room had burned down to glowing ash. He didn't know what time it was but sensed it was close to dawn; over the weeks, as he and Maus had settled into a rhythm, sleeping the night away to awaken with the first rays of sun in the window, he had begun to apprehend the hour in a way that seemed both natural and completely new to him. It was as if he had tapped into some deep reservoir of instinct, a long-buried memory of his kind. It wasn't just the absence of the lights, as he had come to believe; it was the place itself. Maus had sensed it too, that first day, when they had walked to the river together to fish, and later, in the kitchen, when she had told him they were safe.

He sat to draw the boots on over his feet, took a heavy sweater from the hooks, checked the load on the shotgun, and stepped onto the porch. To the east, beyond the line of hills that hemmed the valley, a soft glow was creeping up the sky. During the first week, while Maus slept, Theo had sat on the porch all night; with each new dawn, he'd felt a surprising pang of sadness. All his life he had feared the darkness and what it could bring; no one, not even his father, had told him how beautiful the night sky was, how it made you feel both small and large at the same time, while also a part of something vast and eternal. He stood a moment in the cold, watching the stars and letting the night air flow in and out of his lungs, bringing his mind and body to wakefulness. As long as he was up he would set a fire, so Mausami wouldn't have to wake in an ice-cold house.

He moved off the porch, into the yard. For days he'd done little else but haul and split wood. The woods by the river were full of deadfalls, dry and good for burning. The saw he'd found was no good, the teeth hopelessly dulled with corrosion, but the axe had done just fine. Now the fruits of his labors lay stacked in rows in the barn, with more under the eaves, draped by a plastic tarp.

Those people, he thought as he moved toward the barn door, which stood ajar. The ones in the pictures he had found. He wondered if they had been happy here. He'd found no more photographs in the house, and hadn't thought to search the car until two days ago. He didn't know quite what he was looking for, but after a few minutes in the driver's seat, idly pushing buttons and flipping switches and hoping something would happen, he found the right one. A little door popped open on the dashboard, revealing a wad of maps and, hidden beneath them, a leather wallet. Tucked in the folds was a card with the words UTAH TAX COMMISSION, DIVISION OF MOTOR VEHICLES and, beneath that, a name, David Conroy. David Conroy, 1634 Mansard

Place, Provo, UT. That's who they were, he told Mausami, showing her. The Conroys.

But the barn door, Theo thought; something about the barn door. Why was it ajar like that? Could he have actually forgotten to close it? But he *had* closed it; he remembered this distinctly. And no sooner had he thought this than a new sound reached his ears: a quiet rustling from within.

He froze, willing himself into an absolute stillness. For a long moment he heard nothing. Maybe he'd just imagined it.

Then it came again.

At least whatever was inside hadn't noticed him yet. If it was a viral, one shot was all he'd have. He could return to the house and warn Mausami, but where would they go? His best chance was to use whatever element of surprise he still possessed. Carefully, holding his breath, he pulled the pump on the shotgun, listening for the click as the first round slid into the chamber. From deep inside the barn he heard a soft thump, followed by an almost human-sounding sigh. He eased the barrel forward until it met the wood of the door and gently nudged it open as, behind him, a whispering voice lit up the gloom.

'Theo? What are you doing?'

Mausami in her long nightshirt, her hair spilling over her shoulders; she seemed to hover like an apparition in the predawn darkness. Theo opened his mouth to speak, to tell her to get back, when the door flew open, knocking the barrel of the shotgun with a force that sent him spinning. Before he knew what had happened the gun had fired, blasting him backward. A vaulting shadow leapt past him into the yard.

'Don't shoot!' Mausami yelled.

It was a dog.

The animal skidded to a halt a few meters in front of Mausami, tail tucked between his legs. His fur was thick, a silvering gray with spots of black. He was facing Maus in a kind of bow, standing on his skinny legs, his neck bent submissively, ears folded back against the woolly ruff of his shoulders. He seemed uncertain about which way to look, whether to run away or launch an attack. A low growl rose from the back of his throat.

'Maus, be careful,' Theo warned.

'I don't think he's going to hurt me. Are you, boy?' Dropping to a crouch, she held out a hand for the dog to sniff. 'You're just hungry, aren't you? Looking in the barn for something to eat.'

The dog was directly between Theo and Mausami; if the animal made an aggressive move, the shotgun would be useless. Theo flipped it around in his hands to use as a club, and took a cautious step forward.

'Put the gun down,' Mausami said.

'Maus—'

'I mean it, Theo.' She gave the dog a smile, her hand still extended. 'Let's show this nice man what a good dog you are. Come here, boy. You want to give Mama's hand a sniff?'

The animal inched toward her, backed away, then moved forward again, following the black button of his nose toward Mausami's outstretched hand. As Theo watched, dumbfounded, the dog placed his face against her hand and began to lick it. Soon Maus was on the ground, sitting in the dirt, cooing to the animal, rubbing his face and ruff.

'See?' she laughed, as the dog, shaking his head with pleasure, gave a big wet sneeze into her ear. 'He's just a big old sweetie is what he is. What's your name, fella? Hmm? Do you have a name?'

Theo realized he was still holding the shotgun over his head, ready to swing. He relaxed his posture, feeling embarrassed.

Mausami gave him a forgiving frown. 'I'm sure he won't hold it against you. Are you my good boy?' she said to the animal, vigorously rubbing his mane. 'What do you say? You skinny thing. How about some breakfast? How does that sound?'

The sun had lifted over the hill; the night was over, Theo realized, bringing with it a dog.

'Conroy,' he said.

Mausami looked at him. The dog was licking her ear, rubbing his muzzle against her in a way that seemed almost indecent.

'That's what we'll call him,' Theo explained. 'Conroy.'

Mausami took the dog's face in her hands, smushing his cheeks. 'Is that you? Are you Conroy?' She made him nod, and gave a happy laugh. 'Conroy it is.'

Theo didn't want to let him in the house, but Maus was determined. The moment the door was open he bounded up the stairs, moving through every room like he owned the place, his long nails tapping excitedly on the floor. Maus cooked him a breakfast of fish and potatoes fried in lard and set it in a bowl beneath the kitchen table. Conroy had already taken his place on the sofa, but at the sound of crockery hitting the floor he leapt into the kitchen and buried his face in the bowl, pushing it across the room with his long nose as he ate. Maus filled a second bowl with water and put that down as well. When Conroy was finished with his breakfast and had taken a long, slurping drink of water, he loped from the room and returned to the sofa, where he settled back down with a windy sigh of satisfaction.

Conroy the dog. Where had he come from? It was obvious he'd been around people before; somebody had taken care of him. He was thin, but not what Theo would have called malnourished. His hair was thick with mats and burrs, but he seemed otherwise healthy.

'Fill the tub,' Maus ordered him. 'If he's going to sit on the sofa like that, I want to give him a bath.'

Outside, Theo set a fire to boil water; by the time the tub was ready, the morning sun stood high over the yard. Winter waited at their doorstep, but the middle of the day could be mild like this, warm enough for shirtsleeves. Theo sat on a log and watched while Maus bathed the dog, rubbing handfuls of their precious soap through his silvery fur, using her fingers to smooth out the mats as best she could and picking out the burrs. The dog's face was a portrait of abject humiliation; he seemed to be saying, A bath? Whose idea was this? When she had finished, Theo lifted him from the tub, a great soggy thing, and Maus eased down to her knees once more – it was getting harder each day for her to perform even these simple movements – to wrap him with a blanket.

'Don't look so jealous.'

'Was I?' But she had him, dead to rights; that was exactly how he was feeling. Conroy had thrown the blanket off to give himself a hard shake, sending drops of water arcing everywhere.

'Better get used to it,' Maus said.

It was true; the baby wouldn't be long now. Every part of her seemed enlarged, swollen with some benign inhabitation; even her hair looked bigger. Theo expected her to complain about this, but she never did. Watching her with Conroy, who had finally submitted to her belated and unnecessary attempts to dry him with the blanket, he found himself suddenly and deeply glad, glad for everything. Back in the cell, he'd wanted only to die. Before that, even. Part of him had always struggled with it. The ones who let it go: Theo knew that pull, a longing as sharp as any hunger. To hand himself over; to step into the wild darkness. It had become a kind of game he played, watching himself go about his days as if he weren't already half dead, fooling everyone, even Peter. The worse the feeling was, the easier this deception became, until, in the end, it was the deception itself that sustained him. When Michael had told him about the batteries that afternoon on the porch, part of him had thought: thank God it's over.

And now look at him. His life had been restored. More than that; it was as if he'd been given an entirely new one.

They finished the day and retired with the sun. Conroy took up residence at the foot of the bed; as they did every night, Theo and Maus made love, feeling the baby kick between them. A persistent, attention-seeking tapping, like a code. Theo had found this disquieting at first but did no longer. It was all of a piece, the kicks and jabs of the baby in its pocket of warm flesh, and the soft cries Mausami made, and the rhythm of their movements, even, now, the sounds of Conroy on the floor, watchfully shifting his bones. A blessing, Theo thought. That was the word that came to his mind as sleep eased toward him. That's what this place was. A blessing.

Then he remembered the barn door.

He *knew* he'd dropped the latch. The memory was clear and specific in his mind: pulling the door closed on its squeaking hinges and dropping the latch into its cradle before walking back to the house.

But if that was true, how could Conroy have gotten inside?

In another instant he was shoving his legs into a pair of gaps, wedging on his boots with one hand and pulling on a sweater with the other. All day long, moving in and out of the house, he hadn't once done it.

He'd never looked inside the barn.

'What is it?' Mausami was saying. 'Theo, what's wrong?'

She was sitting up now, the blanket pulled over her chest. Conroy, sensing the excitement, had sprung to his feet and was prancing around the room on his long, tapping nails.

He grabbed the shotgun from its place by the door. 'Stay here.'

He would have left Conroy with her, but the dog would have none of it; the moment Theo opened the front door of the house, Conroy flew into the yard. For the second time in a day Theo crept toward the barn, the stock of the shotgun pressed to his shoulder. The door was still open, just as they'd left it. Conroy dashed ahead of him, disappearing into the darkness.

He crept through the door, the shotgun raised, poised to fire. He could hear the dog moving in the dark, snuffling the ground.

'Conroy?' he whispered. 'What is it?'

As his eyes adjusted, he saw the dog circling the ground just beyond the parked Volvo. Resting on the floor by the woodpile was a lantern Theo had left there, days before.

Bracing the shotgun against his leg, he quickly knelt and lit the wick. He could hear that Conroy had found something, in the dirt.

It was a can. Theo picked it up, holding it by its crinkled edges, where someone had used a blade to open it. The interior walls of the can were damp, smelling of meat. Theo lifted the lantern higher, spreading its cone of light over the floor. Footprints. Human footprints, in the dust.

Someone had been here.

SIXTY-FIVE

It was the doctor who had done it. It was the doctor who had saved her and to whom, in the end, Lacey hoped she had brought some small measure of comfort.

Strange, what the years did to Lacey's memory of the things of that night so long ago, back at the beginning. The screams and smoke. The calls of the dying and the dead. A great black tide of endless night sweeping over the world. Sometimes it all came back to her as clearly as if it were not decades but days that had passed; at other times, the pictures she saw and the feelings she felt seemed small and doubtful and distant, like chips of straw adrift on a broad sweeping current of time in which she floated also, through all the years and years.

She remembered the one, Carter. Carter, who had come to her as she had run from Wolgast's car, shouting and waving; Carter, who had answered her call and swooped down toward her, alighting before her like a great, sorrowful bird. *I . . . am . . . Carter.* He was not like the others. She could see, behind the monstrous vision he'd become, that he took no pleasure in his doing, that his heart was broken inside him. Chaos all around them, the screams and the gunfire and the smoke: men were running past her, yelling and shooting and dying, their fates already written when the world began, but Lacey was in that place no more; for as Carter placed his mouth upon her neck, calling the soft beat of her heart to his own, she felt it. All his pain and puzzlement, and the long sad story of who he was. The bed of rags and bundles under the roadway, and the sweat and soil of his skin and of his long journey; the great gleaming car stopping beside him with its grille of jeweled teeth, and the voice of the woman, calling out to him over the dirty roar of the world; the sweetness of mown grass and the sweating coolness of a glass of tea; the pull of the water, and the arms of the woman, Rachel Wood, holding fast, pulling him down and down. It was his life that Lacey felt inside her, his little, human life, which he had never loved as much as he loved the woman whose spirit he now carried inside him – for Lacey felt that also – and as his teeth cut into the soft curve of her neck, filling Lacey's senses with the heat of his breath, she heard her own voice rising, bubbling past. *God bless you. God bless and keep you, Mr Carter.*

Then he was gone. She was lying on the ground, bleeding, time passing, the sickness starting; that which was to pass between them had found its way, she knew. Lacey closed her eyes and prayed for a sign, but no sign came. As it had been in the field after the men had left her, when she was just a girl. It seemed, in that dark hour, that God had forgotten about her, but then as dawn opened the sky above her face, from out of the stillness came the figure of a man. She could hear the soft tread of his steps upon the earth, could smell the smoke of his skin and hair. She tried to speak but couldn't; neither did the man address her, nor tell her his name. In silence he lifted her into his arms, cradling her like a child, and Lacey thought that it was God Himself, come to take her to His home in heaven. His eyes were hooded in shadow; his hair was a dark corona, wild and beautiful, like his beard, a dense mass of gray upon his face. He carried her through the smoking ruins, and she saw that he was weeping. Those are God's own tears, Lacey thought, yearning to reach out and touch them. It had never occurred to her that God would cry, but of course that was wrong. God would be crying all the time. He would cry and cry and never stop. An exhausted peacefulness swept through her; for a time she slept. She did not recall what happened next, but when it was over and the sickness had passed, she opened her eyes and knew that he had done it; he had saved her. She had found the way to Amy, she had found the way at last.

Lacey, she heard. *Listen.*

She did. She listened. The voices moved over her like a breeze on water, like a current in the blood. Everywhere and all around.

Hear them, Lacey. Hear them all.

And so it was that through the years she'd waited. She, Sister Lacey Antoinette Kudoto, and the man who had carried her through the forest, who was not God after all but human, a human being. The good doctor – for that was how she thought of him; that was the name she used in her mind, though his given name, his Christian name, was Jonas. Jonas Lear. The saddest man in all the world. Together they had built the house in the glen where Lacey lived still – not much larger than the shacks she recalled from the dusty roads and red-clay fields of her youth – but sturdier, and made to last. The doctor once told her that he had built a house before, a cabin on a lake in the woods of Maine. That he had built this cabin with Elizabeth, his wife who had died, he did not say, but he did not have to. The abandoned compound was a bounty, waiting to be harvested. They had taken the lumber from the burnt remains of the Chalet; in the storage buildings they found hammers and saws and planes and sacks of nails, as well as sacks of concrete and a mixer, to pour the posts that would serve as the cabin's foundation and to mortar the fieldstones that the two of them lifted into place to build the hearth. For one whole summer they stripped roofing shingles off the old barracks, only to find that they leaked, the asphalt torn in too many places; in the end they piled sod on top, making a roof of dirt and grass. There were guns, too, guns by the hundreds, guns of every sort and nature; it was not easy, getting rid of so many guns. For a period of time that was how they occupied themselves, dismantling the soldiers' guns until all that remained was a vast mound of nuts and bolts and glossy metal pieces, not even worth burying.

He left her only one time, their third summer on the mountain, to go in search of seeds. He took the one gun he had kept, a rifle, with the food and fuel and other supplies he would need, all packed in the pickup that he had prepared for his journey. Three days, he said, but two whole weeks had come and gone before Lacey heard the sound of the pickup's engine, driving up the mountain. He emerged from the cab wearing a look of such despair she knew it was only his pledge to return that had brought him back to her. He'd driven as far as Grand Junction, he confessed, before deciding to turn around. In the truck were the promised packs of seeds. That night he lit the hearth and sat by it in a terrible, desolate silence, staring into the flames. Never had she seen such pain in a man's eyes, and although she knew she could not lift this grief from him, it was that same night she went to him and said she believed that they should live together from that day forward as man and wife, in every respect. It seemed a small thing, to offer him this love, this taste of forgiveness; and when this came about, as it did in due course, she understood that the love she had tendered was also love sought. An end to the journey she had begun in the fields of her childhood, all those years ago.

He never left again.

Through the years she loved him with her body, which did not age, as his did. She loved him and he loved her, each in their way, the two of them alone together on their mountain. Death came to him slowly over the years, first one thing and then another, nibbling away at the edges, then moving deeper. His eyes and hair. His teeth and skin. His legs and heart and lungs. There were many days when Lacey wished she could die also, so that he would not have to make this final voyage alone.

One morning she was working in the garden when she felt his absence; she went into the house, then into the woods, calling his name. It was high summer, the air fresh and bright, falling over the leaves like drizzled sunlight. He had chosen a place where the trees were thin and the sky was all above; from here he could see the valley and, beyond it, like a great becalmed sea, the wavelike mountains receding to a blue horizon. He was leaning on a shovel, panting for breath. He was an old man now, gray and frail, and yet here he was, digging a hole in the earth. What is that hole, she asked him, and he told her, It's for me. So that when I'm gone you won't have to dig it yourself. It wouldn't do in summer to have to wait to dig a hole. All that day and into the evening he dug, moving small shovels of earth, pausing after each for breath. She watched from the edge of the clearing, for he would have no help from her. And when he was done, the hole having reached a satisfactory dimension, he returned to the house where they had lived so many years together, to the bed he had built with his own hands from heavy joined timbers and lengths of fibrous rope that sagged with the shape of the two of them, and in the morning was dead.

How long ago? Lacey paused in her telling, Amy's and the young man's eyes – Peter's eyes – watching her from across the room. How strange, after so much time, to tell these stories: of Jonas, and that terrible night, and all that had happened in this place. She had stoked the fire and set a pot in the cradle to warm. The air of the house, two low-ceilinged rooms separated by a curtain, was warm and fragrant, lit by the glow of the fire.

'Fifty-four years,' she said, answering the question she herself had posed. She said it again, to herself. Fifty-four years since Jonas had left her alone. She stirred the pot, which contained a stew of this and that, the meat of a fat possum from her trapline and hearty vegetables, the durable tubers, which she had put away for winter. Sitting in jars upon the shelves were the seeds she used each year, the descendants of the ones Jonas had brought in the packets. Zucchini and tomatoes, potatoes and squash, onions and turnips and lettuce. Her needs were small, the cold did not affect her, and she sometimes barely ate for days or even weeks; but Peter would be hungry. He was just as she'd imagined, young and strong, with a determined face, though she'd thought, somehow, that he would be taller.

She became aware that he was frowning at her.

'You've been by yourself . . . for fifty years?'

She shrugged. 'It was really not so long.'

'And *you* set the beacon.'

The beacon; she had almost forgotten. But of course he would ask about this. 'Oh, it was the doctor who did that.' It made Lacey miss him keenly, to speak this way. She broke her gaze away and turned from her stirring, wiping her hands on a cloth and taking up bowls from the table. 'Such things. He was always tinkering. But there will be time for more talk. Now, we eat.'

She served them the stew. She was glad to see Peter eating heartily, though Amy, she could tell, was just pretending. Lacey herself possessed no appetite at all. Whenever it was time for her to eat, Lacey felt not hunger but a mild curiosity, her mind remarking to her in an offhand way, as if to comment on nothing more important than the weather or the time of day, *It would be good to eat now.*

She sat and watched him with a feeling of gratitude. Outside, the dark night pressed down upon the mountain. She did not know if she would ever see another; soon she would be free.

When they were done, she rose from the table and went to the bedroom. The small space was sparsely furnished, just the bed the doctor had made and a dresser where she kept the few things she needed. The boxes were under the bed. Peter stood in the curtained doorway, observing silently, as she knelt and drew them out onto the floor. A pair of army lockers; at one time they had contained guns. Amy was behind him now, watching with curious eyes.

'Help me carry these to the kitchen,' she said.

How many years she had imagined this moment! They placed them on the floor by the table. Lacey knelt once more and undid the hasps of the first locker, the one she'd kept for Amy. Inside was Amy's knapsack, which she'd worn to the convent. The Powerpuff Girls.

'This is yours,' she said, and placed it on the table.

For a moment, the girl simply stared at it. Then, with deliberate care, she drew back the zipper and withdrew the contents. A toothbrush. A tiny shirt, limp with age, with the word SASSY written on it in glittering flakes. A pair of threadbare jeans. And, at the bottom, a stuffed rabbit of tan velveteen, wearing a pale blue jacket. The fabric was crumbling away; one of his ears was gone, exposing a curl of wire.

'It was Sister Claire who bought the shirt for you,' Lacey said. 'I do not think Sister Arnette approved of it.'

Amy had put the other objects aside on the table and was holding the rabbit in her hands, peering into its face.

'Your sisters,' Amy said. 'But not . . . actual sisters.'

Lacey took a chair before her. 'That is right, Amy. That is what I said to you.'

'We are sisters in the eyes of God.'

Amy dropped her gaze again. With her thumb, she stroked the fabric of the rabbit.

'He brought him to me. In the sick room. I remember his voice, telling me to wake up. But I couldn't answer him.'

Lacey was aware of Peter's eyes, intently watching.

'Who did, Amy?' she asked.

'Wolgast.' Her voice was distant, lost in the past. 'He told me about Eva.'

'Eva?'

'She died. He would have given her his heart.' The girl met Lacey's gaze again, squinting intently. 'You were there, too. I remember now.'

'Yes. I was.'

'And another man.'

Lacey nodded. 'Agent Doyle.'

Amy frowned sharply. 'I didn't like him. He thought I did, but I didn't.' She closed her eyes, remembering. 'We were in the car. We were in the car, but then we stopped.' She opened her eyes. 'You were bleeding. Why were you bleeding?'

Lacey had almost forgotten; after everything else, it had come to seem so small, this part of the story. 'To tell you the truth, I did not know myself! But I think that one of the soldiers must have shot me.'

'You got out of the car. Why did you do that?'

'To be here for you, Amy,' she answered. 'So someone would be here when you came back.'

Another silence passed, the girl worrying the rabbit with her fingers like a talisman.

'They're so sad. They have such terrible dreams. I hear them all the time.'

'What do you hear, Amy?'

'*Who am I, who am I, who am I?* They ask and ask, but I can't tell them.'

Lacey cupped the girl's chin. Her eyes were glistening with tears. 'You will. When the time is right.'

'They're dying, Lacey. They're dying and can't stop. Why can't they stop, Lacey?'

'I think that they are waiting for you, to show them the way.'

They stayed that way a long moment. In the place where Lacey's mind met Amy's, she felt her sorrow and her loneliness, but even more: she felt her courage.

She turned to Peter then. He did not love Amy, as Wolgast had. She could see that there was another, someone he had left behind. But he was the one who had answered the beacon. Whoever heard it and brought Amy back – he would be the one to stand with her.

She bent to the second locker on the floor. Stacked inside were manila folders of yellowed paper – still, after so many years, exuding a faint odor of smoke. It was the doctor who

886

had retrieved them, along with Amy's backpack, as the fires had moved down through the underground levels of the Chalet. *Someone should know*, he had said.

She withdrew the first file and placed it on the table before him. The label read:

> EX ORD 13292 TS1 EYES ONLY
> VIA WOLGAST, BRADFORD J.
> INTAKE PROFILE CT3
> SUBJ 1 BABCOCK, GILES J.

'It is time for you to learn how this world was made,' said Sister Lacey. And then she opened it.

SIXTY-SIX

They rode through the fading day, a party of five, Alicia on point. The trail of the Many was a broad swath of destruction – the snow trampled, branches broken, the ground littered with debris. It seemed to grow denser and wider with every kilometer, as if more of the creatures were joining the pod, called out of the wilderness to take their place among their kind. Here and there they saw a stain of blood on the snow where a hapless animal, a deer or rabbit or squirrel, had met its swift demise. The tracks were less than twelve hours old; somewhere up ahead, in the shade of the trees and under the rocky ledges and perhaps, even, beneath the snow itself, they waited, dozing the day away, a great pod of virals, thousands strong.

By late afternoon, they were forced to make a decision: to follow the creatures' trail, the shortest route up the mountain, but one that would take them right into the heart of the pod; or to turn north, find the river again, and make their approach from the west. Michael watched from atop his horse as Alicia and Greer conferred. Hollis and Sara were beside him, their rifles resting across their laps, their parkas zipped to their chins. The air was bitterly cold; in the immense stillness, every sound seemed magnified, the wind like a rush of static over the frozen land.

'We go north,' Alicia announced. 'All eyes.'

There had been no discussion about who would come; the only surprise was Greer. As the four of them had been mounting up to leave, he had come forward on his horse and joined their number without a word of explanation, passing his command to Eustace. Michael wondered if this meant Greer would be in charge, but as soon as they were clear of the ridge, the major turned to Alicia from atop his horse and said, simply, 'This is your show, Lieutenant. Are we clear, everyone?' They all said they were, and that was that.

They rode on. As night was falling, Michael heard, from up ahead, the bright notes of the river. They emerged from the woods onto its southern bank and turned east, using it to guide them through the thickening dark. They had closed up to a single line now, Alicia up front, Greer taking the rear. From time to time one of the horses would stumble or Alicia would pull up, signaling for them to hold and listening intently, scanning the dark shape of the trees. Then they'd press on again. No one had spoken for hours. There was no moon at all.

Then, as a sliver of light lifted from the hills, the valley opened around them. To the east they could discern the shape of the mountain, pressed against a starry sky, and up ahead, some kind of structure, a brooding black shape that, as they approached, revealed itself as a bridge, standing astride the ice-choked river on concrete piers. Alicia dismounted and knelt to the ground.

'Two sets of footprints,' she said, gesturing with her rifle. 'Over the bridge, from the far side.'

They began to climb.

It was not much later that they found the horse. With a tight nod, Greer confirmed that it was his, the gelding Peter and Amy had taken. They all dismounted and stood around the dead animal. Its throat was ripped open in a bright splash, its body stiff and shriveled where it lay on its side in the snow. Somehow it had gotten across the river, probably fording it at a shallow spot; they could see the prints of its last, terrified gallop, coming from the west.

Sara knelt and touched the animal's side.

'He's still warm,' she said.

No one said anything. Dawn would come soon. To the east, the sky had begun to pale.

SIXTY-SEVEN

They were criminals.

By the time Peter put down the last file, rubbing his bleary eyes, the night was nearly done. Amy had long since fallen asleep, curled on the bed beneath a blanket; Lacey had moved a chair from the kitchen to sit beside her. From time to time, as he'd turned the pages, rising to put one file back in the box and remove the next, piecing the story together as best he could, he'd heard Amy muttering softly in her sleep behind the curtain.

For a while, after Amy had gone to bed, Lacey had sat with him at the table, explaining the things he couldn't make sense of on his own. The files were thick, full of information that referred to a world he didn't know, had never seen or lived in. But still, over the hours, with Lacey's help, the story had emerged in his mind. There were photographs, too: grown men with puffy, lived-in faces, their eyes glazed and unfocused. Some were holding a board of writing to their chests, or wearing it like a necklace. Texas Department of Criminal Justice, one board read. Louisiana State Department of Corrections, said another. Kentucky and Florida and Wyoming and Delaware. Some of the boards had no words on them, only numbers; some of the men had no boards at all. They were black and white and brown, heavy or slight; somehow, in the looks of numb surrender on their faces, they were all the same. He read:

SUBJECT 12. Carter, Anthony L. Born September 12, 1985, Baytown, TX. Sentenced to death for capital murder, Harris County, TX, 2013.

SUBJECT 11. Reinhardt, William J. Born April 9, 1987, Jefferson City, MO. Sentenced to death for three counts of capital murder and aggravated sexual assault, Miami-Dade County, FL, 2012.

SUBJECT 10. Martínez, Julio A. Born May 3, 1991, El Paso, TX. Sentenced to death for the capital murder of a peace officer, Laramie County, WY, 2011.

SUBJECT 9. Lambright, Horace D. Born October 19, 1992, Oglala, SD. Sentenced to death for two counts of capital murder and aggravated sexual assault, Maricopa County, AZ, 2014.

SUBJECT 8. Echols, Martin S. Born June 15, 1984, Everett, WA. Sentenced to death for capital murder and armed robbery, Cameron Parish, LA, 2012.

SUBJECT 7. Sosa, Rupert I. Born August 22, 1989, Tulsa, OK. Sentenced to death for one count of vehicular homicide with depraved indifference, Lake County, IN, 2009.

SUBJECT 6. Winston, David D. Born April 1, 1994, Bloomington, MN. Sentenced to death for one count of capital murder and three counts of aggravated sexual assault, New Castle County, DE, 2014.

SUBJECT 5. Turrell, Thaddeus R. Born December 26, 1990, New Orleans, LA. Sentenced to death for the capital murder

of a Homeland Security officer, New Orleans Federal
Housing District, 2014.

SUBJECT 4. Baffes, John T. Born February 12, 1992,
Orlando, FL. Sentenced to death for one count of capital
murder and one count of second-degree murder with
depraved indifference, Pasco County, FL, 2010.

SUBJECT 3. Chávez, Victor Y. Born July 5, 1995, Niagara
Falls, NY. Sentenced to death for one count of capital
murder and two counts of aggravated sexual assault with a
minor, Elko County, NV, 2012.

SUBJECT 2. Morrison, Joseph P. Born January 9, 1992, Black
Creek, Ky. Sentenced to death for one count of capital
murder, Lewis County, Ky, 2013.

And, finally:

SUBJECT 1. Babcock, Giles J. Born October 29, 1994. Desert
Wells, NV. Sentenced to death for one count of capital
murder, Nye County, NV, 2013.

Babcock, he thought. Desert Wells.
They always go home.

Amy's file was thinner than the others. 'SUBJECT 13,
AMY NLN,' the label read, 'Convent of the Sisters of Mercy,
Memphis, TN.' Height and weight and hair color and a string
of numbers that Peter surmised were medical data of the kind
Michael had found on the chip in her neck. Affixed to this
page was a photograph of a little girl, no more than six years
old, just as Michael had predicted. All knees and elbows,
sitting on a wooden chair, dark hair falling around her face.
Peter had never before seen a photograph of someone he'd
actually known, and for a moment his mind struggled to
comprehend the notion that this image was the same person
who was sleeping in the next room. But there was no

question; her eyes were Amy's eyes. *See?* her eyes seemed to say. *Who did you think I was?*

He came to the file for Wolgast, Bradford J. There was no photograph; a rusty stain on the top page showed where one had once been clipped. But even without it, Peter was able to form a picture in his mind of this man who, if what Lacey said was true, had brought each of the Twelve to the compound, and Amy as well. A tall, sturdy man with deep-set eyes and graying hair, with large hands good for work. A mild face but troubled, something moving under the surface, barely contained. According to the file, Wolgast had been married and had had a child; the girl, whose name was Eva, was listed as deceased. Peter wondered if that was the reason he had decided, in the end, to help Amy. His instincts told him it was.

It was the contents of the last file, though, that told him the most. A report by someone named Cole to a Colonel Sykes, US Army Division of Special Weapons, concerning the work of a Dr Jonas Lear and something called 'Project Noah'; and a second document, dated five years later, ordering the transfer of twelve human test subjects from Telluride, Colorado, to White Sands, New Mexico, for 'operational combat testing.' It took Peter a while to put the pieces together, or mostly. But he knew what combat was.

All those years, he thought, waiting for the Army to return, and it was the Army that had done it.

As he put down the final file, he heard Lacey rising. She passed through the curtain and stopped in the doorway.

'So. You have read.'

At the sound of her voice, a sudden exhaustion washed over him. Lacey restoked the fire and sat at the table across from him. He gestured over the piles of paper on the table.

'He really did this? The doctor.'

'Yes.' She nodded. 'There were others, but yes.'

'Did he ever say *why*?'

Behind her, the fresh logs caught with a soft *whump*, blazing the room with light. 'I think because he could. That is the reason for most things people do. He was not a bad man, Peter. It was not entirely his fault, though he believed it was. Many times I asked him, Do you think the world could be unmade by men alone? Of course it could not. But he never quite believed me.' She tipped her head toward the files on the table. 'He left these for you, you know.'

'Me? How could he have left them for me?'

'For whoever came back. So they would know what happened here.'

He sat quietly, uncertain what to say. Alicia had been right about one thing: all his life, since the day he had come out of the Sanctuary, he had wondered why the world was what it was. But learning the truth had solved nothing.

Amy's stuffed rabbit was still on the table; he took it in his hand. 'Do you think she remembers it?'

'What they did to her? I do not know. Perhaps she does.'

'No, I meant before. Being a girl.' He searched for the words. 'Being human.'

'I think that she has always been human.'

He waited for Lacey to say more, and when she didn't, he put the rabbit aside.

'What's it like, living forever?'

She gave a sudden laugh. 'I do not think that I will live forever.'

'But he gave you the virus. You're like her. Like Amy.'

'There is no one like Amy, Peter.' She shrugged. 'But if you are asking what it has been like for me all these years, since Jonas died, I will say that it has been very lonely. It surprises me how much.'

'You miss him, don't you?'

He instantly regretted saying this; a look of sadness swept over her face, like the shadow of a bird crossing a field.

'I'm sorry, I didn't mean—'

But she shook her head. 'No, it is perfectly all right that you should ask. It is difficult to talk about him like this, after so long. But the answer is yes. I do miss him. I should think it a wonderful thing to be missed, the way that I miss him.'

For a while they sat in silence, bathed in the glow of the fire. Peter wondered if Alicia was thinking about him, where she was now. He had no idea if he would see her, or any of them, again.

'I don't know . . . what I'm doing, Lacey,' he said finally. 'I don't know what to do with any of this.'

'You found your way here. That is something. That is a beginning.'

'What about Amy?'

'What about her, Peter?'

But he wasn't sure what he was asking. The question was what it was: What of Amy?

'I thought . . .' He sighed and drew his gaze away, toward the room where Amy slept. 'Listen to me. I don't know what I thought.'

'That you could defeat them? That you would find the answer here?'

'Yes.' He returned his eyes to Lacey. 'I didn't even know I was thinking it, until just now. But yes.'

Lacey appeared to be studying him, though what she was looking for, Peter couldn't say. He wondered if he was as crazy as he sounded. Probably he was.

'Tell me, Peter. Do you know the story of Noah? Not Project NOAH. Noah the man.'

The name was nothing he knew. 'I don't think so.'

'It is an old story. A true story. I think it will be some help to you.' Lacey rose a little in her chair, her face suddenly animated. 'So. A man named Noah was asked by God to build a ship, a great ship. This was long ago. Why would I build a ship, Noah asked. It is a sunny day, I have other things to do. Because this world has grown wicked, God said to him, and it is my intention to send a flood of water to destroy it, and drown every living thing. But you, Noah, are a man righteous in your generation, and I will save you and your family if you do as I command, building this ship to carry yourselves and every species of animal, two of every kind. And do you know what Noah did, Peter?'

894

'He built the ship?'

Her eyes widened. 'Of course he did! But not right away. That, you see, is the interesting part of the story. If Noah had simply done as he was told, the story wouldn't mean anything at all. No. He was afraid that people would make fun of him. He was afraid he would build the ship and the flood wouldn't come and he would look like a fool. God was testing him, you see, to find out if there was anyone who made the world worth saving. He wanted to see if Noah was up to the job. And in the end, he was. He built the ship, and the heavens opened, and the world was washed away. For a long time, Noah and his family floated on the waters. It seemed they had been forgotten, that a terrible joke had been played on them. But after many days, God remembered Noah, and sent him a dove to lead them to dry land, and the world was reborn.' She gave her hands a quiet clap of satisfaction. 'There. You see?'

He didn't, not at all. It reminded him of the fables Teacher had read to them in circle, stories of talking animals that always ended in a lesson. Pleasant to listen to, and maybe not wrong, but in the end too easy, something for children.

'You do not believe me? That is all right. One day you will.'

'It's not that I don't believe you,' Peter managed. 'I'm sorry. It's just that . . . it's only a story.'

'Perhaps.' She shrugged. 'And perhaps someday someone will say those very words about you, Peter. What do you say to that?'

He didn't know. It was late, or early; the night was almost gone. Despite all he had learned, he felt more puzzled than when it had begun.

'So, for the sake of argument,' he said, 'if I'm supposed to be Noah, then who's Amy?'

Lacey's face was incredulous. She seemed about to laugh. 'Peter, I am surprised at you. Perhaps I did not tell it right.'

'No, you told it fine,' he assured her. 'I just don't know.'

She leaned forward in her chair and smiled again – one of her strange, sad smiles, full of belief.

'The ship, Peter,' said Lacey. 'Amy is the ship.'

Peter was still trying to make sense of this mysterious answer when Lacey seemed to startle. Frowning sharply, she darted her eyes around the room.

'Lacey? What's wrong?'

But she seemed not to have heard him. She briskly pushed away from the table.

'I have gone on too long, I'm afraid. It will be light soon. Go and wake her now, and gather your things.'

He was taken aback, his mind still drifting in the night's strange currents. 'We're leaving?'

He rose to discover Amy standing in the doorway to the bedroom, her dark hair wild and askew, the curtain shifting behind her. Whatever had affected Lacey had affected her also; her face was lit with a sudden urgency.

'Lacey—' Amy began.

'I know. He will try to be here before daybreak.' Drawing on her cloak, Lacey gave her insistent gaze to Peter once more. 'Hurry now.'

The peace of the night was suddenly banished, replaced by a sense of emergency his mind could not seem to grasp. 'Lacey, who are you talking about? Who's coming?'

But then he looked at Amy, and he knew.

Babcock.

Babcock was coming.

'Quickly, Peter.'

'Lacey, you don't understand.' He felt weightless, benumbed. He had nothing to fight with, not even a blade. 'We're totally unarmed. I've seen what he can do.'

'There are weapons more powerful than guns and knives,' the woman replied. Her face held no fear, only a sense of purpose. 'It is time for you to see it.'

'See *what*?'

'What you came to find,' said Lacey. 'The passage.'

SIXTY-EIGHT

Peter in darkness: Lacey was leading them away from the house, into the woods. A frigid wind was blowing through the trees, a ghostly moaning. A rind of moon had ascended, bathing the scene in a trembling light, making the shadows lurch and sway around him. They ascended a ridge and descended another. The snow was deep here, blown into drifts with a hard carapace of crust. They were on the south side of the mountain now; Peter heard, below him, the sound of the river.

He felt it before he saw it: a vastness of space opening before him, the mountain falling away. He reached out reflexively to find Amy, but she was gone. The edge could be anywhere; one wrong step and the darkness would swallow him.

'This way,' Lacey called from ahead. 'Hurry, hurry.'

He followed the sound of her voice. What he thought was a sheer drop was actually a rocky decline, steep but passable. Amy was already moving down the twisting path. He took a breath of icy air, willing his fear away, and followed.

The path grew narrower, running horizontally to the mountain's face as it descended, clinging to it like a catwalk. To his left, sheer rock, glinting with moonlit ice; to his right, an abyss of blackness, a plunge into nothing. Even to look at it was to be swept away; he kept his eyes forward. The women were moving quickly, shadowy presences leaping at the far edge of his vision. Where was Lacey taking them? What was the weapon she had spoken of? He could hear the voice of the river again, far below. The stars shone hard and pure above his face, like chips of ice.

He turned a corner and stopped; Lacey and Amy were standing before a wide, pipelike opening in the mountain's face. The hole was as tall as he was, its depthless interior a maw of blackness.

'This way,' said Lacey.

Two steps, three steps, four; the darkness enveloped him. Lacey was taking them inside the mountain. He remembered the tin of matches in his coat. He stopped and struck one, his insensate fingers fumbling in the cold, but as soon as it sparked, the swirling currents of air puffed the flame away.

Lacey's voice, from up ahead: 'Hurry, Peter.'

He inched his way forward, each step an act of faith. Then he felt a hand on his arm, a firm pressure. Amy.

'Stop.'

He couldn't see anything at all. Despite the cold he had begun to sweat under his parka. Where was Lacey? He had spun around, searching for the opening to orient himself, when from behind him came a squeal of metal, and the sound of an opening door.

Everything blazed with light.

They were in a long hallway, carved from the mountain. The walls were lined with pipes and metal conduits. Lacey was standing at a breaker panel on the wall adjacent to the entrance. The room was illuminated by a bank of buzzing fluorescent lights, high above.

'There's power?'

'Batteries. The doctor showed me how.'

'No batteries could last this long.'

'These are . . . different.'

Lacey swung the heavy door closed behind them.

'He called it Level Five. I will show you. Please come.'

The hallway led to a wider space, sunk in darkness. Lacey moved along the wall to find the switch. Through the soles of his wet boots he could feel a kind of humming, distinctly mechanical.

The lights buzzed and flickered to life.

The room appeared to be some kind of infirmary. An air of abandonment hung over all – the gurney and the long, tall counter covered with dusty equipment, burners and beakers and chrome basins, tarnished with age; a tray of syringes, still sealed in plastic, and resting on a long, rust-stained shawl of

898

fabric, a line of metal probes and scalpels. At the back of the room, in a nest of conduits, was what appeared to be a battery stack.

If you found her, bring her here.

Here, Peter thought. Not just the mountain, but here. This room.

What was here?

Lacey had stepped to a steel case, like a wardrobe, bolted to the wall. On its face was a handle and, beside this, a keypad. He watched as the woman punched in a long series of numbers, then turned the handle with a thunk.

He thought at first the case was empty. Then he saw, resting on the bottom shelf, a metal box. Lacey removed it and passed it to him.

The box, small enough to fit in one hand, was surprisingly light. It appeared to have no seams at all, but there was a latch, with a tiny button beside it that perfectly fit his thumb. Peter pressed it; at once the box separated into two perfectly formed halves. Inside, cradled in foam, lay two rows of tiny glass vials, containing a shimmering green liquid. He counted eleven; a twelfth compartment was empty.

'It is the last virus,' said Lacey. 'The one he gave to Amy. He made it from her blood.'

He searched her face to see the truth registered there. But he already knew the truth; more than that, he felt the truth.

'The empty one. That's you, isn't it? The one Lear gave you.'

Lacey nodded. 'I believe that it is.'

He closed the lid, which sealed with a solid click. He slid off his backpack and pulled out a blanket, which he used to wrap the box, then placed it all inside. From the counter he retrieved a handful of the sealed syringes and put these in the pack as well. Their best chance was to make it through till dawn, then get down the mountain. After that, he didn't know. He turned to Amy.

'How long do we have?'

She shook her head: not long. 'He's close.'

899

'Can he get through that door, Lacey?'

The woman said nothing.

'Lacey?'

'It is my hope that he will,' she said.

They were in the field now, high above the river. Peter's and Amy's trail had disappeared, covered by the blowing snow. Alicia had ridden ahead. It should have been dawn by now, thought Michael. But all he saw was the same gray softening they'd been riding toward for what seemed like hours.

'So where the hell are they?' said Hollis.

Michael didn't know if he meant Peter and Amy or the virals. The thought occurred to him, with a vague acceptance, that they were all going to die up here, that none of them would ever leave this frozen, barren place. Sara and Greer were silent – thinking the same thing, Michael thought, or maybe they were just too cold to speak. His hands were so stiff he doubted he could fire, much less reload, his rifle. He tried to take a drink from his canteen to steady himself, but it was frozen solid.

From out of the darkness they heard the sound of Alicia's horse, riding back at a trot. She pulled up beside them.

'Tracks,' she said, gesturing with a quick tip of her head. 'There's an opening in the fence.'

She heeled her mount, not waiting for them, and barreled back the way she'd come. Without a word Greer followed, the others bringing up the rear. They were in the trees again. Alicia was riding faster now, galloping through the snow. Michael heeled his mount, urging the animal forward. Beside him, Sara bent her neck low over her mount as the branches skimmed past.

Something was moving above them, in the trees.

Michael lifted his face in time to hear a gun go off behind him. No sooner had this happened than a violent force slapped him from the rear, shoving the air from his lungs and catapulting him headfirst over the horse's neck, his rifle swinging out from his hand like a whip. For a single instant he felt himself suspended painlessly over the earth – part of his mind paused to register this surprising fact – but the sensation didn't last; he hit the ground with a jolt, landing on his back in the snow, and now there were other things to think about. He had, he saw, come to rest directly in the path of his own horse. He rolled over on his side, covering the back of his head with his hands as if this might actually help; he felt the wild torrent of air as the panicked animal bounded over him, followed by the concussion of its hooves, one impacting just inches from his ear.

Then it was gone. Everyone was gone.

Michael saw the viral – the same one, he surmised, that had knocked him from his horse – as soon as he drew up to his knees. It was crouched just a few meters from him, poised on its folded haunches like a frog. Its forearms were buried in the snow, which glowed with the organic light of its biolu-minescence, as if the creature were partially immersed in a pool of blue-green water. More snow clung to its chest and arms, a glistening dust; rivulets of moisture were running down its face. Michael realized that he was hearing gunshots, an echoing spatter over the ridge and, mixed with this, like the words of a song, voices calling his name. But these sounds might have been signals from a distant star. Like the vast expanse of darkness around him – for that, too, had faded from his mind, dispersing like the molecules of an expanding gas – they might have pertained to some other person entirely. The viral was clicking now, rocking the muscles of its jaw. With a cock of its head it gave a lazy-seeming snap of teeth, as if it were in no hurry – as if the two of them had all the time in the world. And in that moment Michael realized that the place where he kept his fear was empty. He, Michael the Circuit, wasn't afraid. What he felt was more like anger – a huge, weary irritation, such as he might have felt for a fly that had been buzzing around his face too long. Goddamnit, he thought, guiding his hand to the sheath on his belt. I am so tired of these fucking things.

901

Maybe there are forty million of you and maybe there aren't. In the next two seconds, there's going to be one less.

As Michael rose the viral shot forward, its arms and legs extending like the fingers of an open hand; he barely had enough time to shove the blade out in front of him, his eyes closing reflexively. He felt the bite of metal as the viral slammed into him, folding over Michael's body as he tumbled backward.

He rolled to see the viral lying face-up on the snow. His blade was buried in its chest. Its arms and legs were making a kind of paddling motion, clawing at the air. A pair of figures were standing above the body. Peter and, beside him, Amy. Where had they come from? Amy was holding a rifle – Michael's rifle, covered in snow. At their feet, the creature made a sound that could have been a sigh or a groan. Amy drew the stock of the gun to her shoulder, lowered the barrel, and pushed it into the viral's open mouth.

'I'm sorry,' she said, and pulled the trigger.

Michael rose to his feet. The viral was motionless now, its agonal twitchings ceased. A broad spray of blood lay on the snow. Amy passed the gun to Peter.

'Take this.'

'Are you okay?' Peter asked Michael.

Only then did Michael realize he was shaking. He nodded.

'Come on.'

They heard more gunfire over the ridge. They ran.

It wasn't fair, Lacey knew, what she had done. Allowing Peter and Amy to think that she would be going with them. Setting the bomb's timer and leading them to the door to the tunnel, then directing them to stand on the far side. Pulling the door closed as they watched, then dropping the bolts in place.

She could hear them banging on the other side. Could hear Amy's voice, a final time, ringing in her mind.

Lacey, Lacey, don't go!

Run now. He will be here any minute.

Lacey, please!

*You must help them. They'll be afraid. They won't know what
is happening. Help them, Amy.*

All that had happened here, in this place, needed to be
wiped away. As God had wiped the earth away in the days of
Noah, so that the great ship could sail and make the world
again.

She would be His waters.

Such a terrible thing, the bomb. It was small, Jonas had
explained, just half a kiloton – large enough to destroy the
Chalet itself, all its underground floors, to hide the evidence
of what they had done – but not so large as to register on any
satellites. A fail-safe, in case the virals had ever broken out.
But then the power had failed on the upper levels, and Sykes
was gone, or dead; and though Jonas could have detonated it
himself, he could not bring himself to do this, not with Amy
there.

With Peter and Amy watching, Lacey had knelt before it: a
small, suitcase-shaped object, with the dull finish of all
military things. Jonas had shown her the steps. She pressed a
small indent on the side, and a panel dropped down, revealing a keyboard with a small screen, large enough for a single
line of text. She typed:

E L I Z A B E T H

The screen flickered to life.

ARM?   Y N

She pressed Y.

TIME?

For a moment she paused. Then she typed 5.

5:00 CONFIRM?   Y N

She pressed Y once more. On the screen, a clock began to
run.

4:59

4:58

4:57

She sealed the panel and rose.

'Quickly,' she had said to the two of them, leading them
briskly down the hall. 'We must get out of here now.'

903

Then she'd locked them out.

Lacey, please! I don't know what to do! Tell me what to do!

You will, Amy, when the moment comes. You will know what is inside you then. You will know how to set them free, to make their final passage.

Now she was alone. Her work was nearly done. When she was certain Peter and Amy were gone, she freed the bolts and opened the door wide.

Come to me, she thought. Standing in the doorway, she breathed deeply, composing herself, sending out her mind. *Come to the place where you were made.*

Lacey waited. Five minutes: after so many years, it seemed like nothing, because it really was.

Dawn was breaking over the mountain.

The three of them were racing toward the shots. They crested a ridge; below them, Michael saw a house, the horses outside. Sara and Alicia were waving to them from the door.

The creatures were behind them now, in the trees. They tore down the embankment and dashed inside. Greer and Hollis appeared from behind a curtain, carrying a tall chest of drawers.

'They're right behind us,' Michael said.

They wedged the bureau against the door. A hopeless gesture, thought Michael, but it might buy them a second or two.

'What about these windows?' Alicia was saying. 'Anything we can use?'

They tried to move the cupboard, but it was too heavy. 'Forget it,' Alicia said. She drew a pistol from her waistband and pressed it into Michael's hands. 'Greer, you and Hollis take the window in the bedroom. Everyone else stays here. Two on the door, one on each window, front and back. Circuit, you watch the chimney. They'll go for the horses first.'

Everyone took their positions.

From the bedroom, Hollis shouted, 'Here they come!'

*

Something was wrong, Lacey thought. They should have been here by now. She could feel them, everywhere around her, filling her mind with their hunger, their hunger and the question.

Who am I?

Who am I?

Who am I?

She stepped into the tunnel.

Come to me, she answered. *Come to me. Come to me.*

She moved quickly down its length; she could make out the opening, a circle of softening gray, the elongated dawn of the mountain. The first true light of sunrise would hit them from the west, reflecting off the far side of the valley, its fields of snow and ice.

She reached the tunnel's mouth and stepped out. She could see, below her, the tracks and debris of the virals' ascent up the icy slope. A thousand thousand strong, and more.

They had gone right past.

Despair gripped her. Where are you, she thought, and then she said it, hearing the fury in her voice as it echoed over the valley: 'Where are you?' But there was silence from heaven.

Then, from the stillness, she heard it.

I am here.

The virals hit the doors and windows at once, a furious crash of breaking glass and splintering wood. Peter, bracing the bureau with his shoulder, was blown backward, into Amy. He could hear Hollis and Greer shooting from the bedroom, Alicia and Michael and Sara and Amy, too, everyone firing.

'Fall back!' Alicia was yelling. 'The door's collapsing!'

Peter grabbed Amy by the arm and pulled her into the bedroom. Hollis was at the window. Greer was on the ground beside the bed, bleeding from a deep gash in his head.

'It's glass!' he yelled over the report of Hollis's weapon. 'It's just glass!'

Alicia: 'Hollis, stay on that window!' She dropped her empty clip and slammed a new one into place and pulled the bolt. Here they would make their stand. 'Everyone, get ready!'

They heard the front door give way. Alicia, closest to the bedroom curtain, spun around and began to fire.

The one that got her wasn't the first, or the second, or even the third. It was the fourth. By then her gun was drained. Later, Peter would recall the scene as a sequence of discrete details. The sound of her last shell casings ricocheting on the floor. The swirl of gunpowder smoke in the air and the descent of Alicia's empty clip as she reached to pull a new one from her vest; the viral hurling itself toward her through the tattered curtain, the pitiless smoothness of its face and the flash of its eyes and open jaws; the barrel of her useless gun lifting, and the dart of her hand to draw her blade, too late; the moment of impact, cruel and unstoppable, Alicia falling backward to the floor, the viral's burrowing jaws finding the curve of her neck.

It was Hollis who took the shot, stepping forward as the viral lifted its face and spearing the barrel of his rifle into its mouth and firing, spraying the back of its head against the wall of the bedroom. Peter scrabbled forward and grabbed Alicia under the arms, dragging her away from the door. The blood was running freely from her neck, a deep crimson, soaking her vest. Someone was yelling, saying her name over and over, but maybe that was him. Braced against the wall, he hugged Alicia to his chest, holding her upright between his legs, reflexively putting his hands over the wound to try to stop the bleeding. Amy and Sara were on the floor now, too, huddled against the wall. Another creature came through the curtain and Peter lifted his pistol and fired, his last two rounds. The first one missed but not the second. In his arms, Alicia was breathing strangely, all hiccups and gasps. There was blood, so much blood.

He closed his eyes and pulled her tightly against him.

*

Lacey turned; Babcock was perched above her, at the top of the tunnel's mouth. As great and terrible a thing as God had ever made. Lacey felt no fear, only wonder at the magnificent workings of God. That He should make a being so perfect in his design, fit to devour a world. And as she gazed upon him glowing with his great and terrible radiance – a hallowed light, like the light of angels – Lacey's heart swelled with the knowledge that she had not been wrong, that the long night of her vigil would end as she'd foreseen. A vigil begun so many years ago on a damp spring morning when she had opened the door of the Convent of the Sisters of Mercy in Memphis, Tennessee, and beheld a little girl.

Jonas, she thought, do you see that I was right? All is forgiven; all that has been lost can be found again. Jonas, I am coming to tell you. I am practically with you now.

She darted back into the tunnel.

Come to me. Come to me come to me come to me.

She ran. She was in that place but also another; she was running down the tunnel, drawing Babcock inside; but she was also a little girl again, in the field. She could smell the sweetness of the earth, feel the cool night air on her cheeks; she could hear her sisters and her mother's voice, calling from the doorway: *Run, children, run as fast as you can.*

She hit the door and kept on going, down the hall with its buzzing lights, into the room with its gurney and beakers and batteries, all the little things of the old world and its terrible dreams of blood.

She stopped, pivoting to face the doorway. And there he was.

I am Babcock. One of Twelve.

As am I, thought Sister Lacey, as, behind her, the bomb's timer reached 0:00, the atoms of its core collapsed into themselves, and her mind filled up forever with the pure white light of heaven.

SIXTY-NINE

She was Amy, and she was forever. She was one of Twelve and also the other, the one above and behind, the Zero. She was the Girl from Nowhere, the One Who Walked In, who lived a thousand years; Amy of Multitudes, the Girl with the Souls Inside Her.

She was Amy. She was Amy. She was Amy.

She was the first to rise. After the thunder and the shaking, the trembling and the roaring. Lacey's little house bucking and rocking like a horse, like a tiny boat at sea. Everyone yelling and screaming, huddled against the wall and holding on.

But then it was over. The earth below them came to rest. The air was full of dust. Everyone coughing and choking, amazed to be alive.

They were alive.

She led Peter and the others out, past the bodies of the dead ones, into the light of dawn where the Many waited. The Many of Babcock no more.

They were everywhere and all around. A sea of faces, eyes. They moved toward her in the vastness of their number, into the dawning sunlight. She could feel the empty space inside them where the dream had been, the dream of Babcock, and in its place the question, fierce and burning:

Who am I who am I who am I?

And she knew. Amy knew. She knew them all, each to a one; she knew them all at last. She was the ship, just as Lacey had said; she carried their souls inside her. She had kept these all along, waiting for this day, when she would return what was rightfully theirs – the stories of who they were. The day when they would make their passage.

Come to me, she thought. *Come to me come to me come to me.*

They came. From out of the trees, from across the snowy fields, from all the hidden places. She moved among them, touching and caressing, and told them what they longed to know.

You are . . . Smith.

You are . . . Tate.

You are . . . Duprey.

You are Erie you are Ramos you are Ward you are Cho you are Singh Atkinson Johnson Montefusco Cohen Murrey Nguyen Elberson Lazaro Torres Wright Winborne Pratt Scalamonti Mendoza Ford Chung Frost Vandyne Carlin Park Diego Murphy Parsons Richini O'Neil Myers Zapata Young Scheer Tanaka Lee White Gupta Solnik Jessup Rile Nichols Maharana Rayburn Kennedy Mueller Doerr Goldman Pooley Price Kahn Cordell Ivanov Simpson Wong Palumbo Kim Rao Montgomery Busse Mitchell Walsh McEvoy Bodine Olson Jaworksi Ferguson Zachos Spenser Ruscher . . .

The sun was lifting over the mountain, a blinding brightness. Come, thought Amy. Come into the light and remember.

You are Cross you are Flores you are Haskell Vasquez Andrews McCall Barbash Sullivan Shapiro Jablonski Choi Zeidner Clark Huston Rossi Culhane Baxter Nunez Athanasian King Higbee Jensen Lombardo Anderson James Sasso Lindquist Masters Hakeemzedah Levander Tsujimoto Michie Osther Doody Bell Morales Lenzi Andriyakhova Watkins Bonilla Fitzgerald Tinti Asmundson Aiello Daley Harper Brewer Klein Weatherall Griffin Petrova Kates Hadad Riley MacLeod Wood Patterson . . .

Amy felt their sorrow, but it was different now. It was a holy soaring. A thousand recollected lives were passing through her, a thousand thousand stories – of love and work, of parents and children, of duty and joy and grief. Beds slept in and meals eaten, and the bliss and pain of the body, and a view of summer leaves from a window on a morning it had rained; the nights of loneliness and the nights of love, the soul in its body's keeping always longing to be known. She moved among them where they lay in the snow, the Many no more, each in the place of their choosing.

The snow angels.

Remember, she told them. Remember.

I am Flynn I am Gonzalez I am Young Wentzell Armstrong O'Brien Reeves Farajian Watanabe Mulroney Chernesky Logan Braverman Livingston Martin Campana Cox Torrey Swartz Tobin Hecht Stuart Lewis Redwine Pho Markovich Todd Mascucci Kostin Laseter Salib Hennesey Kasteley Merriweather Leone Barkley Kiernan Campbell Lamos Marion Quang Kagan Glazner Dubois Egan Chandler Sharpe Browning Ellenzweig Nakamura Giacomo Jones I am I am I am . . .

The sun would do its work. Soon they would be dead, then ashes, then nothing. Their bodies would scatter to the winds. They were leaving her at last. She felt their spirits rising, sailing away.

'Amy.'

Peter was beside her now. She had no words for the look upon his face. She would tell him soon, she thought. She would tell him all she knew, all she believed. What lay ahead, the long journey they would take together. But now was not a time for talk.

'Go inside,' she said, and took his empty pistol from him, dropping it into the snow. 'Go inside and save her.'

'Can I save her?'

And Amy nodded.

'You have to,' she said.

Sara and Michael had lifted Alicia onto the bed and stripped off her blood-soaked vest. Her eyes were closed, fluttering.

'I need bandages!' Sara yelled. More blood was on her hands, her hair. 'Someone get me something to stanch this bleeding!'

Hollis used his blade to cut a length of cloth from the sheets. They weren't clean, nothing was, but they would have to do.

'We have to tie her down,' Peter said.

'Peter, the wound is too deep,' Sara said. She shook her head hopelessly. 'It's not going to matter.'

'Hollis, give me your blade.'

910

He told the others what to do, cutting Lacey's bed linens into long strips, then twisting them together. They bound Alicia's hands and feet to the posts of the bed. Sara said the bleeding seemed to be slowing – an ominous sign. Her pulse was high and thready.

'If she survives,' Greer warned from the foot of the bed, 'these sheets will never hold her.'

But Peter wasn't listening. He moved to the main room, where among the wreckage he found his pack. The metal box was still inside, with the syringes. He removed one of the vials and returned to the bedroom, where he passed it to Sara.

'Give her this.'

She took it in her hand, examining it. 'Peter, I don't know what this is.'

'It's Amy,' he said.

She gave Alicia half the vial. Through the day and into the night they waited. Alicia had lapsed into a kind of twilight. Her skin was dry and hot. The wound at her neck had sealed, taking on a bruised appearance, purple and inflamed. From time to time she would seem to awaken, emerging into a kind of twilight, moaning. Then she closed her eyes again.

They had dragged the corpses of the dead virals outside, with the others. Their bodies had fallen quickly into a gray ash that was still swirling in the air, coating every surface like a layer of dirty snow. By morning, Peter thought, they would all be gone. Michael and Hollis had boarded up the windows and set the door back on its hinges; as darkness fell, they burned what was left of the bureau in the fireplace. Sara stitched up Greer's head, wrapped it in another bandage made from bed linens. They slept in shifts, two to watch Alicia. Peter said he would stay up all night with her, but in the end his exhaustion got the better of him and he slept as well, curled on the cold floor by her bed.

By morning, Alicia had begun to strain at the straps. All color had drained from her skin; her eyes, behind her lids, were rosy with burst capillaries.

'Give her more.'

'Peter, I don't know what I'm doing,' Sara said. She was worn down, threadbare; they all were. 'It could kill her.'

'Do it.'

They gave her the rest of the vial. Outside it had begun to snow again. Greer and Hollis left to scout the woods and returned an hour later, half frozen. It was really coming down, they said.

Hollis pulled Peter aside. 'Food's going to be a problem,' he said quietly. They had taken an inventory of Lacey's cupboard; most of the jars were smashed.

'I know.'

'There's another thing. I know the bomb was underground, but there could be radiation. Michael says that at the very least it's in the water table. He doesn't think we should stay here much longer. There's some kind of structure on the other side of the valley. It looks like there's a ridge we can use to cut to the east.'

'What about Lish? We can't move her.'

Hollis paused. 'I'm just saying we could get stuck here. Then we're in real trouble. We don't want to try it half-starving in a blizzard.'

Hollis was right, and Peter knew it. 'You want to scout it out?'

'When the snow lets up.'

Peter offered a concessionary nod. 'Take Michael with you.'

'I was thinking of Greer.'

'He should stay here,' said Peter.

Hollis was silent a moment, taking Peter's meaning. 'All right,' he said.

The squall blew through with the night; by morning, the sky was crisp and bright. Hollis and Michael gathered their gear to go. If all went well, Hollis said, they'd be back before nightfall. But it could be as long as a day. In the snowy yard, Sara hugged Hollis, then Michael. Greer and Amy were inside with Alicia. In the last twenty-four hours, since they'd given her the second dose of the virus, her condition seemed to have reached a kind of stasis. But her fever was still high, and her eyes had gotten worse.

'Just don't . . . let it go too long,' Hollis told Peter. 'She wouldn't want you to.'

They waited. Amy was staying close to Alicia now, never leaving her bedside. It was clear to all what was occurring. The merest light in the room made her flinch, and she had begun to strain at the straps again.

'She's fighting it,' Amy said. 'But I'm afraid that she is losing.'

Darkness fell, with no sign of Michael and Hollis. Peter had never felt so helpless. Why wasn't it working, as it had with Lacey? But he wasn't a doctor; they were only guessing about what to do. The second dose could be killing her, for all he knew. Peter was aware of Greer watching him, waiting for him to act. And yet he could do nothing.

It was just past dawn when Sara shook him awake. Peter had fallen asleep in a chair, his head rocked forward onto his chest.

'I think . . . it's happening,' she said.

Alicia was breathing very rapidly. Her whole body was taut, the muscles of her jaw twitching, a fluttering beneath the surface of her skin. A low, effortful moan issued from the back of her throat. For a moment she relaxed. Then it happened again.

'Peter.'

He turned to see Greer, standing in the doorway. He was holding a blade.

'It's time.'

Peter rose, positioning his body between Greer and the bed where Alicia lay. 'No.'

'I know it's hard, but she's a soldier. A soldier of the Expeditionary. It's time for her to take the trip.'

'I meant no, it's not your job.' He held out his hand. 'Give me the blade, Major.'

913

Greer hesitated, searching Peter's face with his eyes. 'You don't have to do this.'

'Yes, I do.' He felt no fear, only resignation. 'I gave her my word, you see. I'm the only one who can.'

Reluctantly, Greer surrendered the knife. A familiar heft and balance: Peter saw that it was his own, the one he'd left at the gate with Eustace.

'I'd like to be alone with her, if that's all right.'

They said their goodbyes. Peter heard the door to the house open and close again. He went to the window and yanked one of the boards free, dousing the room with the soft gray light of morning. Alicia moaned and turned her head away. Greer was right. Peter didn't think he had more than a couple of minutes. He remembered what Muncey had said at the end, how quickly it comes on. How he wanted to feel it coming out of him.

Peter sat on the edge of the bed, the blade in his hand. He wanted to say something to her, but words seemed too small a thing for what he felt. He sat for a quiet moment, letting his mind fill with thoughts of her. Things they'd done and said, and what still lay unspoken between them. It was all he could think to do.

He could have stayed that way a day, a year, a hundred years. But he could wait no longer, he knew. He rose and positioned himself above her on the bed, straddling her waist. Holding the blade with both hands, he placed its tip at the base of her breastbone. The sweet spot. He felt his life dividing into halves: that which had come before and all that would come after. He felt her rise against him, her body clenching against the restraints. His hands were trembling, his vision blurry with tears.

'I'm sorry, Lish,' he said, and closed his eyes as he lifted the blade, gathering all his strength inside himself before finding the will to bring it down.

SEVENTY

It was spring and the baby was coming.

Maus had been having contractions for days. She would be cleaning in the kitchen, or lying in bed, or watching Theo work in the yard, when suddenly she felt it: a quick tightening across her midriff that made her breath catch in her chest. Is this it? Theo would ask her. Is he coming? Is the baby coming now? For a moment she would look away, her head cocked to the side, as if listening for some distant sound. Then she would return her attention to him, offering a reassuring smile. There. You see? It was nothing. Just the one. It's all right. Go back to what you were doing, Theo.

But now it wasn't nothing. It was the middle of the night. Theo was dreaming, a simple, happy dream of sunlight falling on a golden field, when he heard Maus's voice, calling his name. She was in the dream, too, but he couldn't see her; she was hiding from him, she was playing some kind of game. She was ahead of him, then behind, he didn't know where she was. *Theo.* Conroy was yipping and barking, bounding through the grass, racing away from him and tearing back again, urging him to follow. Where are you, Theo called, where are you? *I'm wet*, Mausami's voice was saying. *I'm wet all over. Wake up, Theo. I think my water's broken.*

Then he was awake and standing up, fumbling in the dark, trying to put his boots on. Conroy was up too, wagging his tail, shoving his damp nose in Theo's face as he knelt to light the lantern. Is it morning? Are we going out?

Mausami drew a sharp breath through her teeth. 'Ooo.' She arched her back off the sagging mattress. 'Ooo.'

She had told him what to do, the things she'd need. Sheets and towels to put under her, for the blood and all the rest. A knife and fishing line for the cord. Water, to clean the baby, and a blanket to wrap him in.

'Don't go anywhere, I'll be right back.'

'Flyers,' she moaned, 'where would I go?' Another contraction surged through her. She reached for his hand and squeezed it tight, digging her nails into his palm, gritting her teeth in pain. 'Oh, *fuck.*' Then she turned and retched onto the floor.

The room filled with the tang of vomit. Conroy thought it was for him, a wonderful present. Theo shoved the dog away, then helped Mausami ease back onto the pillows.

'Something's wrong.' Her face was pale with fear. 'It shouldn't hurt like this.'

'What should I do, Maus?'

'I don't know!'

Theo raced down stairs, Conroy following at his heels. The baby, the baby was coming. He'd meant to put all the supplies together in one place, but of course he never had. The house was freezing, the fire had burned down; the baby would need to be kept warm. He put an armful of logs into the cradle, then knelt before it, blowing on the embers so it would catch. He got rags and a pail from the kitchen. He'd intended to boil water, to sterilize it, but it didn't seem like there was time for that now.

'Theo, where are you!'

He filled the pail and got a sharp knife and carried it all up to the bedroom. Maus was sitting up now, her long hair spilling over her face, looking afraid.

'I'm sorry about the floor,' she said.

'Any more contractions?'

She shook her head.

Conroy was back at the mess on the floor. Theo shooed him out and got down on his hands and knees to clean it up, holding his breath. How ridiculous. She was about to have a baby, and here he was, flinching at the smell of vomit.

'Uh-oh,' Maus said.

By the time he'd risen, the contraction was upon her. She'd pulled her legs upward, drawing her heels toward her buttocks. Tears were squeezing from the corners of her eyes.

'It hurts! It hurts!' She rolled suddenly onto her side. 'Press my back, Theo!'

She had never said anything about this. 'Where? How should I press it?'

She was shouting into the pillow. 'Anywhere!'

He gave an uncertain push.

'Lower! For godsakes!'

He curled his hand into a ball and pressed his knuckles into her; he felt her pushing back. He counted the seconds: Ten, twenty, thirty.

'Back labor.' She was panting for breath. 'The baby's head is shoving against my spine. It'll make me want to push. I can't push yet, Theo. Don't let me push.'

She drew up onto her hands and knees. She was wearing only a T-shirt. The sheets beneath her were soaked with fluid, giving off a warm, sweet smell, like mown hay. He remembered his dream of the field, the waves of golden sunlight.

Another contraction; Mausami groaned and dropped her face into the mattress.

'Don't just stand there!'

Theo got on the bed beside her, positioning his fist on the ridge of her spine, and leaned in, pushing with all his might.

Hours and hours. The contractions continued, hard and deep, through the length of the day. Theo stayed with her on the bed, pressing her spine until his hands were numb, his arms rubbery with fatigue. But compared to what was happening to Mausami, this small discomfort was nothing. He left her side only twice, to call Conroy in from the yard and then, as the day was ending and he heard him whining at the door, to let him out again. Always by the time he returned up the stairs Mausami was shouting his name.

He wondered if it was always like this. He didn't really know. It was horrible, endless, like nothing he'd ever experienced. He wondered if Mausami would have the energy, when the time came, to push the baby out. Between contractions she seemed to float in a kind of half sleep; she was focusing her mind, he knew, readying herself for the next wave of pain to move through her. All he could do was press her back, but this seemed to be helping very little. It didn't seem to be helping at all.

He was lighting the lantern – a second night, he thought with despair, how could this go on a second night? – when Maus gave a sharp cry. He turned to see watery blood pour from her, running in ribbons down her thighs.

'Maus, you're bleeding.'

She had rolled onto her back, pulling her thighs upward. She was breathing very quickly, her face drenched with sweat. 'Hold. My legs,' she gasped.

'Hold them how?'

'I'm going. To push. Theo.'

He positioned himself at the foot of the bed and placed his hands against her knees. As the next contraction came, she bent at the waist, driving her weight toward him.

'Oh, God. I can see him.'

She had opened like a flower, revealing a disk of pink skin covered in wet black hair. Then, in the next instant, this vision was gone, the flower's petals folding over it, drawing the baby back inside her.

Three, four, five more times she bore down; each time the baby appeared and, just as quickly, vanished. For the first time he thought it: this baby doesn't want to be born. This baby wants to stay just where it is.

'Help me, Theo,' she begged. All her strength was gone. 'Pull him out, pull him out, please, just pull him out.'

'You have to push one more time, Maus.' She seemed completely helpless, insensate, on the verge of final collapse. 'Are you listening? You have to push!'

'I can't, I can't!'

The next contraction took her; she lifted her head and released an animal cry of pain.

'Push, Maus, push!'

She did; she pushed. As the top of the baby's head appeared, Theo reached down and slipped his index finger inside her, into her heat and dampness. He felt the orbital curve of an eye socket, the delicate bulge of a nose. He couldn't pull the baby, there was nothing to hold on to, the baby would have to come to him. He drew back and positioned a hand beneath her, leaning his shoulder against her legs to brace the force of her effort.

'We're almost there! Don't stop!'

Then, as if the touch of his hand had given it the will to be born, the baby's face appeared, sliding from her. A vision of magnificent strangeness, with ears and a nose and a mouth and bulging, froglike eyes. Theo cupped his hand below the smooth, wet curve of its skull. The cord, a translucent, blood-filled tube, was looped around its neck. Though no one had told him to do this, Theo placed a finger under it, gently lifting it away. Then he reached inside Mausami and tucked a finger under the baby's arm, and pulled.

The body wriggled free, filling Theo's hands with his slippery, blue-skinned warmth. A boy. The baby was a boy. Still he had not breathed, or made the slightest sound. His arrival in the world was incomplete, but Maus had explained the next part well enough. Theo rolled the baby in his hands, bracing his skinny body lengthwise with his forearm and supporting his downturned face with his palm; he began to rub the baby's back, moving the fingers of his free hand in a circular motion. His heart was hammering in his chest, but he felt no panic; his mind was clear and focused, his entire being brought to bear on this one task. Come on, he was saying, come on and breathe. After everything you just went through, how can that be so hard? The baby had only just been born, but already Theo felt his hold upon him – how, simply by existing, this small, gray thing in his arms had obliterated all other ways in which Theo might live. Come on, baby. Do it. Open your lungs and breathe.

And then he did. Theo felt his tiny chest inflate, a discernible click, then something warm and sticky, spraying into his hand like a sneeze. The baby took a second breath, filling his lungs, and Theo felt a force of life flowing into him.

Theo turned him over, reaching for a rag. The baby had begun to cry, not the robust complaints he had expected but a kind of mewing. He wiped his nose and lips and cheeks and scooped the last mucus from his mouth with a finger, and placed him, the cord still attached, on Mausami's chest.

Her face was exhausted, heavy-lidded and worn. At the corners of her eyes he saw a fan of wrinkles that hadn't been there just a day ago. She managed a weak but grateful smile. It was over. The baby had been born, the baby was here at last.

He placed a blanket over the baby, over the two of them, and sat beside them on the bed, and let it all go: he wept.

It was deep night when Theo awoke, thinking: Where was Conroy?

Maus and the baby were asleep. They had decided – or, rather, Maus had decided, and Theo had quickly agreed – to name him Caleb. They had swaddled him tightly in a blanket and placed him on the mattress beside her. The air of the room was still heavy with a rich, earthy smell, of blood and sweat and birth. She had fed the baby, or tried to – her milk wouldn't be coming in for a day or so – and taken a bit of food herself, a mush of boiled potatoes from the basement and a few bites of a mealy apple from their winter stores. She would need protein soon, Theo knew; but there was plenty of small game around, now that the weather had warmed. As soon as they were settled, he would have to leave to hunt.

It seemed obvious, suddenly, that they would never be departing this place. They had everything they needed to make a life here. The house had stood the years, waiting for someone to make it a home again. He wondered why it had taken him so long to see this. When Peter came back, that was what Theo would say to him. Maybe there was something on that mountain and maybe there wasn't. It didn't matter. This was home; they would never be leaving.

He sat awhile, mulling over these things, full of a quiet amazement that seemed to lodge in the deepest part of him.

But eventually exhaustion overcame him. He crawled in beside them and soon was fast asleep.

Now, awake, he realized he'd forgotten all about Conroy. He searched his memory for the last time he'd been aware of the dog's presence. Sometime late, close to sunset, Conroy had started to whine, asking to be let out. Theo had done this quickly, not wanting to leave Maus's side for even an instant. Conroy never wandered far, and as soon as he was done with his business, he'd be scratching at the door. Theo had been so preoccupied that he had simply slammed the door and raced back up the stairs and forgotten all about him.

Until now. It was odd, he thought, that he hadn't heard so much as a peep. No scratching at the door or barking from outside. For a period of days after he had found the footprints in the barn, Theo had kept a watchful eye, never venturing far from the house, keeping the shotgun handy. He had told Mausami nothing, not wanting to worry her. But as time passed, with no other signs, he had let his mind turn toward the more pressing matter of the baby. He'd found himself wondering if he had misread what he'd seen. The footprints could have been his own, after all, the can something Conroy had fished out of the trash.

He rose quietly, taking the lantern and his boots and the shotgun from its place beside the door, and descended to the living room. He sat on the stairs to put on his boots, not bothering with the laces; he lit a piece of kindling off the coals of the fire, setting it to the wick of the lantern, and opened the door.

He had expected to find Conroy sleeping on the porch, but it was empty. Raising the lantern to spread its light, Theo stepped down into the yard. No moon or even stars; a damp spring wind was blowing, bearing rain. He lifted his face into the gathering mist, a light spattering on his brow and cheeks. The dog, wherever he'd run off to, would be glad to see him. He'd want to get inside, out of the rain.

'Conroy!' he called. 'Conroy, where are you?'

The other houses stood silent. Conroy had never shown

more than passing interest in these structures, as if, through some dog sense, he knew them to be of no value. There were things inside, the man and the woman made use of them, what did it matter to him?

Theo advanced slowly down the trace, the shotgun clenched under one arm while, with the other, he swept the area with the light of his lantern. If it started to rain in earnest, he didn't think he'd be able to keep the thing lit. That goddamn dog, he thought. Now was not the time for him to run off like this.

'Conroy, damnit, where did you go?'

Theo found him lying at the base of the last house. He knew at once the dog was dead. His slender body was still, his silvery mane drenched in blood.

Then, coming from the house – the sound traveling with an arrow's swift assurance to pierce his mind with terror – he heard Mausami scream.

Thirty steps, fifty, a hundred: the lantern was gone, dropped on the ground by Conroy's body, he was racing through the dark in his unlaced boots, first one and then the other launching off his feet. He hit the porch at a leap, ripped open the door, and dashed up the stairs.

The bedroom was empty.

He tore through the house, calling her name. No sign of a struggle; Maus and the baby had simply vanished. He raced through the kitchen and out the back, just in time to hear her scream again, the sound strangely muted, as if rising toward him through a mile of water.

She was in the barn.

He entered at a dead sprint, bursting through the door, spinning his body to sweep the dark interior with the shotgun. Maus was in the backseat of the old Volvo, clutching the baby to her chest. She was waving frantically, her words muffled by the thickness of the glass.

'Theo, behind you!'

He turned and as he turned the shotgun was knocked

away, slapped like a twig from his hands. Then something grabbed him, not any single part but the whole of him, Theo entire; he felt himself lifted up. The car with Mausami and the baby in it was somewhere below him and he was flying through the dark. He hit the hood of the car with a crunch of buckling metal, rolling, tumbling; he landed face-up on the ground and came to a stop but then something, the same something, grabbed him, and he was flying again. The wall, this time, with its shelves of tools and stores and cans of fuel. He hit it face-first, glass exploding, wood splintering, everything falling in a clattering rain; as the ground rose to meet him, slowly and then quickly and finally all at once, he felt a crunch of bone.

Agony. Stars filled his vision, actual stars. The thought reached him, like a message from some distant place, that he was about to die. He should be dead already. The viral should have killed him. But this would happen soon enough. He could taste blood in his mouth, feel it stinging his eyes. He was lying face-down on the floor of the barn, one leg, the broken one, twisted under him; the creature was above him now, a looming shadow, preparing to strike. It was better this way, Theo thought. Better that the viral should take him first. He didn't want to watch what would happen to Mausami and the baby. Through the murk of his battered brain, he heard her calling out to him.

Look away, Maus, he thought. I love you. Look away.

XI

THE
NEW THING

To me, fair friend, you never can be old,
For as you were when first your eye I ey'd,
Such seems your beauty still.

— SHAKESPEARE,
Sonnet 104

SEVENTY-ONE

They came down the mountain as the river was thawing, riding on top of the snow. They came down as one, wearing their packs, brandishing blades. They came down to the valley, Michael at the wheel of the Sno-Cat with Greer beside him, the others up top, the wind and sun in their faces. They came down at last, into the wild country they had reclaimed.

They were going home.

They had been on the mountain one hundred and twelve days. In all that time they had seen not a single viral. For days after they had crossed the ridge, the snow had poured down, sealing them inside the lodge of the old hotel. A great stone building, its doors and windows covered by sheets of plywood, set into the frame with heavy screws. They had expected to find bodies inside but the place was empty, the furniture around the hearth of its cavernous front room draped in ghostly white sheets, the larder of its vast kitchen stocked with every kind of can, many still with their labels. Upstairs, a warren of bedrooms, and in the basement, a huge, silent furnace and long racks lining the walls, holding skis. The place was as cold as the grave. They didn't know if the chimney was blocked; at the very least it would be full of leaves and birds' nests. The only thing to do was light a fire and hope for the best. In the office, they found boxes of paper packed away in a closet; they rolled it up for kindling and, with Peter's axe, chopped up a pair of dining room chairs. After a few smoky minutes, the room blazed with light and warmth. They dragged mattresses down from the second floor and slept by the fire, while the snow piled up outside.

They had found the Sno-Cats the following morning:

three of them, resting on their treads in a garage behind the lodge. You think you can get one of these things running? Peter asked Michael.

It had taken most of the winter. By then, everyone was half stir-crazy, anxious to be leaving. The days were longer, and the sun seemed to hold a distant, remembered warmth; but still the snow was deep, rising in great drifts against the walls of the lodge. They had burned most of the furniture and the railings of the porch. From the three Sno-Cats, Michael had harvested enough parts to make one go, or so he believed; it was fuel that was the problem. The large tank behind the shed was empty, fissured with rot. All he had was what was in the Cats themselves, just a few gallons, badly contaminated by rust. He siphoned this off into plastic pails and poured it through a funnel lined with rags. He let it settle overnight, then repeated the process, each time stripping more debris away but also depleting his supply. By the time he was satisfied, he had just five gallons left, which he poured back into the Cat.

'No promises,' he warned everyone. He'd done his best to flush the fuel tank, running gallon after gallon of melted snow through it, but it wouldn't take much to gum up a fuel line. 'The damn thing could kick a hundred meters from here,' he said. Though he knew they wouldn't take this warning seriously.

It was a sunny morning when they rolled the Cat from the shed and loaded up their gear. Gigantic icicles, like long, jeweled teeth, hung from the eaves of the lodge. Greer, who had helped Michael with the repairs – it turned out he'd been an oiler once and knew a thing or two about engines – took a place in the cab beside him. The others would ride on top, on a wide metal platform with a rail. They had removed the plow to cut the weight, hoping to squeeze a few more miles from what little fuel they had.

Michael opened the window and directed his voice to the rear of the vehicle. 'Is everyone on board?'

Peter was lashing the last of the gear to the back of the

Sno-Cat. Amy had taken her position at the rail; Hollis and Sara stood below him, passing up the skis. 'Hold on a minute,' he said. He rose and cupped his hands around his mouth. 'Lish, let's get a move on!'

She emerged from the lodge. Like all of them, she was wearing a red nylon jacket with the words SKI PATROL printed on the back, and small leather boots that fit the skis, her leggings covered to the knees by a pair of canvas gaiters. Her hair had grown back, an even more vivid shade of red, mostly hidden now beneath the band of her long-brimmed cap. Over her eyes she wore dark glasses with leather pieces attached to the lenses, hugging the sides of her face like a pair of goggles.

'Seems like we're always leaving somewhere,' she answered. 'I just wanted to say goodbye to the place.'

She was standing on the edge of the porch, ten meters away, roughly level with the platform on the Sno-Cat. Peter detected, in the sudden, curving grin on her face and the way she tipped her head, first this way and then the other, what she was about to attempt – that she was gauging the distance and angle. She removed her hat, releasing her red hair into the sunshine, and tucked it inside her Velcroed jacket; she took three steps back, bending at the knees. Her hands, at her sides, gave a watery shake, then stilled. She rose on her toes.

'Lish—'

Too late; two quick bounds and she was up. The porch where she had stood was empty; Alicia was lifting through the air. It was, Peter thought, a sight to see. Alicia Blades, Youngest Captain Since The Day; Alicia Donadio, the Last Expeditionary, airborne. She swept across the sun, arms outstretched, feet together; at the apex of her ascent, she tucked her chin against her chest and rolled head over heels, aiming the soles of her boots at the Sno-Cat, arms rising, her body descending toward them like an arrow. She hit the platform with a shuddering clang, melting to a crouch to absorb the force of the impact.

'Fuck!' Michael swiveled at the wheel. 'What was that?'

'Nothing,' Peter said. He could still feel the metallic hum of her landing, chiming through his bones. 'Just Lish.'

Alicia rose and tapped the glass of the cab. 'Relax, Michael.'

'Flyers, I thought we'd blown the engine.'

Hollis and Sara climbed aboard; Alicia took her place at the rail and turned to Peter. Even through the smoky opaqueness of her glasses, Peter could detect the orange thrum of her eyes.

'Sorry,' she said with a guilty grin. 'I thought I could nail it.'

'I don't think I'll ever get used to you doing that,' he said.

The blade had never fallen. Or rather, it *had* fallen, when suddenly it stopped.

Everything had stopped.

It was Alicia who had done it, seizing Peter by the wrists. Freezing the blade in its downward arc, inches from her chest. The restraints had ripped away, like paper. Peter felt the power in her arms, a titanic force, more than human, and knew he was too late.

But when she opened her eyes, it was Alicia he saw.

'If it's okay with you, Peter,' she'd said, 'would you mind closing those shades? Because it's really, really bright in here.'

The New Thing. That's what they were calling her. Neither one nor the other, but somehow both. She couldn't feel the virals, as Amy could; couldn't hear the question, the great sadness of the world. In every respect she seemed herself, the same Alicia she had always been, save one:

When she chose to, she could do the most astounding things.

But then, Peter thought, when had that not been true of her?

The Sno-Cat died within sight of the valley floor. A chuffing and wheezing, followed by a final sneeze of smoke from the exhaust pipe; they coasted a few more meters on the treads and came to rest.

'That's it,' Michael called from the cab. 'We hoof it from here.'

Everyone climbed down. Peter could detect, rising from the trees below, the sound of the river, swollen with runoff. Their destination was the garrison, at least two days of travel in the sticky spring snow. They unloaded their gear and strapped themselves into their skis. They had learned the basics from a book they'd found in the lodge, a slender, yellowed volume called *Principles of Nordic Skiing*, though the words and pictures it contained made the thing itself look easier than it actually was. Greer, of all people, could barely stay upright and, even when he managed it, was always flying off helplessly into the trees. Amy did her best to help him – she had taken to it immediately, gliding and pushing off with a nimble grace – and showed him what to do. 'Like this,' she'd say. 'You just kind of fly along the snow. It's easy.' It wasn't easy, not by a long shot, and the rest of them had suffered more than their share of tumbles but, with practice, had all become at least passably proficient.

'Ready, everyone?' Peter asked, as he snapped his bindings closed. A murmured assent from the group. It was just shy of half-day, the sun high in the sky. 'Amy?'

The girl nodded. 'I think we're all right.'

'Okay, everyone. All eyes.'

They crossed the river at the old iron bridge, turned west, spent one night in the open, and reached the garrison by the end of the second day. Spring was in the valley. At this lower altitude, most of the snow had melted away, and the exposed ground was thick with mud. They traded their skis for the Humvee the battalion had left behind, supplied themselves with food and fuel and weapons from the underground cache, and set out once again.

They could carry enough diesel to take them as far as the Utah line. Maybe a little farther. After that, unless they found more, they'd be on foot again. They cut south, skirting the hills, into a dry country of blood-red rocks rising around them in fantastic formations. At night they took refuge where they could – a grain elevator, the back of an empty semitruck, a gas station shaped like a tepee.

They knew they were not safe. The ones of Babcock were dead, but there were others. The ones of Sosa. The ones of Lambright. The ones of Baffes and Morrison and Carter and all the rest. That was what they had learned. That was what Lacey had showed them when she'd exploded the bomb, and Amy, when she had stood among the Many as they lay down in the snow and died. What the Twelve were, but even more: how to set the others free.

'I think the closest analogue would be bees,' Michael had said. During their long days on the mountain, Peter had given everyone Lacey's files to read; the group had spent many hours in debate. But ultimately it was Michael who had advanced the hypothesis that pulled all the facts together.

'These Twelve original subjects,' he went on, gesturing over the files, 'they're like the queens, each with a different variant of the virus. Carriers of that variant are part of a collective mind, linked to the original host.'

'How do you figure that?' Hollis asked. Of all of them, he was the most skeptical, pressing on every point.

'The way they move, for starters. Haven't you ever wondered about that? Everything they do looks coordinated because it *is*, just like Olson said. The more I think about it, the more this makes sense. The fact that they always travel in pods – bees do the same thing, traveling in swarms. I'll bet they send out scouts the same way, to establish new hives, like the one in the mine. And it explains why they take up one person out of ten. Think of it as a kind of reproduction, a way of continuing a particular viral strain.'

'Like a family?' Sara said.

'Well, that's putting it nicely. We're talking about *virals* here, don't forget. But yes, I suppose you could look at it that way.'

Peter remembered something Vorhees had said to him, that the virals were – what was the word? Clustering. He related this to the group.

'It follows,' Michael agreed, nodding along. 'There's very little large game left, and almost no people. They're running out of food, and running out of new hosts to infect. They're a species like any other, programmed to survive. So pulling together like that could be a kind of adaptation, to conserve their energy.'

'Meaning . . . they're weaker now?' Hollis tendered.

Michael considered this, rubbing his patchy beard. ' "Weaker" is a relative term,' he replied guardedly, 'but yes, I'd say so. And I'll go back to the bee analogy. Everything a hive does, it does to protect its queen. If Vorhees was right, then what you're seeing is a consolidation around each of these original Twelve. I think that's what we found at the Haven. They need us, and they need us alive. I'll bet there are eleven more big hives like it somewhere.'

'And what if we could find them?' Peter said.

Michael frowned. 'I'd say it was nice knowing you.'

Peter leaned forward in his chair. 'But what if we could? What if we could find the rest of the Twelve and kill them?'

'When the queen dies, the hive dies with it.'

'Like Babcock. Like the Many.'

Michael glanced cautiously at the others. 'Look, it's just a theory. We saw what we saw, but I could be wrong. And that doesn't solve the first problem, which is finding them. It's a big continent. They could be anyplace.'

Peter was suddenly aware that everyone was looking at him.

'Peter?' This was Sara, seated beside him. 'What is it?'

They always go home, he thought.

'I think I know where they are,' said Peter.

They drove on. It was on their fifth night out – they were in Arizona, near the Utah border – that Greer turned to Peter, saying, 'You know, the funny thing is, I always thought it was all made up.'

They were sitting by a fire of crackling mesquite, a concession to the cold. Alicia and Hollis were on watch, patrolling the perimeter; the others were asleep. They were in a broad, empty valley, and had taken shelter for the night beneath a bridge over a dry arroyo.

'What was?'

'The movie. *Dracula*.' Greer had grown leaner over the weeks. His hair had grown back in a tonsure of gray, and he had a full beard now. It was hard to recall a time when he wasn't one of them. 'You didn't see the end, did you?'

That night in the mess: to Peter, it seemed like long ago. He thought back, trying to remember the order of events.

'You're right,' he said finally. 'They were going to kill the girl when Blue Squad came back. Harker and the other one. Van Helsing.' He shrugged. 'I was sort of glad I didn't have to watch that part.'

'See, that's the thing. They don't kill the girl. They kill the *vampire*. Stake the son of a bitch right in the sweet spot. And just like that, Mina wakes up, good as new.' Greer shrugged. 'I never really bought that part, to tell you the truth. Now I'm not so sure. Not after what I saw on that mountain.' He paused. 'Do you really think they remembered who they were? That they couldn't die until they did?'

'That's what Amy says.'

'And you believe her.'

'Yes.'

Greer nodded, allowing a moment to pass. 'It's funny. I've spent my whole life trying to kill them. I've never really thought about the people they used to be. For some reason, it never seemed important. Now I find myself feeling sorry for them.'

Peter knew what he meant; he had thought the same thing.

'I'm just a soldier, Peter. Or at least I was. Technically, I'm about as AWOL as you get. But everything that's happened, it

934

means something. Even my being here, with you. It feels like more than chance.'

Peter remembered the story Lacey had told him, about Noah and the ship, realizing something he hadn't thought of before. Noah wasn't alone. There were the animals, of course, but that wasn't all. He had taken his family with him.

'What do you think we're supposed to do?' he asked.

Greer shook his head. 'I don't think it's up to me. You're the one with those vials in your pack. That woman gave them to you and no one else. As far as I'm concerned, my friend, that decision is yours.' He rose, taking up his rifle. 'But speaking as a soldier, ten more Donadios would make a hell of a weapon.'

They spoke no more that night. Moab was two days away.

They approached the farmstead from the south, Sara at the wheel of the Humvee, Peter up top with the binoculars.

'Anything?' Sara called.

It was late afternoon. Sara had brought the vehicle to a halt on the wide plain of the valley. A hard, dusty wind had arisen, obscuring Peter's vision. After four warm days the temperature had fallen again, cold as winter.

Peter climbed down, blowing onto his hands. The others were crowded onto the benches with their gear. 'I can see the buildings. No movement. The dust is too heavy.'

Everyone was silent, fearful of what they'd find. At least they had fuel; south of the town of Blanding, they had stumbled across – actually driven straight into – a vast fuel depot, two dozen rust-streaked tanks poking from the soil like a field of giant mushrooms. They realized that if they planned their route correctly, seeking out airfields and the larger towns, especially those with railheads, they should be able to find enough usable fuel along the way to get them home, as long as the Humvee itself held out.

'Pull ahead,' Peter said.

She drew forward slowly, onto the street of little houses. Peter thought, with a sinking feeling, that it all seemed just like it had when they'd found it, empty and abandoned. Surely Theo and Mausami should have heard the sound of their motor and come out by now. Sara drew up to the porch of the main house and silenced the engine; everyone got out. Still no sounds or movement from inside.

Alicia spoke first, touching Peter on the shoulder. 'Let me go.'

But he shook his head; the job was his. 'No. I'll do it.'

He ascended the porch and opened the door. He saw at once that everything had changed. The furniture had been moved around, made more comfortable, even homey. An arrangement of old photographs stood on the mantel above the ashy hearth. He stepped forward and felt for heat, but the fire had gone cold, long ago.

'Theo?'

No reply. He moved into the kitchen, everything tidy and scrubbed and put away. He remembered, with an icy chill, the story Vorhees had told about the disappearing town – what was its name? Homer. Homer, Oklahoma. Dishes on the table, everything neat as a pin, all the people simply vanished into thin air.

The top of the stairs met a narrow hallway with two doors, one for each bedroom. Peter gingerly opened the first one. The room was empty, undisturbed.

His hope all but gone, Peter opened the second door.

Theo and Maus were lying on the big bed, fast asleep. Maus was facing away, a blanket drawn around her shoulders, black hair spilling over the pillow; Theo was lying stiffly on his back, his left leg splinted from ankle to hip. Between the two of them, peeking from the porthole of its heavy swaddling, was a baby's tiny face.

'Well, I'll be damned,' said Theo, opening his eyes and smiling to reveal a line of broken teeth. 'Will you look what the wind blew in.'

SEVENTY-TWO

The first thing Maus did was ask them to bury Conroy. She would have done it herself, she said, but she was simply not able. With Theo and the baby to take care of, she'd had to leave him where he was for the three days since the attack. Peter carried what was left of the poor animal to the yard of graves, where Hollis and Michael had dug a hole beside the others, moving stones to mark the perimeter in the same manner. If not for the freshly turned earth, Conroy's grave would have looked no different at all.

How they had survived the attack in the barn was nothing Theo or Mausami could wholly explain. Huddled in the backseat of the car with baby Caleb, her face pressed to the floor, Mausami had heard the shotgun go off; when she lifted her face to see the viral lying on the floor of the barn, dead, she assumed that Theo had shot him. But Theo maintained that he had no memory of this, and the gun itself was lying several meters away, near the door – far beyond his reach. At the moment when he heard the shot, his eyes were closed; the next thing he knew, Mausami's face was hovering over him in the dark, saying his name. He'd assumed the only thing that made sense: that she had been the one. She had somehow gotten ahold of the shotgun and fired the shot that had saved them.

This left as the only possibility a third, unseen party – the owner of the footprints Theo had found in the barn. But how such a person would arrive at just the right moment and then escape without being detected – and, most curiously of all, why he or she would want to do such a thing – was un-accountable. They had found no more prints in the dust, no additional evidence that anyone else had been there. It was as if they'd been saved by a ghost.

The other question was why the viral hadn't simply killed them when it had the chance. Neither Theo nor Mausami had returned to the barn since the attack; the body, sheltered from the sun, still lay inside. But once Alicia and Peter went to look, the mystery was solved. Neither of them had ever seen a viral corpse that was more than a few hours old, and, in fact, the passing days in the dark barn had brought about a wholly unexpected effect, the skin drawing more tightly over the bones to restore a semblance of recognizable humanness to its face. The viral's eyes were open, clouded over like marbles. The fingers of one hand lay spread upon its chest, splayed over the cratered wound from the shotgun – a gesture of surprise or even shock. Peter was touched by a feeling of familiarity, as if he were viewing a person he knew at a great distance, or through some incidentally reflective surface. But it wasn't until Alicia said the name that he knew, and once she did, all uncertainty vanished from his mind. The curve of the viral's brow and the look of puzzlement on his face, accentuated by the cold blankness of his gaze; the searching gesture of his hand upon his wound, as if, in the last instant, he had sought to verify what was happening to him. There was no doubt that the man on the floor of the barn was Galen Strauss.

How had he come to be here? Had he set out in search of them and been taken up along the way, or was it the reverse? Was it Mausami or the baby he had wanted? Had he come to seek revenge? To say goodbye?

What was home to Galen Strauss?

Alicia and Peter rolled the corpse onto a tarp and dragged it away from the house. They had intended to burn it, but Mausami objected. He might have been a viral, she said, but he was my husband once. He didn't deserve what happened to him. He should be buried with the others. At least let's give him that.

So that was what they did.

It was late afternoon on their second day at the farmstead when they laid Galen to rest. All had gathered in the yard except for Theo, who was still confined to bed and would, in fact, remain there for many more days. Sara suggested that they each tell a story of something they remembered about Galen – a struggle at the start, since he was not someone any of them except for Maus had known all that well or even much liked. But eventually they managed it, relating some incident in which Galen had done or said something funny or loyal or kind, while Greer and Amy looked on, witnesses to the ritual. By the time they were done Peter realized that something significant had occurred, an acknowledgment that, once made, could not be unmade. The body they had buried might have been a viral, but the person they had buried was a man.

The last to speak was Mausami. She was holding baby Caleb, who had fallen asleep. She cleared her throat, and Peter saw that her eyes were damp with tears.

'I just want to say that he was a lot braver than people thought he was. The truth was, he could barely see at all. He didn't want anybody to know how bad it was, but I could tell. He was just too proud to admit it. I'm sorry I deceived him like I did. I know he wanted to be a father, and maybe that's why he came here. I guess it's strange to say, but I think he would have been a good one. I wish he'd had that chance.'

She fell silent, shifting the baby to her shoulder and using her free hand to wipe her eyes. 'That's all,' she said. 'Thanks for doing this, everyone. If it's okay, I'd like a minute by myself.'

The group dispersed, leaving Maus alone. Peter ascended the stairs to the bedroom and found his brother awake and sitting up, his splinted leg stretched before him. In addition to the broken leg, Sara thought he had at least three cracked ribs. All things considered, he was lucky to be alive.

Peter moved to the window with its view of the yard below. Maus was still standing by the grave, facing away. The baby had awakened and begun to fuss; Maus was rotating back and forth on her hips, one hand cupping the back of Caleb's head where it lay over her shoulder, trying to settle him.

'Is she still out there?' Theo asked.

Peter turned to his brother, whose face was pointed at the ceiling now.

'It's okay if she is,' Theo said. 'I was just . . . wondering.'

'Yes, she's still out there.'

Theo said nothing more, his expression unreadable.

'How's the leg?' Peter ventured.

'Like shit.' Theo ran his tongue along his fractured teeth. 'It's these teeth that bug me the most, though. Like there's nothing where something should be. I can't get used to it.'

Peter let his eyes drift out the window again; the space where Maus had stood was empty. From below he heard the sound of the kitchen door closing, then opening again, and Greer stepped out, carrying a rifle. He stood a moment, then crossed the yard to the woodpile by the barn, balanced the rifle against the wall, took up the axe, and began to split logs.

'Look,' Theo said. 'I know I let you down, staying behind.'

Peter turned to face his brother once more. From elsewhere in the house now, he could hear the voices of the others, gathering in the kitchen.

'It's okay,' he said. With all that had happened, Peter had put this disappointment aside, long ago. 'Maus needed you. I would have done the same thing.'

But his brother shook his head. 'Just let me talk a minute. I know it took a lot of courage, what you did. I wouldn't want you to think I didn't notice. But that's not what I'm talking about, not really. Courage is easy, when the alternative is getting killed. It's hope that's hard. You saw something out there that no one else could, and you followed it. That's something I could never do. I tried, believe me, if only because Dad seemed to want me to so badly. But it just wasn't in me. And you know what's funny? It actually made me glad when I figured that out.'

He sounded almost angry, Peter thought. And yet a lightness had come into his brother's face as he'd spoken.

'When?' Peter asked.

'When what?'

'When did you figure it out?'

Theo's eyes flicked upward. 'The truth? I think I always knew, at least about myself. But it was that first night at the power station when I saw, really saw, what you had in you. Not just going outside the way you did, because I'm sure that was Lish's idea. It was the look on your face, like you'd seen your whole life out there. I chewed you out, sure. It was stupid and it could have gotten us all killed. But mostly I felt relieved. I knew I didn't have to pretend anymore.' He sighed and shook his head. 'I never wanted to be Dad, Peter. I always thought the Long Rides were crazy, even before he rode away and never came back. I couldn't see the sense in any of it. But now I look at you, and Amy, and I know that making sense isn't the point. Nothing about any of this makes *sense*. What you did, you did on faith. I don't envy you, and I know I'm going to worry about you every day of my life. But I am proud of you.' He paused. 'Want to know something else?'

Peter was too astounded to answer. All he could manage was a nod.

'I think it really was a ghost that saved us. Ask Maus, she'll tell you. I don't know what it is, but something's different here. I thought I was *dead*. I thought we were all dead. I didn't just think it, I knew it. The same way I know this. It's like the place itself is watching over us, taking care of us. Telling us that as long as we're here, we'll be safe.' His eyes met Peter's with a haunted look. 'You don't have to believe me.'

'I didn't say I didn't.'

Theo laughed, grimacing through the pain of his bandaged ribs. 'That's good,' he said, flopping his head back down to the pillow. 'Because I believe in you, brother.'

For the time being, they were going nowhere. Sara said that Theo's leg would need at least sixty days before he could even think of walking, and Mausami was still very weak, enervated by her long and painful labor. Of all of them, baby Caleb was the only one who seemed completely well. Just a few days old, and yet his eyes were bright and open, looking about. He had sweet smiles for everyone, but for Amy most of all. Whenever he heard her voice, or even so much as felt her presence as she entered a room, he would utter a sharp and happy cry, flailing his arms and legs.

'I think he likes you,' Maus said one day in the kitchen, as she struggled to nurse. 'You can hold him if you want.'

While Peter and Sara watched, Amy sat at the table and Mausami gently placed Caleb in her arms. One of his hands had come free from the swaddling. Amy bent her face toward him, allowing him to grab her nose with his tiny fingers. 'A baby,' she said, smiling.

Maus gave a wry laugh. 'That's what he is, all right.' She pressed a palm against her chest, her aching breasts, and groaned. 'Boy, is he ever.'

'I've never seen one.' Amy gazed into his face. Every bit of him was so new it was as if he were drenched in some miraculous, life-giving liquid. 'Hello, baby.'

The house was too small to accommodate everyone, and Caleb needed quiet; they carried the extra mattresses out and moved into one of the empty houses across the trace. How long since there had been such activity here? Since more than one house had seen people living in it? By the river, great brambles of bitter raspberries appeared, sweetening in the sun; the water jumped with fish. Each day Alicia returned from the hunt, dust-dressed and smiling, game swinging from a lanyard slung across her back: long-eared jacks, fat partridges, something that looked like a cross between a squirrel and a groundhog and tasted like venison. She carried neither gun nor bow; all she used was a blade. 'No one's ever going to go hungry as long as I'm around,' she said.

It was, in its way, a happy time, an easy time – food plentiful, the days mild and lengthening, the nights quiet and apparently safe, under a blanket of stars. And yet, for Peter, a cloud of anxiety hung over all. In part he knew this was just his awareness of how temporary everything was, and the problems presented by their imminent departure – the logistics of food and fuel and weapons and the space to carry it all. They had only one Humvee, hardly large enough to accommodate everyone, especially a woman with a baby. There was also the question of what they would find at the Colony when they returned. Would the lights still be on? Would Sanjay have them arrested? A concern that might have seemed distant even a few weeks ago, nothing worth worrying over, but seemed so no longer.

Ultimately, however, it was not these questions that oppressed him. It was the virus. Ten remaining vials in their shiny metal container, resting in his pack where he had stored it in the closet of the house where he slept with Greer and Michael. The major was right; there could be no other reason why Lacey had given it to him. Already it had saved Alicia – more than saved her. This was the weapon Lacey had spoken of, more powerful than guns or blades or crossbows, more powerful even than the bomb she had used to kill Babcock. But stored in its metal box, it was doing nothing.

Greer was wrong about one thing, though. The decision wasn't Peter's to make alone; he needed everyone else to agree. The farmstead would be as good a place as any for what he intended. They would have to tie him up, of course; they could use a room in one of the empty houses. Greer could take care of him, if things went badly. Peter had seen that well enough.

He called them together one night. They gathered in the evening around a fire in the yard, all except Mausami, who was resting upstairs, and Amy, who was looking after baby Caleb. He had planned it this way; he didn't want Amy to know. Not because she would object; he doubted that she would. But still he wanted to protect her from this decision and what it might mean. Theo had managed to hobble out on a pair of crutches that Hollis had fashioned from scrap wood; in another few days, the splints would be coming off. Peter had brought his pack with him, the vials inside. If everyone agreed, he saw no reason to delay. They sat on the ring of stones around the fire pit, and Peter explained what he wanted to do.

Michael was the first to speak. 'I agree,' he said. 'I think we should try it.'

'Well, I think it's crazy,' Sara cut in. She raised her face to the others. 'Don't you see what this is? No one will say it, but I will. It's evil. How many millions died because of what's in that box? I can't believe we're even talking about this. I say put it in the fire.'

'You may be right, Sara,' Peter said. 'But I don't think we can afford to do nothing. Babcock and the Many may be dead, but the rest of the Twelve are still out there. We've seen what Lish can do, what Amy can do. The virus came to us for a reason, the same way Amy came to us. We can't turn our backs on that now.'

'It could kill you, Peter. Or worse.'

'I'm willing to take that risk. And it didn't kill Lish.'

Sara turned to Hollis. 'Tell him. Please, tell him how completely insane this is.'

But Hollis shook his head. 'I'm sorry. I think I'm with Peter on this.'

'You can't mean that.'

'He's right. There has to be a reason.'

'Why can't the fact that we're all *alive* be the reason?'

He reached for her hand. 'It's not enough, Sara. So we're alive. What then? I want to have a life with you. A *real* life. No lights or walls, no standing the Watch. Maybe that's for someone else, someday. Probably it is. But I can't say no to what Peter's asking, not while there's a chance. And deep down, I don't think you can either.'

'So we'll fight them anyway. We'll find the rest of the Twelve and fight them. As ourselves, as people.'

'And we will. I promise you. That will never change.'

Sara fell silent; Peter felt an understanding pass between them. By the time Hollis broke his gaze away, Peter knew what his friend was going to say.

'If this works, I'll go next.'

Peter glanced at Sara. But he saw no more arguments there; she had accepted this.

'You don't have to do that, Hollis.'

The big man shook his head. 'I'm not doing it for you. If you want me to agree, that's how it has to be. Take it or leave it.'

Peter turned to Greer, who nodded. Then he directed his eyes to his brother. Theo was sitting on a log on the far side of the circle, his splinted leg stretched out before him.

'Flyers, Peter. What do I know? I told you, this is your show.'

'No, it isn't. It's everyone's.'

Theo paused. 'Just so I understand you. You want to deliberately infect yourself with the virus, and you want me to say, Sure, go right ahead. And Hollis here wants to do the same thing, assuming you don't die or kill all of us in the process.'

Peter felt the starkness of these terms; for the first time he wondered if he had the nerve. Theo's question was, Peter realized, a test.

'Yes, that's exactly what I'm asking you.'

Theo nodded. 'Then okay.'

'That's it? Just okay?'

'I love you, brother. If I thought I could talk you out of this, I would. But I know I can't. I told you I was going to worry about you. I might as well start now.'

Peter turned at last to Alicia. She had removed her glasses, revealing the thrumming orange glow of her eyes, magnified to a sparkling intensity by the light of the fire. It was her consent he needed most of all; without it, he had nothing.

'Yes,' she said, nodding. 'I'm sorry to say it, but yes.'

There was no reason to wait. Too much time to consider the ramifications, Peter knew, and his courage could dissolve. He led them to the empty house he had prepared – the last one, at the far end of the trace. It was little more than a shell; nearly all of the interior walls had been removed, leaving the joists exposed. The windows were already boarded up, another reason Peter had selected it – that and the fact that it was farthest away. Hollis took up the ropes Peter had moved from the barn; Michael and Greer carried a mattress from one

945

of the adjacent houses. Somebody had brought the lantern. While Hollis tied the ropes to the joists, Peter stripped to the waist and lay down on his back. He was suddenly very nervous, his awareness of everything around him almost painfully vivid, his heart beating very quickly in his chest. He raised his eyes to Greer. A silent bargain, struck between them: if it comes to that, don't hesitate.

Hollis finished tying the ropes to his arms and legs, leaving Peter spread-eagled on the floor. The mattress smelled like mice. He took a deep breath, trying to calm himself.

'Sara, do it now.'

She was cradling the box with the virus; in her other hand was one of the syringes, still sealed in plastic. Peter could see that her hands were trembling.

'You can do this.'

She passed the box to Michael. 'Please,' she begged.

'What am I supposed to do with this?' He held the box away from his body, trying to give it back. 'You're the nurse.'

Peter felt a blast of exasperation. Any longer, and his resolve would fail him. 'Will somebody, please, just get this done.'

'I'll do it,' Alicia said.

She took the box from Michael, and opened it.

'Peter . . .'

'What is it now? Flyers, Lish.'

She turned it in her hands to show them. 'This box is empty.'

Amy, he thought. Amy, what have you done?

They found her kneeling by the fire pit as she was dropping the last vial into the flames. Baby Caleb lay against her shoulder, wrapped in a blanket. A sizzling pop flew up as the liquid inside the last vial expanded to a boil, shattering the glass.

Peter crouched on the ground beside her. He was too stunned even to feel angry. He didn't know what he felt at all. 'Why, Amy?'

She did not look at him but kept her eyes focused on the

fire, as if to verify that the virus was really gone. With the fingers of her free hand she was gently stroking the baby's cap of dark hair.

'Sara was right,' she said finally. 'It was the only way to make sure.'

She lifted her eyes from the flames. And when Peter saw what lay inside them, he understood what she had done – that she had chosen to take this burden from him, from them all, and that this was a mercy.

'I'm sorry, Peter,' Amy said. 'But it would have made you like me. And I couldn't let that happen.'

They did not speak of that night again – of the virus, or the flames, or what Amy had done. Sometimes, in odd moments when he recalled these events, Peter felt, strangely, as if it had been a dream; or if not a dream, then something like a dream, with a dream's texture of inevitability. And he came to believe that the destruction of the virus was not, in the end, the catastrophe he had feared but, rather, one more step on the road they would travel together, and that what lay ahead was something he could not know, nor needed to know. Like Amy herself, it was something he would take on faith.

The morning of their departure, Peter stood on the porch with Michael and Theo, watching the sun come up. His brother's splints had come off at last; he could walk, but with a pronounced limp, and he tired quickly. Below them, Hollis and Sara were loading up the Humvee with the last of the gear. Amy was still inside with Maus, who was nursing Caleb one last time before they set out.

'You know,' Theo said, 'I have the feeling that if we ever came back here, it would be just as it is now. Like it's apart from everything. Like no time ever really passes here.'

'Maybe you will,' Peter said.

Theo fell silent, letting his gaze travel over the dusty street.

'Oh, hell, brother,' he said, shaking his head. 'I don't know. It's nice to think it, though.'

Amy and Mausami emerged from the house. Everyone gathered around the Humvee. Another departure, another goodbye. There were hugs, good wishes, tears. Sara climbed behind the wheel, Hollis beside her, Theo and Mausami in the back with their gear. Also in the cargo compartment of the Humvee were the documents Lacey had given to Peter. Just deliver them, Peter had said, to whoever's in charge.

Amy reached inside to give baby Caleb one last embrace. As Sara turned the engine over, Greer stepped to the open driver's window.

'Remember what I said. From the fuel depot, straight south on Highway 191. You should be able to pick up Route 60 in Eagar. That's the Roswell Road, takes you straight to the garrison. There's fortified bunkers about every hundred kilometers. I marked them on Hollis's map, but look for the red crosses, you can't miss them. Nothing fancy, but it should get you through. Gas, ammo, whatever you need.'

Sara nodded. 'Got it.'

'And whatever you do, stay away from Albuquerque – the place is crawling. Hollis? All eyes.'

In the passenger seat, the big man nodded. 'All eyes, Major.'

Greer stepped back, making space for Peter to approach.

'Well,' Sara said, 'I guess this is it.'

'I guess so.'

'Take care of Michael, all right?' She snuffled and wiped her eyes. 'He needs . . . looking after.'

'You can count on it.' He reached in to shake Hollis's hand, wished him good luck, then lifted his voice to the rear of the Humvee. 'Theo? Maus? All set back there?'

'Ready as we'll ever be, brother. We'll see you in Kerrville.'

Peter backed away. Sara put the Humvee in gear, swung the vehicle in a wide circle, and pulled slowly down the street. The five of them – Peter, Alicia, Michael, Greer, and Amy – stood in silence, watching it go. A boiling plume of dust, the sound of its motor fading, then gone.

'Well,' Peter said finally, 'the day's not getting any younger.'

'Is that a joke?' Michael said.

Peter shrugged. 'I guess it was.'

They retrieved their packs and hoisted them onto their backs. As Peter took his rifle from the floor, he spied Amy still standing at the edge of the porch, her eyes tracing the drifting cloud of the Humvee's departure.

'Amy? What is it?'

She turned to face him. 'It's nothing,' she said. 'I think they'll be all right.' She smiled. 'Sara is a good driver.'

There were no more words to say; the moment of departure was at hand. The morning sun had lifted over the valley. If everything went well, they would reach California by midsummer.

They began to walk.

SEVENTY-THREE

At a shimmering distance, they saw them: a vast field of turning blades, spinning in the wind.

The turbines.

They had kept to the deserts, the hot, dry places, sheltering where they could, and where they could not, building a fire and waiting out the nights. Once, and only once, did they see any virals alive. A pod of three. This was in Arizona, a place the map called 'Painted Desert.' The creatures were dozing in the shade beneath a bridge, hanging from the girders. Amy had felt them as they approached. Let me, Alicia said.

Alicia had taken them all. Three of them, on the blade. They found her in the culvert, pulling her knife from the chest of the last one; they had already begun to smoke. Easy, she said. They didn't even seem to know what she was. Perhaps they simply thought she was another viral.

There were others. Bodies, the barest remains. The form of a blackened rib cage, the crumbling, ashlike bones of a hand or skull; the suggestive imprint on a square of asphalt, like something burned in a pan. Usually they came upon these remnants in the few towns they passed through. Most were lying not far from the buildings where they had slept and then departed, when they had laid themselves down in the sun to die.

Peter and the others had skirted Las Vegas, choosing a route far to the south; they believed the city would be empty, but better to be safe than sorry. By then it was the height of summer, the shadeless days long and brutal. They decided to bypass the bunker, taking the shortest possible route, and make straight for home.

Now they were here. They fanned out as they moved toward the power station. The fence, they saw, stood open. At the hatch, Michael got to work, unbolting the plate that covered the mechanism and manually turning the tumblers with the end of his blade.

Peter entered first. A bright metallic tinkling underfoot: he bent to look. Rifle cartridges.

The walls of the stairwell were shot to pieces. Chunks of concrete cluttered the stairs. The light had been blasted away. Alicia stepped forward, into the cool and gloom, pulling off her glasses; the darkness was no problem for her. Peter and the others waited as she descended to the control room, following the point of her rifle. They heard her whistle the all clear.

By the time they reached the bottom, Lish had found a lantern and lit the wick. The room was a mess. The long central table had been overturned, evidently to serve as a defense. The floor was littered with more cartridges and spent magazines. But the control panel itself looked all right, its meters glowing with current. They moved through the rear to the storage rooms and barracks.

No one. No bodies.

'Amy,' Peter said, 'do you know what happened here?'

Like all of them, she was looking in mute astonishment at the extent of the destruction.

'Nothing? You don't feel anything?'

She shook her head. 'I think . . . people did this.'

The shelf that had hidden the guns had been pulled away; the guns on the roof were gone as well. What were they seeing? A battle, but who had been fighting whom? Hundreds of rounds had been fired in the hallway and the control room, more in the barracks, an overturned mess. Where were the bodies? Where was the blood?

'Well, there's power,' Michael declared, sitting at the control panel. His hair flowed to his shoulders now. His skin was bronzed by the sun, wind-bit and peeling at his cheekbones. He was typing into the keypad, reading the numbers that flew down the screen. 'Diagnostics are good. There should be plenty of juice going up the mountain. Unless . . .' He paused, patting his lips with a finger; he began to type furiously again, rose briskly to check the meters above his head, and sat down once more. He tapped the screen with the back of a long fingernail. 'Here.'

'Michael, just tell us,' Peter said.

'It's the system backup log. Every night when the batteries get down below forty percent, they send a signal to the station, asking for more current. It's all completely automated, nothing you'd ever see happening. The first time it happened was six years ago, then just about every night ever since. Until now. Until, let's see, three hundred and twenty-three cycles ago.'

'Cycles.'

'Days, Peter.'

'Michael, I don't know what that means.'

'It means either somebody figured out how to fix those batteries, which I seriously doubt, or they're not drawing any current.'

951

Alicia frowned. 'That doesn't make any sense. Why wouldn't they?'

Michael hesitated; Peter could see the truth in his face.

'Because somebody turned the lights off,' he said.

They spent a restless night in the bunker and set out in the morning. By half-day they had made their way through Banning and begun to ascend. When they stopped to rest beneath the shade of a tall pine, Alicia turned to Peter.

'Just in case Michael's wrong and we're arrested, I want you to know I'm going to say I was the one who killed those men. I'll take whatever's coming to me, but I'm not going to let them have you. And they're not touching Amy or the Circuit.'

This was more or less as he had expected. 'Lish, you don't have to do that. And I doubt Sanjay will do anything at this point.'

'Maybe not. But just so we're clear. I'm not asking, either. Be ready. Greer? Understood?'

The major nodded.

But this warning was for naught. They knew it by the time they reached the final switchback in the road, above Upper Field. They could see the Wall now, rising through the trees, the catwalks unoccupied, no sign of the Watch. An eerie stillness hung over all. The gates stood open and unmanned.

The Colony was empty.

They found two bodies.

The first was Gloria Patal. She had hanged herself in the Big Room of the Sanctuary, among the empty cribs and cots. She had used a tall stepladder, ascending to affix the rope to one of the rafters, near the door. The ladder now lay on its side beneath her pointed feet, freezing the moment when she had put the noose around her neck and pushed off, sending the ladder swooning to the floor.

The other body was Auntie's. It was Peter who found her, sitting in a kitchen chair in the small clearing outside her house. She had been dead many months, he knew, and yet very little seemed to have altered in her appearance. But when he touched her hand where it lay in her lap, he felt only the cold stiffness of death. Her head was tipped backward; her face wore a peaceful expression, as if she had simply fallen asleep. She had gone outside, he knew, when darkness had come and the lights did not go on. She had carried a chair into the yard, to sit and watch the stars.

'Peter.' Alicia touched his arm as he crouched beside the body. 'Peter, what do you want to do?'

He pulled his eyes away, realizing only then that they were full of tears. The others were standing behind her, a silent chorus of witness.

'We should bury her here. Near her house, her garden.'

'We will,' Alicia said gently. 'I meant about the lights. It will be dark soon. Michael says we have a full charge if we want.'

He glanced past her to Michael, who nodded.

'All right,' he said.

They closed the gate and gathered in the Sunspot – all except Michael, who had returned to the Lighthouse. It was just twilight, the sky purpling overhead. Everything seemed held in suspension; not even the birds were singing. Then with an audible pop the lights came on, dousing them all with a fierce and final brilliance.

Michael appeared to stand beside them. 'We should be good for tonight.'

Peter nodded. They were silent for a time in the presence of this unspoken truth: one more night, and the lights of First Colony would darken forever.

'So now what?' Alicia asked.

In the stillness, Peter felt the presence of his friends around him. Alicia, whose courage was a part of him. Michael, grown lean and hard, a man now. Greer, his wise and soldierly countenance. And Amy. He thought of all that he had seen, and those who had been lost – not just the ones he knew of, but those whom he did not – and he knew what his answer was.

He said, 'Now we go to war.'

SEVENTY-FOUR

The last hour before dawn: Amy crept from the house, alone. The house of the woman called Auntie, who had died; they had buried her where she'd sat, wrapping her body in a quilt from her bed. On her chest Peter had placed a photograph he had taken from her bedroom. The ground was hard, it had taken them many hours of digging, and when they were done, they had decided to sleep the night there. The woman's house, Peter had said, would be as good as any-place. He had a house of his own, Amy knew. But he did not seem to want to go back there.

Peter had stayed up most of the night, sitting in the old woman's kitchen, reading from her book. His eyes squinted in the light of the lantern as he turned the pages of her small, neat script. He had made a cup of tea but did not drink it; it sat beside him on the table, untouched, forgotten as he read.

At last Peter slept, and Michael, and Greer, who had traded the watch with Alicia after half-night; she was up on the catwalk now. Amy stepped onto the porch, holding the door so it wouldn't bang behind her. The earth was cool with dew under her bare feet, soft with a pillow of needles atop the hardpan. She found the tunnel under the trunkline without difficulty, dropped through the hatch, and wriggled through.

She had felt him for days, weeks, months. She knew that now. She had felt him for years, since the beginning. Since Milagro and the day of the not-talking and the big boat and long before, through all the years of time that stretched inside her. The one who followed her, who was always nearby, whose sadness was the sadness she felt in her heart. The sadness of missing her.

They always went home, and home was wherever Amy was.

She emerged from the tunnel. Dawn was moments away; the sky had begun to pale, the darkness dissolving around her like a vapor. She moved away from the walls, into the cover of the trees, and sent her mind outward, closing her eyes.

—Come to me. Come to me.

Stillness.

—Come to me, come to me, come to me.

She felt it then: a rustling. Not heard but sensed, gliding atop every surface, every part of her, kissing it like a breeze. The skin of her hands and neck and face, the scalp under her hair, the tips of her eyelashes. A soft wind of longing, breathing her name.

Amy.

—I knew you were there, she said, and wept, as he was weeping in his heart, for his eyes could not make tears. – I knew you were there.

Amy, Amy, Amy.

She opened her eyes to see him crouched before her. She stepped toward him, touching his face where the tears would have been; she put her arms around him. And as she held him, she felt the presence of his spirit within her, different from all the others she carried, because it was also her own. The memories poured through her like water. Of a house in the snow and a lake and a carousel with lights and the feel of his big hand wrapping her own on a night when they soared together beneath the eaves of heaven.

—I knew, I knew. I always knew. You were the one who loved me.

Dawn was breaking above the mountain. The sun was sweeping toward them like a blade of light over the earth. And yet she held him as long as she dared; she held him in her heart. Above her on the catwalk, Alicia was watching, Amy knew. But this didn't matter. What she was witnessing

955

would be a secret between them, a thing to know and never speak of. Like Peter, what he was. For Amy believed Alicia knew that, too.

—Remember, she told him. Remember.

But he was gone; her arms held only space. Wolgast was rising, he was lifting away.

A shudder of light in the trees.

Postscript

ROSWELL ROAD

From the Journal of Sara Fisher ('The Book of Sara')
Presented at the Third Global Conference on the North
   American Quarantine Period
Center for the Study of Human Cultures and Conflicts
University of New South Wales, Indo-Australian Republic
April 16–21, 1003 A.V.

[*Excerpt begins.*]

Day 268

*Three days since the farmstead. We crossed into New Mexico this
morning, just after sunrise. The roadway is in very bad shape, but
Hollis is sure this is Route 60. A flat, open country, though we can see
mountains to the north. From time to time a huge, empty sign by the
roadway, abandoned cars everywhere, some blocking the way, which
makes for slow going. The baby is restless and crying. I wish Amy were
here to quiet him. We had to spend last night out in the open and so
everybody is exhausted and snapping at one another, even Hollis. Fuel
is getting to be a worry again. Down to what we have in the tank plus
one extra from the cache. Hollis says we're looking at five days to
Roswell, maybe six.*

Day 269

*Spirits lifting. We saw our first cross today – a great red splash on the
side of a grain silo, fifty meters high. Maus was up top and saw it first.
Everyone started to cheer. We're spending the night in a concrete
bunker just behind it. Hollis thinks it used to be some kind of pumping
station. Dark and dank and full of pipes. There's fuel stacked in
drums, just like Greer said, which we siphoned off into the Humvee
before bolting down for the night. There's nothing much to sleep on,*

959

just the hard cement floor, but we're close enough to Albuquerque now that no one thinks we should sleep in the open.

Strange, and nice, to be sleeping with a baby in the room. Listening to the little noises he makes, even when he's asleep. I haven't told Hollis my news yet, wanting to be sure. Part of me thinks he already knows. How could he not know? I'm sure it's written all over my face. Whenever I think about it, I can't stop smiling. I caught Maus staring at me tonight when we were moving the fuel and I said, What? What are you staring at? And she said, Nothing. Just, you know, anything you want to tell me, Sara? I did my best to look innocent, which wasn't easy, and told her no and what are you talking about and she said, laughing, Well, okay. That's certainly okay with me.

I don't know why I'm thinking this but if it's a boy, I want to name it Joe, and if it's a girl, Kate. After my parents. It's strange how being happy about one thing can make you just as sad about another.

We are all wondering about the others, hoping they're okay.

Day 270
Tracks all around the Humvee this morning. It looks like there were three of them. Why they didn't try to break into the bunker is a mystery – I'm sure they could smell us. Hoping to make Socorro in plenty of time to lock down for the night.

Day 270 (again)
Socorro. Hollis is pretty sure the bunkers are part of an old gas pipeline system. We are bolted down for the night. Now we wait [illegible]

Day 271
They came again. More than three, a lot more. We could hear them scratching at the walls of the bunker all night long. Tracks everywhere this morning, too many to count. The windshield of the Humvee was shattered, and most of the windows. Anything we'd left inside was scattered over the ground, smashed and torn to pieces. I'm afraid it's just a matter of time before they try to break into one of the bunkers. Will the bolts hold? Caleb cries half the night no matter what Maus does, so it's no secret where we are. What's stopping them?

It's a race now. Everybody knows it. Today we are crossing the

White Sands Missile Range to the bunker at Carrizozo. I want to tell Hollis but I don't. I just can't, not like this. I will wait until the garrison, for luck.

I wonder if the baby knows how afraid I am.

Day 272
No sign tonight. Everyone is relieved, hoping we lost them.

Day 273
The last bunker before Roswell. A place called Hondo. I fear this will be my last entry. All day long they were following us, tracking us in the trees. We can hear them moving around outside and it's barely dusk. Caleb won't be still. Maus just holds him to her chest, crying and crying. It's Caleb they want, she keeps saying. They want Caleb.

Oh, Hollis. I'm sorry we ever left the farmstead. I wish we could have had it, that life. I love you I love you I love you.

Day 275
When I look at the words in my last entry, I can't believe we're alive, that we somehow got through that terrible night.

The virals never attacked. When we opened the door in the morning, the Humvee was lying on its side in a puddle of fluid, looking like some great broken-winged bird fallen to earth, its engine smashed beyond repair. The hood was lying a hundred meters away. They'd ripped off the tires and torn them to shreds. We knew we were lucky to have made it through the night, but now we had no vehicle. The map said fifty more kilometers to the garrison. Possible, but Theo could never make it. Maus wanted to stay with him but of course he said no, and none of us were going to allow it anyway. If they didn't kill us last night, Theo said, I'm sure I can make it through another if I have to. Just get moving and use all the light you can and send back a vehicle when you get there. Hollis rigged a sling out of some rope and a piece of one of the seats for Maus to carry Caleb and then Theo kissed the two of them goodbye and drew down the door and sealed the bolts and we left, carrying nothing but water and our rifles.

As it turned out, it was more than fifty kilometers, a lot more. The garrison was on the far side of town. But it didn't matter because a little after half-day we were picked up by a patrol. Of all people, Lieutenant Eustace. He seemed more perplexed than anything to see us, but in any case they sent a Humvee back to the bunker and now we are all safe and sound, behind the walls of the garrison.

I am writing this in the civilian mess tent (there are three, one for enlisted, one for officers, and one for civilian workers). All the others have already gone to bed. The CO here is someone named Crukshank. A general, like Vorhees, but that's where the similarity stops. With Vorhees you could tell there was a real person in there, behind all that military sternness, but Crukshank looks like the sort of man who's never cracked a smile in his life. I also get the feeling Greer is in a lot of trouble, and this seems to extend to the rest of us. But tomorrow at 06:00, we're going to be debriefed, and we can tell the whole story then. The Roswell Garrison makes the one in Colorado seem flimsy by comparison. I think it's nearly as big as the Colony, with gigantic concrete walls supported by metal struts that extend down into the parade ground. The only way I can think to describe it is to say that it looks like an inside-out spider. A sea of tents and other fixed structures. Vehicles have been coming in all evening, huge tanker trucks and five-tons full of men and guns and crates of supplies, their cabs rigged with banks of lights. The air is full of the roar of engines, the smell of burning fuel, the showering sparks of torches. Tomorrow I'm going to go find the infirmary and see if there's anything I can do to help. There are a few other women here, not many but some, mostly with the medical corps, and as long as we stay in the civilian areas, we're free to move as we please.

Poor Hollis. He was so worn out I never got the chance to tell him the news. So tonight will be the last night for me to be alone with my secret, before someone else knows. I wonder if there's anyone here who can marry us. Maybe the CO can do it. But Crukshank doesn't seem the type, and I should wait until Michael's with us, in Kerrville. He should be the one to give me away. It wouldn't be fair to do it without him.

I should be exhausted, but I'm not. I'm much too keyed up to sleep. Probably it's my imagination, but when I close my eyes and sit very still, I swear I can feel the baby inside me. Not moving, nothing like *that, it's far too early. Just a kind of warm and hopeful presence, this new soul my body carries, waiting to be born into the world. I feel . . . what's the word? Happy. I feel happy.*

Shots outside. I am going to look.

*****END OF DOCUMENT*****

Recovered at Roswell Site ('Roswell Massacre')
Area 16, Marker 267
33.39 N, 104.50 W
2nd striation. Depth: 2.1 meters
Accession BL1894.02

ACKNOWLEDGMENTS

For advocacy, encouragement, counsel, inspiration, expertise, friendship, camaraderie, patience, shelter, sustenance, and the general tossing of meat through the bars, thanks and ponies to: Ellen Levine and Claire Roberts at Trident Media Group; Mark Tavani and Libby McGuire at Ballantine Books; Gina Centrello, president of the Random House Publishing Group; Bill Massey at Orion; the spectacular publicity, marketing, and sales teams at Ballantine and Orion; Rich Green at Creative Artists Agency; Michael Ellenberg and Ridley Scott at Scott Free Productions; Rodney Ferrell and Elizabeth Gabler at Fox 2000; my brilliant and intrepid readers, Jenny Smith, Tom Barbash, Jennifer Vanderbes, and Ivan Strausz; my many wonderful colleagues and students at Rice University; Bonnie Thompson; John Logan; Alex Parsons; Andrea White and The House of Fiction; ACC, best boy ever; IAC, the girl who saves the world; Leslie, Leslie, Leslie.

THE PASSAGE
Reading Group Notes

Justin Cronin: How I Wrote *The Passage*

You write the book that asks to be written, and *The Passage* asked me to write it on a series of long jogs in the fall of 2005, taken in the company of my daughter, Iris, age eight, who rode beside me on her bicycle.

For many years, running has been part of my writing ritual. I do my best creative thinking while running, which I have come to understand as a form of self-hypnosis. It's where I get my ideas, but not just my ideas; on the best days, whole paragraphs seem to drop into my head. I like to say that I write while running; at the computer, I'm just typing.

That fall, four years ago, my daughter asked if she could come along. We had done this from time to time, back when she was first learning to ride a two-wheeler, and I'd always enjoyed it, even if her presence was a bit of a distraction from the mental work I was actually doing. But it was September, blazingly hot, and the novel I was working on was in a bit of a stall. Sure, I said. Get your stuff.

To understand this story, a person would need to know something about my daughter. Iris is simply the most voracious literary consumer I have ever encountered. She reads two or three books a day and has since she was little. She reads while eating, bathing, and walking the dog. She reads while watching television (I'm not sure how), in the backseat of the car, and standing in line at the movies; I have actually seen her reading on a roller coaster. There is always a book somewhere on or near her person, and she goes to sleep every night listening to audio books – in other words, she reads while sleeping, too. Once, just to satisfy my curiosity, I surreptitiously timed the rate at which she moved through the pages and discovered she was reading at twice the rate I do. I am probably the only parent in the history of the world who has uttered this sentence: 'Your mother and I have decided that, as your punishment, you will not be allowed to read a book for the rest of the week.'

In sum, Iris is the reader every writer longs for – when she loves a book, she loves it unreservedly – but she is also the critic we all fear, capable of skewering a novel she doesn't like with the most withering sarcasm. Her verbal parodies of Jane Austen, for instance, a writer I am certain she will someday like but for now considers pompously dull, are scarily dead-on.

That day as we set out, our conversation naturally turned to books and writing, and Iris made a confession: your books, daddy, are boring. She said this offhandedly, as if she were telling me something I probably already knew, which I took to mean that my novels were too grown up for her, and dealt with subjects in which she had no interest. I might have been offended but I was mostly surprised; I didn't know she'd read them. (I was quickly calculating what inappropriate material she would have encountered in their pages.) But when I asked her about this, she said she hadn't read them, not exactly; she knew my books were boring, she explained, from their covers, and the summaries on the flaps. Well, that's literary novels, I explained, relieved. Sometimes it's hard to say exactly what they're about, in so many words. To which my daughter rolled her eyes. That's what I mean, said Iris. Boring.

'Well what do you want me to write about?' I asked.

She took a moment to think. We were running and riding, side by side, moving down the flat, wide sidewalk of our neighbourhood in the autumn heat.

'A girl who saves the world,' she said.

I had to laugh. Of course that's what she'd want me to write about. Not just a town, say, or a small city, but the entire world!

'That's a tall order,' I said. 'Anything else?'

She thought another moment. 'It should have one character with red hair,' said my daughter, the redhead. 'And . . . vampires.'

This was before every teenage girl in America had gone crazy for vampires. I knew absolutely nothing about them, beyond the common lore.

'The redhead I get. Why vampires?'

She responded with a shrug. 'They're interesting. A book needs something interesting in it.'

It was a classic dare, and I knew it. Writer Rule #1 is Never Let Anyone Else Tell You What to Write. But I also knew we had five hot miles ahead of us.

'OK,' I said. 'Let's do it together. We'll work it out together as we go.'

'Like a game, you mean,' Iris said.

'Sure. We can toss ideas around, see if we can work it into a story. Who knows? Maybe it will be good and I can write it.'

She agreed, and across that fall to pass the time of our

afternoon run-rides, we began to formulate the plot of a novel, one hour each day. An orphan girl (her), and an FBI agent who befriends and fathers her (me). A medical experiment in lengthening human lifespan, and a global catastrophe. A hundred years of lost time, and a mountain outpost in California where the last of the human race awaits the end, until a day when a girl – that same girl – appears out the wilderness, to save the human race. Each afternoon after she came home from school we would pick up where we'd left off, and gradually the story and its details came into shape. In the evenings, we'd tell my wife about what we'd come up with, and so she became part of the process too, blessing or dismissing our ideas, offering some of her own to fill the spaces. I kept saying, Isn't this a gas? I can't believe how good our daughter is at this. I had no sense that this was any type of story in particular, literary or commercial, for any particular audience beyond ourselves, and I didn't care; we were just having fun, telling a story around the campfire. Despite what I had said, I had no intention of actually *writing* the thing, writing and talking being in the end two entirely different matters, one much more work than the other.

And then a funny thing happened. As the weeks went by, I began to think this story actually could be a book, and that it was actually a better book, a much better book, than the one I was actually supposed to be writing. And not just one book: saving the world seemed like the kind of undertaking that would take three books to accomplish. The story that became *The Passage* had begun to fill my head, to breathe and walk and talk – to be populated, as someone once said, by 'warm new beings' I actually believed in. Amy and Wolgast. Peter and Alicia (the red-head Iris had requested). Lacey and Richards and Grey and Sara and Michael-the-Circuit – a character who is a kind of boy-Iris, actually, and very much her creation. I had been a literary novelist all my professional life, with a literary novelist's habits and interests; but I had cut my reader's teeth on plenty of genre fiction – adventure novels, science fiction, westerns, espionage. Enough to know that in the end it's how you write the thing that matters, and if you love it. Be interesting, Iris had told me. There's no harm in it, and your reader will thank you. It seemed like good advice. For three months, Iris and I traded ideas back and forth like a ball we were moving downfield; by December, when the cold weather came and her bicycle went into the garage, we had the plot worked out, right down to the final scene. I felt sad, as if something wonderful was ending, and I decided not to let it end; I sat at my computer and began to write an outline, so I wouldn't forget it.

And when that was done, I decided I would write the first chapter. Just to see how it felt.

And so on . . .

For Discussion

How does the opening of *The Passage* set the tone for the novel?

Why did Sister Lacey lie to the other sisters about Amy?

Set in the near future, the author has given us snippets of 'history' between now and the time of *The Passage*. How and why has he chosen to do this in the way he has?

'Nobody's nobody. There's always someone who's interested.' (p.118) Could the powers that be get away with experiments like those on the death row inmates here today?

To what extent do the quotes at the start of each part inform the text?

To what extent is Part One about the 'invisible' people?

'What were the living dead, Wolgast thought, but a metaphor for the misbegotten march of middle age?' (p.225) Does Wolgast still think this after the disaster, do you think?

Do you agree with Grey's concept of time? (p.247)

Why did Bob say he'd never had children? (p.308)

'Why would a viral come home if it had no soul?'
(p.343)

To what extent is the fall of civilization due to the loss
of electricity?

How does Peter set about building a bridge to the past?

Why keep the children oblivious until the age of eight?

'Hope was a thing that gave you pain, and that's what
this girl was. A painful sort of hope.' (p.525) What does
this tell us of the colony?

How does the colony deal with the future?

'The things of your life arrived in their own time, like a
train you had to catch.' (p.565) True, do you think?

What is Amy doing on the bus? (p.650)

To what extent is *The Passage* a novel about faith?

How would you describe Peter and Theo's relationship
and how does it change?

'That what they did, they did for love.' (p.795) Do they?

'You can't overthink these things.' (p.821) Is this the root of the military's problem?

'It was the peace of truth that Peter felt.' (p.844) Is truth what has been lacking from the colonists' lives?

'But you can only hate somebody for so long.' (p.849) Do you agree?

'She did not believe in fate; the world seemed far chancier than that, a series of mishaps and narrow escapes you somehow managed to survive until, one day, you didn't.' (p.866) Is this the only view of fate in *The Passage*?

'I think because he could. That is the reason for most things people do.' (pp.892-3) True, do you think?

To what extent is *The Passage* a novel about hope?

Who, or what, saved Theo and Maus in the barn?

Suggested Further Reading

The Stand
by Stephen King

The Road
by Cormac McCarthy

The Keep
by Jennifer Egan

The Lord of the Rings
by J.R.R. Tolkien

The Angel's Game
by Carlos Ruiz Zafón

The Devil and Daniel Webster
by Stephen Vincent Benét

What happens in the next book?

Read on for an extract from Justin
Cronin's *The Twelve*

Bernard Kittridge, known to the world as 'Last Stand in Denver,' knew it was time to leave the day the power went out.

He wondered what had taken so long. You couldn't keep a municipal electrical grid running without people to man it, and as far as Kittridge could tell from the 26th floor, not a single soul was left alive in the city of Denver.

Which was not to say he was alone.

He had spent most of that morning – a bright clear morning in the first week of June, temperatures in the mid-seventies with a chance of blood-sucking monsters moving in toward dusk – sunning on the balcony of the penthouse he had occupied since the second week of the crisis. It was a gigantic place, like an airborne palace; the kitchen alone was the size of Kittridge's whole apartment. The owner's taste ran in an austere direction: sleek leather seating groups that were better to look at than sit on, gleaming floors of twinkling travertine, small furry rugs, glass tables that appeared to float in space.

Breaking in had been surprisingly easy. By the time Kittridge had made his decision, half the city was dead, or fled, or missing. The cops were long gone. He'd thought about barricading himself into one of the big houses up in Cherry Creek but, based on the things he'd heard, he wanted someplace high. The owner was a man he knew slightly, a regular customer at the store. His name was Warren Filo. As luck would have it, Warren had come in the day before the whole thing broke, gearing up for a trip to Alaska. He was a young guy, too young for how much money he had – hedge fund money, probably. That day, the world still cheerily humming along as usual, Kittridge had helped him carry his purchases to the car. A Ferrari, of course. Standing beside it, Kittridge thought: Why not just go ahead and get a vanity plate that says 'DOUCHE BAG 1'? A question that must have been plainly written on his face, because no sooner had it crossed his mind than Warren went red with embarrassment. He wasn't wearing his usual suit, just jeans and a tee shirt with SLOAN SCHOOL OF MANAGEMENT printed on the front. He'd wanted Kittridge to see the car, that much was obvious; but now that this had happened, he'd realized how dumb this was, showing off a vehicle like that to a floor manager at Outdoor World who probably made less than fifty grand a year. (The number was actually forty-two.) Kittridge allowed himself a silent laugh at that – the things this kid didn't know would fill a book – and he let the moment hang to make the point. *I know, I know,* Warren confessed. *It's a little much. I told myself I'd never be one of those assholes who drove a Ferrari. But honest to god, you should feel the way she handles.*

Kittridge had gotten Warren's address off his invoice. By the time he moved in – Warren presumably snug and safe in Alaska – it was simply a matter of finding the right key in the manager's office, putting it in the slot in the elevator panel, and riding 19 floors to the top. He unloaded his gear. A rolling suitcase of clothes, two lockers of weaponry, a hand-crank radio, night-vision binoculars, flares, a first aid kit, bottles of bleach, an arc welder to seal the doors of the elevator, an assortment of tools, his trusty laptop with its portable satellite dish, a box of books, and enough food and water to last a month.

The view from the balcony, which ran the length of the west side of the building, was a sweeping 180 degrees, looking toward Route 25 and Mile High Stadium. He'd positioned cameras equipped with motion detectors at each end of the balcony, one to cover the street, a second facing the building on the opposite side. He figured he'd get a lot of good footage this way, but the money shots would be actual kills. The weapon he'd selected was a Remington bolt-action 700P, .318 caliber – a nice balance of accuracy and stopping power, zeroing out at 300 yards. To this he'd affixed a digital video riflescope with infra-red. Using the

2

binoculars, he would isolate his target; the rifle, fixed on a bipod at the edge of the balcony, would do the rest.

On the first night, windless and lit by a waning quarter moon, he'd shot seven: five on the avenue, one on the roof of the building across the street, and one more through the window of a bank at street level. It was the last one that made him famous. The creature, or vampire, or whatever it was – the official term was 'Infected Person' – had looked straight into the scope just before Kittridge put one through the sweet spot. Uploaded to YouTube, the image had traveled around the globe within hours; by morning all the major networks had picked it up. Who is this man? everybody wanted to know. Who is this fearless-crazy-suicidal man, barricaded in a Denver high-rise, making his last stand?

And so was born the sobriquet, Last Stand In Denver.

From the start he'd assumed it was just a matter of time before somebody shut him down, CIA or FBI or Homeland. Working in his favor was the fact that this same somebody would have to come to Denver to do this. Kittridge's i.p address was basically untraceable, backstopped by a daisy-chain of annonymizer servers, the order scrambled every night. Most were overseas: Russia, China, Indonesia, Israel, even Sudan. Places beyond easy reach for any federal agency that might want to pull the plug. His video blog – two million hits the first day – had over three hundred mirror sites, with more added all the time. It didn't take a week before he was a bonafide worldwide phenomenon. Twitter, Facebook, Headshot, Sphere: the images found their way without his lifting a finger. One of his fan sites alone had over fourteen million subscribers; on Ebay, tee-shirts that read, 'I AM LAST STAND IN DENVER' were selling for three hundred bucks.

His father had always said, son, the most important thing in life is to make a contribution. Who would have thought Kittridge's contribution would be video-blogging from ground-zero of the apocalypse?

And yet the world went on. The sun still shone. To the west, the mountains shrugged their indifferent shoulders at man's departure. For a while, there had been a lot of smoke in the air – whole blocks had burned to the ground – but now this, too,

3

had dissipated, revealing the desolation with an eerie clarity. At night, regions of blackness draped the city, but elsewhere, lights still glittered in the gloom – flickering street lamps, filling station and convenience stores with their distinctive neon glow, porch lights left burning for their owners' return. While Kittridge maintained his vigil on the balcony, a traffic signal at the corner of the street still dutifully turned from green to orange to red and then to green again.

He wasn't lonely. Loneliness had left him, long ago. He was thirty-seven years old. A little heavier than he'd like – with his leg, it was hard to keep the weight off – but still strong. He'd been married once, though not for years. He remembered that period of his life as 18 months of oversexed, connubial bliss, followed by an equal number of months of yelling and screaming, accusations and counter-accusations, until the whole thing sank like a rock, and he was content, on the whole, that this union had produced no children. His connection to Denver was neither sentimental nor personal; after he'd gotten out of the VA, it was simply the first place he'd landed. Everyone said that a decorated veteran should have little trouble finding work. And maybe this was true. But Kittridge had been in no hurry. He'd spent the better part of a year just reading – the usual trash at first, cop novels and thrillers – but eventually he had found his way into more substantial books: *As I Lay Dying, For Whom the Bell Tolls, Huckleberry Finn, The Great Gatsby*. He'd spent a whole month on Melville, pouring his way through *Moby Dick*. Most were books he felt he ought to read, the ones he'd somehow missed in high school, but he found himself genuinely liking most of them. Sitting in the quiet of his apartment, his mind lost in tales of other lives and times – it felt like taking a long drink after years of thirst. He'd even enrolled in a few classes at the community college, working at Outdoor World during the day, reading and writing his papers at nights and on his lunch hour. He could see himself going on this way for some time. A small but happy life.

And then, of course, the end of the world had happened.

*

The morning the electricity failed, Kittridge had finished upload-ing the previous night's footage and was sitting on the patio, making his way through Dickens' *Tale of Two Cities* – Syndey Carton, the English barrister, had just declared his everlasting love for Lucie Manette, fiancé of the haplessly idealistic Charles Darnay – when the thought touched him that the morning could only be improved by a dish of ice cream. Warren's enor-mous kitchen – you could run a five-star restaurant out of the thing – had been, unsurprisingly, almost completely bereft of food, and Kittridge had long since thrown away the moldy take-out containers that had constituted the meager contents of the fridge. But the guy obviously had a weakness for Ben and Jerry's Chocolate Fudge Brownie, because the freezer was crammed with the stuff. Not Chunky Monkey or Cherry Garcia or Phish Food or even plain old Vanilla. Just Chocolate Fudge Brownie. Kittridge would have liked a little variety, considering there was going to be no more ice cream for a while, but with nothing else to eat besides canned soup and crackers, he was hardly one to complain. Balancing his book on the arm of his chair, he stepped through the sliding glass door into the penthouse.

By the time he reached the kitchen, he had begun to sense that something was wrong, although this impression had yet to coalesce around anything specific. Somehow he failed to notice that the light in the freezer had burned out, so it wasn't until he actually opened the carton and sunk his spoon into a sloppy mush of melted Chocolate Fudge Brownie that he understood.

He tried a lightswitch. Nothing. He moved through the apart-ment, testing lamps and switches. All were the same.

He paused in the middle of the living room and took a deep breath. Okay, he thought. Okay. This was to be expected. If any-thing, it was long overdue. He checked his watch. 11:32 a.m. Sunset was a little after eight. Nine and a half hours to get his ass gone.

He quickly packed a rucksack with what supplies he needed: energy bars, water, clean socks and underwear, a first aid kid, a warm jacket, a bottle of Zyrtec (his allergies had been play-ing hell with him all spring), a toothbrush, and a razor. For a moment he considered bringing *Tale of Two Cities* along, but this seemed impractical, and with a twinge of regret he put it aside, thinking, well, I guess I'll never know how that ends. In the bedroom he dressed himself in a wicking tee-shirt and cargo pants, topping this off with a hunting vest and a pair of light hikers. For a few minutes he considered which weapons to take, finally settling on a Bowie knife, a pair of Glock 19s, and the retro-fitted Polish AK with the folding stock – useless at any kind of range, but reliable close in, which was where he expected to be. The Glocks fit snugly in a cross holster, one beneath each arm. He filled the pockets of his vest with loaded magazines, clipped the AK to its shoulder sling, hoisted the backpack over his shoulders, and returned to the patio.

That was when he noticed the traffic signal on the avenue. Green, yellow, red. Green, yellow, red. It could have been a fluke, but somehow he doubted it.

They'd found him.

The rope, which he'd fixed in place the morning of his arrival, was anchored to a drainage stack on the roof. He stepped into his rappelling harness, clipped in, and swung first his good leg and then his bad one over the railing. Heights were no problem for him, and yet he did not look down. He was perched on the edge of the balcony, facing the windows of the penthouse. In the distance, he heard the sound of a helicopter.

Last Stand In Denver, signing off.

With a push he was aloft, his body lobbing like a softball away from the face of the building. One story, two stories, three, the rope smoothly sliding through his hands: he landed on the balcony of the apartment four floors below. A familiar twang of pain shot upward from his left knee; he gritted his teeth to force it away. The helicopter was closer now, the sound of its blades volleying off the tall buildings of downtown and the empty streets below. He peeled off his harness, drew one of the Glocks, and fired a single shot to shatter the glass of the balcony door.

The air of the apartment was stale, like the inside of a cabin sealed for winter. Heavy furniture, gilt mirrors, an oil painting of a horse hung over the fireplace; from somewhere came a smell

6

of decay. He moved through the becalmed space with barely a glance. At the front door he paused to attach a spotlight to the rail of the AK and stepped out into the hall, headed for the stairs.

In his pocket were the keys to the Ferrari, parked in the building's underground garage, twenty-three floors below. Kittridge shouldered open the door of the stairwell, quickly sweeping the space with the beam from the AK, up and down. Clear. He withdrew a flare from his vest and used his teeth to unscrew the plastic top, exposing the igniter button. With a combustive pop, the flare commenced its rain of sparks. Kittridge held it over the side, taking aim, and let go; if there was anything down there, he'd know it soon. His eyes followed the flare as it made its decent, dragging a contrail of smoke. Somewhere below it caught the rail and bounced out of sight. Kittridge counted to ten. Nothing, no movement at all.

He began to descend. His heart was beating in his throat. Three flares later he reached the bottom; a heavy steel door with a bar and a small square of reinforced glass led to the garage. The floor of the stairwell was littered with trash: pop cans, candy bar wrappers, tins of food. A rumpled bedroll and a pile of musty clothing showed where someone had been sleeping – hiding, as he had.

Kittridge had scouted out the parking garage the day of his arrival. The Ferrari was parked near the southwest corner, a distance of approximately two-hundred feet. He probably should have moved it closer to the door, but it had taken him three days to locate Warren's keys – who keeps his car keys in a bathroom drawer? – by which time Kittridge had already barricaded himself inside the penthouse.

The fob had three buttons: one for the doors, one for the alarm, and one which, he hoped, was a remote starter. He pressed this one first.

From deep within the garage came a tart, single-noted bleep, the sound ricocheting like a bee-bee through the sealed space, followed by the throaty roar of the Ferrari's engine. Another mistake: the Ferrari was parked nose to the wall. He should have thought of that. Not only would this slow his escape; if the car had been facing the opposite way, its headlights would have afforded him a better look at the room. As it was, all he could make out through the window was a distant, glowing region where the car awaited, a cat purring in the dark. The rest of the garage was veiled in blackness. The infected liked to hang from things, Kittridge knew. Ceiling struts, pipes, anything with a tactile surface. The tiniest crack would suffice. When they came, they came from above.

The moment of decision was upon him. Toss more flares and see what happened? Move stealthily through the darkness, seeking cover? Throw open the door and run like hell?

From high overhead came the creak of a stairwell door opening, followed by a sound of voices, murmuring. Kittridge held his breath and listened. There were two of them. Though he knew he shouldn't, he stepped back from the door and craned his neck upward, angling his eyes up the stairwell. Ten stories up, two red dots were dancing off the walls.

He ran like hell.

He had made it halfway to the Ferrari when he heard the first viral drop behind him. There was no time to turn and fire, Kittridge kept on going. The pain in his knee felt like a wick of fire, an ice-pick buried to the bone. At the periphery of his senses he felt a tingling awareness of beings awakening, the garage coming to life. He threw open the door and wedged himself inside, tossing the AK and rucksack onto the passenger seat, slamming the door behind him. The vehicle was so low-slung he felt like he was sitting on the ground. The dashboard, full of mysterious gauges and switches, glowed like a spacecraft's. Something was missing. Where was the gearshift?

A *wang* of metal, and in the next instant, Kittridge's vision was filled with the sight of it. The viral had leapt onto the hood, assuming a reptilian crouch. For a frozen moment, it regarded him coolly, a predator contemplating his prey. He was naked except for his wristwatch, a Rolex fat as an icecube. *Warren?* he thought, for the man had been wearing one like it the day he had taken Kittridge to see the car. *Warren, old buddy, is that you? Because if it is, I wouldn't mind a word of advice on how to get this thing in gear.*

He discovered, then, with the tips of his fingertips, a pair of levers positioned on the undersides of the steering wheel, left and right. Paddle shifters. He should have thought of that. Up on the right, down on the left, like a motorcycle. Reverse would be a button somewhere, on the dash. *The one with the R, genius. That one.*

He pushed the button and hit the gas. Too fast: with a squeal of rubber the Ferrari shot backward. Kittridge knew what was about to happen before it did. As the viral tumbled away, the right rear quarter panel of the car clipped a concrete post; Kittridge's head was slammed into the driver's-side window. His brain chimed like a tuning fork; glittering motes danced in his eyes. But to contemplate this fact, even for a moment, was to die. The viral was rising from off the floor now, preparing to leap. No doubt it would try to take him straight through the windshield.

But something else seemed to catch its attention. With a bird-like darting quickness, it swiveled its head toward the stairwell door.

Fresh meat.

As the viral jumped away, Kittridge swung the wheel to the left and gripped the right paddle, engaging the transmission as he pressed the accelerator. A lurch and then a leap of speed: Kittridge was thrust back into his seat. Just when he thought he'd lose control of the car again he found the straightway, the walls of the garage and its parked vehicles streaming past; allowing himself a quick glimpse in the rearview, he saw the viral tearing into the body of one of the soldiers. The second was nowhere visible, though if Kittridge had to bet, the man was surely dead already, torn to bloody hunks. In school, Kittridge had learned that you couldn't catch a fly with your hand because time was different to a fly: in a fly's miniscule brain, a second was an hour, an hour was a year. That's what the virals were like. Like beings outside of time.

The ramp to the street was at the far end of the lot, which was laid out like a maze; there was no direct route. The soldiers had bought him a moment but that was all: the only safety was

9

daylight. As Kittridge downshifted into the first corner, engine roaring, tires shrieking, two more virals dropped from the ceiling directly in his path. One fell under his wheel with a damp crunch – he almost lost control of the car again – but the other leapt over the roof of the Ferrari, striding it like a hurdler.

He didn't look back.

They were everywhere now, emerging from all the hidden places. They flung themselves at the car like suicides, driven by the madness of their hunger. He barreled through them, bodies flying, their monstrous, distorted faces colliding with the windshield before being hurled up and over, away. Two more turns and he'd be free, but one was clinging to the roof now. He braked around the corner, fishtailing on the slick cement, the force of his deceleration sending the viral rolling onto the hood. A woman: she appeared to be wearing, of all things, a wedding gown. Gouging her fingers into the gap at the base of the windshield, she had drawn herself onto all fours. Her mouth, a bear-trap of bloody teeth, was open very wide; a tiny golden crucifix dangled at the base of her throat. *I'm sorry about your wedding*, Kittridge thought as he drew one of the pistols, steadying it over the wheel to fire through the windshield, point-blank into her face.

He turned the final corner; ahead, a golden shaft of daylight falling down. Kittridge hit the ramp doing seventy miles an hour, still accelerating. The grate was sealed, but this fact seemed meager, no obstacle at all. Kittridge took aim, plunging the pedal to the floor, and ducked his head beneath the shattered windshield.

A furious crash; for two full seconds, an eternity in miniature, the Ferrari went airborne. It rocketed into the sunshine, concussing the pavement with a bone-jarring bang, sparks flying. There was nothing to stop him, he realized; he was going to careen into the lobby of the bank across the street. As he bounced across the median, Kittridge stamped the brakes and swerved to the right, bracing himself for the impact. But there was no need. With a screech of smoking rubber, the tires bit and held, and the next thing Kittridge knew, he was flying down the avenue, into the summer morning.

He had to admit it. What were Warren's exact words? *You should feel the way she handles.*

It was true. Kittridge had never driven anything like it in his life.